Tom Gray
(The Complete Trilogy)

Alan McDermott

Published in 2013 by FeedARead.com Publishing – Arts Council funded

A CIP catalogue record for this title is available from the British Library.

Foreword

The Tom Gray trilogy is a work of fiction. All characters appearing in this work are fictitious (with a couple of obvious exceptions – Osama Bin Laden being one). Any other resemblance to real persons, living or dead, is purely coincidental.

In each book in the trilogy, the character Len Smart mentions the book he is currently reading on his kindle. These are real books by authors whose work I have read and enjoyed, and their names and titles are used with their permission. Please take a moment to search for them on Amazon and sample what they have on offer.

I'd like to thank my family for putting up with me during the many, many months it took to write these stories.

Justice

Prologue

January 21st 2010

Stuart Boyle held the Subaru Impreza at a steady thirty miles per hour as he headed towards the town centre. Red traffic lights halted his progress and he gazed around at the people in the cars, on the buses, walking the streets or sitting in their offices, most of them either at work or heading to work.

He couldn't understand the appeal of working eight hours, doing someone else's bidding all day long for a just a couple of hundred pounds a week. In comparison, he was sitting in a nice motor that took just three minutes to steal and would earn him £500 by the end of the day. That fact that he regularly got caught didn't bother him: it was an occupational risk he was willing to take. Capture was simply an inconvenience, another few hours spent in a cell when he could be out casing his next hit.

No, as things stood, work wasn't for him.

He caressed the wheel of the Subaru he had stolen the night before, wishing he could keep it a bit longer, but he'd already told Sammy Christodoulou that he had it. Sammy wanted it straight away, and you didn't piss around with Sammy. No, best to hand it over, take the cash and see what tomorrow brings. Maybe he'd keep the next one to himself for a few days.

"See what other music they got." he ordered Martin Kyle, who was sitting in the passenger seat.

In the back, Tim Garbutt nodded his head to the current beat and voiced his displeasure when the disc was changed.

"Aww, I was listening to that."

"Stop bleating, Timmy," Kyle said, switching the CD for something with a bit more drum and bass, "my gran wouldn't even listen to that crap."

Boyle laughed, but his eyes were on the black Skoda coming towards them. The thick aerial first caught his attention, and as it neared he saw the white shirts and black epaulettes of the occupants that identified them as police in an unmarked car. The Skoda passed them and in his rear view mirror he watched it continue for another hundred yards before the blue lights illuminated and it performed a u-turn.

Game on.

* * *

"That's Stuart Boyle in the Scooby," PC Trevor Haines told his partner. That was enough for PC Glenn Barker and he hit the blues and twos before spinning the car around in pursuit.

"Hotel Oscar, this is Romeo Tango Two Five, can we have a PNC check on a blue Subaru Impreza, licence number Whiskey Victor Five Three Victor Kilo Mike."

Although it was procedure, the call in was a formality because PC Haines knew for a fact that Stuart Boyle didn't own a Subaru Impreza, nor could he have insurance to drive one because he didn't have a driving licence. In fact, Stuart Boyle had never had a valid driving licence: his driving ban had started before he was even old enough to apply for one and he had a string of motoring convictions, ranging from driving without a licence, driving whilst disqualified and driving without insurance, to theft of a motor vehicle and Taking Without the Owner's Consent. All this despite being just twenty years of age.

"Romeo Tango Two Five, this is Hotel Oscar. The vehicle is registered to a Mr Simon Glover, Winslow Way, Meopham, Kent. It was reported stolen at eight this morning."

"Romeo Tango Two Five, roger that. We believe the driver is a Stuart Boyle, currently disqualified from driving. We are three hundred yards behind it, heading north on Hall Lane, over."

"He's seen us," Haines told his colleague.

"Looks like it. Fasten your seat belt, cos' he ain't one for pulling over," Barker advised. Sure enough, the Subaru was soon doing sixty miles per hour and their Skoda was keeping up but not gaining.

"Hotel Oscar, Romeo Tango Two Five, vehicle failing to stop, continuing west, speed six zero miles an hour. Traffic is light, visibility is excellent, weather is clear, driver is pursuit trained, over."

* * *

As soon as the blue lights illuminated, Stuart was plotting his course home. Once in the network of streets on the Foxwell estate he was confident he could lose them. It was just a case of getting there

8

before they managed to stop him. At this time of day the ring road was the quickest way back, especially in an Impreza.

He hit the accelerator and was soon doing sixty through the morning traffic, weaving between cars and speeding down the centre of the road, forcing other drivers onto the kerb. At the traffic lights he was held up by stationary cars, so he took to the oncoming lane and sped through the junction, narrowly avoiding a collision with a bus coming from his right.

The move held the police up and he gained an advantage, pulling a further hundred yards ahead, but another set of red traffic lights evened things out, and he had to slow in order to squeeze into a gap between a car and a van. The police were right on his tail now, and traffic ahead was stopped, so he took to the pavement, scattering pedestrians as he searched desperately for a clear stretch of road. Up ahead he saw nothing but stationary vehicles, so he turned into a side road and sped along residential streets at twice the speed limit.

He checked his rear view mirror as he took another turn and saw the police car in the distance, and he guessed he had enough of an advantage, just as long as he could maintain it. Another right turn and he was back on the main road, with the ring road only a few hundred yards ahead.

* * *

"Hotel Oscar, Romeo Tango Two Five, vehicle has joined the ring road, heading west, speed now eight zero miles an hour." PC Haines gave the commentary while PC Barker concentrated on the driving.

"Understood, Two Five."

The pursuit carried on for two miles with no sign of the Subaru slowing down. If anything, it was pulling away from the Skoda.

"Hotel Oscar, Romeo Tango Two Five, we believe he may be heading for the Foxwell estate. Do we have any other units in that area, over?" Haines asked. If they didn't get the Scooby contained soon they were sure to lose them, even if they knew who was at the wheel. Recognising Stuart Boyle was one thing, but having proof that he was ever in the car was another matter entirely. He was too clever to touch a car without surgical gloves and his family would provide a watertight alibi, as always. No, their only chance was to catch him at the wheel.

"Romeo Tango Two Five, we have no units available at the moment and Quebec Hotel Nine Nine is on another call, over."

Damn! QH99, the force helicopter, would have been invaluable in this pursuit, especially if they lost sight of the vehicle and the suspects decamped.

* * *

Boyle pulled off the dual carriageway a mile from his home and although it felt like he had slowed considerably, he was still travelling at seventy miles per hour through the light traffic. Behind him the unmarked car was closing, but he had enough of a lead as he turned into the estate. He told Martin to turn the music off and took the first left, then a right and a left again, and with the windows open he could hear the sirens disappearing in the opposite direction. He still wasn't out the woods, though. He was well known among the local constabulary and there was a chance that they might have recognised him. They would also have the chopper up searching for the car, he was sure of that. He had to get home as soon as possible so that his family could swear that he had been in the house all along.

He took the next right into a cul-de-sac, stopped the car and was out and running in no time. His passengers were moments behind him and all three headed for an alley which led to Alba Street and Boyle's house. Had any of them looked back they would have seen the Subaru rolling gently down the slight incline of the street. Slowly at first, but the momentum soon built up and it gathered pace all the time…

* * *

Dina Gray stood outside her sister's door, saying her goodbyes after discussing the upcoming birthday party. Daniel made his way up the garden steps and out into the street, where he looked over the low wall into Sarah's garden and started singing "ten green bottles".

Dina looked up at her son, marvelling at how quickly he had picked up that song. He'd only heard it for the first time at the beginning of the week, and here he was counting down from ten to zero. It was hard to believe that he would be three years old at the weekend: it seemed like just yesterday when he was learning to crawl. Now he could count, he knew the alphabet, he could read a dozen words and loved to sing. She knew he would have lots of fun in the soft play area of the local activity centre next weekend and she was also looking forward to it immensely.

"I really envy you," Sarah said. "I wish I could get my lazy sod of a husband off the beer long enough to get it up, then I might stand a chance of having another little darling like him."

Sharon's own kids were all grown up, and she felt broody every time Daniel popped round, but that didn't stop her volunteering to babysit at every opportunity.

With the front of the garden being elevated, neither Dina nor Sarah saw the Subaru until it was a few feet away. There was barely time to recognise the danger before it hit the wall at only twelve miles per hour. When it hit it wasn't going quite fast enough to demolish the wall, but fast enough to crush the life out of Daniel Gray.

Chapter 1

October 28th 2010

The alarm clock heralded the start of a new day and it came as some relief to Tom Gray, rousing him from yet another nightmare.

In the months since Daniel had been gone he had rarely been able to sleep without dreaming of the incident. At first he had thought it a blessing that he hadn't witnessed Daniel's death, so that he could remember his son as he was the last time he saw him alive, but as the weeks went on he found that each dream saw Daniel dying in more bizarre and painful ways. In all of these dreams he was there, watching it all unfold, but helpless to do anything about it.

The relief soon turned to anguish, though, as he remembered what the day had in store.

As much as Daniel's death had hurt him, he had been able to immerse himself in his work. For his wife there had been no such distraction. She had shunned friends and sat alone in the house day after day, hitting the bottle. He had lost count of the number of times he had arrived home to find her drunk and watching a home movie: Daniel learning to eat with a spoon; Daniel taking his first steps; Daniel saying "Daddy" for the first time...

Every evening was spent consoling her, urging her to get back in touch with her friends and carry on with life, and despite her promises that she would, he saw little evidence of things improving.

The fact that he hadn't spotted the signs for what they were would haunt Tom Gray for the rest of his days, but today more than any other.

It was time to have a shower, shave and head to the office to do the payroll.

In the afternoon he would bury his wife.

Stopping only at a sandwich bar to grab a bacon roll, Gray drove to the offices of Viking Security Services and filled his parking space near the front door. He had started this company a few months after leaving the Army and had been supplying security personnel to domestic and foreign companies for the last five years. His main income came from supplying BGs, or Body Guards, to companies operating in regions affected by the recent upheaval in the Gulf States, although he also provided staff specialising in training private defence teams. His first such contract was supplying advisors to a Saudi prince to train his personal guard and the job they had done had cemented his reputation. Gray currently had a team of five permanent advisors, plus over one hundred other freelance staff on his books ready to take a job at a moment's notice, half of whom were already in the field. Each of them was earning Viking Security Services a commission of £100 a day.

All of the people he employed were either personally selected, having served with them, or came highly recommended by former colleagues still in the forces. If a soldier cut the mustard in his old regiment, he would be pointed in Gray's direction when he left. His insistence on selecting only the best in their field made him the stand-out choice for close protection contracts.

He got out of his BMW cabriolet after putting the roof up to protect the interior from the seagulls which mobbed the area. One of the local residents liked to feed these birds each morning, which meant at least thirty of them would be on the wing, screaming past his office window and shitting all over his car. He wouldn't have minded if they had been little sparrows or blue tits, but seagulls were nothing more than flying rats. They nested on buildings, they ate garbage — often destroying the garbage bag and spreading its contents all over the street in the process — and they made such a racket whenever a rival ventured to within fifty yards of their territory. Perhaps one day they would abandon the city and return to the sea, but as long as this ignorant cow kept inviting them for breakfast, Tom wasn't going to hold his breath.

Inside the office building Tom stopped off at the kitchen to get a coffee to go with his sandwich. He ate after mating the laptop with the docking station on his desk, and once it had powered up he went for a quick look at the BBC news website. The intention was to get the World News section to check on developments in Syria, where he had a team of seven contractors, but before he could navigate to the page the main headline caught his eye:

"Anger at killer driver's sentence."

13

Gray clicked the link and read the article, which told of a 17-year-old youth who received a £500 fine and a twelve-month driving ban for killing his passenger girlfriend when he crashed his car. He had admitted driving without due care and attention rather than face the charge of causing death by dangerous driving.

He thought about Stuart Boyle, the man who had killed Daniel. The police wouldn't give Gray any specific details about Boyle due to the trial, which was starting today, but one officer had admitted he had "previous". They were confident of a conviction, and the fact that Boyle had been remanded in custody at the start of the year suggested their case was good. They had CCTV evidence of Boyle leaving the driver's side door, which was captured by a resident who had installed the cameras after being plagued by the local youths.

Gray would miss the first day of Boyle's trial, which was expected to last all week, but would be in court for the remaining days and the verdict.

Another headline caught his eye

"M1 closed near Luton after crash kills two."

His thoughts immediately turned to his wife. The coroner's verdict was suicide based on the fact that she had removed her seat belt and disabled the air-bag before ploughing into the motorway bridge support at over one hundred and ten miles per hour. Gray didn't dispute their decision, but since her death he had cursed himself daily for not realising she wasn't as strong as him, and he knew he should have seen the signs. His Army training had taught him that death inevitably came for everyone, and when you lose someone close you celebrate their life, not mourn their passing.

On this day, his Army training abandoned him and he cried like he hadn't cried in his thirty-six years.

The funeral was held at the same church where their son was laid to rest. The mourners were equally split between Dina's family and Gray's ex-Army friends, separated by the coffin suspended over the hole in the ground.

Tom's parents had handed him to social services as a toddler and he had been raised by foster family after foster family until he was old enough to join the Army and finally find people with whom he could truly bond. They were his only family now.

To Gray, the service seemed to be over as soon as it had started. He had spent the entire time in his own recollections and heard few of the words spoken by the vicar, not even allowing the late autumn drizzle to penetrate his little world.

Eventually a hand on his shoulder brought him back to the present and he saw that the coffin had already been lowered into the ground. He stood confused for a moment, not knowing if he should throw some soil on the coffin, or say a few words, but thankfully everyone opposite turned to leave and he took that as cue to do the same. He moved to catch up with Dina's mother but his wife's brother stopped and put up his hand. "Now is not the time, Tom."

Tom Gray had a feeling there would never be a right time, because Ruth had made it plain that she blamed him for Dina's death. He had phoned numerous times but Ruth never took or returned his calls. Eventually he had driven to the house to confront her, only to be told that she didn't want to see him. "Mum's taken it hard," Dina's brother had told him. "How could you let Dina get into that state? Didn't you notice something was wrong?"

Gray had offered him no answers and had left without making his peace. That had been his last contact with Dina's family, and now it seemed there would be no more.

"Come on, Tom, let's grab a drink."

Len Smart led Gray to his car and they drove in silence to the pub. Once inside, with pints in front of them, Gray said "I should go to the wake, Len."

"No, Tom, you shouldn't. Give them time, they'll come round, but right now let them grieve."

"I guess you're right."

A dozen of Gray's friends walked into the pub, having followed them from the church. Two headed to the bar to get a round in while the rest pulled tables round so that they were all sitting together.

"How's the business coming along?" Carl Levine asked, although he already knew the answer: he just wanted a topic to take Gray's mind off the day's proceedings.

"Not too bad. I got a contract for three BGs in Afghanistan last week, and another coming up for eight in Iraq, looking after oil workers. I'll be meeting with the oil company in a couple of weeks."

"Sounds good. When you get it, don't forget our old friend Len."

"Don't worry, when the contract's signed, you'll be second on the list."

Len appeared hurt. "Only second? Who's first? Not Sonny, surely."

Simon 'Sonny' Baines was so named because he'd looked like a school boy when he'd enlisted and hadn't seemed to age a day since. Along with his youthful looks he had a penchant for school boy pranks, many of which were at Len's expense.

"No, not Sonny. Me."

"But what about the business? What happens to that when you're running around Baghdad?"

Gray took a mouthful of beer. "It's up for sale. One venture capitalist firm has already shown interest. We haven't discussed numbers yet but my accountant reckons I should be looking for about one point eight million."

"This is a bit sudden. What brought it on?" Jeff Campbell asked.

Gray took another long drink, keeping them all waiting. He had known these men for many years and they had been through a lot together, yet he still felt uncomfortable opening up in front of them. They had shared many things in their time, but rarely their emotions.

"I just can't bear it without them," he finally said, staring into his glass. "If I stay around here it will drive me crazy, I know it. When Dina and Danny were both alive I would think about them on the drive home, and every time I opened the door he would run to me shouting 'Daddy!' Now, when I open the door, there's just silence, and it tears me apart."

His eyes began to cloud and he wiped them before finishing off his beer. As he put his empty glass on the table it was immediately replaced with a fresh pint.

"Whenever I pass his nursery, I think of him. When I go to the supermarket I remember the times we used to go as a family, and I even sleep on the couch because I can't stand to be alone in our bed. When I see a woman and kid in the street, it reminds me of them.

"There are just too many things in my daily routine that make me think about my family. I need a fresh start, get out of the area and throw myself into something that will take up every waking moment. The only thing I know that intense is a stint in Iraq."

"But why sell up?" Colin Avery asked. "Couldn't you just get a manager in for a while?"

"I could," Gray admitted, "but I want a clean slate. I don't want to come back to the old routine; it'll just bring back the memories. This way, once I'm done in Iraq, I can settle anywhere I like." A few nods told him that they thought his plan made sense.

A couple of them asked about positions in the upcoming contract and he began taking the names, but was interrupted when his mobile rang. The display told him it was his solicitor, so he made his excuses and moved to a quieter area of the room. He listened for a few moments, then suddenly exploded into the phone: "You're fucking joking!"

Everyone at the table looked at him, their eyes asking what the problem was. Gray listened for another minute or so before ending the call and resuming his seat at the table.

"They released him," he told his friends, and knocked back a whiskey which was sitting in the middle of the table. "Apparently he offered to plead guilty if they changed the charge to driving without due care and attention. The prosecution accepted the offer and the judge gave him fifteen months, and then released him because he had already served more than half of that on remand."

"Why only fifteen months?" Paul Bennett asked. "Was it his first offence?"

"Fuck, no." Gray spat. "My solicitor said he had forty-three previous convictions for car theft, plus thirty-four other convictions including assault, burglary, possessing an offensive weapon and various drug offences."

"So that's it? He just walks?"

"He just walks," Gray confirmed.

"He's just spent eight months with his own kind, learning new and improved ways of breaking into cars, and now he's free to try them out," Sonny said. "That can't be right."

"This country's too soft on these little shits," Tristram Barker-Fink agreed.

"They should bring back National Service, give them some real discipline."

"...or the birch..."

Other suggestions came thick and fast, including "chop their thieving hands off" and "just shoot them in the fucking head."

"Want us to pay him a visit?" Avery asked, and a few of them nodded their willingness to take part.

"Thanks, guys," Gray said, a faraway look in his eye, "but I think it's gone beyond that now..."

17

Chapter 2

April 12th 2011

Joseph Olemwu desperately wanted some gear, but with no cash he would have to find a different form of currency. Luckily, Albert Tonga accepted mobile phones as full payment, and at this time of night there was always the chance of finding someone to donate one, even if they didn't do so willingly.

He took a large swig of Vodka and passed the bottle to Vinnie Parker. "Robbo told me he did it with Shelly White on Friday," Parker told him before wiping the neck of the bottle and taking a drink. Olemwu nearly choked with laughter, vodka erupting from his nose and clenched mouth.

When he finally recovered he said "Robbo is full of shit. He didn't shag no-one on Friday. I was drinking with him all day and the last I saw him he was puking in the stairwell at midnight. I had to help him to his flat. Fuck me, his mum was pissed off." He smiled at the recollection and imagined the bollocking that would have been dished out.

Marcus Taylor tapped Olemwu and Parker on the arm and motioned towards a figure approaching them. He was at least six inches smaller than any of the boys, perhaps a couple of years older than them at around twenty years of age, wearing glasses and hair cut short with a side parting. He was chatting on a mobile, seemingly oblivious to their presence until he was on top of them. The man stopped when he noticed the three boys and made eye contact for a brief moment, then haltingly walked on past them, keeping them in his peripheral vision.

Olemwu was the first to react. "You looking at me, cunt?"

The man carried on walking, his pace quickening, and the boys trotted to catch up. As they got within ten feet of him he took off through a gate and into the park. The three boys followed, chasing him into the darkness. He had on a light brown jacket and that helped them keep him in view, but they didn't seem to be gaining. As they ran three abreast, the two on the flanks were suddenly confronted by figures dressed entirely in black, who seemed to rise out of the ground barely five feet in front of them. Their momentum carried them towards the men, who took a step to the side and swung baseball bats, catching the boys in the chest. Ribs cracked and they dropped likes sacks of cement.

Neither had managed to get out a cry, but Olemwu had heard the bats striking, as had the man he was chasing. Both stopped, and the man in the brown jacket turned and started walking purposefully towards him, placing his glasses in a protective case. Despite the height advantage there was something menacing in the slight figure that deeply troubled him. He spun round to seek strength in numbers but from the faint street lighting he saw his friends lying in the foetal position, barely able to moan, never mind move. From the sides two dark figures approached him, leaving him nowhere to run.

"Look man, I don't want no trouble. We was just fuckin' wiv 'im, that's all."

The men said nothing, simply moved closer and closer, bats raised and ready to strike. Joseph Olemwu's head spun as he tried to keep an eye on all of them at the same time, and when the blow came he barely saw the blur of the wood before it crashed into his temple. He dropped to the ground, out cold, and the men wasted no time applying plasticuffs to his arms and legs. Sonny Baines put his glasses case back in his jacket pocket and clicked the talk button on his collar mike twice. The three men picked the unconscious Olemwu up and carried him into the darkness, and after a hundred yards Sonny heard a voice in his earpiece. "Seventy yards out, eleven o'clock." Sonny adjusted his heading and saw the transit van when he was within ten yards of it. The driver was scanning the surrounding area with night vision glasses, ensuring there was no-one around to disturb them. Satisfied, he opened the rear doors and Olemwu was bundled in unceremoniously.

"Christ, Carl, could you have hit him any harder? You nearly took his fucking head off."

"He's fine, look," Carl said, giving Olemwu a kick. "He's breathing, ain't he?"

The van pulled out of the park and once on the road the driver turned the headlights on. In the back they settled down for the long journey, using Joseph Olemwu as a footrest.

Chapter 3

Sunday April 17th 2011

John Hammond was preparing his notes for the next morning's Joint Intelligence Committee meeting when Andrew Harvey knocked on his door and walked in without waiting to be beckoned. Normally Hammond would have had something to say about the intrusion, but Harvey was a solid operative, very experienced and above all a man who knew when to stand on convention. If he ignored the unwritten protocol it was often with good reason.

"Something big has come in," Harvey told him. "We're all gathered."

Hammond nodded, locked his workstation and followed Harvey.

In the conference room, Diane Lane used their arrival as her cue to start the briefing.

"In the last thirty minutes, calls were made to all the major newspapers as well as the BBC and Sky news channels to inform them about this new website."

She pressed her remote control and an image of the website appeared on the fifty-inch wall-mounted plasma screen. The banner proclaimed the site to be the home of "Justice For Britain" and in the centre of the page a video was waiting to be streamed. Lane clicked the Play button on the embedded video player and a man appeared on the screen, not overly handsome, the mouth perhaps a little small, but the face under the short chestnut hair had an air of authority. He moved the camera so that it was pointing towards what appeared to be five prison cells, all with their doors open. Each cell contained a single box-like chair upon which sat a shaven-headed figure wearing a white T-shirt and nothing else. They all had tape over their mouths and their arms were outstretched and tied to the cell walls, while their feet were shackled, the chains running through metal rings set into the floor between their legs.

"You are all here," the man began, walking past the cells and addressing the occupants, "because you all have criminal records stretching back years. Despite the courts being lenient with you, you have spurned numerous chances to change your ways. You might have thought that the courts were doing you a favour by just giving you a curfew or community service but it's quite the opposite: If you had committed one crime and learned your lesson, you wouldn't be here. The fact that you have a string of convictions means you have no regard for the law or the people you have plagued over the years. You have shown that you do not want to make a positive contribution to society, and up until now society has had no say in the matter. We have all had to rely on our government to protect us from you, yet they have thrown you back on the street time after time.

"Well, enough is enough. I think you have had all the chances you deserve. I say it is now up to the people of this country to decide what happens to you."

The figure turned to the camera.

"Folks, my name is Tom Gray and the next few days are all about choices.

"Last year, one of these criminals killed my only son and our fabulous judicial system gave him a fifteen month prison sentence and then let him walk free because he had served eight months on remand.

"That was all they thought my son's life was worth."

Gray took a swig of water from a bottle.

"I have created this website so that you, the people of Britain, can have a say in what happens to these five people. Judges throw them back on the streets because the crimes they commit do not directly affect them. If they did, you can be sure the sentences would be harsher. If a judge's son was killed by a joy rider you can be sure he would go down for a long time.

"I have contacted all the major UK news outlets to let them know that I have a device placed at a location which will kill thousands. If one of my colleagues out there lets me know that this website was interrupted for any reason, I will kill everyone in this room, take my own life and the device goes off at midday on Friday. I am the only one who knows where the device is, and its location will die with me."

Gray started to count off on his fingers. "If the government interferes with this website or causes it to stop functioning, I will take my own life.

"If this story isn't shown on all UK news channels, and that includes showing the address of the website, I will take my own life.

21

"If any attempt is made to rescue these criminals by force, I will take my own life."

Gray unzipped his combat smock to reveal a waistcoat fashioned from webbing. Strung from it were three hand grenades, with a cord attached to the pin of the one in the centre. The cord emerged through the lapel of his smock and was attached to a large handle, making it easy to grab.

"In my line of work I have long accepted the fact that death will come, so I do not fear it.

"As the TV and newspapers will no doubt tell you over the coming days and weeks, I spent fourteen years in the Army. My knowledge of explosives is more than enough to create and prime the device I mentioned, so do not doubt its existence."

Gray pulled a photo from his combat smock pocket and studied it for a moment before showing it to the camera.

"Seven months after our son died my wife took her own life, so I have no more family. The choice I had to make was to either live my life in constant mourning, or end it this week while trying to make a difference.

"As you can see, I have made my choice."

He replaced the photo of his family in his breast pocket and buttoned it up.

"I want to remind the Prime Minister that his government came to power on the promise to get tough on criminals. Well, now it's time for him to make his choice: Let the public watch these transmissions through to their conclusion on Thursday night and save the lives of thousands; or try to save these five career criminals."

Gray made a weighing motion with his hands. "Thousands of lives, or five criminals. All I ask is that you let me finish this, let the country decide the fate of these criminals. Consider it the ultimate straw poll.

"To you out there in Britain, the voting starts now. On the left hand side of the screen you will see the profiles and criminal records of the five men here. The first person to be dealt with will be Simon Arkin, aged twenty-one, from Manchester. Simon has sixty seven convictions but has never been behind bars. Instead, the courts gave him community service, which he hasn't carried out.

"If you think he should be set free to commit more crimes, send an email to tom@justiceforbritain.co.uk. Put the word 'Simon' as the subject and the word 'Live' in the body of the email. If you think he has had all the chances a person deserves, replace 'Live' with 'Die'.

Well, do you think he deserves another chance? I know what I think, but what do *you* think?

"Voting closes at seven-thirty this evening and I will be back with a live broadcast an hour later to reveal the results."

The video ended and Lane turned to her colleagues after replacing the image of the website with a photo of Tom Gray.

"This image was sent to us by the MoD. They confirm that Tom Gray was one of theirs but he appears to have understated his role." After glancing at her notes, she continued. "He joined Two Para aged eighteen and after achieving the rank of Sergeant he joined Two-Two Regiment, where he spent his last eight years, including three tours in Iraq which earned him the Distinguished Conduct Medal. We'll have more details when his file arrives."

"He's SAS?" Hammond asked.

"It appears so."

"Which means he probably *will* have the knowhow to create the device he mentioned, so we proceed on that assumption." Hammond massaged his cheeks for a moment. "He mentioned colleagues on the outside. Work that up, see who he has been in contact with over the last six months. Phone records, email account, we need names and addresses for everyone." The Assistant Director General of MI5 turned to Harvey. "Andrew, our main priority is that bomb: Get every available resource looking for it. Once that's rolling, ask the techies to get working on that website. Examine every avenue, give us some options. I don't want them to make a move, just options."

The intelligence officer nodded and left the room.

"Diane, I want reports on each of these boys, and get on to GCHQ and surveillance, see if we can find Gray's location. The techies might get us something but I want to double up on everything."

Lane nodded and walked towards the door. "Will do."

Hammond returned to his office and made a quick phone call before grabbing his briefcase and walking towards the exit. "I'm going to see the Home Secretary," he told Harvey in passing. "Keep me posted on developments."

Chapter 4

Tom Gray watched the counter on his laptop as it crept towards two hundred. The freelance programmer who had created the bespoke software had explained that when a new visitor arrived at the website, the Global.asax file captured their IP address and other items in the ServerVariables collection, wrapped them in an XML message and emailed it to his inbox. His email software then dumped it in a folder which is monitored by a FileSystemWatcher component, which extracted the information and fed it into a web service which returned known information based on the server variables, and then fed it into a database and displayed the results on the screen, which was refreshed every few seconds by a Timer component.

In layman's terms, if someone visited the website, he would know about it, and have a good idea who and where they were.

Gray had contacted the news outlets forty minutes earlier, and as no-one else in the world knew about the website he thought it safe to assume that the first visitors would be the news outlets, the government and the intelligence service.

He flicked back and forth between the BBC news and Sky News until he saw the first of the 'Breaking News' tickers scrolling across the bottom of the screen. Gray checked his watch and saw that his prediction was out by three minutes, which was no big deal. It simply meant he would record more IP addresses than anticipated. If the security services hadn't visited by now, they never would.

With the IP addresses recorded, he would now be able to filter out any votes coming from the same range. In considering possible ploys against him he had reasoned that the authorities might send a few million emails with the word 'Live' in order to rig the vote, but his software would disregard any votes coming from the recorded IP addresses, or any with a certain range. In addition, with the click of a button he could redirect any requests for his website from these IP addresses to any other page on the internet. His choice had been to redirect them to a page on the number10.gov.uk petitions website which was asking the government to reintroduce the death penalty.

Gray also considered the fact that they might try a few ways to influence the results, but this had also been factored in when he had commissioned the software.

He settled down to watch the news, wondering how long it would take them to brand him a terrorist. He didn't have to wait long.

"News is just reaching us that a former SAS soldier is threatening to kill thousands of people unless the government allow him to execute five suspected criminals live on the internet."

A photo of Gray appeared on the screen next to the female anchor, a picture he recognised from his Army days.

"Tom Gray, who spent eight years in two-two Regiment, Special Air Service, has demanded that the government allow him to poll the nation to decide whether or not his captives should live or die. According to a video shown on his website, www.justiceforbritain.co.uk, if the government do not allow him to collect and act on the votes sent in by members of the public he will kill his prisoners and take his own life. If he does this, police will have little or no chance of finding his bomb."

The camera angle changed to show a live video feed on the studio wall. A grey-haired man in his fifties, with heavy jowls and a ruddy complexion, waited patiently for his introduction.

"We are joined now by Home Office spokesman, Adrian Goode. Mr Goode, Thank you for joining us. What is the Home Office's response to this terrorist threat?"

Gray watched the spokesman spend four minute talking a lot but saying absolutely nothing, promising that the government was doing everything within its power to protect the public while giving no indication as to how it would do this. Questions were thrown at him and he answered with prepared statements, never once deviating from the script. It was just what Gray had expected.

He turned his attention to his laptop and waited for the votes to start coming in.

* * *

Andrew Harvey walked into the Technical Operations office and made his way straight to Gerald Small's workstation.

"What have we got?" he asked.

Small continued tapping at his keyboard as he explained their progress. "We have the website host. It's a UK company based in

25

Guildford, and he's either too dumb to know how to hide its location, or he doesn't care."

"Or maybe he wants us to find it." Harvey suggested. "What else?"

"We have gained access to the website's source code. It's written in a programming language I am familiar with, and so far I have discovered a couple of interesting bits of code." Small brought up the first page of interest. "This area here checks to see if it is operating within a date and time range. That range was a couple of minutes before the first call to the BBC and ended forty-five minutes later. It has collected details of every visitor during that time and sent the details to Gray's email address. What he has done with that information, we don't know, but he wanted it for a reason."

"Which means he knows our IP address and can block or monitor our visits?"

Small nodded.

"What about using a different terminal?" Harvey asked.

"We access the outside world via a proxy server, so no matter which terminal you use, it will always show the IP address of the proxy. What we can do is use a different connection." He shuffled his chair to another terminal and opened up a command prompt. After typing for a few moments he declared the job done.

"This terminal uses our failover connection and doesn't use a proxy. It will show up as a residential account if he ever digs that deep."

"Excellent," Harvey said. "So we have anonymous access. What options do we have now?"

Small shuffled back to his own terminal and brought up another page of code.

"This function calls a web service that brings back the results of the votes." Noticing the blank look from Harvey, he dumbed it down. "A web service is a way for two websites to talk to each other. The results are going to another server in South Africa, one we don't have access to. This code here calls that other website and asks it to send the results. This means that if we want to manipulate the results, we could do it here, as the results come back. We could easily add thirty percent to the number of 'Die' votes and show this as the number of 'Live' votes. That way, none of them are killed."

Harvey looked sceptical. "I'm worried that he is making this too easy for us. What other options are there?"

"Well," Small said, rubbing the back of his neck, "we could intercept all emails going to his inbox and delete every third one that says 'Die' before he receives it, I suppose."

Harvey thought about it for a moment. "Okay, that's plan A. Let me know if you come up with anything else." He returned to his own desk and called Hammond to pass on the news.

John Hammond was ushered into the Home Secretary's office and took the seat offered by the minister. The late spring sun hit him square in the face as he sat down and he had to lean to his left to avoid its glare and be able to see Stephen Wells. Hammond was sure the chair had been strategically positioned prior to his arrival.

"John, the PM isn't happy that this has been sprung upon him, especially with a general election just six weeks away. He wants to know what we are doing about it." Hammond's relationship with Wells had been a long and fractured one, and he knew that if things went bad there would be no 'We'. Even if things went their way, it would be the Home Secretary who took all the plaudits, while MI5 would get a brief mention if they were lucky.

"Minister, we have our best resources working on it. As we see it, the priority is locating the device he mentioned. Without that, we cannot make a move on him."

"Do you know where he is?" The Home Secretary asked.

"Not yet. As I said, our priority is locating the device. There is little point in finding Gray and his captives if we can't make a move on him, so while we have a few people searching for his location, our best efforts are concentrating on possible civilian targets. He claims to be targeting thousands of lives, so that narrows it down a bit. We are concentrating on venues that will have large visitor numbers at midday on Friday, and we are in contact with local police forces who are searching all possible targets."

"Do you think this man is capable of killing thousands of innocent people?"

"Does he know how to create a device capable of killing thousands? Possibly. I'd even go as far as probably. Does he have the resolve to detonate it? That's another matter."

Wells leaned forward onto his desk and clasped his hands together. "John, I don't have to tell you how serious it would be if this maniac executes a young man live on the internet, criminal or not." He glanced at his watch. "It's just after midday, giving you seven and a half hours to stop this happening. Find Gray, find his bomb, do

27

whatever you need to do, but put a stop to this, and without loss of life, if you don't mind."

"We may have more time than that." Hammond told him. "On the way over here I spoke to my team. Our techies have access to his website and we have identified a couple of ways to manipulate his figures. If we can swing the vote our way, we might be able to save the life of the first one."

"Might?"

"If he has checks in place to ensure we don't tamper with the site he will spot us messing with the results, but my team are confident that they can intercept negative votes before they hit his system."

"How confident?"

"There are no guarantees, if that's what you mean, but the alternative is to just let the votes come in and hope the people of Britain have utter faith in the justice system."

Wells stared at him for a moment, then said "Do it."

Chapter 5

Hamad Farsi placed two thick files on Andrew Harvey's desk and waited for him to finish his phone call.

"Gray?" Harvey asked after hanging up.

Farsi nodded. "The top one's his M.O.D jacket and the other is what we have on him. Nothing much until six months ago, then it all kicks off. Sells his business for just over a million, cash, when it was worth twice as much. He also sold his house for fifty grand under the asking price, obviously looking for a quick sale. Again, it was a cash transaction. After that he went on a spending spree."

Farsi flicked through the file and pointed out Gray's current account balance.

"Only three thousand left? What the hell did he spend it on?"

"Good question." Farsi said. "We have payments to his web hosting company for a dedicated web server and email exchange server, plus a wire transfer for fifty thousand to a software company in South Africa. There's a hundred and eighty grand to a security firm in Hounslow, and apart from twenty thousand to a software contractor here in London, the rest of the withdrawals were in cash."

"Have you managed to track down the contractor?" Harvey asked.

"He contacted us. Or should I say, he called the police. He recognised his website and apparently didn't know what he was signing up for. I'm going over there in ten minutes. What do you think Gray did with the rest of the cash?"

"Well, a million quid will get you a nice amount of C4, if you know the right people. And in his line of work, he will probably know the right people. Speaking of which, where's the list of acquaintances?"

"Towards the front of the file. We have a list of the people he recruited through his company and Diane is compiling a condensed version based on his phone and email records over the last sixty days."

Harvey skimmed through the file until he came across the mobile phone records. He dialled the number of Gray's phone and he got a response after two rings. "Hello?"

"Is this Tom Gray?" He asked.

"Speaking..."

Harvey put his hand over the receiver and mouthed: "It's him."

"My name is Andrew Harvey, calling from Thames House."

"Hello Andrew. I expected you to call a lot sooner than this. Call me back on my other phone after two minutes." He gave Harvey the new number and broke the connection. Too many people knew this number, or knew how to get it, and he didn't want interruptions all day long. He switched SIM cards and put the old one in his pocket. Ninety seconds later the phone rang again.

"So, what's this all about, Mr Gray?"

Harvey handed the Post-It note containing the new number to Farsi, who nodded and took it over to Lane's desk so that she could contact her liaison at GCHQ. Their communications capabilities far outstripped those of Thames House, and it wouldn't be long before they could get a location from the number.

"Call me Tom. And what it's about is justice for British people, doing what the government have been promising for twenty years now: protecting the innocent and punishing criminals."

"We have a judicial system to take care of that, Tom. What you are doing is not going to change anything."

"Yes it will," Gray told him. "The government have a duty to listen to the people. I am just making sure they hear what is being said."

"Tom, people have tried for years to change things using terror tactics and it hasn't worked. You should know — you used to be on our side of the fight."

"Yes, I noticed it didn't take long to brand me a terrorist, but what options did I have? I could have let it go and accepted the fact that my wife and son are dead and that Stuart Boyle had been punished, but that would mean living a lie, because he hasn't been punished. Did you know that he has been arrested three times since my son's death, each time for driving a stolen vehicle?"

"No, I didn't know that. I haven't seen his file, yet." Harvey admitted.

"Does it sound like he has learnt his lesson? I don't think so. He can't claim to have 'accidentally' stolen three more cars, because that's something you choose to do."

"I agree that he deserves a more severe punishment, but that is not for us to decide, Tom. If everyone took the law into their own hands there would be anarchy, you know that. We have to let the courts decide, that's what they are there for. If you feel badly enough, start a legitimate campaign to get the law changed. It has worked for others in the past, and with your record in the services, people would listen."

"People are listening now, Andrew, and I don't have to spend years fighting an uphill battle while every day reliving the pain of their passing."

There was silence for a moment, and Harvey sensed Gray was once again thinking of his family. He waited for him to continue rather than interrupt his private moment.

"I also considered grabbing him off the street, you know," Gray continued after almost a minute, "taking him somewhere nice and quiet and killing him ever so slowly. Trust me, I thought of that many, many times, but his death would have got a brief mention on the news websites and nothing would have changed. There would be plenty more Stuart Boyles to replace him."

"I still don't think this is the way, Tom."

"Andrew, I appreciate that you have a job to do, and that job is to stop me, but I won't be talked out of this. I accepted your call because I wanted to let you know that trying to mount a rescue would be a bad idea. Apart from the fact that you won't get the location of the device, you will be risking the lives of anyone you send. I know that you will be able to pinpoint my location from the cell phone I am using, and it is only a matter of time before you turn up mob-handed, but I warn you that I have had a few weeks to prepare my defences.

"I have early warning systems set up around the perimeter, including motion sensors and infra-red cameras, so I will know if anyone gets too close. The area around the facility is mined, with only one way in or out of the building. If you send in people to clear the mines, I can pick them off. The roof is covered in razor wire, motion sensors and a few other surprises, making an aerial assault tricky. Even if someone did manage to get in, they have to take me alive, and I will have plenty of warning, which means plenty of time to kill these five and take my own life. This will be done live on the internet, and I will let people know the reason why. The government will then have to explain why they risked the lives of five criminals at the expense of thousands."

"Okay, Tom, I understand your position."

"Good. I'll be in touch."

The phone went dead and Harvey returned it to his pocket on his way over to Farsi's desk.

"We have the location. It's an old factory, Sussex Renaissance Potteries, according to the co-ordinates GCHQ gave me. SO15 are on their way over there as we speak."

"Call them," Harvey said, "and tell them to hang back and observe from a distance. He told me he has prepared his defences and I don't doubt it. After you've spoken to them, get on to the security firm and see what he spent a hundred and eighty grand on."

He had a feeling it wasn't anything that was going to aid their cause.

Tom Gray turned to his array of monitors and checked that each was functioning properly. All twelve screens returned a full colour image and he toggled each between visible light and infra-red. Once he was satisfied that they were all working as required he turned his attention to the motion sensor display. All thirty sensors in and around the perimeter were listed and each had a green tick next to their designation to signify that a test signal was being sent and received every second. Should one sensor not respond to a sent signal, a red cross would appear and an audible warning would alert him.

With the equipment in working order he figured he had at least an hour before anyone turned up at his location, and his warning to Andrew Harvey would prevent them rushing in. With time to kill, he turned his attention to feeding the prisoners. This was done by wheeling a trolley up to each boy's chest so that they could reach the food by craning their neck. He could have released one of their hands to let them eat properly, but he'd decided that if they had chosen to behave like animals, they could eat like animals, too. The food was basic; tinned potatoes and Spam, neither of which he had bothered to heat through.

He pushed the trolley up to the first of the boys, Simon Arkin, and removed the tape over his mouth.

"Eat." He ordered.

"Why're you doing this?" Arkin asked, more than a touch of anxiety in his voice. "What have I ever done to you?"

"Nothing. You did nothing to me. But that's only because I don't live near you. I'm sure that if I lived within five miles of you, you would have had no hesitation in nicking my car or breaking into my house." Gray studied him for a moment. "How many houses did you burgle?"

Arkin averted his eyes as he calculated his answer. "Twenty-eight," he eventually said.

"You see, that's the problem, Simon. You tell me it's twenty-eight, but that's how many convictions you have for burglary. That means you either just lied to me, or you got caught every time you burgled a house. And if you got caught every time, it would have sunk in after the first three or four and you wouldn't have bothered with the other twenty-odd, would you?"

Arkin kept his head bowed, taking it as a rhetorical question.

"So what is it? Were you lying to me about the number of burglaries, or are you really so stupid that you got caught every time and yet kept doing it?"

"About three hundred." Arkin finally admitted. "But it wasn't just me."

"I know, I read your record. So why didn't you give the others up when you got caught? The police knew you weren't acting alone, but they were unable to force you to give up the names of the people who were with you. That's what I am going to change.

"As for you, did you ever spare a thought for your victims? Did you ever stop to think how it might impact them?"

"They were all insured, so they didn't lose anything," Arkin came back, a little too quickly to make the reply sound spontaneous. It was obvious to Gray that it was a line he spouted to anyone who questioned his career choice, be they the police or social workers.

"Well, let me tell you something about insurance companies, Simon. They don't get a call saying 'I've been burgled' and run round to replace everything. They do all they can to put the blame on the home owner, trying to prove that they were at fault for making it easy for the burglar. For example, if you opened a front door, grabbed the keys of a brand new Mercedes and drove it away, the insurance company will say the blame lies with the home owner for not securing the keys properly. They lose their forty grand motor and don't get a penny back."

Gray placed a cup of water next to Arkin's plate and popped a straw in so that he could drink from it. "You know, it's ironic that you never spared a thought for your victims, because now there are three hundred families out there about to vote as to whether you live or die. Not just them, but their friends and families, too. That's thousands of people all voting, and I don't think many will be asking for you to be set free to heap more misery on them. Oh, and don't forget everyone else in the country who has been burgled in their lifetime. I don't think you can count on their votes, either."

Gray left Arkin to his banquet, satisfied with the look of impending doom on his face. He wheeled a trolley into the next cell and again removed the tape from the young man's mouth.

"Why are you doing this to me?" his prisoner asked. Faced with the prospect of repeating his little speech, Gray said "Shut up, dickhead, and eat your dinner."

Once the prisoners had been fed and watered he took a stroll around the outside of the building. The factory had once produced earthenware and stood in its own grounds. He had chosen it because it sat well back from the main road, affording him plenty of notice should anyone approach. The sole remaining building was two stories high and in pretty good repair. Most of the windows had been smashed and Gray had broken the others before boarding them up using two-inch thick planks.

The four sides of the building had been cleared away and there was thirty yards of ground which an attacking force would have to cover. Apart from the chance of being picked off by Gray, they would have to negotiate waist-high razor wire and numerous motion sensors, not to mention the anti-personnel mines. Beyond the open ground there were swathes of knee-high grass and the remnants of the other factory buildings which once stood proud but were now reduced to rubble. If anyone wanted to mount an attack there was little in the way of protection within a hundred and fifty yards of the building.

After checking the perimeter he returned to the building and began removing the feeding trolleys from the cells, which had once been walk-in kilns. At the first cell, Arkin asked to go to the toilet.

"You're sitting on a commode, so just go when you need to. It will get a bit uncomfortable after a while, but this will all be over in five days...if not sooner."

Gray placed a new strip of tape over Arkin's mouth as he began to protest, and went to tend to the prisoner in the next cell.

Chapter 6

Diane Lane walked over to Harvey's desk and handed him a sheaf of papers. "These are his known acquaintances, ordered by last date of contact. The most recent was two days ago, when he contacted the first six names on the list."

Harvey took the list, skipped to the last page and noted that the last entry was number two hundred and four. "That's a lot to get through. Let's take the top ten on the list and hand the remainder over to the local police," he told her.

"My thought exactly. I've been in touch with Scotland Yard and they're disseminating the list to all local forces as we speak." She handed Harvey a thick file. "These are police reports regarding the missing boys. When we speak to these people we need to ascertain their whereabouts at the times the boys disappeared."

"Good work, Diane. Let's go and have a chat with them. You take these three," Harvey said, circling three names, "I'll take these two, Hamad can have numbers three, five and six. Before we go, get onto GCHQ, ask them to monitor all calls and emails, in and out, for the top ten names on the list."

As if on cue, Farsi arrived and made a beeline for Harvey's desk. "I brought the contractor in to speak to Gerald. Much of what he told me went over my head and I thought it best to let him talk to someone who also spoke geek. From what I did understand, a lot of the stuff he asked for was pretty routine, although Gray had some specifications for communicating with a website in Jo'burg."

"Yeah, we already made the South African connection. Gerald's working on it."

Farsi began to remove his jacket but Harvey stopped him. "We've got a couple of his old Army buddies to visit." He jotted down the names and addresses and handed them to Farsi, along with the police reports. "Make a note of the dates and times and see if you can tie either of them into their disappearance." As an afterthought he asked, "What of the security firm?"

"They emailed his order over along with basic descriptions, but they can't go too deep into capabilities and weaknesses as they are only distributors. We will need to go to the manufacturers for those and I don't think it's going to be easy at this time on a Sunday."

"Hand it over to Gerald's team. They must have some kind of technical support service, and if they don't get any joy there, they should go direct to the CEO. We need to know what we're up against and what we can do to get round his defences."

Farsi nodded his understanding, and Harvey stood up and grabbed his jacket. "Let's go rattle some cages."

* * *

The constant beeping of the motion sensor panel heralded the arrival of the authorities. Gray looked at the sensor's designation and it told him the area was covered by camera twelve, so he switched to the bank of monitors and maximised the view for that camera.

There had been several false alarms earlier in the day, caused by local wildlife, but what he saw on the screen was no bunny rabbit: two figures dressed in black were snaking through the grass two hundred and seventy yards from the side of the building, heading towards the cover of a pile of rubble left by the demolition of an old outbuilding. The remaining wall, which stood barely three feet high, offered the best cover available around the main building, and it was for this reason that Gray had deployed a couple of microphones. One was hidden in the rubble to the side of the wall, and the other was embedded in the wall itself. Gray had drilled through the mortar from the side facing the building using a drill bit measured to the thickness of the wall, minus three millimetres, and so it hadn't broken through the other side of the mortar.

In about twenty minutes the two figures would arrive at the wall and he would see if the microphones functioned as well in the rain as they did in the dry conditions when he had tested them.

Sergeant Dave Williams of the Metropolitan Police's Counter Terrorism Command, better known as SO15, reached the wall moments before Officer Ben Knightly. He used his binoculars to scan the area between his location and the building and didn't like what he saw.

"It's just like they said, this guy knows how to set a perimeter. We've got shorter grass for about seventy yards, then open ground for another forty. I say open, but I can see barbed wire and mounds

36

everywhere. There's no way we get across there in a hurry." Williams scanned the front of the building. "We've got three cameras, sweeping in a hundred and sixty degree arc...wait... Shit. One is static, looking straight at us. He knows we're here."

"Do we try another approach?" Knightly asked.

"Hang on." Williams reached for his thermal imaging camera to see if he could detect any heat sources in the building, but he was met with a wall of white blobs, dancing around like some kind of psychedelic waltz.

"He's got some kind of disruption system heating every wall. I can't see a thing in there."

"Now what?"

"We report in and wait for instructions."

Gray watched their approach on the camera and heard every word they said. He couldn't hear the response from their commanders, but at least they appreciated the effort that had gone into his defences. More importantly, the thermal sheets lining the walls worked. If they couldn't see into the room with heat-detecting equipment, they were virtually blind, adding more uncertainty to the chances of a forced entry succeeding.

As a security consultant he was up to date on all of the latest gadgets, and this gave him the edge when it came to defeating them. He had searched the internet for the most state-of-the-art devices which could be used against him, and then trawled through freedom of information documents to see what equipment was available to the various police forces.

Once he knew which thermal imaging camera SO15 would be likely to deploy, defeating it was relatively easy.

The background work had certainly paid off.

He turned his attention to his laptop, and after watching the vote count tick over the million mark he folded his arms and lay back in the chair, the hypnotic hum of the diesel generator helping him to sleep. If they decided to launch an attack, operational sense dictated that it would most likely come in the middle of the night, and he planned to be wide awake for it.

* * *

Harvey peered through the front window of the terrace house but saw no sign of life. He returned to the door and rang the bell again, but after having drawn a blank at the first suspect's home he knew he was wasting his time here, too.

"He's not in," a voice said. It belonged to Tristram Barker-Fink's next door neighbour, a woman in her sixties who was standing in her doorway, arms folded and a cigarette dangling from her lips.

"Do you know where he went?" Harvey asked.

"You the police?" she asked, the cigarette bobbing with every word.

"No, I'm an old friend of Tris. We were in the army together. I was hoping to catch up with him while I'm in town on business."

"I think he went on holiday. He left last week with a holdall and hasn't been back since."

"Did he say where he was going?" Harvey asked, praying that the old cow was as nosey as he hoped.

"No idea, he just left. He doesn't talk much that one, and only has men round..." She left the statement hanging, letting Harvey come to his own conclusions. He realised that he wasn't going to get much from this homophobe, so he told her he would try next time he was in town and returned to his car. Once inside he called Hamad Farsi. "Get anything?" he asked him.

"Len Smart wasn't home, but Carl Levine's wife said he went on a job last week. He told her it was a two-week bodyguard assignment for a visiting dignitary, and she has no reason to doubt him as that's how he earns his living."

"Okay, check that out with Gray's old company, see if Levine is still on their books. If he isn't, get onto all the security firms in the area to see who he's signed up with." Harvey hung up, then called Diane Lane. "What news?" he asked.

"No joy. I've been to all three properties and none of them are there. I got no answer from Paul Bennett, and Jeff Campbell's wife said he was on an assignment. Same with Colin Avery."

"Both two-week assignments for visiting dignitaries, by any chance?" Harvey asked.

"Those exact words," Lane confirmed.

"Then these are our guys. One or two being away is possible, but all eight? I don't think so. Pass their names to Special Branch and tell them it's a priority. We need to find these guys, and quick."

Tom Gray woke after forty minutes and checked his monitors. The two men were still lying behind the wall, but their command structure had moved in, setting up three vehicles in the lane which ran parallel to the building, two hundred yards from the rear wall. Gray guessed they had closed the lane to prevent the press and members of the public from getting too close. They had also set up a perimeter around the area, with men stationed a hundred feet apart and looking out rather than towards the building. Not only did this suit the authorities by keeping nosey civilians and the media at arm's length, it made life easier for him by preventing those same people setting off his motion sensors every two minutes.

He turned his attention to the TV and caught the tail end of the five o'clock news. They were showing a press conference held by Greater Manchester Police, and Simon Arkin's mother was making an impassioned plea for his release.

"I am asking the people of England to vote for my son's freedom. Yes, he may have a criminal record, but he has been to court and he has been punished."

Gray watched as she struggled to compose herself, before she gave up the fight and burst into tears.

"I just want my boy back."

The Chief Inspector reiterated her plea for the population to do the decent thing before they cut back to the studio. Gray picked up his mobile phone and dialled a pre-set number.

The BBC news anchor had just finished reading the headlines at six o'clock when she paused for a moment and listened to the message in her earpiece.

"I'm told we now have Tom Gray from the Justice For Britain website on the phone. Mr Gray, thank you for speaking to us today."

"Hello, Charlene."

"Mr Gray, I imagine the first question the viewers would be asking is 'why exactly are you doing this'?"

"You know, a few people have asked me that today. My answer is, to ensure that when criminals are caught, they are punished."

"But as we have just heard from Mrs Arkin, her son was caught, and he has been punished. We also have a justice system that ensures people are punished appropriately. Why do you think we need to change the current system?"

"I think it needs to change because the word punishment is being used without anyone properly interpreting the definition. Punishment means any change in a human's surroundings that occurs after a given behaviour or response which reduces the likelihood of that behaviour occurring again in the future. This means that to punish someone is to make them think twice about doing it again. As you can see from the list of convictions on the website, none of the criminals I am holding have had any kind of sentence that made them think twice.

"Let's take Stuart Boyle, for instance. After killing my son, he spent less than eight months in custody. If that was meant to teach him a lesson, it failed badly, because he has been convicted of car theft three times since his release."

"But surely killing him is a bit extreme. We don't even have the death penalty for murder."

"Well, that is what this week is all about. Is it too extreme, or has he shown that his only purpose in life is to cause misery to others? If his only contribution to our society is going to be stealing other people's hard-earned possessions, should we have to put up with that? Anyway, I am not the one to decide if he lives or dies; it is the choice of the people. If the people think he should be set free, he will be set free. If they think he should die, he will die."

"Mr Gray, it sounds like you are trying to deflect the blame away from yourself and on to the people of this country, but the fact remains that it will be you that pulls the trigger, as it were."

"I am not trying to shift the blame, Charlene. If I kill any of these boys, then I will be guilty of murder, plain and simple."

"What do you say to suggestions that anyone who votes for the boys to die is an accessory to that murder?"

"I heard the suggestion that voting for a boy to die makes you an accessory to murder, and I think it is ludicrous, something thought up by the government to dissuade people from voting. If twenty million people vote for Simon Arkin to die, what is the government going to do to them? Imprison them all? Fine them all? Every single case would have to go to court and that would cripple the judicial system that everyone suddenly seems to cherish."

"What is your suggestion for dealing with repeat offenders, Mr Gray? Do you think they should all be killed?"

"Actually, Charlene, that's what I called about. The guests you have had on this show seem to think that my only objective is to kill these five people. If that was the case, they would all be dead by now.

What I really want is to get the people of Britain, and more importantly, the government, thinking about introducing punishments that will eradicate recidivism.

"If your viewers go to the website they will find a new link which says 'Justice Bill' at the top of the page. If they click this link they will see my recommendations and will be able to vote as to whether or not they support it or are against it."

The anchor paused a moment as voices passed on the next question. "What recommendations are you making, Mr Gray?"

"First of all, no more hiding behind the Human Rights Act. When a crime is committed, someone's human rights have been violated. The person who commits that crime should have their human rights revoked.

"Secondly, the re-introduction of corporal punishment for second offences. First offences can be dealt with as they currently are, but if someone re-offends they will be birched.

"Next, repeat offenders will be fined the amount in police man hours it cost to bring them to justice. This will mean we can afford more police on the streets.

"For third offences, conscription. Criminals will be drafted into a special regiment in the Army and paid minimum wage, with food and board deducted at source. From their remaining salary they will be given thirty percent and the rest will go towards paying for the police time it took to bring them to justice. On top of that, they will pay compensation to their victims. Finally, they will pay £3000 towards the cost of forming the new regiment. Once these debts have been paid off, they will spend a further five years in the Army on normal salary."

While Gray was reciting his list, the anchor was receiving yet more instructions from her producer. "Mr Gray, what if a second offender cannot pay the amount you are suggesting?"

"Then they are conscripted."

"And what if they don't co-operate once they are conscripted? What if they refuse to follow the Army regimen?"

"Then they are sent to prison for as long as it would have taken to pay off their financial debt, plus ten years. And when I say prison, I mean a real prison, not the cosy hotels we currently have. There are more details of my idea of prisons on the website."

"So what about..."

"Sorry, Charlene, but I have said my piece for today. I will call again tomorrow after the government have given their assessment on my suggestions."

Gray hung up, satisfied that he had handled himself well. He had faced enemy fire, but that was nothing compared to a phone call with a few million eavesdroppers.

With the time approaching six-thirty in the evening he checked the number of votes cast: there were almost four million and it wasn't looking good for Simon Arkin.

Chapter 7

John Hammond walked past Harvey's desk and gestured for him to follow. They headed for Gerald Small's office where they found him deep in conversation with the contractor.

"Gerald, what's the latest?" Hammond asked.

"Alan here has been through the site with me and confirms that there are no booby traps. However, the results aren't counted here. When Gray clicks a button, the website speaks to the South African web service and it sends back the two counts."

"That's right," the contractor said, "Gray told me that he had commissioned other software in Jo'burg and all I had to do was send the IP addresses to his email address when the site first kicked off, and get the votes from this web service."

"Would it be possible to alter this code to change the results in our favour?" Hammond asked Small.

"Sure, that would only take one line of code. However, he gave us easy access to this code, knowing that we would be able to alter it. My guess is that he has other software and this website is just to test us, to see if we interfere with it. I doubt that he is relying on the results this website will display."

Hammond thanked the contractor for his time and asked one of the techies to show him out, then asked Small about the other software.

"That," Small said, "remains a mystery. We got in touch with the company he paid the fifty grand to, but they were simply instructed to source a developer and pass the details on to Gray. They did just that and got five grand for their trouble. We tried contacting the guy they commissioned but there was no reply, so we tried the airlines and he boarded a plane for Manila two days ago, due to return in three weeks time. The ticket was purchased last week."

"Which means we have no idea what traps he has in place for us?" Harvey guessed.

"Exactly." Small confirmed. "We're blind. Once the emails get to his inbox we have no idea what he is doing with them."

"Then we go with the first choice," Hammond said. "Intercept the emails before he gets them and change the odds in our favour. Do it now, we have less than an hour before voting closes."

Small had everything prepared and with a few keystrokes he announced it done. "Every second and third email with 'Die' in the body will now be changed to 'Live'," he announced.

"Why second *and* third?" Harvey asked.

"If we only do the second," Small explained, "the first and second votes will simply cancel each other out and we will be relying on people to send in freedom votes. This way, for every three death votes we turn them into one net freedom vote. If he is watching the figures in real time he will still see death votes coming in, but there will be a surge in freedom votes. He will hopefully put it down to the mother's plea."

"Okay," Hammond said, "while we're waiting for the results, check with the Met, find out how they are doing with the search for the device."

Harvey nodded and on his way to his desk he stopped off at Farsi's station. "Anything in the boys' reports?" He asked.

"There were two cases where the kid who was abducted was with his mates. I think we should get them in and show them some mug shots of our suspects."

"Good idea. Go for it." Harvey saw Hammond heading for his office and stopped him to explain their plan.

"That could be very useful," Hammond agreed. "Gray has no family, so if we can implicate his old army buddies we might have some leverage. He must have some allegiance to them, and they to him, so if we can pin the abductions on them we might be able to convince him to end this."

Harvey saw what Hammond was thinking. "We can tell Gray they will get immunity from prosecution if he gives himself up, otherwise we charge them with kidnapping, ABH, accessory to murder, various offences under the Terrorism Act and send them to jail for life."

"My point exactly."

Harvey turned to Farsi. "Get on to the company he sold and tell them to send over photos of everyone on their books, past and present, then arrange for them to be distributed to the police forces handling these cases."

* * *

44

Harvey was going through the incoming reports from the dozens of police forces around the country. So far they had identified, between them, over a thousand locations that would normally have thousands of visitors at midday on Friday. Many had already been searched and discarded, but at the current rate, there would still be over three hundred to search when the deadline arrived. Shopping centres were being asked to utilise all available staff in searching their own facilities, as were other venues such as exhibition centres and museums. Despite their efforts, though, police were still required to visit each site and give it the once over before it was given the all clear.

Even if all possible venues were cleared before the deadline, there was always the possibility that the device might be mobile and delivered much nearer the time, negating their efforts. The only way to be certain was to get Gray to reveal the location, but he had stopped answering his phone and certainly wasn't going to give that information up readily. If they could just get a break somewhere along the line they might stand a chance of stopping this, but as things stood, Gray still held all the best cards.

He glanced at his watch and saw that the voting would close in ten minutes: time to visit Gerald and see how things were progressing.

At Small's desk he found him staring at the screen. "How's it going?" Harvey asked.

"The numbers are working in our favour. Around seventy five percent of them wanted Simon dead, but that has swung our way now, with seventy five percent wanting him to be set free."

"How does that affect the overall result?"

"That, we don't know. The exchange server is simply a relay, forwarding the emails onto another server, so we don't have a history to look at."

"So we just cross our fingers and hope?"

"Yep, that's all we can do now. Thing is, though, even if we didn't manage to do it in time to save Simon, it should save the lives of the others."

"If he falls for it."

Harvey went to Hammond's office to see what he made of Gray's list of proposed law changes. "Is there anything sensible in his justice bill?"

"On the face of it," Hammond said, "the public will probably lap this up, but some of it just isn't possible — his idea of a real jail, for starters."

"What is he suggesting?"

Hammond looked through the printout to find the details. "Each prisoner will have their own cell, and they will stay in there for twenty-three hours a day. Meals will be served in their cells. There will be one hour of exercise per day, each person in a separate compound, and no contact between prisoners whatsoever. Each prisoner will be given work to do in their cell, and if they meet their daily target they get eight hours pay at minimum wage, minus food and board, plus two hours of television. If they don't meet their daily target they get another day added to their sentence and no pay. Once they have paid off the cost of their prosecution they have the option of moving into the prison population to serve their sentence, or remaining on their work schedule and taking courses to give them a chance on the outside. If they do this, they get extra privileges, such as more TV and more exercise time, and each extra day of work takes two days off their sentence."

"Sounds like he's got it all worked out. Does he say what kind of work they would be doing?"

"To start off with they could assemble pens and other items that require little quality control. The courses will be in areas such as website design, computer maintenance and office skills. Registered charities will be able to commission websites, get their PCs fixed, and so on."

"I guess he wants to revoke their human rights so that they can be forced to work."

"It certainly looks like it," Hammond agreed. "That, and the reintroduction of the birch."

"Reintroduction? I thought the birch was only used on the Isle of Man," Harvey said.

"More recently, yes, but my father told me about the time he was given six strokes on the bare arse when he was a teenager. He was one of the last to get the birch, and the judge told him that if he had been a little older he would probably have been given the cat o' nine tails. My father said it was a very effective form of punishment, and looking back he said it was a shame they abolished judicial corporal punishment in 1948."

46

"Perhaps Gray has a point. When I was at school they had the cane and the slipper, and it made you think twice."

"Yes, Gray mentions that, too. He claims that back in the eighties there was none of the anti-social behaviour that plagues our country today and he thinks it is because schools knew how to discipline kids. These days, teachers can't even shout at their pupils without being sued by the parents."

"Is he demanding that these changes are implemented before Thursday?" Harvey asked.

"No. Again, he wants the people to decide. He wants the government to promise to hold a referendum one year from now, but only if the majority of the votes through his website are for his proposals. He says that holding a referendum gives both opponents and supporters of the changes the chance to put their arguments forward."

"So they should promise him a referendum, and when it's all over they can retract."

"Oh, our Mr Gray thought of that, don't you worry. He said the government can refuse to hold a referendum if they wish, but in doing so they admit that they are happy to let repeat offenders back on the street time and time again. With the whole country glued to this story, and with millions of them having been victims of crime in recent years, I don't think they will be very popular at the upcoming election. If they promise to hold the referendum and retract later, they will be seen to lie to the people."

"It looks like Gray has it all worked out," Harvey said. "Mind you, he has had months to prepare this, and we only have days to stop him."

"That's usually the case, Andrew, but they never think of everything. We just have to find the one flaw in his plan." Hammond rose and put on his jacket. "I'm going to grab some dinner before the main show. I'll be back before eight-thirty."

Hammond left the building and pulled his collar up to combat the evening chill, hoping that his assertion was correct and that there was indeed a flaw in Gray's plan.

In his thirty-seven years in the service he had been through many scrapes and overcome many adversaries, but the vast majority of the time they had been aware of the threat early on and had the time and resources to deal with it. Tom Gray had turned all that on its head, putting them on the back foot from the start and leaving them very little room for manoeuvre.

If there wasn't a flaw in Gray's plan, if this was a no-win situation, then people were going to die and there was nothing he could do about it.

Chapter 8

"Hi.

"Well, it's time to find out what will happen to Simon Arkin. I'm not going to hype this up because this isn't something I'm relishing. I am only doing this because I personally think the government have failed us when it comes to punishing criminals, repeat offenders in particular.

"The results will appear on your page any moment now. There is no need to refresh your browser, it will do it automatically." Gray stared off to the left of the camera, his face illuminated by the reflection of the web page he was studying. He looked over to the right of the camera, then back to the web page. After a few moments of contemplation he addressed his audience once more.

"You will see that the majority of the votes on your screen want me to free Simon Arkin. The results are: Live, four million, eight hundred and six thousand, two hundred and five; Die, three million, six hundred and fifty one thousand, eight hundred and eighty four."

Gray stood and positioned the camera towards Simon's cell. He entered, moved to his right and put his hand out towards the wall. Moments later the single bare bulb suspended over the struggling prisoner flickered into life.

Harvey, Hammond and Small, along with millions of others, watched as Tom Gray stood in front of Simon Arkin, staring at the figure in the chair. Harvey was about to refresh the page, thinking the feed had frozen, when Gray suddenly drew his weapon, an automatic pistol, and fired a single shot. The execution was obscured by Gray's frame, but as he approached Arkin and checked the pulse on his neck, Harvey saw a red patch growing around the slumped figure's heart.

"Shit," Harvey muttered.

On the screen, Gray turned off the light and closed the cell door before returning to speak to the camera. "I have several computers based around the country, each one sending emails at the rate of one per minute, using a different email address each time. These emails are stored in a database which matches the outgoing email database,

49

and checks that each has arrived and that they haven't been tampered with. All of the emails had 'Die' in the body, but they were never counted in the final vote. However, it seems that a number of them have been changed to 'Live' along the way.

"We will never know the actual results, because the Government have interfered with the voting. I asked them not to interfere. In fact, I think I made it pretty clear that they shouldn't interfere, but they ignored my warnings. That is why Simon Arkin won't be going home today."

Gray spent a moment on his laptop, then addressed the camera again.

"Okay, the database has been reset, and voting for the next candidate — Adrian Harper — starts now. Adrian is 19, from Gravesend, Kent, and his crimes include aggravated burglary, assault, and numerous counts of theft of a motor vehicle. It's time to get emailing. Don't forget to vote on my proposed law changes, too. Just click the 'Justice Bill' link at the top of the screen for further instructions."

Gray sat back in his chair. "I will be back at the same time tomorrow, when hopefully the results will reflect the views of the people of Britain, not the views of the government."

* * *

"Shots fired! Shots fired!"

"Understood. Wait one, repeat, wait one." The commander at the scene, Superintendent Evan Davies, had been watching the video feed and heard the report from Sergeant Williams just as the scene unfolded on his laptop. His orders were to observe and report only until he received direct instructions from HQ, regardless of what happened. Headquarters would have seen the shooting, and moments later he got the call he was expecting. "Stand down. I say again, stand down."

"We have shots fired," Davies said, more for protocol than to enlighten his superiors.

"Confirm shots fired, looks like one hostage down. We have no authority to engage at this time, so continue to observe and report only."

"Roger that, observe and report only. Out."

Davies glanced again at the map of the target building and the surrounding area. It was covered with markings showing Gray's defences, and truth be told he was glad their remit was limited to observing and reporting. Davies was ex-Army himself and he knew that a half-decent soldier could prepare formidable defences overnight: Gray had been preparing his for months, and what he saw didn't exactly inspire confidence in a successful outcome.

He had passed these observations on to his superiors and they had acknowledged his assessment, along with his recommendation that this was more suited to the guys at Hereford. He didn't consider this suggestion cowardly, just the optimum way to get things done with the minimum loss of life. His unit had handled many armed sieges with great success, but they had usually been dealing with a single person trapped with nowhere to go, one person who suddenly finds themselves in a situation they never contemplated.

This was a completely different ball game.

* * *

The call from the Home Secretary came three minutes after the shooting, and Hammond took it in his office.

"Tell me I didn't just see a British man execute another British man, on British soil, live on the internet," Wells said without preamble. "The PM is livid."

"Mr Home Secretary, I did explain that the plan to manipulate the votes wasn't guaranteed to succeed, but it was the best — no — it was the only option we had at the time."

"And it got a man killed," Wells shouted down the phone.

Hammond did his best to hold his own temper. "With respect, Mr Home Secretary, even if we hadn't changed the votes, the result would have been the same. The country voted for that young man to die, and I think *that* should concern the PM more, as it shows how out of touch he is with the electorate. At least now the PM can deflect attention from that fact, and spend the next twenty-four hours convincing the population not to sentence the next man to death."

There was silence for a while as the Minister considered the suggestion. "I shall pass that on to the PM, but needless to say he will not want a repeat of tonight's debacle."

The phone went dead and Hammond stared at the handset for a moment before cradling it gently. They now had no way of manipulating the votes, so he had to focus on the two main priorities.

He called Harvey into his office and wasted no time when the group leader arrived.

"Double the efforts on finding that device, and find us something to pin on Gray's associates."

Chapter 9

Monday 18th April 2011

Tom Gray woke just before five in the morning. No-one had made a move on the building and he had managed to grab some sleep just after three o'clock, although the night was far from quiet. Two of his guests had made plenty of noise at around midnight but after ignoring their muffled calls for a while he had eventually shut them up for the night with a few well-aimed blows. Stuart Boyle had also played up for a while but Gray hadn't even entered his cell: he didn't trust himself to show any restraint and now wasn't the time to deal with him. Mr Boyle's day would come, but today wasn't that day.

After checking that the boys were still with him and secure, he scanned his monitors: no sign of any movement except for up at their control vehicle, where a couple of people were standing around drinking hot drinks and looking bored. Not long to go, guys, he thought. This was well beyond their pay grade and it wouldn't be long before the Regiment were called in to take over. It was unlikely that his former colleagues would ever launch an attack, given the consequences and the defences he had put in place, but they need to be ready, just in case the security services discovered his device. While Gray knew they would never find it, they would nevertheless be pursuing that line of investigation rigorously.

He made himself some breakfast and watched the figures on his laptop tick over as he ate. Surprisingly, the Live votes were slightly in the lead, so he checked that his countermeasures were still in place and operational. Everything seemed fine, so he ran a code comparison tool which compared the files on the South African web server with the ones on his laptop: they were exactly the same, which meant the code hadn't been interfered with. Next he ran the duplicate email tool and that appeared to be working, too. If anyone tried to send more than one email from the same email address it would only accept the first as a valid vote: the rest would be recorded on a separate system but not included in the final vote. The same applied to IP addresses, which prevented people from using more than one email account on the same computer. Basically, it was one vote per household. His software had identified over six hundred thousand duplicate emails, which was not unexpected, given the passion some people seemed to have for what was happening.

Gray switched on the news channel and saw a representative from the leading human rights group, Liberty, denouncing his suggestions.

"...is a clear breach of Article Three of the Human Rights Act. How can giving a young person the birch not be considered torture? Article three defines any treatment which causes intense physical or mental suffering to be inhuman, and inhuman acts are defined as torture. I defy anyone to tell me that the birch does not cause intense physical suffering, not to mention the mental suffering that will inevitably go with it."

"So how would you suggest we deal with recidivists, Ms Barker?" the newscaster asked. "As Tom Gray has pointed out, some people have criminal records as long as their arms, and the current system doesn't seem to be helping them at all."

"It sounds like you are in favour of his reforms," the Liberty representative said, much to Gray's amusement.

"Not at all, I'm just trying to engage in an objective debate. You say that corporal punishment is not the answer, so what alternative suggestions do Liberty have?"

Rebecca Barker was clearly annoyed at being put on the spot, and did little to hide her displeasure. "We advocate re-education and community punishments, giving something back to the areas they have affected. Beating criminals has no place in civilised society."

Gray spotted the own goal and watched the newscaster swoop in for the kill. "Are Liberty saying that Singapore, The United Arab Emirates and Saudi Arabia are uncivilised countries?"

"No, of course not," Barker blushed, "but there are thirty other countries that have judicial corporal punishment and some of these are far from civilised nations."

"Such as...?"

"Such as Zimbabwe."

The newscaster nodded, conceding that Barker had made a good choice, but still pressed. "And of course, in Saudi Arabia, persistent thieves have their hands chopped off. This certainly makes it difficult for them to commit the same crime again, yet Tom Gray is not asking the government to go that far."

"Yes, it might prevent a criminal from committing the same offence again, but at what cost? Given one more chance, that criminal might have changed their ways and become an upstanding member of society, but by then he has been robbed of that chance."

"But surely the question is, how many chances does a person need? Is four enough, or seven, or should we go on giving them chance after chance indefinitely? I think Tom Gray's point is that there has to come a time when we say 'enough' and the criminal has to take full responsibility for their actions."

Rebecca Barker was becoming flustered at not winning the argument, so she decided to draw the interview to a close. "We seem to be going round in circles here. Suffice it to say, Liberty's stance is that we strongly condemn any suggestions of re-introducing judicial corporal punishment in the UK."

The newscaster thanked her and introduced the sports reporter, who began with yet another high-profile football manager losing his job after a run of poor results. Gray had little interest in football, so he scanned his monitors and once satisfied that no attack was imminent he prepared a dry breakfast for his guests.

Once they were fed he sat down at the monitors again and scanned the perimeter. Movement on one of the screens caught his eye: a figure emerged from the control vehicle and passed something to one of the men standing around. The man put his cup down on the step of the vehicle and started walking towards the building. Gray kept the camera on him as he closed the distance, and seventy metres from the building the man stopped and held up a large piece of cardboard. On it was written the words "Harvey calling". Gray used the control stick for the camera to move it up and down three times, effectively letting the camera nod his understanding. The figure gave the camera a thumbs-up and Gray watched him retreat before switching his mobile phone back on. It rang within seconds.

"Hello Andrew," Gray said.

"Hello Tom. What you did last night wasn't a very clever move. My bosses are now under enormous pressure to resolve this problem."

"I think it was. I think it showed people that I mean business, and it will remind your bosses what will happen if anyone tries to interfere again. Last night was just a warning, Andrew. The next time I will kill everyone in the building, including myself. That leaves you with the task of finding my device before midday on Friday, and I very much doubt you will."

"That brings me on to my next question, Tom," Harvey said. "How do we know you actually have a device? I believe you, but my bosses and their bosses want proof. If I can't give it to them, they may start to think there isn't a device at all, and that means you lose all of your bargaining power."

In the early days of planning this mission, Gray had expected something along these lines, which was why he had forged close ties with the senior management at a research and development company, a company doing hush-hush work for the Ministry of Defence and specialising in the manufacturing of chemical "deterrents". Having gained their confidence, he had wangled a tour of the facility on the pretence of providing an independent security assessment.

"What you're telling me is that only twenty-four hours into your search and haven't found a thing, and now you want me to hand it to you on a plate, is that right?"

"No, just some solid proof that a device exists."

Gray thought for a moment before answering. "I expect you have been looking for a huge device, haven't you? You're thinking 'he's going to kill thousands of people, so it must be a really big bomb', aren't you? Well, you're thinking too big. Think smaller, think airborne."

"Thanks for that, I appreciate the information, but my superiors will still want proof."

"Fair enough. Have you heard of a company called Norden Industries?"

"Yes."

"If you contact them they will confirm that I have made three visits to the facility."

"Which proves nothing, I'm afraid. I know what they make there, and their stock will be audited on an almost daily basis. If anything was missing they would know about it by now."

"Yes, I saw their audit process, and it is quite thorough in one respect. Their full canisters are checked daily, but it is a visual inspection only, and they don't audit the empty canisters. You take an empty canister, fill it with water, and on a subsequent visit you swap it with a full canister."

Harvey considered the plausibility for a moment, then said "Okay, I'll let my superiors know." He hung up and went straight to Hammond's office, walking in without knocking.

"John, I just spoke to Gray. I managed to get some info about his device but it needs checking out." He shared the information he had gained and waited for Hammond's opinion, which was not long in coming.

"Go down there and see for yourself. Get them to go through the audit process and see if Gray's claim holds water. Let me know as soon as you find out so that I can tell the police to adapt their search."

"Will do. Would you mind calling ahead to explain my visit? It should save time when I get there."

Hammond nodded and Harvey left, grabbing his coat on his way out of the office. After picking up his car from the underground car park he drove north to join the A40 and followed it west until it became the M40. The journey to the facility in the Oxfordshire countryside took just over an hour and after showing his ID he was quickly waved through the gate. The Director of the facility was waiting for him in the reception area.

"Simon Crawford," he said, extending his hand. Harvey shook it and introduced himself before wasting no time in explaining the reason for his visit.

"I need to witness your audit process for myself to determine if there is a weakness that might have been exploited recently. Do you have video surveillance of the storage area?"

"Yes, we digitally record it," Crawford said as he led Harvey to the storage facility.

"How long do you keep the recordings for?"

"Thirty days, in accordance with government regulations."

"When did Tom Gray visit the facility?" Harvey asked.

"He has been here three times. February 8th, February 26th and March 7th."

"So his last visit was more than thirty days ago. Very convenient."

Crawford led him to the storage wing and after passing through two layers of security Harvey was led through a door into an enormous warehouse. Looking left and right he could see over a hundred feet in each direction, and as he followed Crawford he counted off twelve rows of refrigeration units.

"How many fridges are here?" Harvey asked.

"Five hundred and fifty." Crawford said.

"So how many canisters in total?"

"Yesterday's closing count was forty three thousand, six hundred and ten. There will have been a handful more added today."

Harvey walked to a fridge at random and asked Crawford to demonstrate a typical audit. Crawford activated his tablet PC and brought up the stock page relating to the fridge Harvey had chosen. "There should be eighty six capsules in here," he said, and did a swift count to confirm the amount. He then pulled out the first canister. Like all the others, it was a six-inch long cylindrical container with a valve system at the top, rather like a very small SCUBA tank, Harvey thought. It was contained within a Perspex box, and Harvey could see a label on the cylinder. Crawford pulled a pen-like device from his tablet and scanned the barcode, satisfied to see a match on the screen.

"What do you use to generate that barcode?" Harvey asked.

Crawford seemed to squirm at that question and Harvey pressed him on it. "That seems to have hit a nerve," he said.

"Mr Gray asked me the same question, and I told him that it was standard third-party software. He suggested that these labels could easily be replicated and suggested a company which offered a barcode generator with a unique key, so that replication would be impossible."

"And did you take his advice on board?" Harvey asked.

"I passed it along to my bosses, along with his other suggestions, and they took it under advisement," Crawford admitted sheepishly.

"So knowing that the barcode was created using standard third-party software, Gray could easily have made his own, is that correct?"

"I suppose so," Crawford admitted, "but what good would that do him?"

"Off the top of my head, he creates a label identical to one in these fridges. During his first or second visit he steals an empty canister and photographs a label from one of these canisters. He takes the empty canister home, fills it with water, creates the appropriate label and on a subsequent visit he switches canisters, meaning one of these canisters now contains water and Tom Gray is threatening the country with something very nasty. How does that sound?"

Crawford ran through the scenario and matched it with the current security procedures. Harvey watched as the colour drained from his face. "But how would he make the swap?" Crawford asked. "He was accompanied by a member of staff at all times."

"A simple diversion would be my guess. Unfortunately you don't have video surveillance for any of his visits, so we can't say one way or the other that he actually managed to make a swap. With that said, I want you to take a sample from each of these canisters and make sure they contain what they should contain."

"But that's over thirty-four thousand canisters! It will take weeks to test them all because each canister will have to be checked manually to determine the contents."

"Can't you narrow it down to agents that will kill thousands if dispersed at altitude?"

"Mr Harvey, we don't make deodorant or perfume here. *Everything* in this room has that capability."

"Then I suggest you get started," Harvey told him. "I don't care if you have to hire extra staff and work three shifts a day, I want every canister checked. If you have any issues with this, please let me know and my boss will only be too happy to have a word with the Home Secretary and the Defence Secretary. Your career will be over before you can say 'how the fuck did I end up on the dole'."

He walked towards the exit and had to wait for Crawford to gather himself before he joined him and took him to the facility entrance. Once outside, Harvey thought he may have been too harsh with the director of the facility. With this being a government-run facility, his hands were probably tied when it came to the budget, and he probably had request after request denied by his bosses who would then blame him for any shortcomings. This particular incident wasn't going to sit nicely with them.

Still, they were facing a crisis, and there wasn't time to play Mr Nice Guy, so he dismissed the thought and called Hammond to pass on the news. "The threat is credible," he told his boss.

"What did he take?" Hammond asked.

"We don't know if he took anything, yet. However, if he managed to sneak out with a single canister, the results aren't going to be pretty." He described the canisters so that Hammond could pass the information on to the Police, and then got into his car for the drive back to Thames House. A whole day had been wasted looking in the wrong places, which left just four days to search the whole country for a device the size of a can of hairspray. Needle in a haystack just didn't come close.

Chapter 10

Evan Davies climbed out of the command vehicle and went to meet the occupants of the black Land Rover which had just pulled up. He was surprised to see just two figures, the driver and passenger, emerge from the vehicle. The passenger approached and offered Davies his hand. "Major Sean Blythe and this is Sergeant Todd Dennis. We'll be taking over command of this operation."

Davies introduced himself and led them into his command vehicle.

"Have you been in contact with him?" Blythe asked.

"No," Davies said. "We do have a couple of mobile numbers for him, but we just get voice mail every time we try." He brought out a map of the building and surrounding area. "These are the defences we have been able to identify so far," he said, gesturing to the area representing the back of the building. "He has wall cameras mounted here, here and here, each of them multi-directional. In the clear ground he has a maze of razor wire, with a few land mines thrown in for good measure. We have been unable to penetrate any walls using thermal imaging as he has some kind of heated insulation, and directional microphones are just getting white noise from the building.

"The same goes for the two sides of the building, and most of the front as well. The only exception is a path leading up to the main door. The path itself is one metre wide and concrete all the way to the door. The razor wire stops either side of the path, so you have a clear walk up to the front door. Why he left the path clear, I don't know. From what he said on the website, I don't think he's planning on coming out, and I shouldn't think he'd want to give an assault team a clear run at the building."

"He most likely did it so that the hostages that are freed don't blow themselves up on their way out," Dennis suggested, "but we should also view it as a bottleneck. By offering us this route in he is concentrating bodies into a small area, which means a couple of well-placed Claymores and anyone on the path is spaghetti."

"So, going in on the ground is going to be tough, which leaves an assault from above or below," Davies said. "The roof has razor wire all over it, as well as some packages which we can't make out. They

60

could be explosives, we just don't know. There is a large sewer complex under the building, but if you consider the path a bottleneck, the sewer will be a whole lot worse."

Dennis studied the map, frowning in concentration. "It's all academic at the moment, as we can't go in until his bomb is located. However, we need a plan in place for that eventuality. Do you have schematics for the interior?"

"We've requested them, they are on their way over," Davies told him.

"Okay, let me know when they arrive." Dennis folded the map and stuck it inside his leather jacket, excused himself and swapped the command vehicle for his own. He drove off in the direction he had come from, and mentally prepared the briefing for his troops. They were going to like this as much as he did, and he didn't like it one little bit.

* * *

As the man walked into the mosque he got a few cursory glances from those making their way out, but nothing more. He sat on a bench and removed his shoes before striding across the prayer floor towards the Imam's personal quarters, and at the door he was confronted by two young men who moved to block his way.

"The Imam is busy," the first one told him, holding out a hand to stop the stranger.

"He will see me," the man said confidently. "Tell him I bring greetings from Quetta." He was referring to the capital of the province of Balochistan, forty miles from the border with Afghanistan, and the name struck a chord. The guards shared a glance and one of them knocked on the Imam's door before walking in, closing it behind him. A moment later the door opened again and the guard reappeared, gesturing for the stranger to enter.

The Imam stood and came round his desk as his visitor entered the spartan room. The man before him wore traditional Pakistani attire and had a full, thick beard, much like many members of the mosque, but he was certain the man hadn't been to prayers recently. Yet there was something strikingly familiar about the stranger, like a faint memory from long ago, and deep in his mind's eye he found the answer.

"Ahmed?"

61

"Brother," the man said, opening his arms for an embrace which was reciprocated. The Imam then instructed the guard to bring tea and close the door on the way out.

"What brings you back, Ahmed?" The Imam asked.

"I have instructions from our benevolent masters," Ahmed said. "You have no doubt seen the news recently."

"This man holding his own country to ransom? He is a fool."

"Why do you say that, brother?"

"Because he will achieve nothing," the Imam said. "The British government will never give in to his demands."

"They have so far, have they not?" Ahmed pointed out. "They do not attack him because he has put fear in their hearts with his so-called device. And now the time has come to exploit and enhance that fear."

"What do you have in mind?" the Imam asked.

"First I need enough true believers to see this plan through."

"How many do you need?"

"I have a list of men who have been to the training camps and need you to bring them in. We also need as many others as you can find."

"Give me the names and I will bring them to you," the Imam told him. "I can also give you twenty others who are willing to do Allah's bidding."

"Excellent, but time is against us," Ahmed said, "so we must move swiftly. I need these men here by four o'clock tomorrow afternoon. I will reveal the assignment when all are together and, *Inshallah*, we will strike fear in the hearts of these people."

"*Inshallah*."

God willing.

* * *

Tom Gray listened to the news as he scanned his monitors. Nothing was happening outside, and even less was happening on the TV. That was the trouble with a rolling news channel, he thought: unless they had a breaking story it was the same thing over and over again. However, his curiosity was aroused when the newscaster announced an imminent interview with the Home Secretary "...live on air, straight after the weather."

Gray took the opportunity to check on his guests again, then sat down to see what the bloated politician had to say. Stephen Wells was introduced to the viewers and fielded an easy opening question.

"Home Secretary, what progress has been made in the search for Tom Gray's bomb?"

"Police forces all over the country are working day and night to try and locate the device Mr Gray claims to have. Our security services are also working tirelessly to protect the people of this nation. We are confident that we will see a peaceful resolution to this episode."

I'm threatening to kill thousands and he calls it an episode, Gray thought. Talk about playing it down.

"Do we know what kind of bomb Mr Gray claims to have?" the newscaster asked.

"Not at this moment in time, but we are working hard to ascertain just exactly what kind of threat we are dealing with."

The newscaster changed tack, possibly hoping to throw the Home Secretary off his guard.

"What is your response to Mr Gray's proposed law changes?"

The Home Secretary didn't even break sweat. "There are fundamental flaws in Mr Gray's proposals which make them unworkable, I'm afraid. For a start, he wants us to conscript criminals into the Army and give them guns, while we are working hard to take guns out of the hands of criminals. There is also the cost involved in conscription to consider, and we estimate it would run into the tens of millions."

"What about re-introducing judicial corporal punishment?"

"This is the twenty-first century and there is no desire to return to the days of whipping people for stealing a loaf of bread. While the government respects the rights of other countries to use judicial corporal punishment, Britain has a proud history of reform and re-education."

"Does this mean the government will refuse to hold a referendum, even if the people of Britain vote for one through Mr Gray's website?"

"We are currently reviewing the judicial system, and have been for the last few months. While we agree with Mr Gray that something needs to be done, we do not always agree on the way to implement any changes we decide to make. Any changes we make will be with a view to reducing crime and setting higher tariffs for the most serious crimes."

"So does that mean there will be no referendum?" the newscaster pressed. In typical fashion the Home Secretary simply reworded his previous statement, much to the newscaster's, and Gray's, disappointment. The interview continued for a few more minutes, the newscaster switching between simple and searching questions and the politician responding with platitudes and spin.

Gray turned to his laptop while the interview was still fresh in his mind and drafted a response. After an hour of editing he was happy with the copy and picked up his mobile, hitting the speed dial button for the BBC news studio. After a few rings the phone was answered and he gave the password he always used to identify himself. Within seconds was through to the daytime show's producer.

"Hello Paul," Gray said. "I saw the interview with the Home Secretary and just wanted to give my side of the story. Do you have an email address I can send it to?"

"We can put you on the air, Mr Gray," the producer said, thinking of the ratings. However, Gray wasn't in the mood for a series of questions. "No thank you, Paul. Just give me an email address to send it to and you can read it out on air."

"Are you sure? You can make more of an impact with the nation if you..."

"Paul, give me an email address or I call Sky News instead."

Paul Gross reeled off his personal email address and Gray thanked him before hanging up. Within seconds the email was in Gross' inbox and after a quick scan through he forwarded it to the relevant departments with instructions.

Gray only had to wait four minutes before his response was ready to be read out, and he followed every word to make sure it hadn't been edited.

"We have just received a statement from Tom Gray in response to the Home Secretary's earlier interview," the newscaster said. "Mr Gray says '...he would like the nation to hear both sides of the story so that they can make their own choice rather than just accepting the rhetoric the government spew out day after day'."

Gray had wondered if that opening sentence was going a bit too far, but it was too late now.

"The Home Secretary said that I want to conscript criminals into the Army and give them guns: That is far from the truth. My proposal is that conscripts will be non-combatants throughout their probation period, until they have proven themselves and paid off their debt, and all exercises during that time will use blank ammunition. Control of weapons will be ramped up for conscripts, and live fire will only be used after the probation period is up, and only for those conscripts with an exemplary record. Any conscripts who do not abide by the rules will be sent to prison to work out their sentence, which will leave only reformed members of society within the ranks.

"The Home Secretary also states that conscription will cost the nation tens of millions, but as I have already pointed out in my proposal, there were three periods of conscription in the twentieth century: There was the Military Service Act of 1916; the National Service (Armed Forces) Act in 1939; and finally the National Service Act 1948. If conscription could be introduced in the days of paper records, why not now in the twenty-first century? I should also point out that the cost of setting up the new regiment will be recovered from the conscripts' salaries.

"Finally, the Home Secretary said that they prefer reform and re-education to the birch. If reform and re-education work, why are there so many repeat offenders? In 2009, nearly twenty-one thousand offenders who had been convicted or cautioned between twenty-five and fifty times avoided custodial sentences. If they had been birched or conscripted after their second or third convictions respectively this would have prevented between four hundred thousand and one million crimes being committed. Then there are the criminals with more than three but less than twenty-five convictions, and not forgetting the criminals with more than fifty convictions or cautions. If the birch and conscription is introduced it could prevent over four million offences every year. Imagine the saving in police costs, and that is just the ones that were not given a custodial sentence. If my measures were introduced, how do you think the population would react? Would they clamour for these criminals to be set free, or would everyone who has had a crime committed against them in the last twenty years welcome my proposals?

"Finally, Mr Gray wants us to remind you that you can still vote for or against his proposed changes on his website at www.justiceforbritain.co.uk/justicebill. The results will appear on his website tomorrow at midday."

Chapter 11

Hamad Farsi strode over to Andrew Harvey's desk and waited until the group leader finished his phone call.

"Special Branch picked up Marcus Taylor this morning and showed him some mug shots. He picked out Simon Baines."

"Marcus Taylor?" Harvey asked, a look of confusion on his face.

"He was with Joseph Olemwu on the night he was abducted," Farsi reminded him.

"Great news, but it does us no good at all if we can't find these guys. Any news from the security agencies?"

"None. We tried the company Gray sold and while they are still on the books, they haven't had an assignment for the last two months. We also contacted all security firms on our lists and none of them have heard of our guys."

"Have we checked the airports and ferries?" Harvey asked.

"No hits there, either. Unless they got hold of new identities, these guys are still in the country. Gray could have paid for new identities, of course. He has a lot of money unaccounted for, and that's not the kind of thing you buy with a debit card, but some of these guys have families. Do you think it likely that they would abandon them?"

"It's possible, but I doubt it. Let's concentrate our search on guest houses and bed & breakfasts. They may be together or they may have dispersed around the country, so let each establishment know we're looking for one or more men matching their descriptions."

"We can try," Farsi said, "but these guys are used to spending weeks in a hole in the Iraqi desert or a sodden field in Bosnia. They could be anywhere in Britain, and if they don't want to be found they could quite easily make themselves disappear. I think the last place they will choose will be a B & B."

"I know," Harvey said, a little too harshly, "but we have to start somewhere."

* * *

"Sonny, leave that porn site alone and come and butter this bread. These sausages are nearly ready. Oh, and wash your hands first."

Simon Baines clipped Tristram Barker-Fink around the back of the head as he passed. "Cheeky bastard. I was checking the BBC news website."

"Anything new?" Barker-Fink asked as he turned the sausages.

"Nothing in the last hour," Sonny said. "I was looking at some of the readers' comments and there's a lot of support for what Tom's doing. A few nut-jobs want things left as they are but most of them want a change. A couple of them even called him a hero."

"I think they have a point. There must be millions of people who have been victims of crime and millions more who fear becoming victims. This bill of his will make a lot of people feel safer, and it only came about because he is willing to risk everything to see it through. That's some sacrifice."

"If the government agree to implementing it, that is," Sonny said. "If they refuse, this has been for nothing."

"Sonny, if the country vote for this bill there is no way the government can refuse a referendum."

"Of course they can, you know what politicians are like. They can spin it every which way and make it sound like they are doing the country a favour. Look at the expenses scandal: they claim to have cleaned everything up, but then they put a new tax avoidance bill through parliament which closes loopholes for everyone in the country — except MPs, who are still allowed to exploit it. They only care about themselves, and if this bill is going to make life uncomfortable for them, they will drop it like a hot brick."

"We'll see. The results will be in at noon tomorrow and twenty-four hours later we will hear what the PM has to say and this will all be over."

"And in the meantime we're stuck in this fucking barge," Sonny said. "There's no room to move and we can't even stick our heads out the door. It stinks of farts and sweat and all we've eaten is egg banjos, sausage sarnies and fry-ups."

The vessel they were renting was a six-berth narrow boat, although truth be told it was designed more for a family with young children than eight burly soldiers, which explained why two of them had such cramped sleeping quarters while another two slept on the floor.

The Norfolk Broads were relatively quiet at this time of year, and with only one person required to pilot the boat the rest could remain under cover. It had been decided in advance that Carl Levine, with his previous experience of narrow boating, would be the one to show his face, and so he had grown a full face beard and shaved his head. A pair of sunglasses completed the look, which allowed him to be seen on deck without being recognised. It was also his job to procure the food from the local shops, and as his wife forbade him from eating anything high in cholesterol he had chosen everything he had missed in the last five years.

"This is the first chance I've had in the last two years to eat what I want, and I plan to make the most of it," Levine said.

"Why don't you just tell your wife to cook you some decent food?" Avery asked.

"Because my wife doesn't ask me, she tells me. That's the way it is, has been and always will be."

"Carl, I've met your wife and she's a pussy cat," Paul Bennett said. "You keep banging on about her being some kind of monster, but whenever we get together she's always been an absolute diamond."

"Yeah, when you're with her she plays the shy little girl, but once you're gone she chews me a new arsehole for drinking three beers or eating anything containing a gram of fat."

"Then cook something decent when she's at work," Fletcher suggested.

"She can't work," Carl said, "not with what she's got."

"What has she got?" Fletcher asked solemnly, thinking he must have missed some recent news.

"A lazy fucking disposition," Carl said deadpan, bringing chuckles from the others.

"I can't believe you're scared of a woman," Sonny snorted. "If she's always whining, why don't you leave her?"

"For the same reason we don't leave you for whining about the food, and why we don't moan when you snore all night," Carl said from the dining table. "Speaking of food, where are my sausages?"

Barker-Fink brought the pile of sandwiches over and all eight men added their choice of condiments before wolfing them down.

Sonny nudged Len Smart, distracting him from his Kindle.

"What you reading, bookworm?"

"*Fatal Exchange* by Russell Blake. It's about a hot female bike messenger turned judge and executioner."

"Sounds corny," Sonny smirked.

"Stunning would be more accurate," Smart said, returning his attention to the book. "Besides, she'd kick your sorry ass."

"I could murder a beer," Michael Fletcher said to no-one in particular.

"Patience, laddie," Levine said. "A couple more days and you'll get your piss-up."

* * *

At eight-thirty on the dot, Tom Gray sat in front of the web cam and started the video stream. "Ladies and gentlemen, thank you for joining me. I have the results for Adrian Harper."

As with the previous day, he checked the values shown on the website as well as the values sent through his other software. After a moment tapping at the keyboard he looked into the camera.

"As you can see from the results which have just appeared on your screen, the majority of the votes are to free Adrian." He stood up and walked over to the cell holding the second prisoner. After standing in the doorway for a moment, staring at the teenager, he stepped back and closed the door before returning to the camera.

"Adrian will be allowed to leave here on Thursday. The people of Britain have voted and I have found no discrepancies, so I will honour your wishes." After more tapping on the keyboard he addressed the camera one last time. "Tomorrow it is the turn of Joseph Olemwu to learn his fate. Joseph is nineteen years old and has a criminal record stretching back seven years. His speciality is street robbery, but he also has convictions for burglary, assault and possession of a class A drug with intent to supply.

"You, the people of Britain, have already shown that you are unwilling to sentence a man to death. That is understandable, and it is why you have to think carefully about your next choice." Gray held up a weapon and showed it to the camera. There were six thin branches, bound together at the handle. There was more binding up to the halfway point, with the remaining twenty inches allowed to flex independently. "If you think Joseph has had all of his chances, vote 'Die' to the usual email address shown on your screen. If you think he just deserves to be birched, vote 'Live'. If you don't think he deserves either of these punishments, DO NOT VOTE. This will give a true indication of how the people of Britain feel. I also urge you to vote on my justice bill. You can download a copy from this website using the

69

link at the top of the page. Voting on the bill closes at eleven-thirty tomorrow morning, so don't hang around."

* * *

When the transmission ended, Andrew Harvey closed down the browser and turned to his team. "We got lucky today, people, but tomorrow a kid is either going to get birched or shot. Diane, we need that device. He used his position within his old company to gain access to Norden Industries, so maybe he also used that position to gain access to wherever he planted it. Go through his company records to see which businesses he has provided advice to, then search them all." Harvey turned to Farsi. "Hamad, Gray's last visit to Norden Industries was the seventh of March. I want you to put all CCTV from his last address and a fifteen mile radius through facial recognition and see if we can follow a trail. Take it from that date, and use who you need from the training pool to do the same for the other major cities. We need to know everywhere he's been in the last forty days."

Farsi scratched the back of his head. "That's a huge task, Andrew. There must be millions of hours of CCTV to go through."

"I know, I know, but we need something, anything, to get a lead on where he planted that device. Our second priority is finding those who helped him. What's the latest?"

"I passed the assignment to Special Branch as you asked, and they'll be asking plod to make enquiries. They have recent photos of all eight men and local forces will be going to all B & Bs in their own districts. Do you want me to pass it to the media, too?"

Harvey thought for a moment. "Do it. Tell them these people are not to be approached, we just want information on their whereabouts. Diane, get on to GCHQ and ask them if they can trace any signals going into Gray's location. If someone calls him, can we identify the source?"

Lane nodded and went to make the enquiry. She returned a few minutes later to inform him that it could be done.

Harvey thanked her and went to share an idea with his boss. He knocked on Hammond's door and waited to be called in. "My plan," he said, "is to give the mug shots to the media and after a few hours we release a statement saying we have arrested these men. Hopefully this will either get Gray to contact them, or one of them to contact him."

"Or let Gray know that we are desperate," Hammond offered.

"And he'd be right, but I was thinking of giving them time to contact each other and then release a statement saying it was mistaken identity. He must appreciate that that kind of thing might happen, especially with the whole country on alert."

"Okay," Hammond said after a moment, "release the details to the media and announce the arrests four hours after it goes out. Give it another three hours and say it was a mistake. If they haven't been in touch with each other by then, they are unlikely to fall for it. It's getting late, so release the pictures to the media now but leave the arrest announcement until the morning when they are more likely to see it."

Harvey nodded and left to pass on the instructions. At his desk he found several updates on the internal messaging system and he flicked through them, assigning them to the relevant operatives, annotating them with his own notes and instructions. He was coming towards the end of the list when one particular name caused him to search his memory.

Abdul Mansour.

He knew the name but couldn't quite place it, so he searched for his file and brought up the summary page.

Abdul Mansour was listed as having been responsible for training a terrorist cell which was smashed in 2009. The cell had been planning an attack on a shopping centre in the capital using Heckler and Koch MP-5K machine pistols and dozens of homemade pipe bombs, but unwittingly they had taken an MI5 operative into their fold. Two of the terrorists had travelled to Pakistan to one of the many training camps located near the Afghanistan border, and on their return they mentioned that they had met Mansour. He had been unknown to MI5 prior to their visit but by their accounts he was an up and coming figure in the Taliban. It was Mansour who had led their training and he had possessed an extensive knowledge of London, leading the security services to wonder if he was in fact a British national.

Their investigations led them to conclude that Mansour was in fact Ahmed Al-Ali, a student from Ladbroke Grove. His parents arrived in the UK from Pakistan in the late eighties and Ahmed was born a year after they were naturalised as British citizens.

71

Al-Ali had been a bright student with good grades. As a teenager he had been spotted on several anti-war protests and was known to frequent a mosque the security services had taken an interest in. In 2007 he had boarded a flight to Pakistan with minimal luggage and that was the last they saw of him. Sources in Pakistan had no information on him, and it was only a few months later that Abdul Mansour came onto the scene.

His name first came up when a member of the Taliban was captured and interrogated by the CIA. Mansour had been seen with several other high-ranking members and the description offered sounded a lot like Al-Ali, except he was now sporting a full beard. As was typical of the CIA, they decided to keep this information to themselves, and it wasn't until his name had been mentioned in 2009 that MI5 asked them for any information they had on him and the link was made.

However, when the CIA reported Mansour as having been a victim of a drone attack in January 2010, in which several insurgents were killed just inside Afghanistan, his file had been closed. Now, it seemed, the facial recognition software at Heathrow airport had found an eighty percent match for Mansour based on his student ID photograph. The alert had been downgraded due to his current status — deceased — but had been recorded nonetheless.

Harvey passed an annotated version of the alert to the analysts, asking that it be passed to one of the juniors to see what they could find out about the passenger, a Pakistan national named Rahman Jamshed. It would probably come to nothing but it was good experience for them.

He yawned and rubbed his eyes. A glance at his watch told him that he had arrived in the office over fourteen hours earlier. Time to head home and get some rest, he thought, although no matter how tired he was, he knew sleep would not come easily.

Chapter 12

Tuesday 19th April 2011

Sally Clarkson turned on her computer and immediately took the novel from her hand bag, opening it at the book mark. The computer, like all others in the building, held her information in a central repository rather than on the local hard drive. This way, if her computer was corrupted or the hard drive failed, she would not lose any of her work. The downside of this was that it took around five minutes to load the security profile and she used this time to catch up on her favourite detective series. She was just about to find out how Lester Stone was going to escape from the furnace when her computer beeped, announcing that it was ready for her user name and password.

Putting her book to one side, she entered her details and hit the Enter key. A few moments later her profile appeared and she went straight to her email inbox. There were only three messages, none of which were of any importance. She then opened the internal messaging system and saw the message from Andrew Harvey.

Her heart began to race as she read the message and instructions: a real investigation at last. After eight months of learning the service processes and policies followed by filing, classifying and looking for trends in the volumes of available data, she was finally getting to do some real detective work.

Her love of crime stories had begun in her late teens and her personal library of detective novels filled three shelves in her one-bedroom apartment. At the age of nineteen she had applied to be a Metropolitan Police officer and had attended the one-day assessment at Hendon, but during one of the role play scenarios she had shown that she was easily intimidated and didn't have the ability to assert herself in pressure situations.

With her detective career over before it had begun, she had then turned her attentions to the Security Service, hoping to get a role as an Intelligence Officer, but her test scores had been slightly too low for that role. They were, however, good enough to qualify for an Intelligence Analyst position, and she had jumped at the chance.

She sat back and tried to steady her breathing.

Right, where do we begin? The airport, of course. Sally looked up the access page for immigration control and sifted through the entries for the previous day, filtering the results by flight departure point. Within seconds she had the entry for Jamshed, Rahman and looked through the details. He had a six-month visitors' visa and had given his address as Green Street in Forest Gate, a largely Pakistani community.

Sally Clarkson printed out both the airport image and the image of Ahmed Al-Ali and put them in her bag. After checking that she had her smart phone she locked her computer and headed downstairs to arrange her cover details.

* * *

The BBC News channel had been running pleas by the parents of two of his remaining hostages for the previous twenty-four hours and it was beginning to bore Tom Gray. Both sets of parents were saying the same thing; that their son was a good lad and didn't deserve any of this. Yes, proper little saints, Gray thought, as the sequence began again for the umpteenth time. However, once it had finished the newscaster announced that the parents of the other boy, Joseph Olemwu, would be speaking to them live in the studio after the weather report.

Gray had a quick scan of the monitors, and satisfied that there would be no interruptions in the next few minutes he sat back to watch, hoping for something more original from this family.

He wasn't disappointed.

The parents were introduced as Olefina Olemwu and Michael Vincent. The mother was in her late forties and had probably been quite a catch in her youth, but the years hadn't been kind to her. The father, in his fifties with a short white beard and shaven head, sat a good nine inches taller than her. It was clear from the outset that while the mother simply wanted her boy back, the father's only intention was to have a dig at the authorities.

"I want to know what the police are doing to rescue my boy," was his opening statement, before he had even been asked a question.

"Mr Vincent, I'm sure the police are doing everything in their power to try and resolve this without loss of further life," the newscaster said, before turning his attention to the mother. "Mrs.

Olemwu, these must be terribly difficult times for you. What would you like to say to Tom Gray?"

"I want him to think about what he is doing. Joseph may not be an angel but he is loved in the eyes of The Lord just as much as every other person on this planet. It is not for Tom Gray to play judge, jury and executioner: it is God who will guide Joseph onto the proper path."

Before the newscaster had a chance to move on to the next question the father continued his rant. "The police are on Joseph's back day and night, but when this happens they won't do anything. If he was a white kid with rich parents they would be storming that place by now, but because he is just a poor black kid from a council estate they sit on their hands and do nothing."

"Mr. Vincent, if the police were to attack Tom Gray it may well mean the deaths of thousands of innocent people," the newscaster reminded him. "I'm sure this has nothing to do with the colour of your son's skin, or his background."

"You say that, but if it was a white politician's son in there, they would have sent in the SAS, SWAT and God knows who else to get them out. The government just doesn't care about poor black people and this proves it. They are going to sit back while the world watches my son die." Olefina put a hand on her partner's arm to calm him down but he shrugged it off. "This man is a coward but the government is scared of him. He doesn't even have the balls face up to his crimes."

While the newscaster moved on quickly and the producer's voice reminded Vincent to watch his language, Gray smiled and turned on the pre-paid mobile phone which had the BBC news room's number in the speed dial. Once the parents had had their four minutes in the limelight he hit the button, asked for the producer and gave his codeword. Within a minute he was live on air.

"Good morning, Mr. Gray. I understand you are joining us to give your reaction to Mr. Vincent's claims, is that correct?"

"That's right, Sharon. He surely will have noticed that there are five boys here, and only one is black. Therefore his claim that the police are doing nothing because of his son's colour has no merit."

"I was actually referring to his claim that you are a coward."

"Ah. I must admit I found that strange. I am showing my face to the nation, so everyone knows who I am. Does he think I should be braver, like his son, going around in a gang attacking and robbing innocent people, then running off to escape the consequences?"

"Mr. Gray, I think he was referring to the fact that you intend to take your life when this is all over. Isn't that escaping the consequences, too?"

"In case you haven't noticed, Sharon, there is a global recession and Britain didn't escape its effects. The ordinary working people of Britain are feeling this more than anyone, and I don't want to add insult to injury, if you'll pardon the pun, by taking part in a trial which could cost the ordinary taxpayer millions of pounds. This way is much simpler and a whole lot cheaper for the nation."

The news anchor pressed the point. "Couldn't you just plead guilty and avoid a trial, Mr. Gray? Or don't you feel you are guilty of any crimes?"

"Far from it, Sharon. I know I am guilty and deserve to be punished, but once again we come back to the current justice system and the fact that I have been informed that I will face charges under the Terrorism Act. Firstly, I don't consider myself a terrorist and would fight those charges to the bitter end. Secondly, I will also be charged with murder, kidnapping, false imprisonment, assault and a variety of other charges, and even if I plead guilty to all of these charges, the sentence will probably run concurrently. This means that you take the largest penalty and that is all I will serve. I might get thirty years for murder, twenty years for kidnapping, six years for assault, but the most I will serve is the thirty years for the murder.

"I'm sure you're familiar with the phrase 'might as well hang for a sheep as a lamb'. Well, most criminals have this mentality and that is why they commit crime after crime. They know that once they have been caught they can ask for all the other offences to be taken into consideration and their sentence will run concurrently, so they are effectively punished for the latest crime only. My justice bill will do away with this, so that criminals will be punished for every crime they commit."

"So you are saying that you would be willing to plead guilty to a single murder charge?"

"It's not as simple as that, Sharon. The current justice system wouldn't allow the prosecutor to pick and choose the charges I face. That's why it's either a full trial where I can contest some of the charges or I end this as I have always intended, and I have already explained my unwillingness to add to this country's financial burden."

"Moving on, Mr. Gray, the police have given the names of eight people they want to question in connection with your activities. What can you tell me about these people?"

Gray had seen the announcement the previous evening, along with the mug shots of his friends. It hadn't been unexpected, just a little sooner than he had anticipated.

"I can tell you that I know these people, but I don't know why the police want to talk to them. They have nothing to do with this."

"Have they been —"

"Sorry, Sharon, but I came on today to give my reaction to Mr. Vincent's comment. I won't answer questions about these people as they have no connection with what I am doing."

Gray cut the connection before she could start her next question. Had he gotten his point across, he wondered? Only time would tell.

Chapter 13

Andrew Harvey had been at his desk since six that morning. As expected, sleep had been hard to come by and after finally dropping off at three in the morning he'd found himself awake just two hours later. After a quick shower he had set off for the office, grabbing a strong coffee on the way.

As his colleagues began to drift in, he first asked Diane Lane to inform GCHQ to begin monitoring transmissions in and out of Gray's location, then reiterated his request for companies Gray had visited in the last six months. Lane brought the details over twenty minutes later and he saw that there were twelve of them.

"Get this to Special Branch," he told her.

"Already done. There's also a video from BBC news in the archives."

"Gray?" he asked. He had checked the BBC news website earlier that morning but it had contained nothing new. This must have happened recently.

"Yeah. Olemwu's father wound him up and he wanted to have his say."

Harvey found the file in the archives and played it twice. He was hoping that Gray would sound tense, under pressure, losing the plot, but he still seemed as calm and in control as ever. However, it was what he said rather than the way he said it that grabbed him. When John Hammond arrived, Harvey followed him into his office and threw his idea at him.

"I'll have to put it to the Home Secretary," Hammond told him, "but it is all conditional on finding those eight men."

Harvey nodded his understanding and left to speak to Special Branch, asking them to place the call to the BBC. He brought up the BBC news website on his computer and within ten minutes the article appeared next to the Breaking News icon:

Reports are coming in that eight men, believed to be the associates of Tom Gray, have been arrested. The men were taken to separate police stations in London and will be quizzed in connection with the abduction of the five men being held by Tom Gray. Police have revealed no further details at this time.

John Hammond appeared at Harvey's desk. "The Home Secretary has agreed to our suggestion. He wasn't happy, of course, and it is conditional on it happening before anyone else dies."

"Fair enough. I guess another death would make it difficult for him to justify his decision."

Hammond returned to his office and Harvey busied himself as he waited for the call from GCHQ.

* * *

Sally Clarkson drove past the address in Green Street and saw that it was a flat above a clothes shop. She drove on in search of a parking space but these were at a premium, so she pulled into a residential side street and parked outside a semi-detached house. Walking back to the main road, she tried to control her breathing. Easy, girl. All you have to do is knock on the door, ask to see Mr Jamshed and ask him a simple question.

Try as she might, her pulse continued to race, so she found a newsagent and bought a pack of cigarettes and a lighter. Outside the shop she ripped the nicotine patch off her arm, fumbled with the cellophane wrapper on the pack and pulled one out. The first deep drag hit her instantly, making her feel light-headed, and she cursed herself for giving in after three weeks of abstinence. Nevertheless, she smoked the rest of the cigarette and stubbed it out on the pavement. Her pulse was still racing as a result of the nicotine hit, but she felt much more in control, so she made her way to the address.

There was no access from the main street, so she continued along the street until she came to an alleyway leading to the rear of the building. Here she found four kids playing a game which looked like a combination of football and cricket, using an old fruit crate as the wickets. They paused their game as she walked past but were quickly back into their swing as she walked towards the correct building.

She rang the bell and waited for an answer. After a minute she tried again, and was rewarded with the sound of movement behind the door. It was answered by a man wearing shoulder-length dreadlocks.

"Hello," Sally said, flashing her ID and a smile, "I'm Sarah Clark from the UK Border Agency. Would it be possible to speak to Mr Rahman Jamshed?"

Her cover name used the same initials as her real name — and was quite similar — in order for it to be easier to remember.

The man looked at her ID card and shook his head. "You've got the wrong address, lady. There's just me and my daughter, and there's barely room for us two, never mind anyone else."

Sally didn't doubt him: she thought it unlikely that a Pakistan national and a Rastafarian would share accommodation. Which meant that, for whatever reason, Rahman Jamshed had given a false address when he passed through immigration at Heathrow, and that made her heart skip a beat.

After apologising to the occupant for wasting his time she returned to her car, smoking another cigarette on the way. The ten mile drive back to Thames House took well over an hour but it gave her time to plan her strategy.

Her first step was to pull up the CCTV for the arrivals area of Heathrow airport at the time of Rahman Jamshed's arrival. She found him as he walked purposefully through the arrivals lounge towards the exit. Switching to the outside camera she watched him get into a black cab and zoomed in to get the licence plate. After noting it down she got onto the Police National Computer and brought up the owner's details. Armed with his name and address she finally searched the database for his details and got a mobile number, which she called.

"Hello," a cheery voice said.

"Hello Mr. Watkins? My name is Sarah and I am calling from the UK Border Agency. I understand you took a fare from Heathrow yesterday, at around two in the afternoon."

"That's right, an Indian guy. I took him to Kilburn Park tube station."

"Do you know if he went into the tube station, Mr Wilkins?"

"Sorry darling, once they've paid and gone I take no notice."

Sally thanked him and hung up. While Kilburn was predominately an Irish community there were also Indian, Bangladeshi and Pakistani communities in the area, too. Had he gone into the station, or was he staying in the area? She pulled up the CCTV for the entrance to Kilburn Station and opened her packed lunch, knowing that this could be a long day.

Tom Gray was momentarily taken aback when the news anchor announced the arrests of his friends. It had come totally out of the blue and he spent a few minutes considering the implications before coming to the conclusion that it wouldn't affect his plans too much. Having said that, if they had been caught, what had they done to give themselves away? Had they stuck to the mission and the police had just got lucky, or had they been careless?

Andrew Harvey would be in touch, of that there was no doubt, but how should he deal with it? He spent fifteen minutes running the possible conversation in his head before turning his mobile phone on and sitting back to await the call.

But after twenty minutes, none came. He checked the phone in case it wasn't working, but he had a good signal and the battery was fully charged. Should he initiate the call? No, just wait it out.

After another hour had passed he found himself pacing around the room. Why hadn't he called? Was he waiting to verify their identities? Did he want to speak to them before he called? Had they escaped? No, if they had escaped they would...

He slapped himself on the forehead and went to the laptop, bringing up the dead-drop email account and signing in. Both he and his friends had the user name and password to this free account and it had been set up four months ago using false details. A few emails had been sent to various websites asking for information, not because they were pertinent but simply to keep the account from lapsing. Since Sunday afternoon they had created dead-drop emails every 8 hours to stay in touch, but rather than sending them to each other and creating a trail, the emails were saved as drafts. His friends would save a draft with 'Many' as the subject and Tom would read it before discarding it. When Tom wrote a draft he would use 'One' as the subject.

Tom had read the last draft email from them at eight that morning and it had contained the code word that told him everything was okay: Furniture. If he had read "Bathroom," he would have known something was amiss. When he signed in now he found a draft which had been saved forty minutes earlier. He opened it and read the message:

'Furniture — what's going on? It isn't us.'

Gray discarded the draft and created one of his own:

'Furniture — proceed as planned.'

He saved the draft and signed out, relieved that they were sticking to operational procedures, but unhappy at Harvey's subterfuge. Unhappy, though not surprised, and he realised he could turn this to his advantage. He called Harvey's mobile and it picked up on the second ring.

"Hello Andrew."

"Tom. How can I help you?"

"I understand you are holding some friends of mine," Gray said.

"Not us, Tom, Special Branch."

"Why were they arrested? What are they supposed to have done?"

"You know what they did, Tom. We have an eye witness from the Olemwu kidnapping who placed Simon Baines at the scene, and we're waiting to interview another witness to Mark Smith's abduction. We know there's no way you could have done this alone."

Gray remained silent for a few moments, then said "So what happens to them now?"

"Simple. They'll be charged with aiding and abetting, kidnapping, false imprisonment, assault and any other charges that come to light during their interviews. That's before we even get to the offences under the Terrorism Act."

"I coerced them," Gray said lamely.

"Sorry, Tom, that won't wash. Even if I believed you, you couldn't explain that in court as you will be dead by the time it goes to trial. I'm afraid they will have to take their own chances and live with the consequences, as will their families." As he spoke the last words, Harvey hoped they had the desired effect. There was a noticeable pause before Gray responded.

"I want you to let them go, Andrew. Release them and give me assurances that they will never be charged. I've lost my family; they don't deserve to lose theirs."

"If you end this now, agree to come out and give us the location of the device, I'll see what I can do."

"Andrew, if you look through my justice bill you will see that at every stage I am raising revenue to allow more policing, so I am not going to waste a couple of million of taxpayer's money on a trial."

"What if I can guarantee that the only charge you will be faced with is murder?"

There was another pause before Gray asked "I only face murder and my friends go free? No charges, ever?"

"I can't guarantee that there will be no charges for your friends. They might have to face a token charge just to placate the families of the boys you are holding."

"I'll think about it and get back to you."

Gray ended the call and turned the phone off, the beginnings of a smile on his face. A glance at his watch told him he had a few minutes before it was time to announce the result of the justice bill, so he checked the monitors for signs of anything out of the ordinary. What he saw was that the black Land Rover had returned, and climbing out of the driver's side was Sergeant Todd Dennis.

The sight of Todd was a welcome one. A solid NCO, Gray had been his squad leader in Iraq and had been most impressed with his attention to detail and his knack of making the right decision, especially under pressure. That same man was now tasked with finding a way through his defences, and it was reassuring to know that he was not one for taking unnecessary risks.

With nothing else requiring his immediate attention he turned to his laptop to check the results. As had been the trend over the last twenty-four hours, the people were overwhelmingly in favour of a referendum, and he prepared the web cam to share the news.

"Ladies and gentlemen, thank you for joining me today. As you can see from the figures on your screens, the vast majority of you, over seventy percent, are unhappy with the current justice system and want the government to implement my justice bill.

"This, however, is just the first step. You, the public, have told the government what you want, and it is now up to them to decide if they want to listen to you. They may choose to ignore your voice, or they may, with an election looming, choose to give the people what they want by promising to hold a full referendum on Thursday, the third of May, next year.

"To the government I say, make your choice wisely. If you agree to a referendum and renege once this is over, you will be showing the people that you cannot be trusted. You can of course choose to refuse a referendum, in which case you will be showing the people that you are happy with the way criminals and their victims are being treated. I don't want you to make your decision to try and placate me; that is not what this is about. It is about whether or not you are willing to listen to the voice of the people.

"Prime Minister, you have had plenty of time to read through the bill and seek the opinions of your advisors. However, I will give you

83

another twenty-four hours to let the nation know your decision. I would like an announcement to be made at midday tomorrow on the BBC news channel.

"I will be back at the usual time this evening with the results of the votes for Joseph Olemwu."

Gray turned off the Web cam and after checking the monitors again he prepared lunch for his guests. When he removed the tape from Olemwu's mouth, the boy immediately began pleading with him.

"Man, you gotta let me go. My arms and legs are killin' me. I'm gonna get deep vein frombosis or somin'."

"That's the least of your worries," Gray told him. "It's your turn tonight."

"Look, I don't wanna die, man. All I did was nick a few phones and shit. You can't kill me for that."

"It's not up to me. It's up to all the people who have had their phones nicked by little shits like you."

"That's bullshit," Olemwu spat, showing his true colours. "You'll be the one pulling the trigger, so it's your fuckin' choice."

Gray seemed to consider the statement for a moment before replying. "You're right, I suppose. Even if they vote for you to die, I still have the choice of either pulling the trigger or not. I have the chance to do the right thing, because I am the one who has to live with the consequences."

"That's right," Olemwu said, beginning to glimpse hope. "You can do the right thing, man."

Gray rubbed his chin and feigned contemplation. After a while he said "Hmmm. Let me ask you something. When you went to court for the first time, did they send you to prison?"

"No, man, they just gave me a fine and a curfew."

"And did you obey the curfew and stop 'nickin phones and shit'?" Gray asked, mimicking the boy's accent.

Olemwu hesitated with his answer. "No, I —"

"No," Gray interrupted, "you had a choice between taking your punishment and going straight, or carrying on with your old ways, and you chose to break the curfew and continue mugging people. So why should I change my ways when you weren't prepared to change yours?"

Olemwu again struggled for an answer. Gray gave him five seconds to come up with one, but when nothing was forthcoming he ripped off a new piece of tape and put it over the boy's mouth. "It's not all your fault, Joseph. If the courts hadn't been so lenient you might not be here now. However, you *are* here and must face the consequences, just as I will. In the meantime, it won't hurt you to miss a meal. Somehow I always think better on an empty stomach; let's see if it works for you."

He wheeled the trolley into the next cell and prepared to remove the tape from Mark Smith's mouth. "You say one word, the tape goes back on and you starve. Understand?"

The youth nodded his head and Gray ripped the tape off, taking a little of his fledgling moustache with it. Smith began to curse but held his tongue when Gray gave him a stern look. The trolley was wheeled up to Smith's chest and a straw placed in the glass of water, and Gray moved on to Stuart Boyle.

"Not a word," Gray warned him, and ripped off the tape.

"Mister, I'm sorry —"

Gray's balled fist was a blur, and it caught Boyle on the side of his right eye, just below the temple. The boy went limp and Gray put a new piece of tape over his mouth.

"You never fucking learn," he said, wheeling the trolley out of the cell.

With lunch served, Gray turned his phone on and called Harvey.

"Hello Andrew."

"Tom. Have you made your decision?"

"Yes I have. I have decided that as I have just heard from my friends, you were lying to me, and therefore I can't trust you, so the deal is off."

Harvey was confused. He had heard nothing from GCHQ, so how could they have been in touch? Email? Unlikely, as they were monitoring all incoming traffic through his Internet Service Provider. It must be a dead drop email. Damn! How could they not think of that?

"We must have the wrong guys, then," he offered, trying to sound as apologetic as possible.

"Don't insult me, Andrew. You tried to suck them out and it didn't work. I don't like it when you treat me like an idiot."

Harvey held his mobile to his chest as he thought of a reply. "I'm sorry, Tom. However, the offer still stands. We are going to catch them sooner or later, and they are going to face some pretty stiff charges."

"No they aren't, Andrew. Your little stunt has raised the stakes, so if you want me to come in you get me a guarantee that they face no charges whatsoever."

"I'll see —"

"Also," Gray interrupted, "I want the Home Secretary to go live on TV and announce the amnesty. I only face a charge of murder, and they face no charges whatsoever. I also want it to stipulate that we will never face any civil charges, whether filed by these boys or their families. The Home Secretary has to have a copy of the agreement delivered here to me, and a duplicate delivered to the BBC so that they can show it and its contents. I won't have him going back on his word."

"We can make that request, but we can't tell him what to do, Tom. You have to understand that."

"Finally, I am going to put this to the public and let them vote on it."

"Tom, there's no need —"

"In the meantime, anything I do to these boys between now and the time I come out has no bearing on the agreement. If the public vote for Olemwu to die, he will die. If they vote for him to be birched, he will be birched."

"You're asking a lot, Tom."

"That's what happens when you piss me off. Just think yourself lucky that the rest are still alive after your little stunt."

The phone went dead and Harvey cursed to himself as he marched to Hammond's office.

"John, I just spoke to Gray," he told his boss. Hammond sat silent as Harvey went over the conversation and couldn't hide his disappointment when his subordinate had finished.

"The Home Secretary is going to have a conniption fit," he finally said. "How the hell could you forget a dead drop email?"

"I underestimated him," Harvey admitted sheepishly.

Hammond glared at him. Eventually his demeanour mellowed. "At least he has gone for the offer, even if it does have caveats. I just have the simple task of squaring it with the Home Secretary."

As he picked up the phone he gestured with his head for Harvey to leave the room. Harvey was only too happy to oblige. He went to his desk and called Simon Crawford at Norden Industries. While it was possible that the Home Secretary would agree to Gray's conditions it would be preferable to find the device first. If not find it, then at least identify it.

"Mr. Crawford, anything to report?"

"Not yet, Mr. Harvey. So far we have checked over four thousand cannisters but everything is in order. We have three shifts working around the clock and my bosses are not happy about the expenditure."

"Then you should point out that if they hadn't scrimped in the beginning, we wouldn't be doing this. Four thousand cannisters a day is not enough, Mr. Crawford. Is there any way you can intensify the search?"

"I'm afraid not, Mr. Harvey. It is not a case of personnel, but the facilities to check the contents of the cannisters. We simply can't process any more cannisters than we currently are."

"What about spreading the load around other facilities?" Harvey asked.

"There are no other facilities that can handle these compounds. Unless we consider private facilities..." He left the question hanging but Harvey dismissed the idea.

"No, we can't have this going public. Just get back to me if you have any news."

He cut the connection and went to see Gerald Small.

"Any hits from the CCTV?" he asked the technician.

"Nothing yet," Small told him.

"How far have you got?"

"We're doing quite well, actually. I have created virtual machines and loaded an instance of the facial recognition software on each. This lets us divide the work up between the twelve instances, so we are scanning a dozen times faster than we normally would. However, there are a lot of images to go through."

"Can't you make more virtual machines?" Harvey asked.

"Not that simple, I'm afraid. It's a case of processor power, and we are near the maximum as it is. Any more and the whole lot will crash."

Harvey wasn't about to second guess the expert, so he took his leave and went to speak to Special Branch. He had just instructed them to release the statement announcing that they had arrested the wrong people when Hammond summoned him into his office.

"Well, I can't say that was the most pleasant conversation I've ever had," Hammond said. "An election around the corner and there I was asking him to commit political suicide."

"Did he agree to it?"

"Yes, reluctantly, and at a cost. He made it quite clear that heads will roll when this is over. Yours and mine for a start. He also wants us to try and get a hostage freed, as a show of good faith." Hammond sat back in his chair, rubbing his temple. It was a while before he spoke again.

"The deal only stands once Gray agrees to it. We have until then to find an alternative resolution that will save our necks. What progress are we making?"

"Gerald is working hard on tracking Gray's movements in the hours and days following his visit to Norden Industries. If we can follow his tracks we might be able to locate the device. There's little point using police resources to look for his friends now, so we can concentrate them on searching the most likely targets."

Hammond wrung his hands, looking around the room as if for inspiration. "The boys from Hereford say the only way in is to introduce a sleeping agent into the building and move in when it takes effect. However, the chances of being discovered while they try to introduce it are extremely high, given his CCTV coverage. Even if they did manage to deliver it, Gray has been well trained in resisting interrogation and chances are he could hold out long enough for the device to go off. That leaves finding the device as our only option.

"As the deal isn't valid until Gray accepts it, we take advantage of that. We need to find his friends, and we squeeze them for every bit of information they have. Gloves off, if you get my meaning."

Harvey nodded his understanding and left Hammond's office, pulling out his mobile. He thumbed through his recent numbers and called Gray. "Hello Tom."

"Andrew. What did the Home Secretary say?"

"He has agreed to your demands, Tom. He will provide immunity from prosecution for your friends and you will only face the charge of murder. The deal is valid once you accept it."

He paused a moment, considering the best way to phrase the next request. "There is a condition, Tom. He wants you to free a hostage, to give him some political leverage."

"Well, that's up to the public. I'd better go and let them know. In the meantime, I want you to deliver the agreement personally. I'll see you in four hours."

"We need a decision about the hostage now, Tom, otherwise the deal is off. His words, not mine."

88

Gray hesitated for what seemed to Harvey an interminable time. "Okay, you can have one. I will send him out in the next ten minutes, but he has to learn a lesson before he leaves."

"Tom, don't do anything —"

The phone went dead and Harvey put it back in his pocket before sitting at his desk and putting his head in his hands. Sally Clarkson came up and stood next to him waiting patiently for him to notice her, but he was in a world of his own, so she gave a little cough to grab his attention.

"Hi. Andrew Harvey?"

"Yes."

"I'm Sally from downstairs."

This meant nothing to Harvey and his look said as much, so she explained the purpose of her visit. "Sorry. I was assigned the Rahman Jamshed case. I've found something. Well, it might be something, it might be nothing, but, um, well, it seems like he might be up to something."

Harvey grabbed his jacket and put it on. "I'm sorry, Sally, but I haven't got time for this. Just send me a summary and I'll get back to you."

He headed for the exit, desperate for some fresh air and a chance to clear his head.

"But Mr. Harvey —"

"Enough!" Harvey shouted, grabbing the attention of the entire room. All eyes upon him, he put his hands up in apology. He thought for a second of explaining himself, but instead he turned and left the office, the beginnings of a headache forming at the base of his skull.

Chapter 14

Tom Gray dialled the number for the BBC news producer and told him about the latest developments. Within ten minutes he was once again the main story.

"We're hearing about startling developments in the Tom Gray saga," the news anchor told her audience. "Mr. Gray has just informed us that the Home Secretary has agreed to offer immunity from prosecution for all those accused of helping him in his venture. In addition, Mr. Gray has been told that he will only face a single murder charge if he hands himself in and reveals the location of his bomb. In return, Mr. Gray has agreed to release a hostage. At this moment in time we do not know which one it will be, but we will bring that to you as soon as possible.

"We hope to speak to a Home Office spokesperson shortly to see if we can get more details about the agreement. We will also be speaking to our Home Affairs correspondent, John Lythe. Join us again after the weather and news from where you are."

As the announcement was made there was a lot of back slapping and a few high fives on board a narrow boat in Norfolk. One or two wanted to go and grab a few beers to celebrate but Len Smart, always the voice of reason, put paid to that idea.

"Let's see what they have to say," he told them. "Tris, drop Tom an email, see if this is just another ruse."

Tristram Barker-Fink logged into the email account and saw no new messages, so he prepared a draft, saved it and logged out. "He isn't due to check for another three hours, but if this is another wind up, Tom will let us know. I'll keep checking every fifteen minutes."

They all gathered round the small TV and cranked up the sound. After enduring the local travel news and a piece on a local farmer's albino lamb, the focus returned to the main studio.

"You're watching the BBC news at one o'clock. The main headlines: The Home Secretary is prepared to offer immunity from prosecution if Tom Gray gives himself up; Three NATO soldiers are killed in Sierra Leone as tensions rise; and fuel prices are set to rise as the budget kicks in.

"But first to our main story. The Home Secretary has offered immunity from prosecution for the eight people alleged to have been involved in the abductions of Tom Gray's hostages. He has also offered to disregard all charges against Tom Gray with the exception of a murder charge relating to the death of Simon Arkin. In return, Tom Gray has agreed to release one hostage immediately. We don't know who that will be, but will keep you updated on that development.

"The Home Secretary is in our London studio. Home Secretary, thank you for joining us today. Can you explain the reasoning behind this offer?"

The Minister appeared on a large screen off to the anchor's right. "Hello. The reason I made this offer is to avoid any further loss of life, plain and simple. I have personally negotiated the release of one of the hostages, and Mr. Gray has agreed to hand himself in to the authorities if I can guarantee that these eight individuals face no charges. I have looked at their service records and they have served their country proudly in hostile conflicts around the world. I can understand their allegiance to Mr. Gray, however misguided, and have agreed to his request that no charges will be brought against them.

"In terms of Tom Gray himself, I feel it necessary that he face the courts in order to restore faith in our judicial system. I have listened to Mr. Gray's arguments that an expensive trial would not be in the public's best interest and his insistence that he would fight any charges under the Terrorism Act. Having weighed this up, I decided to make the offer so that he could be brought to justice."

"Which hostage will he be releasing?"

"That we don't know, but we expect it to happen in the next few minutes."

"How do you balance your decision with the government's policy of not negotiating with terrorists?" the anchor asked.

The Home Secretary, already briefed on the questions he would be asked, gave the prepared reply. "We stand by our policy of not negotiating with terrorists. In this particular case we are not giving in to his demands and letting him go, we have achieved a situation whereby Mr. Gray will be handing himself in and facing the consequences of his actions."

"Will Mr. Gray be handing himself in immediately?"

"That was our initial request, but Mr. Gray informed us that he would like the people of Britain to make the decision. I therefore expect he will be making an announcement on his website in the near future."

"But what if he were to harm or kill another of his hostages in the meantime? How would that affect the agreement?"

"The agreement does not come into force until Mr. Gray accepts it. Until he does that, we will concentrate all of our resources in resolving this without injury or further loss of life. With this in mind, I urge the people of Britain to abstain from voting on the fate of Joseph Olemwu and the other boys being held by Mr. Gray."

"It sounds, Home Secretary, like you have given him Carte Blanche to do as he pleases with Joseph Olemwu."

"That couldn't be further from the truth, Sharon. If I hadn't made this offer to Mr. Gray we would be in the same situation as we find ourselves now, but I am confident that this agreement can end matters early and justice will be seen to be done."

"One final question, Home Secretary. Will you be releasing a copy of this agreement to the media?"

"Yes, a copy will be made available within the hour."

"Home Secretary, thank you for joining us today."

As the news anchor moved onto the next story after promising more on those developments, Len Smart reiterated his stance. "Sounds like the real deal, but we wait to hear from Tom before we do anything."

They kept one eye on the news channel, waiting for news of Tom's announcement, while his website was loaded on the laptops. After seven minutes the website performed an auto-refresh and the video was ready to stream. Tristram Barker-Fink hit the Play button and sat back so the others could crowd round.

"Ladies and gentlemen, the Home Secretary has made me an offer and I want to once again put it to the people. The offer is to grant immunity from prosecution for the eight men accused - and I stress accused - of helping me in this week's events, if I turn myself in. In addition, I would only face a single charge of murder carrying a full life sentence, meaning I would face no charges under the Terrorism Act and avoid a lengthy and expensive trial.

"These eight men are indeed friends of mine. I have known them for many years and feel confident that a jury would find them not guilty of any charges they are likely to face. However, a trial would not only be an ordeal for them and their families, it would also damage the reputation of our beloved Regiment.

"I said at the start of the week that I would take my own life when this was over as I have already lost my family. However, in order to protect the families of my friends, I will entertain the Home Secretary's offer while leaving the final decision to you, the people of Britain.

"If you think I should hand myself in, send an email with Adrian as the subject and Live in the body of the message. If you think I should refuse the offer and take my own life on Thursday, replace Live with Die.

"When I started this venture I only had the software set up for six rounds of votes: One for each of the boys and one for the justice bill. In order to allow you to vote on my fate I will be releasing Adrian Harper, which is why you must put his name in the subject of the email, not mine.

"Voting starts now and ends at six o'clock tomorrow evening. I will reveal the results an hour later."

The video ended and Michael Fletcher got up to stretch his legs. "Whose turn is it to cook?"

"Yours," the others chorused.

* * *

Tom Gray phoned his solicitor, Ryan Amos, and asked him to take a look at the agreement, just to ensure that it was genuine and it covered the points the Home Secretary had promised. Amos was only too willing to help, having grown close to Gray and his family over the past four years. Tom faxed the document to him and received a call within five minutes to say it was genuine.

"Just to make sure, Ryan, I will only be charged with the murder of Simon Arkin and that's it?"

"Yep, just the one murder charge relating to the death of Simon Arkin, that's what it says."

"And the eight men named on the document will never face any charges relating to what went on in the last two weeks?"

"None whatsoever," Amos confirmed.

"What about any civil proceedings against any of us?"

"There won't be any, according to this."

"Great. Thanks for your help, Ryan."

"Tom, wait. You are going to need help when this is over. Do you want me to be there when you come out?"

"The public haven't voted yet, Ryan. I may not make it out at all," Gray reminded him. "If I do come out, though, then yes, I would like you to be here with that copy of the agreement. As you can see, I've already signed it, just in case. Will that be a valid document in a court?"

"Yes, if you give yourself up before the deadline of seven tomorrow evening, it will be."

"Okay," Gray said, "I'll give you a ring tomorrow. Bye, Ryan, and thanks for everything."

Gray hung up the phone and picked up a small sack before entering Adrian Harper's cell. The boy had been dozing, but lifted his head at the sounds of the door opening, squinting against the light which invaded the dark room.

"Time to go home," Gray said, as he covered the boy's head with the dark cloth bag. "I'm going to untie you now. If you make any sudden moves I'll stab you through the heart. Do you understand?"

Harper nodded like a jack-in-the-box in an earthquake and Gray removed the shackles from his feet and the ropes from his wrists. Harper let out a moan as his hands fell to his side for the first time in days, his triceps burning in protest at the slightest movement.

"Get up," Gray said, and he watched as Harper tried and failed to stand on his own two feet. His legs collapsed beneath him and he lay on the floor whimpering. Gray grabbed him under the armpits and lifted him to a standing position, dragging him towards the exit.

"Hold on here," he said, and moved Harper's hands to the frame of the cell door. "If you let go I'll leave you where you drop and you stay in here."

Harper gripped the wood with all of his might, summoning every last ounce of strength to keep himself upright. When he'd been committing a burglary or evading the police in a stolen car, he'd had a heightened sense of — not fear, but excitement — the thrill of the prospect of being caught. This was totally different, this was fear he had never known, the knowledge that his very life was at risk, not just his liberty.

As Gray had expected, Harper gripped the frame but swung up against the inner wall of the cell in order to support his own weight. He seized the moment and, grabbing the heavy door, slammed it closed on Harper's hands.

The boy collapsed to the floor, his screams muffled by the tape over his mouth.

"Oh, sorry," Gray said, not even trying to sound apologetic. "Let me help you."

He took hold of Harper's hands and, ignoring his protestations, began dragging him towards the entrance to the building.

"I guess you won't be able to break into any homes for a while. Too bad. Still, it gives you time to reflect on what happened here this week."

He didn't know if the boy was even listening, but as he reached the inner door he let go of Harper's hands and grabbed his head, putting his mouth close to the boy's ear.

"This is your last chance to go straight, so don't waste it. The law is going to change and you don't want to be on the wrong side of it."

In order to leave the building they had to go through two doors. Gray had built a wall around the inside of the main entrance, so anyone who made it through the front door would find themselves in a room only four feet deep and ten feet wide, with a sturdy door off to the left. It was secured from the inside by a metal bar which lay inside four strong brackets, two on the door itself and one on the frame each side.

He lifted the bar out, struggling slightly with the weight. It certainly wasn't going to be knocked out of place from the outside, he was sure of that. After dragging Harper through the inner door, again ignoring the muffled screams, he looked at a small screen on the wall which showed a picture of the exterior. There was no sign of anyone lying in wait for him, not that he expected them to.

This door had the same locking mechanism as the inner door, and both opened outwards. This made it doubly difficult for anyone on the outside trying to break it down. He removed the steel bar and pushed the door open, taking in a deep breath. All his preparation, all his planning over the last six months, and he hadn't taken into account the stink of shit and piss that would invade every inch of the building. Chemical toilets would have eliminated the odour better than the wooden boxes they had been sitting on, but then it must have been a lot worse for them than it was for him, sitting atop the excrement all day long in a cell whose door was hardly ever opened. No, it was better this way. He just wished he'd thought to bring a can of air freshener.

With one last tug he pulled Harper into the daylight and left him lying on the concrete path. "Don't move, someone will come and collect you in a minute. If you roll off to either side you will land on top of a mine, and that would be a shitty end to your day."

Looking towards the command vehicle he saw four men making their way towards him, arms outstretched to show they weren't armed. When they got within fifty yards Gray told them to stop and do a three-sixty to see if they had any concealed weapons, but there were none. He motioned for them to continue and closed the door, re-inserting the steel bar. On the screen he watched as they each grabbed a limb and carried the boy clear of the building at a jog, then he went back inside, closing and securing the inner door.

Yes, a can of air freshener would be wonderful.

* * *

Sally Clarkson sat at her desk, hands shaking with anger. How could he be so rude? She had gone to Andrew Harvey armed with vital information and he had treated her like...like the junior analyst she was. Still, he could have at least listened to what she had to say.

After following the trail from Heathrow to Kilburn Park she had brought up the CCTV archive and watched Rahman Jamshed walk towards the station entrance. He had stopped outside the telephone box and put his hand in pocket as if searching for loose change, but once the taxi had moved off he had walked to the junction and turned right into Alpha Place. Once he had turned the corner he was out of CCTV coverage, and two hours of scanning the local streets had produced no results.

This was someone who didn't want to be followed, that was for sure. The question was, what was he up to, if anything? That was the question she had wanted to ask Harvey, but he had been unwilling to listen to her. She felt a wave of self-pity wash over her but knew that she couldn't give in to that emotion, so she mumbled "Bollocks to you, Andrew Harvey," and got down to work.

She brought up the file on Abdul Mansour/Ahmed Al-Ali and looked through his history prior to leaving for Pakistan in 2007. There was a list of known associates and after cross-referencing them she found only two who still lived within three miles of Kilburn Park station. Jotting down their details, she looked for further links with the area but the only one she could establish was the mosque near

Willesden, about two miles from the station as the crow flies. It once ranked quite highly on the watch list but its status had been downgraded in the last year.

Armed with the three addresses, she left the office and went to seek authorisation to perform a surveillance under the Regulation of Investigatory Powers Act (RIPA). After explaining the reason for the surveillance she was given permission and went to the car park to collect her Fiat Punto. Throwing her handbag into the passenger seat, she put the key in the ignition and turned it.

Nothing.

Damn! Not today!

Her battery had been losing its charge overnight for the last week and she had an appointment with her local garage at the weekend, but that didn't help her at this particular moment, so she went to the back of the car and retrieved the jump pack, a small portable battery designed to provide a jump start when there was no vehicle and set of jump leads available.

She connected the jump pack, climbed in and turned the key. The engine caught at the second attempt and she removed the connections before returning the pack to the boot.

As she drove north she formulated her plan. With it being a working day she didn't expect much response from the residential addresses, and besides, with its previous history she expected the mosque would be more likely to produce results. If she got no result there she would park up close to one of the private dwellings and observe any comings and goings.

It took nearly an hour to reach her destination, road works and a minor shunt hampering her progress. As she drove past the target building she was expecting golden minarets or a dome at the very least, but all she saw was a red brick building that could easily have been the headquarters of a small insurance company rather than a place of worship. She drove on until she found a side street to turn around in, then drove back and parked fifty yards from the entrance.

Her watch told her it was just after two in the afternoon. She had no idea what time prayers took place, so she looked up the details on her smart phone. According to the first website she found it would be within the hour, so she opened the window a fraction to let in a breeze and sat back in her seat to wait it out.

The mosque was in a largely residential area with a few shops at the end of the street, and as a consequence footfall was light. A few mothers passed by, children in tow or riding their pushchairs, but generally the street was quiet for the first half an hour. She checked her reflection in the mirror and once again told herself it was time to lose a few pounds. Her face was growing increasingly rotund and her short hair did nothing to hide the fact. If she didn't do something about it while she was in her early twenties it would get much harder as the years passed.

As the time approached the top of the hour people began making their way into the mosque. Most arrived on foot but it was the party of four that pulled up in a battered Nissan that caught her eye. As the front passenger climbed out there was something very familiar about him. She couldn't tell if she had been drawn to the large nose or if she had seen him somewhere before. Still racking her brains, she grabbed her smart phone and took a quick photo. Almost as an afterthought, she took pictures of the others exiting the car and then prepared an email before sending it to a colleague back in the office.

As more visitors arrived she decided to take snaps of as many as she could. Those walking away from her toward the entrance offered no clear shot but some stopped outside to chat with friends, affording her some decent pictures. She had around twenty images by the time the reply came back from the office and her heart skipped a beat as she read it.

The man with the large nose was Sami Hussain and the reason he had looked familiar was that he was a known acquaintance of Ahmed Al-Ali. She had not taken much notice of his profile in her earlier search once she saw he now lived in Coventry, over ninety miles from the mosque. While there was no law against making such a long journey to attend prayers, the fact that his travelling companions lived even further north, one in Derby and the other two in Chesterfield, suggested something was brewing, especially as two of them were on the watch list.

Sally opened the window a little more and fished in her bag for the cigarettes, lighting one with a slightly shaking hand. Her nicotine craving satisfied, she prepared another email and attached the other images she had taken. The street was quieter now that prayers had begun and she took the opportunity to get out and stretch her legs. After crossing the road she strolled past the entrance to the mosque, throwing a casual glance through the glass pane in the door. As she did, one of the two men standing inside saw the movement from the corner of his eye and watched as she continued past and out of view.

She wasn't sure if she had been noticed until she heard the door open behind her. Were they following her? She wasn't sure, and certainly wasn't going to turn around and find out, so she casually continued on to the end of the street and walked into a convenience store where she purchased more cigarettes. As she came out holding the unopened pack she saw no sign of anyone suspicious, so she crossed the street and returned to her car, all the time making a conscious effort not to look at the mosque.

As she climbed back inside the car her phone beeped and she checked the message. Her colleague had run the images through the database and had identified three more people who were on the watch list. One of them lived in London but the other two had travelled a considerable distance from the south-west coast, and the message told her to report in and await further instructions.

Sally was preparing the report when a yellow coach pulled up outside the mosque and around thirty men abruptly left the building and climbed aboard. As they filed out she caught sight of Rahman Jamshed marshalling the men onto the coach and she added this to the message. There were more details she wanted to add but the last person climbed on and the coach pulled away, driving past her. She put the phone on the passenger seat, put her seat belt on and turned the ignition, but the engine simply stuttered.

"NO!" she screamed. She tried again and after coughing and spluttering, as the battery offered the last ounce of its charge, the engine finally caught. She saw the coach disappearing in her side mirror and did a three-point turn in order to catch up. As she followed it through traffic, she managed to add more details to her report each time they stopped at traffic lights. As they crossed the Thames, she sent the message, including their current heading and the licence number and description of the coach.

They continued south for another ten miles before heading east, with Sally maintaining her observations from three cars behind. Signs for Biggin Hill Airport came and went and she found herself on the M25, where she let the coach pull ahead, confident of keeping an eye on it. At Junction Five, the coach pulled off onto the Sevenoaks Bypass and Sally pulled a little closer while still allowing two cars to be between her car and the target vehicle. After another three miles, the coach suddenly pulled into a lay-by and she was forced to either pull in too, or carry on and wait for them to catch up. When they moved off they would have to continue down the same road, so she decided to carry on. At the next junction, she drove round the roundabout until she could see the dual carriageway from the overhead island and she parked on the grass verge so that she could spot them when they passed.

Keeping one eye on the approaching traffic, she called the office to update her colleague.

Chapter 15

Malik Zarifa walked down the aisle of the coach and stood over Abdul Mansour's seat.

"Brother, we are being followed, just as you predicted. It is the woman I saw at the mosque."

"Are you sure it is her?" Mansour asked.

"I am certain. As we left I saw her parked nearby and the same blue Fiat has been behind us since."

"Are there any other vehicles following?"

"I have seen none."

"Okay, thank you, Malik." Mansour got up and spoke to the driver, instructing him to pull into the lay-by that was coming up. When they parked up he watched the Fiat continue past and told the driver to open the door. He climbed out and strode to the Nissan waiting for him, and the driver wound down the window.

"We are being followed by a blue Fiat," Mansour told the driver. "Drive ahead and check the next junction to see if it is waiting for us."

The Nissan pulled off and Mansour pondered the situation. If it was just this woman following, she would be waiting ahead for them to pass by. If there were others following, she would be called off and another car would take her place.

The Nissan returned twenty minutes later, having driven to the next junction, then back to the previous junction before completing the circuit back to its starting point.

"The car is waiting at the overpass," the driver told him. "There is a single passenger, a woman."

"Very well. When the coach sets off, wait three minutes then follow it. The driver will lead her to a secluded area and I want her captured alive. We need to know what she knows."

The driver nodded and Mansour walked back to the coach, checking his watch. He climbed aboard and told everyone to disembark, and as they did he gave instructions to the driver. When the last person climbed off, the coach driver set off and Mansour and his men only had to wait a couple of minutes before the other bus arrived. As they boarded, Mansour watched the Nissan set off and they followed a minute later, turning off the dual carriageway at the next junction.

Sally's instructions had been specific: If they move off, follow them and give a running commentary until other units can join her; if they don't move off, sit tight. For a long time she thought it would be the latter but suddenly the coach came into view. She made sure it had the same registration number before rejoining the dual carriageway and tucking in four cars behind it. For four miles they continued south, then she followed the coach onto a B road. Traffic quickly thinned and she found herself directly behind the coach, so she dropped her speed to let it pull ahead a little. The scenery became increasingly rural, the road twisting and winding through the countryside, but she was able to see the top of the large coach above the hedges and allowed herself to drop even further back.

Grabbing the phone from the passenger seat she hit the speed dial and spoke to her colleague. "We're on the B2017, heading towards Five Oak Green," she said.

"Hang on," she was told, and a moment later the team leader was on the line.

"Sally, good work so far. I want you to hang back and take no chances. We have two ground units en route and they should be with you within the hour. The chopper had a maintenance issue but it's on its way now."

"Will do," she said, but as she spoke, the coach pulled up a couple of hundred yards ahead. "Wait, they've stopped."

"Hold your position," the team leader told her.

The road was extremely narrow and she pulled as far onto the grass as she could, but half of the Punto remained on the road. "Now what?" she asked.

"Hold there, we will have air coverage in fifteen minutes."

"Okay," she said, and ended the call. A yellow light on the dashboard grabbed her attention: the fuel reserve warning.

"Shit." She had only filled the car up two weeks previously, then she realised the driving she had done today was not part of her normal daily routine and that would have taken its toll. Her backup would arrive within the hour, but what if the coach set off before they arrived? Even if it stayed still, she still had to drive home, and hadn't noticed a petrol station on her journey down. With no choice but to reserve her fuel, she turned the ignition off and sat in silence.

For a few minutes there was no movement, no sound except the occasional bird call. As she kept an eye on the coach in the distance she saw the red car approaching in her door mirror. She was confident that she had left enough room for it to pass, so she was seriously pissed when it crawled by and took her door mirror off. The car parked up just in front of hers and the driver got out, surveying the damage he had caused. As he did, Sally saw the glint of metal in his waistband.

All thoughts now turned to self-preservation. Her hand shot to the ignition and for the final time her car let her down. The man was already at her door, tugging at the handle, but as was her habit she locked the door every time she got in, the result of a friend having been car-jacked the previous year.

She grabbed the phone but before she could hit the speed dial a bullet shattered the side window, the round flashing by her right ear and burying itself in the passenger door. Sally let out a scream and covered her ears, the sound of the blast still resonating.

The gunman unlocked the door through the broken window and opened it, grabbing her by the hair and sticking the barrel of the gun into her temple.

"Out," he ordered, and Sally shakily complied, tears now running down her cheeks.

The gunman reached into her car and grabbed the phone and her handbag before dragging her towards the Nissan, the rear door already opened from the inside by a passenger. The gunman pushed her inside and the passenger dragged her the rest of the way in before placing a hood over her head and pushing her to the floor well.

The driver got back in and they sped off towards the coach. When they reached it he beeped his horn and the coach driver emerged, gave them a wave and disappeared back inside, heading for the back seats. After puncturing a can of petrol he splashed the contents over the seats as he made his way towards the entrance. At the door he flicked his Zippo lighter, got a good flame and threw it as far into the interior as he could manage before running to the open passenger door of the Nissan. He got in and slammed the door, the car speeding away as the first flames began licking the windows of the coach.

* * *

The satellite navigation system told Andrew Harvey to turn off the A23 at the next junction and led him towards Tom Gray's location. After popping over to the Home Office building to collect Gray's document, he had driven down the M23, his headache increasing in intensity with every mile. His watch had told him he had over an hour to spare, so he pulled in at Pease Pottage services and grabbed a coffee and some max-strength pain relief tablets. That was thirty minutes earlier and he could now feel the headache waning.

When he got to within half a mile of his destination, he came across the first cordon that had been set up, a police car blocking the road and a detour sign pointing towards the country lane on his right. His eyes followed the arrow and he saw that several news agencies had sent outside broadcasting units, their vans lining the side of the road as far as the eye could see, cameras pointing at Gray's building in the hope of catching any unfolding drama.

Harvey pulled up and waited for the officer to approach before flashing his identity card and explaining the purpose of his visit. The officer had to call his superiors to get clarification, but after a minute or two the police car was moved aside and he was waved through. Beyond the police car was another, its nose pointing towards the entrance to Gray's compound which lay six hundred yards down the road. As he drove down the lane, he saw Gray's building off to the right, all but the roof hidden by the hedges which surrounded the entire compound. When he pulled up at the command centre he was greeted by Evan Davies.

"Mr. Harvey, Major Blythe is expecting you." He led Harvey into the vehicle where the Major, wearing civvies, stood with a phone in his hand. They waited for him to finish his conversation before Davies made the introductions.

Harvey held up the document he was carrying. "I have to go and give it to him," he said.

Blythe nodded. "While you're there I need you to gather as much information as you can," he said. "We haven't been able to get very close, so I need to know what defences he has on that path, if any. I also want you to try and get inside, let us know about any weapons he has, the layout, where the prisoners are being held, where he sits, what equipment he has, everything."

"I hear he released one of the boys," Harvey said. "Where is he?"

"He was taken to hospital. He seemed healthy enough, apart from the smashed hands. I think it was Gray's way of making sure he didn't go straight back to burglary."

"Didn't you manage to get anything out of him before he left?"

"Nothing," Blythe said. "He was in his cell all day, and all he could hear was mumblings from the other hostages. He couldn't even hear Gray when his cell door was closed, which was most of the time."

"He must have seen something when he walked out."

Blythe shook his head. "Gray put a hood over his head before he released him, and he didn't walk out. He'd been sitting on a box for the last four days and couldn't stand up, so Gray dragged him out by his hands, and as he'd just had them crushed, you can understand that he was a bit more focused on the pain than his surroundings."

Harvey could indeed imagine the pain he was in, having broken a wrist in a motorcycle accident while on holiday the previous year. "I'll get all the information I can," he said. He pulled out his mobile phone and called Gray.

"I'm here, Tom."

"Have you got the agreement?" Gray asked.

"Right here. Want me to bring it in?"

"Sure, come on over. Don't hang up, just walk nice and slowly up to the front door."

Harvey nodded to Blythe and left the vehicle. Turning left into the compound, he strolled up to the front of the building. When he was twenty yards from the main door, Gray told him to stop. "Put the phone and agreement on the ground and remove your jacket."

Harvey did as he was told, then picked up the phone. "Turn round slowly and raise your shirt." Again Harvey complied. After following further instructions to raise his trouser legs to reveal his ankles, he was told to approach the door. He did so, slowly, trying to identify any dangers on the path or off to the side. He saw nothing. There were mounds in the dirt either side of the path but he recognised the three-pronged triggers sticking out of them as belonging to anti-personnel mines rather than Claymores. These mines would only go off if someone stood on them, whereas Claymores could be detonated remotely.

The door opened as he got to it and before him stood Tom Gray, one hand out ready to accept the agreement, the other clutching the trigger to the grenades on his waistcoat. Harvey kept the document by his side. "Aren't you going to invite me in?" he asked, manoeuvring his body to get a better view inside the building.

"Nice try, Andrew, but I'm not about to compromise my combat effectiveness by letting you know what I have in here." He clicked his fingers and gestured towards the agreement again. Harvey handed it over and Gray made to close the door.

"Wait," Harvey said. Gray paused to listen, face impassive. "Why did you do that to Harper? I thought we had a deal, and the public certainly didn't vote for that."

Gray shrugged. "If he had lasted to the end of the week, he would have been birched — which would have been a deterrent — or killed. As he left early, that was my reminder that he should change his ways. He won't be in a position to break the law for a while, and that means he will have time to reflect."

"The Home Secretary won't be pleased," Harvey told him.

"Perhaps. But everyone living near Adrian Harper will be a lot safer for the next few months, and that's who I care about, not some bloated politician who takes credit for others' work."

Gray went to close the door and Harvey took a step forward, sticking his foot in the gap. "Why did you ask me to come down here? Why not someone else?"

Gray pushed the door open and threw Harvey a look which told him to move back quickly or suffer the consequences. Harvey took the hint, retreating a couple of steps.

"I wanted to see who I was up against," Gray said. "There's only so much you can find out about a person over the phone. Looking a man in the eye, seeing the way he carries himself, you can learn a lot about an adversary."

"And what, exactly, have you learnt?"

"Well, your appearance suggests that you pay attention to detail, you obviously keep fit, and you seem calm under pressure. That tells me that you shouldn't be underestimated."

Harvey's expression didn't change, he just stared at Gray, taking his own chance to weigh him up.

"See you soon," Gray said, and closed the door.

Harvey walked back to the command vehicle, collecting his jacket on the way. Blythe was waiting for him, and wasn't impressed that he was back so soon.

"Well, that taught us a lot," he said, disappointment etched all over his face.

106

"If that had been you in there, would you have let me in?" Harvey asked, not even waiting for a reply. "He knows why I wanted to look around inside because he isn't as stupid as you might think he is. You should bear that in mind, because if you underestimate him it could cost lives."

"I don't underestimate him by any stretch of the imagination. I know his reputation within the Regiment, and he is highly regarded. I'm just frustrated that we can't seem to gain any advantage. Did you learn anything there?"

"I couldn't see inside. Behind him, all I could see was a wall. I don't know if you go through the door and turn left or turn right, so you would have to split your forces straight away.

"Outside, all I saw were anti-personnel mines, nothing that could be detonated remotely."

"He has had plenty of time to adapt them for remote detonation," Blythe reminded him.

"True, but the triggers are level with the ground. If they were to inflict damage to anyone on the path, they would be angled towards it."

Blythe noted the clever observation, regretting having been so short with him earlier, but before he could comment Harvey took his leave and began the journey north, hoping the rush hour traffic would allow him to be back in the office in time to see the result of the voting.

As he made his way up the M23, he thought about what Gray had said, that looking a man in the eye told you something about him. He had to concede that there was some truth in it, because having met Gray he now realised how focused he was. There was no sign of anxiety that would have marked him as unpredictable. Gray was a man in control of his destiny. It was then that Harvey realised the true purpose of the meeting: it wasn't so that Gray could weigh up Harvey, it was the other way round.

Chapter 16

As the coach pulled up to the barn the door was opened by the farmer and the driver pulled up inside. Abdul Mansour was the first off and the rest of the passengers followed, taking in their new surroundings as the barn door closed to hide them from prying eyes. One side of the barn was stacked to the roof with hay, the other side straw, and at the far end there was a pile of logs cut into eight inch lengths. The wood was stacked three feet high and protruded from the wall by a yard and a half.

The farmer introduced himself as Flynn — Mansour didn't know if it was his first name or surname, nor did he care — and pointed to the logs. "Let's shift this lot," he said to Mansour, who struggled to understand his heavy Irish accent.

He had been reluctant to use the IRA after they had double-crossed the Syrians back in the eighties, but his masters had insisted that they were the only option with time against them, so messages had been exchanged and two million dollars had been transferred to their account. Despite his misgivings, Mansour wasn't about to do anything to jeopardise his rise to greatness, which so far had been meteoric.

Ahmed Al-Ali had always been a devout follower of Islam and had attended the mosque near Kilburn since his parents moved to the area when he was just nine years old. The next few years had been distinctly uneventful, with nothing more interesting than a couple of fist fights to break up the cycle of school, prayers, homework and sleep, until the death of the Imam just after his sixteenth birthday.

The old man had been loved and respected by the community and his passing had saddened them all. Hundreds attended the funeral to pay their respects, and afterwards the topic of conversation had turned to who his successor was going to be.

The answer had come just a few days later in the form of Amir Channa. His initial teachings followed on from those of the previous Imam, but there had been gradual introduction of political themes, subtly at first to allow him to gauge the reaction, becoming more intense as time went on.

As Ahmed was approaching his seventeenth birthday, the Imam had asked him to attend a protest organised by the Stop the War Coalition and that was when he had been introduced to Nazeem. He hadn't offered a surname and Ahmed had never asked: He suspected Nazeem wasn't even his real first name.

Where Channa was the prospector, tasked only with finding the rough diamonds, Nazeem was the jeweller who shaped them into something beautiful. He took Ahmed under his wing and fed him stories from back home, of the struggle against the infidels, the oppression of the faithful in their own land.

Ahmed had been a willing apprentice and quick to learn, and after three short months he had made such progress that he'd been offered the chance to go to the homeland and make a proper contribution to the fight.

"I want you to think about it carefully," Nazeem had said. "It will mean saying goodbye to your family forever."

Ahmed had agreed without hesitation. He was an only child and his father had ensured a strict upbringing. There had been no love, only beatings when he showed any disobedience. From the age of three he had been given chores to do and there was a leather strap waiting if they weren't done properly and in time. There was always a surreptitious hug from his mother afterwards, her semi-sweet voice begging him to obey his father before giving him more chores to complete.

And so, with less than a hundred pounds in his pocket and a few changes of clothes in his bag, Ahmed Al-Ali had taken the Pakistan International Airways flight to Quetta, changing planes in Lahore. He had been met at the airport, driven the six miles to the capital of the Balochistan province and dropped at a house which was nothing more than a shack made from corrugated iron. He'd been fed and given a bed for the night, and before dawn he was awoken by yet more strangers and driven out of civilisation and into the wilderness.

The journey took him past mountains and over the border into Afghanistan. Their vehicle turned off the main road onto a dirt track, which ended hours later at the base of a mountain range. For another four hours he had been guided at an unrelenting pace through the hills by a man who hadn't spoken more than a handful of words all day. After being handed off to another guide waiting in the hills, he'd arrived at the camp an hour later.

At first he had been treated like any other recruit, sharing a tent with seven others and helping with the cooking and guard duty. However, he took to the AK-47 like he had been born with one, able to hit a target the size of a human head from four hundred yards, considered the maximum effective range of the weapon. He'd also showed an aptitude for explosives, able to create an Improvised Explosive Device within ten minutes.

When an American patrol had been ambushed and captured, they had been taken to the camp and Ahmed was given his first major test by the Mullahs. They asked him to dispatch one of the three captives and handed him the Marine's handgun, but instead he had taken out his knife and slit the soldier's throat, maintaining eye contact until he took his last breath. That demonstration of ruthlessness elevated him in their eyes, and he was no longer considered the coddled outsider.

From that moment on Ahmed had adopted the name Abdul Mansour, casting off the final tie to his previous life. The name meant 'servant of God and is victorious', which he thought an apt description.

The first sortie he took part in had not gone well, with sixteen of the twenty men in the team being killed while attacking a supply convoy. Air support had been called in and the Apache helicopters had decimated them, but Abdul had completed his part of the mission, destroying the fuel tanker before leading the survivors to safety.

With so many men lost, Abdul had been promoted and given a team of his own, which he led to many successes due to his astute tactics, tactics which had impressed the Mullahs so much that he was involved in all further planning.

It was Abdul Mansour who had seen the beginnings of the Tom Gray saga and had come up with the plan to deal a blow to the infidels on their own soil, and after listening to his idea they had immediately put things into motion.

Now here he was, less than ten miles from his target and about to share the plan with his men. First, though, he had to ensure that the weapons they were going to use were fit for purpose, so he instructed his men to move the logs as the Irishman had ordered.

With the wood gone Mansour saw a trapdoor with a rusty ring as a handle. Two men lifted the door and the Irishman went down the stairs followed closely by Mansour. Shelves ran down the sides of the cellar, three on each side and all filled with wooden boxes. Flynn gestured to Mansour to give him a hand and they lifted a box off a shelf and placed it on the floor. Using a crowbar, the Irishman took the lid off to reveal a dozen AK-47s wrapped in wax paper. Mansour took one out and examined it, checking the mechanism before deftly stripping it down and inspecting the barrel. The rifle had been well looked after and he nodded his head.

"What about the rest?"

Flynn pointed to five other boxes. "The rest of the AK-47s, ammunition, the grenades and the C4."

"I'll need a pistol."

"That wasn't on the list," Flynn said, sounding like a dodgy plumber, "but I'll throw in a Browning."

Mansour feigned appreciation. "Thanks. And the Rocket Propelled Grenades?"

The Irishman led him to the back of the cellar where a long box lay on the floor supported by two-inch blocks of wood to protect it from damp.

"Four RPGs, as requested."

Mansour opened the box and pulled out an RPG-22 he had become familiar with back home.

"These are single shot weapons. We requested RPG-7s."

"This is all we got," Flynn said with a shrug.

"Then we will need twice as many."

"As I said, this is all we got."

Mansour cursed inwardly, his reticence in using these people fully justified. Still, it was too late to do anything about it now: Their time would come. He shouted to his men to come down and get the boxes.

"I'll need lots of cleaning kits," he told Flynn, who pointed at a cardboard box on a shelf. Mansour carried it upstairs and got the more experienced men to supervise the weapon stripping and cleaning, helping those who had never seen an AK-47 before. While they did this, Mansour asked Flynn to show him the getaway vehicles.

The Irishman took him around the back of the barn where seven cars were parked. All were saloons around three years old and in good condition.

"Where did you get them?" Mansour asked.

"All stolen in the last couple of days and fitted with plates that relate to similar vehicles, so you shouldn't get stopped by the police ANPR units." The Automatic Number Plate Recognition system was the bane of the illegal driver, able to read a number plate and run it against information gained from several agencies, letting the police officers know with a couple of seconds if it was stolen or the driver had no insurance.

Flynn headed for the farm house and Mansour returned to the barn, telling his twenty-seven men to gather round so that he could explain their mission.

"Brothers, we have been given a unique opportunity to hit the infidels on their own soil and we must strike in the next twenty-four hours. The beautiful irony is that the hard work has already been done by one of their own."

He looked at the men to see if anyone understood what he had in mind, but all he saw was blank faces, so he laid out the plan in simple terms.

"You have all seen the news story about Tom Gray, have you not?"

Nods all round.

"Then you know that he has planted a device somewhere in this country, a device that he claims will kill many people."

"Are we going to look for his bomb?" One asked.

"That won't be easy," another pointed out. "If the police can't find it, how do we get our hands on it?"

Willing, they certainly were; intelligent, they were not. "We do not need to find the device, we simply need to prevent Tom Gray from giving away its location." He let the words sink in, eventually seeing realisation dawn. "We expected to have until Thursday to complete our mission but news of this agreement has brought the deadline forward. We must strike tomorrow, and strike hard. Once Gray is dead the country will panic. No-one will go near a city centre on Friday and that will hit their economy hard. There won't be thousands of deaths as Gray predicted, but it will strike fear in the hearts of the people and their anger will be directed at their government for failing to protect them."

He studied the men, his voice conveying the solemnity of their mission.

"What we do tomorrow, we do for Allah. He has given us the courage in our hearts to complete this deed, and we do so in His name. Not all of us will survive the next twenty-four hours, and those that make the sacrifice will have their reward in *Jannah*, the Garden of Heaven. Those that do make it live to do Allah's work another day."

He was pleased that none of the faces showed any signs of unease.

"We are not facing one man. He is surrounded by police," one said. "How are we going to get to him?"

"Yes, we need to know what we are facing. How many people are protecting him?" another asked.

Mansour was glad that some were already thinking tactically. "The police are there to keep civilians and the media out of harm's way, not to protect him. Our attack will be the last thing they expect."

"Are they armed?"

"How many are there?"

The questions came thick and fast, so Mansour held up his hands for silence. "I will explain the plan and take your questions later.

"Firstly, the British media have given us all of the information we need. They have shown the number of police surrounding the area and from those pictures we know that they are carrying arms. Those men are SO15, their Counter Terrorism Command, and they know how to shoot. However, it is easy for us to get within two hundred yards of them and still find cover."

He knelt down and drew a square on the dirt floor with his finger. "There are hedges running down two sides of his compound, here on the left and to the south. To the right the land rises away from his building then slopes down, forming a ridge. This gives us the high ground.

"Along the south side of the compound there are several media vehicles and in the bottom left hand corner, here, there are two police vehicles. There are men stationed around the building, thirty yards apart, forming a semi-circle from here to here, covering the south and east. Finally, in the top left-hand corner we have the command vehicles.

"We will approach from the east and two cars will park at the head of the media vans, here. In these cars will be the six men who will take up their position on the ridge. The rest of the cars will carry on, one parking at the other end of the line of media vans, the rest parking near the two police vehicles here.

"I will be in the last car to arrive and will be carrying two of the RPGs, which I will use to take out the police cars. Everyone else in these four cars will follow up and kill any survivors and then split up, ten going for the command vehicles, the rest towards the media vans."

"Do we kill the reporters?"

"Not unless you have to. I will assign four people to round them up and put them in one vehicle while the rest fire at the police in the field from behind the hedge. We will use the reporters as a shield, which should limit the amount of return fire.

"Once the first shot is fired, the first six men we dropped off will move to the ridge and lay down fire. Of the ten men heading for the command vehicles, four will position themselves along the hedge here and keep the police in the compound pinned down while the remaining six will attack the vehicles themselves."

"I need two volunteers who are able to ride these motorcycles," he said, pointing to a couple of dirt bikes leaning against bales of straw. "You must be able to ride off-road at high speed." Several hands went up. "Okay, you will all have a go later and I will pick the best two."

He grabbed an RPG and held it up. "Who has fired one of these before?"

Only one hand went up this time. "Okay, Zulfir, you will be in the team on the ridge. That gives you a clean shot at his front door and we are counting on you to provide a way in. On my signal you will take the doors out and everyone will move in. Fire and move, fire and move. Half of you will provide covering fire while the other half move ten yards closer to the building. The rest will then move ten yards past your position and cover you while you do the same. You keep doing this until you have cleared a path for the men on the bikes. They will approach from over the ridge and ride to the door, dismount and run inside.

"Once Gray is dead you all return to your vehicles and disperse. Make sure that when you exit your vehicles, you leave the engines running."

Mansour looked around at the men before him. Some were older than his twenty-one years, the majority younger, but all looked pumped up, eager to get going. It was time to bring them back to reality.

"After we have finished preparing the weapons I will assign your positions, then we will practise our attack, again and again, until you all know your responsibilities. Finally, we will pray to Allah and thank him for this opportunity."

At that moment the barn door opened a crack and Flynn squeezed through the gap. "Someone's coming," he said.

Mansour went to the door and saw the red Nissan approaching. "It's okay, they're with us."

The Irishman opened the door fully to allow the car in and closed it behind them. The driver got out and pulled a sobbing Sally from the back seat, the hood still in place.

Mansour looked at her hands and legs, which were shaking like leaves in a hurricane. This woman was scared, well outside of her comfort zone. She should be easy to crack.

"Take her to the cellar," he said in his native tongue. "Tie her hands and legs and keep a guard on her. I will deal with her later."

As Sally was taken away, Mansour called Zulfir over.

"You are the only one who knows how to fire the RPG, but I don't like to put all of my eggs in one basket. I will assign five others to be with you on the ridge and you must show them all how to fire the weapon, just in case anything happens to you."

Zulfir nodded, not even slightly offended by the suggestion that he might not be able to complete the job. "Yes, brother."

Chapter 17

Andrew Harvey was halfway back to London when he got the call and he activated his hands free set.

"Harvey."

"Andrew, what's your position?" Hammond asked.

"I'm on the M23, about seven miles south of the M25."

"You need to turn around. We have a situation. Punch this location into your satnav."

Hammond gave him the post code and Harvey saw that it was close by. "What's the problem?"

"One of our analysts, Sally Clarkson, was tailing suspects when she went off grid."

Harvey's heart missed a beat at the sound of her name. A couple of times during the day he had thought about the way he had dismissed her, deciding an apology was definitely in order. Now she appeared to be in dire trouble and it was all his fault.

"I gave her that assignment," he said. "I thought it was a false alarm, given Mansour's status, but she obviously found something. Do you have any details?"

"Looks like Rahman Jamshed turned out to be Abdul Mansour after all. She found him at a mosque in Willesden where he boarded a bus with about thirty others, a few of which are on our watch list. She tailed them to her current location but by the time help arrived she was gone and the coach was in flames."

"They must have transferred to another coach, they can't all be on foot. Can we get a chopper up to search the area?"

"Already there, but there were just a few cars in the area, nothing that could hold thirty people, and thermal images showed no-one hiding in the nearby fields."

"Okay, I'm on my way. Send me everything she reported in."

The satnav told him to leave the motorway at junction nine, then led him through B roads for forty minutes until he came across the fire engines. Two surveillance units were already on hand and a Scene of Crime Officer was dusting the Fiat's door for finger prints. Harvey approached the SOCO first.

"Got anything yet?" he asked, flashing his ID.

The SOCO looked at the card, shook his head and returned to his work, so Harvey went to speak to his colleagues.

"What do we know so far?"

"We know Sally has been taken at gunpoint," John Collins told him. He began giving a rundown of the events but Harvey stopped him.

"I listened to the recordings on the way down. I know she got to here, now we need to know where she went. What's the story with the coach?"

"Booked yesterday from Duckitt Travel and paid cash when they picked it up this morning," Collins said. "The owners weren't happy when they heard what happened to it."

"I'll bet. So who rented it?"

"Mohammed Ali. That's the Muslim equivalent of John Smith."

Harvey stared at the coach, the flames now extinguished and the firemen going through the damping down process. "There were thirty men on that coach, and they've disappeared. They had to transfer to another vehicle, be it another coach, or three mini-buses, or seven cars. Have you checked other hire companies?"

Billy Emerson shook his head, and Harvey called Farsi, throwing his colleagues an admonishing look. "Hamad, we need to find any coaches rented today. Look for anything booked yesterday, particularly anything booked by a Mohammed Ali and paid in cash. We know he booked one with Duckitt Travel, we need to see if he booked any others elsewhere. It might by a single coach or multiple mini-buses. Whichever it is, it will probably be self-drive.

"Can you also send me Mansour's file? I read the summary, but I need to know all I can about this guy."

He pocketed the phone and started to say something to Emerson, but caught himself in time. It wasn't up to these guys to investigate all the possibilities, it was his, and the last thing he needed to do was alienate anyone else. "I think they came down here and noticed they were being followed, so they stopped, picked her up and carried on. That means they were heading south, which is where we need to concentrate our search."

He strode over to the burnt out coach and eventually found the Sub Officer. "Can you tell us anything?" he asked.

"Nothing much at the moment. An accelerant was used, probably petrol, but you'll be hard pressed to get any prints or DNA. This was an old coach, lots of combustible material used in its construction. That's why it went up so quick."

As he spoke, the roof at the rear of the coach collapsed, debris falling into the interior. Harvey thanked him and returned to the surveillance team. "There's nothing for us here and I'm starving. Let's head south, find a café and grab a bite. I think it's going to be a long night."

Chapter 18

Abdul Mansour took the men with weapons experience aside and gave them their instructions.

"Take them into the field and run them through the drill. Show them how to hold a rifle, how to aim, how to squeeze the trigger rather than pull it, how to change the magazine, how to clear a blockage, everything. They need a three month course in the next three hours."

He stared into the field, imagining the scene they would face.

"Give them some targets to aim at. Policemen, Gray's building, police cars, everything."

The seven men nodded in unison, ideas forming in their minds.

"Start them all off as if they were getting out of their vehicles and give them their positions. Do you remember the instructions I gave?"

More nods.

"Okay. There are thirty-one of us, including myself. Three of you will go right, taking nine men towards the media vans. Two of you will take another eight towards the command vehicle. There will be two on the bikes, and the remaining two of you will be among the six on the ridge. I will take an observation role near the coach. When the path is cleared for the bikes I will blow a whistle twice, two long blasts. When it is time to retreat, I will blow multiple short blasts.

"Any questions?"

There were none.

"Good. Mahmood, I want you to take the ones who can ride a bike and see what they can do. Find me two who can cover two hundred yards in the quickest time."

Mahmood nodded and Mansour left them to their duties, heading off to speak to his hostage. As he entered the barn he saw the two guards playing around, laughing and aiming at each other with their new weapons. He strode over and delivered a punch to the larger of the duos' head, sending him sprawling. The man lay on the ground massaging his jaw, staring at him with incomprehension.

"Who is looking after the girl?" Mansour roared.

"The Irishman said he would watch over her," the other guard said meekly.

"And what do you know about this man? Would you trust him with your life?"

The guard shook his head. "No, brother."

"This isn't a holiday, Sami, this is war. If I give you instructions you follow them or people die."

"I'm sorry, brother."

Mansour grabbed Sami's gun and checked the chamber before showing it to the guard. "You were pointing a loaded weapon at one of your own men. How many times have you used one of these?"

"Never, brother. I was given it just now."

Mansour was furious. Under different circumstances he would have taken them aside and shown them the error of their ways with a bullet to the head, but he needed every available man for the mission ahead. Instead, he removed the magazine and ejected the round from the chamber before handing the weapon back.

"Get everyone outside, the training begins now."

As the men filed outside he went down into the cellar where he found Flynn with his hand inside the hostage's blouse. The Irishman, so immersed in the moment, didn't hear him arrive.

"Do you mind if I speak to my prisoner?" Mansour asked.

Flynn jumped, embarrassment etched on his face, but he soon regained his composure. "Just getting to know her." he said, a smile forming.

"Don't bother, she won't be around for long."

Flynn looked at the woman, admiring the body. Maybe carrying a couple of pounds too many, but still attractive. "Now that would be a waste," he said. "Why not leave her to me when you've finished? You're a guest here, and it's always wise to keep your host happy. Besides, we can call it payment for the Browning."

Mansour considered the statement and recognised the veiled threat. There was no telling what this snake would do if he refused his request, and he couldn't afford any complications at this late stage.

"Fine. Once I have finished with her she is all yours."

Flynn patted him on the shoulder on his way out of the cellar. "Be gentle with her, I don't like damaged goods."

Mansour bit his lip. The insolence of this man knew no bounds! He forced the thought from his mind and concentrated on the woman. She still wore the hood, so he had no idea what she looked like. Her bag was on the cellar floor, so he picked it up, looking for some form of identification. He found the two images of him, one taken during his days as Ahmed Al-Ali, the most recent taken at the airport. He also found her wallet and an ID badge said her name was Sarah Clark.

I don't think so, he thought to himself. The UK Border Agency weren't known for covert surveillance, which meant this badge was a forgery, and only the Security Service would be able to create something like this.

He studied the picture, and the face staring back was rather plain. Did the Irishman know what he was going to be getting? Probably not, but then he doubted he cared, the pudgy fifty-year-old lucky to get any kind of female attention at all.

"What's your real name?" He asked her, but got no reply. She was breathing heavily, her body shaking, possibly because of her pawing by Flynn, most likely because of the situation in general. Mansour wasn't about to put her at ease, preferring to deal with the frightened child inside her. He drew his knife and placed the sharp point of the blade into her throat.

"I asked you a question and I am not noted for my patience," he said, pressing the point in a little harder, drawing a drop of blood.

"Sarah Clark," she whimpered.

Mansour moved the knife down her chest between her open blouse and sliced through the front strap of her bra, then moved the material to reveal her right breast. He placed the blade beneath the mound of flesh.

"Try again."

"Sally!" she screamed. "Sally Clarkson!"

Mansour kept the knife in place. "And who do you work for, Sally. If you tell me it's the UK Border Agency, I will slice your breast off."

"The Security Service," she cried, bursting into tears.

"MI5? I didn't know they employed anyone so incompetent. What is your role?"

"I'm an... an analyst."

"What does that involve?"

"Data mining, looking for trends, things like that," she said, her voice still trembling.

"So why did they send you to follow me?"

Sally told him the whole story, from Harvey's outburst right up to the moment of her capture. Mansour believed her, and wasn't happy with the confirmation that the intelligence agencies knew of his presence in Britain. They would certainly be looking for him as well as the woman, but the only clue they had was her last location, which was over forty miles away. Still, it didn't do to underestimate the enemy.

The authorities would certainly have aircraft up looking for them, so doing the training out in the open was perhaps not the best idea, but he had to weigh up the risk of detection against the need to familiarise the men with their mission.

He decided to give them forty minutes, then get everyone inside for further weapons training. After ensuring that the woman was securely bound to the wooden chair she was sitting on, he went outside to oversee the training.

As he stood in the centre of the field watching as his recruits carried out the instructions they had been given he tried not to allow the frustration to show on his face. This was only their second attempt but still they faced more of a threat from each other than the police. The field was roughly the same size as Gray's, and bales of straw had been set up to represent the enemy, with a tractor taking on the role of the target building.

It was unfortunate that he couldn't test their proficiency with the weapons, instead having them shout BANG! BANG! to simulate each round being fired. If he allowed any rounds to go off the sound would travel, and although they were isolated here, there was always the chance someone would hear the reports.

He shouted for them to stop and the men obeyed, remaining in their current positions. He strode to the group advancing from the ridge — actually a line of straw bales — and pointed out their mistakes. "You are too close together. You three are supposed to give covering fire while the other three advance, but look at their position now."

The men looked, but the expressions on their faces told him they saw nothing. "Your field of fire is too small. You can only point your weapon three inches this way and three inches that way. Any more than that, and you will hit your own men." He instructed the men to move apart by another ten yards and the three in the firing positions immediately noticed the difference.

"Syed, Irfan, show me your weapons."

The men handed over the rifles and Mansour looked at the fire selector. "What setting is that?" he asked Syed, handing the weapon back. The recruit checked and confirmed that it was set to fully automatic.

122

"I want all weapons on semi-automatic tomorrow." He held up the other weapon in the firing position. "Breathe, aim, squeeze, breathe, aim, squeeze. Firing single shots will preserve your ammunition and give you greater accuracy. If you just spray the enemy on fully-automatic you will exhaust a magazine in seconds and give them the advantage, allowing them to close on your position while you reload."

He handed the rifle back to Irfan. "Back to your start positions, let's do it again."

This time they did better, but in his heart he knew that there was very little chance of any of them surviving the assault. Allah would receive them and would show His gratitude, and then He would put steel in the hearts of others to take their place.

A drop of rain landed on his face and he started at the heavens, watching as the grey clouds moved slowly towards them. The weather forecast was for light rain over the next two days, which suited him perfectly. The police protecting Gray would be demoralised and he would attack with men pumped up for the mission.

He instructed his men to go through it one more time, then return to the barn, while he himself went to see how the five volunteers were getting on with the bikes.

Mahmood pointed out the two most promising riders and Mansour summoned them over.

"What are your names?" he asked.

"Kamran."

"Nadeem."

"I hear you handle those bikes well," he said to them, and watched the smiles appear on their faces. "Are you willing to take on the role tomorrow?"

They both nodded, smiles remaining in place.

"And do you believe in your hearts that what we do tomorrow needs to be done?"

"Of course, brother. This is *jihad*."

Mansour knew they were applying the translation commonly used by western civilisations — holy war. In fact, *jihad* meant "struggle", notably the struggle to defend Islam. Still, if it helped them to complete their mission it didn't matter how they interpreted it.

"Allah has chosen you for a reason," he said, and saw their chests puff with pride. "When you get to the entrance of the building you will be facing a man with years of combat experience. Neither of you have ever held a weapon, so you would prove no match in a gun fight.

That is why I want you to wear an explosive vest and detonate it once you get inside."

He didn't quite get the reaction he hoped for, with both of the men losing their smiles, but a moment later first one, then the other, nodded.

"I will do this for Allah," one said.

"Allahu Akbar," the other proclaimed. *Allah is the Greatest.*

"Allahu Akbar," Mansour agreed. "Come, it is time to pray."

Chapter 19

Tom Gray removed his laptop from the table and placed it on one of the feeding trolleys, then pushed the table into Joseph Olemwu's cell, parking it up against the left hand wall.

"It's time, Joseph," he said, removing the tape over his mouth before unlocking the shackles on the boy's ankles. Olemwu waited until both feet were free, then kicked out, catching Gray on the chin with the bridge of his foot. Gray staggered backwards but gathered himself immediately, the boy's weakened leg muscles having failed to deliver a telling blow.

"You really are a dumb fuck," he said, massaging his jaw. "You should have at least waited until I untied your hand. Now what are you going to do?"

Olemwu's silence told him he hadn't thought that far ahead. He had tried talking his way to freedom earlier in the day, but once he'd realised that this approach wasn't going to work he had resorted to the only other thing he knew — violence — and his rational thought process had once again abandoned him.

Gray untied the rope connecting Olemwu's left wrist to the ring on the wall, then grabbed his arm and picked him up, swinging him around so that he was bent double over the table. Once his wrists had been tied to another ring he wrapped his belt around the boy's legs and secured it tightly just above the knees. With the preparations complete, he wheeled the trolley into the cell and focused the laptop's built-in web cam so that it showed Olemwu lying across the table, his toes just about touching the floor and three-day-old faeces crusting the crack of his bare backside.

His watch told him he had a few minutes until the broadcast was due, so he left the cell to escape the smell, closing the door behind him. Olemwu kicked off big time, shouting, swearing and thrashing about, but he ignored the commotion and climbed the stairs to the first floor, stopping at one of the windows. Although it appeared to be completely boarded up from the outside, the bottom panel was hinged, allowing it to be swung upwards. The three-inch gap would allow him to lay down suppressing fire, should the need arise.

He opened the panel and put his face to the gap, breathing deeply. The cool evening air was like nectar and he drank deeply, savouring the taste of the countryside.

All too soon it was time to speak to the nation again, so he put the panel back in place and made his way downstairs to where Olemwu was still causing a huge fuss. He entered the cell and Olemwu immediately began pleading with him, begging for mercy.

"Fat chance," Gray said.

Gray hit the Play button on the laptop's streaming software and took a couple of steps backwards.

"People of Britain, the results of the votes for Joseph Olemwu should be on your screens now. As you can see, only thirty-seven percent of the voters want Joseph to die, the rest wanting to see him birched.

"So be it."

He disappeared off the screen for a moment and returned with the birch in his hand.

"Normally I would tell you to send the children out of the room at this point, but if you have kids over twelve years of age you should let them watch this so that they know what they might face if they decide to break the law."

Olemwu began pleading again, his voice high-pitched and strained, but Gray ignored him and delivered the first stroke. The boy screamed and a thick weal immediately appeared on his buttocks. The next blow landed an inch lower.

"OW!"

Tears streamed down Olemwu's face and he sobbed like a three-year-old, but Gray continued regardless, opening up the first weal with his third stroke. He cursed inwardly, not intending to draw blood. The purpose of the exercise was to show the effect of the birch as a deterrent, not its ability to wound, and this could turn people against its reintroduction. He gave Olemwu another three strokes, taking care to hit undamaged skin each time, then put the birch down and turned to face the camera.

"As you can see, Joseph — who considers himself a bit of a hard man — didn't like that very much, and if this punishment is reintroduced I am convinced it will make criminals think twice. Once Joseph is free I'm sure there will be lucrative newspaper offers to sell his story, but if he tells you that it wasn't painful or effective I would take his answer with a pinch of salt. All you have to do is remember him as he is now, crying like a baby.

"While I tend to his wound, I want you to continue voting on my future. Do I give myself up, or end it here on Thursday? The choice is yours."

He turned off the Web cam and pushed the trolley out of the cell, then untied Olemwu's left wrist and carried him back to a sitting position on his home-made commode, causing him to shriek with pain. He arched his back in an effort to get his backside off the box but Gray pushed him back down and jerked his arm towards the ring on the wall, tying the rope securely. Once the shackles were back on Olemwu's ankles he removed his belt from around the boy's knees.

"You said you were gonna treat my wounds."

"Yeah, but then I remembered the kick on the chin, and now I can't be bothered. Don't worry, though, you will be free in a couple of days, maybe sooner."

"But this will get infected," Olemwu sobbed.

"You really want me to treat it? You really want some antiseptic on it?"

"Yes!" the boy shouted.

"Fine." Gray left the cell and returned a moment later carrying the boy's underwear. He went round the back of the box and told the boy to lean forward as far as he could. Olemwu complied as best he could and Gray applied the antiseptic to the boxer shorts and rubbed it into the wound.

The scream was ear-splitting, much as Gray expected, but he carried on applying it nevertheless.

"What the fuck are you putting on there?" Olemwu shouted.

"Salt," Gray said casually. "It has antiseptic qualities and I'm fresh out of Savlon."

Olemwu continued cursing but Gray had heard enough and ripped off a piece of tape, securing it over the boy's mouth.

"Ungrateful sod," he said, leaving the cell and closing the door behind him. It was time to prepare his dinner, but first he headed upstairs for a bit more fresh air.

127

Chapter 20

Wednesday 20th April 2011

Andrew Harvey woke just before six in the morning and after getting his bearings he turned on the television set in the small room of the bed and breakfast in Crowborough. The three men had stopped here to have dinner the previous evening and had been ordered to remain in the area after reporting in to Hammond.

"Find a place to rest up," Hammond had said. "If we get any news about Sally I want you ready to move at a moment's notice."

But there had been no news, just waiting, and late in the evening they had booked into separate rooms for the night.

Harvey turned to the BBC News channel, which was predictably still focusing on the Tom Gray saga. Live video from their correspondent at the scene showed the old factory building in the background as he explained what had happened during the night, which was absolutely nothing. However, he was looking ahead to the prospect of Gray handing himself in to the authorities, and he began speculating as to whether or not the government would agree to hold a referendum on Gray's justice bill.

"What choice have they got?" Harvey said to himself, and went to take a shower. Afterwards he shaved and dressed before calling the office for an update, only to be told the trail had gone cold. There were no hits with the other coach hire companies, with only a few dozen vehicles out on hire and the vast majority of those to regular customers. Of the remaining six, five had been pulled over by armed police officers only to find the drivers and passengers were legitimate travellers on day trips, and the other one had been involved in a traffic accident on the M5 and had been towed to a garage, it's passengers a group of casino staff returning from a day trip to the races.

They had also been unable to trace her phone, suggesting it had been turned off or destroyed, and an aerial search of the surrounding area had turned up nothing.

Harvey asked for updates on the Gray case and was told that Crawford from Norden Industries had reported over nine thousand cannisters checked, but that still left over twenty-five thousand with only twelve hours to go.

They were also drawing a blank in the search for Gray's accomplices.

Twelve hours, he thought, but only if Gray came out this evening. And even if he didn't, if he stayed in until Thursday, what difference would it make? One more criminal would get his just desserts and maybe a handful of people would really give a shit.

Meanwhile Sally Clarkson, who had no field experience, was missing, assumed kidnapped by a terrorist cell. They just didn't have the people to deal with both, and as far as he was concerned, the Gray saga could run its course.

Sally was his priority now.

Why did Mansour have to turn up this week, of all weeks? If only he'd waited another few days they would be fully resourced again. At the moment there just weren't enough people to deal with both Gray and...

As the realisation hit him, he picked up his phone and dialled Hammond's mobile.

"John, I don't think it is a coincidence that Mansour turned up out of the blue. I think he's planning something in the next forty eight hours."

"What's his target?"

"That I don't know," Harvey admitted, "but fourteen months after being reported dead he suddenly appears on our radar, a mere twenty-four hours after Gray goes live on television. I think he knew we would be throwing everything at the Gray problem, allowing him to sneak in quietly and carry out his plan, whatever it is. If it hadn't been for Sally being so tenacious he might have slipped clean past us."

"There's been no traffic on the wires recently," Hammond said. "If something had been planned we would have got a sniff of it by now."

"I know, and that's what bothers me. None of the intelligence we have suggests an attack is imminent, yet everything points to him trying to exploit this window of opportunity. The only thing I would put any money on is that the target is somewhere near here, because they were heading towards the south coast when Sally was tailing them."

"I concur. We'll work up possible targets from Tunbridge Wells down to Brighton and check with our American cousins to see what information they've forgotten to share with us."

"Okay," Harvey said. "Once you've prioritised the targets let me know and we'll head to the most likely. Oh, and speak to Hamad, see if he managed to get any hits on rented coaches."

Harvey hung up and caught the introduction of the Shadow Home Secretary on the news channel.

"Let's speak now to Michael Conway, who's just taken a seat in our Westminster studio. Thank you for joining us. Can you give us your reaction to Tom Gray's justice bill?"

"Over the last three years we have been looking at crime statistics and frankly they make shocking reading. As Mr. Gray has pointed out, in the last ten years this government has allowed over one hundred thousand career criminals to escape custodial sentences and this is something we vow to change.

"We have been working on a set of proposals during this time and much of what Mr. Gray has asked for has already been covered. We have identified several locations to hold what we call super-prisons, each housing up to five thousand prisoners. To put that into context, the current largest prison in the UK, Wandsworth, holds less than seventeen hundred prisoners.

"Within these super-prisons we are looking into the possibility of implementing Mr. Gray's suggestion that prisoners are kept in solitary confinement, and in parliament last year we brought up the idea of prisoners being forced to work."

"There are arguments that the government should be focusing on the causes of crime rather than building even more prisons. Do you think opting for an immediate custodial sentence is the right answer?"

The politician adjusted his posture and rearranged his jacket. "We are not advocating immediate custodial sentences, I need to make that absolutely clear. What we plan to do is look at another of Mr. Gray's proposals and examine the feasibility of clawing back some of the cost of policing. If we do this, a large percentage will go towards crime prevention in schools.

"We are confident that this approach will actually *reduce* the prison population in future years."

"What about his other proposals?" the newscaster asked. "Do you agree with the reintroduction of corporal punishment?"

"This issue has divided our party, I must admit. What we do propose is a one year trial, and after that we will look at the results. Our ultimate aim is to eradicate recidivism, and we are determined to investigate all avenues."

Harvey watched for another couple of minutes, then turned the television off. Despite the rhetoric, he knew that the Shadow Home Secretary was only saying what he thought the country wanted to hear in the run up to the election. He wasn't the first politician to do a u-turn, and he certainly wouldn't be the last.

Needing something he could trust beyond doubt, he collected his colleagues and went down for a full English breakfast.

* * *

Sally Clarkson was jerked awake by the sound of the bedroom door opening. She knew instinctively that she was naked and tried to curl up in an attempt to hide her modesty, but her hands and feet were tied to the corners of the wooden bed frame and memories of the previous evening came flooding back.

Flynn had brought her here shortly after Mansour had questioned her. She had been dragged up the narrow stairs and bundled onto the bed, where the Irishman had removed her hood. He had tied rope around her right wrist and she'd struggled when he tried to attach the other end to the bed frame, but several agonising punches to her kidneys and thighs had subdued her. Before long, all four limbs were secure and Flynn had left, only to return a few minutes later with a pair of scissors, which he'd used to slowly cut the clothes away from her body in some kind of sick, perverted strip tease. He'd taken his time over this, a full fifteen minutes, his breath quickening with each piece of flesh revealed.

In contrast, once she was naked he had stripped off his own clothes as if they were on fire. He'd climbed clumsily on top of her, entering her painfully and thrusting wildly until reaching his climax a minute later.

He'd gone downstairs after that, returning a couple of hours after night had fallen for more of the same. This time he'd lasted longer and had left her with an aching body and the lingering odour of sweat and beer.

Finally alone again, sleep had not come easily, drifting in and out of semi-consciousness as she tried to foresee a way out of the situation, but it looked hopeless. She didn't have the strength to break her bonds and it was unlikely he would free her, but the most damning realisation was that he had removed her hood, allowing her to see his face. She knew it was highly unlikely that she would live to tell anyone what he looked like. Her only hope was to survive as long as possible in the hope that someone would find her.

As Flynn came through the door she tried to force a smile onto her face, hoping to convince him to keep her around for a little while longer. The smile appeared more like a grimace, but it did nothing to dampen his ardour. She could see the bulge in his trousers as he came to stand next to her and he followed her eyes, a sneer appearing on his face as he unzipped his pants and began to caress himself.

"What are you waiting for?" she asked, as alluringly as she could manage. "Don't waste it." She thrust her pelvis towards him, catching him off guard. He hadn't expected compliance, and he found himself suddenly embarrassed, standing before her with his dick in his hand.

The sneer was replaced by a look somewhere between confusion and anger, and he rushed from the room, tucking his manhood away.

Sally cursed to herself. How stupid could she be? He didn't want a girlfriend, he wanted someone to dominate, someone he could control and use at his leisure. Instead of prolonging her life she had no doubt brought the end closer.

All she could do now was wait and hope she hadn't pissed him off too much.

* * *

Tom Gray pushed the trolley into Joseph Olemwu's cell and removed the tape from his hostage's mouth.

"Hungry?"

Olemwu shot him a filthy look. "When I get outta here I'm gonna fuck you up, old man."

Gray was hurt and it showed on his face. He'd been called many things in his time, but *old*?

"Suit yourself." He wheeled the trolley out and stood in the doorway, studying the boy before him.

"I have to ask, what have you learned from the last few days?"

Olemwu continued to stare, his expression still hostile, but Gray gave him a few minutes to reply and rephrased the question when none was forthcoming.

"Has this experience taught you anything?"

"Yeah, it taught me to hate white fuckers like you," Olemwu spat.

"Hmm. I was thinking more along the lines of 'crime doesn't pay'. You could have easily found a job, but you prefer to inflict misery instead. Even after all you've been through these past few days, your attitude still stinks.

"I had hoped to scare some sense into you, but it looks like you're a lost cause."

"So what, you gonna kill me now? That's your answer to everything."

"No," Gray said, "I'm not going to kill you. I'll let you go when this is all over, because I think you're just angry at the moment. When you get home, spend a couple of days with your mother, listen to what she says, and think about what you want from your life.

"If you choose to carry on as you have so far, you will be in prison or dead within a very short time, and that would devastate your mother. Your father...," he shrugged, "I'm not so sure."

"I don't need you tellin' me how to live my life."

"That's fine," Gray said, his voice calm. "I just wanted you to know that I'm giving you another chance."

He pulled off a length of tape and placed it over the boy's mouth. "Think about it."

Gray left the cell and closed the door before turning the sound up on the television. It was approaching midday and the government was due to announce its decision on his justice bill.

He considered giving Boyle Olemwu's food but the thought was fleeting and he tucked into the Spam and cold potatoes as he watched the news channel. The weather girl said he could expect rain for much of the day, but the forecast for the weekend was a return to the bright sunshine the country had enjoyed over the last few weeks.

Sounds good, he thought. Maybe a trip to the beach when this was all over.

The newscaster read out the main headlines, the first of which was an interview with the Home Secretary.

The politician sat in the Westminster studio and didn't look all that comfortable to Gray. When he began his announcement, he realised why.

"Unfortunately, Sharon, we have not been able to make a decision on a referendum at this time," he said. "The legal implications have to be considered and we don't want to make a promise to the people that we might have to break."

Why not? Gray wondered. It wouldn't be the first time.

"We have a legal team looking into the possibility of implementing some or all of Mr. Gray's proposals, but we cannot guarantee that any changes can be made to current legislation."

"What are the sticking points?" the newscaster asked.

"Well, the Human Rights Act is fundamental in ensuring we live in a fair society, and it isn't as simple as repealing it. The Act was introduced to prevent people having to seek redress at the European Court of Human Rights, which takes up a lot of time and money. Even if the Act is torn up, people would still be able to take their case to Strasbourg and we would be bound by any judgement handed down.

"The only alternative would be to opt out of the Convention, but as the European Union itself is about to join as a party in its own right, it would mean pulling out of the EU as well.

"So you see, this isn't as simple as Mr. Gray would have us all believe."

"Which aspects of the Act are you most concerned about?"

"Protection from torture and mistreatment is the only real sticking point. The reintroduction of the birch would be a breach of Article three."

"We had the Shadow Home Secretary on the programme this morning and he seems convinced that this wouldn't be a problem."

The Minister couldn't wait to score a few political points at his counterpart's expense. "I think you'll find that if you look at the current polls, my learned friend's party are in a very poor position. The comments you heard this morning were those of a party desperate for votes in the upcoming election, a party who hasn't thought the situation through, a party destined to disappoint the electorate if they ever get to power."

"What about the part of the Act guaranteeing protection from slavery and forced labour? Isn't Mr. Gray asking that prisoners be forced to work while they are incarcerated?"

"Not quite, Sharon. For one, he is suggesting that those who are willing to work will have their sentences reduced. In addition, the Act doesn't apply to prisoners carrying out work as part of their sentence."

The newscaster nodded, looking at her notes. "When can we expect a decision, Mr. Home Secretary?"

"We believe we can make an announcement late on Friday." he said.

"We expect this situation to be over by then. Won't that be too late?"

"Not at all. Mr. Gray pointed out that we were not making a decision to appease him, we are making a decision based on the will of the people, and we want to make sure it is one that is right for the people."

Gray turned the television off and picked up his mobile, selecting a pre-set number.

"Harvey," the voice said.

"Hello Andrew."

"Tom. What can I do for you?"

"The Home Secretary isn't taking me seriously, Andrew. You know what that means."

The phone went silent in Harvey's hand and he checked to make sure he still had a signal, but Gray came back on the line a few moments later.

"Andrew, the next sound you hear will be Stuart Boyle."

Gray placed the phone on the feeding trolley and pushed it into Boyle's cell so that Harvey could hear everything. From the corner of the room he picked up a contraption that looked like a giant nutcracker, two three-foot lengths of metal hinged together at one end, and he noted the look of fear in Boyle's eyes.

On the day Boyle had arrived, Gray had explained the reason for his abduction.

"My name is Tom Gray, father of Daniel Gray and husband to Dina Gray. On January twenty-first last year you killed my son — which in turn led to the death of my wife — and at some point in the coming days you are going to pay for that."

"What are you going to do to me? Are you going to kill me?" the boy had asked, the fear and panic in his voice palpable.

"No," Gray had promised. "Death is too quick, too easy. If I put a bullet through your head you won't suffer at all, you'll just cease to be.

"No, you aren't going to die, no matter how much you beg me."

He had explained the purpose of the implement and placed it inside the room so that Boyle could see it every waking moment. He hadn't said when it would be used, only that it wouldn't be straight away.

Now the time had come.

Gray placed the device around Boyle's left arm, a couple of inches above the wrist, holding it there while studying his captive's face. The boy was shaking, his eyes as big as saucers, and he was trying to say something. Gray removed the tape covering his mouth.

"Please, Mister, I'm so sorry..."

Gray clamped his hand over Boyle's mouth and put his lips close to the boy's ear so that Harvey couldn't hear what he was about to say.

"Save it," he growled softly. "Sorrow isn't something you can express with a single word, it's something you feel inside. My solicitor told me that you were laughing and joking with your family when you walked free from court seven months ago. You even went on to commit more crimes, showing no remorse whatsoever for the pain you inflicted.

"You think you're sorry? Oh, believe me, you will be."

Gray grasped both handles and squeezed them together with all the strength he could muster, crushing Boyle's radius and ulna like he was breaking into a crab claw. The sound emanating from Boyle's mouth barely managed to drown out the sound of the bones cracking.

Ignoring the screams, Gray transferred to the other side, inflicting similar damage to the right arm.

Boyle was a mess, snot and tears streaming down his face.

"Had enough?" Gray asked, his voice calm.

Boyle could hardly control his movements, only barely able to nod his head once.

"Yes," he whimpered.

"Tough."

Gray turned his attentions to Boyle's legs, shattering first the right tibia and fibula, followed by the left.

Once he'd finished he picked up the phone and walked out of the cell, leaving the babbling Boyle to deal with the pain in his own way.

"That was for failing to meet the deadline. If I don't hear an announcement about the referendum on the news by six this evening, he's really gonna start hurting."

"Whatever you did, you just went too far," Harvey said. "The Home Secretary put his neck on the line to arrange this deal, and you're doing all you can to jeopardise it."

"The same Home Secretary that took all the credit when I released the hostage, adding a couple of points to the government's rankings in the latest MORI poll? Christ, with a couple of minutes of spin, this will be forgotten by the end of next week. He's got plenty of time to make up a story."

"I hardly think —"

"Have you got kids, Andrew?"

"No," Harvey said.

"Well, let me tell you, if you put a thousand fathers in my position, right now, half of them would do what I've just done."

"What about the other half?"

"The other half would have killed him by now."

"I don't think so, Tom. Think about it, how many kids are killed each year? It must be hundreds, but this is the first time anyone has taken the law into their own hands."

"That's rubbish," Gray said. "There will have been quite a few revenge beatings over the years, but very few, if any, make the news. And besides, this hasn't been about a personal vendetta, it has been about raising awareness of the inequalities of justice and getting the law changed so that appropriate sentences are handed down and the courts take into account the suffering of the victim for a change."

"You sound convincing, Tom, and many would believe you, but I'm beginning to think that this was all about getting even with Stuart Boyle from the start."

Gray sighed. "Andrew, we've already been through this. I could have grabbed him any time I liked, and I reckon I could have got away with it if I'd put as much thought into it as I have into what I'm doing now. One thing I will concede, though, is that he was never going to just walk out of here. Whether this ends today or lasts until tomorrow night, he was always going to get a gentle reminder about his future conduct."

Harvey had to admire the composure of the guy. He'd just mangled the kid, yet he sounded like a Sunday school teacher who'd just chastised a four-year-old for wearing a cap in church.

"That didn't sound gentle to me," he said.

"Relax, I just gave him some thinking time, that's all. He won't be able to do much for the next couple of months except reflect on what happened here this week, and hopefully he will come to the right decision as to where his future lies."

"It sounds like he needs medical attention," Harvey said, Boyle's moans clearly audible in the background. "I think it would be best to let him go now."

"He'll be fine. In the meantime, I'd advise you to pass my message on to the Home Secretary."

Gray turned the phone off and returned to Boyle's cell. He wasn't doing very well, the noise subsiding but his body shaking with the amount of adrenalin coursing through his veins. Gray checked him for shock but saw none of the signs: His pulse was fast yet strong; his skin wasn't cold or clammy; and his breathing, while rapid, wasn't shallow.

"You'll live," he said, and put a new piece of tape over his mouth. He turned to leave the cell but stopped in the doorway, looking over his shoulder. With malice aforethought, he turned back and gave Boyle a Chinese burn, just to make sure he got the message.

Chapter 21

Carl Levine steered the narrow boat slowly towards the bank and cut the engine as it glided up to its mooring. He jumped ashore and tied it up securely, then climbed back on board to make sure everyone was ready to leave.

"It's pissing down outside," he said as he entered the cabin, even though this was obvious from the rhythmic drumming on the roof of the boat.

"Good, gives us an excuse to keep our hoods up," Tris Barker-Fink observed.

The eight men packed away the last of their belongings and sat down to wait for the minibus, which turned up just after half past one in the afternoon. While Levine went to hand the boat back, the others took their baggage and climbed aboard, Jeff Campbell taking the seat next to the driver.

The driver was a Geordie in his early thirties, with receding hair and a photo of two kids stuck to the middle of his steering wheel. He smiled and introduced himself as Barry, but as he studied his passenger, his expression changed, concern registering on his face. As their mug shots had been all over the media for the last thirty-six hours, Campbell was expecting just this kind of reaction, and he put his hand inside his jacket pocket.

He withdrew his hand slowly and it took all his will power to stop himself from exploding with laughter: Barry looked like he was torn between running for his life and shitting his pants, having recognised his fares. The look changed to confusion when Campbell revealed a wad of notes.

"Here we go, Barry," he said, counting off five hundred in twenties. "That's a little tip for you. The thing is, I'm going to need your mobile, and I'm afraid we can't be stopping along the way, so if you need to go, go now. One of my friends will escort you to the toilet."

Barry shook his head, mouth still dangling open, so Campbell asked about the fuel situation. It turned out they had nearly a full tank, and Barry assured him it would last them all the way to Leeds.

139

"Sorry, Barry, change of plans. I know we said Leeds when we ordered the bus, but we're actually going south. Just a precaution, you understand."

Barry nodded this time, but when he learned of their new destination he still didn't think they would need to stop for diesel. He was still staring at Campbell, expecting him to pull out a weapon at any moment.

Jeff smiled. "Chill out, Barry. We're not ruthless killers, and we aren't going to hurt you. Just concentrate on the driving and it'll all be over in a few hours. You'll probably be interviewed by the papers afterwards, as well as the news channels. Should earn you a few extra quid."

Barry seemed to perk up at that idea, and it helped him find his voice.

"Did you really kidnap all them thieves?" he asked.

"We can't talk about that, I'm afraid."

"Why not? I thought they were going to let you off, like."

"Maybe," Campbell said, "but we haven't got anything in writing yet, and anything you tell the police could be held against us."

"Fair enough," the driver said, "but if it *was* you, then me and about twenty million others would love to buy you guys a pint. You're the bees knees, real fucking heroes. Not just because of what you did for that Tom guy, but just for being in the SAS. Man, you guys rock. You're like fucking Superman or summut."

"No we're not," Paul Bennett said from the seat behind the driver. "We're just well trained, well disciplined and very fit. We don't leap tall buildings in a single bound, or take on a thousand armed enemy and kill them with a small knife and a single mag of ammo. That's the stuff of books and movies."

Barry turned to face him, undeterred. "Well, *I* think you're heroes. I've been burgled and had me satnav nicked twice in the last four months. What's happening to these toe rags is fucking brilliant, I mean it. There's even a petition on the government website to let Tom off if he turns himself in. I tell ya, the whole country loves 'im, except for the fucking criminals. There's already over a million signatures on it, and it's growing all the time."

"A million?" Campbell asked, quite incredulous.

"Aye. And me and the wife have signed it, and me mates at work. Listen, I fancy meself as a writer. I'd love to hear some of your war

140

stories for me book. It's a bit like them other SAS stories but better, like."

At that moment Carl Levine returned from the boat office and climbed in the back, but Campbell motioned for him to get back out, and he joined him outside the bus.

"You sit up front with the driver," he said.

"Why?" Levine asked.

"Because you are the least likely to be recognised if anyone is coming towards us."

Levine realised this was good thinking on Jeff's part, particularly if they went through any cameras capable of facial recognition. It was good to see that the old team was still on the ball.

Barry set off as soon as Levine put his seatbelt on and immediately began to press him for anecdotes. He turned to look at the smiling Campbell, who simply offered a shrug which said 'I told you we should have tied him up and left him on the boat'."

Carl Levine sat back and thought about the conflicts he had been involved in, from Northern Ireland to Iraq and Afghanistan. He'd risked life and limb on more than one occasion, had fought his way out of impossible situations, and suffered some serious injuries in his time.

After weighing everything up, he knew this was going to be the most difficult three hours of his life.

* * *

A few minutes after Harvey had relayed Gray's message to Hammond, his boss was back on the phone.

"We've got a possible location," Hammond said without preamble. "The chopper spotted a coach at a farm house near Cuckfield and there's a lot of heat sources inside the barn."

"Give me the address," Harvey said, and Hammond relayed the details which he punched into his satnav.

"I'm about fifteen minutes away. Who else is en route?"

"We have Sussex Armed Response vehicles on the way. They should get there at about the same time."

"Okay. I'll let you know what we find."

Harvey cut the connection and let the speed of his Vauxhall creep up to eighty as he barrelled past other vehicles on the A23. He'd been out filling the car when Gray's call had come in, not because he was short on fuel but simply as an excuse to get out of the stuffy bed and breakfast and clear his mind. Some people liked the solitude of a hot foamy bath to do their thinking, others liked background music to get the mental juices flowing, but with Harvey it was driving.

While his focus should have been on finding Sally, he would suddenly find himself thinking about Gray again. He didn't know why, but something was niggling away at the back of his mind. He thought it might be because he was trying to imagine what Gray had done to Stuart Boyle, but he dismissed that idea. No, something wasn't adding up with this whole affair, but he struggled to put his finger on it.

Before he knew it he was off the dual carriageway and less than two miles from his destination, so he cast aside all thoughts of Tom Gray and focused on the job in hand.

The Tactical Firearms Unit had made good time and were waiting a few hundred yards from the farm, which lay just over a small rise. The officers were already out of their vehicles; two Volvo estates and three unmarked cars. Most were donning their gear and checking their weapons, while a senior officer gave instructions.

Harvey climbed out and introduced himself, and was told that a scouting team had already been sent out. "One is heading up that hill there to get a view of the back of the farmhouse," Chief Inspector Roberts said, pointing to a figure dressed in black making his way to the vantage point. Harvey could just about see the chimney of the farmhouse from where he stood, so the armed officer should have a good view of the entire farm once he reached his position.

"Do we know how many are in there?" Harvey asked.

"Thermal imaging from the chopper shows thirty-six. We did a drive-by in an unmarked car but saw no-one outside. Two officers are following the hedgerow to the gate, and once my men are suited up we'll send two unmarked cars to the other end of the lane. At the moment we only want to maintain a perimeter and gather as much intel as we can. If needs be, we'll call in backup."

"What about to the east of the farm? Have you got any men there?"

"There's nothing to the east except fields," the Chief Inspector said. "If anyone makes off that way we can quickly round them up, and the chopper will keep tabs on anyone making a run for it."

Harvey looked up and for the first time heard the faint buzz of the force helicopter as it maintained its position above the area. The sound was barely audible out in the open air, so it was doubtful that anyone inside could hear it.

"Are you patched in to the chopper?"

"We have comms and video feed," the officer said, and offered Harvey a seat in his car, out of the rain. He produced a tablet PC, its seven-inch screen showing exactly what the chopper observer was seeing. A touch screen menu on the right allowed them to toggle through the light spectrum, from visible to infra-red.

"It uses a microwave frequency to provide real-time images from the eye in the sky, really handy for this kind of operation."

"I didn't know they could actually look into buildings," Harvey said. "I mean, I've seen them on cop shows on TV, but all they showed was the outline of buildings. They were never like this."

"That's the old technology. This works on the principal of Capability Brown's dictum that nature abhors a straight line. Special software takes each image apart pixel by pixel and anything which represents a straight line, such as the wall of a building, or a window, is ignored. Only heat sources with irregular shapes are displayed. There's actually more to it than that, but you get the idea."

"You normally just see stuff like this in the movies."

"Well, you'd be surprised at how many movie ideas become reality. Some say the first flip-up mobile phone was modelled on the communicators from Star Trek."

Harvey studied the screen, which showed white blobs representing the body heat of the people inside the barn. A few appeared to be stationary, others moving around slowly, as if mingling at a party.

"No-one seems to be isolated," he observed. "I would have expected Sally to be kept apart from the rest of them."

"I had the same thought, but we found no other heat sources apart from those in the barn. She might be in the main house, or it could mean she's..."

He left the statement hanging, and Harvey knew he didn't think there was much hope of finding Sally alive. Nevertheless, if they went in, it had to be on the assumption that she was.

"Do you have any thermal cameras of your own, or are you relying on the chopper images?"

"We haven't the budget for them at the moment, but we hope to get some in the next financial year."

Fat lot of good that will do us now, Harvey thought.

"What information do we have about the bus?"

"Hired four weeks ago, paid by credit card and collected two days ago," Roberts told him.

"Doesn't sound like our guys, unless it was a cloned or stolen card. Even then, they would probably use it much closer to the time to avoid detection. This doesn't add up."

Harvey tapped his fingers on the side of the seat, deep in thought. "I'll need a gun," he said. "If this goes down soon you'll need every available man."

"My men can handle anything they are presented with," Roberts said, dismissing the idea.

"Have it your way." Harvey got on the phone to Hammond and three minutes later the Chief Inspector got a call from his superiors. It only lasted a few seconds, and after hanging up he opened the car's armoury and grudgingly handed over the Austrian pistol, a belt holster, two single-stack magazines and twenty 9mm rounds.

After loading the magazines, Harvey pulled the slide back to ensure it was clear, inserted a mag, hit the slide release to chamber a round and applied the safety. It took less than a minute to thread the holster onto his own belt and he stowed the weapon, all the time keeping an eye on the images coming from the tablet PC.

Two of the unmarked cars set off to take up their positions further up the road, and the officer on the hill reached the crest, lying up in the rain sodden ground. After a quick scan through his binoculars he reported back to the scene commander.

"Only two windows on this side of the building, both have their curtains closed. I can't see any movement."

"Acknowledged. Charlie team, what's your status?"

"Charlie team in position, one hundred yards from the farm entrance. No sign of movement from here."

"Roger that."

"Now what?" Harvey asked.

"We wait. Once we know what we're up against we can then make a decision. First, though, we need to identify exactly who we're dealing with."

"Well, we can't do that sitting in here. I'm going to take a closer look."

"I can't allow that, Mr. Harvey."

Harvey already had his hand on the door release. "If we wait for them to come out, we could be sitting here for days. Let me get in close and ID them, then you can decide what to do."

Roberts was about to object again, but Harvey stopped him short. "If you want to sit and read the Health and Safety manual, that's fine, but while there's a chance my colleague is in there I want to go and take a look. You can either tag along, or I can call my boss again. I don't want to have to do that because it could cost you your job, but we have good reason to believe an attack is going to take place in the next twenty-four hours and there simply isn't time to do things by the book."

Roberts knew it wasn't an empty threat, and that there was more to be gained from playing along than making waves. There was certainly a lot to lose if he stood in the spook's way, and he hadn't risen this high by making bad decisions.

"Okay, on your head be it. The chopper has done a three-sixty of the area and the best way to approach is from up on the hill, where Simpson is keeping watch. There's a large window on the ground floor and a smaller window on the first floor. Once you've had a good look at the house and the barn, get back here, preferably without losing the element of surprise."

Harvey let the last comment slide: If he'd been in Roberts' position he would probably have said something a little more cutting.

"I'll need comms," he told the officer.

"We haven't got any. They are issued at the station and we don't carry spares."

Harvey thought for a moment. "Give me your mobile number."

He typed in the digits as Roberts recited them and hit the Call button. "Answer it and leave the connection open," Harvey said, climbing out of the warm car and into the teeming rain, turning his collar up as drops ran down his neck.

The climb would have been a doddle in dry weather but the underfoot conditions made walking a nightmare, and he slipped a dozen times before he reached the summit. He tapped Officer Simpson on the shoulder and began the climb down the other side, the descent a lot faster than the ascent. When he reached the bottom he moved as fast as the conditions would allow to the wall of the house and crouched down under the window. With his right hand he drew his weapon and with his left he reached into his pocket and pulled out his phone.

"I'm at the window but I can't hear anything," he whispered into the handset.

"Roger that," Roberts replied.

Harvey stuck his head up, looking for a gap that would afford him a glance into the room, and he found one in the bottom right hand corner. He peeped through but saw no sign of movement, so he moved to the end of the wall and gauged the distance to the barn. It appeared to be no more than forty yards away, maybe four or five seconds on a good day, but the rain had turned the ground to thick mud and it wouldn't be easy going.

He decided to take the long way round, moving first behind a tractor, then finding cover behind a Land Rover a few yards away. He stopped to survey the area, but saw no movement from either the barn or the house. The next piece of cover was a muck-spreading machine, and once he made his way there he had only open ground to the barn. The distance was down to about twenty yards and he covered it as fast as he could, nearly losing his balance twice.

He was at the rear of the barn, which was solidly built from slats of wood nailed vertically to a wooden frame. Finding a way to look inside wasn't going to be easy. He quickly checked the planks but couldn't find a gap between any of them, so he headed round the side, hidden from any prying eyes in the house. Here he had more time to explore, and found a knot hole at waist height. Peering inside, he was met with a wall of darkness, but he could hear muffled voices. He moved further along the wall, all the time checking for the slightest gap, and he eventually found one right on the corner. He knelt down to look through the two-inch hole and clearly saw the occupants.

Holstering the gun, he stood up and spoke into the phone. "Pull your men back. These aren't the people we're looking for."

"Who's in there?" Roberts asked.

"I don't know, but unless our targets managed to age forty years and have a sex change in the last twenty-four hours, this isn't them. It looks like some sort of local produce fayre. They're probably inside because of the rain."

Rather than risk climbing back up the hill, Harvey walked out of the farm's main entrance and caught a lift back to his car.

Chapter 22

Abdul Mansour had been putting his men through their paces since six that morning and they all knew their responsibilities. After nine hours of practice it was time for a meal — the last one for most, he knew — and then they would begin the last leg of their journey.

With no suitable cooking facilities available, they had sent two cars into town to purchase soft drinks, cold meats and bread. Not the most elegant of banquets, but it was enough to give them the energy they would need in the coming hours.

Mansour ate his share while once again studying the men around him. The ones who had weapons experience had done a good job teaching the novices, and now every man could change a magazine within five seconds and all knew the drill for clearing a blockage. It was unfortunate that they couldn't conduct any live fire exercises, as that would have given him a true indication of their ability to handle the rifles, and he expected many to panic when the time came, but he had chosen the best to lead the fire from the ridge, and as long as they cleared a path for the riders that was all that mattered. The rest would rain down chaos and confusion, and the under-manned police force would not know which way to turn.

Popping the last slice of cold mutton into his mouth, he went down to the cellar to add the finishing touches to the two vests the riders would wear. The C4 explosive was in place, as were the detonators. All he needed to do now was attach the wiring from the detonators to the wire leading to the vibration device of an unregistered pay-as-you-go mobile phone, so that when he called the number the electrical charge would instead set off the smaller charge, which would trigger the bigger explosion.

He could have attached them earlier, but even though no-one knew the number, these modern dialling machines could accidentally trip across the numbers and set of the vests prematurely.

With the numbers pre-programmed into his own unregistered phone against the colours each rider would be wearing — black and red — he made the connections and carried the vests up the stairs. As he reached the top he heard the sound of a ringtone and placed the vests carefully on the floor, his body tensing as the anger took a hold.

"Who has a phone?" he shouted, and all eyes turned to him, then slowly they all turned their heads to look at one of the men at the back of the barn.

Mansour strode over and snatched the phone from him, looking for the Off switch. He couldn't immediately find one, so he thrust it back into the man's hand.

"Turn it off, now!"

Ibrahim Mohammed sheepishly took the Smartphone and did as instructed, then handed it back to Mansour.

"I said no mobile phones, didn't I?"

He looked around the room and the general consensus was that Ibrahim had fucked up badly, and it showed on their faces.

"Who else has a phone?" Mansour demanded.

No-one spoke, so he turned to Ibrahim. "Why did you bring this?" he asked, barely trying to disguise the anger in his voice.

"I didn't bring it, brother, it belonged to the woman."

Mansour almost turned purple, the vein in his temple throbbing. "How stupid can one person be?" he shouted. "Every secret service agent in this country is looking for that woman, and you turn on her phone and lead them straight to us!"

"I'm sorry, brother, I —"

Ibrahim didn't manage to finish the sentence due to the knife protruding from the front of his throat. Mansour withdrew the blade and watched as he collapsed to the floor, clutching at the wound, blood pouring between his fingers.

Abdul watched until he took his last breath, then turned to the others.

"That is the last time anyone disobeys me. Is that clear?"

There were nods all round, and their expressions told him that they were obviously shocked at the sudden explosion of violence. This didn't bode well for the coming battle, but there wasn't time to do anything about it.

"Everyone, pack up your things and be ready to leave in the next five minutes. You two," he said, pointing to the riders standing next to their bikes, "come with me and I will show you how the vests work."

The men followed him and he dressed each one in turn, then showed them how to operate the trigger. It was a small device, much like a lipstick container, with a red button on the top. A twenty-inch length of wire ran from the trigger to the first of the detonators, then spread out like a spider's web to connect to the other detonators embedded in the twenty packs of explosives, ten on the front of each vest and another ten on the back. Each block of C4 was the size of a Snickers bar and he had studded them all with nails in order to cause the maximum amount of collateral damage.

"Put your jackets on and keep them zipped up. We don't want anyone seeing the explosives before we even get there."

Mansour turned to address the others. "I want to make sure you all know the route. Sami, where do we meet up?"

"At the Hare and Hounds pub on the A272."

"Good. Zulfir, how do we get there?"

"Follow the A22 to the Black Down roundabout, then take the first left towards Haywards Heath. At the next roundabout take the first left, signposted Newick, then follow the signs for the A272 for another six miles."

"Excellent. Has everyone got that?" Everyone offered a single nod.

"I want a couple of cars between each of us, and those in the back seats should keep your heads down as much as possible. They will probably be looking for a coach, but if they see thirty men in convoy it could give us away.

"Brothers, our time has come. Be strong, be brave. Allah will be watching over us.

"Allahu Akbar!"

"*Allahu Akbar!*" they chorused.
.

* * *

When the call came in Harvey was just leaving a convenience store, having picked up a sandwich for a late lunch. He was still pissed that he had been forced to return the Glock, but as he had separated from the Tactical Firearms Unit he could hardly go gallivanting around the countryside with a weapon they were responsible for.

The display said the call was from Hammond and he hit the Accept button.

"We've found Sally," his boss said. "She's at a farm seven miles north of Eastbourne."

"Another wild goose chase?" Harvey asked, not relishing another crawl up a muddy hill.

149

"Not this time. Her phone was activated for just under three minutes, then went dead again. GCHQ pinpointed her location and the TFU are on their way. Meet them at these co-ordinates."

Hammond began to reel the numbers off but Harvey stopped him. "John, the Armed Response Vehicles are all well and good for domestic stand-offs, but this is different. We need someone with a lot more experience in hostage situations. The boys from Hereford, to be exact."

"I've already been in touch with them, but it will take them five hours to deploy, and there are signs that Mansour and his team have been at the farm but the chopper only saw two faint heat sources, which means they've moved on. If Mansour is going to make his hit today, five hours is just too long."

"What about the team deployed to tackle Gray? He's probably going to be coming out in the next four hours, so is it really necessary to have them there?"

Hammond was silent for a while, weighing up the options, but he came to the same conclusion as his subordinate.

"Okay, I'll get in touch with their CO and get back to you. In the meantime, take these details down and get moving."

Harvey asked him to wait while he got back into his car, then punched the location into the satnav. He was looking at a thirty minute drive, and the SAS would be facing a slightly longer journey.

"I want to meet up with the Tactical Firearms Unit on the way and grab some of their kit," Harvey said. "Their tablet PC link to the local police chopper will be handy for a tactical overview. It would also help if you can get hold of a handheld thermal camera for the take down. I think I saw one mentioned in one of the daily reports from SO15. Can you check on that?"

"I'll call them and find out. If they haven't got one, we'll source one from somewhere," Hammond promised.

Harvey asked him to make sure the Sussex Police Helicopter got above the scene as soon as possible, then set off through the driving rain.

The timing of the discovery couldn't have been worse, the streets and lanes packed with parents picking their kids up from school. It was bad enough in fine weather, but during downpours it was always bedlam, with three times as many vehicles on the road, and most of them people carriers.

What he thought would be a half-hour journey was going to take at least twice as long, and he still had to meet up with the Tactical Firearms Unit. First, though, he had to get out of this traffic jam and onto open road.

He called Roberts and arranged to meet a couple of miles away, and the officer was waiting when he pulled up to the hotel car park. Harvey got into the police car and Roberts handed him a tablet PC, making sure Harvey knew how to use it.

"I'm sorry about earlier," Harvey said as he was getting out. "I was a bit harsh going over your head."

"Don't mention it. Roles reversed, I would probably have done the same myself."

Harvey conceded the point and ran back to his own car, sending spray flying as he sped onto the main road.

During the journey he received a call from Hammond, who gave him new co-ordinates for the rendezvous and confirmed that the team he was meeting had already picked up the thermal camera from SO15.

Traffic had thinned with the end of the school run and he managed to catch up a little time, but still arrived ten minutes behind Blythe and his men.

He wasn't surprised to see only eight of them, as he had been a fan of the SAS since he purchased a copy of Bravo Two Zero in the early nineties. There had been no internet for him to do more research on them when he was thirteen, but he had found a plethora of books at his local library and had read everything from their formation by David Stirling in 1941, their exploits in the Dhofar rebellion, right through to the Iranian Embassy siege on the fifth of May 1980 and their much understated presence in the Falkland conflict of 1982.

They were all parked up in a field a mile from the target, their two Land Rovers hidden from view by an overgrown hedge which lined the road. Harvey's car had struggled to join up with them after entering the field, its tyres more suited to concrete than sodden wet grass.

The men before him represented two four-man patrols and had been through the rigorous counter revolutionary warfare training, which included expert training in close quarter battle, hostage rescue and siege breaking. Rather than the black uniform normally associated with the SAS, they wore normal fatigues, the disruptive pattern material more suited to the current surroundings.

A glance up through the stinging rain confirmed that Hotel nine-hundred, the Sussex Police Helicopter, was on station.

"What's the plan?" he asked Blythe.

"Willard has gone ahead with the thermal imaging camera and will let us know where the x-rays are, and the best angle from which to approach the building. We'll be setting off to join him in the next few minutes."

"Okay. Wanna take a seat in your Land Rover and view the aerial picture?"

Blythe nodded and they escaped the rain, ensuring the tablet PC didn't get wet. The picture showed one very faint heat sign in the barn and only a couple of faint sources in the farm building itself. Two of the white blobs appeared to be lying down, with only one moving around. Looking further afield, they saw hedges on three sides of the farm that would provide them cover from view, at least until they made the assault, but there were no further signs of human life. A few animals were seen, but nothing large enough to be a person in disguise.

"Looks like they already left," Blythe said, "but one of these two prone figures could be your colleague."

"Then we go in and get her."

"Not we," Blythe told him, "us. You stay here and set up a road block, see if we can catch the others."

Harvey looked surprised, like he'd just been slapped in the face. "The girl in there is my responsibility," he said. "I'm not here to organise the traffic cops."

"You're not coming with us, period. We don't work like that. We work hard and train hard, and I'm not having one of my operations going tits up because some spook thinks he's John McLean."

"But —"

"No buts, you stay here. You'll have comms and you can keep us updated on their positions using the chopper view, but you're not joining the take down."

Harvey pulled out his phone and hit the speed dial for Hammond. "John, can you get on to the MOD and have a word —"

Blythe grabbed the phone from his grasp and put it to his ear, ignoring Harvey's protestations. "This is Major Sean Blythe, who am I speaking to?"

"Sean, it's John. We spoke earlier."

"Well John, we have a problem. As the team leader, we go on my say-so, and my say-so only. Either tell your boy to pull his neck in and let us do our job, or we withdraw and he can go in by himself."

"Let me speak to him."

Blythe handed the phone over, no emotion on his face. Harvey took it and listened to his superior.

"Andrew, you asked for these people because you know they are the best at what they do. It's time to swallow your pride and let them get on with their job."

It wasn't his pride that was the issue, it was the knowledge that once this was over, his ten-year career would be, too. If he could come out of this with some distinction he might be able to salvage something, but as Hammond pointed out, these were the best men for the job, and he was more likely to be a hindrance than a help. He realised that his desire to take part in the operation was not driven by the hope of saving Sally, but for his own selfish reasons, despite feeling responsible for her current position.

Besides, it was the Gray affair that had caused all the problems, and nothing he did in the next four hours was going to make up for the fact that he had been unable to prevent loss of life or injury to the hostages. That it was Gray who had put the Home Secretary in such an awkward political position wasn't his fault, but he knew he would be the one to take the blame.

"You're right, John. I'm sorry."

Harvey hung up and apologised to Blythe, too, who brushed it aside as if the little episode had never taken place.

"I want you to organise road blocks for a twenty mile radius. They can't have got that far in the last hour, so we start at twenty miles and squeeze it until we have them cornered."

"Road blocks have already been set up," Harvey told him. "That's the first thing our team did."

"What radius?"

"That I don't know," Harvey admitted.

"Then find out, and make sure it's big enough that they couldn't have slipped through already. We need — "

He held up a finger as he listened to the message coming through on his earpiece. After a moment he tapped his throat microphone twice to acknowledge the message, then shared the details with Harvey.

153

"Willard says there are no x-rays moving in the barn, but the door is open and he can see a coach. That suggests they left in other transport. Pass that on to the police, they might just be looking for one vehicle.

"He also has two heat sources in the house, one on the ground floor and one on the first. The one on the first floor appears to be lying down. That's probably Sally."

"I agree."

Blythe handed over a comms set and showed Harvey how to use it, then gathered his men together and told them what they were up against. Within minutes they were on their way to meet up with Willard at the Lying Up Point, sticking close to the hedge in single file.

The LUP was behind a hedge three-feet high, roughly five hundred yards from the barn, to the right of which lay the farm house. They found Willard crouching down, viewing the scene through the budding foliage.

"Echo one," Blythe said through his throat mike, using Harvey's call sign. "We're at the LUP. Do you have an update on x-ray one's position?"

"I have you on the screen, and x-ray one is on the far side of the main building."

X-ray one was the designation of the heat source that was mobile, the one least likely to be Sally. X-ray two was the figure on the first floor, while x-ray three was in the barn. While Blythe and his team had their own thermal imaging camera and were able to see which floor x-ray one was on, they only had a two-dimensional view of him, and no depth perception. Harvey, in turn, could only see where he was in relation to the inner walls. Together, however, they could build up a three-dimensional picture of the target's exact location.

"We need to take him alive so that we can find out what Mansour's target is."

"If he co-operates, he'll live," was all Blythe would commit to, then he spoke to the four men who would make the initial approach. "Take yourselves down the hedge line until you have the barn between yourselves and the farm house, then move across and clear it. Once the barn is secure we will move on the house."

Edwards, Monk, Frost and Wickens moved off at a trot and within two minutes they signalled that they were in position.

154

The other four would remain in reserve at the LUP, with Mitchell manning the HK417 medium range sniper rifle.

"Echo one, any sign of movement in the barn?" Blythe asked.

"Negative," Harvey replied, so he gave the word to move in.

The four men pushed their way through a gap in the hedge and covered the ground quickly, lining up against the side of the barn. Monk took the lead, rounding the corner and rushing through the opening, rifle raised covering the right-hand side of the building. Edwards was next through, the barrel of the MP5SD suppressed sub-machine gun following his eyes as he scanned for signs of movement. They were followed quickly by Frost and Wickens, who moved past them and made their way to the back of the barn where the heat source was known to be.

Frost raised his fist when he saw the feet sticking out from the front of the bus and as he moved in closer he kept his gun trained on the prostrate figure, even though the pool of blood around its head suggested it wasn't going to put up much of a fight.

"X-ray three is dead," he reported, and the others crowded round, two checking the body for signs of life and booby-traps while the others kept their weapons trained.

"Building clear," Frost said. "Where is x-ray one?"

"Still on the far side of the farm house. Move in now."

Frost responded with two clicks of the throat mike and signalled to the others to move out. The plan was for Wickens and Frost to set charges on two of the ground floor windows. They would detonate the first and send through CS cannisters, and while the target was reeling from this they would detonate the second charge, further disorientating him, allowing two of the team to burst through the door and make the take down.

They were just setting the first shaped charge when the call came through.

"X-ray one is on the move, heading upstairs."

Flynn had been torn between emotions since his encounter with the woman earlier that morning. His personal porn collection swayed towards the dominance and submission genre, and when this young filly had landed in his lap he thought it was Christmas and all his birthdays come at once. Last night had been the first chance he had ever had to play out his fantasies, but this morning she had shattered those dreams.

At first he'd felt shame, like someone had walked in on him in mid-masturbation. In effect, that is what she had done, jumping into his fantasy without invitation and catching him unawares.

Next had come anger, a burning desire to punish her for ruining his morning. Not just this morning, but the days and weeks ahead. He had planned to keep her alive for as long as possible, but after this morning's performance he wasn't so sure.

The final emotion had been lust, his loin leading his head, telling him to keep her around, just smack the confidence out of her. This emotion had won the day, and he had laid into her just after nine that morning, punctuating each slap with an instruction.

"*Don't...*"

Whack!

"*...ever...*"

Slap!

"*...speak...*"

Smack!

"*...to me...*"

Whack!

"*...again!*"

She had laid there sobbing, her left eye beginning to swell and blood running from her nose where she had moved her head mid-slap. She wasn't a pretty picture when he left her, and he realised he had done exactly what he asked the rag-head not to do: damage her. After taking himself away to calm down he had returned an hour later and was pleased to see her cowering this time. Regardless, she was still in a state, so he had untied her and allowed her to clean herself up, all the time demeaning her to make sure she understood that she was his slave now, that there was no friendship or pity involved. He made her change the bedding and scrub the mattress, getting rid of the piss-stained sheet and the smell that went with it.

After tying her up again he had left her alone, but parted with a warning that he would be back for more later, and return he did, but only to release her left hand so that she could eat a meagre lunch. He knew this would increase her anxiety, and it appeared to work.

Leaving her for a couple of hours longer, he settled down to watch one of his favourite DVDs to get himself in the mood, but he was interrupted by the sound of the cars leaving in a hurry. He would have to dispose of the coach himself, but that wasn't a problem. That can be done later this evening, he thought. It was simply a case of driving it to the outskirts of the town two miles away and leaving it running. Some local piss-head would have it away in a matter of minutes, and no doubt it would be burnt out by the morning.

Once they were gone he concentrated again on the movie. After years of practice he could bring himself close to climax again and again without going over the edge, and he was almost delirious as he climbed the stairs for the final explosive moment.

As squad leader, Frost would make the ultimate decision, and there just wasn't time to hold a Chinese parliament and get the opinions of the other three. They could try to make a noise and coax him downstairs again, but that would put him on his guard, and an x-ray on edge was not conducive to a good day. On the other hand, if they forced an entry while he was upstairs he would have time to arm himself and either kill the hostage or kill one of his men, neither of which options he could accept.

Peering through the kitchen window he saw a mobile phone on the counter, and it gave him an idea, which he shared with the team.

He took off his respirator and put his ear to the glass in the back door. From the other end of the house he heard the muffled shouts, which wasn't good for the hostage but it should keep the x-ray occupied for a few moments. The door was old, paint flaking all around the frame, so he was very gentle when he tried the handle. At first he thought it was locked, but when he applied a little pressure it gave with a creak.

Heart in his mouth, he was aware that the shouting had stopped. His hand went to the trigger guard of the MP5SD, ready to rush, but a moment later the verbal abuse started up again, much to his relief.

Removing one of his gloves, he crept into the kitchen and closed the door, then picked up the phone, flicking through the menu to the Sounds option. He selected Ringtones, then chose the current tune and put it back on the counter top near the sink before retreating to a position behind the kitchen door.

A moment later he heard the sound of footsteps as the target rushed down the stairs and burst into the room, grabbing the phone. He had his back to Frost, so he couldn't see the look of confusion, but when he pounced he saw the surprise on the x-ray's face.

"Down on the floor! Now!"

Flynn spun round and stared in amazement at the soldier pointing the silenced weapon at him.

His first thought was that he was truly fucked.

His second was that it was the rag-head's fault.

His third thought was to grab for the knife in the sink, and it was the last thought he ever had.

The first bullet smashed through his temple and pierced the brain as it continued its journey. By the time it hit the far side of the skull it had lost so much momentum that it wasn't capable of breaking through the other side, so it just bounced around like a fly in a jar, shredding the brain even more.

The second bullet, fired less than a second later, wasn't necessary, but training dictated a double-tap and that's what the x-ray got.

The other three members of the team burst in as he shouted his warning but Flynn was on the floor before they got through the door, so they hurdled over him and raced through the kitchen door.

"X-ray one down," Frost reported, his voice just a little taut after his first kill.

The squad cleared the house room by room, ending up in the master bedroom, where they found Sally still tied to the bed, tears running down her face. They didn't know if they were tears of fear or joy, but as with most traumatic situations they knew they would continue for some time. They untied her and gently wrapped her in the bed sheet before escorting her down the stairs and into the front room, seating her on the sofa.

"House clear, x-ray one down, hostage safe," Frost said over the comm link, his voice steadier now that the burst of adrenalin had been spent. "She has a few injuries but nothing life-threatening. I'm more concerned about her mental state."

Chapter 23

Twelve miles from their destination, it might as well have been twelve thousand miles, because if he spent another minute in Barry's company, Carl Levine was sure he would kill him. The last three hours had been an absolute nightmare, and he'd lost count of the number of times he's said "That's classified". Still, Barry was relentless, desperate for a first-hand account of a battle — or even a minor skirmish — for his book.

Eventually Levine had caved in, and told him about the time he and three others had parachuted into Taliban territory in Afghanistan. They had marched forty miles in two nights carrying a hundred pounds of kit each, then attacked an enemy stronghold, killing over a hundred and fifty men and rescuing a British soldier before carrying him the forty miles back to the pick-up point.

Barry was lapping it up, but the others in the back could barely contain themselves. They knew for a fact that Carl had never been to Afghanistan, and that no self-respecting squad leader would ever take three men on such a suicidal operation. Even when Paul Bennett started ribbing Levine about his exploits, Barry just thought it was friendly regimental banter.

Their destination was a holiday cottage two miles from Gray's stronghold. As with the narrow boat and the minibus, it had been paid for on a credit card belonging to one of their non-military friends, so it was unlikely that it would be traced back to any of them. Their friend had been given the cash plus a little extra for his trouble, along with a family holiday that would end at the weekend, giving him the perfect reason for not informing the authorities about the purchases.

They planned to stop off in the nearby town to stock up on beer and snacks, and the local takeaways would be providing the catering that evening, but when they reached a point roughly a mile from the cottage, the minibus negotiated a bend and they found themselves confronted with a police roadblock a hundred yards ahead. The officers looked to be concentrating on cars coming from the opposite direction, but they couldn't take any chances.

"Heads up," Levine said, and everyone craned to see what the problem was. Having identified the danger, the men in the back averted their gaze, not so much that they aroused suspicion, but enough to make identification a little harder. They had discussed the possibility of being stopped on the way and had decided that it wouldn't be the end of the world; they would go along quietly. All they had to do was hold out until seven-thirty that evening, and after all the interrogation training they had been through, being questioned by plod didn't even come close to scary.

"Just chill, Barry, and act normally," Levine said.

There were two police cars creating a chicane, with officers at either end allowing traffic to flow first in one direction, then the other. They followed the line of traffic as it crept towards the officer on point duty, Levine silently praying that they be allowed to pass unhindered.

It wasn't to be.

The armed officer raised his hand just as Barry was about to follow the car in front through the gap, then he signalled to his colleague at the other end of the roadblock to allow his stream of traffic to start moving.

"What do we do now?" Barry asked through clenched teeth, his gaze fixed ahead and his hands gripping the steering wheel in the ten-to-two position.

"First," Levine said as jovially as possible, "we drop the ventriloquist act. If you notice, they are only checking the cars coming from the other direction."

Barry seemed to relax slightly as he saw that Levine was correct, but he was still ill at ease.

"What if they recognise us?"

"Why would they recognise you, Barry? Have you had your face plastered all over the front pages this week?"

"No, but I mean, the rest of you...and how can you be so cool, like?"

"We've been in tighter spots than this," Levine said, trying to keep a smile on his face despite the temptation to throw Barry through the windscreen. "It's only a cop, for fuck's sake. It's not like the Sussex branch of Al-Qaeda just swarmed into view."

The quip helped him loosen up a little, but he was still gripping the wheel tightly and staring at the officer, who was facing the other direction.

"Just a couple more minutes and we'll be through," Levine said softly, doing his best to relax the driver, but Barry was having none of it. When the policeman turned to see how much traffic he was holding, he caught sight of Barry and knew instantly that something was amiss.

With a quick word into his radio, he approached the minibus, his right hand on the grip of the Heckler and Koch MP5 he was carrying, forefinger extended along the side of the trigger guard.

"Barry, chill, for fuck's sake," Levine urged. "Just answer his questions and we'll be on our way."

The officer gestured for Barry to wind down the window and he peered inside, taking in the scene.

"Is this your vehicle, Sir?" Constable Stuart Fisher asked.

"Yes, officer," Barry said, and Levine could hear the tension in his voice. The policeman also sensed it, and the alarm bells started ringing.

"Turn the engine off and step out of the vehicle, please," he said, and Barry turned to look at Levine, his eyes imploring him to do something. Carl simply nodded his head. "Go on, then. Do as the officer says."

Barry climbed out gingerly and Levine knew the game was up when the driver raised his hands above his head in surrender.

The cop told Barry to assume the position up against the side of the bus and he reached in and took the keys from the ignition, then told Levine to step down and move around the front of the vehicle, all the time keeping a watchful eye on him.

Another officer trotted up, having been summoned earlier, and he covered the two men while Fisher opened the back door and told everyone to get out. He stood back as they did so and immediately recognised three of the faces as they exited the vehicle.

"Lie face down on the ground and spread your arms and legs," he shouted, all the time covering them with his weapon.

"Hotel Sierra, this is Tango Foxtrot Two-Five."

"Go ahead, Two-Five."

"I believe we have the eight suspects we're looking for in connection with the Tom Gray kidnappings."

"Roger that, please hold."

The other officer ordered Barry and Levine to the rear of the vehicle and instructed them to lie down next to their friends, then radioed the officers at the other end of the roadblock to bring up their handcuffs and some plasticuffs, temporary plastic binds used when no cuffs were available. Barry moaned at having to lie on the wet tarmac with the rain bouncing down all around him, but he got little sympathy.

Fisher read each of them their rights and all acknowledged him, except for Barry.

"I'm not one of them," he pleaded. "I'm just the driver. They hired me to bring them here."

"He's telling the truth," Levine said, glad of the opportunity to be rid of him, but Fisher was having none of it.

"Two-Five, be advised, we have no available units at this time. You are requested to escort them to the command centre outside the old Sussex Renaissance Potteries building on the B3387."

The officer recognised that as the location of the old pottery factory in which Tom Gray was holed up, and it wasn't very far away. The only problem was how to transport them. Two other armed officers ran over and they began securing their suspects, and he used this time to come up with a plan of action.

His decision was to load them back into the minibus, and he climbed into the driver's seat while one of his colleagues sat in the back to keep an eye on the prisoners.

"Isn't this against health and safety regulations?" Paul Bennett asked whimsically. "Shouldn't we have seatbelts or something?"

"Shut it," the officer in the back chided. "No talking."

Ideally Fisher would have kept the prisoners separated so that they couldn't formulate a defence against any upcoming charges, but without the manpower it was impossible. Besides, he thought, they had been hiding out together for a while now, which meant they had already had more than enough opportunity to get their stories straight. Couple that with the short journey time and he didn't think it would make much of a difference.

Thankfully, none of them felt like talking, and they arrived at the outer perimeter within six minutes. Having radioed ahead, they were waved through the checkpoint and drove the last few hundred yards to the command vehicle, where they found Evan Davies waiting for them.

"Just leave them in the vehicle," he told Fisher as he climbed out. "Someone will be here shortly to pick them up."

"Can you arrange transport to take us back to the roadblock?" the officer asked.

162

"No need. These guys will be transferred to another vehicle soon, then you can take the minibus back."

Davies looked through the windows and put names to faces for all of the passengers apart from Barry.

"Who's that?" he asked Fisher.

"Claims to be just the driver."

"Let him go," Davies said.

"Sir?"

"Release him," Davies said, emphasising each syllable.

"But Sir, he might be an accomplice. Shouldn't we at least —"

"We have our orders," the Superintendent broke in. "Someone will be along in thirty minutes to collect the eight suspects. It's out of our hands now."

"Do you want me to go down to the station with them? I am the arresting officer, after all."

"I doubt they'll be going anywhere near a police station," Davies told him. "The orders came from the very top, so we just do as we're told. Get the driver out and stick him in the command vehicle for now. You can take him with you when you leave."

Fisher did as instructed, but with a sense of betrayal: This was the biggest arrest of his career, and no-one would hear about it. It probably wouldn't even be a factor when he came up for promotion and that really pissed him off, and in turn he was a little aggressive as he dragged Barry from the back of the minibus.

Levine wasn't impressed with his manner. "Take it easy," he said. "The guy's done nothing wrong. Wrong place at the wrong time, that's all."

"Shut the fuck up," Fisher snarled. "You should be more concerned about your own safety."

Levine snorted. "I think we can handle a couple of hours in a police cell."

"You should be so lucky," Fisher said as he slammed the door closed.

"What's he talking about?" Levine asked.

"No idea," the officer in the back of the van said. "Just keep quiet."

* * *

Harvey had watched the whole affair at the farm house on the video link provided by the helicopter and heard every word through his

163

comms unit. When the confirmation came in that Sally was alive he was relieved beyond measure, and called the emergency services, just to be on the safe side.

"Ambulance on its way," Harvey confirmed. "I'm coming in."

He gunned his motor which resulted in him fishtailing around on the wet grass. He soon realised that slowly was going to be the quickest way out of the field, but once on the open road he floored the accelerator and was outside the farmhouse in no time.

Blythe was waiting at the back door by the time he arrived, having jogged in from the LUP. Harvey took off his comms gear and handed it back. "Thanks."

"Keep it," Blythe said. "You have comms to the police manning the roadblocks, and you can guide us in if they find anything. Meanwhile, we'll head back to our vehicles and wait to hear from you."

"What about Gray? Is that assignment over?"

"It is for us. We would be unlikely to get the orders to take him down at this late stage, and the more pressing need is to find these terrorists. It's better to stay here, in the centre of the search area, so that we can deploy in any direction at a moment's notice."

"That's good to hear," Harvey said. "Nice take down, by the way. Was there no way of taking him alive, though?"

"I don't second guess the squad leaders. If x-ray one had complied he'd still be with us, but he made his choice, and we don't take any chances. At least he got a warning shout, and that is not something we do every day."

Which is why they had built up such a fearsome reputation, Harvey thought.

He remembered the Balcombe Street siege in December 1975. Four suspected members of a Provisional Irish Republican Army Active Service Unit were chased through London after shooting through the windows of a Mayfair restaurant. This led to a six-day standoff in a block of flats, during which the four suspects held a married couple hostage. Negotiations were going nowhere, so knowing the suspects were following the events on the news, the authorities leaked information that the SAS had turned up to end the siege. The terrorists promptly freed the hostages and surrendered.

"I'll go and speak to Sally, see if she can give us a clue as to what Mansour is planning."

He found her sitting on the couch, the bed sheet wrapped tightly around her, rocking gently back and forth.

The marks on her face looked superficial, but the real damage would be the psychological scars. She would get all the help she needed from the service, that was for sure, and eventually she would forget this episode, or at least learn to live with it. For now, though, he wanted her to recollect as much as possible.

"How are you holding up?" he asked her.

"I'm fine," she said, but he could tell she was far from okay. Although she was looking at him, her focus was elsewhere.

"Sally, did they mention their target at any time?"

She shook her head. "They spoke in Urdu, but used a few English words here and there. You know, words they don't have in their own language."

"Which words? Do you remember any?"

"I heard AK-47 a couple of times, but that's about it. They took me into a cellar somewhere but weren't with me for long, only about twenty minutes. After that it was Flynn..."

Her voice tailed off as the recent memories came flooding back, but Harvey couldn't allow her to dwell, not just yet.

"What about Mansour? Did he speak to you?"

"Yes, he came in and told Flynn to leave, but he didn't say what his target was, he just wanted to know what I knew — what we knew — about him."

Her eyes started to cloud over. "I told him everything, everything I knew..."

The tears came now, so he sat beside her and put a comforting arm around her shoulder.

"You did what you had to do," he assured her. "Most people would."

The words didn't seem to comfort her, the tears still coming thick and fast.

"I doubt the information you gave him would do him any good," he said. "What exactly did you tell him?"

She managed to get herself under a semblance of control. "I told him I was with the Service, and that we knew about his arrival."

"That's it?"

Sally nodded.

"Then that's nothing he wouldn't have already guessed." He ran his palm up and down her arm. "It's okay, Sally. No-one will blame you for any of this. We're all just so relieved that you're okay."

She nodded again, and blew her nose on the bed sheet.

"Are you sure Mansour didn't say anything at all about his target? How about the others?"

"Nothing, really. Well, there was one thing..."

"What?"

"I'm sure it was nothing..."

Harvey wanted to shout at her to spit it out but knew that would be counter-productive. Instead he cajoled her gently.

"You never know, Sally. Even a single word could be significant."

"Well, there were a few of them standing at the top of the cellar stairs and I heard the word 'grey' a few times. At first I thought they were probably talking about the weather, what with the sky being grey for the last few days, but later it occurred to me that it might be Tom Gray they were talking about."

"Yes, we already made the connection," Harvey said. "We think the timing of his arrival in the UK was meant to take advantage of the fact that vast resources are being focused on the search for Gray's bomb."

"No, not that, although it makes more sense, I guess..."

"If you have another theory, please share it," Harvey said, even though he was sceptical of any ideas she might have.

"I was just thinking, maybe Gray is the target."

Harvey thought about it, running through all possible connections between the two men but finding none. Gray had already left the army by the time Mansour came on the scene, and thinking back to both men's profiles he was pretty sure that their paths hadn't crossed in recent years.

"I can't see any reason why he would target Gray," he said. "What would he gain?"

"At first I asked myself the same thing, but it boils down to one question: What would happen if Tom Gray was to die today? Think about it, why haven't we stormed the place yet?"

"Because," he began, hoping to enlighten her, "if we did, he would take his own life and the device he planted would..."

His voice tailed off as he made the connection. By killing Gray, Mansour would deprive them of all hope of finding his device. It was so simple, yet he hadn't even considered Gray as one of Mansour's possible targets; it was Sally who had actually figured it out.

Harvey put the SAS comms unit to his ear and was about to share his findings with Blythe, but the airwaves were already full of chatter, and he realised the revelation had come just too late.

Chapter 24

Tom Gray was watching the BBC news channel, waiting to see if the Home Secretary would make his announcement on the justice bill before the second deadline passed. There was still an hour to go until the six o'clock target but there was always the chance of an early press release, so he sat back to wait for it.

He'd checked on Stuart Boyle frequently, just to make sure he hadn't gone into shock. The last thing he wanted was the little shit dying on him. No, he wanted him to live a long time and remember this day for the rest of his life.

On his last visit to the cell there had been no significant sign of internal bleeding, no signs of clammy skin or a fast but weak pulse, so he had left him to his crying. After checking that his other guests were still with him he sat down for a final snack of Spam and potatoes, which he heated through on a Hexamine stove. Not the heartiest meal he'd ever prepared, he thought, and not really fitting the occasion, considering that this evening he would be celebrating in style with his friends.

And there was plenty to celebrate.

It had been a long week, with broken sleep and the constant feeling that the whole thing was about to go pear shaped, but in the end he'd achieved his goal: to get the country clamouring for a change in the law.

That he was able to exact his revenge on Stuart Boyle without recrimination was the cherry on the cake.

The original idea had been bandied about in the pub on the day of his wife's funeral, but no-one had really taken the suggestion seriously.

However, the seed had been planted.

Over the coming days, as he'd put more and more thought into it, he'd realised that it might just be feasible, and he had got the guys together for a night in to see what their thoughts were. Naturally, some were sceptical at first, but as each obstacle was thrown in their path and they managed to find a way to overcome it, they parted that evening with a fledgling plan that developed quickly over the coming weeks.

There had been no doubt from the outset that they were taking a huge risk. While a lot of things could be controlled, others relied on assumptions: that the world believed Simon Arkin was actually dead; that they would fall for the fake mines around his perimeter; that people believed he was willing to take his own life; that they would offer him the chance to face a single murder charge if he gave himself up.

That had been the biggest worry. If they hadn't come up with that offer he would be facing life in prison with no chance of parole. Even if he did manage to get released he would be a very old man by the time he got out. His friends, many with families, faced a similar fate if that part hadn't come off, but when Olemwu's father called him a coward it gave him the opportunity he was looking for. Of course, there was no way of knowing that Vincent Olemwu would make that remark, but there had been four other ways they could have steered the security service around to offering that deal, all of which were superfluous now. One had been to make sure his eight friends were implicated, and all that took was to contact them frequently in the days leading up to the first webcast. To be doubly sure, they'd picked up a couple of the boys when they were with friends, so that they would be able to identify them. Gray guessed the security services would try to use emotional blackmail, and giving them the ammunition had been easy.

At first he'd insisted that he carry out the whole thing himself as he really had felt he had nothing to lose and he hadn't wanted his friends giving up their liberty. Sure, he'd wanted to create a trail to the others, but they would all have watertight alibis when they eventually handed themselves in. His friends had understood his reasons but had insisted on taking part. Besides, Campbell had argued, the only way they could truly be implicated was if they were seen to take part in the abductions. He'd reluctantly agreed, but on the condition that they each took a hundred grand in cash and stashed it away in case the excrement hit the twirly wind machine.

He smiled as he thought of the justice bill that the country had voted overwhelmingly to support. The suggestion that the whole country get a say in whether or not the law was changed to come down harder on repeat offenders had been a touch of genius on Michael Fletcher's part. Originally it was to have been Tom who would demand a review of the current system, but putting the vote to the people had been an inspired idea. The decision from the government on the future referendum might not be in yet, but something would be done, he was sure of it. The opposition party was already jumping on the bandwagon, but whether or not they kept their word if they came to power remained to be seen. One thing was for sure: If they made a promise and went back on it, the country would never forgive them.

His favourite part of the new bill was the reintroduction of National Service, though he wasn't too sure the birch was such a good idea. It certainly hadn't had much effect on Joseph Olemwu, apart from making him an even angrier young man. Even now, a day after administering the punishment, Olemwu had still been defiant when he'd visited his cell.

No matter, he lived the gang culture and that would seal his fate in the not so distant future. Another black youth stabbed or shot in the streets, and barely a handful of people would give a shit.

All he had to do now was make a final webcast to accept the Home Secretaries offer and he would walk out the door. There was always the chance that the public wouldn't vote for him to surrender himself, but one click of the mouse had activated a command on his South African server which had disregarded all incoming emails and instead sent back the results showing that the people wanted him to give himself up. Moments after he left the building the police would enter and find Simon Arkin alive and well, and the sole charge he was facing would be dropped, making him a free man.

They would certainly be surprised that Arkin had survived his "execution", when in fact all it had taken was a blood pack and a blank round. The trickiest part had been to get the struggling boy to slump when the shot was fired, and this had been achieved by having a drip attached to his right arm, hidden under the long sleeve of his T-shirt. The drip was activated by a button which he had taped to the wall right next to the light switch, and as he'd entered the room he'd hit the button a couple of times, administering a dose large enough to render him unconscious but not large enough to kill him.

Wouldn't that have been ironic: faking the boy's death and actually murdering him in the process! Fortunately he had an ex-colleague who now worked as an anaesthetist at a large hospital, and getting just the right amount of Propofol to knock him out for a couple of minutes hadn't been a problem.

He'd stood in the doorway, blocking the camera's view until the boy was under, then fired the "fatal" shot before going to complete the illusion by checking his pulse.

170

The final part of the plan was to give the authorities a big enough reason not to launch a rescue mission, and so one of his last acts as the Managing Director of Viking Security Services had been to use his connections to arrange a free security appraisal of Norden Industries. The purpose was not to actually take anything, but to come up with a feasible scenario that would convince them that he actually had a weapon. The one he'd come up with would have kept them occupied for a few weeks, never mind just the few days he needed.

One concern was that any agreement they made would be conditional on him giving the location of the device, so he'd really created one which would take thousands of lives, with the emphasis on small and airborne. They'd not be best pleased when they discovered that it was a small incendiary device hidden under a beehive in a nearby apiary. If it went off, thousands of lives would indeed be lost: the lives of thousands of small, airborne insects. He'd been careful never to say that thousands of *people* would die, so technically he had told the truth. If they chose to interpret his words differently, that was their problem.

Had it all been worth it?

It had been a gamble, that was for sure, and some might have argued that if he'd simply beaten the shit out of Boyle he would have probably got a few months inside, maybe a suspended sentence because of the mitigating circumstances. However, he had wanted to punish Boyle *and* do something about the judicial system. When the judge had allowed Boyle to get away with eight months on remand after depriving him of a family, he had seen that as a huge slap in the face. Crippling the boy and walking away scot free was going to be the perfect "fuck you" to Justice A. B. Benson.

Even if his justice bill never saw the light of day, he hoped this last week would at least let the government know that soft sentences were not palatable, and that people would no longer accept them.

As he polished off the last of the Spam he thought about how pissed off Andrew Harvey would be. He'd really given him the run around; having him search the country for a device he would never find; leaving a trail to his friends, one that he wouldn't be able to follow to its conclusion; and getting him to come all the way down here just to deliver a document.

When Harvey found out that this really *was* mostly about revenge, he wasn't going to be adding him to his Christmas card list, but hurting a spook's feelings wasn't going to cause him to lose sleep.

171

He sat back in his chair, looking forward to a few beers later, and satisfied that he'd thought of everything.

Everything apart from the fucking smell.

* * *

As Abdul Mansour approached the line of media vans along the side of the road, he was glad to see that the two lead cars and pair of motorcycles were already parked in their designated positions.

So far, the journey from the farm had been without incident, and as planned he was bringing up the rear of their little convoy. They had followed his instructions and kept other cars between them up until the last couple of miles, but as traffic thinned out they found they were the only vehicles on the road. No matter, they had reached their destination, and in moments he would be firing the first shot in what he hoped would be his greatest victory so far. Hoped, because no matter how good the tactics, no matter how good the planning, there was always the unexpected.

Admittedly, they'd only had a day to practise their attack, but even if they'd had a month there would still be countless obstacles waiting to trip them up: An over-zealous policeman could have stopped a car for having a tail light out; a pedestrian could have walked in front of one of their cars; police reinforcements could have been brought in to contain the crowds for when Gray turned himself in, resulting in a greater opposing force; the RPGs might not work; the motorbikes might...

There wasn't time to dwell on what might or might not happen.

Another car pulled into position at the head of the news vans, the occupants remaining inside awaiting his signal. They received cursory glances from the media folk, but nothing more.

He was seventy yards from his destination now, and the first of his vehicles was rolling to a stop.

It was all in Allah's hands now.

Sixty yards from his intended position, and it seemed Allah wasn't in the best of moods.

No sooner had the first car stopped when a policeman approached, MP5 held across his midriff. He got to within ten yards of the vehicle when the occupants leapt out and began spraying hot metal in his general direction.

Damn them!

172

He specifically told them not to open fire until he had given the signal, which was firing off the first RPG round, and he definitely instructed them not to select automatic fire!

Their bullets were flying high and wide of the mark, while the officer returned fire more accurately, laying down single rounds as he retreated hastily. Within seconds he was being covered by two of his colleagues who were crouching behind their vehicle, and two of Mansour's men went down in quick succession. Another had expended his entire magazine within a few seconds and was struggling to get a replacement from his jacket pocket when two rounds caught him in the chest and another threw up a crimson spray from the back of his head as he fell.

The attack was falling apart before it had even started, and the police were quickly gaining the upper hand. The two remaining cars had stopped dead, leaving him twenty yards further away than he would ideally have liked, but still well within range of the police cars.

"Everyone out, now!" he shouted. "Lay down fire while I get into position!"

All four men in the car jumped out of the passenger side doors, keeping the vehicle between themselves and the incoming fire. As the other three added to the volley of fire being directed towards the police cars, he slung the first of the two RPGs onto his shoulder, raised the rear sight to manually cock the weapon and took careful aim.

Perhaps Allah was looking out for him after all, he thought, as the angle he was forced to fire from exposed the rear of the first police vehicle, which wouldn't have been the case if he had stopped where he'd originally planned.

Despite the staccato buzz of gunfire all around him, he took a breath and exhaled slowly before pressing the trigger. The High Explosive Anti-Tank round, or HEAT round, found its mark, penetrating the side panel of the Volvo before detonating a millisecond later over the petrol tank. The force of the explosion threw the car four feet into the air, and the policemen taking refuge behind it were flattened by the overpressure, the lightning-fast shockwave literally crushing their internal organs.

The driver of the other vehicle was calling in the attack to his superiors when the grenade hit, but his report was cut short as searing hot shards of shrapnel shredded the vehicle, a piece of the rear wheel arch removing the top half of his head.

"Move to your positions," Mansour shouted. "You lot, make sure they're all dead, then attack the command vehicle. The rest of you, come with me."

A bullet flew past his ear and he ducked instinctively. It had come from the direction of the field and he realised that the armed officers surrounding the building had run over to investigate the initial explosion and were looking to exact revenge for the deaths of their colleagues.

Mansour reached into the car, grabbed the other RPG and slung it over his shoulder, then grabbed his AK-47 and began putting rounds down to suppress the incoming barrage. His first shot missed by a hair's breadth but the second found its mark, the policeman crumpling to the floor clutching his stomach.

His men had already begun the process of rounding up the reporters and their technicians, and were herding them all towards the middle media van. Through a gap in the hedge he saw that the six men lying at the ridge were already engaging their targets and he instructed five of his men to leave the reporters to the others and take positions at the hedge to help keep the police under pressure.

His men were now attacking from three sides, and he saw two more of the enemy go down, but at the cost of six more of his own people.

All he had to do now was keep the enemy totally pinned down and let Zulfir destroy the door to the building. Once he'd done that it would be time to signal the riders.

* * *

At the sound of the first gunshots, all eight men turned as best they could to look through the rear windows of the minibus, but with their hands cuffed behind their backs it was no mean feat. Their view was also obscured by the policemen, who were peering down the road to where the battle was now raging.

"What the fuck's going on?" Paul Bennett asked, a touch of concern in his voice. It wasn't the thought of being present when the bullets were flying, it was being present when the bullets were flying while being trussed up like a turkey and unable to defend himself that bothered him.

"I don't know," their guard said, opening the back door to go and investigate.

174

"Wait!" Levine said. "That's gunfire, and it sounds like AK-47s. They aren't police issue. You have to let us go, now."

"Just wait here, I'll see what's going on."

"We can help, trust me," Levine persisted.

"Look, there's no way I'm letting you go. Just sit tight, I'll be —"

Over five hundred yards away, Parwan Chaudhury flew backwards, the 9mm round from the police MP5 catching him five inches below the chin and travelling through his body to decimate his spine. As he fell, he was completely unaware that the penultimate bullet he'd fired had missed its intended target but had found another place to land. The bullet travelled far beyond the maximum effective range of the AK-47, but as it hit the officer's right eye it had enough momentum to pass through and lodge in the soft tissue of his brain.

Their guard fell backwards into the aisle of the minibus, blood pouring from the eye socket. Paul Bennett's training kicked in, and from the rear seat he quickly manoeuvred himself over the body and fell onto it, fumbling blindly around the dead officer's waist for his handcuff keys. Another bullet slammed into the rear door of the bus as he groped around the belt, and he took it as a sign to get his arse in gear.

Colin Avery also offered some gentle encouragement.

"Get a fucking move on, Bennett."

Bennett eventually located the key but found it tricky to insert it into the lock, the rigid steel bar of the Hiatt handcuffs hampering his efforts. It took three attempts, during which he dropped the key twice, before he managed to unlock one of the cuffs. Quickly removing the other, he in turn released Colin Avery and handed him the key, then grabbed the MP5 and a spare magazine from the dead man's belt.

As he opened the rear door and jumped out he saw, then heard, the explosion at the other end of the lane.

Avery jumped down beside him. "Just like the good old days," he said. "But I think we're going to need a lot more than one weapon between the eight of us."

"Then let's go ask the nice policeman," Bennett suggested, and they sprinted over to the command vehicle. Bennett was first up the stairs and as Fisher opened the door to see the source of the explosion, Bennett pushed him to the floor and burst into the cramped vehicle with Avery following close behind.

"Knock knock," Avery said.

Davies was busy informing his superiors about the attack, and when the two prisoners rushed in brandishing the machine pistol he thought his time had come. He raised his hands slowly, as did Fisher, who still lying on his back.

"Don't shoot," Davies said. "Just go with your friends. No-one else needs to die."

Bennett was confused for a moment, then the realisation dawned. "You think these people have come to rescue us?"

Davies nodded. "Obviously. Why else would they be attacking us?"

"We don't need to be rescued," Bennett pointed out. "We'll be walking free in a couple of hours."

"Then who are they after?" Fisher asked.

Avery offered a hand and helped him to his feet. "I don't know," he said, "but we have to stop them."

"What have you done to Bainbridge?" Fisher asked.

"Who's Bainbridge?"

"He was with you in the bus," he said. "How did you get his weapon?"

"Bainbridge is down," Avery said without emotion. "They shot him. Speaking of weapons, what have you got in your arsenal?"

Davies used his head to gesture towards a cabinet on his right.

"Put your hands down," Bennett said, "we're on the same side."

Davies did as he was told, and opened the gun cabinet. "We have three more MP5s and four Glocks," he said, studying the contents.

"We'll take them all." Avery took off his jacket and laid it on the counter, then grabbed the weapons and ammunition and placed them on top before bundling it up.

"I'll distribute these," he said, lugging the makeshift holdall out of the door.

"I assume you've called in backup," Bennett said to Davies, and the Superintendent nodded.

"Good. When they get here, let them know we're the good guys," and he ran out to join the others.

Barry had been sitting in the back of the command vehicle throughout, not saying a word, just taking in the surreal scene. He had been thinking about how he could incorporate Levine's Afghan heroics into his book, but now he was about to witness first-hand the SAS in action, and it would give him an ending that would put any previous fictional work to shame. All he had to do was live through it...

176

* * *

When Gray heard the faint sound of the first gunshot he dismissed it, but when it was followed up by the distinctive Clack! Clack! Clack! of an AK-47 on automatic fire and his motion sensors suddenly went berserk, he switched his attention to the monitors. The sensors were being tripped by the armed police running to the southern corner of the field, so he switched to the camera covering that sector just in time to see two men in the lane fall to the ground.

He could see at least twenty people firing towards the two police cars, and his immediate thought was that they were complete amateurs. They stood like the hero in an action movie rather than shooting from cover, and they were wasting ammunition at an astonishing rate. As the third man fell he caught sight of the man at the rear of the line of cars firing the RPG, destroying the police vehicles.

The attackers split up, some heading up the lane towards the command vehicle, the others towards the media vans. He saw a policeman collapse in the field, and panning his camera to the left he saw that there were people on the ridge two hundred yards from the building. He was flanked on three sides now, and that only meant one thing: He was their target.

Why, he had no idea, and there wasn't time to worry about it. All that mattered for the moment was repelling their attack. If only he'd brought more weapons than the 9mm Browning and the ancient ex-army issue L1A1 Self Loading Rifle, he'd have half a chance, but he only had a magazine of ammunition for each, figuring that if he had to use them it would be to warn anyone approaching the building rather than for full blown defence.

He removed the Browning magazine containing the blanks and inserted one containing thirteen live rounds, then loaded the SLR with a twenty-round mag and ran up the stairs to the window affording him a view of the hostiles on the ridge. They currently presented the greatest danger to the police officers in the field and had to be taken out first.

Gray removed the bottom board from the window and stuck the barrel of the SLR through the gap. His first round fell short so he adjusted his aim slightly and squeezed the trigger again, this time hitting the attacker in the shoulder. Not a kill shot, but it put him out

177

of action and he moved on to the next target. His next shot was a clean kill but he had drawn attention to himself, and rounds began to pepper the boards around his head. He ducked to the left, restricting his field of fire but still giving him a shot at two of the hostiles at the far end of the ridge.

While this firing position reduced his visible profile, it also meant he couldn't see Zulfir at the other end of the ridge, preparing his RPG and taking aim at the main door of the building.

The HEAT round hit high, punching a hole in the wall above the door and projecting debris throughout the interior. A breeze block the size of a loaf of bread smashed into the computer table, destroying his laptop and ricocheting into the bank of monitors, while other smaller fragments of concrete shrapnel fizzed around the room. A splinter buried itself in Gray's buttock, stinging like a hornet, and he fell to the floor, the concussion from the explosion disorientating him momentarily.

He shook his head and opened his mouth wide to equalise the pressure, then pushed himself up and surveyed the damage. His equipment had been decimated but the generator was still going, though all it had to feed now was the lights.

The round had come from the ridge, of that he was sure, and when he returned to the window he saw his assailant preparing to take another shot, the weapon already poised on his shoulder. Grabbing the rifle he took a snap shot but the bullet went wide. His next effort went high but the third smashed into the man's forehead, throwing him backwards, but not before the grenade left the tube.

Gray threw himself to the floor and covered his ears as the projectile arched towards the building, finding its mark and demolishing the front door.

As the sound of the explosion died down, Gray heard two long blasts on a whistle coming from the right, and he identified the person responsible as the one who'd fired the first RPG at the police. This was undoubtedly the leader, and therefore his priority target.

Priority, that was, until he saw the motorcycles enter the field behind the ridge. The riders raced towards the rising ground and swept over the crest, making a beeline for the path leading to his door.

There was now no doubt in Tom Gray's mind that he was the intended target, and it seemed that the men on the bikes were intent on finishing him off at close range. He checked the inner wall and was glad to see that it remained intact, although there were signs of damage, a large circle of bricks protruding outwards like a huge blister. It wouldn't take much more to breach it, so the men on the bikes had to be stopped before they got close enough to try. As he raised his rifle again and took aim he saw the biker in the black jacket slump forward onto the handlebars, and the bike skewed from side to side before tossing the rider and settling on the sodden ground.

A glance to his left and he saw three figures in civvies running into the field, MP5s raised and pouring lead ahead of their advance.

Gray squinted as he thought he recognised them.

Bennett?

Avery?

Fletcher?

What the hell were they doing here?

The sight of his friends rushing towards the ridge had caught him totally by surprise and he'd almost forgotten about the other rider, who was powering onwards and only twenty yards from the door. He raised the rifle and snapped off a few rounds, and while some missed, others pinged off the bike in a shower of sparks but failed to do any significant damage. The rider was also in his friends' sights, but Nadeem was wiser than Kamran and he played the throttle, first speeding up, then braking before instantly applying the gas again, just as Mahmood had shown him. Mahmood had said this would make it harder for anyone firing at him to get a proper lead. Nadeem had no idea what that meant, so Mahmood had explained that when aiming at a moving target you had to fire in front of it so that the target and bullet arrived at the same point at the same time. If the target was moving at a constant speed this could become quite easy with practice, but by speeding up and slowing down it made life for the shooter much more difficult.

It certainly worked for Nadeem, and he made it to the entrance. However, once the bike had stopped he became a sitting duck for the experienced soldiers and took several rounds in the back as he hurdled over the debris that had once been the front door to the building. The impact punched him up against the inner wall and he collapsed in a heap, his left hand having been millimetres from the trigger of his vest.

* * *

179

Mansour was standing in a gap between two media vans when he saw Nadeem go down and was proud that he'd managed to get as close as he had.

Allah would truly reward him.

Digging the mobile from his pocket, he thumbed through the contacts list, selected *Red* from the list and hit the Call button.

Nothing happened.

Wait a moment...

Still nothing.

Incredulous, he was checking that he had a signal when the explosion came, shaking the ground beneath him. The shockwave shoved him backwards but he just about managed to keep his feet. The hedges surrounding the field were buffeted and satellite dishes were blown from the roofs of the media vehicles, and he saw that everyone else on the battlefield was stunned into inaction by the violence of the blast.

As the dust settled he saw that the building had sustained a huge amount of damage. A hole the size of a bus had been blown out of the front wall, part of the roof had collapsed at the rear corner, and the majority of the boards covering the windows on the upper floor had been blown out. It was hard to imagine anyone inside surviving the explosion, certainly not anyone near the blast point.

While everyone was recovering from the impact of the blast, Mansour ran past the media vans and jumped into one of the cars, performed a neat three point turn and sped off down the lane towards the nearest village. He had said that he would signal with several short blasts of his whistle when it was time to retreat, but he needed time to make good his escape, and his men, Allah praise them, would provide him with it, keeping the enemy at bay and preventing them from pursuing him.

He knew there would be roadblocks all around the area but that didn't concern him. All he needed to do was reach the village and make a couple of phone calls.

* * *

Gray watched the rider disappear beneath him and lost the shot, but when he saw his friends offer a couple of double-taps each, then move on, he knew the x-ray was dead. He turned his attention back to the

180

leader and saw him standing next to the rear door of a Sky News van, and he swung the rifle round, taking aim.

He was certainly a cool customer, Gray thought, standing in the midst of a battle and still finding time to make a phone call, but he was about to cancel the guy's tariff permanently.

He had a bead on the target and was increasing the pressure on the trigger when his world collapsed.

The explosion was like nothing he'd ever experienced. His head seemed to contract and he felt a free-falling sensation as the gantry on which he was kneeling disappeared beneath him. Everything became silent and the drop happened in slow motion, tumbling downwards into the grey mist of brick dust thrown out by the blast. He thrust an arm out in a feeble attempt to grab at the ceiling but it slowly receded before being consumed by the cloud of debris.

He fell for what seemed an eternity, as if the floor no longer existed and instead he was making the journey straight to hell, spiralling downwards relentlessly.

He didn't feel the moment of impact.

There was light, streaming in through the hole that suddenly appeared in the roof, then an instant later there was just darkness.

* * *

Jeff Campbell and Tristram Barker-Fink were through the gaping hole before the dust even settled, while Sonny Baines, Len Smart and Carl Levine rushed to see to Bennett and the other two who had led the counter-attack.

They each tended to one of their friends, but Sonny soon felt a hand on his shoulder.

"Fletch is gone," Smart said, and moved on to inform Levine. Sonny took the news stoically, simply nodded and turned his attention back to Avery and his injuries. Blood was seeping from his ears and his left leg was bent up underneath him, and Sonny was grateful that he was unconscious.

"We need medics," he shouted over to Levine.

"No chance. They aren't going to send an ambulance crew into the middle of a battle."

"Fair enough," Sonny said, grabbing Avery's weapon and the spare magazines. "Let's go end it."

181

He ran to his left and Smart and Levine followed him as he reached the top of the ridge, level with the two remaining attackers. The six pounds of metal in his hands spat twice and the nearest hostile lay motionless. Beyond him the other target appeared, raising himself to his knees as he swung his AK-47 round. The movement was all too slow and he was pushed backwards by the force of the impact, both bullets catching him in the sternum.

With the ridge clear, the three men spread out and headed towards the hedge marking the boundary of the field. Incoming rounds peppered the ground around them, but the intensity dropped as one by one the attackers exhausted their meagre supply of ammunition.

Sonny saw four men pile into a car and shoot off in the opposite direction from the burning wreckage of the police vehicles and he chased them with a couple of short bursts from the MP5. The rounds shattered the back windscreen but the driver kept his foot on the gas, screaming round the corner out of sight. Sonny had no way of knowing if he'd manage to hit anyone, but it didn't matter, because a bullet flashed just over his head to remind him that there were still plenty of hostiles remaining.

The incoming rounds were coming from the lane leading up to the command vehicle, so he laid down some covering fire while Smart and Levine advanced, firing as they moved. When they dropped to a kneeling position and continued to pepper the hedge with accurate fire, Sonny ran past them and took out one of the hostiles with a head shot. Two more shots came his way, then he saw the remaining two shooters jump up and run towards the burning vehicles, their empty weapons discarded by the roadside. As far as Sonny was concerned, an unarmed foe was simply a foe capable of arming himself again, so he had no qualms about giving them both the good news in the back.

The only remaining opposition came from the direction of the media vans, and Sonny burst through the hedge and approached from the lane, swiftly changing out his magazine as he moved, the weapon sweeping from side to side as he searched for his next kill. Levine and Smart were at his six and they spread out across the road, advancing slowly.

A figure ran out from between two vans and stopped dead, surprise written all over his face. The AK-47 in his right hand clattered to the ground and he raised his hands, but didn't find anyone in the mood for taking prisoners. With one friend dead two more seriously injured and Tom Gray unaccounted for, the three men didn't even have to exchange glances to know what the others were thinking. Each fired a double tap and the enemy headcount decreased by one more.

Smart went left, Levine and Sonny to the right, and they moved slowly but with purpose down the line of vehicles. They cleared past two before they encountered and dispatched another hostile, then came towards the larger vehicle near the middle of the queue. The rear door was open and Smart could see people packed inside like sardines, and as he reached the edge of the preceding van he understood why they looked terrified.

"Drop it!"

The command came from a boy barely eighteen, his AK-47 trained on the hostages. Smart saw his two mates approaching the kid from the rear and did as he was ordered, hoping to attract his fire. The plan worked and the youngster swung the rifle towards him, but didn't even get close to getting Len in his sights, the front of his face blowing outwards before he clattered to the floor.

Smart indicated for the people to remain in the van and kept guard as the other two continued to clear each vehicle in turn, but when they returned three minutes later he gestured for everyone to climb down one at a time, all three men keeping a keen eye out for any possible hostiles squirreled among them.

Once the area was secure Sonny jogged back to the command vehicle and instructed them to call in the paramedics, then trotted over to the building to see what had become of Tom. Policemen were already tending to the wounded, including Bennett and Avery, making them comfortable until the ambulances arrived.

He climbed over the rubble to where Campbell, Levine, Smart and Barker-Fink were tossing debris to one side.

"Where's Tom?" he asked.

"Under this lot," Campbell said. "Give us a hand."

Sonny scrambled over to them and saw a finger poking out from the side of the debris, and he joined them in tossing half bricks and wooden stakes towards the side of the room. It was a couple of moments before he realised that only three of the prisoners' cells remained standing, the two closest to the front door having been completely demolished. No sound was coming from any of the remaining cells, but he wasn't going to lose sleep over it.

All he cared about was getting Tom out.

They continued the excavation for another couple of minutes until finally his head and chest were clear, and neither looked particularly pretty. His entire head was purple and swollen, and his right cheek had been sliced open revealing the jawbone beneath. His chest was a mass of blood, and Levine fought in vain to find a pulse.

Campbell pushed him aside and began to administer CPR, but Sonny backed off, knowing it was far too late.

As he clambered towards the entrance he saw the rain had stopped and a thin ray of sunlight forced its way through a hole in the clouds, but nothing was going to brighten up his day.

The scene around him was chaotic. Some of the media people in the lane were howling and comforting each other while others had grabbed cameras and were filming all they could, no gory scene left unrecorded. One tried to make his way through the hole in the building but Sonny grabbed him by the collar and swung him round before smashing his nose with his forehead.

The cameraman collapsed in a heap, clutching his face and trying to stem the flow of blood.

"Fucking parasite," Sonny spat. "You want to be on my battlefield, you carry a rifle, not a fucking camera."

He kicked out at the figure on the floor, who took the hint and scuttled away, leaving a hundred thousand pounds worth of video equipment lying on the ground.

The sound of sirens in the distance shook Sonny from his rage and he went to see how the living were getting on, starting with Bennett.

Chapter 25

"Emergency, what service do you require?"

"Ambulance! My aunt has collapsed and isn't breathing. She's seventy years old."

"What is your address?"

Mansour read out the details from a gas bill on the table. "Please, come quickly!"

"Okay, someone will be with you in seven minutes. In the meantime, have you administered CPR before?"

"No, but my brother has. He's doing it now," Mansour said, and pretended to pass further instructions to his non-existent sibling. He was actually sitting in the lounge of the cottage, which he'd chosen the night before as he'd reconnoitred the area. He'd selected it because it was isolated and he could park his vehicle behind it, away from prying eyes. The old lady on the floor may well have been someone's aunt, but it wasn't a heart attack she was suffering from, it was severe blood loss caused by the gaping wound in her throat.

While he waited for the ambulance to arrive he put the corner of a tablecloth over his handset and dialled the pay-as-you-go mobile phone he had purchased at the airport and given to the Imam, Amir Channa, at the mosque.

"Brother, I have finished work and need a lift home," he said. He knew full well that GCHQ would be listening to all calls coming from the immediate area — or at least he expected them to be — hence the reason for disguising his voice and using code.

"Okay," was the simple reply, and that told Mansour that the pre-arranged pick-up was still on. The Imam would now give the SIM card from the phone to one of his trusted followers and have them take it on a bus ride and drop it into someone's bag, leading them far from the mosque should the phone call ever be flagged up. The phone itself would be tossed into a garbage bin, ready to be taken away and crushed.

He sat back in the chair and took the chance to reflect on the past few days. That his idea had been accepted by the elders was an achievement in itself, but to carry it out with so little notice and under the watchful eyes of the world's media was bound to elevate his status. The audacity of the raid would become the stuff of legend, and his name would become known and feared throughout the western world.

Of course, he regretted the fact that many of his men had died, and that the rest would surely be captured, but they had served Allah well and their rewards would be waiting for them in *Jannah*.

He stood and went to the window, glad to see that the rain had finally stopped and the clouds were dispersing. It was as if Allah had sent the downpour to help him complete the mission, and now that it was over he was showing his gratitude with the beautiful rainbow on the horizon.

While he was appreciating the natural phenomenon he caught sight of the ambulance approaching in the distance, and he stepped through the front door and waited at the garden gate, waving his arms frantically as it approached. The vehicle pulled up and both the driver and passenger got out and headed to the rear to get their AED, the Automated External Defibrillator, from the back. Mansour followed them and climbed in, the pistol already in his hand. The driver sensed him climbing in and was about to tell him to get out when the barrel of the gun was pointed in his face.

"Do as I ask and you might live," Mansour said calmly.

The paramedics dropped their equipment and raised their hands.

"We have to deal with an emergency," the female said, her voice quivering.

"Sadly, you are too late the save the old lady," he said. "Now, can you both drive this thing?"

The couple nodded, the woman close to losing control but the man holding it together better.

"You," Mansour said, pointing to the male, "take her coat off and strap her into the stretcher, nice and tight."

The female paramedic almost fainted when he gave his instructions and had to be helped onto the bed by her colleague, who uttered soft words in an attempt to soothe her.

With the female secured he ordered the man to climb through the small gap into the driver's seat, then put on the woman's high-visibility jacket. It was a snug fit but would help with the illusion, and he completed the look with a disposable cap and surgical mask.

"What is your name?" Mansour asked.

"John."

"Drive, John," he said, "and turn on the siren."

The medic did as he was told and Mansour took a seat on the free stretcher, his gun trained on the driver.

"Where are we going?"

"South," Mansour told him. "Head for the A23, then join the A27 westbound towards Worthing. There will be police roadblocks on the way but I want to go through them. Use whatever excuse you need, but if you reveal my presence the first bullet will be yours and your friend will be next."

He searched around inside a box and found some tape and a bandage which he used to cover the woman's mouth. He felt sure the man would obey instructions but this female was such a wreck, she might start screaming at any moment.

Sure enough, not ten minutes into the journey as they approached the dual carriageway, they came across the first police checkpoint. Traffic was backed up three hundred yards and John asked what to do next.

"Do what you would normally do," Mansour said, exasperated. "Use the other lane, get to the head of the queue and drive through."

Oncoming traffic pulled over as the driver rushed towards the police cars, and John frantically thought of a way to let the police know he was in trouble. Sadly for him, and to Mansour's great relief, the police manning the point ushered him through and they continued onto the A23 southbound towards Brighton.

"Good, good," Mansour said, more to himself than the driver.

Traffic was heavy but the blues and twos soon shifted anything in front of them, and soon they reached the outskirts of Brighton and turned onto the A27.

"There is a lay by just after the tunnel ahead and a black Volvo should be waiting. Pull in behind it."

The small parking area appeared three miles along the road, and the car was indeed parked up. The paramedic pulled in and stopped close to the back of it, and Mansour told him to silence the siren.

"Get in here," he said, and gestured for John to climb through the gap.

"Lie down."

The man did so, and Mansour quickly strapped him into the other stretcher, then searched his pockets and found his wallet.

"Nice family," he said, examining a photo. "It would be a shame for anything to happen to them, which is why I suggest you lie still until someone arrives to free you. If I am followed today I will know it was you who told them where I was, and my followers will exact my revenge."

He took John's driver's licence from the wallet and stuffed it into his trousers. "I now know where you live, John, so lie down and wait to be rescued. When that time comes, tell them that Abdul Mansour will be back one day, and they should tremble at the thought."

With that, he jumped out of the ambulance and into the waiting car, which sped off towards Shoreham airport and the waiting Cessna which would fly him first to a small airport outside of Paris, then on to Tirana in Albania, where he would take a different mode of transport home.

His threat to return was an empty one, and he knew it. His profile would be raised to a whole new level internationally and it would be almost impossible to get into the West again after this, but in the months and years to come they will be expecting another attack and that would only enhance his reputation and compound their fear.

He would only relax completely once he was back home in Quetta, but for now he closed his eyes and savoured the victory a little more.

Epilogue

He woke and immediately felt confused. It took some time for his brain to kick into gear, but even then he could only focus on objects, not take in any detail. He stared at the ceiling fan above his head, humming gently as it spun slowly. He saw it, but it didn't register as a fan, just movement, hypnotic and calming.

Movement from the corner of his eye broke the spell and a man appeared next to him. The man was talking but he didn't hear the words, just saw the lips moving. As quickly as he'd appeared the man was gone again, leaving him to stare at the fan some more.

Sleep, his body said.

He desperately wanted his head to clear but putting a thought together was like trying to swim through treacle. He wanted to remember something, anything, but all he could concentrate on was the fan, mesmerising, round and round and round...

Sleep.

He closed his eyes to help his concentration levels but nothing came, just an image of the fan, turning relentlessly.

Then sleep.

When he opened his eyes again the room was darker, the afternoon sun giving way to twilight. The fan was still there and the man had returned. No, not the same man. This one was taller, different hair, white complexion, not olive-skinned like the other.

He realised that his ability to think had returned and immediately searched for answers inside the fog that was his memory.

Nothing.

The man stood over him, arms behind his back.

"Good morning, Tom," he said, his accent suggesting public school and privilege.

"Where —"

The word had barely escaped his lips when the pain from his jaw shot to the top of his skull. He winced, then tried again, gently this time.

"Where am I?"

"My, how original," the man said. "I must say, I expected more from you."

He introduced himself as James Farrar and had an air of condescension about him: Gray took an immediate dislike to the man.

Tom repeated his question despite the pain it caused.

"Subic," Farrar replied.

Gray searched his memory for the name, and it came after a moment.

"Manila?"

"Close. The nearest town is actually Olongapo, but Manila isn't that far away. Couple of hours in a decent vehicle, if you can find one in this God-forsaken country."

"How —"

"Tom, you really are disappointing me. Where am I? How did I get here? What do you want from me? At least you seem to know your own name, which is a start I suppose. Well, let me save you some time.

"The where, as I already mentioned, is Subic Bay Freeport. Our colonial friends left in 1991 and the locals turned it into a thriving business area, but the Americans retained a small interest, including this house. It was once the billet of an admiral, you know."

Gray was unimpressed. He didn't care if Lord Nelson himself had slept in the very same bed, he just wanted answers.

"The how was a Hercules transport plane which picked you up from Farnborough all those weeks ago. The —"

"Wait. What do you mean, all those weeks ago? How long have I been here?"

"Almost two months now. I must say, you really were a mess when you arrived, and I wouldn't trust the local medical staff as far as I could throw them, but they seem to have done a pretty decent job on you."

Two months? What the hell had happened to him? His recollection was still hazy, but he caught a glimpse of himself at a window, a rifle in his hands...

"You had a broken leg, two broken arms and a multitude of internal problems. I'm afraid your looks have gone, too."

Gray's hands went to his face. "Get me a mirror."

Farrar handed one over and Gray examined himself. His hair was unkempt and at least three inches longer than he would have maintained it, and a moustache adorned his upper lip, while the rest of his face was clean shaven.

But it was the shape of his face that shocked him.

His nose had been broken and was flattened across the middle of his face, and the top of his right ear was missing. A curved scar ran from the bottom of the ear down to the jaw line, and his brow jutted well over his eyes, giving him a Neanderthal appearance.

He looked like an old boxer, and not a very good one.

"What the fuck happened to me?"

"You had a particularly nasty accident which caused the scar and the small nick on the ear. The rest," he smiled smugly, "was all our work."

"What? You did this to me? Why?"

"We did it because you would still have looked like Tom Gray, and I'm afraid Tom Gray is dead."

He let the words sink in and was glad to see that Tom was struggling to handle the bombshell he had just dropped.

"I don't understand..."

"No, I didn't think you'd be able to. After all, it isn't every day someone dies."

Gray's head was swimming, and another glance in the mirror did him no favours.

"Is this hell?"

Farrar roared with laughter. "Good Lord, no. Well, it depends on whether or not you like billions of mosquitoes and cockroaches the size of your dick. But no, you aren't dead. Tom Gray is, but you aren't."

Perhaps it was the medication, he thought, but Gray just couldn't get his head around Farrar's cryptic comments. Farrar noticed the continuing confusion and decided to put him out of his misery.

"Your little escapade caused a lot of embarrassment to Her Majesty's government. When news first reached us about the explosion there was utter panic, as you can imagine. Everyone thought you were dead and a biological weapon was unaccounted for.

"Then we found out you were alive but barely able to breathe, never mind talk, so we concentrated our efforts on your colleagues."

"What did you do to them? Where are they?"

"Relax, they are fine. In fact, you should be grateful to them. They refused to co-operate until the Home Secretary promised to honour the agreement, which he did, live on TV. It was only then that they

191

revealed your little subterfuge, and that was a huge kick in the teeth for the security services, chasing their tails for days, looking for a bomb that never existed. The chumps at MI5 had taken a battering and wanted to come out of it smelling of roses, so they put out a statement to the press, saying the device had been made safe and no-one was in any further danger."

Farrar rubbed a handkerchief around his neck to soak up the sweat that was building, while mumbling something about the "bloody humidity".

"But why am I here? You said the Home Secretary honoured the agreement."

"That's right, he did, and was all ready to jail you for life for the murder of Simon Arkin."

"But Arkin wasn't dead," Gray said. "I mean, I didn't kill him. I remember that much."

"Oh we know that now, your friends told us right after the Home Secretary's TV announcement. The rescue services found evidence of the blood pack, but there wasn't enough of Simon left to establish a time of death. Therefore, you were going to face the murder charge and life in prison."

"So what changed?"

"Your friends decided that, as free men, they would tell their story to the newspapers, and they stressed the *whole* story, unless the government admitted that Arkin died in the blast. They would mention the fact that there never was a bomb, contrary to what the security service had said, and that Simon Arkin was alive until the explosion killed him."

"That still doesn't sound like a good enough reason to fake my death."

"True, and it wasn't even considered at that point. But when half a million people brought London to a standstill for a fortnight protesting for your freedom, we came to a compromise: You disappear, new identity, new country; and they wouldn't go to the press."

"Half a million people?" he said, amazed at the support he had gained.

"That was the conservative estimate. They camped out in the streets for thirteen days in all, and there were similar protests all over the country. Oh, and a seven-million signature petition."

"So why not just release me? Why the new identity?"

"Because you were becoming a hero, and there was the danger that you might continue the fight for a change in the law. We simply couldn't allow that to happen, so an announcement went out that you had died and you were whisked off to Farnborough."

"Do I get a say in this?"

"Of course. You can go along with it and get a generous salary for the rest of your life, or," and his demeanour changed instantly, "you can tell the world that you're still alive and we will happily remedy that within twenty-four hours."

Gray yawned, despite the news he'd just received.

"I can see you're still tired," Farrar said. "We'll talk later."

"But who attacked me? And what happened to the kids in the cells?" Gray asked, stifling another yawn.

"We've got plenty of time for all that, trust me. I'll give you all the details tomorrow, including your new role."

"New role?"

"When you're on the payroll, you have to earn your money. I'll explain it all in the morning."

Farrar clicked the button on the intravenous feed to dispense a little morphine and watched as Gray's eyes struggled to focus. After a minute they finally gave up the fight.

"Goodnight, Sam Grant."

Resurrection

Prologue

Friday 13th April 2012

If only he hadn't written that note!

Arlan Banting's infatuation with Maritess Cabanag had been going on for over a year now, and despite being one of the more popular boys in school he had always been shy around the girls, never comfortable in forming close ties with his female classmates. It had taken months for him to pluck up the courage to invite her to Font's and Mon's Restaurant in Barangay Seaside, and another two weeks to save up enough dinner money to pay for their date, but it had been worth it. He'd discovered that he had more in common with Maritess than he could have ever wished for: they both loved the same music and films, and both played the guitar. Maritess also had the voice of an angel and wrote her own lyrics, which Arlan would put to music before they recorded their efforts on an ancient tape recorder.

One of Arlan's immediate dreams was to buy a decent video camera so that he could record one of their sessions and then send it to all of the many talent shows airing on TV, but having a distinct lack of cash went hand in hand with living in Isabela City.

It had been a first class city in the early sixties, but after the Moro rebellion razed the plantations it was relegated to a fifth class province within a decade, and though it had a population of over eighty five thousand people, nobody lived in Isabela City: they simply existed.

Nobody, that is, except the criminal gangs who operated with near-impunity.

They consisted primarily of members of Abu Sayyaf, a military Islamist separatist group operating in Bangsamoro (from the Malay word Bangsa, meaning nation of people, and Moro, which refers to the Muslim population of the Philippines). Bangsamoro is an area comprising the Zamboanga Peninsula and the islands of Jolo and Basilan, the capital of which is Isabela City. They controlled everything from the police and local judiciary to protection rackets and drugs, but their main source of income came from kidnapping. They had raised some hefty ransoms over the years, which replaced the donations they'd once received from their Muslim brothers overseas. Al-Qaeda in particular had been only too happy to help in their struggle for an independent province in the early days.

As Arlan strode through the city he regretted his decision to pass the note to Maritess rather than giving it to her after class. If only he'd waited another twenty minutes he wouldn't have been kept behind after school to explain his actions to the principal, and he would have been able to take his normal route home in time to babysit his younger sister while their mother went to her evening job. As it was, the only way he would keep to his schedule was to take a detour down Veterans Avenue. His normal route home took him right at the bandstand followed by a left onto the Rizal Avenue extension, then onto La Piedad and finally down Lower Lanote Road and into a side street where his shanty house sat among a hundred others.

This circuitous route added an extra thirty minutes to his journey home but it meant he could avoid the Jolo Bar, a hangout for members of the Arroyo gang. Unlike the Abu Sayyaf gangs who collected money on behalf of their masters on Jolo Island, the Arroyo gang were in it for themselves. They would sit at the tables outside the bar, drinking San Miguel beer and smoking imported Marlboro cigarettes rather than the much cheaper locally produced version. Anyone who happened within thirty yards of them was fair game, as Arlan had found to his cost earlier that year. A group of five of them had stolen his meagre savings and beaten him for good measure. When his mother had reported the incident to the police they had promised to give it their full attention, then promptly binned the report once she'd left the station.

Like everyone else in Isabela, the police rarely ventured close to the Jolo Bar – unless it was to collect their weekly payoff for turning a blind eye.

Arlan was glad to see that no-one was occupying the chairs outside the bar, but still he quickened his pace, and was about four yards past the entrance when a hand on his shoulder stopped him in his tracks.

"Saan ka pupunta?"

Where do you think you're going?

Arlan knew the answer to the question was nowhere, and he turned to face the man who'd grabbed him. In fact there were four of them, all in their early twenties and most with cigarettes hanging from their mouths. The one with his hand still gripping Arlan's shoulder put his face closer and the stench of stale beer on his breath made Arlan wince. The man's teeth were already in the process of turning brown and Arlan suspected he hadn't seen a tube of toothpaste in his life. He recognised him as the man who had beaten him back in January, and the others had called him Dindo.

"This is our street. You have to pay if you want to walk here."

Arlan nodded and dug into his pocket, producing his lunch money. He got fifty pesos a day, roughly one U.S. dollar, and for the last few months had managed to save thirty pesos a day towards his camera. He'd spent forty pesos today, deciding to treat himself to a proper lunch, so he thrust the ten peso note towards the man, who sneered at it and swatted it out of his hand.

"You call that payment? What's in the bag?"

"Only my school books, po," Arlan said, using the word to show respect for his elders. He had no respect whatsoever for these people, but if it helped him avoid another beating, it was worth a try.

One of the others grabbed the bag from his shoulder and rummaged through it, throwing out text books, pens and pencils. When he came across a photo of Maritess he sniggered and showed it to his friends.

"Who's this? Your sister?"

"No, po, my girlfriend."

"Liar," Dindo said. "She's too good for a peasant like you. Maybe you should bring her down to the Jolo and let her meet some real men."

Dindo grabbed his crotch with his free hand and began rotating his hips back and forth, moaning sounds emanating from his nicotine-stained lips.

Arlan knew a beating was just around the corner, no matter what he did, and the disrespect they were showing towards his first love drove him to actions he'd never considered in his wildest dreams. Before he knew it, his right hand bunched into a fist and flew at Dindo's face, connecting with his left cheek. Unfortunately, Arlan was built for playing the guitar, not street brawling, and the blow bounced off harmlessly. Dindo's face registered shock, not at the force of the impact, but at the sheer impudence of the gutter rat.

"Putang ina mo!! Papatayin kita!!"

But before Dindo could carry out his threat and kill the son-of-a-bitch, someone else had an idea along similar lines, though it was Dindo and his friends who were the targets.

The jeepney is the ubiquitous form of public transport in the Philippines. Originally made from surplus jeeps left behind after the

Second World War, they were transformed to carry larger numbers of passengers. This particular jeepney had been hijacked just a couple of streets away, and as it drove past the Jolo bar four AK-47 rifles appeared through the glassless window on the side of the vehicle and began blazing away at the men standing by the entrance. Despite their aim being below poor, the close proximity guaranteed hits, and the men in the vehicle saw three of their targets fall instantly. Two tried to run but got less than a couple of steps before they too crumpled to the ground.

The jeepney stopped and a young man climbed out of the back and strode confidently towards the prostrate figures.

One of them was clawing at the air and begging for help, but mercy and compassion were not in his assailant's vocabulary. Instead, he placed a sheet of paper over his victim's face and used a four inch knife to staple it to his forehead, before calmly climbing back inside the jeepney, banging on the side to tell the driver to move off.

Arlan Banting's last action was to crawl towards the discarded photo of Maritess, the bullet wounds in his chest and arm making it a painful journey. It was inches away from him but every movement sent shockwaves through his body, and when he finally collapsed his finger fell still over her heart.

Chapter 1

Saturday 14th April 2012

Sam Grant had become a familiar figure in the Vista Real subdivision on the outskirts of Manila. Having paced out the route from his front door, around the houses and back to his start position he knew it was roughly half a mile, and so his aim was to do ten circuits a day.

Almost a year after breaking both legs in the explosion it was a tall ask, but he was determined to get back into the old routine. For the first few days he had jogged round a couple of times before the muscles in his calves screamed for mercy, but a month later he was comfortable at three miles and pushing it at four. An easy five was his ultimate target but he knew that was still a couple of weeks away at least.

After nearly seven laps of the compound the sweat had completely soaked his sando, which was the Philippine equivalent of the sleeveless T-shirt. Completing the ensemble was a pair of bright blue shorts and his New Balance sneakers, all of which had been purchased in Manila.

He'd arrived in the country wearing nothing more than a hospital robe and for the first six weeks that was all he'd needed, having been bedridden due to the multiple fractures in his legs. His left arm had also suffered, as had his chest, but it was the face that took the most getting used to. When he'd first seen his new look he had been horrified, but as the swelling from his injuries and the subsequent surgery went down he found himself staring at a totally different person. His eyes seemed sunken due to the heavier brow, and his nose looked like it had been lifted off a local, flat against his face instead of sticking out proudly as it had once done. He had tried growing a full beard to hide the crescent shaped scar which covered his right cheek but the climate made it itch intolerably, so he settled for a goatee and moustache and simply put up with people staring at it. Time being the healer it was, the scar was already receding, but he knew he would wear it for the rest of his life.

James Farrar had told him to use it as a reminder as to why he was here in the Philippines, but then James Farrar was a dickhead.

From the moment he'd met Farrar, Grant had taken an instant dislike to him. He didn't know if it was the condescending attitude, or the pin-striped suit, or just that he stank of green slime. Of course, he couldn't be sure Farrar was from the Royal Intelligence Corp because one of his favourite games was point-blank refusing to give Grant any information.

After their first brief meeting, Farrar had popped by a couple of months later, totally unannounced, just to check on his progress. Since then, he had only made a phone call every couple of months, which suited Grant down to the ground. If Farrar wasn't willing to answer his questions, then the less contact they had, the better.

He waved at Mr Lee as he passed the house on the corner and got a wave in return. The Philippines might not be the most modern country in the world, but the people were generally nice and the whole neighbourhood had made him feel welcome when he'd moved in.

Prior to living here he'd stayed in the house in Subic Freeport, but there was only so much to do there, and he had craved a busier life. On Farrar's second visit he'd requested that a bag of belongings be brought over from the U.K. The holdall he'd asked for contained just over a million pounds sterling, the proceeds from the sale of his home and business, and was stored at his solicitor's office in London.

Farrar wasn't pleased at the idea and made his feelings known, but Grant had insisted that he needed his own place to live and money to set up a small business to keep himself occupied. Farrar had eventually relented on the condition that the money be banked and Grant could only have access to forty thousand pesos per month. Any withdrawal over that amount would have to be sanctioned by Farrar himself. Grant had agreed, and the bag was delivered to his quarters by diplomatic courier three days later, followed by a phone call from Farrar who took great delight in telling him that the government salary he'd been enjoying was coming to an end, since he was now able to support himself. Grant wasn't even slightly concerned at losing the miserly allowance and told Farrar as much, causing even greater animosity between the pair.

The house he'd bought, with Farrar's consent, was a two bedroom up and down, with a decent garden and covered car port. He could have bought something ten times the size and still have half of his money in the bank, but as he was going to be living alone he didn't see the point.

As he approached his house he saw Alma appear from the front door, hosepipe in her hand ready to water the plants. He blew her a kiss as he passed and continued round the corner and onto lap eight.

Alma had happened out of the blue, and it had been the last thing he'd expected.

He'd been out shopping for kitchen appliances for his new home when she'd caught his eye, and he'd found himself smiling at her. More surprisingly, she'd smiled back from behind the counter and before he'd even thought about it he'd found himself standing before her, lost for words. Then came the realisation that she might have been smiling simply because that was what she was paid to do: put on her customer service face.

"Um, I'm looking for a washing machine," he had said feebly.

The smile had remained in place, and the amount of eye contact he'd got went well beyond customer care, so he'd chanced his arm and invited her for a coffee after work. She'd readily accepted, which he'd found amazing, and after they had arranged a time for him to pick her up, he'd left the shop looking for the hidden cameras, convinced it was some kind of sick reality TV gag.

He'd then walked straight back in and purchased the white goods he'd originally gone in for.

The date at a local coffee shop had gone well. Alma spoke English very well, although there was a hint of an American accent, a result of the U.S. presence up until November 1992, when the American flag was finally lowered in Subic for the last time.

He'd been conscious about his looks all evening, though Alma either hadn't noticed or hadn't cared. She'd wanted to know about his past, and he'd had to think quickly.

A year earlier he'd been Tom Gray, widower. A few weeks later he was Tom Gray, terrorist. The next thing he knew he was waking up in an Admiral's bedroom in the Philippines with a new name, a new face and an explicit warning from Farrar: tell anyone about his previous life and he would be dead within twenty four hours. So he'd spent the evening telling her about Sam Grant, entrepreneur.

The story he'd told was of a man who'd lived in London all his life, taking various part-time jobs before starting his own small business selling T-shirts online. A raft of other websites soon sprang up, and it was while on holiday in Manila the previous year that he'd seen the lack of online shopping sites and decided to corner the market.

The latter part was true, as he'd tried to order some sneakers over the internet and found it impossible, so he'd rented an office, furnished it with half a dozen computers and hired some developers to create the sites. He now had a dozen customers signed up to sell their goods through his web portals, offering them the software and hosting for free in exchange for five percent of each sale.

Sales had taken a while to pick up, he'd explained to her, but the business was starting to pay for itself.

He'd been in the process of creating the warehouse and distribution side of the business when he'd met Alma. She was twenty seven and had been working in the department store for a couple of years, having travelled up from the southern islands to stay with relatives in Manila, and having previously worked in a wholesale company she had plenty of contacts that would help him in his quest to start selling direct to the public. That revelation had prompted him to offer her a job with his company at double her current wages, and she had accepted without a moment's hesitation.

They'd parted that evening without so much as a goodnight kiss, Grant heeding the words of an ex-pat he'd met in a bar when he'd first arrived in Manila.

"It takes time to court a good Filipina," he'd said. "You should never try anything on the first three dates."

It wasn't until he'd got into the taxi to take him home that Grant had thought about his wife and son. Was he being disrespectful towards them by flirting with another woman? All it had been was coffee and a chat, yet deep down he knew that he wanted a whole lot more.

He'd wrestled with his conscience during the days leading up to their second date, and had come clean with Alma about the fact that he was previously married. He'd lied when he'd said wife and child had both died in a car crash several years earlier, but at least she now knew about them.

It wasn't the third but the fifth date before he kissed her, by which time he'd come to terms with the fact that he had to move on, no matter how much he missed his family. Their relationship had moved on at an advanced pace from that first kiss, with consummation following soon after and Alma moving in with him a few weeks later.

She had certainly made her mark on the house, adding a woman's touch to his barrack-style minimalism. Pictures now adorned the walls and a sensible spread of ornaments brightened up the living room. She had also introduced him to Filipino cooking in a big way, with Sinigang Na Hipon, fresh prawns and vegetables in a sour tamarind broth, being his favourite dish. The food had certainly piled on the pounds, which was one of the reasons he wanted to get back into his five-miles-a-day routine.

The muscles in his calves were beginning to cramp as he neared the end of the eighth lap but he felt confident that he could get another in before calling it a day. He tried to ignore the pain as he pounded the road, instead reflecting on the great shape his new life was taking. All would be wonderful if he could just cut James Farrar out of it.

He turned the corner into his street and saw the black SUV parked up in his driveway, and he used that as an excuse to cut his exercise short. As he strolled up to the vehicle the driver's side window hummed as it descended and Farrar's face appeared, looking ridiculous in aviator sunglasses.

Speak of the Devil, Grant thought, and his shit-filled illegitimate son will appear.

"Get in," Farrar said, polite as ever.

Grant climbed into the passenger seat and the blast from the car's air-con hit him like a frozen sledgehammer, chilling him to the bone – much to Farrar's delight. Grant appreciated air-conditioning and had it in every room in his home, but nothing as ferocious as this.

"We have some work for you," Farrar said without preamble.

"What kind of work?"

"I'll give you the details later. Just be ready to board a plane in five days time. That should give you plenty of time to sort out your affairs here."

Grant stared at him for a moment, the anger building.

"No thanks," he finally said, and made to open the door. Farrar was apoplectic.

"What do you mean 'No'? You'll do as you're damn well told."

Grant turned back to him. "Not until I get some answers."

"Such as...?"

"I want to know who I'm working for."

"You are working for Her Majesty's government."

"I gathered that, but which branch," Grant asked, exasperated.

"That's need to know."

"Yes, and I need to fucking know."

"No you don't," Farrar said. "All you have to do is follow instructions. Now, there are rumblings of terror cells operating in Europe and we want you to go and do what you do best."

"You're not listening, Farrar. I want some answers before I do anything for you."

Farrar sighed and angled himself to get a better view of Grant. "It wouldn't do you any good to know who my bosses are. We're so black, even the prime minister doesn't know the full extent of what we do, and you won't find us in the Yellow Pages. All you need to know is that we are the cutting edge of anti-terrorism and we have a proactive agenda. We like to stop attacks while they are in the planning stage, and do it in such a way that they don't know that we know, if you know what I mean."

Grant's expression barely changed, waiting for Farrar to elaborate.

"We take down cells at the earliest possible stage, causing accidents so that the men at the top don't know we're on to them. Their people die in car crashes, in street robberies, all manner of different ways, but crucially they are explainable accidents. However, you can only have so many of your people die in a crash before it becomes suspicious, and so we need to think of more ingenious ways. That's where you come in.

"Your little stunt last year was well thought out, and we need that kind of lateral thinking to enable us to ramp up the body count. We're taking down our fair share of terrorists, don't get me wrong, but there are just too many others willing to replace them."

"Then go for the main men, not the foot soldiers," Grant said, despite his reticence to engage in conversation with the man, his training and planning skills kicking in before he had a chance to stop himself.

"You see, that's what I mean. You hear the problem and immediately have the solution."

"Don't try and blow smoke up my arse, it won't work. Besides, I'm out of that whole business now. You'll have to find someone else."

"This isn't up for discussion, Sam. You either do as we ask, or things get very uncomfortable for you."

"What are you going to do?" Grant laughed. "Come and visit me every day? I'm a free man."

"I was thinking more of having the lease on your company offices cancelled, or maybe retracting your Barangay clearance to operate a business. That puts your staff out of work and your business goes down the pan. I can also stop all withdrawals from your bank account, leaving you without a pot to piss in."

Farrar nodded toward Alma, who was just finishing up with the hose. "Do you really think your dolly bird will hang around when she finds out you can't support her anymore?"

He enjoyed the pained look on Grant's face at the thought of losing his bed warmer, a look that swiftly turned to anger.

"I'll do one job, but with conditions," Grant said, more than a touch of hostility in his voice. Farrar started to object but Grant cut him off. "I want some of my old team with me. Sonny Baines, Len Smart and Tristram Barker-Fink all helped come up with the plan last year, and I want their help again."

"Impossible. The fewer people involved the better."

"It's not negotiable, Farrar. As you've already said, they don't need to know who they're working for; they just need to follow instructions. I'm sure you'll have front companies that can employ them at proper contractor rates, so make it happen."

Farrar wasn't accustomed to having people dictate terms to him, and was determined to make that clear. "It's out of the question. We have no idea where these people are. It could take weeks to track them down."

"That's bullshit. I could call their mobiles and be talking to them in a couple of minutes. The only reason I haven't spoken to them in the last year is because you told me not to. I've done everything you asked of me, so it's time you gave me something in return."

Farrar considered the request a little more and decided the time was right to accede to Grant's demand. "Okay, you can have Smart and Baines. Unfortunately, Tristram bought it in Iraq a few months ago."

"How?"

"I don't have all the details," Farrar said. "All I know is he was doing some bodyguard work and his client was attacked by a large force. The agency he worked for couldn't give us any further information."

Grant gazed out of the window, staring at nothing in particular as he thought about his good friend. Tris had served with him in the regiment and they had shared a couple of tours in Iraq, and Grant had subsequently hired him when he was managing director of Viking Security Services. When Grant – in his previous incarnation as Tom Gray – had first come up with the notion of kidnapping five habitual criminals in order to force the government to come down harder on repeat offenders, it was Tris who had been the most supportive, helping mould the initial spur-of-the-moment idea into a solid, viable plan. Tris had also been one of the people to administer CPR when he'd been seriously injured in the explosion that had brought his four-day siege to an abrupt end, and he had never been able to thank him.

In fact, Grant hadn't spoken to any of his friends since his arrival in the Philippines. He'd been tempted, obviously, but he knew that Farrar would be monitoring all of their incoming calls. If he'd tried to contact them, Farrar would have known about it.

Farrar's main concern, however, was that Grant might reveal the fact that he was actually Tom Gray, a man for whom the people of Britain had held a two-week protest demanding his release from custody. The official line was that Tom Gray had died from his injuries, when in fact he had been spirited out of the country to prevent him causing the government any further embarrassment. Grant had long ago considered the implications should the world find out that Tom Gray was still alive, and it didn't look rosy. Farrar would certainly follow through with his earlier threat to have him killed, at the very least. He might even go as far as to terminate all others who knew about him, and that included some good friends back in England.

Although he hadn't asked to be placed in this predicament, Sam Grant knew he had to deal with it, and had been doing quite a good job up until the last few minutes.

He turned back to Farrar, a steely look in his eyes. "I want Sonny and Len here before we set off, plus full details of the operation. We'll travel together and I'll brief them on the journey."

"Don't push your luck, Sam. You may be good at what you do, but you're not indispensable."

They sat staring at each other for a full minute, and it was Farrar who backed down first. "Okay, I'll give you the details on Monday and get Baines and Smart here by Tuesday evening. Just be ready to fly on Thursday afternoon."

"How long will I be gone?"

"It shouldn't take more than a couple of weeks. It all depends on how quickly you can devise and then execute your plan. We'll give you the target, you do the rest."

Grant nodded and opened the door, glad to get back out into the warm evening air. He didn't look back as he headed towards the house and he heard Farrar reverse off the driveway and disappear towards the subdivision gates.

Inside the house he found Alma preparing *pulutan* for the evening's game of *Tong-its*, a rummy-like card game the locals enjoyed playing, especially for money. The stakes were never high but it made for a good night's entertainment, particularly when accompanied by a few San Miguel beers, his neighbours and a table full of *pulutan*, drinking-food to soak up the alcohol. Grant had always been one to drink first and eat later, but he had slipped comfortably into the habit of picking at the array of small dishes throughout a drinking session. Popular dishes included *Sisig*, which consisted of ground pigs' ear and liver, and *Tokwa't Baboy*, toasted tofu and boiled ham in garlic-flavoured soy sauce. Alma had become famous with the local men for her generous servings, and there was never an empty chair on card night at the Grant household.

Grant hugged Alma from behind as she washed the rice in a large pan to get rid of the starch. He stood a good eighteen inches taller than her, and had to stoop to kiss her affectionately on the neck. He then checked the supply of San Miguel and saw that he was down to less than a crate, so he grabbed a five-hundred Peso note and headed towards the door.

"Just gonna get some more beer," he told her, and got a smile in reply.

Like many Filipinas, Alma didn't drink; they tended to leave that to the Filipino men. She enjoyed the card evenings immensely, though, as it meant the wives would join their husbands in the house. The men would sit out in the garden while the ladies spent the evening inside, usually doing cross-stitch while sharing the weeks' gossip.

Grant returned from the local shop within five minutes, his arms straining under the weight of two crates of San Miguel. The beers went into the drinks fridge, which he'd bought specifically for Saturday nights, and then he headed to the bathroom to have a shower.

The guests began arriving just after eight that evening, with Mr. Lee the first as always.

"Sam, how are you? How's business?"

"Booming," Grant said. "How's the Lee empire coming along?"

Albert Lee had a string of shops in all the major malls dotted throughout Manila, and seemed to open a new one every time they met. "I'm meeting with two companies next week. If either of them

209

can provide a suitable delivery service I will be in a position to sign up to your website."

Grant was happy at the news, but it reminded him that he had to make arrangements for his office manager, Alfredo, to take over for a fortnight. He also had to break the news to Alma, but thought it best to wait until they were alone.

The evening began well, with each of the five guests doing their best to outdo each other in the business stakes. One would announce that he had secured a new contract with a major supplier, and another would trump that with an international order. The banter was light-hearted, but Grant wondered if they would put so much effort into their work if they didn't have their Saturday night bragging rights to look forward to.

Grant himself wasn't one for getting into pissing contests, no matter how good-natured, so he settled for soaking up information about the current trading conditions. He just learned of a new competitor in the online market who had been canvassing his friends when the need to pee grabbed him, so he excused himself and made his way to the CR, or Comfort Room, the Filipino term for the toilet. On his way past the living room he saw Alma in tears, being comforted by her friends.

"What's wrong?" he asked, taking a seat next to her, but Alma was too consumed with grief to answer.

"Her brother died today," a friend said. "She just got a phone call from her mother."

Grant wrapped his arms around Alma and hugged her tight. He knew she had a brother and a much younger sister as she was always talking about them, and was always sending a few Pesos home to help them out. She was so proud of her brother for being near the top of his class despite his poor background, and now that bright light had been extinguished.

"How did it happen?" Grant asked her friends in a hushed voice, but all he got was shrugs in response. He wasn't about to push Alma in her present state, so he let the question lie. A friend appeared with a glass of water and Grant offered her the seat next to his girlfriend, then he went outside to call an early end to the game.

His guests were understanding and went inside to offer Alma their support, but by this time she had regained a little control and assured them she would be okay. After making some more consoling noises their friends began to drift off into the night, leaving the couple alone.

Alma began to open up, and she replayed the brief conversation she'd had with her mother. "Arlan didn't come home from school at the usual time and Mama was really angry. She thought he'd gone out with his girlfriend, but when Maritess called asking to speak to him she got worried and called the police. That was when she found out that he'd been shot. The police said it was a robbery, but Arlan had nothing worth stealing..."

Her words tapered off as the tears came again, and just after midnight she finally drifted off to sleep in his arms.

Chapter 2

Sunday 15th April 2012

Grant woke up on the sofa alone, a thin ray of sunlight blinding him as it broke through a gap in the curtains. He immediately remembered the events of the previous evening and went in search of Alma, eventually finding her in their bedroom. She was packing a holdall with clothes and a few toiletries and she looked up at him as he appeared in the doorway, her eyes still red.

"Kumusta?" he asked.

"I'm okay," she said, resuming her packing. "But I have to go home for the funeral. I'll be back in a couple of days."

Grant moved into the room and gave her a hug. "I understand. I'll come with you."

"Are you sure? What about the office? Who will run things while you're gone?"

"It's fine. Alfredo can manage."

"It's not really safe in Isabela City," Alma said, concern etched on her face. "Maybe you should stay here, I'll be back soon."

"Darling, if it isn't safe, I'm definitely coming."

Alma smiled and kissed him on the cheek.

"How do we get there?" Grant asked her.

"We can take a flight to Zamboanga City and then take the boat across the Basilan Strait to Isabela. There's a plane leaving just after two this afternoon."

Grant checked his watch, added on three hours to get through the Manila traffic and realised he only had an hour and a half to get ready. "Call and book the tickets and book a taxi," he said. "I'll go and take a shower."

He finished washing in less than five minutes and as he dried himself he realised he would have to call Farrar to let him know where he was going. After getting dressed he punched the speed-dial number and the call was answered on the second ring.

"What?"

There's no end to this guy's manners, Grant thought. "I'm taking off for a few days," he replied. "I should be back late Tuesday night, maybe Wednesday."

"Taking off? Where to? This is no time for a holiday!"

Grant explained the situation but Farrar was unfazed by the news. "My condolences and all that, but you're staying put. She can go down there herself."

"I wasn't calling to ask your permission; I'm letting you know so that you can tell Len and Sonny that the key to my house will be with my next door neighbour. Tell Sonny to introduce himself as cousin Bob and they can make themselves comfortable until I get back."

"You really are the most insolent, jumped up —"

Grant ended the call and turned the phone off. He considered leaving it in the house while he was away, but he needed to be available should Alfredo have any problems at the office, so he tucked it into his jeans and began filling his sports bag with enough clothes for three days. In went socks, underpants, T-shirts and shorts, along with a spare pair of jeans and his toiletries: shaving kit; toothbrush and toothpaste; and soap. The final item was his bottle of Off Lotion insect repellent.

Farrar might be an arsehole, but he was right about the bloody mosquitoes.

The taxi arrived early to take them to Ninoy Aquino airport, which was just as well as traffic was exceptionally heavy, even for Manila. They got to the Cebu Pacific Air desk and picked up their tickets with a couple of minutes to spare, then rushed through the departure lounge to the boarding gate.

Grant was glad to see that the plane was an Airbus A319 rather than some ten-seater turbo-prop, and he enjoyed a snack on the flight, his first bite of the day.

An hour and a half later they arrived in Zamboanga City and took a taxi to the port, where Grant opted for the MS Weesam Express as it took just forty-five minutes to make the crossing and had air conditioning, as opposed to the normal ferry which took an hour longer and would leave him at the mercy of the late afternoon sun.

Once they disembarked they had a choice of vehicles to take them to their destination. Grant declined the offer of bicycles and motorcycles, both with sidecars capable of carrying two passengers, and chose instead to splash out an extra hundred pesos on a taxi.

The journey to the house where Alma grew up took just fifteen minutes, and as with the rest of the journey she sat in silence, looking out of the side window at nothing in particular. He did the same, not wanting to interrupt her thoughts, knowing full well what she was going through. It was almost two years since his son had died at the hands of a car thief, and less than a year later he had lost his wife, too, so he appreciated that there were moments when it was appropriate to talk and times when he should leave her to her reflections.

The only time she spoke was towards the end of their journey.

"Mama doesn't know about...us," she told him. "Can I introduce you as my boss?"

Grant assured her he was fine with that, but pointed out that it would be awkward if they were going to sleep under the same roof. Alma hadn't thought that far ahead, and was grateful when he offered to stay at a local hotel.

When they arrived at their destination he was surprised to see around thirty people sitting outside in the street. Most were playing cards, piles of money in the middle of the tables. The house itself was more like an old allotment shed, with the front wall made of two wooden doors nailed horizontally onto a makeshift frame. The inside was no better: the floor was bare concrete; cheap plasterboard lined the internal walls; and the only sign of technology was a portable television on a wooden sideboard.

In the centre of the small living room a couple of tables had been shoved together and on top was an open casket. Toddlers were chasing each other around it, laughing and giggling, while parents sat around the edge of the room chatting and eating. In the small kitchen towards the back of the house three women were preparing yet more food, and looking round he wondered where they could possibly put it. Every available inch of space was already taken up with bowls of rice; pork, chicken and fish dishes; and copious amounts of soft drinks.

Alma was staring at the peaceful face of her sibling when a woman in her late forties entered the room and came towards them.

Alma threw her arms around her. "Mama."

They hugged for some time before Alma's mother noticed the stranger staring at them. Introductions were made and Grant found that she spoke very little English, but Alma translated and Grant replied with some of the Tagalog phrases he had learnt over the last few months.

214

A plate heaped with rice and pork was suddenly thrust into his hand and he was ushered outside to a spare seat. Alma remained inside to catch up with her family, so he got stuck in. One of the locals at the table spoke passable English and sparked up a conversation, though Grant was more interested in the food than chit-chat. He answered questions about his past as truthfully as he could, though at times he had to be economical with his words.

A police car pulled up and he watched the sole occupant get out. He gave Grant a curious glance as he passed, then walked into the house. Through the open door Sam saw him cuddle Alma, a little too passionately for his liking, so he polished off his food and went inside on the pretence of grabbing a second helping. Alma stopped him on his way to the table and introduced the officer.

"This is Lorenzo," she said. "We went to school together."

Grant shook his hand. "Sam," he smiled, wondering what it was they'd done together *after* school.

"Lorenzo was just telling me that Arlan wasn't killed in a robbery."

The officer gestured for her to keep her voice down. "That's what I believe," he said softly. "There was a message attached to one of the other victims which tells me he was caught up in a gang war."

"Arlan wasn't in a gang," Alma said with indignation.

"I know. We think he was just in the wrong place at the wrong time."

"What was the message?" Grant asked.

"It said 'Basilan belongs to Abu Sayyaf'."

"Who's he?"

"Not a He," Alma said. "Abu Sayyaf is a Muslim independence group."

"More like terrorists," Lorenzo said. "And they want complete control of the region. There have been many gang killings in the last few months and we believe they want to eliminate all of their competition."

"But why was Arlan's death reported as a robbery?" Grant asked.

"Because certain members of the police would prefer that Abu Sayyaf incidents are not reported to the mainland. It might affect their income."

"I don't understand."

"The senior police officers receive payments from Abu Sayyaf and turn a blind eye to their activities," Lorenzo said. "Their crimes are attributed to others and they are allowed to operate as they wish."

"Are all policemen on the payroll?" Grant asked Lorenzo quizzically, and the Filipino resented the suggestion.

"No," he said, a little too loudly, drawing looks from others in the room. He noticed the attention and dropped his voice a little. "Some of us actually believe in the role we've been given. That's why I wanted Alma to know the truth." He looked at both of them in turn. "Don't tell anyone what I just told you."

Grant and Alma nodded solemnly.

"Where are you staying in Isabela?" Lorenzo asked him, his voice back to its normal level.

"I was hoping to find a hotel for a couple of days," Grant said, although sensing a history between these two he was no longer sure he wanted to let Alma out of his sight.

"I know a good hotel not far from here," Lorenzo said. "I can take you if you like, but we have to be quick; the reception closes early."

Grant looked at Alma and she nodded at him. "Go, I'll come and get you in the morning."

He grabbed his bag and followed Lorenzo to the car, and as they pulled away he looked back at the house and saw Alma in the doorway, offering a surreptitious wave which he returned through the open window.

"Alma tells me she works for you," Lorenzo said as they drove sedately through the evening traffic. "What does your company do?"

"We build websites for online shopping."

The concept was lost on the policeman, so Grant explained the principle.

"Does it make a lot of money?" Lorenzo asked.

"At the moment we only make about a million pesos a month, which is just about enough to break even. Hopefully we can start showing a healthy profit in the next twelve months."

Lorenzo whistled, impressed with the figures although he didn't appreciate the fact that it barely covered Grant's outgoings. The numbers were still going round in his mind as he helped Grant check in to the hotel, and after he made a mental note of the room number he left his charge to settle in for the evening.

"I suggest you stay in your room tonight," he told Grant. "The streets of Isabela are not safe for a stranger, especially after dark. Abu Sayyaf are everywhere, and you would make a good trophy for them."

Grant agreed to the suggestion. He took the stairs to the first floor and found room one zero eight, and once inside he realised that his idea of 'good' differed hugely from Lorenzo's. The bedding had seen better days – not to mention a lot fewer stains – and the toilet was functional in that there was a pot to sit on but no cistern to flush his bodily fluids away. Instead, a bucket full of water and a large ladle had been provided. His morning ritual for the next couple of days would consist of shit, scoop, shower and shave.

The television offered only local channels, so he settled on the bed, wishing he'd brought a book along, but at the same time thankful for the insect repellent.

In the street below, Lorenzo sat in the patrol car looking up at the second floor. He toyed with the phone in his hand as he wondered what exactly there was between his old girlfriend and this foreigner. It didn't make sense for a company owner to accompany a member of staff to their home town for a funeral unless it was more than just a working relationship.

When Alma had announced that she was going to Manila to stay with family just after her twenty-fifth birthday he had been devastated. He had been trying to cultivate a romance between them for the previous three years, building on their friendship. He would visit her in the evenings and often bring his guitar to jam with Arlan, though she rarely took up his offer to meet on the weekends, insisting that was family time.

Then she'd dropped the bombshell, dashing all of his dreams. He'd tried to persuade her not to go, to stay with him, but she'd wanted more for her family and saw Manila as the place to find a better opportunity. He'd relented after a while, convincing himself that she would be back within a few weeks, but as the months wore on her letters told him she was doing well and really enjoying the new challenge. Whenever he had written to her he'd casually joked about her new man but she had always assured him that she wasn't looking for a boyfriend.

That was, until three months ago.

Her letters had suddenly become less frequent and a lot shorter, until they had stopped completely four weeks ago. Now she was back, and with a foreigner in tow.

He had told the truth when he'd told Sam that he hadn't taken bribes from Abu Sayyaf.

However, there was always a first time.

He punched in a number and waited a moment for the recipient to pick up.

"Pare, I have something you might be interested in..."

Chapter 3

Monday 16th April 2012

Grant didn't know if it was the lack of air-conditioning or the food he'd eaten at Alma's house, but he woke up just after midnight covered in sweat, the thin cotton bed sheet sticking to his naked body. He headed into the bathroom and stood under the weak shower, allowing the tepid water to slowly wash away the layer of perspiration. As he dried himself he realised after five minutes that he was no longer towelling off water: he was back to the layer of sweat that had replaced it. Giving up on the fruitless exercise, he walked back into the bedroom where he grabbed a local newspaper and used it to fan himself.

He turned on the television, knowing that trying to get back to sleep would be futile. The music from a talent show blasted into the room and he jumped for the remote, turning the volume down to an acceptable level. After flicking through the channels he settled on cock fighting, although he saw more adverts than action. That was the trouble with TV in the Philippines: they showed four minutes of the program followed by five minutes of advertisements.

Grant was just learning how to get bigger breasts when he heard a knock at the door and he immediately assumed it was someone coming to complain about the television being too loud. He dashed into the toilet and grabbed a towel to wrap around his waist, then opened the door a little and peered through the crack. As he did so he was shoved backwards and four men ran into the room, weapons raised and pointing at him. Two of the men had handguns, the other two rifles which he recognised as American M16s.

"On the floor!" one shouted. Gray complied, a little too slowly for their liking, and he got a rifle butt in the shoulder for his troubles. He sank to his knees, still holding the towel, and weighed up the men before him.

Three of them were about five feet six tall, about average for Filipinos, while the one who'd struck him dwarfed them by a good fourteen inches. The rifle looked like a toy in his huge hands and he was the only one without facial hair. Grant decided to designate him 'Ox', because the dumb-looking giant probably couldn't spell it, but he looked like he could lift one.

Grant considered fighting his way out, but they had too much distance between them, whether by training or chance, he didn't know. Any attempt to take one of their weapons would afford the others enough time to give him the bad news, so he decided to wait and see what they wanted: The longer he managed to play this out, the more he could learn about them, in particular their strengths and weaknesses.

It didn't take long for them to reveal the reason for the visit.

"We are Abu Sayyaf," one of them said, and Grant decided he was the leader of the little group. "You will come with us."

"What for?" Grant asked, feigning fear. Back in his Army days he'd been taught that by acting submissively in these situations his enemies would most likely be more lenient, whereas someone who was antagonistic would be watched more closely and treated with more aggression.

"You will be our hostage. You are a rich man and will pay us a million dollars."

"I haven't got a million dollars," Grant said, incredulous. "I just work in an office."

"Liar!" The shout was punctuated with another blow from the rifle butt, this time to the back of the head. He collapsed, his vision blurred and bells ringing in his ears. "We know you are a businessman and have a company in Manila. You will pay us!"

One of the men grabbed his clothes from the chair and threw them at him.

"Put your clothes on," Leader shouted, while another emptied Grant's bag out onto the bed. After handing the mobile over to his boss he put the rest of the belongings back in the bag and swung it over his shoulder.

Grant dressed slowly despite their prompting, pretending to fumble with his clothes as he desperately thought of a way out. Leader had backed away to the door, covering him with his pistol, and Grant realised that there would be no escape while they were in the room. The situation got worse a moment later.

"Anton, tie his hands," Leader said, and one of the men stepped forward and produced something from his pocket. It looked to Grant like the flex from a lamp, and he put his hands out, palms facing each other. Anton was having none of it, and he gestured with his own hands to show that he wanted Grant to place one wrist on top of the other. These guys have had practice, Grant thought as he followed Anton's instructions.

With his hands secure they ushered him into the hallway, but even here they were too spread out for him to take them all down, even if his hands had been free. Once down the stairs he saw that the reception desk was empty, and Ox used the muzzle of his rifle to urge Grant through the front door where a battered Toyota saloon was waiting.

Leader opened the boot and told him to climb inside, and he looked round for a possible alternative. There was a sprinkling of people on the streets and he considered crying out for help, but his captors were either blissfully unaware of the onlookers or, more ominously, they didn't care. If it was the latter, then attracting their attention was unlikely to do him any good, so he complied once more.

The lid slammed down, blotting out the meagre street lighting. The air inside the cramped compartment was stifling. The car then took off and his whole body rattled as they navigated the uneven streets, his head crashing against the lid of the boot every time they hit a pothole. By the time they reached the outskirts of town a trickle of blood was already running down his forehead, and things only got worse once they hit the dirt roads leading out of Isabela City.

Grant knew the situation wasn't going to improve anytime soon, but one advantage he had was that they didn't know about his military past. They thought he was just a businessman, and he would happily keep up that illusion until the time came.

The pace of the car slowed but the jostling continued for another thirty minutes, then abruptly stopped. Grant heard and felt the occupants climbing out and the doors slamming shut, and a moment later the boot was opened. Grant closed one eye to protect his night vision, expecting light to come flooding in, but the night was pitch black. As he was being dragged out of the car he realised that the reason for the utter darkness was that they had driven deep into the jungle, and not even the night stars could penetrate the tree tops.

Blood dripped from his forehead into his eyes and he wiped it away with his wrist. He then stretched his legs, glad of the chance to straighten them again after his short confinement, but no sooner had he got the circulation going than Ox once more prodded him with the rifle, suggesting he fall in behind Leader who was striding into the darkness. As he set off the lights of the car lit the men up, then reversed and disappeared back in the direction of the main town.

"Emilio, you watch our backs," Anton said as he fell in behind his giant comrade.

After those few words they walked in silence for three hours, fording a shallow stream before heading to higher ground where the going was tougher on Grant. His calves began to burn as they took a circuitous route up the hill but fortunately Leader was also in the mood for a break and ordered everyone to rest up. While his captors dumped their gear and sought a comfortable place to sit, Grant collapsed into the foliage and began massaging his legs. He hadn't had a drink of water in hours and knew from his jungle training days in the regiment that dehydration was his most dangerous enemy right now. Unless he got that under control he would be in no fit state to walk much further, never mind find a way to escape.

"I need a drink," he shouted over to Leader, who immediately came over and clamped a hand over his mouth.

"Keep your voice down. The Sundalos are everywhere."

Grant waited until the sweaty palm had been removed then asked what Sundalos were, a lot more quietly this time.

"They are the Armed Forces of the Philippines. They want to deny us our right to an independent Muslim state."

Grant was encouraged by the fact that they were surrounded by the Army and it showed on his face, but his hoped were soon dashed.

"They are incompetent, but even an idiot with a gun can be dangerous. They don't care who they shoot at, as long as they fire in our general direction. Sometimes they hit us, sometimes our hostages. I don't think you should look at them as your saviours: they are more likely to kill you than rescue you."

With a grin, Leader returned to his small backpack and took a swig from a half-full bottle of water before throwing it over to Grant, who gulped it down. It was warm and did little to quench his thirst, but it would keep him going for an hour or two.

A few minutes later they heard faint voices coming from below them on the hill, and Leader whispered for everyone to start moving again. No-one was sure if the voices belonged to soldiers or civilians but they were taking no chances, and climbed ever higher while making as little sound as possible. Even Grant, who would have been as clumsy as possible if it meant alerting a rescue team, did his best to keep the noise to a minimum.

They trudged on for another two hours until Leader suddenly raised his hand for those behind him to stop. Everyone dropped to a knee, even Grant. He cursed himself for letting his training take over but none of the others seemed to care; they were more intent on finding out what Leader had come across.

After an interminable three minutes Leader stood again and opened his arms. From the darkness two men appeared, both carrying rifles, and they each hugged Leader.

"*Salam alaikum!*" they said as they kissed each other on both cheeks. Grant's guards joined in the greetings and when they'd finished one of the newcomers came and stood over him. He considered Grant for a moment and then rattled off some Tagalog to his companions. They grabbed Grant under his arms and lifted him to his feet, then pushed him forward. Once again Leader took point and it was only a few minutes later that they arrived in the camp.

In fact, the camp was little more than a clearing in the jungle, the remnants of the smaller trees they'd chopped down to create it still littering the ground. Larger trees were dotted around the centre and all of them had hammocks swinging between them, some with more than one occupant. Over to Grant's right he saw a small tent capable of housing two, maybe three people at a push, and to his left he saw a group huddled together on the ground.

There were four Filipinos, a Chinese couple and three westerners, and Ox poked him with his rifle, gesturing that he should join them. He took a seat next to the white trio and the first thing he noticed was their poor condition. The two males were undernourished, their faces having an almost skeletal appearance. Both wore shorts and T-shirts which looked like they hadn't been washed in months and one man had a festering sore the size of a golf ball on his neck. The woman seemed in better health, though her clothes were just as ragged. Her shoulder-length blonde hair fell about her face and clearly hadn't seen shampoo in a long time, but underneath all the dirt he could see a rather striking woman. Despite his circumstances something stirred inside him, something he hadn't felt in years.

She grabbed his arms, her grip surprisingly strong.

"I'm Vick," she said. "Vick Phillips."

"Vick?" Grant looked confused.

"Short for Victoria," she explained.

"Ah, I see. Sam. Sam Grant. How long have you all been here?"

Vick gestured to the men. "Robert Moore and I have been here since January and Eddie Halton arrived about three weeks later."

"What about the others?" he asked, looking beyond the trio.

"The Chinese couple have been here for about two months and don't speak a word of English, and the Filipinos..."

Her words drifted off and her eyes glazed over as she stared towards the rising sun as it broke the horizon.

"The locals don't have the same value as we do," Moore explained. "They tend to have a couple of weeks to come up with payment or they are just taken away and never come back. We heard one of the guards joking about how one man's head bounced and rolled down the hill. That seems to be their favourite way of dealing with people."

No wonder they all look petrified, Grant thought. He wasn't afraid of death, but he didn't like the idea of it coming by decapitation.

"Have you heard anything about us?" Vick asked. "On the news, I mean?"

"I don't really follow the local news. I mostly read the BBC news website."

Vick look at him, imploring him to continue.

"Sorry, but I haven't seen anything about you, any of you. Are you sure the government know you're here?"

"Of course they do. We spoke to the British Embassy the day we were kidnapped and Jonjon has sent them messages every week."

There was no way of sugar coating it, so Grant settled for: "I'm sorry..."

An awkward silence followed, during which Grant took the opportunity to assess his captors. There were fifteen guards that he could see, some adorned in U.S Army combat trousers, boots and smocks while others wore a mishmash of army gear and civvies. He didn't see anyone who looked over the age of thirty, and three of them looked like they should still be in school. Two things they all had in common were that they wore bandanas in varying shades of red and each carried small arms, including M16 rifles and pistols. Almost all had bolos — long knives similar to machetes and used for hacking a path through the jungle — hanging from their waists. A couple even had hand grenades dangling from various bits of webbing. A couple of Multi-shot Soviet RPG-7s were propped up against a tree next to a box of High Explosive rounds, representing their heavy arsenal.

"We'll be moving out soon," Vick said, watching the Abu Sayyaf members pull down their hammocks and gather their belongings.

"Where are we going?"

"Somewhere else," she said flatly. "We never have a destination, we just march until sundown."

That made sense to Grant. Alma had told him that the island of Basilan was only about forty miles across, and with the AFP constantly hounding them Abu Sayyaf would have to stay mobile to avoid detection.

His stomach growled and he realised that he hadn't had a bite to eat since the previous evening. "What about breakfast?" he asked. "Have you already eaten?"

"Ha!" Halton snorted. "We're lucky to get a handful of rice once a day. Once we had a tin of sardines between twelve of us and we thought it was Christmas and our birthdays all rolled into one."

His accent marked him as American, whereas Grant could tell that Vick and Moore were definitely British.

"And now that you've joined us," Halton continued, "our portion just got smaller."

"I don't think Sam chose to be here, Eddie," Vick chastised. "Given the choice, I'm sure he would prefer to be tucked up in bed right now."

Halton continued muttering while he scratched his beard but Grant shrugged the comment off, instead returning to his assessment of the setup.

As he scanned the encampment two figures emerged from the tent and Leader joined them, handing over Grant's mobile phone. They exchanged a few words and then Leader came over and ordered Grant to get to his feet before handing over the phone. "Call your office and tell them we want one million dollars for your release."

"I already told you, I haven't got a million dollars. The company barely brings in a million pesos a month."

"Then you must get it somewhere. Call your embassy, call your family, I don't care. The price is one million dollars."

Grant toyed with his phone, weighing up his options. Just one look at the other prisoners told him this wasn't a situation he wanted to endure for any length of time, but he was telling the truth when he said his company didn't have that kind of money. He had about five hundred thousand dollars in his personal account, but to get access to that he would have to go through James Farrar, and he wondered briefly if decapitation would be a better alternative to another conversation with that snake. Sadly, he knew he had little alternative and he thumbed through his call history and dialled the number.

"What?" Farrar snapped, unhappy at being woken at such an ungodly hour.

"I have a problem and I need access to my account," Grant told him.

"What's wrong? Your bed warmer got a bun in the oven?"

"Farrar, for once I want you to stop being a sarcastic prick and listen. I am being held by Abu Sayyaf and I need all the money in the account, plus another half million dollars."

There was silence as Farrar took in the news and it seemed an age before the reply came, exploding into Grant's ear.

"You really are the most incompetent shit I've ever had the misfortune to deal with."

Grant allowed him that cheap shot. "Will you get the money?"

"It isn't our policy to negotiate with terrorists," was the frank reply.

"You don't have to negotiate, you just have to pay them," Grant said menacingly through gritted teeth, his patience with Farrar exhausted. Leader sensed the call wasn't going well and grabbed the phone from Grant's hand.

"I am Bong Manalo. Who is this?"

"James Farrar."

"Well, James Farrar, we want one million dollars for the safe release of Sam Grant. You have until the end of the day to agree to pay or we will deliver his head to you."

Manalo killed the connection and pushed Grant back to the ground before striding back to the men standing at the entrance to the tent.

"Who're the guys he's talking to?" Grant asked, nodding towards the trio.

"The taller one's name is Zandro Calizo, but they call him Jonjon. He's the main man. The other one is his second-in-command, Abel Guzman. Neither of them speaks English, so Bong acts as an interpreter."

As she spoke there were raised voices from the trio, with Bong and Jonjon shouting at each other and Abel trying to calm them both down. Grant caught the word *Sundalos* a few times and got the gist of the conversation: keep your voices down or you'll bring the soldiers down on us.

Bong eventually backed down and stomped off in a huff, taking his frustration out on anyone who got close enough, but it seemed

226

everyone knew to keep out of his way when he was in this kind of mood.

The packing up moved at double-quick time and when they were ready to move off the group of prisoners was told to get to their feet. It was only then that Grant saw them tethered to each other by the ankle in groups of three. One of the younger terrorists came over and released Eddie Halton, then used a fresh piece of twine to tie him to Grant, turning a bad day into a really shitty one.

They were lined up in their little groups and flanked by eight guards they moved off into the jungle, the mosquitoes taking their turn to heap misery on them.

"You know, your voice sounds familiar," Vick said to the back of Grant's head. "I've heard it somewhere before, I'm sure of it."

"Yeah, that happens a lot," Grant said, not happy that she'd brought it up. Farrar may have changed his name and looks, but the voice remained the same, the voice which had been broadcast worldwide a year earlier.

"People say I sound like the guy in that advert," he offered.

"Which advert?"

"You know, the one for car insurance."

He left her with that vague answer and concentrated on putting one foot in front of the other in time with Halton.

* * *

James Farrar put his phone back on the bedside table and tousled his hair, trying to shake off the remnants of the previous nights' sleep. He hated Mondays as a rule, and to start one this way wasn't going to do anything to help his mood.

He'd met some ill-disciplined people in his time, he thought, as well as his fair share of imbeciles, yet Grant was the only one who fell into both categories. Only an idiot could get himself kidnapped four days before a mission, one that had been manufactured especially for him. Well, perhaps manufactured was the wrong word, but they had been awaiting an opportunity to get Grant out into the field and one had presented itself in the shape of a small-time arms dealer who was looking to provide weapons to terrorist cells in Pakistan.

Hakan Farli was a Turkish national who had spent a few years selling small arms in his country of birth but was now hoping to step up to the big time. In order to do so he had spread the word about the

227

services he offered, but unfortunately for him he had spread it too far and showed up on the MI6 radar in Islamabad while meeting with suspected terrorists. A full background check was done and the data sent to London where it was disseminated to all the other security services, and within hours a copy had been sent to James Farrar who saw Farli as the perfect opportunity to send Grant out into the open.

The plan had been simple: Grant, who would now be accompanied by Len Smart and Sonny Baines, would be tasked with tailing Farli with a view to causing an 'accident'. However, they themselves would be tailed, and the terrorist cell Farli was going to meet would be informed of their mission. Several of Farrar's men would be on the ground to record the moment the cell took them out and that video would then be shown to the other surviving co-conspirators as proof that Tom Gray was once and for all dead.

Of the eight men who had helped Tom Gray carry out his terrorist act — there was no other word for it in Farrar's opinion — Colin Avery and Michael Fletcher had died in Abdul Mansour's attack and two had passed away in the subsequent eleven months. Farrar had been telling the truth when he'd told Grant that Tristram Barker-Fink had died in Iraq, but what he hadn't shared was the fact that it was Farrar's team who had leaked the route Tris and his principal would be taking. After the IED had been planted at the roadside by the insurgents it came down to just waiting for their convoy to pass.

Paul Bennett had been involved in a tragic motorcycle accident while he was doing over eighty miles-per-hour on the motorway. No other vehicles were involved in the incident, but only a select few knew that the people in the car following him at the time worked for Farrar. A portable heat gun had been focused on the back wheel of the bike for just a few hundred yards, its beam intense enough to compromise the integrity of the tyre wall and cause the fatal blowout.

That left just Carl Levine, Jeff Campbell, Baines and Smart to eliminate. Oh, and of course Sam Grant, he reminded himself.

Farrar would have happily let Grant rot in the jungle for a couple of years, but there was growing pressure to tie up all the loose ends as soon as possible. Besides, there was an agreement in place to show a video of Grant to his friends, with new footage to be provided every fortnight, as proof that he was still alive and that the government were sticking to their side of the bargain. He could of course just inform the Abu Sayyaf leadership that the man they thought was Sam Grant was in fact a British agent, but selling his death at the hands of terrorists to his friends would be difficult and raise too many questions. What was he doing there? What was done to try and get him out? Well, they could hardly send in the SAS to rescue a man who should be dead, but...

Stumbling upon the possibility of killing three birds with one stone he did a quick mental calculation that told him it was close to midnight in England. A bit late to be calling, he thought, but if he'd had his sleep disturbed, why not pay it forward? He picked up his phone and dialled the first number. It answered on the second ring. "Hello?"

"Len, it's James. I need to tell you about a change in the contract."

"You're not cancelling it, are you?"

"No, it has become a recovery mission, that's all I can tell you at the moment," Farrar said, not needing to point out that it was an unsecure line. "Tickets will be waiting at the KLM desk at Heathrow and you'll be met at the airport when you get here."

"What's the terms?" Len Smart asked.

"Same daily rate as we discussed, plus five thousand on completion."

"And the terrain: how should I pack?"

"It'll be mostly jungle," Farrar said.

"I'll need some equipment when I get there."

"I'll provide everything you need," Farrar promised.

"Okay, see you tomorrow."

That's how it should be done, Farrar thought: No quibbling, no arguments, just get the instructions and be ready to move. If only Grant could be like that. He ended the call and gave the same instructions to Sonny Baines, who also readily agreed. It was a shame they had to die, but when you dance with the devil...

His next call was to the office.

"It's me. I need you to track a mobile phone," he said and read out the number. "It should be somewhere in Mindanao. I want an exact fix and constant updates on its movement."

With the wheels in motion he cranked the air conditioning up a notch and jumped into the shower to prepare for what he knew was going to be a long day.

Chapter 4

Monday 16th April 2012

"What do you know about our brothers in the Philippines?"

That had been the simple question, and Abdul Mansour had answered honestly: very little.

It had been asked at a meeting just over the Afghan border from his home in Pakistan and he had told them what he knew, which was that Abu Sayyaf had had some notable successes in the past, including the kidnapping for ransom of several foreign nationals, and of course the ferry bombing in 2004 which had killed over a hundred people. There had been other minor incidents in recent years but nothing that had made international headlines. Beyond that he knew little of their current strength or future strategy, and said as much.

"They are more concerned with internal and regional feuds than striking out against their oppressors," Azhar Al-Asiri had told him. "They need some proper leadership in order to focus their attention."

Al-Asiri had long been both Osama Bin Laden's deputy and the brains behind Al-Qaeda but had nowhere near the charisma of the man he called the Sheikh. He had been happy to let the Amir front the organisation while secretly pulling the strings from behind the scenes.

In fact, it was Al-Asiri who had suggested taking things to a global level. Bin Laden's initial fight had been against the presence of American soldiers on Saudi soil, but it was Al-Asiri who had planted the idea of aiding fellow Muslims in their grievances, wherever they may be. There had been financial support for Abu Sayyaf in the early days but that had dried up as their hierarchy had fragmented, splintering into separate groups.

"Our aim is to unify these pockets of resistance once more and turn them into a formidable ally, but we cannot do that with money and weapons alone. I would like you to go there and do for them what you have done for me here.

"You will take them the weapons they need and show them how to use them. More importantly, you must get them to launch attacks against our enemies as soon as possible."

Mansour hadn't questioned the need for an immediate strike. He'd simply accepted the mission without hesitation, honoured to have been chosen for such a task.

"You will not have long," Al-Asiri told him. "You will leave in seven days and I need you to return before the middle of May. I have a major offensive in mind and I want you to take part in the planning."

Following Bin Laden's death the previous year Al-Asiri, in his early fifties, had taken over the reins, as had been widely anticipated by the western world. However, they were quick to dismiss him as a lamb to Bin Laden's lion, a sparrow to his eagle, and it pleased him that they had written him off so readily. So far he had done what his detractors had expected, which had been nothing whatsoever.

At least, so they thought.

His focus had been on building up an army of generals, men who would go into the world and train others so that one day they could launch a co-ordinated attack that would leave the infidels trembling at the mention of his name.

One such general was Abdul Mansour, whose rise through the ranks had been meteoric. From a humble British background he had quickly proven himself an excellent soldier, carrying out numerous raids against the occupying U.S. and British forces in Afghanistan. His crowning moment, however, had been his attack on the stronghold of Tom Gray in England the previous year. The intention had been to prevent Gray revealing the location of a device set to kill thousands of people, and it had cost the lives of thirty young martyrs. The device had been found in time by the British authorities, but the audacity of the raid in such a short time had cemented his name in Al-Qaeda history. Mansour had come up with the idea himself and seventy-two hours after putting forward his proposal to the elders he was in the middle of the battle, taking several lives including that of Gray himself.

Upon his return to Pakistan he had received a hero's welcome and quickly been elevated up the ranks, going from foot soldier to tactician, from student to teacher. The recruits he trained were in awe of his achievements and he taught them that nothing was impossible if you trusted Allah with your life. Many men had passed through his hands, soaking up his courage and strength as well as his knowledge, and his exploits had come to the attention of the very highest in the organisation.

To his great regret, Mansour hadn't been able to meet Osama Bin Laden in person. A meeting had been arranged in Abbottabad but the U.S. Navy Seals struck two days before Mansour could be introduced to his master. That had been a personal blow, but he'd soon found that Azhar Al-Asiri was a more than fitting replacement, and it was Al-Asiri who had been instrumental in his successive promotions.

Mansour began overseeing the training of all new recruits and Al-Asiri was impressed with the results. He was even more impressed with Abdul's suggestion of a series of co-ordinated strikes around the world, something which fit his global ambitions, and had considered it for many weeks before convening a meeting between the highest ranks of the organisation. The idea was discussed and agreed, with generals dispatched to a variety of countries to make their preparations.

Azhar Al-Asiri had personally chosen Abdul for what he considered the toughest assignment, which was why Mansour was now sitting on the rain-soaked deck of a Banca heading for the island of Jolo, alongside his companion Nabil.

Nabil Shah was Mansour's lieutenant, an excellent soldier in his own right and good friend over the last few years. Although older than Mansour, Shah had no qualms about taking orders from his general, a man who had proven himself in battle time and time again. Indeed, he thought it a privilege to serve him.

The journey had been long and arduous, beginning with a four hundred mile drive from Quetta south to the port of Karachi. It had taken a full ten hours to reach their first destination, travelling not only on main roads but also on rough tracks which often limited the speed to a mere ten miles an hour. At the port, they had been whisked aboard a freighter and given a cramped cabin for the seventeen day trip. On nearing the port of Zamboanga Abdul, Nabil and their cargo had been transferred onto this vessel for the final leg of the journey. The boat looked like any other Banca but boasted two giant Tohatsu outboard motors which could be swung into place at a moment's notice, making it easily capable of outrunning the local navy patrols. In addition, there was a box of shoulder-launched missiles on board which would discourage, if not sink, any of the Hamilton Class cutters that might manage to get in too close.

A lesser person might have taken the easier route of either flying to their destination or travelling most of the way overland, but Mansour was not only highly regarded within his own organisation: he was also known and sought throughout the world. Crossing just one border was a huge risk, so he had no hesitation in taking such a circuitous route. He'd filled his time using his 3G tablet PC to read up on Abu Sayyaf and their exploits over the years, using both the internet and files provided by Al-Asiri.

Known to everyone else as Abu Sayyaf — meaning "bearer of the sword" — they called themselves Al-Harakat Al-Islamiyya, "Islamic Movement" and were founded in the early 1990s when they split from the Moro National Liberation Front (MNLF). Their first leader was Abdurajak Janjalani, a veteran of the fight against the Soviet occupation in Afghanistan, and their first major attack claimed the lives of two American evangelists in 1991. Shortly afterwards they claimed responsibility for the bombing of M/V Doulos, a Christian missionary ship docked in Zamboanga City Port.

Their attacks weren't limited to foreign nationals, as the Ipil raid in April 1995 proved. Desperate for funds, they had attacked the predominantly Christian town of Ipil in Zamboanga Del Sur, looting shops and banks while firing indiscriminately at civilians. Fifty-three people were killed in the attack and upwards of thirty — mostly women and children — were taken hostage as they retreated.

Another attack in 1999 had claimed the lives of six Christians when their jeep was attacked. Some of the victims were shot while others were hacked to death with bolos.

In the last decade their favoured method of attack, however, was bombings. From 2002 they had hit populated locations with the intention of causing as many casualties as possible. Targets included a karaoke bar in Zamboanga (killing three, including an American soldier), as well as a FitMart store in General Santos City where they killed fifteen.

In 2003 twenty-one people died when a waiting shed at the front of Davao airport was blown up, and on Valentine's Day 2005 they hit separate targets in General Santos City, Makati and Davao City, where they claimed eight lives.

Recent attacks had been sporadic, with only the attack on Tubigan village in Maluso, Basilan making international news. Eleven people died that day as up to seventy members of Abu Sayyaf raked houses with gunfire and set them ablaze in the pre-dawn raid.

In order to carry out these attacks, Abu Sayyaf needed weapons, and weapons cost money. In the early days they received funding through Mohammad Jamal Khalifa, a brother-in-law of Osama Bin Laden. Bin Laden had been a colleague of Janjalani during their

Afghan Mujiheddin days and had provided his personal financial support until 1995 when Khalifa's connection to Abu Sayyaf was uncovered.

Having cut their ties with MNLF and by association the Malaysian group Jemaah Islamiyah in 1991, they had foregone their access to the major Al-Qaeda funding that had been channelled into the region, so they stepped up their kidnapping campaign as a way of supporting themselves. They had taken hostages in 1993 and 1996 (the latter managing to escape after thirteen days) but kicked it up a gear at the start of the next decade following the death of Abdurajak Janjalani. Instead of retaining his ideological focus they fell into kidnapping, murder and extortion in a big way under the rule of Janjalani's younger brother, Khadaffy.

There were four separate abductions in 2000, starting with several teachers and students from two schools in Tumahubong, Basilan. Father Rhoel Gallardo and three of the teachers were found murdered in May that year, the bodies showing indications of torture. Following that was the Sipadan kidnapping in which twenty-one people were taken from a dive resort in Malaysia, with most of them being released within a few months. During that time TV evangelist Wilde Almeda and some of his Jesus Miracle Crusade "prayer warriors" turned up at the Abu Sayyaf camp in Jolo, Sulu, to pray for the hostages. Unfortunately, they themselves became captives and were held until being rescued by the military nearly four months later.

American Jeffrey Schilling became a hostage under totally different circumstances in August 2000, reportedly walking into their camp following an invitation from one of the Abu Sayyaf members who was related to his wife. Abu Sayyaf demanded a ransom of $10Million but he managed to escape and was picked up by a local military patrol in April the following year.

In 2001 one of the highest profile kidnappings took place when twenty foreign nationals were grabbed from tourist resort Dos Palmos Beach in Palawan, including three Americans: Martin and Gracia Burnham, and Guillermo Sobero. A fortnight later a request was made for a Malaysian intermediary to negotiate a ransom payment but instead they came under attack from AFP soldiers. After managing to evade the soldiers, Sobero was taken into the jungle and beheaded, a move designed to show that Abu Sayyaf were taking the situation seriously, even if the Philippine government were not.

It was over a year later that Martin Burnham and Ebidorah Yap, a Filipino nurse, were killed when the AFP launched yet another attack. Martin's wife Gracia was wounded in the leg but survived, and a subsequent investigation showed that it was AFP bullets which had been to blame for all three casualties.

Following the botched rescue the U.S. Army sent six hundred military advisors as part of Operation Freedom Eagle (later to come under the Enduring Freedom umbrella). In addition the CIA sent elite paramilitary officers of the Special Activities Division (SAD). As a result, kidnappings fell to an all time low, but not before they abducted six Jehovah's Witnesses and their Muslim guides in 2002. Two of the preachers were beheaded and some of the captives managed to escape before the rest were rescued by government troops in May 2003.

Khadaffy Janjalani himself was killed in action in 2006 and in 2007 Jainal Antel Sali Jr., known to all as Abu Sulaiman and Khadaffy's likely successor, was killed by the AFP.

Mansour had soaked all of this information up during his journey, and his conclusion was that the kidnappings had probably tailed off because of the relentless pressure being applied by the U.S. and Philippine forces, as well as a lack of continuous leadership.

No matter, he thought, as he saw the island of Jolo appear on the distant horizon. Their days of limited funds would soon be over thanks in no small part to the cash he was bringing, as well as the promise of continued financial support for years to come.

The man he was due to meet was called Abu Assaf, the current head of the Abu Sayyaf organisation. Mansour had very little information about the man, except that he was in his forties and had stepped into the vacant position after the previous leader was shot by a raiding party led by a U.S. SAD team four months earlier. He was glad that he was going into the initial meeting with no preconceptions: he preferred to form his own opinions based on what he experienced, not what he had heard from others.

"It has been a long journey," Nabil said, gazing out towards the horizon.

"Our journey is just beginning," Mansour replied. "Once we arrive it is imperative that we get them to strike as soon as possible. I will remain here while we plan the attack, but after that I will be moving on. I would like you to stay here and show them how to organise themselves against the infidels."

Shah nodded, showing no emotion, though deep down he was proud to be offered the opportunity to prove himself again.

It was over an hour before they neared the shore: unsurprisingly, it wasn't a commercial port they drew up to but simply a deserted beach. A group of men was waiting and as soon as the anchor went out they waded into the water and began unloading the boxes he had brought. One man was supervising the transfer and Mansour made a beeline for him.

"*Salam alaikum!*" the man said, and Mansour returned the greeting.

"I am Jun," he said. "We go soon."

It was obvious to Mansour that he wasn't much of a conversationalist, and equally apparent that there were not enough men to carry all of the baggage he had brought. Jun saw this too, and ordered half of the consignment to be camouflaged and appointed two armed guards to watch over it. The rest of the boxes were picked up and Jun led the way into the jungle, with Mansour and Shah following in his footsteps.

The march to the camp was slow going, mainly due to the weight of the boxes but also because they were avoiding known tracks, instead relying on Jun to cut a way through the dense vegetation with his bolo. This turned out to be the most intense part of his journey, knowing that somewhere on this small island there were close to two hundred U.S. and Filipino troops who would just love to get their hands on him, and here they were crawling along at a snail's pace.

They stopped twice on their way to the camp, the second time for over an hour as a patrol ventured close. They crouched in silence as the soldiers made camp just thirty yards away and started cooking up their lunch. Mansour could see a few of the Abu Sayyaf were itching to take them on but Jun threw them looks which warned them to just stay quiet. Eventually the patrol moved on and they were able to make the last mile and a half without further encounters.

It was hardly recognisable as a camp. The only distinguishing feature was the number of people gathered in the small clearing, with no permanent structures to suggest they would remain here for any length of time.

Abu Assaf came to greet them effusively, arms spread wide and a toothless smile on his face, then ushered them over to a log next to a small fire. Three large fish were cooking over the flames and a pot of rice bubbled away on a small gas stove. Mansour suddenly realised that he hadn't eaten in over twenty hours and graciously accepted the invitation to dine.

"I understand you have gifts for us," Assaf said in excellent English, the accent British.

Mansour nodded and led him over to the boxes arranged at the centre of the clearing. The first one he opened was the size of a family suitcase and contained nothing but cash, over two million American dollars in twenties and fifties, and Mansour was glad to note that Assaf's reaction was muted appreciation. There were no signs of greed on the man's face, just a look that said "this could come in handy."

The next box to be opened revealed dozens of brand new M16 rifles still wrapped in protective wax paper. "Rather than AK-47s, we decided to provide weapons your enemies use because this way you can make use of any captured ammunition," Mansour said.

He gestured to a couple of boxes and explained that they were full of 5.56mm rounds for the rifles, then opened the next container.

"Claymore mines," he said, lifting one out to show it to Assaf. "These will help with setting up defensive perimeters and discouraging your enemies from following you," he explained when he saw the look of confusion.

He smiled as he pointed to the next three boxes. "These will be the difference between a struggle with the AFP and driving them out of the land," he said. Releasing the catches on one of the lids, he swung it open to reveal a Dillon Aero M134 Mini-gun. The six-barrelled weapon fired 7.62mm bullets at an astonishing fifty rounds-per-second, fed from a 4400-round magazine.

"In the other boxes I have grenades, C4 explosive, ammunition for the M134 and twenty single-shot RPG-27s. Bear in mind, this is just a down payment on the support we are willing to offer you."

"What are you asking in return?" Assaf asked, clearly satisfied with the gifts.

Mansour placed an arm around his shoulder and led him away to a quiet spot at the edge of the clearing. "We want only what you want: to drive the infidels from the land. To do that you must become a force to be reckoned with, and I will show you how. The days of cowering in the jungle will soon be over for Abu Sayyaf."

"We do not cower," Assaf said harshly, aggrieved at the suggestion.

"Perhaps not, but while the AFP and the Americans wander calmly through your towns, you are sleeping up here in the hills. That is the first thing we need to change."

"How do we do that? There are barely a hundred of us."

"Don't you have any men on the surrounding islands that you can call on?" Mansour asked.

"There are perhaps another hundred spread throughout the Sulu Sea, but they have hostages and are trying to negotiate their release."

"Bring them all here," Mansour said. "You have no more need to risk the lives of your men for mere money: we can provide all you need."

Assaf nodded, making a mental note to pass on the order while Mansour continued with the questions.

"When was the last time you launched an attack on the infidels?"

"Attack? We can barely defend ourselves, never mind launch an attack. Besides, there are American soldiers here — elite American soldiers."

"Who have a strictly non-combatant role, as I understand," Mansour smiled. "Tell me everything you know about their base."

"I know much about their base," Assaf said, "but attacking it would only cause them to double their efforts against us. It would be counterproductive."

"Far from it, my friend. An attack on their base may indeed make them bring the fight to you, but it would also show Jemaah Islamiyah that Abu Sayyaf are no longer the poor relation they think you are. Your Indonesian brothers will sit up and take notice of you once again, and by reuniting with them the Muslim movement within the region will become stronger than you could ever imagine."

"They will not join with us. They refuse to even talk to us, so how will this one attack change their mind?"

"It is quite simple," Mansour said. "I will act as your emissary to explain that they can join us and share the glory — as well as the support we will provide — or they can fend for themselves and we will no longer provide them with training, weapons or funds."

"They are proud people," Assaf argued. "They will not submit to threats and intimidation."

"As are we all, brother, but any man who puts his own pride before the will of Allah is not worthy of calling himself a true believer. I will give them one chance, and one chance only. Naturally, I shall be very diplomatic in my approach."

Mansour could see that Assaf was still not convinced, but he was confident in his own ability to bring the two groups together.

"Let me worry about Jemaah Islamiyah, brother. All you need to do is help me plan the attack on their camp."

Chapter 5

Monday 16th April 2012

Sam Grant found the going hard enough without having to keep step with Halton, whose bare feet were constantly slipping on the wet jungle floor. A rain shower had hit an hour earlier and the remnants were still falling from the dense canopy above, even though the clouds had long since gone. While it cooled him down and provided some much needed drinking water, it also turned the floor to gloop which his trainers were struggling to cope with, despite the decent tread on the sole. The camber of the route they were taking didn't help, either, and the undulating terrain meant they were either climbing or descending, rarely walking on level ground.

Things got much worse when they came to a river and Bong signalled for everyone to break for food. Most made their way to the bank and took in as much water as they could, while Vick and Moore waded into the water to give themselves a quick wash. They did so without removing any garments, and Grant guessed this was due to shyness on their part. Once they'd finished they sat down next to Grant and Halton.

"It's really hard washing yourself with all your clothes on," she said. "I nearly got a beating the first time I stripped down to my bra and panties. I haven't taken these off since," she said, fingering the ragged material of the khaki blouse. "Apparently it makes the Muslim men uncomfortable or something."

"What's your story, Sam Grant?" asked Moore.

Before he could answer, Ox came and stood in front of him and rattled off some Tagalog that Grant barely understood, although he did catch the word "Sapatos" — shoes. Feigning ignorance, Grant simply shrugged but it wasn't enough to deter Ox, who grabbed one of his feet and hoisted it into the air.

"Akin 'to," Ox said. *These are mine.*

Rather than get into a confrontation Grant slipped off his sneakers and handed them over. Ox snatched them and walked off to try them on, leaving Grant with not so much as a 'Salamat'.

"You'll get used to that," Halton said. "What's yours is theirs, period. You'll be lucky to hold on to that T-shirt for much longer."

Sure enough, Ox was back moments later. He whipped off his grimy sando and threw it at Grant, holding out his hand for the Lacoste T-shirt in exchange. Again, Grant handed it over without complaint and Ox trotted away to show off his new attire. Grant considered ditching the stinking rag but knew he would be grateful for it when the mosquitoes got into full attack mode. He did, however, start to imagine the things he would do to Ox should the chance present itself.

"So?" Vick asked.

"So what?" Grant replied, confused.

"What's your story?"

"Oh yeah, sorry. My mind was elsewhere." He told them about the death of Alma's brother and his abduction from the hotel, and when asked for his reason for being in Manila he gave them the same story he'd told his girlfriend when they had met. Throughout the monologue he was acutely aware of Vick staring at him, a look of fierce concentration on her face. When he finished he stared back at her and she blushed when she realised what she had been doing.

"I'm sorry, but you just look so familiar," she explained.

"There's an exhibit in the British Museum called Neanderthal Man. Maybe you saw me there."

She shrugged off his weak joke and the look of concentration returned, and Grant was thankful when their dinner was served: a pile of rice on a large leaf. Everyone tucked in, grabbing handfuls of the bland food and shoving it in their mouths as fast as they could manage. It was a free-for-all, with plenty of shoving and pushing, and the leaf was picked clean within a couple of minutes. Grant had managed to get one decent handful and could have easily outmuscled the others to get more, but their condition was much worse than his and he figured they needed the nutrition more. If he was going to be here any length of time he would have taken all he could, but he was determined not to be in it for the long haul: Either Farrar would come up with the money, or he'd fight his way out.

Halton suddenly reached down to his ankle and began undoing the twine.

"What are you doing?" Grant asked, worried that his companion was about to do something stupid.

Halton shouted "Ebbs ako," and the nearest guard looked at him and nodded his head.

"I'm going to park my breakfast," he told Grant, and wandered away from the group grabbing a couple of large leaves on the way.

"They just let you wander off on your own?" Grant asked, clearly surprised. "Aren't they worried that you'll run off?"

"You have to stay in view," Vick explained. "If you disappear into the jungle they'll come after you with their bolos. You don't want that to happen, trust me."

Grant assured her he would do no such thing. "You've heard my story. What about you?" he asked.

"I'm a travel writer," she said. "I was doing a story about Apulit Island in Palawan and was enjoying an evening on Rob's boat. He has a charter company on the island and a few of us were on the sunset cruise when they struck."

"How many others were there?" Grant asked.

"There were seven of us in all: Rob and I plus five Filipinos. They transferred us onto their boat and brought us here."

"Are the others here?"

He could see the pain in her eyes when he asked the question, and suddenly wished he hadn't.

"There were two couples and one of them had a daughter, Carmen. She was only three..." Her voice tailed off as the tears came, and Grant guessed this wasn't the first time she had cried since being here.

"They threw Carmen overboard on the second day," Moore explained, putting an arm around Vick's shoulder and cradling her head against his chest. "She had been crying, probably because she was so hungry, and when her mother couldn't settle her down one of them just grabbed her and tossed her over the side like she was a bag of rubbish."

"Christ!" Grant said, astonished that anyone could be so deliberately brutal towards a child.

"The mother dived straight in after her," Moore continued. "Before they could stop him, the father jumped, too. We were about halfway through our journey at the time, which meant they were about a hundred and fifty miles from land."

He didn't need to elaborate for Grant to understand what he was trying to say: there was no way they could have survived.

"The other two made it here with us, but after ten days the husband was taken for a walk and never came back. When the wife couldn't arrange her ransom she was taken for a walk, too."

"What about Eddie?" Grant asked, nodding in the direction of the squatting figure ten yards away.

"He's just a tourist, and a pain-in-the-arse one at that," Moore said. "We all know the future doesn't look rosy but he bitches about it all day long. You'll learn to tune him out after a few weeks."

"I hope it isn't going to take that long," Grant said. "Do they honour the ransoms that are paid?"

"Yes, so far. There was a German guy here last month and he managed to arrange his ransom within a few days. He even sent a food package for us a week later, but all we got from it was a note. Bong had the rest."

"Bong's English is good," Grant noted.

"He was educated at De La Salle, the best university in Manila." Vick said, having regained her composure. "Comes from a well-off family who kicked him out of the house when they heard he was hanging out with Muslim friends, and he came down here to teach them a lesson. His friends introduced him to Jonjon and he signed up there and then."

"Did he tell you this?"

"God no, it was Dindo," she said, lowering her voice and gesturing towards one of the younger captors. "He drops by every night and slips me some food when the others are asleep. I think he has a crush on me."

Grant wasn't surprised, given her looks. "Bong doesn't seem very friendly. Are they all like that?"

"To be honest, most of them treat us as well as can be expected. Bong is the exception, though. I think there's a little power struggle going on there."

"How so?"

"He's told us on more than one occasion that we are being treated too well, and that when he takes command things will become a lot tougher for us. I think the conflict stems from their goals: While Bong is fighting for an independent Muslim state, Dindo thinks Jonjon and Abel are in it for the money, pure and simple."

Grant glanced upstream where the senior Abu Sayyaf members were gathered and the power struggle became a little more even as a plume of red erupted from Jonjon's chest, spraying blood all over Guzman's head and neck. The report from the bullet followed a millisecond later.

"Sundalos!"

243

As the shout went up, their captors grabbed their weapons and began returning fire, spraying bullets into the undergrowth in the general direction of the initial round on the far bank of the river. As bullets began peppering the area, Vick and the rest of the hostages tried to make themselves as small as possible but Grant knew it was just a matter of time before one of them was hit. He sought a defilade position and saw one a few yards away, a slight depression behind the rotting trunk of a fallen tree. He grabbed Vick and began pulling her towards it, then remembered that she was still attached to Moore.

"Move!" he shouted at them, but Moore had frozen, his body shutting down in response to the assault. Grant leaned over Vick and grabbed him by the ear, twisting it as hard as possible. Moore had no option but to follow, and Grant pulled them to the safety of cover.

The fire intensified on both sides, and Grant realised that Bong's warning about the AFP was true: they were more likely to kill the hostages than rescue them. Fire from both sides was indiscriminate, and Grant wondered how many of the AFP had their eyes opened during the attack. Bullets strafed the log and a cry went out as one of the Filipino hostages took a round to the calf, a round that would have done serious damage to Vick or Moore if he hadn't dragged them to safety.

Grant gauged the incoming fire and estimated that there were five or six attackers as best, suggesting a small recon patrol: an extremely stupid recon patrol, given the circumstances. In their position he would have laid up and called in reinforcements rather than try to take on a much larger force, especially one holding hostages.

One of the guards went down with a wound to the throat but he was ignored by his compatriots as they continued to repel the attackers. A couple of grenades were lobbed across the narrow river, one landing harmlessly short but the other bouncing its way into the vegetation, taking out two AFP soldiers.

Grant nearly jumped with fright when a body landed next to him and he turned to see Halton cowering by his side, trousers still around his ankles.

"Unbe-fucking-lievable! Whose side are they on, for Christ's sake?"

Grant ignored him, instead concentrating on one of the Abu Sayyaf who had picked up the loaded RPG. His stance was all wrong, and as he fired he lost his balance, falling flat on his backside. Luckily for all concerned — except the AFP — the explosive head went where he had aimed.

Crump.

A tree took the brunt of the impact, cracking the trunk in two, but the AFP got the message and their attack petered out as they retreated back through the jungle, firing sporadically as they ran.

With the battle having lasted barely more than a couple of minutes a sense of calm returned to the jungle, but the Abu Sayyaf members were still pumped up, keeping a close watch on the far bank. The silence didn't last long, however, as the Filipino woman who'd been hit in the leg began to make the transition from shock to pain. Her cries were ignored by the guards, who were more intent on dealing with their own fallen, two of whom were clearly dead. The other casualty was one of the younger Abu Sayyaf who had sustained a flesh wound to the arm, and he showed it off proudly, pleased with his new battle scar.

Bong began barking orders and the two bodies were wrapped in hammocks, ready to be carried away. Others were instructed to see to the hostages and they began by ensuring everyone was tethered to at least one other person. When they got to the injured woman they seemed at a loss as to what to do. Her screams were intensifying all the time and any attempts to treat the wound simply increased her hysteria.

After a couple of minutes Bong purposefully strode over to them and surveyed the situation. It was clear to everyone that the woman was not going to be able to walk on the injured leg, and the noise she was making would only serve to alert the AFP as to their whereabouts. He rattled off more orders in Tagalog and the tether was removed from the woman's other ankle.

Grant watched the proceedings but had no idea what was being said, the words spitting out like automatic weapon fire. Bong gestured with his arm and the hostage who had been cradling the casualty was suddenly dragged away, and his own screams began to drown out those of the woman Grant assumed to be his wife or girlfriend. He was kicking and screaming as they pulled him clear, and Grant suddenly knew what was coming. He grabbed Vick and cradled her head into his chest just as Bong lowered his rifle and ended the woman's pain with a single shot to the head. Her partner collapsed in tears, howling with grief, and Bong was clearly not in the mood to put up with it. He pointed the rifle at the man and barked out more instructions, but the heartbroken hostage either wasn't listening or didn't care. His cries continued for a moment as he stared at his loved one, then stopped as rage moved to the top of the emotional table. His face contorted and he clambered to his feet, anger etched on his face. Bong shouted at him to back off and raised his rifle to reinforce the threat, but the man kept coming, fists clenching as he approached. Another warning, but the advance continued, the man cursing venomously as he moved nearer.

"Bahala Ka!" *Suit yourself.*

The rifle spat one more time and the man collapsed in mid-stride. Abel Guzman came over and began remonstrating with Bong, who stood his ground and argued back, vehemently defending his actions. Everyone stopped what they were doing to watch the confrontation, which escalated when Guzman pushed Bong in the chest and he stumbled backwards, losing his footing on a tree root and splashing into the river. Apoplectic, he jumped up and ran for Abel, grabbing him round the throat and pinning him to a tree. Guzman tried to prise him off but Bong had too firm a grip, so he fumbled for a weapon as his face began to turn scarlet. He reached towards his bolo but Bong swung a knee up, deflecting his hand away from the handle of the knife. With his last remaining strength he tried to claw at Bong's face but his reach was half an inch short and his life ebbed away moments later.

Bong let him drop and spat on the corpse before cursing in deep, deep Tagalog. He turned and looked at his men, daring any to challenge him for the leadership, but none seemed in the mood, even though they were brandishing weapons.

Their tacit approval accepted, he gave orders to pack up while he himself took the cell phones from the fallen leaders and claimed their tent as his own.

Grant was once again tied to Halton, and was thankful that his companion had managed to dress himself once more, though his sarcasm hadn't deserted him. "Just another day in paradise."

"And it's about to get a lot worse with Bong in charge," Moore said. He turned to Grant. "Thanks. If you hadn't moved me, I'd hate to think what would have happened."

"Don't mention it. Just make sure you take cover next time the bullets start flying."

"That wasn't your first time in a gunfight, was it?" Vick asked.

"What do you mean?" Grant replied, but he was already aware of what she was implying. When the firefight had started, all of the hostages – and a couple of their captors – had frozen, dropping where they were. He had been the only one to seek protection. His army training had kicked in once more and while it may have saved his life again it was beginning to get noticed. If Vick and Robert could spot it, it wouldn't be long before one of the guards did, and that would make him dangerous in their eyes.

"I mean you knew how to react when they started shooting at us."

"Self-preservation, I guess," Grant shrugged, trying to play down the incident, but Vick wasn't ready to accept such a weak response.

"If it was self-preservation, why didn't you just look after yourself? Why did you drag Rob and I behind the tree?"

"I suppose I wasn't really thinking straight," he said, knowing it wasn't far from the truth. Thankfully her questions stopped when they were ordered to get up and prepare to move out.

Lined up in pairs, they were given the bodies of the dead to carry and the formation moved off once more. Grant had the feet end of the hammock over his right shoulder and Eddie Moore, walking in front of him alongside Vick, carried the head end. For a man who had been used to carrying sixty-pound packs into battle it was still a bit of a struggle for Grant, especially in his stocking feet, but Moore was in shit state already without having this additional burden literally thrown on his shoulder.

Twenty minutes into the march, Moore had already stopped twice for a short rest and to change his grip, and Bong wasn't best pleased at the pace being set. He told one of his subordinates to take over on point and came back down the line to see what was causing the hold up.

"Pick it up!" he shouted at Moore, who had dropped his end of the hammock so that he could massage his shoulder.

Grant laid his end on the floor and told Bong to let him have a rest. "Can't you see he's in no condition to carry this kind of weight?"

Bong advanced towards him menacingly, despite the height disadvantage. Grant, having learned a lesson less than half an hour earlier, adopted a submissive posture rather than standing up to the man. It didn't prevent him getting a whack on the back with the flat edge of a bolo, but it helped to keep up the pretence.

Bong was readying himself to deliver another blow when one of the phones in his pocket chirped.

He dug it out and stabbed the Connect button.

"Ano?" *What?*

He spoke for a couple of minutes, then ended the call with a simple "Sige." *Okay.*

"We are taking a boat ride," he announced to the prisoners, and after a brief scan round to get his bearings he resumed point duty, leading them downhill towards sea level.

"Do they often move you from island to island?" Grant asked Moore as they once again picked up their load.

"No, we've always been here."

Grant considered the implications. The AFP were on this island, which meant that if he could get away from the Abu Sayyaf he would have someone he could turn to. The next island, wherever it may be, might not contain any friendly forces at all, which meant escape would need to entail slipping away from his captors *and* stealing a boat *and* crossing an ocean. If he was going to end this any time soon, he would have to do it before they were loaded onto the boat.

Through a gap in the trees he saw the Sulu Sea in the distance and estimated that it would be a couple of days at their current pace before they reached the coast. Not much time, but it was all the time he had to come up with a plan.

* * *

James Farrar toyed with the phone as he considered the best way to word his message to Grant. When he called the cell phone he was certain it would be answered by one of the Abu Sayyaf, so he would demand to speak to Grant to make sure he was still alive and well. Two things that bothered him were that the message would have to be concise, and that their conversation might be on speakerphone.

The message he wanted to get across was that no money was going to be paid and that Baines and Smart were on their way to get him out, but how to say that in a way that only Grant would understand? He got up and made himself a cup of coffee, all the time trying to formulate a couple of short sentences that would carry the message.

It was almost an hour later that he picked up the phone and dialled Grant's number.

"It's James Farrar," he said as soon as the connection was made. "I want to speak to Sam."

"Do you have the money?" Bong asked.

"We're putting it together but it will take a few days. In the meantime I want to speak to Sam. I want to be sure he's still alive."

A moment later he heard Grant's voice. "James, have you —"

Bong snatched the phone away. "You have heard his voice. Call me in three days to arrange the transfer."

"I want to speak to him, let him know that everything is okay."

There was silence for a moment. "You give me the message, I will pass it on," Bong said.

Farrar had expected as much. "Can't you just put me on speakerphone? He must be terrified and will want to hear a friendly voice."

He heard mumbling as Bong tried to find the setting on the unfamiliar phone, but eventually he was instructed to relay his message.

"Sam, it's James. I hope you're bearing up under the pressure. I have asked a specialist company to handle the transfer. They are called Baines and Smart and they deal with hostage situations all the time, so I thought it best to let them do things their way. It might be a little expensive but I'm sure you understand."

"Yes, James, I understand."

Bong took the phone off speaker. "You have passed on your message," he said. "Call me in three days with the arrangements."

"Wait, I have instructions from Baines and Smart. They want me to call every eight hours to ensure he is still alive."

"No," was the simple reply.

"Then they won't make the transfer," Farrar said. "I'm not about to send more people in there so you can take them hostage, too. Either you let Baines and Smart handle it and follow their instructions, or the deal is off and you get nothing."

Farrar held the phone to his ear, praying the bluff wasn't called, and the interminable silence was eventually broken. "I will call you once a day at three o'clock in the afternoon."

The phone went dead in his hands and Farrar realised he'd been holding his breath waiting for the response. Exhaling loudly, he went to the kitchen, uncorked a bottle of red wine and grabbed a glass, then settled on the sofa.

So, Grant's phone would be active every day at three in the afternoon, which should give Baines and Smart the opportunity to pinpoint his location, and hopefully Grant got the message that help was on its way: the last thing he wanted was the sonofabitch ruining

249

his plan by escaping before the others arrived. There was always the chance that the man holding the phone might split off from the others but there was nothing he could do about that, and he wasn't one for worrying about things beyond his control.

After polishing off half of the wine he headed for bed, making a mental note of the equipment he would need to source in the morning. They would need weapons, a device to track him with, and some form of communications, both for the mission and to report in to him. Happy in the knowledge that he could have everything he needed delivered to the office he set the alarm for five and climbed into bed.

* * *

Grant pondered the message Farrar had sent him and kept coming back to the same conclusion: Sonny and Len were going to attempt a rescue mission.

While it was good news in one respect, he would have much preferred Farrar to stump up the cash. His friends were more than capable of pulling it off, especially if he was able to assist them somehow, but there was always the chance of a hostage or two getting hit in the melee. Paying the ransom was by far the best option, and the money could always be replaced, probably within a year the way the company was performing.

He pushed the thought aside. Focus, he told himself. Sonny and Len were probably already on their way, which meant they would be arriving in the Philippines in the next twenty-four hours. Adding time for a briefing and the trip down to Basilan, he reckoned they could be on the island by Wednesday morning. Unfortunately he and the others would reach the shoreline at roughly the same time, which meant his friends would end up scouring the wrong island for him.

He gave himself two priorities, the first of which was to slow their progress somehow. The second was to get his hands on a weapon.

Chapter 6

Tuesday 17th April 2012

Simon "Sonny" Baines was shaken awake as turbulence tossed the Boeing 777-200 violently around the skies. Next to him, Len Smart was reading a detective mystery on his Kindle, oblivious to the chaos around him. It wasn't until an overhead locker broke open and disgorged its contents into the aisle that he tore himself away from the gripping story.

His watch told him that they were still six hours from Manila, having left Amsterdam's Schiphol airport an eternity earlier. The flight from Heathrow had been a short hop and after a three-hour stopover they had climbed aboard. An hour into the flight they'd had breakfast, which Sonny topped off with a scotch before falling into a deep sleep. Smart envied him the ability to sleep on planes, something he had never been able to master. A freezing hillside in the middle of winter was no problem, but not an airplane seat. It didn't matter if it was a civilian airliner or a military transport, he just couldn't nod off, no matter how tired he was.

"Do you think Tom will be joining us on the pickup?" he asked Sonny.

"He's got a new name now," his friend reminded him in a low voice.

"Yeah, right. It's hard to get used to the idea after knowing him as Tom for ten years. I wonder what name he's chosen."

"I guess we'll find out soon enough. What are you reading?"

"*Black Beast* by R. S. Guthrie."

"Any good?"

"Brilliant," Smart said, and promptly turned his attention back to the Kindle. Sonny shoved a pair of headphones over his ears and scanned the channels on the in-flight entertainment console, settling for an episode of Mr. Bean, but as the plane cruised over central Asia he quickly lost all interest in the show. Instead he recalled the last time he had seen Tom. It had been in the ruins of the old pottery factory that had been transformed from fortress to rubble in an instant during the attack by Abdul Mansour and his men. Tom's plan to reform the justice system had been audacious, and had almost succeeded. It also nearly cost him his life.

It would be good to see his old friend again, Sonny thought, and closed his eyes to sleep away the rest of the flight.

It seemed just moments later when Len woke him. "We'll be landing in fifteen minutes," Smart said, stowing his Kindle in his rucksack. Sonny paid a quick visit to the toilet and then stopped by the galley to chat up the stewardesses. Despite being in his mid-thirties he looked ten years younger, and hadn't seemed to age a day since joining the SAS as one of their youngest recruits. The name Sonny soon stuck, and he used his boyish good looks at every available opportunity, with varying degrees of success. On this occasion he struck out and resumed his seat, staring out of the window as they approached Ninoy Aquino International Airport. After touching down they made their way through immigration and picked up their luggage, a suitcase each packed with items most of which they were never likely to use. It was just easier to throw some jeans and T-shirts into a case than explain why they were arriving for a holiday without a change of clothes.

As promised they were met at the exit. A Filipino in a white shirt and black trousers held up a card with their names as they fought through the crowd of taxi drivers looking for a chance to charge unsuspecting foreigners ten times the normal fare. Len and Sonny introduced themselves and were led out into the sunshine, and the first thing that hit them was the smell, an odour which seemed to be a combination of sewage and rotting food. As they walked to the pickup area the heat added to their woes, and they were thankful when they climbed into the air-conditioned SUV.

It took close to an hour to get the three miles to their destination, near the British Embassy in Makati. Manila has some of the most congested roads in the world, despite government efforts to keep the traffic flowing. Vehicle number plates end with a number, and each day two of those numbers were banned from the road. Despite this measure, journeys were most often made at a steady crawl at best. Along the way they had to contend with a variety of ancient trucks, buses and cars, and now and again they would spot a brand new vehicle that seemed very out of place. At each set of traffic lights their transport was assaulted by vendors or beggars, often seven-year-old girls carrying a baby and dressed in rags, holding out a hand in the hope of a dollar or two.

The SUV pulled into an underground car park below a thirty-storey office block. The driver opened the door for them, then led them to an elevator which took them to the seventeenth floor. The door at the end of the corridor proclaimed the office to belong to Knight Logistics Management, and they were shown into the reception where a lady in her fifties asked them to take a seat. A few moments later a connecting door opened and Farrar ushered them into his office, pointing towards a sofa as he sat on the corner of his desk. They dumped their luggage and took a seat.

"Gentlemen, thank you for coming at such short notice," he said. The pleasantries out of the way, he laid out the details of the mission. "Sam Grant has been kidnapped by Abu Sayyaf, a Muslim terrorist group operating in the southern Philippine islands. I want you to get him out."

"Who's Sam Grant?" Smart asked.

"Ah, sorry, I forgot you didn't know. Sam Grant is the name Tom Gray goes by these days." He paused to let the news sink in, pleased to see that it had come as something of a shock. If they'd recognised the name it would surely mean they'd been in contact with him, something he'd strictly forbidden.

I guess that answers the question: 'Is Tom coming with us?' Len thought. "How did he get kidnapped?" he asked.

"I don't know all the details," Farrar admitted, "but whatever happened, I'm beginning to wonder if he's up to the job he's been chosen for."

"Tom still has what it takes," Sonny said quickly. "If he was kidnapped it was because he knew that trying to fight his way out was a waste of time, but he'll be working on an escape, I guarantee it."

"Does he know we're coming?" Len asked, changing the subject in an attempt to diffuse the tension creeping into the room.

Farrar shared the message he'd relayed the previous evening, and they agreed that in all likeliness, Tom knew a rescue was going to be attempted.

"You said you'd have some equipment for us," Len said, and Farrar walked over to a closet and retrieved a long sports holdall. Inside they found two Heckler & Koch MP5SD suppressed sub-machine gun, a pair of Beretta M9 pistols and two American M4 Carbine rifles with under slung M203 grenade launchers. In addition there were ammunition, night vision goggles, a smart phone and a communication set comprising throat microphone and earpiece.

"These comm units use 2048 bit encryption and flash-burst the messages, so they're very hard to intercept or decrypt." Flash-bursting meant compressing the whole message into a tiny blob of data and sending it when the user finished talking, so rather than anyone being able to hear their real-time conversation, any eavesdroppers would simply hear a millisecond burst of static.

"The phone will give your current location as well as the location of Sam's phone." He opened an application on the phone and they saw a map of the Philippines, with a green dot flashing over their current location in Manila and a red cross on one of the southern islands. The map lacked topography, showing just the land masses as brown to the sea's blue. A scale on the right hand side of the screen showed the distance between the two locations..

"How up to date is Tom's location?" Len asked.

"Sam's location," Farrar said, emphasising the new name, "will be real-time just as long as his phone is turned on. Abu Sayyaf have agreed to call me at three in the afternoon each day, so we know it will be updated at least once every twenty-four hours."

He used his thumb and forefinger to expand the image with the red cross and hit a symbol at the top of the screen, which showed a dot-to-dot red trail. "These are Sam's movements since they first made contact with me. It looks like they traversed the high ground and are heading towards the coast."

"Do we know the enemy strength? Numbers, weapons, anything at all?"

"Nothing whatsoever. You'll be going in blind with just a cross on a map as your guide. Is there a problem with that?"

Smart and Baines looked at each other and had the same thought: this was a clusterfuck waiting to happen.

"What is it with people's perception of the SAS?" Sonny asked. "Why does everyone think we're invincible super heroes? We only get the job done because we do our homework and know what we're facing, not by jumping in with our eyes closed and nothing but a mean expression and a huge set of balls."

There was no animosity in his voice. A touch of sarcasm, perhaps, but no animosity. Farrar, however, chose to take it completely the wrong way.

"I'm beginning to wonder if anyone from your beloved regiment is capable of conducting a real mission these days," he said, eyes directed towards Sonny. "In case you didn't know, I called you as soon as I found out that he'd been kidnapped. That was only twenty-eight hours ago, and considering we don't have any assets down there, and given the fact that I haven't been able to have a private conversation with him to get any first hand intel, it is impossible to know anything about what you will be facing. But then, you'd know that if you were smart."

"He's Smart," Sonny said, pointing to Len, "I'm pragmatic, and this has nothing to do with being capable of conducting a real mission, this is about the seven Ps: Proper Prior Planning Prevents Piss Poor Performance."

Len put a hand on his friend's arm to calm him down. "We've been in worse situations," he said to Sonny, then turned to Farrar. "We'll do it, but the price just went up. Thirty thousand on completion. Each."

"Twenty," Farrar countered.

"Twenty five."

"Done. There's a plane waiting to fly you to Zamboanga but you'll have to make your own way from there. My driver will take you back to the airport and show you through the diplomatic channel so you'll avoid having to check in the bag. My secretary will provide you with the necessary passes."

He stood and ushered them out of his office, handing Sonny the bag after they'd collected their own luggage, and as promised there were two name badges waiting for them on the secretary's desk, each complete with a recent photo.

"My number is programmed into that phone, which uses satellite rather than 3G, so you should have a signal wherever you are," Farrar said. "I'll keep you updated if there are any developments."

The driver was waiting in the hallway to take them back to the car park.

"I would have done it for the original five grand," Sonny said to Len as they walked towards the elevator.

"For Tom, I would have done it for nothing," Len replied.

* * *

When he was alone in his office Farrar checked his watch and calculated the time it would take them to arrive on Basilan and make

255

their way into the jungle. The ideal scenario was for them to be within sight of Grant before he gave their location away, but unless they fed him regular updates he doubted he would get to know when they were close enough. He decided to wait until Bong called him tomorrow for his three o'clock conversation with Grant and break the news then. He would then have the location and could guide them in to what would surely be an ambush.

It wasn't as if they were likely to manage a rescue in the meantime, not with the ammunition he'd supplied. Any soldier with as much time on the range as the SAS had would be able to tell if all of the explosive propellant had been removed from a bullet, so the powder in the rounds he'd given them had been replaced with plain old sand. Figuring that they would have no reason to fire their weapons until they got into a battle with Abu Sayyaf, he had no concerns about them discovering his little subterfuge until it was too late. The only thing that could scupper his plans was if they found Grant as soon as they landed on the island, but if the AFP and U.S. special forces had trouble locating anyone from Abu Sayyaf, he was damn sure a couple of ex-soldiers — no matter how good they once were — would find it a struggle to locate them.

With Baines, Smart and Grant out of the way he could then turn his attention to the two remaining conspirators, Carl Levine and Jeff Campbell. They would demand some kind of explanation as to why their friends had disappeared, which was the reason he'd videotaped the conversation they'd just had. That would keep them quiet for a while, giving him the chance to put together a plan to eliminate them and close down the operation. After that he would finally be free to return home to England and be rid of this terrible climate once and for all.

He knew he would have to be quick, though, as having five friends die within a year would be seen as too much of a coincidence, especially when these five knew something that could cause serious embarrassment to the government. The deaths of Barker-Fink and Bennett would arouse little suspicion on their own, but when Baines and Smart disappeared along with Grant he was sure Campbell and Levine would begin asking questions. This made their demise all the more critical, so he went to his computer, entered his password to open the secure file and began reading up on the preparations for their deaths.

He knew that Campbell had booked a holiday in Florida for himself, his wife and his three children and would be leaving in nine days, so he was the priority target. The surveillance operation had noted a few of his most common habits, including the darts night at his local pub, the Wheatsheaf, every Wednesday evening. He also went jogging at seven o'clock every morning, and these two opportunities were the ones the team were currently working on. The last updates to his file were his U.K. team's three suggestions for the take-down. Dismissing the first two — a hit-and-run accident and a common pub fight — as too obvious and risky, he pondered the third option. They wanted to fake a burglary and kill him in the process. A man of his nature would surely try to defend his family, the team suggested, and they could kill him when he tried.

Farrar wasn't so sure. If Campbell didn't resist and just let them take his possessions, the team would have no reason to kill him. If they did kill him under those circumstances, his family would surely know that he was the real target and they would have to be silenced, too, which was something he didn't want to contemplate. Not yet, at least.

Adding a note to the team to come up with some other options by the end of the day, he closed Campbell's file and moved on to the next one.

Levine, too, was a creature of habit. Twice a week he went skydiving at the local airport and the team had managed to get one of their number into his Tuesday evening sessions. Like Levine, their man was an ex-paratrooper and through that common bond they had become friends over the last four weeks. Their report said he was now in a position to gain access to Levine's rig with a view to sabotaging it. Farrar didn't understand the intricacies of how they intended to rig the parachute, but they assured him that both the main and reserve would fail to operate on the last dive of the day. Their man would cry off that last jump, claiming to have a prior engagement, and as he had used a false name — belonging to a real ex-para he'd served with — and the licence plates on his car were also false, there was nothing but a description to link him to the death. Once he'd shaven off the full beard and had a haircut, the authorities would be searching for a ghost.

Farrar was satisfied with the plan and gave the go-ahead to implement it the following week.

Another few days, he thought, and he could finally get a proper roast beef dinner. For now, though, he had to be satisfied with a half-decent shepherd's pie from the local English pub.

Chapter 7

Wednesday 18th April 2012

Sam Grant woke as yet another mosquito helped itself to a drink from his exposed arm. Instinctively he tried to swat it, and that was when he remembered the handcuffs. They had been produced as the sun fell the previous evening, and he had been shackled to a tree and left to sleep in a sitting position. When he asked what he was supposed to do if he needed the toilet he was simply told to hold it until the morning. With that, his vision of a night escape had vanished, leaving him with not only dented optimism but also a very full bladder.

When one of the guards stirred close by Grant called out to him.

"Ihi ako," he said, letting the man know he was desperate for a piss.

The guard rubbed his eyes and then dug into his pocket for the keys, and as he ambled past Grant he dropped the key by the base of the tree and continued on to answer his own call of nature. After a little fumbling Grant managed to free himself and stood up on legs filled with pins and needles, a product of his awkward sleeping position. Still, he managed to move a few steps to the edge of the clearing and finally relieve himself. The thought occurred to him that he was losing a lot of fluid and not taking much in, and if he didn't change the ratio soon he was going to start feeling the effects.

However, that wasn't the most troubling thought rattling around in his head.

The previous evening, in line with Muslim tradition, the bodies of Jonjon and Abel were buried as soon as was practical. Grant and the others had been given the task of digging the grave while the Abu Sayyaf washed the dead and shrouded them in hammocks, these being the only white material they had.

With the bodies laid to rest, their heads pointing towards Mecca, the pace of the march had picked up considerably and the beach was no more than five hours away: they would reach it long before Sonny and Len could get into the area. His only hope was that they would lie up close to the shore and wait until nightfall before boarding the boat, but that was far from guaranteed.

Movement near his foot caught his eye and he saw a six-inch long black millipede slink past his toes. He followed its path and watched it crawl inside a fallen tree trunk, where he noticed the particularly sharp remnants of a branch that had been snapped off, probably when it was felled. The stub of the branch gave him an idea, and he knew what he had to keep an eye out for.

He rejoined the group, most of whom were already awake and preparing for another day in the jungle. Halton in particular was in good voice.

"Who's Dina?" Vick asked, catching Grant totally off guard.

"What made you ask that?"

"You were saying the name over and over in your sleep," she said. "You must have been dreaming."

Grant knew which dream she was referring to. It was one he had at least three times a week and it never varied. He is in the car with Dina driving and Daniel in the back seat, all three of them heading towards the beach for a mini break. He is enjoying the beautiful sunshine and Daniel's singing when the song suddenly stops and the sky darkens, thundery black clouds blotting out the sun. He looks in the back seat and Daniel is flopping from side to side, his eyes lifeless. He turns to tell Dina but she is removing her seatbelt, foot planted on the accelerator and their speed building with each passing second. He tries calling out to her, telling her not to do it, to stay with him, but her focus is on the approaching bridge spanning the motorway. He screams her name again and she is smiling now, not at him, but at the bridge support looming large. He tries to reach across to her but his own seatbelt is so tight that he can't move a muscle.

"DINA!"

With that final scream the dream ends, a split second before they crash headlong into the concrete pillar.

"Dina was someone I knew once," he said. "It was a long time ago."

"The name's familiar," she said, curiosity once more etched on her face.

"It's not that unusual. I went to school with three girls called Dina," Grant lied. He could see Vick racking her brains for a glimmer of recollection but he wasn't about to help her. Instead he stood and did some stretches to try to eliminate of some of the muscle knots he had

260

accumulated during the night. In the distance he heard the sound of a light aircraft, and moments later his captors began shouting for everyone to move to cover. Grant followed everyone's lead and jogged into the trees. He squatted down, head up in search of the plane. It passed over a minute later, a single-engine Cessna T41-B.

"They fly over every few days," Moore told him nervously.

"Yeah, and every time they fly over we get attacked a few hours later," Halton added.

Grant ignored the morale officer's whining and considered how he could turn this to his advantage. In the undergrowth he searched around for something that could be used as a weapon and found the perfect item — a twig the thickness of his thumb with a point at one end where it had been cut from a tree. It even had a growth on either side, so his hand wouldn't slip down the shaft when he used it. He slipped the eight-inch shiv into his sock and pulled his pant leg over it for concealment, careful to make sure no-one noticed his movements.

Once the sound of the engines died away, Bong instructed everyone to get up and start packing away, seemingly desperate to leave the immediate area. Even though trees had been cut down to make the clearing, they were only the younger plants — the canopy overhead remained in place, just as it had in the other camps they had forged. Grant thought it unlikely that they would have been spotted from the air, but the others obviously had differing opinions and their eyes scanned the jungle as they stuffed possessions into their packs, weapons always close at hand.

Within ten minutes they were on the move again, and Grant tried to keep pace with Dindo while at the same time trying not to make it too obvious. It meant Halton had to move at the same speed, which did nothing for his demeanour.

Grant found it unnerving that now and again Vick would turn and look at him with a puzzled expression, and he wondered how close she was to guessing his true identity. Given the current situation it might not be that big a problem, he thought, especially if she didn't make it out of the jungle. However, if she managed to secure her release and shared the news with others, he knew Farrar would make him disappear again, but this time permanently.

After five hours they were within smelling distance of the sea and Grant thought his wish was going to come true when Bong ordered everyone to make camp. Through a gap in the trees he could see the beach about half a click away, a sheltered cove with a golden, sandy

261

beach. He was thankful that there was no sign of a boat, adding to his hope that they would wait until dark to transfer to the next island.

As a fire was prepared and rice thrown into a pot he realised how hungry he was, but was more intent on scanning the surrounding jungle for signs of anyone approaching. Whether it was the AFP or his two friends, he wanted to be close to one of his captors when it all kicked off. Dindo unwittingly obliged, drawn to the group by the allure of Vick's beauty. He stood off to one side of her, glancing her way now and again, and both Grant and Vick knew that he was trying to get a glimpse down the front of her tattered T-shirt. Vick did nothing to obscure his view, lest he become embarrassed or angry. The last thing she needed was to lose her only real supply of nourishment, so she leaned forward a little, giving Dindo a better view of her cleavage while she chatted to Moore.

Grant judged the time to be about midday, which meant it would be another few hours before Sonny and Len were likely to turn up. With that thought still in his head, his heart sank as he saw a large banca appear at the mouth of the cove and throw out its anchor. Bong ordered everyone to prepare to move out and the guards starting packing everything away. The rice which was bubbling away in the pot was dumped unceremoniously onto the fire, extinguishing the flames while at the same time dealing yet another blow to the hostages' morale.

Grant frantically sought a way to avoid boarding the boat, but the only way he saw that happening was if he was dead, so he stood when ordered to and took his place in the line as they marched the last few hundred yards to the beach. A small motorised inflatable had been dropped over the side and was chugging towards the shore when they reached the sand and the first of the hostages were ordered to climb aboard, which they did awkwardly with their legs tied together. When the first four were in they were joined by two guards who ferried them to the banca, then they returned to escort the next lot across. Grant, Vick, Moore and Halton were the last hostages to climb into the dinghy and Sam wondered if it would be possible to overpower the crew once onboard, but again his idea was dashed as he climbed onto the larger vessel and saw four more armed men watching over the group of hostages already aboard.

Resigned to the journey, he sat down next to Halton and prayed they had a well-stocked galley on board.

Chapter 8

Wednesday 18th April 2012

Sonny gazed out of the tiny window at the sea far below and wondered what the fishing would be like in those waters. The island of Jolo was just a few minutes away and yet another glance at his watch told him that it was approaching seven in the evening. The return journey from Farrar's office to the airport had been as torturous as the initial drive over, and once they'd passed through the diplomatic channel the news had been broken that the plane was suffering a technical fault in the avionics. The resulting delay meant they didn't arrive in Zamboanga City until five in the afternoon, by which time Farrar had been in touch with the latest developments.

"I got the call from Abu Sayyaf but they didn't use Sam's phone, so we have no way of updating his current position. However, he did manage to tell me he was on a boat heading south-west, which means his most likely destination is Jolo." He'd pronounced it 'Ho-lo' just as the locals did. "Once you touch down in Zamboanga you can catch a connecting flight to Jolo. Be warned, though: there is a U.S. base close to the airstrip and I don't think they'd take kindly to you turning up armed to the teeth. Once you arrive, flash your new credentials, bribe them, do whatever you have to, just get the hell out of there before the military take an interest in you."

With that advice ringing in his ears, Sonny had booked them two seats on an AirPhilExpress DHC-8 for the thirty-five minute flight.

The plane touched down on the single airstrip and taxied to the gate, where any concerns they had about customs inspections proved unfounded. Once outside they flagged down a battered taxi and asked to be taken to the Bud Dajo trail.

Bud Dajo is a volcano rising out of the centre of the island to a height of just over two thousand feet. Its last eruption was over a hundred years ago, and while it was considered active there was little chance of it going off in the next few days.

It was dark by the time they reached the beginning of the trail, and as expected there were no other visitors to worry about. They paid off the taxi driver, who insisted he would be happy to wait for them, but Sonny declined the offer. He even offered his services as a guide up the mountain but Sonny insisted they knew the way and he reluctantly drove off into the night.

Once the headlights had disappeared they began changing, swapping their tourist clothes and comfortable shoes for field uniforms made from Disruptive Pattern Material, and sturdy hiking boots. The DPM had an IRR (Infra-Red-Reflective) coating, which made the wearer less likely to be spotted by anyone using night vision devices aimed at detecting infra-red signatures. Donning their own night vision goggles and cradling their suppressed MP5SDs, they set off up the trail, maintaining a moderate pace to ensure they didn't alert anyone to their presence.

Having studied a Google map of the island, they'd agreed that the most likely landing place for Sam and the others would be the north end of the island, and from there they would most likely head inland, so the plan was to get to high ground and from there make a night sortie to try to locate their friend. Should that fail, they would wait until they got an update the following afternoon and close in on the latest location.

It was midnight by the time they got to within a hundred feet of the summit and found a good location for their Lying Up Point. After snacking on sandwiches they'd purchased at the airport they cleaned their weapons and set off back down the side of the conical volcano, this time heading north. With their M4 assault rifles slung over their shoulders they walked slowly, Sonny on point with his Heckler & Koch at the ready. Ten yards behind him Len scanned the area to their sides, occasionally turning to check their six. An hour into the search they came across a building and stopped twenty yards short to check it out. It was built on stilts, with the floor raised three feet off the ground. There appeared to be no sign of movement. After a ten minute wait, Sonny edged closer while Len covered his advance. It took another few minutes to cover the ground, then Sonny popped his head round the corner and returned to signal the all clear. Len joined him and saw that they'd come across a storage hut, piled a couple of feet high with coconuts. With no sign of any targets they took a quick drinks break before Len took his turn on point.

For a further two hours they snaked their way through the jungle without coming across anything larger than a cockatoo and finally they agreed to head back to their temporary camp and get some shuteye.

Daylight was barely four hours away, and they took a more direct route back up the mountain, little realising that at one point they passed within two hundred yards of Sam as he once again tried to get some sleep with only a tree for a pillow.

* * *

It had taken just over six hours for the boat to cover the one hundred and fifty kilometres from Basilan to Jolo. When they arrived at the deserted beach just after dark they were again transferred ashore using the inflatable. If the banca had a galley on board Sam and the other hostages were not on the dining list, and once they began the march into the jungle he knew it would probably be the next day before they got another bite to eat. All the while he kept close to Dindo in anticipation of an AFP attack, hoping he could take out the young Muslim with his hidden shiv and grab his weapon to aid his escape. Unfortunately, no such attack took place, and at around eleven in the evening they arrived at yet another temporary camp, but one which was vastly different from the others he had been in.

The first difference was the number of terrorists he saw, close to two hundred by his estimate. There were also boxes galore and all of the weapons on view looked like they'd just come from the factory. As they entered the camp they passed a huge pot of rice and a selection of cooked meats, although he couldn't tell which animal they'd come from. Given his current hunger he wouldn't have cared if it had once been a horse's arse, and their spirits were raised when they were told to sit and bowls of rice and meat were handed round. It wasn't exactly a banquet but he could see from the smiles on the faces of the other hostages that it was the best they had eaten in a long time.

Grant was watching a group of men who were gathered around a box deep in discussion, torches masked with red tape illuminating a drawing of some kind. It looked to him like one of the many Chinese parliaments he had taken part in while on operations, when his small squad would evaluate a situation and all offer their opinions, regardless of rank. He popped another piece of horse arse into his mouth just as the group broke up and started to walk towards the huddled hostages, causing him to stop mid-mastication.

Two of the men were taller than the others, their attire different and their features Arabic. Grant's entire body froze as he started at the face

265

of the man he'd been researching for the last nine months, the man who had effectively ended the life of Tom Gray.

After he'd left his hospital bed in Subic Freeport, the first thing Grant had done was get internet access. Farrar had agreed to it and had provided the laptop, but only after reminding him that his old life was over and he shouldn't try to contact anyone from the past. Having learned a lesson from the Tom Gray saga, where communication had been done with dead-drop emails — those that were written and saved as drafts but never sent, therefore never leaving an electronic signature — Farrar had set up security privileges on the machine so that it refused to load the websites of any email providers. Grant also suspected it contained a key-logging program, which would record every stroke on the keyboard. Unfortunately, his knowledge of computers wasn't advanced enough to check for such software, and searching for help online would just alert Farrar to his intentions if any were installed. Instead, Grant had worked on the assumption that everything he did was being monitored.

The first search string he had entered into Google was "Tom Gray", and wasn't surprised to see the search engine's announcement that there were "about 3,500,000,000 results". His first port of call was the BBC news website where he first discovered the name of the man suspected of attacking him. Abdul Mansour had also been suspected of killing a pensioner in a near-by village as part of his escape plan, although he had spared the lives of an ambulance crew he'd taken hostage. According to their testimony, it was so that they could let the world know who had been responsible for the attack. Grant then did a search for Abdul Mansour and judging by the number of search results returned, Grant guessed he'd gotten the message across. He found reports on Mansour's background, from growing up as Ahmed Al-Ali in Ladbroke Grove, London, to his reported activities in Afghanistan and Pakistan both before and after the attack in Sussex.

Grant immediately recognised Abdul Mansour and had to use all his willpower not to stare at him as he came to a stop and surveyed the hostages. His whole body was tense, not with fear but with the rising anger he felt at meeting the man who had tried to kill him. He'd anticipated this day would come, but not under these circumstances. He'd expected to be the hunter rather than the prey, or at least be armed with more than a pointy stick when they met.

Mansour stood over the group and played the light over them. His eye was drawn to Grant.

"We have no more need for these people," Assaf said. "Guarding them will be a waste of men, and we no longer need the money they will bring us." He gave some orders and his men moved in.

"Not so hasty, my friend," Mansour said, holding out his arm. "They have more than just a monetary value. After we attack the base on Friday night, the Army will come at us in numbers, but they will be handicapped if we still have these hostages. They put a high value on human life and that is a weakness we will exploit."

"Besides..." He was staring at Grant, who saw the same look Vick Phillips had been giving him for the last couple of days.

"What's your name?" Mansour asked.

"Sam."

Mansour searched his memory for the name but came up blank. "You look familiar."

"He gets that a lot," Vick said, but her comment was ignored.

There was something about this man that had Mansour looking back over the last few years, yet nothing would come to mind. He gave up the mental search but took a moment to weigh the man up. By the look of him he must have been picked up quite recently, and many in that position were usually still in a state of shock at this stage, yet he had an air about him, something that said he wasn't too uncomfortable in these surroundings.

"What do you do for a living?" he asked Grant.

While his new looks might hide his past, Grant knew that his voice would be the one giveaway and he tried to keep his answer as short as possible.

"I make websites."

There! That voice! He recognised it from somewhere, but just exactly where, he didn't know. He asked a few more questions but each time Grant answered in as few syllables as possible, and Mansour guessed there was a reason for this, but what? Had they met before?

The more he stared, the further away the truth seemed to be, so Mansour walked away. He was sure the answer would come to him, but if it didn't arrive soon he would have to do something about this "Sam".

Once he'd gone Vick inched closer to Grant.

"Tom," she whispered.

Grant turned to face her and immediately realised what he'd done.

"I knew it! You're Tom Gray!"

267

Grant gestured for her to keep her voice down, knowing that denying it would be futile.

"Oh, my God! I thought you were dead!"

"That was the plan," Grant said. "How did you know?"

She took a moment to compose herself, still shocked at the discovery she'd made. "I may be a travel writer but in order to pay for my trips I write for several publications. When you released your justice bill last year I was one of those opposed to it, and wrote an article explaining why it was a non-starter. I did a lot of research on you, including watching your appearances on the news over and over again. That's where I knew your voice from."

"That's it?"

"No, the voice was only part of it. When you saved me from that bullet I knew you were no ordinary business owner, and I saw the look on Abdul Mansour's face when he walked up to you. I think he's close to recognising you, too. Maybe it's a good job the explosion altered your appearance somewhat."

"You know who he is?" Grant asked.

"Are you kidding? After he attacked you his face was all over the news. He's more notorious than Osama Bin Laden."

"Look, you have to forget about Tom Gray. I mean, you have to forget about me being Tom Gray. It's complicated, but if you tell anyone I'm alive, they'll kill the both of us. Now eat your food."

"But who would want to kill you?" she persisted.

It was a conversation he didn't want to have, but she had to know the danger she had stumbled into, a danger greater than her current situation.

"Think about it. The government announced my death to the whole world. How happy do you think they'd be if you proved they had lied, eh? They know where I am right now, and if you ever mention my name and link me to this place they will know you are telling the truth. Oh, they'll dismiss you as a crackpot, saying it was post traumatic stress disorder or something similar brought on by your ordeal, but they won't risk someone believing you and reigniting the fire."

"They wouldn't do that," she insisted. "That only happens in books and films, not real life. The British government doesn't murder its own people."

"Don't be so naïve. Government as a whole might not sanction it, but individuals will do all they can to hold on to their power. If anything threatens their position they will do all they can to eliminate the danger."

"Then why did you agree to the name change?"

"I didn't agree, not at the time. I only found out about it when I woke from a coma two months after the attack, and by then the choice was either to accept the new life or go back to sleep permanently. They even performed plastic surgery to make me look even less like Tom Gray. I'm banished from the U.K., I can't contact anyone from my past, and I didn't get a real say in any of it. If they can do that to someone who had such a high public profile, they wouldn't hesitate to silence someone who — and I mean no disrespect — they've never heard of."

"But I don't understand. Why keep you alive if you are such a thorn in their side?"

"That was one of my first questions, and it seems some friends of mine had them over a barrel. I don't know the full details, but they negotiated a deal whereby I get a new life and the government's lies aren't exposed. I guess it would have been easy enough to get rid of me, but to silence my eight friends too would have been a red flag to the conspiracy theorists."

"I see," Vick said. "That's gotta suck."

"As I said, I didn't have a choice. And if we don't get out of here sharpish it's going to suck a whole lot more."

"What's your plan?"

"Not a plan, as such. A couple of friends are on their way to get me and we just need to be ready when they get here."

"Baines and Smart! I knew those names were familiar! They were part of your team last year, weren't they?"

"That's right, and hopefully they'll be here sometime tomorrow. When it all kicks off you need to do exactly as I say, you understand?"

Vick nodded and Grant reminded her to tell no-one, but she wasn't going to let it lie.

"I'm a writer, Tom, and this is absolute gold. I can't just pretend I don't know about the story of the century."

"Just leave it," Grant said, throwing her a look and signalling the end of the conversation. A few minutes later his guard arrived with the handcuffs and he settled down to another night of broken sleep.

Chapter 9

Thursday 19th April 2012

While Grant's sleep was disturbed by the constant feeding of the indigenous insects, Abdul Mansour was kept awake by the gnawing sensation that comes from being one step away from total recall.

The fact that he couldn't put a name to the face had weighed heavily on him, and with it came a sense of foreboding. He wasn't a superstitious man, but he trusted his instincts, and right now they told him that there was something dangerous about this man.

These thoughts troubled him throughout his morning prayers and continued as he ate his breakfast, and once he'd finished he decided that the best thing to do would be to rid himself of the man, just to be on the safe side. However, having made that decision he found himself reluctant to go through with it.

Looking over at Grant, he knew he was so close to the truth, yet it was always a few inches from his grasp. If he killed the man and then subsequently made the connection it would be too late to do anything about it, yet his head said the man had to go.

After another hour of going round in circles he opted to settle the matter once and for all.

"Brother," he said to Abu Assaf, "the prisoner, Sam Grant, troubles me deeply. I feel it is not safe to keep him alive."

"Troubles you? In what way?"

"I don't know," Mansour had to admit, "but it would be safer for all of us if he was no longer with us."

Assaf shrugged and called over one of his men. "Bong, take Grant into the jungle and dispose of him. Do it quietly."

Bong Manalo nodded and went to find a couple of helpers, and together they approached the group of prisoners. Having already finished their breakfast, the hostages were lounging around in anticipation of the inevitable daily march through the jungle.

Bong stood over Grant and ordered his compatriots to remove the tether attaching him to Halton.

"Get up," Bong said, "you're coming with us."

Grant did so, warily. "Where are we going?" he asked.

"For a walk."

Grant looked down at Halton, who averted his eyes and dropped his gaze to the ground. The simple gesture told Grant all he needed to know: This was one of those walks Vick had told him about, where four go out but just three come back.

He thought quickly and decided not to make a fuss here, not with a few dozen armed men to deal with. Instead he would go quietly and take his chance with his three escorts. Two of them carried their brand new M16 rifles while Bong was holding his bolo and had a pistol tucked into a hip holster. For his own part, Grant could feel the shiv up against his right calf and knew the time to use it was drawing close.

As they walked towards the edge of the clearing, Vick returned from her visit to the toilet in time to see Grant being led away. When she asked Halton what was going on she got the same response he'd given Grant and she immediately chased after the small group.

"No!"

She was quickly grabbed from behind and dragged back to the group of hostages, but she managed to scream one more time before a hand across the mouth silenced her and a bolo appeared at her throat.

"If you make another sound you will take a walk as well. Do you understand?"

With tears running down her face she nodded, never taking her eyes off Grant's back as he finally left the clearing and was led down a track and out of sight.

* * *

After grabbing a couple of hours sleep each — one napping while the other took watch — Sonny and Len set off back down the mountain in search of their friend. They retraced their route from the previous night for about a kilometre before peeling off to the right towards another hill. The sensible thing for Abu Sayyaf to do would be to seek the high ground and that was where Sonny and Len expected to find them, though as the landscape undulated relentlessly it was hit and miss as to which hill they should target.

An hour into their trek, Sonny wasn't sure if the sound he'd heard had been a woman's distant scream or just another of the animal sounds that continually assaulted the ears. The noise had come from his left and he looked back to see if Len had heard it, too. His friend

271

indicated the direction the sound had come from and that told him that it wasn't his imagination.

Sonny took the lead and upped the pace slightly, balancing speed with the need to remain undetected. The origin of the sound he'd heard would be around a click-and-a-half away, he figured, which meant close to the top of the hill they were now approaching. Once within sight of the summit he slowed the pace and Len closed the formation, the pair inching closer while scanning the bush ahead for signs of movement.

Sonny's hand went up and Len froze, following the direction of Sonny's finger as he indicated two figures approaching fifty yards ahead. They both recognised their friend from the videos they'd been shown, and they guessed the man holding the long knife was his captor. Moments later two armed men came into view and the four continued their slow march towards the bottom of the hill. As the men passed, Sonny and Len gave them a thirty-second start before moving onto their tail.

They followed for another hundred yards before their targets stopped and Grant was shoved onto his knees. The two armed men moved aside to give the man with the knife some room, their rifles hanging loosely by their sides, muzzles pointing towards the ground.

Sonny indicated these two and showed which one he intended to take out, leaving the other to Len. They would then both concentrate on the man with the knife.

With his target in his sights, Sonny applied pressure to the trigger until the firing pin was released to send the round on its way.

Nothing.

A click, but nothing more. He quickly cleared what he assumed was a misfire and took aim again, but once more he got nothing more than a click as the firing pin hit the dud bullet.

Len had been waiting for him to take the first shot, taking that as the signal to take out his own target, and when he heard Sonny clearing his weapon for a second time he looked over to see what the problem was. All he got in response was a shrug and a finger to indicate one more attempt. Len nodded and took aim again but the shot he was waiting for never came.

Another glance over and he saw that Sonny had abandoned the silenced MP5 and was now readying his M4 Carbine. Sonny indicated that Len should try to take out the armed men and he would support him if things got loud.

Accepting the lead role, Len got a bead on the target farthest from him, exhaled and took the shot.

Click.

"What the fuck..?"

One weapon misfiring was unusual, but two just never happened. They'd stripped the guns down the previous evening and all of the moving parts were in perfect working order, which left just the ammunition. He ejected the next cartridge in the breach and used his knife to pry the round from the casing, expecting black powder to pour out. Instead he ended up with a tiny pile of sand in the palm of his hand.

He could hear their friend's voice through the half-dozen trees separating them and knew time was running out. Inching sideways, he crept towards Sonny and told him what he'd found.

"Is all the ammo the same?" Baines whispered.

"Not sure."

To answer his own question, Baines ejected a round from his own M4 and prised the bullet free, revealing yet more powdery sand.

"This was done deliberate," Baines said. "The question is: why?"

"No time for that now," Len said, discarding all of his weapons except for his knife. "We'll have to go hand-to-hand."

Baines put a hand on his shoulder. "What about playing rabbit?"

Len considered it for a moment, then nodded and made to get up. Baines grabbed his arm and pulled him back down.

"Rabbits are young and fit, not old, fat and bald," he said to Len. "Let me be the bunny, you catch them as they follow me."

"Cheeky sod," Len said, but had to concede that he'd put on a few pounds in the last year, and while he was not exactly bald, his hairline had been receding since just after puberty and there was nothing he could do about it. Sonny often joked that he looked more like a managing director than a soldier, but then occasionally he thought Sonny was a pillock, which evened things out.

Len crawled back from their vantage point to seek a decent hiding place, and after finding a tree trunk wide enough to hide his frame he indicated which direction Baines should run and got into position.

* * *

Grant marched slowly down the hill with his two armed escorts behind him and Bong leading the way. After a couple of hundred

273

yards Bong stopped and one of the guards put a hand on his shoulder and forced him onto his knees. Grant didn't offer any resistance as he'd anticipated the action and saw it as the chance to grab his shiv from his sock. With his hand on the shank he sat facing his executioner.

"You don't have to do this," he said, glancing over at the two armed guards who had moved off to the right-hand side of the track. They were at ease, their guns pointing to the ground, but they could bring them up and have him in their sights within a second. "The money is on its way, why don't you just wait for it and let me go?"

Bong remained impassive. "I have my instructions."

No emotion, just the simple acknowledgement that taking this life would mean no more to him than taking out the garbage or mowing the lawn.

"Why don't you come with me, all three of you? You could share the money between you. You won't have to live in the jungle anymore and no-one will tell you what to do." He added just the right amount of panic to his voice, letting them believe to the end that he was a man with no fight in him.

"I don't care about money. All I care about is a free Muslim nation, and Allah will provide that."

"Then why kidnap me if you don't want the money?"

Bong sighed like a parent trying to explain the workings of the internal-combustion engine to a three-year-old. "The money we made from you was supposed to help our cause, but now we have more than enough."

Grant looked over at the other guards. "What about you two? Wouldn't you like a million dollars between you?"

"They don't speak English," Bong said. "And even if they did, their loyalties lie with Allah. Now, have you anything else to say?"

"Yes. That man in your group, the foreigner: he's going to get you all killed. Believe me, I recognise him from the television and he was responsible for an atrocity in England last year. He recruited thirty local men and got them all killed while he got away."

Bong let out a snort of derision. "You think I fear death? No! It is coming to all of us and I will embrace mine so that I can finally fulfil my duty to Allah!"

He looked at his bolo and ran a finger along the sharp edge. "You should embrace yours, too."

274

As Bong took a step forward, Grant prepared himself. The bolo was hanging at Bong's side now, and he would have barely a second to get in close enough to use the shiv before his enemy had time to pull it back and counter the strike. Still, a second was a long time when the target was oblivious to the threat you posed. At least, that is what his training had taught him.

One more step...

A shout of pain pierced the jungle and all four of them looked towards the source of the noise in time to see a uniformed figure stumbling away from them. Grant recognised the gait and immediately knew that it was a diversion, one which his captors were falling for. The two guards immediately began firing as the retreating shape blended into the surrounding jungle, and a moment later they were off in chase. Bong raised his bolo, pointing at his two compatriots.

"Stop! Let him go!"

As he took a step towards them, Grant saw the chance and struck. He sprung up onto his feet and threw his left shoulder into Bong's armpit, lifting him off his feet, while his right hand came round and plunged the point of the stick into the Filipino's neck. His momentum carried them for a couple of steps before he tripped on a tree root and they collapsed in a heap. Grant lay on the arm holding the bolo while he grabbed for the pistol in Bong's holster. He met no resistance: Bong was too busy dealing with the damage to his throat to bother about anything else.

With the pistol in his hand Grant swivelled towards the other two targets, flicking the safety off as he brought the weapon round in anticipation of them bearing down on him. He was surprised to see that they hadn't even noticed his attack, intent as they were on chasing their prey through the jungle.

He looked back down at Bong, who was clutching at the wound in his neck. He figured that the terrorist might survive if he got help quickly, and that wasn't something he wanted to happen.

"Live by the sword, die by the sword," he whispered, and brought the bolo down hard, the sharp blade severing a few of Bong's fingers on its way to embedding itself in his spinal column. With one down and two to go, he set off in pursuit of the remaining threats. They were about twenty yards ahead, still pausing and firing every few steps, and he made up the ground quickly. He was within ten yards and had one of them in his sights when the leader passed a tree and an arm flashed out, catching him in the throat, sending both man and rifle clattering to the ground. The second terrorist stopped too, stunned at what he'd seen. He then saw a uniformed figure appear from behind the tree, stooping down to collect the weapon on the jungle floor. Raising his own rifle, he got the stranger in his sights and his finger began to squeeze the trigger.

Len saw the rifle being aimed at him and grabbed for the weapon at his feet, expecting to get the bad news any second. When the double-tap came he tensed for the impact, but none came. Instead, the remaining terrorist collapsed like a sack of bricks. As he went down Len saw Sam Grant standing a few yards beyond the body.

"I see the timing's still there," he said, and gave his old friend a huge embrace. Sonny came jogging back through the jungle.

"Typical. I'm the one that gets shot at and Len gets all the hugs."

He ignored the look he got from Smart and instead grasped Grant's hand and slapped him on the shoulder in a more macho welcome. "Good to see you, Tom," he said.

"It's Sam now."

"Yeah, Farrar told us. It's going to be hard to get used to calling you Sam after all these years."

"We can discuss that later. Right now we have to get moving. There's a couple of hundred heavily-armed terrorists about half a click from here and all that shooting will bring them down on top of us."

While Sonny and Len collected the weapons and ammunition from the fallen, Grant trotted back to Bong and went through the dead man's pockets looking for more ammunition. He found a spare clip, along with the mobile phone the Filipino had taken from him. When he rejoined the others, Sonny led them back in the direction of their LUP on the adjacent hill.

They moved quickly, desperate to put as much distance between themselves and anyone following. After a kilometre they stopped for a two-minute breather and checked their tail to see if anyone had latched on to it, but there was no sign of a pursuit.

"While I'm glad to see you guys, what the hell made you decide to turn up at a firefight without any weapons?"

"We had weapons, more than enough to do the job," Len said. "Trouble was, the ammo Farrar gave us was no good."

"What do you mean by 'no good'?"

Sonny removed the projectile from one of the 9mm MP5 rounds and handed the cartridge over to Grant, who immediately recognised the problem. "Are they all like this?"

"All the ones we've tried have been, and I can't see it being an accident."

Grant let the sand trickle through his fingers. "The question is: why? Why send you all the way here and then give you duff kit?"

"It looks like he didn't want the rescue to succeed," Len offered.

"Possible, but then he could have just left you two at home and refused to pay a ransom. It doesn't make sense."

"Maybe he was just sold some dodgy ammo," Sonny said.

"Possible, but I doubt it."

"Then let's go and ask him," Len said to Grant. He was about to get up when he spotted the red dot moving up from Sam's shoulder to his temple.

"We've got company," he said, and turned slowly to look in the direction of the laser sights.

"Let me see those hands. NOW!"

The good news was that the voice was American. The bad news, they realised, was that they had a whole lot of explaining to do.

The trio got to their feet, hands in the air.

"Walk towards me, slowly."

They did as instructed and six figures emerged from the bushes, their camouflage having worked a treat. Five of them were Filipinos, while the sixth stood a foot taller.

"What the hell are you doing running around the jungle armed to the teeth?" the tall man asked as he approached, weapon still trained on them. When he got no answer he instructed his men to gather up the weapons and frisk their prisoners. The quick body searched produced two knives, a couple of 5.56mm magazines and their mobile phones and comms gear.

After a quick conversation in his radio the leader of the group motioned with his gun. "Okay, get moving."

"Where are you taking us?" Grant asked.

"Our base is just a few clicks from here. My boss wants to ask you a few questions."

* * *

277

At the first sound of gunfire Assaf had sent his aide and a dozen men to investigate, and they returned twenty minutes later.

"They are dead, all three of them. The prisoner is gone."

"The sundalos?" Assaf asked.

"I don't think so. Edgar was shot but Bong and Manny were killed with knives. The sundalos are cowards: they don't like to get in that close."

Mansour was disturbed by what he was hearing. It seemed his instincts had been right all along, and he cursed himself for not disposing of the man with his own hand.

"Is it possible that the prisoner killed them?" he asked.

The aide considered the possibility. "By himself? Unlikely. Two were stabbed and one was shot in the back of the head. I can't imagine how he could do that, especially when they managed to fire so many shots. He must have had help."

Mansour frowned. If it wasn't the local soldiers, then who had come to his rescue? And what was so special about this man that someone would send in a team to retrieve him?

These concerns were soon pushed aside as he remembered having discussed the upcoming attack on the base in the man's presence. Should he bring this to Assaf's attention? He decided not to: Assaf would surely want to cancel the attack, and there was a schedule to maintain. Instead he took Nabil's arm and pulled him to one side.

"The attack will go ahead tomorrow, as planned, but there is a chance they may have been forewarned. You should expect heavy resistance."

"If Allah wills it, they will all be sleeping in their beds. If not, I am ready to fight for my place amongst the virgins."

"Allah will reserve a special place for you, I am sure of it."

They rejoined Assaf. "How are the preparations for the attack coming along?" Mansour asked.

"The vehicles have been purchased and we will be fitting them for the mini-guns this evening. Everything else is in place and the men know what is expected of them."

"I would still like to get the team leaders together to go through the attack one more time."

Assaf nodded and sent his aide to gather them together around the map table, which was nothing more than four crates pushed together to form a square.

278

"When the mounted unit goes in, you will have some extra company," Mansour said. "The Americans have a fondness for all things living, so we will place one of the white prisoners in each vehicle. We will need to ensure they are prominent, but not so much that they interfere with the mission. Any suggestions?"

He was hugely disappointed by the lack of response. How on earth were these people going to think on their feet in the middle of a battle if they couldn't come up with a solution to this simple problem? But then, the raid didn't have to succeed: it just had to be audacious and act as a warning to the western world.

"Nabil, what would you suggest?"

"The trucks we will be using have an open bed at the back. We could lash a board to the back of the cab so that it is pointing to the sky. We can then strap the prisoner to the board standing up, facing forward. They would be vulnerable to any incoming fire, which should cause our enemies to think twice before shooting."

"I like it. Take some men and oversee the modifications to the trucks. Once they are completed we need to finish off the defences, so you will need to be quick."

Nabil selected a couple of armed men to guide him down the mountain and another couple to help carry the mounting for the mini-gun and they set off through the morning heat. It was a three hour trek to the compound where the trucks were being stored and he was soaked with sweat by the time he arrived, but he shrugged off the inconvenience and dived straight into the work.

The Dillon could be supplied with a DVRM-1 support assembly for mounting the weapon on the back of a vehicle, but aside from being bulky it was designed for use with the HMMWV, or Humvee class of vehicle. Instead they had brought along a couple of MK16 naval post mounts, designed primarily for naval deployment but which was capable of being mounted on any flat bed. All it required was an area of two feet by two feet — which the Datsun pickups had with room to spare — and Nabil began by marking out the bolt holes before drilling them out. He then used a rivet gun to secure the feet in place and moved on to the post for the prisoner. They settled on a couple of planks six feet long by eight inches wide and lashed them to the back of the cab vertically.

Once the modifications had been made they drove the trucks to a clearing a couple of kilometres from the base of the hill and climbed back to the camp. Mansour was standing with a group of others around one of the boxes and he was explaining how the Claymore mines worked when Nabil joined them.

"You are just in time," Mansour said. "I have been told that the perimeter foxholes have been completed. After you have eaten, I would like you to check them and start laying the defensive mines."

"Certainly," Nabil replied. A belly full of food was just what he needed, and afterwards he went to inspect the work that had been done.

The first foxhole he came across had half a dozen soldiers sitting around it and showed how much work remained to be done. It was barely a scrape in the ground and the occupant couldn't have been more conspicuous if he'd painted himself fluorescent orange.

Nabil instructed one of the men to gather the others from around the perimeter and while he waited for them to return he gave the remaining soldiers instructions as to what he expected.

"This hole needs to be at least three feet from front to back and six feet wide. It also needs to be deep enough so that you can stand up in it with just your head and shoulders visible."

He marked out the size with a stick and told them to start digging. While two took to that task Nabil showed the others how to create a roof for the hole using branches lashed together with thin strips of bark. The finished product looked like a coffee table, with an eight-inch leg in each corner. Nabil placed it over the finished hole and it had enough of a gap on the right-hand side that the occupants could get in without removing it. The final step was to camouflage it and he used cuttings from nearby bushes and ferns to disrupt the outline while allowing those inside a good field of fire.

Nabil pointed to one of the soldiers. "Go and get another thirty men and tell them to bring shovels. The rest of you, follow me. I will mark out the location for the other foxholes and I want four men working on each one. These have to be in place before we launch the attack tomorrow, so you will have to work fast."

He paced out the distance to the next hole to ensure they weren't too far apart: If the enemy managed to overcome one of the positions he wanted the neighbours to be able to cover the gap. Once he'd done a complete circuit of the hill and returned to the original hole he had marked out ten positions and work had begun on each of them.

Next up was the laying of the Claymores. Unlike conventional mines which are designed to be buried underground, these anti-personnel devices are command-detonated and directional, meaning they could target a certain area. The operator would wait until the enemy were in the kill zone before hitting the plastic detonator switch, sending around seven hundred 3mm steel ball bearings out to a distance of a hundred yards, much like a giant shotgun. Anyone caught in the sixty-degree blast radius could kiss their shredded ass goodbye.

Nabil showed the men how to prepare the mine and disguise it, then ensured that the detonation wire leading back to the foxhole was buried under the dead leaves and other fallen debris on the jungle floor. Once back at the foxhole he demonstrated the trigger before attaching it to the wire, effectively priming the weapon.

Evening was drawing in as he finished the lesson. "We need to make every hole the same as this one," he said, "and we don't have much time. After tomorrow's attack the enemy will come at us in great numbers, and these defences will be the only thing between survival and annihilation."

Leaving them with that thought he returned to the camp for his evening prayers. As he neared the plateau he heard the familiar sound of gunfire coming from the opposite side of the hill. He flicked off the safety on his M16 and headed towards the noise.

Chapter 10

Thursday 19th April 2012

Sister Evangelina Benesueda was concluding afternoon prayers, guiding the children through the Lord's Prayer for the second time that day. She had been running the tiny school virtually single-handed for nearly a year since arriving from Manila and the work had been the most rewarding of her life.

It lifted her heart to see the happy faces of the orphans as they followed her lead, a few of them grappling with the English words but the majority comfortable with the new language.

> *"...Thy Kingdom come.*
> *Thy will be done in earth,*
> *As it is in heaven.*
> *Give us this day our daily bread.*
> *And forgive us our trespasses,*
> *As we forgive those who trespass against us..."*

As they neared the end of the prayer Evangelina heard a commotion outside the front door and became wary. In a predominantly Muslim region, her Christian teachings attracted a lot of negative attention. This was the reason she had hired a local ex-policeman to stand guard outside during school hours, and it sounded like he was in a confrontation with someone.

She was walking towards the door just as it came crashing in and half a dozen armed men strode into the classroom. They were all brandishing bolos and two or three of them were already bloodied. Through the open door she could see her guard laid out on the floor, blood seeping from several wounds.

She saw the men eyeing the youngsters and ran to place herself between them, arms outstretched.

"They are just children!" she screamed, but her protests were cut off as a bolo arched through the air and connected with the side of her head, cleaving a gaping wound above her temple. A second blow caught her on the back of the neck as she fell and the last thing she saw was the kids being dragged, kicking and screaming through the classroom door.

* * *

Camp Bautista is located next to Jolo's domestic airport runway and is home to the 3rd Marine Brigade, Philippine Marine Corps. Within the base is another compound which houses U.S. troops, predominantly National Guardsmen. In addition, there is a detachment of the CIA's Special Activities Division.

In the battle against Abu Sayyaf, the U.S. military had been given a strictly advisory role, assisting the local armed forces in terms of strategy and occasionally logistics. This directive hadn't sat too well with Colonel Travis Dane, commanding officer of the Special Operations Group which was the elite paramilitary element of SAD. As a man of action, sitting around in a comfortable office while just a few clicks away there were bad guys waiting to be killed was anathema to him. Being limited to arming and training the local soldiers had done nothing for his already formidable demeanour, leading the indigenous troops to give him the name Angry Dog. He was rather proud of his new tag and made sure everyone used it, even his own men. Perhaps because they shared his frustrations, he wasn't as hard on them as he was the rest of the world.

"Dog," Scott Garcia said as he entered the office. "The guys we found are in the cells."

The Colonel got up from behind his desk and followed the sergeant over to the stockade.

"What do we know about them?"

"They're British, but they won't give me their names. One of them claims that Abdul Mansour is on the island preparing for an attack on the base."

"Abdul Mansour? *The* Abdul Mansour, here on Jolo?"

Garcia shrugged. "So he claims."

As they entered the guardhouse the two Filipino guards snapped to attention.

"At ease."

Dog saw the three men sitting in the single cell. A pile of personal belongings was on a table, including their phones. Dog powered them both up before thumbing through the contact lists in search of clues.

One phone contained several Manila numbers and a few belonging to mobiles, while the other contained a single entry: Farrar.

"You want to tell me what you were doing in my jungle?" he asked the trio through the bars.

"We came to get our friend," Len said, indicating towards Grant.

"So what's your friend's name?"

The question was met with silence.

"Okay, tell me about Abdul Mansour."

"He's here on the island and is planning to attack one of the bases tomorrow night," Grant said.

"This is the only base on Jolo," Dog told him. "We have a few people scattered across the island doing humanitarian work, but this is the main camp. So tell me how Mansour came to be on Jolo."

"I don't know. I was captured by the Abu Sayyaf on Basilan last week and they brought me here yesterday. Mansour was already in their camp."

"And he told you he was going to attack this base?"

"He didn't tell me personally, I overheard a conversation."

"How can you be sure it was Abdul Mansour?"

"His face has been all over the news for the past year. I'd recognise him anywhere."

Dog's expression conveyed his scepticism. "Sorry, but I don't buy it. Mansour is a big-time player and if you told me he was going to attack the White House I might believe you, but to come to the poorest part of the world to attack a base housing less than a hundred U.S. personnel is not his style."

"Whether you believe me or not, it's going to happen," Grant said, exasperated. "You can either prepare for it, or ignore the warning and explain to your bosses why everyone under your command is dead."

Dog let out a laugh. "I hardly think a few dozen poorly-armed terrorists are going to wipe out an entire base."

"I'd say the number was closer to two hundred, and their weapons looked brand new. I think your intel needs updating."

The size of the enemy force was clearly news to Dog, and it took a moment to process the new information. His team consisted of just half a dozen men, himself included, with the rest of the U.S. contingent made up of eighty National Guard Engineers. There were also over a hundred Filipino Marines assigned to the base. While they might be closely matched on numbers, he felt sure that training and experience would be the deciding factor. That was, if there was such a strong opposing force and they were actually planning an attack.

"We'll need to check this out," he said. "You said you were held in their camp: where is it?"

"Not far from where he found us," Grant said, nodding towards Garcia. "Head south for about one click, then start climbing. They're on a plateau about a hundred yards from the summit."

He took his sergeant aside. "Scott, does that sound plausible?"

Garcia pulled his operations map from his pants pocket and found the location. "He could be telling the truth. Those directions put them on Hill 178, and we've had a few skirmishes in that area, though we've never managed to get close to the top. Drones haven't managed to tell us much, either."

"Take your team and see how close you can get. Avoid contact if you can, just give me numbers." Dog lowered his voice to a whisper. "Before you leave, stop by the command centre and get close-up shots of these guys using the CCTV, then have them sent to Langley."

Garcia nodded and left the room.

Dog sat on a desk and folded his arms. "So, assuming you're telling the truth, I still need to know who you are. We're usually the first to be notified about kidnappings and there's been no reports of a white male being taken, not for a few months anyway. Why would that be?"

"Maybe because I didn't contact the embassy," Grant shrugged.

"But you have had contact with the outside world," Dog said, and turned his attention back to the phones. The operating system was unfamiliar so it took him a moment to find the call log.

As he was fiddling his way through the menus the door banged open and a five-foot storm barrelled into the room.

General Tomas B. Callinag, commanding officer of the 3rd Marine Brigade had a reputation that made Dog look like an excited puppy. While Dog begrudged his unit's non-combatant role, Callinag resented their very presence on Philippine soil.

"When were you going to tell me about these prisoners?"

Dog stood lazily to attention, knowing his insubordinate actions would further rile the officer but caring little.

"I was just about to send a runner to inform you, sir."

Callinag dismissed the excuse with a wave of his hand and stood in front of the cells staring at the occupants.

"Who are they? What are they doing on Jolo?"

"I was just in the process of establishing that, General. Would you mind if I continued?"

The Filipino shot him a look before moving away from the cell and settling into a chair behind the desk.

"You say you were kidnapped last week," Dog continued, "which means you could only have been communicating with someone called Farrar. And why did they let you keep your mobile, I wonder? It looks to me like you guys are members of Abu Sayyaf."

"They didn't let me keep it," Grant said indignantly. "I took it back when I escaped."

"Okay then, tell me about Farrar."

"He's just someone I met in Manila. One of my captors saw his name in the phone and called him, that's all."

"So how come your friends have a phone with just one contact in it: Farrar?"

Grant knew he had already said far too much, and just started at the wall indicating an end to the conversation.

Garcia popped his head round the door and nodded to Dog before disappearing as quickly as he'd appeared.

"Gentlemen, you might as well tell me who you are now. Your mug-shots are currently being analysed at CIA headquarters in Langley and they will be able to cross-reference your details with every friendly intelligence agency in the world. Why don't you just —"

He was interrupted by the chirping of Grant's phone, and the display told him who was on the other end of the call.

"Let's see what Farrar has got to say about all this, shall we?"

"Put it on speakerphone," Callinag said, "I want to hear this, too."

* * *

When the notification appeared on his laptop screen, Farrar clicked the message and saw that Grant's phone had been activated. Strangely, the device he'd given to Smart and Baines appeared to be in exactly the same location. Did it mean they had successfully rescued him already, or had they been captured by Abu Sayyaf, too?

He decided that the only way to find out was to call Grant's phone and see who answered.

"Hello?" he heard when the call was connected. Farrar didn't recognize the voice but it was definitely Filipino.

286

"Where is Bong?" he asked.

"Bong isn't here," the voice said. "Who is this?"

"It's Farrar. Is Sam still with you?"

"Yes, Sam is here, and so are two of his friends."

Excellent, Farrar thought, giving himself a mental high-five. Knowing he had to temper his excitement for a little longer he took a couple of deep breaths.

"I think you should know that Sam and his friends are mercenaries working for the British government. They were sent to kill your leaders."

"Farrar, you bastard —"

Smart's words told Farrar that his last statement had sealed their fate and a genuine smile appeared in his lips for the first time in weeks.

"Goodbye, Sam. I can't say it's been a pleasure knowing you."

Farrar hung up the mobile phone and removed the SIM card, placing it in his pocket. He called his driver and told him to have the car ready in ten minutes, then asked his secretary to book him onto the next flight for London Heathrow.

With Grant and the others out of the way he had a few hours to shut down the Manila operation before heading home to Oxfordshire. The staff would be transferred to other duties and the offices would be handed back to the leasing company, all details which the attaché at the British Embassy would handle on his behalf. His sole concern was to get home to his apartment and pack his bags.

Picking up just his laptop and jacket he walked out of the office for the last time, without giving his secretary so much as a 'goodbye'.

On the drive to his apartment he tossed the SIM card into the street where a thousand tyres would crush it to dust within the hour. When he arrived he told the driver to wait while he went inside to collect the few personal items he'd brought with him from the U.K., mainly clothes and books.

With his suitcase packed it was time to head to the airport, where his ticket was waiting at the Emirates Airline desk, and in the First Class lounge he relaxed with a twelve-year-old malt.

As he sipped the whiskey he was thankful that the end of the operation was in sight. Just another couple of weeks and his career progression would advance another step closer to the top.

* * *

287

When the phone call ended Callinag demanded to know why the British government were sending kill squads to his island. The reply was rather succinct: "That's bullshit!"

"We'll find out soon enough," Dog said, stepping in to calm the situation. "Once your files come back we'll know what to do with you."

"I want to talk to you," Callinag said, and Dog followed him out of the guardhouse.

"The bastard set us up," Smart whispered once they'd gone, his anger apparent.

"Why, though?" Baines wondered.

"Pretty obvious, really," Grant said. "Very few people outside the government know that I'm still alive, and every single day brings the threat that one of us might break the news. It's something I've thought about for the last year, and I know what I would do if I was in their shoes: Get rid of us, permanently."

"We considered that, too," Smart admitted, "but they can't kill us all. We agreed that if one of us dies in suspicious circumstances, the others would go to the papers with our story."

"What if the deaths were above suspicion? Farrar told me that Tris died while on a mission in Iraq, and that happens in our line of work, so it didn't raise any alarm bells with me at the time. That means, of the seven of us that survived the attack last year, there are only six of us left. If Farrar had succeeded in getting us captured and killed by Abu Sayyaf there'd be just three."

"Two," Baines corrected him. "Paul came off his bike a couple of months ago."

"Fell off, or knocked off?" Grant asked.

"The back tyre blew while he was bombing up the motorway. Witnesses said there was no-one near him at the time. Trust me, we checked."

"So with us out of the way there's just Jeff and Carl left, and the secret will die with them."

"That's if they accepted that our deaths were not suspicious," Baines pointed out.

"Of course they wouldn't be suspicious. They can hardly blame the British government if we were killed by terrorists in the Philippines, can they?"

The considered their position for a while, but no matter which way they looked at it they kept coming back to the same conclusion.

"Farrar's trying to bury the evidence — namely us," Smart said.

The others agreed, and the discussion turned to their options. Baines wanted to turn the tables on Farrar but Grant was quick to point out that it was a waste of time.

"Farrar must have been taking orders from someone in power, someone near the top of the political ladder. If we take him out they will just replace him with someone else to finish the job."

"So we take the fight to them?" Smart asked.

"It's that or spend the rest of our lives on the run."

Baines began suggesting a plan of attack, the first stage of which was to grab Farrar and find out who was pulling his strings, but Grant was quick to dampen his enthusiasm.

"One step at a time. First we need to get out of here."

The thought brought them all back to reality. With their photos winging their way to Langley it was only a matter of time before Baines and Smart were identified.

Grant was another story.

If the CIA cross-referenced with the British security services it was possible that a match might come back, but more likely the U.K. government wouldn't want to share the fact that Tom Gray was still alive.

They were considering their next move when Dog and Callinag returned.

"So, Mr. Baines, Mr. Smart, we now know a lot more about you than we did thirty minutes ago," Dog said. He focused on Grant. "You, however, remain a mystery."

Grant simply looked away, not wanting to engage the man, and Dog was content to deal with the other two for the moment.

"Quite a past you guys have," he said, reading from a printout. "Served in the SAS; saw action in Iraq; freelancers for the last five years; and co-conspirators with Tom Gray in the spring of last year."

He looked up from the page. "If you'd tried that stunt in the States you'd be on death row right about now. How come your government let you walk?"

"I guess the PM is a sucker for a pretty face," Baines quipped.

Dog ignored the comment and turned his attention back to Grant. "What about you? You're obviously British, and friends with these guys, yet your picture isn't listed on any database and the name Sam doesn't bring back any matches. How do you explain that?"

Grant maintained his silence, much to Callinag's annoyance.

"Answer the question!" he shouted, but Grant didn't so much as flinch.

"Don't worry, General, Langley is passing their details over to the Brits, so we should have a match real soon. In any case, they'll no doubt be sending someone to take them off our hands." He flipped a lazy salute to the superior officer and took his leave.

* * *

It was four hours later when the reply from Langley came through. Dog looked at the printout and wondered just who the hell this man was, given that the page simply contained the name Sam Grant and the words TOP SECRET in big, bold letters. No matches in the CIA database — or any other database for that matter. NSA had turned up blank, as had the FBI, leaving just the concise response from the Brits.

Orders from Langley were to await their collection by a British team, ETA thirty-one hours.

Back in his office, and with his interest aroused, he spent the next two hours researching Baines, Smart and the whole Tom Gray affair, but there was no mention of a Sam Grant.

There was, however, a strong likeness between Grant and the image of Gray on his screen. Could this be the man sitting in his cell? It would explain the secrecy, especially as Gray was certified dead.

Internet searches for Sam Grant returned nothing that related to his prisoner, adding further weight to his burgeoning theory.

He printed off a photo of Tom Gray and was heading over to the guardhouse when one of his troopers caught up with him and flashed a salute.

"Sergeant Garcia has just reported in, Dog! He's taking heavy fire on hill 178!"

"Casualties?"

"One dead. He's pulling his team back."

Dog grimaced. Callinag wouldn't be happy that one of his men was down.

"Okay, tell Harrison to take two squads in support."

The trooper nodded and ran off to relay the order, while Dog abandoned his trip to the cells and instead headed towards the command centre.

"What's the latest?" he asked as he entered.

290

"Garcia's pulling out. Confirmed one dead, one injured: a bullet to the leg. It's slowing their withdrawal."

Dog grabbed a headset. "Bravo One, Charlie Two, what's your situation, over?"

"We're half a click from the base of hill 178, no pursuit at this time, over."

"What's the enemy strength, over?"

"Upwards of thirty, small arms and mortars, over."

It didn't sound like a typical skirmish: the numbers suggested a much larger concentration of enemy than they normally encountered.

Dog gave Garcia co-ordinates to an exfiltration point and ordered a medivac team to meet them there. With the team now out of danger he crossed the square to the guardhouse, formulating a plan as he walked.

Dusk was approaching, heralding a shift-change for the ubiquitous flying insects. He was thankful for the Army-issue repellent that would keep them at least eight inches from his skin, for a while at least.

Inside the stockade he took his usual seat on the corner of the desk and pulled out the printout he'd made, which had Tom Gray's photo and some notes he'd garnered from the internet. Now and again he would look up at Grant, then back to the page.

"So, it looks like you did some time in the SAS, too, Sam Grant."

He glanced over to the cell but the prisoner remained impassive. Time to crank it up, he thought.

"It also says you're single. Well, you are now that your alcoholic wife rammed herself into a bridge!"

Grant's jaw hardened at the remark, but it was Baines who gave the game away by leaping from his seat and grabbing the bars.

"She wasn't an alcoholic, you worthless shit!"

Dog dismissed the two Filipino soldiers on guard duty and once they were gone he strode over to the cell. "Calm down, son, I didn't mean anything by it. I was just fishing, and I think I just caught me a Tom Gray."

He looked at Grant, who offered no denial. Baines also turned to Grant and shot him an apologetic look.

"So what happens now?" Grant asked.

"Well, a team is en route to pick you up and take you back to England. In the meantime, why don't you explain what you're doing here, and what was that phone call from Farrar all about?"

"Wait! Who exactly is coming to pick us up?"

Dog shrugged. "All I know is a team from the U.K. are on their way and they'll be here the day after tomorrow."

The three men looked at each other. After a few moments it was Grant who made the decision and he told Dog the entire story, starting with Abdul Mansour's attack the previous year. He explained how all three came to be on Jolo and ended on Farrar's phone call and the implications it held for all three of them.

"I know you don't agree with what we did last year, but if you hand us over to them you'll be signing our death warrants."

"That's where you're wrong. What you guys did took balls, but I couldn't say that in front of the General."

"Then let us go."

Dog shook his head. "No can do. The best I can offer is to pass your concerns back to Langley and let them decide."

Grant sprang to his feet. "Are you fucking listening to me? If you mention the name Tom Gray to anyone, you'll be next on their list!"

Dog considered the statement, and with the story he'd just heard he knew it made sense.

"Okay, so I don't tell Langley. But that doesn't leave me with many options."

"Well, we're fresh out of options, too," Grant said. "So I'll make this simple: if you hand us over to them, I'll tell them you know my real identity."

He let the threat hang for a moment.

"Now find a way to get us out of here!"

Chapter 11

Thursday 19th April 2012

When the Emirates flight touched down in Dubai, Farrar was one of the first to disembark from the first class section. After the short walk to his connecting flight he turned his phone on and checked for messages. He was a nervous flyer and had happily complied with the stewardess once she informed him that it could interfere with the flight instruments.

There were seven voicemails, all from his boss, which suggested they weren't welcome home messages. His call was answered on the second ring, the voice exploding in his ear.

"Where the hell have you been?"

"I was on a flight, sir. What's the emergency?"

"What's the emergency? Well, let's see. The last communication I had from you said our three problems had been eliminated. So why did I receive a request for information about them from our American cousins? How do you explain the fact that they are being held at a U.S. base on a remote southern Philippine island?"

Farrar's head was spinning. How could they still be alive? Did they escape, or did Abu Sayyaf let them go? As he pondered the likelihood of both scenarios, a third popped into his head: they hadn't been with Abu Sayyaf when he'd called.

"Are you still there, Farrar?"

His boss's voice brought him back to the moment. "Yes sir, still here. I'll catch a flight back and sort this out personally."

"Don't bother. I've sent a team to do the job. I couldn't wait around all day waiting for you to return my calls. You just get back here and report to my office as soon as you land."

"Yes sir, I'll be there in....," but the line was already dead, and a sinking feeling in the pit of his stomach told him his future was heading in the same direction.

Damn you, Tom Gray!

He sat in the lounge fuming for what seemed an eternity, until self-preservation took over. Perhaps all was not lost. There was still a

293

chance to redeem himself by personally making sure the remaining two hits were executed as planned. His failure in the Philippines could be explained away and once this mission was over he would make damn sure the next went without a hitch.

Once he boarded the plane he declined the offer of champagne, preferring instead to keep a clear head while he fabricated an explanation for his superiors.

* * *

"What makes you think Grant is telling the truth?" Dog asked Garcia towards the end of the debriefing.

He'd given his sergeant a rundown of the information received from Langley, but had stopped short of revealing Grant's true identity.

"These people were dug in, and dug in well." Most of the encounters with the terrorists had taken place as they moved from one temporary base to the next, but this latest battle suggested a more permanent encampment.

"It still doesn't mean an attack is imminent, or that Abdul Mansour is on the island."

Garcia had to agree, but said the shift in the enemy's Standard Operating Procedure suggested they were hunkering down.

"Maybe they just got sick of running," Dog offered. "Either way, it plays into our hands. We don't have to chase them all over the island and we can keep them contained on that hill indefinitely. If necessary we can starve them out."

"They're bound to have hostages," Garcia pointed out. "We'd be starving them, too."

"I've taken that into account. We offer food in exchange for the hostages and eventually they run out of bargaining chips."

He could tell by the look in Garcia's eyes that something was bothering him and asked him to speak his mind.

"Well, they might refuse an exchange and instead start killing hostages until food is delivered. Their regard for human life isn't all that great."

It was something Dog had considered, too, and to be fair to Garcia it was probably the most likely outcome. Grant's recollection of his time with Abu Sayyaf suggested they had just three western hostages and a handful of Filipinos. The locals would probably be the first to go, the American and two Brits being too valuable to simply kill.

294

Having said that, they were quite willing to murder Grant and probably would have, had he not had any help. His planned execution came at a time when they thought a million dollars was on its way, which suggested their need for money wasn't as great as previously thought.

So what made them toss away a million bucks?

The question brought him back to Grant's sighting of Abdul Mansour, and he knew in an instant that the man was telling the truth. He shared his thoughts with Garcia, who concurred.

"He could be telling the truth about an attack, too," Garcia said.

Dog nodded. If Grant was right, a couple of hundred terrorists were about to come charging out of the jungle. He'd need more than a handful of battle-hardened soldiers, some National Guard bridge builders and a heap of — in his opinion — poorly-disciplined Filipinos if he was going to repel them successfully.

"Do we wait for them to launch an attack, or try to stop them before they get here?" Garcia asked.

"We don't have the men to go out and face them. In fact, we are going to be hard pushed to mount a solid defence within our own perimeter. I'll call SOCPAC and see what resources they have available."

He rose from his chair and gestured for Garcia to follow him.

"Before I call this in I want to see if Grant knows what we will be facing," Dog said as they crossed the square to the stockade.

The prisoners were just finishing up a meal when they entered, and Dog waited for the Filipino guards to clear away their dishes before dismissing them.

"Sam, you said an attack was about to take place on this base, and we believe you," Dog said. "We need to know what we're up against."

"How many men, what weapons they have available, anything you can tell us," Garcia added.

Grant told them what little he knew about the enemy's strengths. He had seen them brandishing new M16s and there were several ammo boxes dotted around the camp. There were also the multiple-shot RPGs, but he had no idea how many rounds they had for them. That was all he could be certain of. One or two of the boxes looked like they might contain more RPGs but he hadn't seen the contents, so he couldn't be sure.

"What else?" Garcia pressed.

"There were a few other containers but they were nondescript and could have contained anything from food to a small generator. Apart from the weapons, there's a couple of hundred bad guys and Abdul Mansour.

"How does that stack up against your defensive capabilities?"

"We're slightly outnumbered, but we know how to build a perimeter," Garcia said confidently.

Baines wasn't impressed. "I've seen Abdul Mansour in action, and he knows how to plan a co-ordinated attack at very short notice. Last year he took thirty kids off the streets, gave them AK-47s and managed to get through Tom Gray's defences, which included well-trained armed police officers. Imagine what he could do with two hundred armed men who've already seen their share of battle.

"So tell me, how many skilled troops do you have?"

"Six with combat experience," Dog replied, "plus another seventy National Guard and a hundred locals, give or take. They can all handle a weapon."

"That may not be enough. Can you draw on anyone else in the region?" Smart asked.

"I'm heading over to speak to Special Operations Command Pacific. We'll have all the men we need by the time tomorrow night comes."

He got up to leave, but Grant had some final words of warning.

"Don't underestimate him. Get them to send the best they have, and lots of them."

* * *

When Nabil climbed back to the camp he found Mansour and Abu Assaf were waiting for him. The gunfire had lasted barely three minutes, and the battle was over by the time he'd got there.

"A small patrol," he reported when they asked what had happened. "I estimate five or six men. We killed one that we know of, and took no casualties of our own."

Assaf shrugged off the incident. "We have these skirmishes all the time," he told Mansour. "It is nothing new."

"Perhaps," Mansour mused, but something told him all was not well. "How often do patrols come into this area?"

Assaf had to think about the question for a moment. "The last time they ventured this close was about three months ago," he admitted.

296

"Most of our encounters are in the lower regions, in the valleys and flatlands towards the edge of the forest."

As the last of the twilight gave way to darkness, Mansour made his decision. "The prisoner who escaped must have alerted the enemy, which is why they sent a scout party. We must bring forward the attack before they can prepare their defences."

"You want to attack them in daylight?" Assaf asked, his expression suggesting he wasn't entirely happy with the idea.

"No, we must hit them tonight." He turned to Shah. "Nabil, have you prepared the defences?"

"Everything is in place."

"Good, good." To Assaf he said: "Nabil will lead the attack. Gather your senior men and we will assign them their targets."

Assaf called one of his men over and told him to assemble the others.

"I must leave tonight," Mansour said. "Please ensure the transport is ready to go in three hours."

Assaf handed a phone to another soldier and told him to contact the boat owner with the updated schedule. As he did so, a group of men arrived at the camp with nine children in tow.

Nabil looked at Mansour questioningly. "What are they doing here?" he asked.

"Just a little insurance, my friend. There is no telling how they will retaliate, and a few adult hostages might not be enough to stay their hand. They will think twice if they know there are children in harm's way."

Nabil wasn't happy with the idea, but was not about to question Mansour's decision. Instead he offered to lead the briefing and with Mansour's blessing he went off to prepare the map of the base.

"The boat is on its way," Assaf told Mansour. "I will have my men escort you to the rendezvous point."

Mansour thanked him for his hospitality. "May Allah watch over you; I pray he doesn't need too many martyrs tonight."

"Thank you, my brother. Will we see you again?"

"No. I cannot make this journey again, but I will send others in my place. You can be assured of our continuing support."

He saw that Nabil was about to begin the briefing so he said a quick farewell.

"Once the attack is over I want you to make your way to Sumalata as planned."

Sumalata, set in a bay in one of the seventeen thousand Indonesian islands, was a three-hundred mile journey due south.

"The vessel that brought us here should be able to make the journey in less than a day. I will have someone waiting onshore at one o'clock in the morning for the next seven days. If you don't arrive by then I will assume Allah's need was greater than mine."

After a brief hug, Mansour — carrying his bag and an M16 — joined the four armed men ready to guide him through the pitch black jungle. The Sundalos never ventured into the jungle at night, one of them explained, but that did not prevent them from taking their time. One man took point a hundred yards ahead, ready to raise the alarm if necessary, but the trek passed off without incident.

As Abdul Mansour climbed aboard the banca he saw the sky on the horizon light up as mortars hit their targets, followed moments later by the signature *CRUMP!* and the chatter of distant small arms fire. Saying a prayer for his friend, he gave the order to cast off and began the next leg of his mission.

Chapter 12

Friday 20th April 2012

While Len and Sonny slept soundly on their bunks, Sam Grant lay awake staring at the ceiling. Despite the events of the past few days, it wasn't Farrar or Abdul Mansour that occupied his thoughts, but rather Vick Phillips.

In the short time spent in her company he had seen an inner strength that he'd found alluring, even more so than her considerable physical attributes. She had obviously been deeply affected by the death of the Filipino girl and her parents shortly after her capture, and the constant run-ins with the local forces must have taken their toll, too. Still, she remained resolute, determined not to let the situation completely overwhelm her.

If only Dina had managed to find such courage following Daniel's death, they might still be together, but she simply hadn't been prepared to deal with the tragedy. Her life had been an easy one, brought up with private schooling and all the privileges her parents could bestow, whereas he had been dragged up on a South London council estate and had fought to survive from a very early age. They were as different as could be, and it came as no surprise when Dina's parents objected to the engagement. The fact that he was coming to the end of his military career went some way to appeasing them, and when his business took off his star rose a little higher, but there was always the underlying class gap that he couldn't seem to overcome.

He had loved Dina, of that there was no doubt, but they were from different worlds. She had never been more than dutiful in the bedroom. It was as if love-making was just a necessary — and not entirely pleasant — part of the pregnancy process. Following the birth of their son Daniel the passion had almost completely disappeared, with her focus turning to the needs of their child.

The short relationship with Alma had been much the same to this point. The physical aspect aside, his own passion had been on the wane as with every passing day he realised just how little they had in common.

With Vick, though, it was different. They had only spent a couple of days together, but during their snatched conversations in their rest periods he had felt a real connection. They were both physically active, enjoying running and cycling, and they had similar tastes in music, books and films. An only child, she had never married and had infrequent contact with her parents, who had retired to Australia a few years earlier. She had been offered the chance to go with them but had turned it down in order to continue her career in journalism.

He tried to push thoughts of Vick out of his mind. He was with Alma now, but as he considered their relationship the realisation hit him: he could never return to his Manila home. His life in the Philippines was over, and Alma was not the kind of person who would be suited to a life on the lam. He would do what he could to ensure that she was taken care of financially, but he knew he could never see her again.

His thoughts once again turned to Vick, and he knew it would not be fair to drag her any further into his business. Despite his feelings for the girl, he knew he had to steer clear of her lest she become embroiled in the fight which lay ahead.

His priority was to get out of the cell. After that he had to get word to Jeff and Carl to let them know they were in danger. Beyond that, he didn't know, but he wasn't willing to spend the rest of his life looking over his shoulder.

He was in the process of figuring out the next step when the first mortar round hit the fuel dump a hundred yards from the guardhouse. The shockwave almost picked the building up, and all three were thrown from their bunks. Len and Sonny instinctively scrambled for their weapons, but they soon remembered where they were and realised they had nothing to protect themselves with.

The solitary guard rushed to what was left of the window and looked out at the devastation just as another shell fell in dead ground.

"You have to let us out of here!" Grant shouted. "Those rounds are getting closer!"

The guard ignored him and stuck his rifle through the broken window frame, desperately searching for a target. The sound of small arms fire could be heard between mortar blasts, and the tree line beyond the runway sparkled with each incoming bullet.

"Hey! You have to let us out!"

Len and Sonny joined in, all three trying to get the guard's attention, but his focus was on the attackers. He let off a five-second burst towards the trees but all he managed to do was empty his magazine. As he fumbled for another he suddenly became aware of the prisoners shouting at him.

"Let us out!"

He grabbed the keys from his belt but rather than open the cell he simply looked from the men to the keys, back and forth, wondering if it was such a good idea. Before he could make a decision another mortar round burst a few yards away, showering the hut with red-hot shrapnel. The guard, standing too close to the already shattered window, took the brunt of the force. His shredded body hit the opposite wall and bounced to the floor a few feet from the cell.

Grant tried to grab the keys but they were tantalisingly out of reach. He looked around for something he could use to extend his reach but nothing seemed available, so he whipped off his T-shirt and tried to snag it on the keys in the dead guard's hand. Again and again he tried, but with no luck.

The next shell to land in the camp gave him the help he needed, destroying the guardhouse door and sending chunks of wood in his direction. Grant grabbed a piece around three feet long and finally managed to wrest the keys from the corpse.

He opened the cell and they poured out, looking for weapons. The guard had his M16 but there was nothing else in the room.

"We need to find the Colonel," Len said, snatching the weapon up and inserting a fresh magazine taken from the Filipino's pocket.

The others followed him to the door and they took in the situation. A truck was on fire away to their left, caught in the blast that devastated the fuel dump. Three other buildings were also alight and others had suffered bomb damage. Several Filipino soldiers were firing blindly into the tree line from behind whatever cover they could find, while a few lay dead, having been caught out in the open during the initial barrage.

Sergeant Garcia was trying to get a defence organised and the American troops were doing their part, but his efforts were hampered by the inexperienced local troops, who ignored his orders and continued to fire ineffectively at targets they couldn't see.

Grant pointed to a building with several antennae on the roof. "Comms building," he said, and they all moved towards it at speed. They had to break cover twice but made it safely to the building just as Dog emerged with his rifle. The surprise on his face was obvious but there wasn't time for explanations.

"We need air support," Grant said as he led the group behind the shelter of the building. "The fire is coming from the trees. What have you got in the air?"

"Nothing local. I called it in but SOCPAC say it will be at least forty minutes before they can get anything overhead."

"We'll be lucky to last ten minutes," Len said, a feeling shared by the others.

"What about heavy weapons?" Grant asked.

"We have mortars but they don't have the range to be effective."

"So how come theirs can reach us?" Sonny asked.

Dog led him to the side of the building and pointed towards the chain link fence separating the base from the runway. "On the other side of the airstrip there's Junk Town, built from scraps of corrugated iron and anything else the locals can lay their hands on. They must be holed up in there."

"We need to clear them out. Can you spare a couple of men?"

Dog got on the radio and two of his troops were with them within thirty seconds. The pair couldn't have been more different. One looked like he'd come straight from a Mr. Universe contest, while the other had a similar frame to Sonny — only without the good looks.

"Harrison, Keane, I need you to clear Junk Town. You're looking for mortar teams, number unknown."

"I'll go with them," Baines said.

"I can't sanction that. You stay here."

"Sonny was a CRW instructor for three years," Grant said. "No-one does house-to-house better."

Dog thought for a moment, then nodded. He had been through the Counter-Revolutionary Warfare programme whilst on secondment to Hereford a few years back, and knew how good you had to be to pass the course, never mind teach it.

To Keane he said: "Grab their weapons from the command room and bring three comms units."

The soldier disappeared and was back within a minute, doling out the equipment as well as ammunition. Len handed Grant the M16 as well as a spare magazine, preferring the Heckler & Koch. With everyone geared up, Keane led Harrison and Baines to the main gate to make their circuitous approach to the shanty town. Meanwhile, Dog surveyed the chaos inside the camp.

"We need to help the Sarge get the defence organised," he said, nodding towards Garcia.

They ran from cover and Dog sprinted over to Garcia, who was still struggling to get the Filipino marines to conserve their ammunition and pick their targets. A few National Guardsmen were scattered around the camp, but not as many as Grant had expected to see.

Smart peeled off to the right while Grant took the left and dropped himself between two Filipino soldiers. The shock on their faces barely had time to register before he broke into tutor mode. He tried explaining that they should conserve ammunition but got blank stares in return, so he mimed the actions as he spoke.

"Ba-ba-ba-ba-bang! No good!" he said, making the universal "cut-it-out" motion with his arms. "Bang....bang...bang, good!"

To force the point home he checked chamber on his weapon and squeezed off three staggered, aimed rounds towards the jungle.

"Okay?"

He got nods in return and slapped them on the back before moving on to the next panicking soldier. This one understood English, negating the need for sign language, and Grant took a moment to catch his breath.

As he gulped the cordite-filled air he felt something wasn't quite right.

Images of his previous encounter with Abdul Mansour flooded his mind, and he knew what the problem was. He got on the radio.

"Colonel, who's manning the front gate?"

"No-one! What you see is all we got. Most of the locals live off base and one of the first buildings to be hit was the accommodation block housing the National Guard. Barely ten people made it out."

He was astounded that the Filipino troops were not on base with an attack imminent but this wasn't the time to discuss it. "It's a feint. Mansour doesn't attack head-on: he draws your resources and exploits the weak points."

A moment of silence, followed by: "I'll send someone back there."

"I'll go," Grant replied, and he grabbed the soldier he had been sheltering with.

"Come on!"

Together they ran across the open ground towards the laundry building. From there it was a left turn to the main gate fifty yards away, but something caught Grant's attention as he peered around the corner. It wasn't coming from the gate, but rather from behind him. He turned in time to see the outline of a pick-up truck blazing down the runway, headlights out but a stream of fire erupting from the rear of the vehicle. The accompanying buzz-saw sound told him what was approaching.

"Colonel, mini-gun!" he screamed into the radio as the lance of fire devastated wooden buildings and shredded the wire fence, but Dog had already seen and heard the danger and the net was suddenly alive with his own warnings to get the fuck down.

The truck on the airstrip continued to rain havoc on the camp, puncturing the fuel tank of a jeep and killing the two soldiers who were taking cover behind it. With those deaths they were down to a couple of dozen men, and the number was falling fast as more mortar rounds found their target. From the truck an RPG round shot into the compound and took out the command building, sending flames high into the sky.

Grant got the pick-up in his sights but held fire as the truck moved closer and was illuminated by the fires burning all around him. A plank of wood rose from behind the cab and he could see a figure strapped to it. He couldn't see the face but the white skin and fair hair told him it was certainly not a local, which meant it was one of their prisoners, and only one of them had short, fair hair. He quickly got on the radio.

"Colonel, they have one of their hostages tied to the truck." As an afterthought he added: "His name is Eddie Halton and he's American."

Dog began barking the order to cease fire but the local soldiers were in a shooting frenzy, finally having a target they could see. Rounds peppered the truck, puncturing one of the tyres and sending it fishtailing for a moment before the driver got it back under control. It sped down the runway and out of sight, hidden by the airport terminal building. The respite didn't last long as it did a one-eighty and began the return journey, the Dillon spewing fifty rounds a second into the base.

With one tyre shot out it was a job to control the vehicle as it reached fifty-miles-per-hour, but when both wheels on the passenger side were rendered useless by incoming fire it began to slow and yaw like an aeroplane fighting a side wind. The driver tried his best to keep it straight. His efforts ended when a bullet punched through the side window and continued through his neck, entering three inches below the right ear and exiting the other side, destroying his larynx on the way through. He choked to death on his own blood before the vehicle came to a halt.

The two terrorists in the back continued the assault on the camp. One was preparing the second of six RPG-27s while the one manning the Dillon kept his finger on the trigger, despite the warnings he had received from Nabil. At fifty rounds per second, the 4400 bullets in the belt-fed magazine would be exhausted within ninety seconds of continuous fire. Nabil's instructions were to fire short bursts of around three to four seconds to make sure the ammunition lasted the entire assault, but in the heat of battle it was easy to forget such things. Eight seconds after the pick-up rolled to a stop, the belt feed relinquished its last round. As it did, the RPG round darted towards the mess hall, blowing a huge hole in the side of the building.

The hostage strapped to the back of the cab was doing nothing to deter retaliatory fire, so the terrorists grabbed two of the single-shot RPGs apiece and jumped over the side of the cargo bed. They headed away from the base, sprinting over the grass towards the chain link fence separating the runway from Junk Town. They both threw their weapons over the top of the fence and began the ascent, but as they climbed one was hit in the small of the back and he lost his grip, dropping several feet before landing in a screaming heap. The other, feeling the bullets whizzing through the air around him, scrambled up the fence and launched himself over the barbed wire atop it.

Without stopping to check on his friend he picked up two RPGs and dashed into the middle of the town, just as Sonny and the two Americans approached it from the left.

* * *

From the cover of a food kiosk, Keane surveyed the entrance to Junk Town. Not the official name, it was so-called because each dwelling was made from whatever material the inhabitants could find. Walls were made from reclaimed bricks and stone, while the majority of roofs were constructed from corrugated iron. A few had plastic roofs, while some had nothing more than sheets of polyethylene to protect the occupants from the elements.

Two armed men stood at the mouth of the alley leading into the dark village, their rifles hanging loosely in their hands. One was acting as spotter for the concealed mortar teams while the other simply stood and admired the fireworks display emanating from the base.

Keane turned to the others and let them know what they were facing. Sonny swapped places and gauged the distance to the targets

305

and the ground to be covered. Seeing nothing to hinder the take down, he turned and indicated that he would clear the way using his silenced MP5SD. He got nods in return, pushed the stock of his rifle into his shoulder and broke cover at a crouch.

He approached from their three o'clock and got to within twenty five yards before they spotted him. As they brought their guns up he straightened and double-tapped them both before they even had a chance to get a shot off. Keane — peering around the corner ready to offer covering fire if things went noisy — saw the men drop and signalled Harrison to follow him. They trotted over and helped drag the bodies out of sight, and once again Sonny took the lead as they headed into the maze of makeshift streets.

The attack on the base had brought the population out of their houses, presenting Sonny with a host of false targets. Fortunately for Sonny, they had about enough to spend on clothing as they did on accommodation, and to a man they wore little more than flip-flops and shorts, with T-shirts for the women. He motioned them aside as he passed, the barrel of his MP5 flicking left and right as he searched for anyone carrying anything more threatening than a penknife.

Sonny heard the familiar *WHOOMP!* as another mortar shell shot into the sky and the sound told him the launcher was close. Ten yards ahead he saw a side street open up and motioned towards it. The smell of rotting food and untreated sewage assaulted his nostrils but his focus was on what lay around the corner. As he approached, a figure appeared carrying a rifle and Sonny immediately got a couple of rounds off. The first missed by a gnat's hair but the second caught the target on the forehead, grazing the skin and ricocheting off the bone beneath. A third round found its mark and the figure crumpled, but not before managing to shout a warning.

"Shit!" Sonny cursed. The last thing he need was the situation to go loud with so many bystanders around.

He rushed to the corner and sneaked a peek, just in time to see the mortar team grabbing their rifles. He hit the first with a double-tap but the second was quicker to his weapon and returned fire, causing Sonny to retreat back around the corner. The firing stopped and he counted to five before sticking a quarter of his head out, but the target had gone.

"One went this way," he told Keane. "You two go straight on, see if you can cut him off."

The two Americans continued down the main alley while Sonny followed the fleeing terrorist. The side street ran for seven yards before turning right, and the mortar had been set up at the corner. He glanced around but saw no-one except a woman consoling a young girl.

The unmistakeable chatter of M16s could be heard a couple of streets away, which told him that Keane and Harrison must have found the target. He followed the sound, stepping round the mother and child and on to the next corner where he once again stopped to clear the turn. He saw his quarry disappear around the next corner, rejoining the main thoroughfare and following in the footsteps of his new team mates. Sonny sprinted after him, knowing that he had to catch up before the shooter got on their six.

Training told him that he should stop at the junction and clear it, but with fellow soldiers in danger he took the risk and barrelled around it, a move which saved his life. The target was standing in wait with his rifle pointed at the corner, ready to destroy any face that appeared. As Sonny exited the side street the rifle spat, but the man behind the trigger wasn't expecting a fast-moving target and his reactions were a little slow, the bullet flying harmlessly wide.

Sonny's training gave him the edge in the encounter. Still moving at speed, he brought his weapon up and put two rounds into centre mass. The man fell instantly and Sonny stopped, took a few steps towards him and put another round through his forehead to make sure the threat was fully neutralised.

From further down the alley he heard yet more gunfire and headed towards it, taking a lot more care when he got to any side streets. With bullets flying just outside their front doors the locals had retreated to the relative safety of their ersatz homes and he had the street to himself, so when the rifle appeared from his right he spotted it instantly.

Getting a bead on the target, he took up the tension on the trigger. Another ounce of pressure and the rifle would spit once more: he just had to wait for a face to follow the gun into the open. A second later he got his wish and a lesser man would have pulled the trigger under the circumstances, but Sonny had no equal when it came to distinguishing friend from foe in high-pressure situations. He dropped the barrel and drew in a fetid breath.

"I heard shots," he said.

"We took out another mortar team two streets over," Harrison told him. "We carried on to the other end of the town, it's clear."

Sonny told Keane to stay put and asked Harrison to follow him.

"There's a couple of boxes of mortar rounds back here," he explained as they jogged back to the initial contact point. "Let's put them to good use."

They retrieved the ammunition and lugged it back to where Keane was waiting, his M16 pointing into the air and trying his very best — and failing — to look like the archetypal U.S. Army poster boy.

When the figure emerged from a side street ten yards behind Keane, time slowed for Sonny. He saw the weapon in the man's hand and immediately went for his own gun, at the same time shouting a warning. He wasn't about to drop the box of live shells he was carrying and lost a second and a half placing it on the ground. By this time the RPG was almost on the target's shoulder and Sonny stood, grabbing the MP5 which was resting on top of the box and bringing it up in one smooth motion. His first round left the barrel before he'd even pulled the stock of the rifle into his shoulder and flew a couple of inches wide. The next hit the mark but didn't take the man down, the bullet shattering his left collar bone and throwing him off balance. Another squeeze of the trigger and Sonny expected the man to hit the deck, but the firing pin fell on an empty chamber.

Instinctively he reached for the spare magazine, even though he knew he wouldn't have time to load it. He had just removed it from his pocket when the shot came.

* * *

With the main threat from the mini-gun on the runway over, Grant realised that there was no more fire coming from the tree line, and the mortars had also stopped. Just as it looked like the attack might be over a blast of heat hit him in the back and sent him sprawling. He looked up to see the main gate hanging from its hinges and approaching fast was a second pick-up. It crashed through the twisted metal and came at him on a collision course but he managed to roll himself up against the side of a building just as it sped past. The Filipino soldier had less luck, the truck running over his left leg and snapping it like a twig. His screams of agony were cut short when the gunner in the rear opened up with the Dillon, cutting him in half.

Grant snatched up his rifle but held his fire when he saw that once again there was a hostage strapped to the back of the cab. His heart skipped a beat as he thought it might be Vick, but as the truck passed into the light cast by the numerous fires he could see that the human shield was male, which meant it had to be Moore.

The truck had entered the main square and was driving in a counter-clockwise circle, the gunner and his companion in the back letting loose with all they had. Two soldiers sought cover by diving through a hole in building's wall but the Dillon followed them and sliced through the thin wood as if it were tissue paper. An RPG round followed for good measure, destroying more of the wall and bringing the roof crashing in. Another RPG round was quick to follow, this one completely destroying the guardhouse.

With the enemy in the tree line forgotten, the Filipino soldiers turned their attention to the truck. Grant knew it was only a matter of time before Moore was hit, so he had to neutralise the threat. His main concern was that the guy behind the Dillon was standing just inches from Moore, and with the vehicle constantly moving and jolting it was not going to be an easy shot.

Decision made, he went for the truck's wheels and engine block, emptying a whole magazine into the front of the vehicle as it swung its nose towards him. The tyre on the passenger side immediately went flat but it did little to kill the speed. The truck continued on its course, showing its back end to Grant, and he went for the rear tyres, puncturing them both. In the back of the truck his actions hadn't gone unnoticed, and an RPG with Grant's name on it was thrown over the terrorist's shoulder. He had his finger on the trigger when Dog took him out with a single, clean head shot.

With his steering becoming erratic, Nabil Shah knew that it wouldn't be long before he became a sitting duck. He gunned the engine and headed for the gate but found Grant standing in his way, inserting a fresh magazine into his rifle. This was the man Abdul had been so concerned about, and killing him was the least he could do for his master. Foot hard to the floor, he drove straight at Grant in the hope of knocking him down as he made his exit.

He didn't get within five yards.

Grant walked the line of bullets from the bottom of the windscreen to the top, shattering the glass and almost splitting the driver down the middle. The truck veered wildly and buried itself in the remains of a shower block, slamming the gunner against the back of the cab where he slumped onto the deck of the cargo bay.

Grant ran over to finish the gunner off from close range but when he pointed the rifle over the side wall he saw just the terrorist Dog had taken down. Before he had time to wonder where the gunner was he took a punch to the right temple that floored him. It felt like he'd been hit by a grizzly bear, and when he managed to look up his hazy vision told him he wasn't far wrong.

When the pick-up had hit the wall, Ox had jumped over the other side and snuck around the back of the vehicle. He now stood next to Grant and was reaching down for the M16 he had dropped.

Groggy, Grant pulled his knees up and kicked Ox square in the chest, knocking him backwards. He rolled onto his side to reach for the weapon but Ox was on him quickly and stamped on his arm. He brought his other foot crashing down on Grant's face, smashing his nose. With blood pouring and tears in his eyes Grant struggled to get his act together. He knew that if he didn't move quickly he would be dead in moments, and any action was much better than inaction.

He got up on one knee and launched himself at the blurry figure in front of him, managing to get both hands around Ox's waist. He pumped his legs and lifted with all the strength he could muster, hoping to catch the man off balance, but Ox grabbed his wrists and easily managed to pull him off. A knee in the face followed and Grant collapsed, spent. He was simply too dazed to put up any more resistance and Ox could see it. He picked up the rifle and aimed it at Grant's head, no emotion on his face whatsoever. A volley of fire followed, and Grant's face was covered with blood.

It had come from Ox's chest, ripped open as Len put half a dozen rounds through his spine. Smart put his hand out and helped Grant to his feet.

"Can you still handle a weapon in that state?"

Grant wiped the blood — both his and Ox's — from his face and assured him he could. With the pick-up destroyed the firing from the tree line had recommenced, pinning down the few remaining defenders. It wasn't long before he heard the faint sound of a mortar shell leaving the tube and he braced for the impact, but the explosion came from the tree line. Round after round crept along the edge of the jungle, with a couple of RPGs adding to the pyrotechnic display. As a result, the incoming fire petered out, giving Grant time to take stock of the situation.

Less than a dozen men were left standing in the camp, with scores of dead littering the area. Fires burned in the majority of the buildings and not a single vehicle was left serviceable.

While others began tending to the wounded, Grant gingerly helped Moore down from the pick-up. He had suffered several gunshot wounds and was in shit state, but none of the injuries seemed life-threatening. A couple had passed straight through his right arm without hitting bone but one had lodged in his right femur.

"Lie still," Grant said. "We'll get you to a hospital as soon as possible."

"Is E.. Eddie o..o..kay?" Moore asked, his breath staggered as shock set in and adrenalin pumped through his body.

Grant got up and saw a couple of soldiers at the pick-up on the runway. The way they cut his bindings and caught him as he collapsed like a sack of potatoes told him the worst. There was no way to sugar coat it.

"Sorry Robert…"

"Moore closed his eyes, taking in the news. After a few moments they flashed open and he grabbed Grant's arm.

"Abu Sa..Sayyaf," he stammered. "They ha..have more hos...hostages. Kids."

A Filipino joined them and administered morphine, then went to work with his supply of bandages taken from the remains of the medical unit. They applied tourniquets and once Moore was stable Grant left him in the soldier's care.

He found Dog surveying the grisly scene in the accommodation block.

"Why the hell did you let the soldiers go off base when you knew we were about to face an attack?"

"It wasn't my call," Dog said. "I shared your intel with the General but he dismissed it. He said Abu Sayyaf are cowards and wouldn't dare attack his base."

Grant was about to comment on the typical officer arrogance but thought it best not to offend the Colonel. He felt a hand on his shoulder and found Sonny standing next to him.

"Damn, these boys are quick on the draw!"

"We cowboys have a reputation to keep up," Harrison beamed.

"There I was staring down the launcher of an RPG with my dick in my hand when Harrison whips out his SIG P226 and puts a bullet between the man's eyes from twenty-five yards." He patted his new best friend on the back. "We gave them a taste of their own mortars and sent them packing."

Len joined them and interrupted the back-slapping session. "We gotta go."

Grant looked at Dog. "Colonel?"

Dog shifted his focus from the dead to those who had survived. Some went about their work like automatons while others just stood and stared at the carnage, the shock of battle still to sink in. There was no celebrating the fact that they had managed to repel the attack; just the realisation that they'd evaded death's reach by the narrowest of margins.

"You guys saved a lot of lives today," he finally said. "Go. Get as far away as you can."

"What will you say when they arrive to pick us up?"

"I'll tell them you're missing, presumed dead."

Grant thanked him, but decided to push his luck further. "We could do with some gear."

"What do you need?"

With daylight only a few hours away there wasn't time to get the equipment Sonny and Len had stashed at the LUP. He gave Dog a list, including hand guns, knives, ammo, three sets of NVGs and some DPMs to replace his jeans and filthy sando.

"That tells me you're not planning to leave the island," Dog said, letting his expression tell Grant what he thought of the idea.

Grant didn't try to deny it. "How do you think the General is going to react when he gets here to find his base has been destroyed? Colonel, you know him a lot better than I do, but would I be far wrong if I said he'll want to launch a retaliatory strike within the next twenty-four hours?"

Grant took the lack of response as a Yes. "They still have a female British hostage, and Moore told me they are also holding some kids. If the local troops go in, they will all be in real danger and you know it."

Dog indeed knew. No matter how much training he provided the local troops it was all forgotten the moment they got a sniff of the enemy. The hostages would be stuck in the middle of indiscriminate fire with no way to protect themselves, and casualties would be a certainty.

"We got news of a raid at a small school late yesterday evening. The nun and a guard were killed and nine kids were snatched." A father himself, Dog couldn't bear to think what they were going through. He certainly couldn't let Callinag go in with all guns blazing.

"What's your plan?"

312

"Short version? Rescue the hostages and kill any fucker who tries to stop us. We'll work the rest of the details out on the way."

That brought a brief smile from Dog, but it was tempered by the thought of just three men — no matter how well trained — going up against a camp full of Abu Sayyaf. Sure, they'd taken losses tonight, but there was no way of telling how many. There could still be upwards of a hundred and fifty of them dug in, and with the advantage of the high ground, too.

If his team hadn't been handed a non-combatant role as part of Operation Freedom Eagle, if they had been allowed to do things their own way, he knew he wouldn't be staring at a pile of bodies right now. He also knew he wouldn't get authorisation to launch a rescue mission of his own, even if he did paint it as an attempt to capture Abdul Mansour, and SOCPAC wouldn't let him interfere with any action Callinag decided to take.

Still, there was more than one way to circumvent direct orders. He called his entire team and they were standing before him within a minute. He introduced them to the trio. Garcia, Harrison and Keane they already knew. Evans and Shaw rounded off the SAD complement.

"You guys up for a hunt?" Dog asked his men quietly.

Their reaction was exactly what he expected, every one of them thrilled at the prospect of a proper mission for a change. He spelled out his idea.

"Keane, take these three and get them kitted out with whatever they need. Once they're geared up tell them how to get to the trail, then come running three minutes later to tell me they escaped. I'll order the five of you to go after them. We'll do it nice and loud so it squares things with Callinag when he asks where my team is."

Nods all round.

"Meet up at the mouth of the trail and Grant will give you the details of the mission. He's been inside the camp, so listen to what he says."

His men indicated that they had no problem with that directive.

"They have kids in there," Dog said. "They are the priority. Other hostages second, Abdul Mansour third."

The thought of a group of kids in the middle of a firefight cooled their bravado a little, if anything making their mission that much more critical.

"What about afterwards?" Evans asked. "I mean, what about these guys?"

Dog considered it for a moment. "You didn't find them. You were looking for them and came across the camp where you were fired upon. You're allowed to use deadly force in self defence, so that's how we'll report it."

No-one had any questions, so Keane led the trio to the armoury to grab the equipment they needed. At least a couple of shells had hit the building but fortunately none of the ammunition had taken a direct hit. Grant selected a box of 9mm rounds for the Heckler & Koch machine guns as well as two boxes of 5.56mm for those using the M16s. After picking a SIG P226 for himself he told the others to look for smoke and fragmentation grenades, which they found in a locked cabinet. He also spotted a box of flares and some grenades for the under slung M203s. He helped himself to a few of each.

"What about knives?" Grant asked.

"We'll have to scavenge for the rest, including your fatigues," Keane told him. He led them to the SAD hut which was separate from the National Guard accommodation. It too had sustained damage, but Keane was able to find a spare set of clothes for Grant in Harrison's locker. He also raided the foot lockers and found a pair of boots for Grant and two knives, which he gave to Len and Sonny.

"Shit!"

Keane's NVGs had been damaged in the raid, the delicate equipment not being able to stand up to the pounding they'd taken. Another pair was completely smashed but they found two sets which were functioning.

Grant finished changing and began jotting down a note on a small piece of paper.

"The trail begins around five hundred metres from the camp," Keane told them. "Take a right out of the gate and you'll see it on your right hand side. It's nothing more than a dirt track, so keep your eyes peeled. Once you get into the trees, go on for another fifty metres and we'll meet you there soon."

Grant handed him the slip of paper and asked him to pass it to the Colonel, then the trio grabbed their gear and jogged up the road, finding the track near where Keane had said it would be. They followed it into the outer reaches of the jungle and occupied their time by filling their magazines with the ammunition they'd brought along.

"I thought we were going to be heading back to warn Carl and Jeff," Len said, concerned that his friends in the U.K. were still in danger and unaware of it.

"I asked the Colonel to call Timmy Hughes in Singapore," Grant said. "He'll ask Timmy to gives the boys the heads-up and expect a call from us. If we make it out of here, that is."

"Which brings me on to my next question," Len said. "Why exactly are we here? Is it the kids, Abdul Mansour, or the girl?"

Grant had known these two men for too long — and had been through too much with them — to even think about lying. As a father who had lost his own son at a tender age, he couldn't in all conscience sit back and let those kids go through a major attack. He also blamed Mansour for putting him in this position in the first place. Without his interference, Grant would be a free man in his own country rather than a fugitive. Without a doubt, though, the main driving force was Vick Phillips, and he admitted as much.

"Do you still want to tag along?" he asked them.

"Do bears shit themselves when they see me in the woods? Of course I'm coming along!"

Sonny also agreed, and they continued their preparation for another fifteen minutes until they caught sight of the American team approaching.

"Sorry we're late," Harrison said in his Texas drawl. "The General turned up just as we were ready to leave. He brought a shit-storm along for good measure."

"Why?" Grant asked. "He was told that an attack was imminent and he ignored the warning. Even if you don't think a threat is credible you prepare for it, you don't order all of your troops off base."

"Yeah, it's the Colonel's problem now," Len said.

"It will soon be our problem," Keane said. "Callinag wants to hit them at first light, which is why he wasn't happy with us disappearing like we did."

"How long does that give us?" Sonny asked, and was told they had a little over four hours.

"There must be about a hundred Abu Sayyaf hightailing it back to their camp right now," Harrison said. "If we can get on their tail we should be able to take a few out."

"We could," Len agreed, "but that might alert them to our presence. I say we let them get back, let the adrenalin wear off and take them while they sleep."

Jones asked what they would do if they weren't in a hurry to get back and a quick discussion on possible scenarios took place. Grant asked for a map of the area and wanted to know the likely route Abu Sayyaf would take during their retreat.

"If we stay on this track, are we likely to run into them?" he asked.

"Not for some time, if they take the shortest way home," Garcia told him, indicating the markings on his map. "There is a network of tracks throughout the area, and they are most likely to follow this route."

He traced a line from the airstrip to the top of Hill 178, and then drew another from their current location to the same destination point.

"We remain roughly seven hundred metres from them until we get to this point." He indicated a spot a kilometre from the terrorist camp, and Grant could see the two tracks converging.

"I say we get a sprint on and get there first. The fewer people in the camp, the better our chances of securing the hostages."

With everyone in agreement they divided up the ammunition, checked their pockets and pouches to make sure they didn't rattle as they ran, and then set off at a shade over jogging pace. The dirt track soon gave way to denser jungle and what was once a clear path became nothing more than a narrow channel through the undergrowth. The sound of fixed-wing fighters could be heard overhead and Grant hoped they'd been informed about the hostages plus the fact that friendly forces were in the area. If they hadn't, it could turn very hot, very quickly.

The Americans, being familiar with the route, each took a turn on point, remaining a hundred yards ahead of the others. They would stop at regular intervals to switch point man and listen for any sign of the enemy, but the first leg of their journey went without incident.

After an hour and a half they reached the spot where they would begin to close on the enemy and Grant suggested a two-man patrol take the NVGs and scout the area ahead. While they did, he and the others took the opportunity to catch their breath. Although he'd been fit for most of his life, a ninety minute run through the jungle in oppressive heat was taxing enough for anyone, and he was glad to see he wasn't the only one suffering.

He brushed aside some dead leaves and used a stick to draw in the soft earth.

"As I remember it, the camp is circular, roughly seventy yards across. The perimeter is lined with trees and there are more trees dotted throughout which they use to rig their hammocks. The hostages were being held over here but that may have changed.

"At the back of the camp the hill continues on to the summit, so we should be able to approach from these three sides." He used the stick to indicate possible entry routes.

Sonny and Shaw returned after twenty minutes, and the news was both good and bad.

"There isn't a lot of sound coming from the area, which suggests they aren't back yet, but those who stayed behind are nicely dug in. There's a track leading up to the camp and we saw movement from a couple of fox holes either side of it. If we go in that way we'll be torn apart."

"We could try skirting to the left or right of the track and get to the camp that way," Len said, but Sonny explained that they had tried that and spotted another fox hole not far from the first.

"My bet is that they have a ring all the way around the camp," he said, although he admitted that they hadn't had time to verify it.

"Are they two up in each hole?"

"It looks like just one," Shaw said. "I would have expected two, but maybe they sent the majority of their people on the assault."

Grant was acutely aware that time was short, and they had to make a decision.

"We can't hang around forever. Their wounded might be slowing them up but that doesn't mean we have all night. I say we clear those two holes, go straight up the middle and surprise the hell out of anyone still in the camp."

He waited for dissenters but there were none.

"Okay. Sonny, how close do you think you can get to them?"

"We can get to within fifty yards easily. Any closer and we risk detection."

Grant asked who was comfortable with a head shot from that distance and two of the Americans declared it an easy take down.

"Ever use the MP5 before?" he asked them. They had in fact used the naval variant, so they were given the task of clearing the way.

"Once the track is open I need you to get as close to the camp as possible and report numbers and locations. We'll be right behind you and when we know where the x-rays are we split into two-man teams."

He paired everyone up, with Len and Sonny working together while he would accompany Evans.

317

"We need to keep this as quiet as possible, otherwise we'll have them crawling out of their holes and they'll be coming at us from all sides. Once it goes noisy get those NVGs off straight away because I'll be popping flares. Hopefully it won't come to that: I'd much rather cure their SBA while they're sleeping."

"SBA?" Harrison asked, puzzled.

Sonny smiled. "Still Being Alive."

Shaw and Garcia took the NVGs and silenced weapons and made their way to their positions. The area ahead of them was bathed in a sea of light-green twilight as the optical core of the NVGs magnified the light from the barely-visible quarter moon and allowed them to see distinct shapes impossible to distinguish with the naked eye.

"When you get into position and have a target, send me two clicks," Garcia whispered. "I'll respond with the same when I'm eyes-on."

They split up, one either side of the dirt track leading up to the plateau. On their bellies they crawled towards their targets, ever mindful to clear away any fallen twigs or dry leaves that could create noise and give their location away. This cautious approach meant it was six minutes before they were on target.

Shaw brought up his weapon and trained it on the figure beneath the canopy and sent the signal to his sergeant, getting two clicks in reply. There wasn't a lot to aim at through the eight-inch gap, especially as he could only see the top half of the head, but as a former marine he knew how to shoot. All marines needed to attain the rank of marksman, the lowest grade required to exit initial training. Shaw had not only beaten the minimum required score but also exceeded that needed to earn the sharpshooter badge, his skills giving him the honour of being called an expert. He saw the current shot, a four-inch target from fifty metres, about as difficult as hitting a buffalo's ass with a banjo, especially as the fool thought it a brilliant idea to smoke while on lookout. He was lit up like a Christmas tree, just inviting a bullet.

Shaw was happy to oblige.

Five seconds later his night sights showed a puff of green exit the back of the head and he signalled the kill to Garcia, who responded in kind a few seconds later. They waited to see if the alarm had been raised but they heard nothing to suggest they had given the game away.

"Clear," Garcia said into his comms unit, and the others moved up cautiously to join them. By the time Grant arrived Shaw was already approaching the camp. Keeping his head just below the edge of the plateau he manoeuvred towards a tree and used it to hide half of his profile as he slowly rose to view the scene. He took six seconds to take in the details before slowly drawing back, making no sudden movements likely to draw him to anyone's attention.

Garcia watched as Shaw relayed the details and as he had the only other pair of NVGs he translated the signals for the others. With the camp being circular, Shaw represented positions analogous to a clock face.

"Hostages are at the four o'clock, ten metres in, two guards on them. Five more in the centre of the camp, talking around a fire. Between eight and ten o'clock there are seven or eight sleeping. Three sleeping at one o'clock, and four more sleeping at three o'clock.

"There's a mini-gun fifteen metres in, and it's pointing towards the track, two up."

"Any sign of Mansour?" Grant asked. Garcia relayed the question over the net but the response from Shaw was a shrug of the shoulders.

Twenty four targets didn't represent a massive force, but with almost half of them awake it was going to get noisy a lot earlier than Grant wanted. The obvious first targets were the guards on the hostages and the two manning the Dillon, a thought he shared with the others.

"Agreed," Garcia said. He hit the throat mike so that Shaw could hear his instructions. "I'll take the two on the hostages and Shaw can take out the mini-gun. After that we both go for the five in the middle. If we can take them down without waking the others we'll clear the rest. If at any time the alert goes out, the rest of you pick your targets.

"Grant and Evans, you go right. Baines and Smart go left. I'll take Harrison down the centre along with Keane and Shaw.

"Any questions?"

There were none, just two clicks from Shaw to acknowledge the instructions.

"Good luck, gentlemen."

Chapter 13

Friday 20th April 2012

The overriding principle behind any plan is KISS: Keep It Simple, Stupid! That was what Grant had always been taught, and what they were about to attempt was as simple as they could make it, under the circumstances. As with any plan, there was always the unexpected that simply couldn't be factored in, and that was why the ability to adapt instantly often meant the difference between death and survival.

Grant was less than ten seconds into his latest mission when it all went to shit, and that ability kicked in.

Just as they entered the camp, a guard left his defensive position and tracked along the side of the hill in search of a cigarette from his friend in the adjacent hole. Finding him with a bullet in the forehead, he shouted a warning that brought everyone to their feet.

With their cover blown, Shaw kicked off the assault, taking out the two men who were readying the mini-gun. As he did so, Garcia dispatched one of the men guarding the hostages, but the other was quicker to the danger and managed to duck down behind the prisoners. He raised his weapon and fired over the heads of the children in the direction of the attackers, spraying bullets in a sweeping arc.

Grant shouted his own warning to those wearing the NVGs and popped one of the flares, bathing the scene in an artificial light which cast deep shadows and gave the camp an eerie feeling. With one eye closed to protect his own night vision he ran to the right, firing as he went. He managed one hit but the element of surprise was lost and their targets had gone to ground.

He got to the tree line and popped a smoke grenade, lobbing it beyond the group of hostages, then continued his run to get round the back of them. The remaining guard was lying on his back and switching out magazines when Grant got to him, and he smashed the butt of his rifle into his face, knocking the fight out of him. Grant drew his pistol, held it to the man's forehead and grabbed him around the throat.

"Where is Mansour?" He screamed into the bloodied face. The reply was muted but he understood the single word: "Wala"

Mansour was gone.

Grant put a round between the man's eyes.

"Tom!"

Vick was on her feet and picking her way through the crowd of children who were cowering on the ground, and the sight of her made Grant hesitate for a second. Despite her being his main reason for taking part in the assault he was caught off guard and forgot himself for a brief moment. It was only the sensation of a bullet whizzing past his head that shook him out of his reverie.

"Get down!" he shouted, spinning towards the trees. Before the flare gave up the last of its light he saw figures climbing the hill towards the camp, firing as they advanced. Evans was already engaging them and Grant joined in, pinning them down. He grabbed a fragmentation grenade and lobbed it towards them but instead of landing and exploding it ricocheted off a rock and detonated harmlessly beyond them. Evans had more luck with his M203. He aimed at the ground to the right of a tree and the resulting blast dismembered the man standing behind it.

"We need to clear a path and get these kids out of here," Grant said into his mike. It wasn't quite a shout but it conveyed the urgency of the moment. He turned and sent another flare rocketing towards the leafy canopy and as he did he saw a figure approaching through the bank of smoke. The Dillon, still on its tripod, was cradled in his right arm, and he was dragging the belt-fed magazine behind him. Grant brought up his rifle and was a millisecond away from dropping him when the smoke parted and he made out Harrison's features.

With a huge grin that said: 'I always wanted one of these,' he stopped at the top of the slope and let rip into the jungle. Smaller trees disintegrated as he swept the muzzle of the weapon from side to side, and the incoming fire stopped abruptly as the attackers were cut down.

"We have the kids and an exit," Grant said over the net. "Everyone, on me!"

He screamed for the adults and children to get down the hill, he and Evans urging them along with helpful shoves; in the heat of battle, there just wasn't time for niceties.

On the other side of the camp Len and Sonny were being pinned down by fire from in front and from their left. Keane eased the pressure with a couple of well-aimed M203 rounds and was readying a third when a bullet caught him in the chest and he fell backwards, his gun slipping from his dead hands.

"Keane is down!" Shaw shouted, pouring more fire onto the enemy. A couple of grenades followed and the response from the Filipinos dwindled, allowing them all the opportunity to crab their way over to Grant. More smoke grenades were thrown to mask their retreat and soon the only gunfire came from the few remaining Abu Sayyaf, shooting blindly into the haze in the futile hope of hitting targets long since out of their line of sight.

Vick had assumed the lead and was guiding the other hostages down the hill when Grant screamed for her to stop. He had come across one of the defensive positions and the plastic triggers for the Claymore mines were all too familiar. He called Sonny over.

"Trace this to the mine and watch out for trip wires. We'll take them with us, just in case."

They slowly gathered the wire in as they walked down the hill, keeping a keen eye out for signs that they were rigged to explode automatically.

Shaw and Garcia had remained near the top of the hill and as a couple of faces peered over the edge they did nothing, in the hope of sucking more targets into their sights. Unfortunately one of the terrorists raised his weapon with the aim of hitting a fleeing figure and both men were forced to open up, cutting him down. They got a barrage of incoming fire in return. The shooters were lying flat inside the camp while extending their arms over the edge and spraying lead indiscriminately. Fortunately their aim was too high to endanger life and Shaw sent a fragmentation grenade arcing into their midst in order to silence them.

The explosion brought an end to the immediate battle.

Grant and Sonny reached their mines without killing themselves or anyone else and they deactivated their respective devices.

"Take point," Grant said to Garcia as he joined up with them. "We need to get these kids out of here before the others turn up." He took a moment to get his bearings. "They'll be coming from the north, so we need to head west. Are there any towns that way?"

"No, there's nothing. We'll have to track west and head north after a couple of clicks. That'll bring us out near the airport and we should be able to avoid any contact."

"Okay, you lead the way." Grant called the men together and allocated their positions. "Shaw, you stay on our right flank and keep your eyes peeled. Harrison, Evans, take the rear and cover our retreat with the mini-gun. The rest of us will help keep the kids quiet."

The adult hostages were having trouble with this as most of them were as frightened as the children, but with Grant, Sonny and Len there were now almost enough adults to take care of one child each. The men were assigned to the larger children, leaving the smaller ones for the women just in case they had to carry them at any point.

One more adult would have been perfect, but it took at least two people to carry the Dillon along with its magazine and power unit. Even with a quarter of its rounds expended, the entire unit still weighed close to two hundred pounds.

Grant gathered them all together and explained the situation, choosing words he hoped the young ones would understand.

"We're taking you home to your parents now, but there are some bad men looking for us, so we have to be very quiet."

He was sure the pained expressions on their faces were due to having this ugly foreigner address them, but Vick leaned over and whispered in his ear.

"They're orphans."

Grant let loose a quiet expletive. "Okay, then we'll take you back to the orphanage."

This didn't go down well, either.

"It was run by one woman, Sister Evangelina. She was hacked to death in front of them."

Of all the battles he'd taken part in, Grant had a feeling this was one he was not going to win.

"You tell them," he whispered back. "Just make sure they know to keep quiet."

Vick had obviously gained their trust during the short time they'd been together. The children nodded, a few smiling, when she explained that they were going to take them somewhere safe and give them some hot food and a soft, comfortable bed.

"But you all have to stay close to your grown-up and do as they say," she emphasised, "and be very, very quiet."

More nods, and she declared them ready to go. Grant sent Garcia on ahead and gave him a two minute start before leading his charges into the darkness. Daylight was still another two hours away and their progress was slow to begin with. The moon was struggling to penetrate the treetops and what little light got through cast shadows across their path, so they didn't know if their feet were about to fall on shade or a hole in the ground.

Garcia reported in every two minutes, letting everyone know that he was still alive as well as reporting any hazards or obstacles the kids might have trouble with. For their part the children behaved as well as Grant could have hoped, but their first challenge lay just yards ahead.

He heard the river before he saw it. When he reached the bank he saw that it was at least twenty feet across, and although the surface water wasn't racing there was always the undercurrent to consider. Garcia was waiting for him.

"Should be fine for us to cross, but the kids might find it more difficult."

Grant agreed, and offered a solution. "Form a chain and help them across?"

"That works for me. I'll send Harrison ten yards downstream, just in case one of them gets away from us."

They explained the plan to the others, who were much happier to have the help of the soldiers rather than make the crossing by themselves.

Harrison set the mini-gun on its tripod and walked a few yards down the bank, where he eased himself gingerly into the river before wading out towards the centre. By the time he reached the halfway point it was lapping above his navel, which equated to neck-high for the adult Filipino hostages, never mind the children.

Shaw remained in the trees, keeping an eye out, while the other five men entered the water and formed a line from one bank to the other. Grant could feel the undercurrent constantly tugging at his calves and knew it wouldn't be long before they started to cramp up, so he beckoned to the first person.

The Chinese male was the first across, followed by his wife a minute later. One by one they crossed the river until there was just Vick and two of the children remaining.

Shaw's voice came over the radio. "We've got company."

"Where and how close?"

"This side of the river, a hundred metres and closing. I see eight…no, make that twelve."

Grant knew there wasn't much time before they were spotted, and he had to get the remaining people across. He urged Vick to send the next child over quickly, but his actions told her something was wrong. In a panic, she was a little too forceful with the young girl and rather than guide her into the hands of Grant she virtually pushed her into the river. The girl lost her footing immediately and her head went under the water, reappearing a few feet further downstream.

"Help her!" Vick pleaded to Harrison. Everyone else held their breath, as if doing so might prevent her cry from carrying to the enemy, but Shaw confirmed the worst.

"They heard us," he said. "Get them across, I'll cover you."

He immediately began picking off the targets one by one using the silenced weapon, but as each went down another two seemed to appear from nowhere. With their numbers swelling and their advance quickening, they began returning fire in all directions, still not sure where the attack was coming from. They soon got an idea when Shaw switched to the mini-gun and sent a six second burst in their direction. Over a dozen were killed and the rest hit the jungle floor seeking whatever cover they could find. A few had the nerve to return fire but their vision was limited to a few feet and their bullets flew wildly. Shaw picked up on their muzzle flashes and began picking them off with the Dillon, firing a short burst before shifting his aim and hitting them again, until finally they got the message and held their fire.

Harrison had plucked the girl from the current and carried her over to the far bank where she was reunited with the others. Vick, meanwhile, was shaken by the incident and Grant had to climb out of the river to get the remaining child. After passing her over to Sonny he went back for Vick.

"Come on," he said, taking hold of her arm. "This is the last hurdle. Once we're across we'll be home free."

She followed his lead, refusing to release her grip on his hand until they reached the safety of the opposite bank. Shaw was still pinning the enemy down whenever he saw any sign of movement and Garcia told him to join up with them. Rather than leave the Dillon to the enemy, Shaw firstly emptied the magazine in their direction before pressing the latch on the safing top cover and opening it, which put the weapon into 'safe' mode. He then extracted a pin from a fragmentation grenade and jammed it between the latch and its housing. The sergeant took up the defence while he navigated his way to the other side, and when the grenade exploded it tore off the latch, rendering the weapon unusable. Grant had calmed Vick down enough to get her to let go of him and was waiting with the Claymores when he climbed up the bank.

"Let's get into the jungle and leave an obvious trail," he said. "I'll set the first one up after a hundred yards and the other fifty yards after that."

They set off once again, this time at a faster pace. When they came to a good spot, Grant stopped and urged the others to continue onwards. Garcia pulled out a device and began punching keys.

"Just marking the position on my GPS," he said when he saw Grant's quizzical expression. "If it doesn't get tripped in the next hour we'll come back and disarm it once reinforcements arrive."

Grant secured one end of the tripwire around the trunk of a tree and pulled it across the path they had created before securing the other end in the trigger mechanism. He then covered the mine itself with detritus from the surrounding area and moved on to set up the next one.

With both traps set they jogged after the others, happy in the knowledge that if they were still being pursued the mines would at least slow their efforts, if not halt them altogether.

After another twenty minutes the first signs of morning broke through the trees, bringing with it a downpour. A muffled explosion from their rear signalled one of the traps being sprung and that told them they had a sizeable lead on those following. Grant saw it as the ideal time to take a short rest and he showed the kids how to catch rainwater in leaves to quench their thirst. It had been a long time since any of them had taken on liquid and he decided to let them drink their fill before moving on again.

Vick was standing a few feet away from him, her face pointing towards the heavens as she enjoyed the impromptu shower. Despite the setting — or perhaps because of it — she struck Grant as the most beautiful creature he'd ever seen, and in that instance he knew he could never bear to let her go. He also knew that it would be unfair, even irresponsible, to drag her into what was undoubtedly going to be a titanic struggle to reclaim his former life.

His thoughts were interrupted when she came over and put a gentle hand on his arm.

"I'm sorry for making all that noise at the river," she said. "I just panicked."

Grant told her not to worry about it. No-one had been hurt and they were almost out of danger. It was a bittersweet thought, as he knew it would mean saying goodbye for the last time.

"I haven't even thanked you for saving our lives," she said, and kissed him softly on the cheek.

"Come with me."

The words were out of his mouth before he knew it, and he couldn't tell who was more shocked by them. For the first time in his life his heart had been battling his head, and that simple peck on the cheek had been the clincher.

Vick saw the look of panic on his face and regained her composure before he could retract the request. "Okay."

Grant was about to backtrack, to make an excuse for the outburst, when Sonny interrupted and told him that Garcia wanted a word with them. He grabbed his weapon and they walked over to the sergeant, his thoughts still jumbled.

"The Colonel has been in touch. He said that Callinag has sent out the first of his patrols and they should be in the area pretty soon."

"That's not good," Grant said. "If they see us it is going to raise a lot of questions and we can't afford to hang around to answer them."

"I know, the Colonel explained your situation. I was going to tell you a few minutes ago but I didn't want to interrupt your reunion." He nodded towards Vick with a knowing smile and Grant wondered if his feelings for her were as obvious to everyone else. Their sly grins confirmed the worst.

"Bollocks to you lot! What else did the Colonel say?"

"Your friend has arranged to pick you up ten miles off the west coast of the island. He'll be there in forty eight hours." Garcia read off the co-ordinates to the remaining Claymore so that Evans could transfer them to his own device before handing his own GPS over to Grant.

"Your rendezvous is the first number in the list," Garcia said, explaining how the device worked. "I've named it Timmy so you know which one it is. Just select it from the list and it brings up a map showing your current location and the destination."

Grant took the device, hit the Back button and saw two other items on the list: Meeting and Sleep. "What are these?"

Garcia explained that Sleep represented a small cave four miles to the south that they could hide in until they were ready to head out to sea. It was an area of little activity and so the chances of being found were slim. "The Colonel is making arrangements for a boat to be left at this location," Garcia said, bringing up the Meeting co-ordinates.

"It will be delivered at ten tomorrow evening, which will give you roughly six hours to get on station."

Grant stowed the device in his pocket and thanked them for helping with the rescue.

"You've got a good team here, Sergeant. I'm sorry about Keane."

There was naturally a professional rivalry between all armed forces units, each believing themselves to be the best. However, deep down it was begrudgingly accepted that the SAS were the true masters of special warfare, and so Garcia recognised the short statement as praise indeed. He too would miss Keane, but like Grant, his years as a professional soldier had prepared him for such events.

"It comes to all of us," he said philosophically.

Grant asked Sonny and Len to give him a moment while he squared things with Vick. He still couldn't understand why he'd made her the offer, but it was something he couldn't go through with. Vick saw the look on his face as he approached and guessed what was coming.

"Don't you dare try and leave me here," she warned him. Grant put up his hands to placate her but she was going to have her say, whether he liked it or not.

"You just asked me to come with you!"

"This isn't your fight, Vick."

"Don't give me that!" she shouted. "I've been stuck in this jungle for three months and my government did nothing!"

He tried to keep his voice level rather than engage in a shouting match. "Vick, where I'm going it will be dangerous. I can't ask you to be part of that."

"Dangerous! What would you call the last few hours? A walk in the park? Tom, I'm coming with you!"

"It won't be the same kind of danger, Vick. Here you know who your enemies are. Back in England you'll have no idea until it is too late."

"I can handle it," she said, defiantly.

"Like you did at the river? You nearly cost that child her life and your actions gave away our position to the enemy."

Vick didn't like the accusation but had to admit that she'd not covered herself in glory. The tension of the last quarter of a year began to bubble to the surface and the thought of endangering the child's life finally broke her resolve. As the tears came Grant placed a gentle hand on her cheek and rubbed them away with his thumb.

"Vick, I love you, but where I'm going —"

"What?"

Grant looked confused, while Vick suddenly perked up. "What?" he asked in return.

"You said you loved me."

"No I didn't."

"Yes you did, Tom Gray! You said 'Vick, I love you'!"

As he struggled to rewind the last few seconds in his mind she took advantage of his bewilderment and grabbed his face, planting her lips onto his. He wrapped his arms around her and returned the kiss, his argument for leaving her on the island crumbling with every passing moment.

Sonny walked past and slapped Grant on the shoulder.

"Get a room, guys. Better yet, I know a good cave not far from here…"

Grant realised that he'd been outflanked and outmanoeuvred, but a part of him knew that he hadn't really been putting up much of a fight.

"I'm serious," he said as he held her close. "The next few weeks are going to be tough. It may even be months before this is all over."

"I don't care, I'm coming with you."

He slipped an arm around her shoulder and they set off in pursuit of Len and Sonny.

"So what's your plan?" she asked.

"Plan A is to take a shower. After that I want to find the people who are trying to kill me."

It was Vick's turn to look confused. "A couple of days ago the government was sending someone to rescue you." She pointed up the trail towards his friends. "I take it that was these two. What's changed?"

"It's a long story."

Vick smiled. "I've got all night."

Chapter 14

Friday 20th April 2012

Azhar Al-Asiri finished the Asr, or afternoon prayer — the third of five he would perform that day — before picking at a plate of flat bread and Sajji, a lightly-spiced leg of lamb cooked by roasting it next to an open fire. The food was good, freshly prepared by his 'family' in the home situated in the Pashton Abed district of Quetta, Pakistan.

The people he lived with weren't actually blood relatives, nor was the dwelling a single apartment. Instead it was three apartments connected by hidden doorways, and his family consisted of a daughter, Nyla, and two grandchildren. Nyla was in fact the widow of a martyr who had given his life to the cause, and her two children: the girl, Hifza; and her son, Mufid, played an integral part in ensuring Al-Asiri remained anonymous.

His accommodation could have been more opulent, but that would have attracted unwanted attention. His preference was to live in simple surroundings, just another face in a city of two million. That wasn't to say he placed all of his trust in this simple ruse. The buildings surrounding him were home to his loyal supporters, and lookouts were posted in a wide radius to give notice of any unwanted visitors. They ranged from the young boys playing football to the old man smoking and drinking coffee outside the café, all keeping an eye out for government troops or foreign snatch squads.

Each of the lookouts carried a simple early-warning device. It was the size of a matchbox and had a button in the middle, which, when pressed three times in rapid succession would send a signal to Al-Asiri's home. This would allow him time to get down to the cellar where a network of tunnels led to various exfiltration points. By the time his enemies got to his home he could be emerging from one of eight different shafts and be spirited away by his loyal followers.

A glance at his watch told him it was almost time to check for messages. Wary that telephone calls could be traced and Web traffic could be tracked by IP address, Al-Asiri kept no such instruments on the premises. Instead all communications went through a computer in the basement of a jewellers shop half a mile from his apartment.

The shop had a CCTV system that would be expected in any such establishment, but as well as monitoring the shop and its customers it was used to keep an eye out for uninvited guests.

Access to the rear of the shop was through a metal cage. The employees would use a security card to open the outer door and once inside they would use the same card to release the inner door. The outer door had to be closed before the inner would operate, preventing more than two people entering the room at the same time. The card system also recorded the movement of staff and prevented them sharing a card. If an employee swiped his way into the workshop, his card would not allow anyone else entry until he had swiped his way out again. Once through the cage, the employees then had to negotiate a heavy wooden door which finally granted access to the workshop.

All of this could be explained away as security for the valuable stock, but the real purpose was to deny quick entry to the cellar which lay beneath the workshop floor.

The communications room was constantly manned throughout the day. Each shift lasted twelve hours and the room had everything the occupant required to see them through to the handover: a toilet, and food and water which were replenished four times a day.

It was to this communications centre that Al-Asiri sent his 'Grandson', Mufid.

As always, he wrote his message on a small piece of paper, rolled into a tight tube and placed it inside a small plastic receptacle similar to a medicine capsule. The boy placed the capsule under his tongue and took a walk to the jewellers', ready to swallow the evidence if anyone tried to halt his progress.

The trip was uneventful, and ten minutes later he handed the capsule over to his uncle, who disappeared into the back. A few minutes later he returned with an identical capsule which Mufid took back to the apartment.

Al-Asiri read the note before setting fire to it in an ashtray. Two more teams had reported in, making five in total. Only one remained outstanding: Abdul Mansour's, but given his location Al-Asiri didn't expect to hear from him until he was closer to civilisation. It wasn't as if he could simply walk into an internet café in the middle of the jungle, and Abdul knew better than to make contact via an insecure phone. It was more likely that he would see his handiwork on the

331

news channels before he received a report, and knowing his young general, it would be something spectacular.

He reflected on how far the young man had come in such a short time, and it saddened him that he couldn't quite trust him fully. Mansour had arrived in Pakistan at a tender age and had been quick to show his allegiance, dispatching a captured U.S. soldier with chilling efficiency. The transition from taking parts in raids to planning and leading them had been swift, and his execution of the attack on Tom Gray's fortress had been masterful.

However, he still had doubts about someone so young being so capable.

His enemies would love nothing more than to have an agent infiltrate the organisation, and it seemed a little strange that Mansour should arrive on the scene with skills not normally seen in a teenager from a poor area of London. He had since shown himself to be a natural born killer, but according to background reports he had previously been involved in nothing more serious than a few playground fights.

So where did he acquire these skills? That had been the question on his mind for the last two years, and at first he'd suspected that it had been courtesy of the British security services. However, discreet surveillance had shown no signs of any communications with anyone outside the organisation. In fact, all they had seen was a devout Muslim, apparently true and loyal to the cause.

He had approved Mansour's plan to attack Tom Gray as a way of testing his credentials. If the attack had been foiled it may have suggested that Mansour had tipped the security services off and they had baulked at the idea, but he had actually succeeded, killing Gray and denying him the chance to tell the government where his bomb was. That they found it in time was perhaps luck, maybe good police work, but who had Mansour actually killed? Tom Gray: a terrorist in his own government's eyes; a couple of his associates; and a handful of police officers. Would the British government have allowed that toll in order to protect Mansour's true allegiance?

After all this time he still hadn't come to a conclusion about his young general, but the result of his Asian mission — and more importantly Mansour's next assignment in the U.K. — would offer the defining answer.

* * *

Farrar had been sitting outside the office for nearly twenty minutes when the door opened and the familiar figure of the Home Secretary stormed out, his face like thunder. Farrar's boss stuck his head out and told him to enter, then offered him the warm seat recently vacated by the Minister.

"You've got a reprieve," Charles Benson said without preamble. "It seems our friend Mr. Gray is a much more resourceful character than I gave him credit for. The team we sent to collect him has reported him missing."

Missing? Farrar perked up at that news.

"It seems there was a little altercation with the locals and he managed to escape, along with his two acquaintances."

"What about a search of the island? They can't have got very far."

Benson dismissed the idea with a flick of the wrist. "We haven't got the resources or jurisdiction. The reason I brought you back in is that you've known this man for over a year. You've been through every inch of his file, spoken with him, observed him. What are his intentions?"

Farrar considered his answer carefully. If he admitted to having no idea, his usefulness would immediately evaporate. Better to play the subject-matter expert.

"He's got two things on his mind: the first is revenge; the second is survival. Given the events of last year I'm afraid we cannot discount the former."

"Last year he had the advantage of anonymity, plus a sound financial footing. Do you really think he'll come after you?"

The question left Farrar under no illusion: the trail stopped with him.

"That's a possibility, but it's a long way home. As you said, he has no money. I also know he hasn't got a passport, and he'll need both to get back to the U.K. That gives us plenty of time to set up border protocols across Europe and beyond.

"He will have to seek help from others, and we have a comprehensive list of former acquaintances, from his Army days up to his time as Managing Director of Viking Security Services. I'm confident that anyone he contacts will be on that list."

"That sounds like it could be a long list. We can't possibly monitor everyone on it," Benson observed.

"True, but his buddies in Britain aren't going to be a lot of help to him right now. He's going to need someone in the local area and only two people spring to mind. One is in Vietnam, the other in Singapore."

Benson nodded. "What of the remaining two, Levine and Campbell? Are plans in place to deal with them?"

"They are. We expect those problems to go away within the next fortnight."

"Why so long?"

"We have to work to their patterns," Farrar explained, "otherwise suspicions will be aroused."

Benson sat back in his chair and folded his arms. "Consider this your last chance, James. If this mess isn't cleared up soon you can kiss your career goodbye. We cannot simply blame this on the previous government, no matter how appealing it sounds. I want an end to the whole Tom Gray saga, or you will be the one to take the fall."

Benson picked up a pen and opened a folder, signalling the end of the meeting. Farrar got up from his chair and let himself out of the office, the threat still clear in his head. As he stepped from the government building into an April shower he knew that failure wouldn't simply mean spending the rest of his life in prison: his very life depended on killing Tom Gray.

Redemption

Prologue

Saturday April 21st 2012

Ben Palmer placed the bloodied knife on the table and removed the tape covering Kan Tek Kwok's mouth.

"I know that you've been passing sensitive material to Alphaco," he said, his voice calm. "Just tell me what you shared with them."

It was, in fact, a lie. He neither knew that Kwok was selling trade secrets to his client's rival technology firm, nor did he care. His remit for the current assignment was simply to extract information, and in this particular field he had no equal.

"I swear..."

It wasn't the answer Palmer was looking for. He placed the tape back over Kwok's mouth and picked up the knife, which he'd found in his subject's kitchen drawer. It was probably fine for slicing vegetables but it had taken a lot of effort to cut through the man's fingers. Still, he thought, it all added to the effect.

Palmer ran the knife down Kwok's bare stomach and over the two marks created by the Taser. The file he'd been given showed the man lived alone, and fortunately he hadn't been entertaining that evening. After getting him to answer the door, Palmer had stunned him with the electroshock device. While he was still reeling from the shock, Palmer had flipped him over and administered an injection between his shoulder blades. He had then closed the curtains while the neuromuscular-blocking drug — derived from Curare, a relaxant which left the recipient unable to move any of his voluntary muscles — took effect. Unlike other varieties — such as Suxamethonium chloride, which also affected the involuntary muscles such as the diaphragm — this derivative allowed the patient to breathe unaided. The result was that Kwok was unable to put up any resistance whatsoever, but could still feel every ounce of the pain being inflicted.

"I can make this last all night, Kan," he said, moving the knife down to Kwok's bare genitals. "It would be better to tell me now, while you can still father children."

Palmer placed the blade on the man's penis and applied a little pressure while making a sawing motion – not enough to break the skin, but sufficient to bring a look of horror to Kwok's face.

"I'll count to five," Palmer said. He got to four when his phone rang and he knew it was work-related — less than a dozen organisations and governments had this number, and his circle of friends could be counted on one hand.

"Think about it," he said to Kwok, and hit the Accept button. "Palmer."

* * *

James Farrar had been through Tom Gray's file twice, but as he'd already suspected there were just two associates known to be in Asia. In order to prioritise them he had been in touch with the Government Communications Headquarters to get a breakdown of recent calls made to their known numbers, specifically anything from the island of Jolo. Within twenty minutes GCHQ had come up with the information he wanted.

Farrar closed down Gray's electronic file and opened the one for Timothy Hughes. Once it had passed through security protocols and loaded, he looked for the current address. Minimising the file, he opened another screen and searched for resources in the area. The results showed that the nearest was in Japan and currently working a case, and Farrar didn't have the authority to pull him off it for his own needs.

What he could do, though, was bring in some outside help. Given the sensitivity of the mission, it would have to be someone he could trust, and that narrowed it down to just one man. Despite this, he was reluctant to mention Tom Gray's name. After careful consideration, he decided to limit the mission to locating and, if possible, eliminating the quarry: Len Smart, Simon Baines and one other, as yet unidentified.

Farrar looked up the number in the database and dialled.

"Palmer," he heard when the call was connected.

"Ben, it's James Farrar. I have an urgent job for you."

"Sorry, gonna be a bit busy for the next few days."

Farrar cursed silently. Palmer was the only man he could turn to, the only one he could trust. He had performed other jobs for the organisation and Farrar knew that operational secrecy was a given.

"How much are they paying you?" he asked the freelancer.

"Three hundred..." Palmer replied, and Farrar knew from previous negotiations that he had to add "thousand" to the end. He also suspected that Palmer had doubled the fee he was currently earning, but that wasn't his concern. All that mattered was getting him on board.

"I'll give you five hundred if you can start now."

The offer brought a pause in the conversation. "Sterling," Palmer said eventually.

"Dollars," Farrar insisted.

Another pause, then: "Write this down." He gave Farrar an internet URL consisting of letters and numbers, one that couldn't be guessed or stumbled upon accidentally. Palmer also gave him a twelve-digit code to enter when he got to the website.

"Once you're in, enter the job details and hit send. You can also upload files and images. Don't worry, it's secure."

"How secure?"

Palmer explained that it used 2048-bit encryption and a one-time 28-digit key, which meant even a supercomputer would spend a lifetime trying to unscramble the garbled message.

"I'll have access to the message in an hour. Please make sure the money is transferred to the usual account before then."

The phone went dead in Farrar's hand. Now that he had secured Palmer's services, all that remained was to get his hands on half a million dollars. As an idea came to him, it brought a smile along for company. He still had control of Tom Gray's Manila bank account, which had a balance a shade over the sum he needed. The smile grew as he considered the irony of using Gray's money to pay the man sent to kill him, and he thumbed through the list of contacts in his phone in search of the account manager for the Philippine National Bank.

* * *

Palmer put his phone away and looked down at Kwok. The man had tears streaming down his face and a pool of urine had formed between his legs.

"You got lucky," he said, extracting another hypodermic needle. Kwok had overheard his conversation, but that was the least of Palmer's worries: he had seen his face, and that sealed the man's fate. Palmer stuck the needle into his subject's carotid artery and delivered double the normal dose. As he waited for the drug to take effect, Palmer straightened his wig and considered an explanation for his current employers. He settled on reporting that Kwok had been innocent and collecting the fee, which he had tripled for Farrar's benefit.

Kwok's breathing was becoming laboured and Palmer prepared to leave, replacing the hypodermics in their case and stowing it in the inside pocket of his jacket. He sat there for another minute until Kwok took his last breath, then he left the house, quietly closing the door behind him. As he walked to his car he removed the bloodied surgical gloves and screwed them into a ball before wrapping an elastic band around it to stop them unravelling. The ball was discarded down a storm drain, along with the hairpiece.

He drove the car to a secluded wooded area and removed the false licence plates which he had stuck over the originals. He wiped them down before digging a shallow hole in the undergrowth and burying them.

No loose ends.

Palmer drove back to his rented apartment, curious to see what the urgent mission entailed.

Chapter 1

Sunday April 22nd 2012

The radar indicated a small vessel a mile ahead, apparently stationary in the water. According to his GPS it was within fifty metres of the rendezvous point and the captain made a small course correction to intercept it.

"Just where you said they'd be, sir," he said to Timmy Hughes, who had just entered the cabin.

"Anyone else around?" Hughes asked.

"Nothing larger than a canoe for twenty miles."

Hughes stepped onto the deck and switched on the Carlisle & Finch searchlight, playing its beam out over the bow of the twenty-metre yacht. It was a couple of minutes before he located the small craft and its four occupants. Using hand signals he indicated for the captain to slow their approach and a few minutes later they pulled alongside the craft. Hughes threw out a rope and it was caught by one of the males, who tied it to a ring on the wall of the inflatable. Hughes walked the rope to the stern and tied it off, allowing his visitors the chance to climb onto the swim-deck attached to the transom.

First aboard was the familiar figure of Len Smart and Hughes gave his old friend a hug.

"Good to see you, man."

"You too, Timmy. You haven't changed a bit."

Hughes grabbed an inch from his own midriff. "Maybe a couple of pounds heavier."

He looked over the transom at the others. "Who are your friends?"

Len leaned over and gave Sonny a hand up. "This is Simon Baines. He joined the regiment shortly after you left."

The men shook hands.

"Looks like you're doing okay for yourself," Len observed. "Nice boat."

"Business has been great for the last couple of years," Hughes said. "I struggled at first because everyone was going to Viking Securities, but once Tom Gray sold up, the company lost its reputation. They raised their prices and cut the wages for the people in the field, so a lot of the contractors came to me instead. I approached all of Viking's clients and offered to do the same work for a twenty percent discount and the rest is history."

The final two passengers had clambered aboard, and the male came over to shake his hand.

"Hello, Timmy."

The voice was familiar, but not the face. It was a few moments before realisation hit him.

"Tom?"

"I hear you've been stealing my clients," Gray said with a grin, his amusement increased by the look on Hughes's face.

"But you're dead. It was all over the news."

"It's a long story. I'll tell you over some food."

Once Hughes got over the shock of seeing a ghost from the past, Gray introduced his female companion. "This is Vick."

Hughes held out a hand while simultaneously straightening his short-cropped brown hair. For a man approaching his mid-forties he still had the looks and physique the ladies found appealing.

"Welcome aboard," he said in his most charming voice.

Hughes led the party down to the main cabin and offered them seats while he went to the galley. He was back moments later with a champagne bucket full of beers on ice.

"Something for the lady?" he asked Vick, but she was already reaching for a beer. He disappeared again and was back five minutes later, this time carrying a plate of bread, butter and cold meats.

"So, tell me how you happen to be in the middle of the Sulu Sea a day after a terrorist attack on Jolo."

"You hear about that?" Gray asked, making himself a sandwich.

"It was all over the local news."

Gray gave him a rundown of events over the last year, starting with his injuries in Abdul Mansour's attack and the government's subsequent subterfuge in declaring him dead while spiriting him out of the country. He glossed over the following year and took up the story at his kidnapping in Basilan.

Vick was nursing her third bottle of beer and the alcohol — combined with her first full stomach in months — was taking its toll. Her head was on Gray's shoulder and her eyes told the others in the cabin that sleep wasn't far away.

Hughes sat back in his chair and took a swig of his beer. "I've alerted Carl Levine and Jeff Campbell to the danger and they are taking their families into hiding. There's nothing to stop you calling the media in London and letting them know that you're still alive." he said.

Vick looked at Tom through tired eyes. "Tim's right. You could just call the newspapers and this would all be over."

"It's Timmy," Hughes corrected her with a smile.

Gray sighed. "You have to think like James Farrar. He's sitting at home listing the options open to us, and going to the press is right at the top of the page. If I was him I would have a blanket DA-notice on anything mentioning my name"

DA-Notices — called D-Notices until 1993 — come in five varieties, with DA-Notice 05 dealing with British security and intelligence. Although they are advisory requests and not enforceable by law, it would be a very brave editor who chose to ignore one.

"What about social media?" Sonny suggested. "Get yourself all over Twitter and Facebook. They can't sensor that, can they?"

"Trust me, they'd find a way. Besides, I don't have accounts, and if I create one and claim to be alive, who's going to believe me? There must be a few million crackpots on the web, and I'd just be the new nutter on the block."

"So what have you got in mind?" Hughes asked.

"I haven't got a plan as such, but the first step is to get back to England, and that isn't going to be easy without a passport. Even with one, you can bet every port will be keeping an eye out for us."

"Sounds like you're going to have to sneak in," Hughes said. "I may know just the man."

He disappeared up the carpeted stairs and Gray made himself another sandwich. He took in the sumptuous surroundings and for a fleeting moment considered cruising around the South China Seas for a few weeks, but the urge to get his life back soon put a stop to such thoughts.

Hughes returned with a handful of towels and put them on an empty chair. "There's a shower just down the hall," he said, pointing towards the stern. Vick was quickest to react and disappeared through the door, grabbing a towel on the way.

"Do you think it's a good idea to be taking her along?" Hughes asked when Vick was out of earshot.

"If you think you can talk her out of it, be my guest," Gray said.

"Stubborn?"

"She'd prefer tenacious."

"Then she's in for quite a trip," Hughes said. "I've told the captain to head to Port Kelang in Malaysia so I can introduce you to Arnold Tang. He specializes in getting people into the UK."

"A people smuggler? Nice company you keep."

"He's actually a respectable businessman. He just happens to have his fingers in lots of pies."

"How long will it take to get there?" Smart asked.

"About fourteen hours," Hughes said. "This little beauty will do sixty knots without breaking sweat."

"No, I don't mean how long to Port Kelang. I mean how long will it take to get to the UK?"

"Ah," Hughes said, finally understanding the question. "That, I don't know. I'm sure Arnold will let you know tomorrow."

"More importantly, how much is it going to cost us?" Gray asked.

"I'll get mates-rates, but it'll still be pushing seventy thousand for the four of you."

Gray explained his cash situation, but Timmy wasn't concerned. "Once you get this all sorted you should be able to get access to your money. You can pay me back when you do." Hughes rose from his seat and opened a small safe built into the wall. He handed an envelope to Gray.

"Here's five grand. That should keep you going once you get back to the UK."

"I don't know how to thank you," Gray said. "I really appreciate it."

"You could thank me by taking a shower before you mess up the sheets in your cabin," Hughes smiled.

Vick entered the cabin wearing nothing but her towel. All heads turned and Gray's remained fixed on her. She may have looked good in the jungle, but having scrubbed up she had the presence and beauty of a movie star. Her damp, blonde hair fell about her shoulders and she smiled at Gray.

"Shower's free," she said. Gray simply nodded, struck dumb by the vision in front of him. It took him a moment to realise that he was staring.

"I'll go next," he said, averting his gaze.

As he picked up a towel Sonny offered some friendly advice, accompanied by a huge grin.

"Better make it a cold one."

Gray shot him a look before disappearing down the hallway. The bathroom was not as large as he'd expected but it had a spacious shower stall. He climbed in and turned on the water, letting it soak him for a few minutes while the heat took some of the stress out of his muscles. By the time he had washed and shampooed his hair, his body felt relaxed for the first time in days.

He returned to the main cabin to find that Vick was no longer there.

"She's gone to bed," Smart said when he saw Gray. "Timmy told her where to find some clothes and she turned in."

"I could do with some myself," Gray said, and Hughes told him to help himself from the closet in the master bedroom. After saying his goodnights, Gray went in search of some shorts and a T-shirt to wear in the morning, then found the cabin Timmy had assigned him.

He climbed into the bed naked and within moments the rhythmic bobbing of the boat began rocking him to sleep. What seemed like seconds later he felt the bed covers move and he sat bolt upright, fully awake. Lying next to him on the bed was Vick, wearing just a T-shirt which barely extended below her hips. She smiled at Gray and put an arm around his neck, pulling his head towards hers. The kiss was long, their tongues exploring deeply. The love-making that followed was gentle, unrushed, and afterwards Gray collapsed next to her, spent. Vick placed her head on his shoulder and ran her finger lazily across his chest. He made to say something but Vick placed a finger on his lips, relishing the silence.

Within a few minutes he heard the change in her breathing which signaled the transition to sleep, and he wasn't long in following her.

Chapter 2

Sunday April 22nd 2012

Tom Gray woke to find himself alone in the bed, and for a fleeting moment he wondered if he had dreamed the events of the previous evening. Those fears were allayed when Vick opened the cabin door, clearly fresh from the shower and again wearing nothing but a towel. She stooped and kissed him on the cheek.

"Good morning. Sleep well?" She asked.

"Like a log. What time is it?"

"Two o'clock. Timmy says we should be in port by eight this evening."

Gray ran a hand up her leg but she swatted it away. "Later," she said with a smile. "I'm starving."

Vick slipped into a T-shirt and shorts and brushed her wet hair. Even without any make-up Gray thought she looked beautiful, her tanned skin perfectly complementing her blonde hair.

"Don't be long," she said as she left the cabin in search of food, and Gray realised just how hungry he was. After a quick shower he wandered on deck, where he found everyone sitting round a fully-laden table. He took a seat, said his good mornings and dived into a plate of sausages and eggs.

"So how is your friend going to get us to the UK?" Gray asked Hughes.

"I don't know the details of the entire route, but I expect entry through the port will be in the back of a truck."

"That's not a guaranteed way in," Sonny said, concerned. "I've seen the documentaries on the telly and there are lots of ways of detecting stowaways. They can detect minute concentrations of carbon dioxide in the back of the trucks, and that's just for starters."

"He has a very high success rate," Hughes said. "I'm sure he's got everything covered."

Gray hoped his friend was right; otherwise the closest he would get to redemption would be Dover.

It was five hours later when they cruised up the narrow channel, passing a jungle-covered island on the left and industrial units on the right. As they pulled up to the dock Gray saw a black SUV with tinted windows parked up, and as the gangway was lowered one of the rear doors opened.

The melon-shaped passenger who climbed out weighed around two hundred and fifty pounds and was wearing smart trousers and a white shirt. By the time he climbed the gangway, circles of sweat had appeared around his armpits.

Hughes was waiting to welcome him aboard. "Arnold, thank you so much for coming."

"Not at all," Tang Ben Lee smiled. He'd adopted the name Arnold and told anyone who asked that it gave him what he liked to call "international appeal". In actual fact, it was due to ignorant foreigners reading his name as they would in the West and addressing him as Mr. Lee, which was his given name. His contempt for westerners came despite having studied at Oxford University, which was where he'd acquired his accent.

Hughes led him to the stern where the others were sitting at the table, the onboard lights illuminating them as the sun began to sink below the horizon. He made the introductions before placing a glass of expensive cognac in front of Tang. The Remy Martin Louis XIII cost upwards of fifteen hundred dollars a bottle and was reserved for a select number of guests.

"I understand you want help with transporting some goods to England," Tang said.

Hughes gestured to his four companions. "That's right, Arnold."

"These people?" Tang asked. "What's wrong with Malaysian Airlines?"

"They lost their passports," Hughes said with a smile, but Tang didn't reciprocate.

"I'm not happy with this situation, Timmy," Tang said. "I don't usually meet the cargo, for obvious reasons."

"Don't worry, Arnold, I can vouch for them. I trust them enough to pay for their trip."

Tang let his displeasure show on his face as he mulled it over. If he allowed these people to travel through his network there was a chance that they might expose his role should they ever get caught. But then again, they *already* knew about his involvement.

347

On the flip side, there was a lot of money to be made from this shipment, and Arnold Tang knew how to have his cake and eat it. An idea came into his head, one that would solve the problem, and he pulled out his phone before speaking quickly in Cantonese. The conversation lasted just a few seconds.

"The initial part of the journey will be by boat," he told the group at the table, "which leaves in eighteen hours. It will be two weeks before you reach South Africa, so make sure you bring enough clothes and food for your journey. You'll be fed on the ship but I can't guarantee the quality of the cuisine. Once you reach Durban you will be taken by cargo plane to northern Africa and across Europe by truck. You should reach the UK in three weeks."

"We have concerns about crossing the border," Gray said. "How do we get around their detection methods? I understand they can detect even the smallest concentration of carbon dioxide. Is that true?"

"The vehicle you will be travelling in is equipped with CO_2 re-breathers that direct the exhaled gasses through a filter canister containing a carbon dioxide absorbent, in this case a form of soda lime. Even the most accurate probe placed next to the filter gives inconclusive results."

That went some way towards allaying their fears, but the questions kept coming. "How do we fly from South Africa to North Africa without passports?" Sonny asked.

"You do not need to worry about the logistics," Tang said. "I have people in place all along the route to ensure you reach your destination, and my delivery rate is unparalleled. All you need to do is follow instructions until you reach England. Once you get there, you are on your own."

He turned to Hughes. "The fee will be one hundred and twenty thousand."

"That's a lot of money, Arnold. I thought perhaps…"

"It is one hundred and twenty thousand because you put me in this awkward position. Just be grateful I am willing to help you."

Hughes considered the options and after a glance at Gray he agreed to pay the money. "Okay, I'll transfer it once my friends reach their destination."

Tang's face lost what few signs of geniality remained. "I want the money within three days or your friends will never see England again."

"Arnold, I am laying out a lot of money which my friend here is going to repay once he gets home. If you are confident enough to guarantee his arrival, what is the harm in waiting until delivery is complete?" Hughes sat back in his chair and took a sip from his beer. "On the other hand, if you can't be sure he'll get there, I will have to take my business elsewhere."

Tang was beside himself with anger. No-one dictated terms to him, not even his own mother, because she knew what it meant for a Chinese person to lose face. Just a few moments earlier he had planned to have the four passengers thrown overboard once the money had been transferred, but now he would have to guarantee their safe passage lest this *gweilo* insult him further by going to a competitor. He took a few deep breaths to disperse the adrenalin coursing through his body before replying.

"Once they reach the UK they will call you to confirm their arrival. You will then transfer the money."

"Deal," Hughes smiled, offering his hand to shake on it, but Tang ignored the gesture.

"If the money isn't in my account an hour after that phone call, you'd better pray that you're already dead."

While Hughes digested the threat, Tang rose from his seat and polished off his brandy. "The ship leaves at three tomorrow afternoon. It is the *Huang Zhen* on dock C6."

With that, he took his large frame down the gangway and climbed back into his vehicle, which left immediately.

"Nice chap," Len said, sardonically.

"I didn't realise it was going to take so long to get home," Vick said, not relishing a fortnight on board a ship. Having gone from sleeping in the jungle to the comparative luxury of Hughes' boat, she was reluctant to endure any further hardship, but there was no way she was letting Tom Gray out of her sights.

"It'll give us a chance to come up with a plan," Gray said.

"So what do we take with us?" Vick asked. "I don't want to sound stereotypical, but I've got literally nothing to wear."

"I'll send the skipper into KL first thing in the morning," Hughes said. "Let me know what you need and he can pick it up."

"KL?" Len asked.

"Kuala Lumpur," Hughes explained. "It's about thirty miles from here."

Vick began scribbling a list while Sonny passed the beers around. "We might as well enjoy these while we can."

* * *

Arnold Tang sat in the back of the SUV, his anger growing with every passing second. Having built up a small empire both at home and abroad, the last thing he needed was for it all to come crashing down, which is what would happen if anyone found out about any of his less than legitimate enterprises.

He pulled his back-up mobile phone from his pocket and inserted a SIM card with one hundred Ringgit of pre-paid credit. He then looked up a number on his main phone and dialled. When the connection was made he was very brief, speaking in his native language.

"A consignment of four will be delivered in three weeks. Once they arrive, give them a phone and make them call this number." Tang read off Hughes' mobile number and got the recipient to read it back.

"After they make the call, get rid of them." He turned the phone off and removed the SIM card before opening the window and throwing it into the street. As for Hughes, he would wait until the money was transferred before deciding the man's fate.

* * *

James Farrar was in the middle of preparing his Sunday roast when his mobile rang. He wiped his hands and checked the display, which told him it was Todd Hamilton, head of the team watching Carl Levine.

"What is it?" Farrar asked, although the weekend interruption suggested it wasn't good news.

"They've gone," Hamilton said.

"Who's gone?"

"Levine and his family. We saw no sign of them this morning so we sent a couple of team members in with Watchtower brochures. There was no answer."

Farrar was puzzled, and a feeling of dread beginning to build in the pit of his stomach. "Have a poke around, make sure they're gone."

"We've been all around the ground floor and checked through the windows. There's no sign of any activity in the lower rooms and they never sleep this late."

350

Farrar put him on hold and wondered what the hell could have had spooked Levine and caused him to up sticks during the night. He checked the call log with GCHQ and was told that, as requested, they had been looking for contacts from the Philippines. There had been no calls or emails originating from that country. As they reiterated the criteria he had specified, the thought struck him that he hadn't updated the monitoring information following Gray's disappearance. All he had been expecting over the last year was for Gray to contact his old friends from his new home in Manila, but now that he was on the run he could be anywhere in the region.

"Alter the search to check for any and all calls, regardless of origin."

It was a few moments later when he got the bad news. "There was a call on Friday the twentieth to Levine from Singapore."

As the number was read out Farrar was already moving to the living room. He sat down at his laptop and entered his password before loading the file belonging to Timmy Hughes. The number he'd just been given matched the one on record.

Damn!

He asked about all calls to Jeff Campbell and his Sunday got a whole lot worse.

Farrar ended the call and took Hamilton off hold. "What about Campbell? Have you been in touch with the other team?"

"Not yet," was the reply, and it wasn't the one Farrar wanted to hear. He hit the End button and found Matt Baker's number.

"What's the situation with Campbell and his family?" Farrar asked once the call was answered.

"All quiet here," Baker said nonchalantly.

Farrar was furious at the man's casual attitude to the situation, despite Baker not being aware of all the facts.

"Where exactly are you now?" he asked, as calmly as he could.

"I'm parked at the end of their street. I can see the house from here."

"I want you to go to the house and make sure they are still inside," Farrar said.

The phone went quiet for a while before Baker's voice said: "Just did a walk-past and I can't see any movement in the house."

"I didn't ask for a fucking walk-past! I want to know, in the next two minutes, if there is anyone in that house!"

Baker began spluttering but Farrar cut him off. "I don't care how you do it: just find out if they are home. Knock and ask for a cup of sugar, try to sell them double-glazing, just *let me know if they're still there!*"

At times he regretted having made Baker a team leader. The man was young and keen, never shirking his duty, and he executed the end game skilfully. It was just a shame that he often focused all of his efforts on the kill at the expense of the operational fundamentals.

Baker was back on the line ninety seconds later. "There's no answer," he said.

"Did you try the windows?"

"I looked through but couldn't see anyone. No sound from the TV or radio, either."

Farrar couldn't believe what he was hearing. Just a few days earlier he'd been looking to wrap up the operation by the end of the month, and now he had five fugitives and no idea where to start looking.

He told Baker to remain where he was and report in if the family came back, but he wasn't holding out much hope. A year ago Levine and Campbell had managed to evade the authorities despite a nationwide search, and Farrar had just six men under his immediate control. It was nowhere near enough, and his options were limited. There was one person who could help, but it was a phone call he didn't want to make.

He paced the room, trying to come up with an alternative, but there was nobody else who had the infrastructure he needed. Reluctantly he picked up the phone and dialled her number.

* * *

Veronica Ellis concluded the meeting and sent the staff on their way. She was sitting at the head of the conference table contemplating the notes she'd taken when her cell phone rang and she looked at the caller ID.

It was the last person she'd expected a call from.

"Hello James. To what do I owe the pleasure?"

Their break-up two years earlier hadn't been the most amicable. The relationship had been deteriorating for some time, both blaming each other for focusing more on work than each other. However, the clincher for Ellis was finding Farrar in bed with one of his interns.

"I need access to one of your resources," Farrar said.

352

"Yes, I'm fine," she said sarcastically. "Thanks for asking."

"Veronica, this is a professional call on an urgent matter. I need help in finding two individuals and their families."

Same old James Farrar, Ellis thought. What she ever saw in the man, God only knew. Still, it made her response all the more satisfying.

"Impossible. We are stretched as it is, and we have more work coming in every day. Why else do you think I'm in the office on a Sunday?"

"Veronica, either you find someone to help in my search or I get the Home Secretary to order you to assign someone. It makes no difference to me, but I'd prefer this to be handled in the spirit of co-operation."

Ellis was not normally one to succumb to threats, but she knew that Farrar had access to the minister and would use that influence if necessary. Having taken over from John Hammond as Assistant Director General of MI5 following the Tom Gray fiasco, she was well aware that the service was still under the microscope. The last thing she needed was more scrutiny from the upper echelon.

"I can give you one man, that's it."

"That's all I'm asking for," Farrar said, his voice more pleasant having gotten his way.

"Send me the details and I'll get someone to work it up. What's the rush, anyway? Is it something we should know about?"

"It's nothing to concern you or your department. I just need information as to their whereabouts. We know they were in London in the last twenty-four hours."

Ellis knew she wasn't going to get anything more from him so she ended the call without a goodbye and dialled Andrew Harvey's internal number.

"My office," she said when the call was answered, and set off to meet him.

Harvey had been the section lead when Hammond had handed in his resignation, taking full responsibility for the service's failure to end the Gray saga in a manner which put the government in a good light. She had stepped into the hole that had been left at the top of the organisation on what was supposed to be an interim basis, but her ambitions reached beyond being a stop-gap.

Her first act had been to deal with the others responsible for the debacle, and while there was no evidence of Andrew Harvey, Diane

Lane or Hamad Farsi being guilty of negligence at the disciplinary hearings, Ellis was quick to ensure they were never given anything more important than analysis work for a while. This hadn't sat well with Lane, who resigned within a few weeks, but Harvey and Farsi still reported to their desks dutifully each morning. Ellis knew that they were very capable operatives, as their performance over the subsequent months proved. There did, however, seem to be some resentment towards her, as if it were her fault that Hammond was ousted. It wasn't something that concerned her, though. Adding yet another string to her considerable bow was far more important than making friends with the staff.

This latest request had piqued her interest, though, and if anyone could dig deep enough to get to the real story it was these two.

Harvey knocked on the door and walked in when called, standing at ease in front of her desk.

"What's your workload like at the moment?" Ellis asked.

"Manageable," he replied.

"Good. I have something extra for you. We need to locate a couple of people."

"What are their names?" Harvey asked.

"We don't know yet. The details will be with us shortly and I'll pass them on to you."

"What's the urgency?" Harvey persisted.

"I don't know that, either. I'll pass the information on as soon as it arrives."

Harvey nodded, her last statement telling him that this was an external request. He left the office wondering why she had bothered asking about the amount of work he currently had assigned to him. Normally she would just dump things in his lap regardless of his other commitments, and this suggested the new task needed someone's full attention.

He resumed his seat and from the opposite desk Hamad Farsi asked why he had been summoned.

"The Oberstgruppenführer wants me to find two people."

"Who?"

Harvey gave a replay of the brief conversation and asked for his colleague's opinion.

"Sounds very strange," Farsi said, but clammed up when he saw Ellis approaching with a printout in her hand. She asked them to follow her as she passed their table and led them into the conference room, closing the door behind them.

"I've just been told who you're looking for," she said. "It has come through as eyes only, so it doesn't go beyond the three of us."

She placed the sheet of paper on the desk and Harvey read the names before passing it to Farsi.

"I know these people," he said. "I interviewed them after the attack last year."

"Yes, they jumped out at me, too," Ellis admitted.

Farsi studied the names. "You just want us to find them?" he asked.

Ellis's eyes betrayed a conspiratorial glint. "That's the request that came in, but I'd like to know *why* someone wants them found. I don't like being kept out of the loop, and if these people are involved in something I think we should know about it."

"So let's start with who made the request," Harvey said.

"His name is James Farrar," Ellis said. "I don't know who he works for, though."

"Yet you're granting his request for information? Isn't that contrary to every protocol we have?"

Sharing her past with her subordinates was not something Ellis was comfortable with, but she had little choice if she wanted their help in getting some answers.

"We used to work together over the river," she said, referring to the Secret Intelligence Service building on the opposite bank of the Thames. "We were... involved for some time, but shortly after we broke up he left Six to join another organisation. Our paths have crossed a few times since but he'd never tell me who he is working for now."

"And you want us to find out?" Farsi asked.

"Discreetly," Ellis confirmed.

Chapter 3

Monday April 23rd 2012

It was just after ten in the evening when Timmy Hughes walked down the gangway of the Sterling Lines and walked through the Saf Yacht Club to his waiting Bentley. The ten mile drive south took a leisurely twenty minutes and he parked in the Atrium car park just a couple of hundred yards from his apartment just off Orchard Road.

The streets were still alive despite the hour, with the majority of the revellers tourists taking in as much of the city as they could manage in a single day. As he approached the apartment building the throng had thinned out to just a few locals. He was digging for the keys to the lobby when he felt a dig in his back and a figure appeared next to him, a sports jacket draped over his right hand.

"Hello Timmy," the stranger said. Hughes didn't recognise him but the accent was from his own neck of the woods, just north of London. A second dig in the ribs told him that the man was carrying more than just a Carl Gross coat.

"You know the drill. Nice and cool, stay calm and follow me to my car."

The hire car was waiting just around the corner and Hughes was told to drop his bag and get into the front passenger seat.

"Roll down the window. There's a set of cuffs under the seat. Put them on your right hand."

Hughes again complied and was then told to thread the other cuff through the door handle and attach it to his left hand. After checking it was tight the stranger climbed into the driver's seat and set off through the light traffic.

It was a forty-minute drive to the Sungei Buloh wetland reserve in the Lin Chu Kang area and they made the journey in silence after it became clear to Hughes that his questions were going to go unanswered.

When they reached their destination Ben Palmer handed Hughes the keys to the cuffs, told him to get out and then followed him through

356

the passenger side door. Hughes found himself in an industrial estate, deserted because of the late hour.

"Move," Palmer said, indicating with his silenced pistol that they should head into the darkness. They walked for a minute before Palmer told Hughes to stop and get down on his knees.

Hughes refused. Instead, he turned and faced the gunman. If this man wanted him dead, it would have happened by now, which meant he needed something from him. That gave him the advantage.

"Care to tell me why you're going to kill me?"

Palmer had the gun pointed at centre mass. "On your knees," he repeated.

Hughes was five yards from him and moved closer, hoping to cut the distance in half so that he would have a chance to go hand-to-hand, but Palmer put his left hand behind his back and grabbed the Taser tucked into his waistband. He hit Hughes in the chest with the barbed dart and kept his finger on the trigger, delivering fifty thousand volts down the thin wire. Hughes dropped to the floor and Palmer gave him another jolt for good measure.

"It's much easier if you do as you're told," he said, standing over Hughes. "Now, tell me where Len Smart is."

"Never heard of him."

Palmer delivered another shock to jog his memory. "I don't like it when people lie to me," he said calmly. "You've been in contact with Smart and Simon Baines. Where are they?"

"Go fuck yourself."

Palmer brought the pistol up and shot the prostrate man in the kneecap. When Hughes screamed and reached for the wound, Palmer kicked him in the temple, knocking him out cold.

Hughes regained consciousness a few minutes later and immediately reached for the wound, but his arms wouldn't obey the command. He lay there helpless, staring up at the night sky, the stars magnificent in the cloudless night.

For the first time in his life, Timmy Hughes felt truly frightened.

Palmer could see it in his face, and welcomed the sight.

"I'm not gonna bullshit you, Timmy. You're gonna die. It's just a matter of how long it takes, and that's up to you. Now, where are Baines and Smart?"

He removed the tape covering Hughes's mouth and got a face full of spittle in response.

Palmer wiped it away. "Okay, have it your way." He pulled a small bottle from his jacket pocket and unscrewed the lid carefully before pouring a couple of drops on his victim's hand. The sodium hydroxide solution immediately began to burn through the skin and Hughes screwed up his face as he fought to battle the pain.

Palmer gave him a few moments to consider just how much suffering was still to come.

"It's going to hurt a whole lot more when I put it on your knee," Palmer said, holding the bottle over the open wound. "After that I'll do your eyes, one at a time."

Hughes knew there was nothing he could do except hope for a swift end. He wasn't afraid of death, and he knew that there was little point in delaying the inevitable, but he wasn't about to give up his old friends so easily.

"They've gone," he said.

"Where?"

"Home. Back to the UK."

Palmer considered this for a moment. If the British security services were after these people, it was unlikely that they'd be on a commercial flight. "How are they getting there?"

"I don't know."

Palmer poured a quarter of the solution into the hole made by the bullet and Hughes screamed with every ounce of breath in his lungs, but the hand placed over his mouth stopped the noise travelling. Palmer waited until there was nothing left but whimpering and tears.

"Let's try again. How are they getting back to England?"

"I don't know," Hughes whispered, and Palmer shook his head, positioning the bottle above his left eye.

"No, wait! Wait! Sammy Li!"

Palmer moved the bottle and looked into Hughes's eyes. "Tell me more."

"I handed them over to Sammy Li in Malaysia. He said he would get them home."

"Who's Sammy Li? Where do I find him?"

"I don't know where he lives, but he is a regular at the Atlanta Club in Kuala Lumpur."

Hughes prayed that this stranger would fall for his ruse and end up searching for a fictitious target. Unfortunately for him, Palmer wasn't about to take his word for it. He took out his phone and hit a pre-programmed number.

"It's me. I need information about a Sammy Li from Malaysia. He might be involved in people smuggling."

He turned to Hughes. "I have access to several security services throughout the world. If you are lying to me..."

He returned his attention to the call, listening intently before thanking the other party and hanging up.

"Sammy Li comes up blank, but I was given another name. Care to guess what it is?"

Hughes knew the game was up, and any more procrastinating would only lead to more pain. He felt bad for letting his friends down, but this man would get the information out of him eventually. Besides, their boat had already set sail, and the chances of this man getting through Tang's security screen and having enough time to question him seemed remote at best.

"Arnold Tang," he said, and closed his eyes, waiting for the bullet. He felt the tape being placed over his mouth, but the shot didn't come. Instead, Palmer emptied the bottle onto his exposed throat and stood back quickly.

Hughes began gagging and spluttering, trying his best to expel the corrosive solution, but Palmer had mixed it at such a high concentration that it burnt through the skin in seconds and poured into his larynx. Screaming was impossible with his voice box destroyed, and moments later his heart gave out under the overwhelming assault on his nervous system.

"That's for lying to me," Palmer said, and strolled back to his car. Once inside he pulled out his phone and dialed the number he had called earlier.

"You were right, it's Arnold Tang. Tell me about him."

* * *

Farrar looked at the screen and what he saw wasn't encouraging. Arnold Tang had long been suspected of being involved in a variety of illegal activities, but there had never been enough evidence to bring a prosecution. From gambling dens to fraud, the accusations had been levelled and immediately withdrawn, mainly due to his powerful connections.

It was also reported that Tang had two personal bodyguards who travelled everywhere with him, meaning it wouldn't be easy for

Palmer to get in close enough to do what he did best, and he said as much to the contractor.

"What about posing as a customer?" Farrar suggested.

The line went silent while Palmer considered the suggestion. The reply wasn't what Farrar wanted to hear.

"I don't do undercover. You hired me for my skill set, and I don't go outside my comfort zone. That's how mistakes happen. Just give me the names of some known associates and I'll have a quiet word with them."

Farrar looked through Tang's profile and found two men suspected of being heavily involved in the trafficking operation. He started to read out the details but Palmer cut him off.

"From now on, no details over the phone. Go to the website and enter this code."

He read off a series of numbers and got Farrar to repeat them.

"Leave a message and I'll call you tomorrow," Palmer said, and hung up.

Farrar did as instructed and gave the names and addresses of Tang's men. He ended the note with instructions for when Palmer located his targets:

When you find Baines and Smart, find out what 'Saturday the ninth of April, option three' means. It is vital, repeat, vital that you get this information.

Farrar hit the Send button and then called Veronica Ellis for an update. He found her in a less than accommodating mood.

"We just started looking yesterday," she said when he asked how things were progressing. "You have to realise that last year they managed to evade a countrywide manhunt when every police force in the nation was looking for them. If these people don't want to be found, it will be almost impossible with such limited resources."

Farrar knew that her point was valid, but he wasn't about to cut her any slack. "Can't you draft anyone else in to help?" he asked.

"In order to fund some extra overtime I would need to know more about the operation, otherwise I can't justify it."

"It's beyond your pay grade, that's all you need to know."

The statement didn't sit well with Ellis, but Farrar's next words almost had her screaming venomously down the phone.

"If you can't get this done with the resources you have, I'll send over the names of six of my operatives. You can set them up with accounts and give them grade one access."

Ellis took a few deep breaths as she formulated an appropriate response: one that didn't require Farrar to go and fuck himself. She knew that denying him access to the network would simply send him scurrying to the Home Secretary, but the more she considered the request, the more she could see it work in her favour.

"I guess that's the only way we're going to find them," she said, feigning disappointment. "Email the names, I'll fill out the paperwork and have the accounts set up within the hour."

"No!" Farrar said, a little too quickly. If the accounts were set up through the proper channels, it was possible that his bosses might find out about them and start asking some awkward questions. The last thing he wanted to do was alert them to the fact that Campbell and Levine had skipped town from under his nose. Even worse was the fact that he now needed to bring MI5 into the mix. Despite his earlier bluff about making a complaint to the Home Secretary, that was the last thing he wanted to do.

His men weren't really cut out for this kind of work, but he wanted to have something in place, just in case Palmer failed to deliver.

"Just... keep this below the radar. I don't want other agencies interfering with this case."

Intrigued, Ellis promised to do all she could, but made it clear that his latest request meant it might take some time to put things in place.

Farrar thanked her and hung up, and Ellis went straight to Gerald Small's office, grabbing Harvey and Farsi on the way. They found the technician tucking into a sandwich in front of a bank of monitors, each one displaying network activity.

"Busy?" Ellis asked.

Small pulled his feet off the desk and scrambled into a proper sitting position.

"I...erm, was just...someone was trying to hack the network. I was just running a trace."

"Calm down, I'm not the posture police. I need you to come with me," Ellis said, and the head of the Technical Operations department dutifully followed her to the conference room, throwing Harvey a look that asked what was going on. He got a shrug in response.

Once inside, and with the door closed, Ellis explained the situation.

361

"I need you to create six new network accounts, all with grade one access."

"Sure," Small said, wondering why this couldn't have been done in his office. "Just send me the requisition forms and I'll set them up."

"It's not quite that simple," Ellis said. She was worried that too many people were being dragged into her little conspiracy, but she had no choice but to involve Small: without him, she had little chance of discovering what Farrar was up to.

She gave Small a summary of recent events, including Farrar's request to find Campbell and Levine, his reticence in sharing any further details and the request for network access.

"Am I right in thinking that every request, every search made through our accounts is audited and reports made available to the JIC?"

Small confirmed that she was correct. Every database search and VOIP — or Voice Over IP — telephone call was recorded and the Joint Intelligence Committee had access to these reports. It was a way of ensuring that the information held on their systems was not abused in any way.

"Is there a way to spoof an identity so that their searches appear under someone else's name?"

Small thought about it for what seemed an age. "I suppose it *could* be done," he eventually said, "but it would take a couple of days to set up."

"What will it involve?" Ellis asked.

"I'll have to create a virtual server and route their requests through it. I'll also need to write a Windows service that intercepts the request. At that point I can switch principal identities."

"Before you forward the request with the new identity, can you make a note of every search they make?" Ellis pressed.

"That shouldn't be too hard," Small said. "I can set up a separate database to record everything they are looking at. You'll want to view the results real-time, I suppose?"

"If you can, that would be great."

"No problem. I should have it all in place by Thursday morning."

With that matter dealt with, Ellis asked Harvey for an update on the search.

"When they went into hiding last year they had friends pay for everything so that they couldn't be traced," he explained. "That doesn't seem to be the case this time. None of their known acquaintances have any credit or debit card payments that suggest a planned disappearance."

"Are you saying they haven't left a single trace?"

"No, we have the use of their debit cards at an ATM, but that was late on the evening before the search started, and it was at South Mimms services on the M25. It's at the junction with the A1, which means they could be anywhere north of London by now."

"If they actually headed north," Farsi pointed out. "Let's assume they know the card transactions will be picked up: do you think they'd use an ATM on their actual route?"

Harvey had to concede that his colleague was right. "Then they could have headed in any direction, which gives us even less to go on than we had a minute ago."

Ellis knew that with a cold trail it would be almost impossible to locate their quarry. "What about phone conversations: they must have spoken to someone in the last few days."

"That's where it gets interesting," Harvey said. "We asked GCHQ for a list of all calls to and from their known numbers in the last two weeks and got a couple of interesting hits."

"Interesting how?"

"Most of the calls in the preceding days were mundane, but Levine got one at midday the day before they disappeared. The number was an unregistered mobile originating from Singapore. A minute later Levine called Campbell and that was the last call either of them made."

"Do we have transcripts?" Ellis asked.

"They came through this morning and we've been working up a lead," Farsi said. "The call from Singapore was brief. The caller introduced himself as Timmy and said he had a message from the Sarge."

"The Sarge?" Ellis asked.

"We're working that up, just waiting for the MoD to get back to us," Harvey said.

"What was the message?"

"That's the interesting bit. All he said was 'Saturday the ninth of April, option three.'"

"That was just a couple of weeks ago," Ellis said. "What's the significance?"

"Actually, the ninth of April this year was a Monday. We think he was referring to the same date last year."

Ellis couldn't make the connection and asked them to spell it out.

"That was the day Tom Gray's eight associates went into hiding, and five days later his website went live," Farsi explained.

"So this Timmy has told them to do what they did a year ago, which is disappear. Could option three be an alternate hideaway they were planning to use?"

"It could be," Harvey admitted. "Unfortunately, we expected Tom Gray's death to be the end of the matter, and no-one thought to question them about any other preparations they'd made."

Ellis thought for a moment. "So we don't yet know where they are, but someone has told them to go into hiding. Have you checked the whereabouts of the other four members of Tom Gray's team?"

"Paul Bennett was killed in a road traffic accident at the start of the year and Tristram Barker-Fink died while on a security detail in Iraq. Phone records suggest the remaining two, Baines and Smart, took a contract job in Manila last Monday. We checked the number they were called from and it's no longer in use, so we've asked the British Embassy to check it out for us."

"Have you got a recording?" She asked.

"Not available, according to GCHQ, though they did send over the auto-transcript. The contact in Manila was someone called James, no surname mentioned."

"If we find Baines and Smart, they should be able to tell us what option three was," Ellis pointed out.

"It could be our best chance of finding Levine and Campbell," Farsi agreed.

"Then let's concentrate on the leads we have," Ellis said. "Find out all you can about Timmy and the Sarge, and track down Baines and Smart."

Chapter 4

Monday April 30th 2012

Vick woke once more to the smell of body odour and curry and began having second thoughts about tagging along with Tom Gray. Oh, for a hot shower and a soft comfortable bed rather than a stinking mattress on the floor of the cargo container they shared with more than a dozen others. Even an hour in the sun would have been appreciated, but the captain had made it clear that anyone sticking their head above deck would be dealt with severely, and she suspected that in the people-smuggling trade, severely often meant permanently. That meant two weeks in the lower hold and goodbye to her tan. At least there was a chiller unit pumping cold air into the compartment, otherwise the heat would have quickly become unbearable — perhaps even fatal — given the temperature in the Indian Ocean, especially during the earlier part of the journey.

She looked down at Gray, who was still sleeping, as were most others in the cramped container. She ran her finger over the crescent-shaped scar on his cheek and tried to imagine what it must have been like to be in that building when it blew up around him.

Vick had asked Gray to share the whole story with her, from the death of his son to his arrival on Basilan. He had tried to gloss over certain events but she'd insisted on hearing all of the details, even from Sonny's and Len's perspectives. It had certainly passed the time, but with another week to go until they reached Africa she was beginning to wonder if she'd made the right decision. There had been nothing to stop her from just going to the British embassy in Singapore, explaining her story and getting a flight home, but her heart had told her to stick with Tom.

After a quick visit to the toilet, a Porta-Cabin like structure located just outside the container, Vick returned and rummaged through one of their bags to find something to eat. They were served hot food twice a day but there was a limit to the amount of curry she could eat, so she found a tin of ham and tucked in.

Gray woke next to her and yawned, immediately regretting the action.

"Christ, it stinks in here."

"You've just noticed?" Vick asked, trying to ignore the smell as she chewed.

Gray ignored the jibe and went to relieve himself. When he returned he grabbed a fork and helped Vick to finish off the cold meat.

"Last night I thought of a way we could locate Farrar, but it's a risk," Gray said.

"What's your plan?"

"We need someone on the inside, and I think I may have just the person."

"Anyone I know?"

Gray shook his head. "An old adversary."

"Then yes, it does sound risky. Care to tell me more?"

"I met him for just a few moments, but something about him told me he was honest and could be trusted," Gray said.

"How do you know he isn't involved in the whole thing?" Vick persisted. "What if he just turns you all in?"

"It was something Farrar told me last year. I remember he said something disparaging about MI5, which suggests they weren't involved in all this."

Vick wasn't convinced, but it was Gray's call and he had made a few good ones in the last couple of weeks. Having said that, she'd have been a lot happier if Gray had packed an air freshener, and she told him as much.

"Yeah, I never have one when I need one," he sighed.

* * *

Azhar Al-Asiri prepared for one of his infrequent jaunts into the outside world. As always, he strapped on the bullet-proof vest and over that went the padding to add the appearance that he weighed a hundred pounds more than he actually did. The ensemble was completed by the full-length black *burqa*, transforming him from Al-Qaeda leader to humble wife.

Outside, the vehicle was waiting. The Toyota Land Cruiser appeared to be ancient, but under the hood was a finely-tuned V10 engine, and the side panels were armour-plated. Al-Asiri stepped out into the street for the first time in weeks and made the short walk to the car, looking to any casual observer like a harmless octogenarian. He took a seat in the back and cranked the window a little: not so much that he would be exposed to any incoming small-arms fire, which the bullet-proof glass could easily handle.

The drive was a short one and within ten minutes they arrived at the hotel, where his fellow passenger helped him out and escorted him through the lobby to the small elevator. They rode in silence up to the third floor and when the doors parted, Al-Asiri waited until his bodyguard checked the hallway for danger. After getting the all-clear, Al-Asiri followed him to room 317, where they found two men, one sitting on the bed, the other on a chair.

Al-Asiri recognised one of them as part of his security detail, which meant the balding man in his fifties had to be Professor Munawar Uddin. Although he'd never met the man, Al-Asiri had been financing his work for the past five years, and as reports suggested the project was almost complete, he wanted to get the latest update in person.

He removed the *burqa* and waited for the shock to pass from Uddin's face.

The professor had been told nothing about the purpose of his visit, just that he would be away from his facility for as short a time as possible. The last thing he'd ever expected was to meet the leader himself.

Al-Asiri offered his greetings, dismissed the escorts and took a seat in the chair opposite the professor.

"I understand the project is nearing completion," he said when they were alone in the room. "Tell me about the latest test results."

Uddin took a moment to gather himself before explaining that the experiments carried out on Bonobos — once known as the pygmy chimpanzee and more closely related to man than apes — had shown a ninety-three percent success rate.

"The virus we have developed successfully targeted the male Y chromosome in all of the test subjects. A few suffered testicular azoospermia, which is a complete lack of sperm in the semen, while the majority suffered a highly-reduced Y chromosome sperm count, roughly two percent of all sperm produced."

Al-Asiri was pleased with the update, but wasn't about to celebrate a victory quite yet. "What are the chances of similar results in humans?" He asked.

"The genetic differences between the two species are negligible, and the process of spermatocytogenesis is virtually identical."

367

The look Al-Asiri gave Uddin suggested a simplified explanation might be in order. "The formation of sperm starts with cells called spermatogonia. The spermatogonium splits to form two spermatocytes, which in turn split to become spermatids. These spermatids mature to become the spermatozoa."

Al-Asiri nodded for him to continue, though he didn't pretend to understand the whole process.

"Consider the spermatogonia to be templates: they are not in infinite supply, and so when they split some remain in the basal compartment to create further spermatogonia, while the others move to the adluminal compartment to enter the spermatidogenesis stage, the next step in the production of the spermatozoa."

"At what stage do the subjects become affected?" Al-Asiri asked, beginning to grow impatient.

"W...well," Uddin stammered, acutely aware of the need to get his point across, "at the initial spermatocytogenesis stage we have found a way to latch on the spermatogonia containing the Y chromosome, which produces male offspring. The virus destroys these cells, leaving just the female X chromosome spermatogonia. Eventually only X chromosome sperm will be produced by the subjects, which means all offspring will be born female."

"How soon is eventually?"

Uddin swallowed, knowing the answer was not going to be accepted with good cheer.

"It could take months, perhaps a year," he said, awaiting the backlash.

None came. Instead, Al-Asiri seemed quite happy with the timeframe.

"What about delivery methods," the head of Al-Qaeda asked.

Uddin was happy for the subject to be changed and breathed a sigh. "The virus is a hybrid of Influenza A and so can be passed from person to person through airborne transfer. The lifespan outside of the host is an impressive one hour in the air, with a reduced period of around thirty minutes on door handles, work surfaces and other non-porous surfaces. On contact with skin and other porous surfaces, such as paper, the virus will die within a few minutes, but if anyone comes into contact with an infected surface and then touches their eyes, nose or mouth, they will be susceptible."

"What about introducing it into the water supply?" Al-Asiri suggested. "Surely that would have the greatest reach?"

"From the very start of the project, the delivery method was a primary consideration. Your idea was one of the first we looked at, but investigations showed that most modern water purification processes use ultraviolet light to eliminate bacteria, viruses and mold from the sewage. Our virus would not be able to withstand such exposure to the UV radiation."

"Then what do you propose?"

Uddin explained that the virus had an incubation period of four to five days, following which the subject would experience mild flu-like symptoms which would last two, perhaps three days at the most.

"Introducing the virus into a densely populated area would have the maximum effect. Perhaps you could send infected subjects onto the London underground to spend the rush hour riding the tube, or have them attend an indoor concert."

Al-Asiri filed the suggestions away for later consideration, but he had a more pressing concern. "What about the selectivity issue?" He asked. "Can you guarantee that only westerners will be affected?"

"There are no guarantees, but the differential allelic gene expression resulting from X-chromosome —"

"Enough!" Al-Asiri said, his patience worn thin. "Just give me a number. Are you one hundred percent sure that it will affect only westerners, or just ten percent?"

Uddin considered his answer carefully. While there had been extensive research in this area, it had yet to be proven conclusively that a particular race could be identified – never mind targeted – at the genome level. Nevertheless, his work with a variety of cell samples was had managed to produce the desired results in seventy-seven percent of trials, a figure he shared with Al-Asiri.

The response was quiet contemplation for a few moments before Al-Asiri declared the number high enough for the project to go ahead.

"Prepare as much as you can over the next ten days," he said, rising from his seat. "I will be in touch with you after I have made other preparations."

He made sure his disguise was in place before leaving the scientist in the hotel room and making his way back to the car. Once settled, he reflected on how far things had come in the last few years, and how close their biggest victory now appeared.

It was a shame that they would never be able to claim responsibility for it.

Veronica Ellis strode purposefully into the Technical Operations office, her mood destroyed by yet another phone conversation with James Farrar.

"Any idea when it will be ready?" she asked Gerald Small, her tone a little harsher than she normally used on the staff.

The technician continued tapping away on his keyboard.

"Almost there."

Another few keystrokes and he declared the job done.

"The next time he logs on to his computer, his account profile will be pulled from the central server. When this happens, the key logging application will extract itself and begin running. I'll place an icon on your desktop that gives you a breakdown of every key he presses in real time."

Ellis thanked him and apologised for her abrupt manner. The thrice-daily calls from Farrar were beginning to grate on her nerves, especially as he now had three times the manpower working on the search.

The accounts he'd requested had been set up a few days earlier and she had been through their searches only to find that they were simply duplicating much of the work her team had already done. None of their network activity had given any clues as to who they were working for, which was why she had requested that the key logging software be installed on their workstations. Unfortunately, it wasn't standard software in the MI5 inventory and so she'd asked Small to code it up himself. Being more of an infrastructure specialist rather than a developer, it had taken Small a couple of days to get a working version ready to deploy.

"Please let me know once it is activated," she said as she left the office.

Her next port of call was Andrew Harvey's station, where she found him involved in a heated phone call. She waited for him to finish and then asked for an update on the two men they were concentrating on: The Sarge and Timmy.

"We've been through the records of all eight men involved in the Tom Gray episode, and between them they served under five sergeants in the SAS. So far we've had no luck with four of them."

"What about the other one?" Ellis asked.

"The other one was Tom Gray himself," Farsi said, from the opposite desk, "so we kinda ruled him out, with him being dead and all."

Ellis conceded that it was a fair call. "What about Timmy? Did you manage to identify him?"

"We've had seven hits and we're working through them now," Harvey told her.

"Diplomatically, I hope," recalling the conversation he was having when she arrived at his desk.

It took Harvey a moment to realise what she was referring to. "Oh, that. Just some dickhead at the British Embassy in Manila. I've been waiting for news about Knight Logistics Management, the company Smart and Baines were supposed to be working for. I sent the request in over a week ago and he's still dragging his feet."

"Want me to have a word with them?" Ellis asked.

"No, it's okay. I've put a flea in his ear and he promised to get back in touch later today."

"So how long before we can identify Timmy?"

"We've eliminated four so far," Farsi told her. "Of the other three, one left the country a few years ago and we think he might be the one we're looking for. His name is Timothy Hughes and he served with Levine eight years ago."

"Who was his sergeant at the time?" Ellis asked, hoping the pieces would just drop into place.

Her momentary excitement evaporated when Farsi told her that it had been Tom Gray.

"Any idea where Hughes is now?"

"We already sent out a request to the British High Commission in Singapore," Harvey said. "They came back with an address and I've asked them for all information they have on him."

"Let's hope they don't take as long as Manila," Ellis said.

Harvey was about to respond when his phone rang. He took the call and indicated for Ellis to hang around. After a minute he asked the caller for all phone records and emails for the last month and hung up.

"That was the Commission in Singapore," he said. "The good news is: they've found Timmy Hughes."

"And the bad news…?"

"He's in the morgue. It looks like a professional hit."

* * *

James Farrar rubbed his temples as he digested the news he'd just received from the British Embassy in Manila. Why hadn't he considered the fact that MI5 might make a connection between Levine and Campbell and tie them to Baines and Smart?

Yet another sleepless night was beginning to take its toll, and he'd been unable to come up with a quick and satisfying answer, instead telling the attaché to just stall any further requests for the time being.

The last thing he needed was Ellis and her team poking around in his operation, and he decided to nip that activity in the bud.

"Veronica," he said with his most pleasant voice when she answered his call. "I understand you are doing some investigation into Simon Baines and Len Smart."

"And just how would you know that, James?" Ellis asked, her curiosity aroused.

"Well…obviously…I want to be kept abreast of developments, and as you haven't done a very good job of finding my two fugitives I decided to look through the logs to see what your team had been doing all this time."

Farrar was relieved at having come up with such a good excuse, yet angry for leaving himself wide open like that. In future he would think it through before calling Ellis: She was nobody's fool and one day he was going to dig himself a hole too deep to climb out of.

"We've been doing what you asked," Ellis said, indignation in her voice. "We know there is an obvious link between all four men and we want to —"

"Forget about them," he interrupted. "Baines and Smart have nothing to do with this case, so stop wasting valuable time on them and concentrate your efforts on finding Levine and Campbell."

"James, we have to investigate all possibilities if —"

"Veronica, I want you to *drop it*!" He shouted. "*Now!*"

Farrar took a few moments to calm himself, the phone shaking in his hand. "I'm sorry," he eventually said. "This whole case is being closely watched by the Home Secretary and he wants results sooner rather than later. I can't have you sending your people on wild goose chases when resources are so limited."

It was Ellis's turn to pause, and for a moment Farrar thought she'd already hung up. Her voice came back, the tone one he recognised from their time together: Compliance, but not wilful. "Okay, James, we'll ignore Baines and Smart and concentrate on your two suspects."

Farrar started to thank her but found himself talking to a dial tone.

Great, he thought. Just when the day couldn't get any worse, a quick chat with Veronica and it turns to complete shit. He was wondering for the umpteenth time how they'd managed to stay together for so long when his phone rang. The caller simply gave him a twelve-digit number before hanging up.

Farrar recognised Palmer's voice and logged into his computer, and then brought up the website he had used earlier in the week. After entering the code he was redirected to a page with a short message that improved his mood a little:

Sorry about the delay in replying, was waiting for the right moment. Spoke to subject 1 yesterday. Knows that they travelled by boat (Huang Zhen) to Durban but no onward itinerary available. Subject 2 confirmed same. Additional: there are now 4 (four) passengers heading your way. Names unknown.

Farrar wondered where the hell this fourth person had come from, but the more pressing issue was how to track them once they reached South Africa. He opened a new browser and searched for a website offering shipping itineraries. Once he found one he entered the name *Huang Zhen* and found that it was due in to Durban on the seventh of May, a week from today. That was plenty of time for Palmer to get to South Africa and head them off.

He wrote a quick note in reply to the message and hit the Send button.

* * *

Ellis was still fuming when Small knocked and entered her office. Before she could even begin to complain about the intrusion he gave her some much-needed good news.

"Farrar logged on and the software has been activated."

He hit a couple of keys on her laptop to minimise the open files and clicked the icon he had placed on her desktop. A new window filled the screen and Ellis soon found some human-readable data.

"What are these other characters?" She asked Small, pointing to what appeared to be random keystrokes. He told her that they were non-alphanumeric keys, such as Backspace or Shift.

"I can filter them out if you like, but it will take time and you'll have to wait until he logs out and back in again."

"Never mind," she said. "I can make it out."

Near the top of the screen she saw what looked like a website URL suffix, but the random characters before it didn't look like any internet address she'd ever seen, and she dismissed it as a coincidence. Small, however, had found it more curious. He grabbed the mouse and highlighted a series of characters.

"This is the first website he visited after logging on," Small explained. "I've been there and found just a textbox and Submit button." He moved down the screen and selected a twelve-digit number. "It looks like this was his login. I tried entering the same code but it simply redirected me to a porn site."

"Do you think that was Farrar's intended destination?" Ellis asked.

"I shouldn't think so," Small said. "After logging in he went to another website and did a search for '*Huang Zhen*'. I retraced his steps and saw the itinerary for a cargo ship."

"Is he expecting a delivery?" Ellis asked.

Small nodded and pointed to a section of text further down the screen:

Passengers arriving Durban May 7ᵗʰ 3PM. Meet them, get the information and ensure no onward journey.

Ellis read the succinct message a few times, and a couple of questions popped into her head: who were the passengers; and who was being sent to meet them?

"Any idea who's behind the website?" She asked.

Small shook his head. "First thing we tried, but whoever it is, they know how to cover their tracks. I've got one of my guys working on it, but I'm not hopeful."

"Then we need to know who these passengers are. What was the port of origin for the *Huang Zhen*?"

"Port Kelang in Malaysia," Small told her. "It left there last Monday."

South-east Asia again, Ellis thought. First there was Timmy Hughes in Singapore, then Baines and Smart in Manila. Now Farrar seemed to be tracking some people who'd recently departed from Malaysia, and all this in the last couple of weeks.

She called Harvey and asked him to bring Farsi to her office. When they arrived, she also told them about Farrar's request to stop searching for Baines and Smart.

"And you're going to do as he says?" Farsi asked.

"Of course not," Ellis said. "Those two are the key to finding the others. What we must do is try to keep any searches off the record."

The operatives nodded, and Ellis gave them a rundown of the information gleaned from Farrar's computer and laid out her findings.

"It could be just a coincidence," Harvey said. "Maybe Farrar has more than one thing on the go."

"I agree," Farsi said. "There was that terrorist attack in the southern Philippines last week. Maybe he's working that up."

The attack on Jolo had slipped Ellis's mind. Although it had been flagged to her department and was being investigated, there was nothing to suggest a threat to Britain. The CIA had jurisdiction and had shared some of their data — it had, after all, been an American base which had come under attack — and her team of analysts had created a summary report for her. It suggested Abdul Mansour had been responsible for the attack, although there was no concrete evidence, just an eye witness statement, but they were working hard to confirm his location with several other agencies around the world.

Ellis conceded that Farrar might be working a different case, but it couldn't hurt to go over the Jolo data one more time.

"Andrew, get over to the Asia desk and have them send everything we have relating to the attack on Camp Bautista. Once that's organised, contact our friends across the pond and ask them for the very latest information. The stuff we have is at least three days old."

Harvey nodded and left to carry out her orders.

"Hamad," Ellis said, turning to the other operative, "get a manifest of the *Huang Zhen* and see if you can find a connection with anyone we have on our radar."

Farsi followed Harvey out of the room, leaving Gerald Small alone with the boss.

"One thing puzzles me," he said, his eyes still on the short message Farrar had sent. "If he has his own team, why isn't he communicating with them through normal channels? Why go through the trouble of setting up an untraceable website?"

Ellis hadn't picked up on that fact, but the more she thought about it, the more intriguing she found it. "An outsider," she said, and began pacing the room, throwing ideas around in her mind. Why would he use an outside contractor? Whoever it was, they were interested in some people originating from Malaysia, which placed them in the same area as Timmy Hughes. And the fact that Hughes was linked to Levine and Campbell meant that whoever had taken him out could well be looking for them, too. It could of course be a coincidence that Hughes was taken out by a professional just a few days after contacting Levine, but the more she thought about it, the more unlikely it seemed.

Ellis knew that in order to confirm her suspicions, she had to discover who Farrar was in contact with. "You said that whoever created the website covered their tracks: does that make finding them impossible, or just very difficult?"

"As I said, I have someone working on it. We might get lucky if the host has been careless, but at this moment in time I wouldn't hold my breath."

It wasn't what Ellis wanted to hear, but she was determined to either verify the connection or dismiss it as an avenue of investigation.

"How about gaining access to Farrar's files? Would you be able to do that undetected?"

Small thought about it for a moment, not wanting to offer hope if there was none. He knew the network inside out, but as several agencies had access to the core functionality a lot of it was compartmentalised. Gaining access to a sub-net would be no easy task, but as he'd never even explored the idea before, it didn't mean it would be impossible.

"I can try," he said, the excitement of the challenge plain to see.

"Go for it," Ellis smiled.

Chapter 5

Tuesday May 1st 2012

Ben Palmer's Emirates flight touched down at King Shaka International Airport just after five in the afternoon. An hour later, he climbed into an airport taxi which ferried him twenty-two miles to the Alteron hotel, a three-star establishment a couple of miles from the container port. A larger, more opulent choice of accommodation was available to him, but he preferred the low-key lifestyle while working. His cover as a British businessman would probably stand up to close scrutiny in one of the four- or five-star establishments dotted around the city, but he much preferred to be off the radar.

The hotel had been booked in advance, and after signing in at reception he took the stairs to the second floor and found the single room was as pleasant as could be expected for the price. He dropped his baggage on the bed and took a quick shower before opening his laptop and logging in.

The first thing he did was to visit the proxy server. As he was using the hotel's internet connection, he couldn't be sure that they weren't logging every website he visited. To be on the safe side, he routed all requests through the proxy, so as far as any snoopers were concerned he would only appear to have visited one website.

Once signed in, Palmer went straight to his own website and composed a short email, which was encrypted and sent to a friend named Carl Gordon. Palmer's knowledge of computers was limited to the end-user experience, while his profession required a deeper understanding and ability. Knowing at an early stage that he wouldn't be able to learn enough to work alone, he had recruited a student a few years earlier. He'd scoured the web for court schedules, looking for anyone facing charges under the Computer Misuse Act 1990. Gordon had been caught hacking into the servers of a utility company threatening to cut the power to his shared accommodation and had been slapped with a hefty fine. Palmer had been in court listening to the case and afterwards he met up with Gordon and agreed to pay the fine in exchange for some well-paid ad hoc work in the future. The kid had jumped at the chance and they had worked together ever since, although Gordon had never discovered Palmer's real name. All subsequent communications had simply been signed 'B'.

An hour later he received a text message which simply said: "Hi, Billy. Fancy a drink later?"

It was Gordon's signal to say the work had been completed. Palmer replied, saying he would try to meet up but wasn't making any promises. What he was actually saying was that Gordon's fee would be transferred to the usual account within the hour.

Palmer logged into his own website and looked at the information his specialist had managed to find in the shipping port's system. He had requested the manifest for the *Huang Zhen* as well as the name of the haulage company that was scheduled to collect the container, and he found everything he needed on the screen.

After searching for the website of Wenban Freight Management he made a mental note of the livery, glad to see that the dark blue cab with lightning strikes on each door would be easy to recognise. It wasn't a large company, and there was no online freight tracking system, which suggested their paperwork would be hosted internally rather than on a server Gordon could get access to. That meant he had the choice of either visiting the office to see where the container would be heading next, or simply following the truck to see where it dropped it off.

With six days to go before the ship arrived, there was more than enough time to check out the setup at Wenban.

He also had plenty of time to find a place to dispose of his targets.

* * *

Andrew Harvey was ploughing through the raw data the CIA had sent over and he had the feeling it was going to be a long day. The vast majority of the reports had already been couriered to Thames House a few days earlier and compiled into the summary which had been presented to Ellis, but he had to go through each one, just in case a relevant slice of information had been missed. It was the report highlighting the sighting of Abdul Mansour that got his attention.

A statement from the Special Operations Division commander, Travis Dane, mentioned that one of three western prisoners had claimed to have seen Mansour in a local Abu Sayyaf camp the day prior to the attack. There were no further details as to who the

378

prisoners were, and the summary had assumed that they had escaped from Abu Sayyaf.

Having not heard of any hostages being taken in recent months, he did a search for known abductions in the region and found three, two British and one American. They could be the prisoners in the statement, he thought, but as he read more the timings seemed off. Two of the prisoners had been strapped to the attacking vehicles, suggesting they couldn't have fingered Mansour the previous day. That left one — Victoria Phillips — but despite a thorough search he found no mention of her in the CIA documents.

Harvey put in a call to the British Embassy in Manila, though he wasn't expecting a whole lot more co-operation than he'd previously received. His heart sank further when the familiar voice came over the phone, but he kept his composure and politely asked if there was any information available about her disappearance and release.

"I can confirm that we were informed of her disappearance at the start of the year," the attaché admitted. "I haven't been informed about her release, though. She certainly hasn't been in touch with us."

"Are you sure?" Harvey asked, astonished. If he'd been held by terrorists, the first thing he'd want to do was get to British soil, and that would require a passport.

"Positive," came the reply, along with a little indignation. "If she contacted the embassy, I would know about it."

"If you say so," Harvey said. "What about the other matter, the one I called about last week?"

"I've got someone working on it," the attaché said, "but things work a little slowly around here. Once I have something, I'll be in touch."

The phone went dead and Harvey wished the same on the attaché.

His next call was to the American Embassy, where he was put through to his CIA counterpart, Doug Wallis.

"Andy, how are you?"

Harvey didn't usually take kindly to people shortening his name, but Wallis was such an affable character, and when seeking information it was a good idea to let the little things slide.

"Good, thanks, Doug. How's the family?"

Wallis gave him the usual sob story about how his wife just couldn't get settled in England, no matter how much shopping she did. Harvey knew the story could go on indefinitely so he cut his friend short.

"I'm just looking for some information about the attack on Jolo last week."

"We sent that over yesterday," Wallis said. "Didn't you get it?"

"Yeah, we got it, but I'd like to know more about the prisoners. We can't seem to locate one of them, a woman named Victoria Phillips."

"I don't recall any of them being female," Wallis said, sounding confused.

"Are you sure?"

"Positive. There was certainly no-one named Victoria, anyway."

Harvey rifled through the papers on his desk. "I can't see any reference to the prisoners anywhere," he said. "Are you sure you sent that information over?"

"No, they won't be on anything we passed to you," Wallis said casually. "That report was classified Internal Eyes Only."

"Any particular reason?" Harvey asked, curious as to why the identities should have been withheld.

"No idea," Wallis told him. "That's what we got from Langley, no explanation as to why."

It wasn't unusual for agencies to withhold certain sensitive information from each other, but it seemed strange that the names of three people rescued from terrorists should be considered classified, especially if two of them were British.

"Is there any chance you can tell me the names?" Harvey asked, knowing what the answer would be. He had, however, planted the seed.

"Sorry, pal, no can do."

"That's okay, Doug, I understand. Hey, fancy a beer later?"

The question was a signal they both used when they wanted something off the record, and Harvey was relieved when Doug agreed to meet up later that evening. He was, however, slightly frustrated that he would have to wait another few hours to get the information.

He walked round to Farsi's desk to see how he was getting on with the analysis of the *Huang Zhen* manifest. His colleague had been compiling a list of companies who had used the ship to transport their goods abroad. Once finalised, each company would be run through the internal search engine to find matches to persons of known interest.

"Anything yet?" Harvey asked, but a shake of the head told him all he needed to know.

"Nothing so far, but I've only been through a quarter of the companies. The *Huang Zhen* is a ULCV, or Ultra Large Container

Vessel. This beast is carrying close to two thousand containers for just over twelve hundred companies. It's going to take some time to get through them all."

Harvey sympathised with his friend. If only investigations were like the movies, he thought, they'd just have to wait for that one clue to drop into their laps and the mystery would be solved. Back in the real world, it was relentless hours of data analysis which usually won the day. It was just a shame the men in power didn't appreciate that fact; otherwise they would provide more people to get the job done. As it was, the vast majority of staff had been assigned to identifying threats associated with the upcoming Olympics, which left Harvey and Farsi doing work the analysts would normally power through in a few hours.

To make matters worse, the equally under-manned UK Border Agency was forcing staff to take holidays in the months leading up to London 2012 so that they would have all hands on deck for the games. It meant queues would be shorter during July and August, but it left them woefully short-staffed in the lead-up, something that had been flagged up on several occasions. The politicians, however, refused to believe that anyone posing a threat to the UK would turn up prior to the games, instead expecting them to arrive when they were in full flow. This short-sightedness was a constant thorn in the security services' sides, but it was something they'd learned to live with.

The culmination of this was that resources were stretched in just about every critical service and all of the major newspapers had picked up on the fact. Their coverage, in Harvey's eyes, was an open invitation to attack the country, and he was one of the few people who could do anything about it.

Harvey shook the thought off and went back to his desk, where he found an internal message which informed him that a secure fax had been received.

He took a walk down to the communications office and handed over his identity card, despite knowing the receptionist and her recognising him from multiple previous visits. The rule was simple and rigorously enforced: no valid, current ID; no entry.

After a quick inspection of his card he was given a smile and offered a seat while the receptionist placed a call through to the inner office. A moment later a junior clerk appeared and handed over the communication.

Harvey saw that it was the call records he'd requested from the High Commission in Singapore. As well as a list of calls made to and from Hughes's registered mobile number, there was a handwritten note at the bottom of the page:

A second mobile was found on the body, unregistered. Here is a list of calls we extracted from the SIM:

There were just four entries underneath the note, and Harvey had a feeling that one of them would be significant. He rushed back to his office and compared the numbers with those of Carl Levine and found a match on the last entry. The mobile number Hughes had called from also matched the incoming phone records they held for Levine.

Any suspicions they had that this was the Timmy they were looking for were now confirmed, and he asked Farsi to cross each of the company owners with the names on Hughes's call log.

"I know it's a major pain, but if we can tie Hughes to that ship somehow..."

"Then what?" Farsi asked.

"I'm not sure," Harvey admitted. "But I have a feeling there's a lot more to Farrar's request for help than just finding Levine and Campbell."

* * *

People were beginning to drift out of the office and a glance at the clock told Harvey that it was almost six-thirty in the evening. He'd taken half of the manifest from Farsi and was also running company names through the computer, but for the last few hours he had come up empty.

When he met Wallis, it was usually at seven in Armando's restaurant a few streets away, which meant he'd have to make a move soon. He locked his half of the manifest in a drawer and grabbed his jacket as he headed for Ellis's office to deliver his end-of-shift report. He found her gazing intently at her monitor.

"I'm done for the day," he said when Ellis looked up. "We haven't been able to come up with anything that says the *Huang Zhen* is linked to Levine and Campbell, but we still have a lot of companies to go through."

Ellis stretched and stifled a yawn. "Nothing coming from Farrar, either," she said. "It's as if he's given up the search."

"Should we do likewise?" Harvey asked, hoping for — and getting — a negative response.

"No, we carry on. There's a link in Asia, I'm certain of it. That was Abdul Mansour's last known location and now Al-Qaeda chatter has gone off the charts."

"As happened just before 9/11," Harvey mused.

"Exactly," Ellis said. "A lot of it is rubbish — a smokescreen — but the sheer volume makes it near impossible to pick out the relevant stuff."

She rubbed her temples and let out a sigh. Harvey could see she was under an enormous amount of pressure, as were they all, but as head of the organisation she bore the brunt. He wanted to cheer her up by letting her know about the meeting with Wallis, but if he mentioned it she would no doubt ask what information he had shared in the past. That wasn't a conversation he wanted to get into right now.

"I'm heading home," he said, and Ellis nodded as he made for the exit.

Outside, the sky had clouded over once more, heralding yet more rain in what had already been the wettest May in recent years. It was only a ten minute walk to Armando's and he arrived just as the heavens opened. Inside, he found a table near the back, and the drinks arrived just as Wallis dashed through the door.

"I'm beginning to see why my wife wants to go home," he said, bringing a smile to Harvey's face. He knew that Doug loved his current assignment, and the more his wife complained, the more determined he was to stay.

Wallis hung his coat on a stand and sat opposite Harvey. They enjoyed their drinks in silence for a moment, Wallis favouring a pint of bitter to Harvey's lager.

"So what have you got for me, Doug?"

Wallis savoured his beer before putting the glass on the table and leaning closer to Harvey.

"The order to keep it under wraps came from the Home Secretary himself," Wallis said, and saw the expected surprise on his friend's face. It quickly turned to curiosity.

"So who were the prisoners?"

"The one he was concerned about was Sam Grant."

Harvey made the quick transition from curious to confused. He'd never heard the name, and was certain he hadn't seen it in any recent reports.

"Who is this Grant guy?"

"We don't know. Colonel Travis Dane, commander of the Special Activities Division on Jolo sent his picture over to Langley and all they got back was the name and an order not to share with anyone, not even you guys."

Harvey wondered why the minister would want to withhold information from his own security services, and the obvious answer was that it wasn't an operation that he wanted the Intelligence Services Commissioner to know about. The commissioner is responsible for service oversight and can visit any of the security services at his discretion, requesting documents or information relating to any case. Each year he reports his findings direct to the Prime Minister. This report is then laid before parliament and subsequently published.

If the Home Secretary didn't want this case becoming public knowledge, it could only mean one thing. But who would carry out such an operation? It would have to be someone with access to the system. He made a mental note to check with Gerald Small to see if any of the sub-nets fit the bill, but one leaped immediately to mind.

Farrar.

Ellis had said that even she didn't know who he worked for, which pointed to his role being covert. And if it *was* Farrar, did this mean that this Sam Grant was one of the passengers he was expecting?

"Who were the other prisoners?" He asked.

"Simon Baines and Len Smart," Wallis said.

"Are you sure?" Harvey asked, a little louder than he intended.

Wallis nodded. "I read through the report just before I left the office. According to Dane, one of his troops caught three armed men wandering around the jungle and brought them in for questioning. They wouldn't talk, so Dane sent their pictures to Langley, who sent back the details. All they got for Sam Grant was a name, a photo and that's it."

"Do you have the report with you?" Harvey asked, more in hope than expectation.

"Sorry, buddy. You know the deal, completely off the record, and that means no hard copies."

Harvey understood. "So what happened to the prisoners? Where are they now?"

"Dane said the three of them went missing during the attack. The guard house was hit and they must have escaped. Apparently your people were pissed when they turned up to collect them."

"*My* people?" Harvey asked, once more confused. "Are you sure they were from Five?"

"Langley assumed they were, but the look on your face tells me otherwise."

"They certainly weren't sent by anyone I know," Harvey said, but he didn't add that it once again pointed to James Farrar.

He recalled that the *Huang Zhen* had left Malaysia on Monday the 23rd, while the attack on the base had taken place just three days earlier. That meant Baines and Smart would have had three days to travel to Port Kelang. His search through Hughes's file had shown that he owned a yacht, but could it make the journey in that time? He'd have to wait until he got back to the office to work that one out, and the introduction of the mysterious Sam Grant into the mix meant he wasn't prepared to wait until the morning.

"I have to go and check a few things out," he said as he rose. "Thanks for the info, Doug. I owe you one."

"Big time," Wallis agreed.

It took Harvey less than five minutes to jog back to Thames House, and once in the office he went straight to his desk and logged onto his computer. He was waiting for the security settings to synch when Ellis approached him.

"I thought you'd gone home," she said.

"I've got some new information," Harvey told her. "I need to do a search for Sam Grant."

The welcome screen appeared and he began typing into the internal search engine.

"Where did you get the name?" She asked as they waited for the results to come back.

"A completely anonymous and deniable source," Harvey told her with a smile. "I could tell you but then I'd have to kill myself."

The screen showed six results and they went through each one, Harvey looking for anything that could link him to the current investigation. The first four were quickly dismissed, but when trying to open the fifth record he was shown a dialog box which requested a password. He entered his account login and a flashing message filled the screen:

Access Denied.

"Okay," Ellis said, looking at Harvey. "You got my attention. Who is this guy?"

"I've got no idea. However, find Sam Grant and we find Baines and Smart."

He gave her a breakdown of the information he'd got from Wallis but stopped short of revealing his identity, despite Ellis asking more than once. She suggested they try to access the file using her credentials, which had a higher level of access. When they got to her office and repeated the process, the outcome was the same.

"If the Home Secretary personally gave the order to withhold Grant's file from the CIA — and from his own people — then it smells of black ops to me," Harvey said. "That means we're dealing with a team who have the minister's ear, a team who are off the official grid but still have access. And if Grant was with Baines and Smart on Jolo, that team would not want you looking for that particular pair, even if they were solid leads to finding Levine and Campbell."

He looked Ellis in the eye. "So who does that sound like?"

Ellis had to agree that it pointed the finger fair and square in Farrar's direction, but it wasn't conclusive.

"We need to pin this to him," she said, rubbing her palms together as she concentrated.

"Then what?" Harvey asked.

It was a very good question, one she hadn't got round to considering. If the passengers were in fact the mysterious Grant and the two men Farrar didn't want her searching for, what was she to do about it? If she interfered in an order signed by the minister himself, she knew she could kiss her career goodbye. On the flip side, she had proof that Farrar had ordered someone to intercept them, and the phrase *'ensure no onward journey'* sounded very much like a kill order. If these people were who she thought they were, could she stand idly by and allow a state-sanctioned hit on British citizens? She knew she wouldn't allow another nation to get away with it, so why shouldn't those same standards apply to her own government?

"First we confirm that Farrar is behind this," she said.

Harvey nodded. "How do we do that? If Farrar is involved, he'll just deny any knowledge of Sam Grant."

Ellis smiled. "To catch a rat, you have to become a rat."

* * *

386

James Farrar was wading through the reports his team had produced. So far they had checked hundreds of bed & breakfast establishments for cash-paying families checking in on the 22nd of April, but there were still thousands to be done. There were also numerous camp sites, caravan parks and boat rentals to be eliminated, and all of this in the next few days. At the current rate, his targets would die of old age before he found them.

He wished he could bring in the police, but that was out of the question. The last thing he wanted was this hitting the newspapers, and all it would take would be one loud-mouthed copper to open his mouth to the wrong person.

He was still fumbling for ideas when his mobile rang. The display told him it was Ellis and he prayed that she had some good news. He answered using the most pleasant voice he could muster.

"Veronica, how are you?"

"Tired," Ellis said wearily.

You and me both, Farrar thought, though he didn't say as much. "I hope you're calling to let me know you've found what I'm looking for," he said, not wanting to be too specific over an unsecure line.

"Not yet, but we have been given a lead, a name. Trouble is, we can't follow it up."

"Why the hell not?" Farrar asked, dropping the pretence of amiability.

"I can't access his file," Ellis said. "It's password protected. I was calling to ask if you could have a word with the Home Secretary and persuade him to release it to me."

"Whose file is it?" Farrar asked as he prepared to enter the name into the search engine.

"Sam Grant," she said, and Farrar almost dropped the phone. Where the hell did she get that name from?

"Are you there, James?"

"Uh...yeah, just doing a search now." He brought the screen up as he tried to figure out who the hell knew about Grant. He did, of course, and the Home Secretary. Besides them, there was the request from the CIA a few weeks earlier. Farrar had been on a plane back from Manila when the request had come in, otherwise he would have handled it himself and sent them a completely different name. In his absence, all they had been given was a photo, which was what they had in the first place. Giving them the name should have been no big deal, either: It was a fictitious name in a sealed file that was only accessible to a handful of people, and the CIA had been given explicit instructions not to share with anyone. Unfortunately, it seemed that the Americans hadn't been as tight-mouthed as they should have been.

"I'm getting a password prompt, too," he said. "Looks like I'll have to ask the minister for access. I can't promise anything, though. If I can't see the file, there must be a good reason."

Ellis sounded disappointed as she asked Farrar to do his best.

"I will," he assured her, "but I need to know what information you have about this man. If it can lead us to Levine and Campbell I can put that forward as a case for releasing the file."

"Nothing beyond the name," Ellis told him.

"Okay, then who gave you the name?" He asked, hoping to confirm that it had come from the CIA.

"One of my operatives got it from an undisclosed source."

"Which operative?" Farrar pressed.

"That's not important, James. Please just let me know when you've spoken to the Home Secretary."

The phone went dead in his hand and Farrar swore half a dozen times before typing his password into the box.

Whatever was in this file, he had to find it quickly.

* * *

Ellis still had her hand on the receiver when the key-logger began spitting out new characters. She copied and pasted them into the password dialog before hitting the Enter key. A moment later a picture appeared, underneath which was the name Sam Grant.

"James Farrar, you're a lying shit!"

They read through the brief biography and found nothing out of the ordinary. In fact, it appeared decidedly sterile. Born in London during the early seventies, worked for a few small companies after leaving school, single, no driving licence, lived in rented accommodation until his sudden move to Manila a year earlier.

"It looks like a legend," Ellis commented.

"And a poor one at that," Harvey confirmed. "I'll have someone check these firms, but I'll bet they're no longer trading, if they ever existed in the first place."

Legends are cover stories created when an intelligence operative is required to go under cover. It creates a believable personal background should anyone do any checks into the operative's history.

Ellis nodded and scrolled down through the entries. If the bio was brief, the last entry was even more succinct: Deceased.

The entry was dated Thursday the 19th of April 2012, a day before the attack on Camp Bautista. Harvey wondered how that could be: According to Wallis, the three prisoners had escaped during the attack, and he told Ellis as much.

"Then to paraphrase Mark Twain," Ellis said, "it looks like reports of his death have been grossly exaggerated."

Harvey studied the picture, which also appeared to be contrived. It was like a collage of facial elements, with a large flat nose that didn't seem to naturally fit with the size of the face. Despite this, there was something familiar…

The image disappeared as Ellis clicked the History link to see who had been responsible for each of the entries. The last recorded user, the person who had declared Grant dead, was none other than James Farrar.

"So Farrar thinks Grant is dead, but when the CIA requests his details, a team from the UK is sent to pick up him and his friends. We know that team wasn't one of ours, so I'm guessing Farrar is behind that, too."

"It certainly looks like it," Harvey agreed, "which is why he doesn't want you looking for Baines and Smart. He already knows where they are and has someone waiting for them when they arrive in Durban."

Ellis nodded, having come to the same conclusion. "I want you to go out there," she said. "Find them and bring them home."

Harvey told her that he was happy to oblige, but was also aware that there could be some serious fallout. "I don't think the Home Secretary is going to be too happy if we interfere with one of his operations," he warned her.

"I know," Ellis said, "but when I joined the service I vowed to protect Britain from all threats, foreign and domestic. We don't know why Farrar is looking for these people, but whatever it is they're supposed to have done, they are still entitled to a fair trial. It isn't up to the Home Secretary to decide who lives and dies."

"Not even in the interest of national security?" Harvey asked.

"If it was national security, we'd have heard about it," Ellis said indignantly.

Harvey suspected the real reason she was taking this course of action was that she had been left out of the loop by her superiors. She might also be looking to settle an old score with Farrar, but whatever her motive, they were reading from the same page.

"I'm going to need some help over there," he said. "We don't know if it's just one man or a whole team waiting for the *Huang Zhen* to arrive. The only thing that we're certain of is that someone will be waiting to kill those passengers."

"Then you'll need to establish that as your priority. You'll be looking for someone who's just entered the country and is booked into accommodation until the seventh of May. Cross reference flights from Malaysia with hotel reservations and run any matches through the system."

Ellis brought up a new screen and searched for information on their people in South Africa. She was rewarded with the bio for Dennis Owen, whose cover was that of a senior advisor in the UK Trade & Investment department.

"I'll let him know you're coming," She said. "Draw up a list of anything you're going to need and choose your legend. Farrar may be watching the airport departure lists and I don't want to have to explain what you're doing over there."

Harvey nodded and went to his station to book his flight. He chose one the following evening to give himself time to try to discover just who was waiting for Baines and Smart in Durban. He was too pumped up to sleep and knew an all-nighter was on the cards, so he set the search running and grabbed his jacket before heading out of the building. He was back twenty minutes later with a large coffee, two sandwiches and a selection of chocolate bars, once again thankful that there was no-one waiting for him at home.

The list of passengers was ready and waiting for him and he immediately filtered out those who were in transit as well as all South African nationals. It was entirely possible that whoever he was looking for could be a resident but he had to focus on the leads he had. If Farrar was using a contractor, it was highly likely that they would be British.

The filtered list contained just over seventy promising matches and Harvey began the process of comparing them — one by one — with names held on their system.

* * *

Tom Gray stared at the ceiling of the container and for the umpteenth time he wondered what he was going to do to James Farrar once he got his hands on him. Vick was having yet another nap, while Baines was busy cheating at a game of patience and Smart was once again engrossed in the new Kindle he'd purchased in Kuala Lumpur.

"What are you reading now?" Sonny asked.

"*The Bones Of The Earth* by Scott Bury. It's a historical fantasy."

"Sounds good."

"I'd say it was closer to exceptional," Smart said, and returned to his book.

Vick woke and stretched, doing her best to stifle a yawn in case she breathed in too much of the fetid air. She got up to get the circulation moving in her legs before sitting back down and rummaging in the bag for some food.

"What time is it?" She asked.

"Three in the morning," Sonny told her. "That means about a hundred and thirty something hours until we get to Durban, so go easy on the food."

Vick soon realised what he meant. They had brought along enough tins and drinks to last them well beyond the two week journey, but boredom had seen her snacking constantly and there was barely enough left for the next couple of days. Despite this she broke open a tin of peach slices and tucked in with a fork.

Her actions hadn't gone unnoticed by one of her fellow passengers. A young Chinese man stood and walked over to her, gesturing at the food and pointing towards his own chest. Vick instinctively cradled the food close to her chest while turning her back on him. This did nothing to dissuade the man and he began to raise his voice, gesturing towards the bag.

"What's he saying?" Grant asked Sonny.

"How the hell should I know?"

"I thought you took language lessons in the Regiment. I know I signed off at least three of your requests."

"That was because the teacher was so pretty. During the lessons I only picked up the most important phrases."

"Which were?" Len asked.

"'Give me a beer', obviously." This brought appreciative nods from the other two former soldiers. "There was also 'fancy a shag', and of course, 'kill him'."

"Why do you need to say that in other languages?" Vick asked.

Sonny grinned: "I don't. I just need to know when someone is saying it in my presence."

Their idle chit-chat was beginning to incense the Chinese passenger and he stepped in among the group and reached down into the bag. Baines grabbed the man's wrist and pulled it towards him while at the same time getting to his feet, twisting the arm as he did so. The hungry stranger lost his battle with gravity and landed on his back, and Baines was on him in an instant. He put one knee on the man's chest and grabbed him around the throat.

"That's not very polite," Baines said, as he squeezed with just enough force to bring some colour to the face.

A howl erupted behind Baines and Gray touched him on the arm, indicating towards a woman who was quite clearly pregnant. "Let him go, Sonny."

Baines hesitated for a moment but then climbed off. Gray handed the man a tin of Spam and gestured for him to disappear.

"Wonderful," Baines said. "That takes us about ten hours closer to starvation."

"Don't be daft," Smart said, his eyes still focused on his book. "They'll be serving breakfast in a few hours."

"Don't get me wrong, but while highly original, curry for breakfast does lose its appeal after a while. I'd rather eat a Pot Noodle."

To change the subject, Smart put down his Kindle and asked Gray if he'd decided on a plan of action.

"I'm still torn between two options, but I'm swinging towards public exposure."

"We dismissed that idea a couple of weeks ago," Baines pointed out. "They'll have DA notices out and no paper would dare run the story."

"I agree that if we just called the BBC or a newspaper they wouldn't run the story, but there are other ways."

He explained what he had in mind but the others were not totally convinced that his plan would work. However, they'd had the same reservations a year and a half earlier but had come so close to pulling off a masterful plan.

"I know it's risky, but the alternative doesn't guarantee results, either."

Plan B was to gain control of a television news studio and tell the world what James Farrar had been up to on behalf of the government.

392

However, they would eventually have to hand themselves in, and they couldn't be sure they would be allowed to see the light of day again.

The others agreed with him, and so they spent the next few hours developing Gray's favoured option, suggesting and dismissing ideas until they had what they thought was a workable solution to their problems.

"It all hinges on you convincing your man to help us," Smart pointed out. "Fail to do that and we fall at the first hurdle."

Gray was well aware that the initial plea for help was crucial to their success. If he couldn't pull it off, there would be no option but to revert to the back-up plan. "Then I'd best be at my most persuasive," he said, determination in his eyes.

Chapter 6

Thursday May 3rd 2012

Ben Palmer crept through the darkness towards the chain link fence surrounding the Wenban Freight Management compound, even though he knew there was no camera coverage to record his approach.

His initial recce the previous day — a drive-by followed by a walk-past — had revealed just three CCTV cameras covering the vehicle park, all static. Negotiating them wouldn't be a challenge, but he had no idea what kind of security they had in place to protect the main office building. To get to the office, he first had to get through the fence. It wasn't particularly high but was topped with razor wire, so going through seemed the most prudent option.

A quick look around showed no sign of life, either from the tyre yard thirty yards to his left or the warehouse on the other side of the road, which looked like it had long been abandoned.

He pulled a pair of cutters from his jacket and began snipping away at the wire next to a supporting post, starting at the bottom of the fence and working his way upwards until he had created a twelve-inch gap. He put the cutters aside and pulled the broken part of the fence towards him so that he could squeeze underneath. He stopped when he heard a sound close by, and strained to detect the direction it had come from. A glance to either side showed no signs of movement, but he waited a couple of minutes, just to be sure.

The compound was quite a distance from the nearest populated town, so he assumed the noise was probably some kind of nocturnal animal scratching around for food. He turned his attention back to the fence and was beginning to roll it upwards when a hundred and seventy pounds of Boerboel came bounding towards the fence, barking for all it was worth. Palmer barely had time to roll the fence back into place before the guard dog began clawing at his fingers, shredding the skin and destroying his surgical gloves.

Palmer fell on his backside and used his feet to prevent the dog from crawling through the gap he'd created, at the same time reaching for his Taser. By this time, the hound had managed to get its head through the small gap and was attacking Palmer's feet, though the thick rubber soles of his boots prevented any serious injury. The animal still came at him, inching through the hole while snapping and snarling, saliva dripping from its mouth.

Palmer finally managed to get the Taser free and fired into the dog's shoulder, delivering a charge which at first appeared to have no effect but which eventually brought it to the ground. He kept his finger on the trigger while he extracted a syringe, and he cut the charge just before he stabbed it into the back of the dog's neck with shaking hands.

With the animal incapacitated, he lay on the ground to catch his breath, wondering where the hell it had come from. He'd looked for a kennel during his earlier observations but there had been nothing whatsoever to point to a guard dog patrolling the compound. The manager must have kept it inside during the day, probably to stop it attacking the staff, judging by its demeanour.

Palmer decided to keep the Taser handy, just in case there were any more surprises. He also had to get the dog back inside the compound so that his little visit went unnoticed. He moved the animal aside and crawled through the gap he'd made, and it took some considerable effort to pull the mutt through after him. He eventually got it clear of the hole and dragged it behind a stack of pallets, then used his feet to obliterate the trail leading to his entry point.

With the dog hidden, Palmer wiped the sweat from his face and neck, and then pulled out his lock-picking tools. The main office was bathed in darkness and he stepped carefully, listening intently for the slightest sound that could indicate another dog, or even a night watchman, though the latter seemed unlikely given the amount of barking the dog had done.

He reached the door and found that his first hurdle was a padlock which secured a deadbolt just above the door handle. It took less than fifteen seconds to defeat it, and another thirty to open the Yale lock. He eased the door open gently, looking for any sign of an alarm but finding none.

Once inside the wooden structure he found a couple of untidy desks, both with computers at least a dozen years old. He ignored those, instead looking for hard copies of movement schedules. He found these in the single filing cabinet, and using a small torch with a green filter over the glass to diffuse the beam he flicked through the records searching for anything relating to the seventh of May. He was thankful that the operation was small, with less than a dozen vehicles, which meant he was able to find what he was looking for within a minute.

There were just seven entries for the coming Monday, and two of them were pickups for Arnold Tang's company. His little chat with Tang's lieutenant hadn't revealed the fact that there would be more than one consignment arriving, which left Palmer having to decide which container his targets were likely to be in. The first one was a standard forty-foot high-cube container with a declared gross weight of forty-five thousand pounds, while the second was half the size and lighter by around seventy percent.

Palmer knew that his targets were just four of twenty people making the journey to the UK, so he discounted the smaller container and checked the details of the other one. It was due to be offloaded just before seven in the evening, with delivery to an import/export company the following morning. This suggested that the container would be parked up overnight, most probably within the compound.

After taking snaps of both records with a compact digital camera, he carefully placed all of the documents back in their respective folders and closed the cabinet, wiping down any surfaces he had touched. At the door he did the same before closing it quietly and re-attaching the padlock. The dog was still where he had left it, and he was pleased to see that it was still breathing; the last thing he needed was a dead dog broadcasting his incursion.

At the fence he smoothed out the soil around the gap and pulled a pallet up to the post before squeezing through the hole. He then moved the pallet over the hole to prevent the dog from scratching around and bringing it to anyone's attention. He then used small lengths of wire to fasten the fence back to the post as best he could. It wasn't a permanent solution, but if it prevented detection for just a few days it would serve its purpose.

He made his way back to the main road and waited until there was no traffic in sight before sprinting to the main entrance, where he quickly checked the condition of the security. A large, rust-free chain and combination lock secured the two metal gates, and he made a mental note to add industrial-strength bolt cutters to his ever-growing shopping list.

Palmer ran back to his car, which he'd parked behind the tyre yard, then drove back into town, stopping off at a bar to grab a beer. He stayed there for just ten minutes, and once he reached his hotel he made a point of getting close enough to the receptionist that she could smell his breath as he asked for a morning wake-up call. This helped keep up the pretence of the travelling salesman out enjoying the local nightlife.

When he got to his room, he booted his laptop and logged into his proxy server before searching his contact list for the number of an old friend. He called using an unregistered pre-paid phone he'd bought earlier in the day.

"Sean," he said when the connection was made. "It's Ben. I was in town and thought I'd look you up."

"Hey, it's good to hear your voice, man."

They chewed the fat for a couple of minutes before Palmer explained that he needed to do some shopping while he was in town.

"No problem," Sean said. "I'm having a *braai* this weekend. Wanna join me?"

"Just like old times. Sure, sounds great."

They arranged to meet at the farm just after midday on Saturday and Palmer ended the call. He spent the next thirty minutes finding a van rental company with a vehicle large enough for his purposes before turning the lights out and grabbing some sleep.

* * *

Andrew Harvey's KLM flight touched down just after nine-thirty in the evening, and an hour later he was met in the arrivals lounge by a man wearing a suit despite the temperature being close to eighty Fahrenheit.

Dennis Owen was in his early thirties and had the bearing of a man who did more in life than simply offer advice on trade and industry matters. His hidden remit was to get detailed background information on companies looking to invest in the UK in order to ensure there were no skeletons in closets that might embarrass the country. The last thing the government needed was a repeat of the Quatromain fiasco a few years earlier. It transpired that the money men behind that corporation were subsequently prosecuted for drug-trafficking, which was a particular embarrassment for the Secretary of State for Business, Innovation and Skills, who had personally signed off the deal.

Owen offered Harvey a confident handshake. "Welcome to South Africa."

"Thanks," Harvey said, stifling a yawn. The twenty hour journey had taken a lot out of him, despite managing to grab some sleep on the flight following the two-hour stopover in Amsterdam's Schiphol airport. "Did you have any luck with the seven names I sent you?"

"I've got a friend in the local police force and he did some checking, but none of them have any records here at all," Owen said, as he led Harvey out of the airport terminal in direction of the car park. He stopped at a BMW saloon and once inside he handed a printed sheet to Harvey. "These are the supposed itineraries of your suspects. I also got the name of the haulage company collecting the containers you're interested in. They're a small firm called Wenban Freight Management."

Hamad Farsi's efforts had paid off. He'd made the connection between Timmy Hughes and Arnold Tang, which in turn led to the discovery that one of Tang's companies had two consignments on the *Huang Zhen*. They hadn't yet been able to get into the Durban Port Authority computers to find out who was collecting the containers, which was why they'd asked Owen to get the information. While they now knew who would be collecting the consignments, they still had no idea where they were going to be dropped off.

"What about the company?" Harvey asked. "Any ties to Arnold Tang?"

"None that we could find. It looks like your typical small business. They've been in operation for six years and grown from a couple of vehicles to ten during that time. Tax records and company accounts suggest this expansion has been financed using their own capital, and their income is consistent with a haulage company of that size."

"That's good. They should have no problems co-operating with us."

"You'd think so, but we spoke to them this afternoon and the owner is reluctant to give us any information about his customers without a warrant."

"Fine, so get one," Harvey said.

"Not so easy," Owen told him. "I asked my friend but he said the police will want documented evidence before they apply to the courts. We might have better luck with customs, though. If we let them know the container might contain illegal immigrants, they could check it at the port."

Harvey thought about it, but soon dismissed the idea. "If we do that, we lose whoever's here to meet them," he said. If he was going

398

to play his part in disrupting Farrar's plans, he wanted concrete evidence of his involvement in any wrongdoing, and having the person or persons sent to carry out the kill order would be a good start.

It was forty-five minutes later when they arrived at the hotel and Owen dropped Harvey off outside.

"I'll be back for you at seven in the morning, then I'll drive you down to Durban. Your room is booked and paid for."

Harvey thanked him and dragged his suitcase into the foyer. It was aesthetically mundane, though that mattered little to Harvey as he planned to do nothing more than sleep for the next six hours.

* * *

Azhar Al-Asiri threw open his arms to welcome his young general home.

"*Salam alaikum*!"

Abdul Mansour returned the greeting and took a seat at the small table. It was the first time he had been to Al-Asiri's home and the humble surroundings were exactly as he would have fashioned for himself.

"How was your journey?"

"Fine," Mansour said as he accepted the offer of tea, though fine was being generous. Once he'd received news that his lieutenant, Nabil Shah, had been killed on Jolo, Mansour had made his way home from Indonesia. He had spent most of the journey on a fishing vessel and it had been several days before he'd stopped throwing up. Even now he wondered if the smell would ever leave him.

"I am glad you are back, my friend. Tell me about your latest mission."

Mansour explained how he'd delivered the weapons and money to the Abu Sayyaf leader and provided training in their use, but as for the attack itself, he only knew what the television and newspapers had reported. Over a hundred American and Filipino soldiers had been killed in the firefight at Camp Bautista, although Abu Sayyaf had lost a couple of hundred men in a reprisal attack immediately afterwards.

As for the overall mission, he had convinced the leaders of Jemaah Islamiyah — Abu Sayyaf's Indonesian counterparts — to enter into talks aimed at creating a Muslim alliance. The promise of more weapons and money had been extended to the Indonesians, with a view to them controlling most of maritime South-East Asia.

399

"You have done Allah a great service," Al-Asiri told him. "However, the fight must continue at pace. Tell me, how would you feel about going back to England one last time?"

"I will go wherever you ask," Mansour said with heartfelt conviction.

"As I thought," his master smiled as he leaned back into his chair. "Your mission will be to simply provide training to a new group of martyrs. You will not be exposed to danger yourself."

"What do they need to know?"

"You will show them how to create explosive devices. These are young men who have not come under the scrutiny of the security services, and to use the internet for their research would be to wave a red flag at a bull."

"How can we be sure that they are not being watched?" Mansour asked. "The last thing we should do is underestimate our enemies."

"I have people with access to this information," Al-Asiri said confidently. To his lasting regret, he hadn't been able to get anyone into the security services themselves, but there were other agencies that were party to certain information, and airline no-fly and watch lists were just two ways of knowing if MI5 were interested in an individual.

"What would you have them attack?"

"There are multiple targets across the UK," Al-Asiri told him. "In addition, co-ordinated attacks will take place in the US and Canada. Timing will be of the utmost importance."

"Are these military targets, or infrastructure?" Mansour asked, intrigued.

"Sperm banks," Al-Asiri said, and smiled at Mansour's confused expression.

"I'm sorry, I do not understand. How will this further the cause?"

Al-Asiri explained how his research team had developed a virus that would kill off Y chromosome sperm, and spelled out his vision for the future. "The next generation of British and American children will be predominately female, which in years to come will reduce their fighting capability. The small percentage of males born will carry the new gene, which means the cycle continues in ever decreasing circles. The only chance to produce male offspring is through inter-racial breeding."

Mansour looked at Al-Asiri and did well to hide his true feelings. His facial expression portrayed fascination, but inside he began to wonder if the old man had gone completely mad.

"You plan to breed them out of existence?"

"Exactly," Al-Asiri told him. "In a hundred years, America and Britain as we know them will be nothing more than a page in the history books. Our Muslim influence will spread throughout their lands until ultimately the whole world kneels before Allah!"

Mansour had to marvel at the audacity of the plan, but it was flawed on so many fundamental levels.

"How many sperm banks are there in the UK and US?" He asked, hoping his master would recognise the scale of the operation he was proposing.

"Many hundreds," Al-Asiri told him, "but we do not need to destroy them all. We have a website ready to go live, and it will proclaim the formation of the Campaign for Natural Birth. It is a fictitious Christian organisation seeking the abolition of medically-assisted pregnancy on the grounds that it is God alone who decides the birth of every child.

"We will bomb a small number of sperm banks in each country and CNB will claim responsibility for these actions, warning that more attacks will come unless they are closed down. They will also claim that anyone donating to one of these banks makes themselves a viable target."

Mansour could see the sense in that approach, and if nothing else it would tie up the security services in both countries for quite some time. Nevertheless, he still had major concerns about the overall plan, and he wasn't sure how much criticism he could level at his master's idea.

"That still leaves them with a very large stock pile. I'm not sure these efforts will deliver the results you are looking for. I am also concerned that the bombers will give away the fact that a Christian group wasn't actually behind the attacks."

"That is why you are here," Al-Asiri told him, his demeanour a lot less convivial than moments earlier. "I have given you the tools and explained the effect I wish to achieve. It is now up to you to make it work."

Mansour sat in silence, the enormity of the task weighing heavily on his shoulders. His rise through the Al-Qaeda ranks had been meteoric, but fail this mission and all of his efforts would have been in vain.

Al-Asiri saw the blank, almost pained expression on his general's face and offered a powerful incentive. "As you know, since the Sheik died and I took over his mantle, I delayed in filling the vacant place on the inner council. There was a reason for this.

"I have been watching you develop over the years, and your commitment to the cause, your courage and skill all point to you one day making a great leader."

Al-Asiri paused to let the words sink in. "Complete this mission and take your place on the council."

Mansour's excitement was tempered by his concerns over Al-Asiri's mental state. He had hoped to one day become a regional commander, but he'd envisaged that being many years in the future. To have it handed to him on a plate at such a tender age was a blessing from Allah himself, though it meant being led by a man who was obviously cartwheeling towards senility.

The seed of a plan popped into Mansour's head, one that would need to be nurtured, but for the time being he gave his leader the reaction he desired.

"Of course I will take on the challenge," he smiled. "Tell me what plans you already have in place."

Chapter 7

Friday May 4th 2012

"I'm bored!"

Alana Levine sat with her arms folded, staring at the caravan floor. "Wish I could have brought my iPhone."

Her father was drying dishes in the tiny kitchen area and he slammed down the cup in his hand, smashing it into a dozen pieces. "How many times do I have to tell you?" He snarled.

Sandra Levine grabbed her husband by the arm. "Carl, leave her alone. What do you expect from a thirteen-year-old?"

Carl Levine took a couple of deep breaths before gathering up the shards of porcelain and dumping them in the trash. After getting a look from his wife he went to sit next to his daughter and put an arm around her shoulder.

"I'm sorry, darling, but we couldn't bring anything that could be traced, I told you that."

"I know, but I could use it to just play games," Alana pouted, bottom lip thrust out like a diving board.

Levine sighed. He had been through this a dozen times, explaining how SIM cards could be tracked even when the phone was not in use, and that even without the card it might be possible for those with the right technology to locate the device.

"I'll make it up to you when this is all over, I promise."

"But when will that be?" She asked.

Carl Levine didn't have an answer to that one. A year earlier he had a schedule to keep to, but this time it was simply a case of waiting to hear from his friends. He didn't have any way of communicating with the outside world, and all the money they had was being spent on food and fuel. While they still had a few hundred pounds between them, the money wasn't going to last forever. It was a blessing that the caravan they were staying in was owned outright by Tom Gray's solicitor and the ground rent was being paid by direct debit, otherwise their finances would be stretched even further.

"Hopefully not too long," Levine said.

"Is it going to be like last time, with the reporters hanging round the house and school?"

Levine promised her that it wouldn't be a repeat of the previous year, when the press had camped outside their house for a fortnight in the hope of a story. They had even tried to interview his daughter as she entered the school grounds, and the following day he had escorted her to the entrance of the school building. On leaving the playground he'd stopped to speak to the press, but not to give then the story they'd hoped for. Reading from a prepared statement, he'd given them what he considered their final warning.

"Yesterday, several members of the press tried to manhandle and harass my daughter into giving them an interview, something I, as her father, find deeply offensive. I reported this matter to the police and asked them to provide her with an escort every day but they say they don't have the resources, despite my insisting that adults were laying their hands on my vulnerable child.

"As the police refuse to do anything about this situation, I will be forced to take the matter into my own hands should anyone try to interfere with my daughter on her way to or from school, using all force necessary to protect my child."

Levine smiled as he remembered that statement going out on all the news channels, with commentators asking why the police were leaving a twelve-year-old girl to the mercy of a mob of reporters, and the anchors quick to point out that none of the reporters worked for their particular franchise. Within a few hours a police escort was arranged for the next few days until the media eventually gave up their efforts.

"I'm sure it won't be like last time," he told her, even though he himself had no idea how it was going to play out. He kissed his daughter on the head and went back to his kitchen duties.

"I think she's missing her friends," his wife said, and Levine could quite understand. It wasn't easy for him, sharing a small space with not only his wife and daughter, but Jeff Campbell and his wife, too. For Alana, it must be doubly difficult, especially with no company her own age to keep her occupied.

He once again hoped that whatever was happening, it would be over soon, for his daughter's sake if nothing else. When the call had come, the last thing on his mind had been creature comforts, and he certainly hadn't been expecting to be holed up in this tiny box for more than a couple of days. It was now approaching two weeks, and he still no idea why they had been told to go into hiding.

Campbell was just as concerned, highlighting the fact that during their enforced holiday they hadn't been mentioned on the BBC news channel. That suggested the police weren't the ones they were hiding from, but if not the police, then who?

Following the attack a year earlier, and with Tom Gray lying critically injured in hospital, they had been briefed by a representative of the Home Office. He'd explained that the knowledge they had regarding the whole affair — the fact that no bomb existed and that Tom Gray hadn't actually killed any of his hostages — could be highly embarrassing to the government if it were ever leaked. In return for their silence, the government would allow Tom Gray to be spirited away with a new identity and the six survivors would face no criminal proceedings.

Levine and the others had been given a few minutes to consider the proposal, and on face value it seemed an acceptable offer. It meant staying out of prison, and keeping their mouths shut was second nature to members of Two-Two Regiment.

It wasn't until a couple of days later that they had gotten together and discussed some of the less favourable scenarios, and it was then that they realised what they had signed up for. The knowledge they held was always going to be damaging, be it to the current government or future ones, and all that stood between complete secrecy and a national security fiasco was their individual integrity.

In effect, they were relying on the government to trust six men who had only a few days earlier held the country to ransom.

Following that epiphany they had promised each other that if one of them were to disappear or die under suspicious circumstances, the others would take their stories to every available media outlet. The death of Tristram Barker-Fink in Iraq had been a shock to them all, but there was no way they could blame that on anyone but the terrorists who took out the convoy he was travelling in. A few weeks after Tristram's death, Paul Bennett's followed, crashing his motorbike at high speed. Independent witnesses saw his tyre explode while he doing more than eighty miles per hour, with no other cars within fifty feet of him. The police report also cited mechanical failure as the reason for the crash, the tyre having blown out.

Both of these losses were put down to misfortune, but since they got the call to go into hiding, they were beginning to have second thoughts.

Levine went to sit next to Campbell. "It's been a while since we heard from anyone," he said quietly. "What if we're the only ones left?"

"I was thinking the same thing," Campbell agreed, "but there's no way of knowing. I also don't like the idea of being in the same place for so long."

"Me neither. The longer we stay in the same place, the easier it will be to track us down."

Both men thought about their predicament, with their focus being on the other family members.

"We could send the girls away and wait it out," Campbell suggested, and Levine liked the idea, though he had concerns as to where they would be safe. Hotels and guest houses were out of the question, and there was no way to get them out of the country.

"We could get them a tent and they could stay in a field close by," Campbell offered, and Levine concurred.

"I think that might be the best option. I also think that any threat will come at night, so the girls can stay here during the day and slip out when it gets dark."

"Sounds good to me," Campbell said. "I'll send the missus into town to buy a tent and they can start using it tonight."

While the men broke the news to their wives, Alana resumed her ritual of staring out of the window. For the first time, she noticed movement in the next caravan and saw that a family estate car was parked next to it. A young boy, no older than seven, was helping his parents unload bags and boxes and take them inside, but it was the sight of the girl that caught her attention. She was roughly the same age as Alana, and rather than helping her family she was leaning against the car, her attention focused solely on her mobile phone.

* * *

Andrew Harvey sipped his mineral water in the hotel bar and looked at the photo in his hand.

He'd arrived in Durban after a six and a half hour drive and gone straight to the address of the first person on his list. Gerry Ainsworth, forty six years of age, served in Northern Ireland as an eighteen-year-old Green Jacket, left the Army five years later and had various jobs since, mostly in sales. Currently running his own business which purported to sell diving equipment.

406

After grabbing a sandwich Harvey had parked himself in the bar while he waited for Ainsworth to return from a day of canvassing potential clients, and it was just after six in the evening when his target finally walked through the lobby.

Harvey was disappointed to see that the man had gained at least forty pounds since his passport photograph had been taken, and he wheezed under the weight of the sample bags he was carrying. There was simply no way Ainsworth could be the hit man he was looking for.

With one name eliminated he asked the receptionist to call him a taxi to take him to a local bar, and while he waited he called Owen to see how he was getting on with his suspects.

"Nothing from the first one," Owen told him. "I asked his hotel receptionist where he might be and she said he'd taken a taxi to the International Convention Centre. I checked that he'd signed in and watched him come out about an hour ago. Looks like he's really here for the gardening exhibition."

Harvey agreed to meet up with Owen for dinner at the hotel of suspect number three and hung up. His taxi arrived a few minutes later and he told the driver to forget about the bar and just to take him to the Fairview hotel. When he arrived at his destination he found Owen waiting for him in the bar, with two cold beers sitting in front of him. He took a seat that gave him a good view of the entrance.

"It's not going to be easy to check the others out now that the weekend has arrived," Owen noted.

Harvey had been thinking the same. If their suspects were here to ply their trades, they would be unlikely to do so over the weekend, and Harvey explained that probably meant him and Owen spending the next two days shadowing each one in the hope of finding something out of the ordinary.

"Are you ready to tell me who's arriving on Monday?" Owen asked.

It was a question which had come up during their drive from Johannesburg earlier that day, but Harvey had simply explained that some British subjects were arriving on the seventh and that persons unknown were waiting to intercept them. He hadn't said who was on the ship for fear of opening a can of worms: if word spread that he was looking for Baines and Smart it could eventually reach the wrong ears, and the fewer people who knew he was about to crash a government-sanctioned party, the longer his career was likely to last.

However, he had been so pre-occupied with keeping them from Farrar's clutches that he hadn't considered how he was going to get them back to the UK, and for that he knew he was going to need Owen's help.

"Does the name Tom Gray ring any bells?"

"Are you kidding?" Owen laughed. "I'm hardly likely to forget him." He looked Harvey in the eye, his tone more serious. "You're not going to tell me he's on the ship, are you?"

It was Harvey's turn to offer a smile. "No, but he did have some help, remember?"

"Yeah, a few of his Army buddies were involved, weren't they?"

"That's right," Harvey said, "and two of them are on their way here."

He gave Owen a rundown of events over the last two weeks, starting with the request for help in finding Levine and Campbell and all the way up to the discovery that James Farrar was looking for two of the men on the ship, too.

"This Farrar, is he looking for the rest of Gray's team?"

"These *are* the rest of the team," Harvey explained. "Two were killed in the attack last year, and two have died since."

Owen thought about this for a moment. "Sounds like this Farrar is looking to eliminate the whole team."

"That's the conclusion we came to."

"Do you know why?" Owen asked.

"That's what I plan to ask Baines and Smart."

Owen tapped him on the arm and nodded towards the door. "How do you want to do this?"

Harvey watched Alan Skinner enter the bar and order a Southern Comfort, then browse a menu as he waited for the barman to pour the drink.

"You keep him occupied," Harvey whispered as he stood, "and I'll check his room."

He left the bar as Owen took a seat next to their target and struck up a conversation. Harvey knew Skinner's room was on the second floor and he was glad to see that the hotel hadn't upgraded to key cards. He had the lock open in seconds and slipped into the room, searching for anything out of the ordinary. He found a diary and flicked through it, only to find appointments with various companies around the world. The suitcase, cupboards and drawers offered nothing to contradict the suggestion that Skinner was anything other than a travelling salesman, and he headed back downstairs a frustrated figure.

As he walked past the entrance to the bar he paused and waited for Owen to notice him, and when he did so Harvey offered a quick shake of the head and disappeared towards the entrance. His companion followed a minute later.

"It's not our guy," Owen said, pre-empting Harvey, who concurred.

"Let's call it a day and pick them up first thing," Harvey suggested. "If we get to their hotels early enough we can catch them before they go out."

"You don't sound convinced," Owen said, detecting a note of dejection in Harvey's voice.

"I'm not. These are the best leads we have, but what if the one waiting for the ship to arrive isn't using the same passport for the hotel as they did for the flight? What if they have more than one identity?"

"That's what I'd be inclined to do."

Harvey knew there was no point trying to investigate the other sixty-something people on his list. There simply wasn't time, and besides, none of them had been flagged on the system as being of any interest.

"Want me to drop you at your hotel?" Owen asked as they climbed into his BMW.

"Later. First I want to take a look at Wenban Freight Management."

Chapter 8

Saturday May 5th 2012

Ben Palmer steered the rented Mercedes Sprinter van down the dusty trail towards the remote building, his back taking a pounding from the rough ride over potholes and ruts.

Sean Littlefield's place was a farm in name only. It had been years since any animal or crop had been within a few miles as Littlefield made his living from a completely different source. He was standing at the door when Palmer's van pulled up to the house, a pair of tongs in his hand.

"How's you?" He smiled.

"I'm good, Sean. Jeez, can't you get yourself a place near a decent road?"

Littlefield slapped him on the back and led him through the entrance. "This place is perfect, man. I can see people coming from miles around in any direction."

Having once been a prominent member of the Afrikaner Weerstandsbeweging under the leadership of Eugène Terre'Blanche was reason enough to be prudent when it came to unannounced visitors. His activities during the apartheid years — being suspected of attacks and murders against non-whites — was another.

Inside, the house looked just like Palmer remembered it, except that the antique furniture had gathered an extra layer of dust.

"Still no woman in your life?" He asked, but Littlefield waved him away. At close to sixty, he had long since abandoned the idea of sharing his remaining days with anyone but himself.

The barbeque was already going and a couple of huge steaks were sizzling away nicely. Palmer took a seat and accepted a cold beer while Littlefield prepared a salad.

"So what brings you here?" The host asked, and Palmer explained the need for a few sensitive items. Littlefield rubbed the stubble on his chin as he went through the list.

"Sounds like you're planning a party," he smiled. "The gun is no problem, but I'll need to visit a friend for the rest."

"Can you get them by tomorrow night?" Palmer asked, and Littlefield assured him he could.

With business out of the way Palmer was able to relax. He polished off his beer and accepted another, and they spent the next two hours swapping stories of their exploits since they'd last met. More accurately, Palmer told the stories while his friend listened intently, his days of action far behind, though the desire still burned inside.

"So what's the latest job?" Littlefield asked as he tidied up the dinner plates.

"More of the same, really. Just gotta get some information from a couple of ex-soldiers and their two friends, then dispose of them."

It didn't sound all that exciting, but it was more action than the old man had seen in a few years.

"Need a hand?" He asked. "I mean, it's not going to be straightforward with four people to control."

Palmer smiled. "You pining for the old days, Sean?"

"You know it."

The old man had a point, Palmer thought. He may not be able to out-sprint a fleeing fugitive as he used to during his days in the South African Police, but the years hadn't robbed him of his mean streak. Palmer preferred to work alone, but he knew it would be handy to have someone on lookout, or a second gun should it come to that. Help with carrying four lifeless bodies wouldn't go amiss, either.

"I can't promise you any fireworks, Sean, but you're welcome to tag along."

* * *

Abdul Mansour had done nothing but think in the two days since his meeting with Azhar Al-Asiri. This very evening his new position would be announced to the whole of the organisation, and coupled with the mission he had been given, he had seen the opportunity to elevate himself to greatness beyond his wildest expectations.

Once, he would have been satisfied to have his loyalty and dedication recognised by his elders, but as his reputation grew, so did his aspirations. Becoming a general had been a magnificent honour, but it was just another step on his path to ultimate glory. His sights had then been set on the rank of regional commander, which also meant a place on the council, allowing him the chance to share in the highest level of decision making.

411

However, one goal reached simply meant a new one to strive for, and following his promotion that meant only one thing.

Azhar Al-Asiri, still in his early fifties, was not an old man by any means. He could carry on as their glorious leader for another thirty years if Allah wished it, but Abdul Mansour wasn't prepared to wait that long. He'd asked to meet the scientist to gather more information, such as a suitable alternative method of delivery and any conditions which would lessen the effect of the virus. This meticulous attention to detail had pleased Al-Asiri and he'd readily agreed, unaware of Mansour's true motive.

As the building drew near it looked just like the grain wholesaler the sign above the entrance proclaimed it to be. Sacks of maize were piled up beside the main door, and local vendors were busy bartering for their stock for the coming week.

Mansour was driven round the back of the large building — more a warehouse than a shop — and found the rear entrance open, a man waiting for him. Mansour climbed from the vehicle and when the driver made to follow him, he signalled that he would go in alone.

Inside, all he could see was the silhouette of the man leading him down the narrow corridor. His guide suddenly stopped and fumbled against the wall, and Mansour heard a faint *click* as a chink of light appeared through a door off to his left.

Mansour stepped through and found himself in an antechamber. Through toughened glass he could see people inside the laboratory wearing protective suits complete with breathing apparatus. One of them noticed his presence and entered an inner door into a chamber, where jets of what looked to Mansour like steam filled the small area for a few seconds. Extractors sucked the vapour from the air and moments later Professor Uddin emerged and removed his headgear.

"Thank you for taking time to see me," Mansour said after greeting him. "I appreciate that you are very busy."

Uddin assured him that is was no inconvenience, and Mansour noted how nervous the scientist was. Al-Asiri had told him that Uddin had been like a lamb in a lion's den when they'd met at the hotel, and Mansour was glad to see the same reaction.

"The Emir tells me you are doing some fine work here," Mansour said as Uddin led him to a small office. "He is delighted with the progress you have made."

Uddin seemed to relax a little at the praise, but Mansour soon took the smile off his face. "However, he would prefer you to do more testing on the virus before we unleash it on the world. He is not completely satisfied with the figures you presented to him."

"We…er…"

Mansour waved off any attempt at an excuse. "I spoke to the Emir and we agreed that this operation should only go ahead when we are completely confident of success. As that isn't currently the case, we are going to postpone it while you conduct further tests."

Uddin looked worried, but Mansour allayed his fears. "The Emir is not angry with you, but he does think it prudent to wait. He had wanted to use an upcoming window of opportunity, but others will come along."

The professor let out a sigh, grateful that he hadn't incurred Al-Asiri's wrath.

"Despite this, the window remains open, and the Emir wants to make full use of it. Tell me about the other variants you and your team have been working on."

Uddin explained that the vast majority of time had been spent on Al-Asiri's pet project, but they did have another strain of the virus that was much more aggressive.

"It is a natural variant of Reston Ebolavirus, which originated in the Philippines. Reston has been found in several indigenous animals, from crab-eating macaques to pigs, although as yet it hasn't claimed any human lives. Our strain has been genetically modified to enhance the cytopathic effect — the breaking down of cellular tissue."

"Why not just use Ebola itself?" Mansour wondered aloud.

"Governments from all over the world — governments with much better resources than we have here — have been trying to find a cure for Ebola Zaire since it was first discovered in 1976. They have tried and failed, and only recently the US military cut funding to two private companies searching for an effective antidote.

"If they cannot find it, there is very little chance of us stumbling across the answer. Even with our own creation, we are not yet able to reverse the effects."

"What does it do to those exposed to it?" Mansour asked.

"It causes irreparable damage to the liver and kidneys," Uddin told him. "Failure takes place just forty-eight hours after infection, leading to major haemorrhaging and eventually death within the next twenty-four hours."

"What about an antidote?"

"We have been unable to prevent death once the subject has become infected," Uddin said. "Those subjects who were given the vaccination prior to infection did survive, but they suffered severe damage to their organs. We need to do a lot more work on this before we can be confident it is ready for use."

"It seems to me that it is ready now," Mansour smiled.

"I agree it has the effect we were looking for," Uddin said, "but until we are able to control it, we cannot consider using it. With international travel so common, a strain this virulent could reach almost every major population before it was ever discovered. It would create a pandemic within weeks."

Mansour was impressed with the projected reach, but the target he had in mind would only claim around a thousand lives. Al-Asiri's vision of breeding westerners out of existence was flawed at even the most fundamental level: it wasn't the people that were the issue; it was the people leading them, the policy-makers who determined which countries were to be invaded, which villages were to be bombed. He had no real issues with the people of Britain or the United States: they simply followed their leaders like sheep. No, more like lambs being led to the slaughter by warmongers fuelled by greed. They dressed it up as a crusade to rid the world of tyrants, but their sole agenda was to get cheap access to the Arab world's oil supply.

The internal conflicts in Libya and Syria epitomised this. When Tripoli used deadly force to put down the uprising, the US and Britain mobilised troops immediately and were instrumental in the fall of Gaddafi. Yet the troubles in Syria started at around the same time, and eighteen months later the UN were still dithering and threatening worthless sanctions. Russia and China were the major suppliers of arms to Damascus and were vetoing any resolutions at the UN, and the western powers conveniently used this as the main reason they couldn't take any decisive action to stop the massacres. Mansour knew that even if the eastern superpowers voted in favour of military action, the cost of an invasion would greatly outweigh the financial gain to the likes of Britain and America. They would continue with the rhetoric while waiting for the next oil-rich country to implode.

"My target is a building which is protected against chemical and biological attacks. However, they would be expecting an attack to come from the outside, not within the building itself. If it were released in such a place, would it be able to escape?"

414

Uddin admitted that without schematics of the defences, he couldn't offer any guarantees, but he did think the efficacy of the virus would be severely diminished. "The air within such a building would most likely be filtered through sophisticated scrubbers, ultraviolet lights and a host of other defences. It could be destroyed within minutes."

"What if the filtration system was inactive during the initial release and no-one was allowed to leave the building. Would that make a difference?"

"It certainly would, but it would depend on the size of the building and the number of people within it. The more people, the less effective the defences would become, but eventually the virus would become so prevalent that everyone within the building would succumb."

The news was exactly what Mansour wanted to hear, and he instructed the professor to prepare as much of the virus as possible within the next few days. "I will also need a way of transporting it via aeroplane and through customs without arousing suspicion. What would you suggest?"

The professor looked nervous. "I have to reiterate that this virus is not ready to be used. If just one person were to get out of the contaminated area, there is no telling how fast it could spread. The incubation period — the delay before the onset of symptoms — is two days, but the virus can be passed to others within a few hours through close contact.

"I really think you should reconsider, at least until we have a working anti-virus."

Mansour's glare told Uddin that any further dissension would not be tolerated, and the professor reluctantly stood and picked up an inhaler from a shelf. "This is capable of storing the virus for seventy-two hours," he said, his voice edgy. "If you press here, it works just as it should."

As promised, a small cloud of mist shot out when the cartridge was pushed into the device. "When you first insert a new canister, it breaks the initial seal and works like a normal inhaler. However, if you were to hold it pressed in for a count of ten, you activate a second valve which releases the entire contents of a hidden compartment in one continuous burst."

"You mean it can be activated and left unattended?" Mansour asked, and Uddin nodded.

"We tried to design it with built-in latency to give the person activating it a chance to clear the area," Uddin told him, "but that introduced too many extra components which would show up on security scanners, such as airport X-Ray machines."

Mansour liked the simplicity, and it should easily pass a cursory inspection at any border. The fact that it required someone to sacrifice their life to deliver the virus was not a problem: There were plenty of true believers willing to take on the task in the name of Allah.

"What kind of coverage will I get from one canister?" Mansour asked.

Uddin thought about it for a moment, searching for a suitable comparison. "If you were to activate one canister in a large airport baggage hall, it would infect everyone in a ten metre radius in moments, and it would travel to all adjoining areas within five minutes. It would take less than an hour for the entire airport to become contaminated."

The projection once again pleased Mansour, especially as the target he had in mind was similar in size to a major airport terminal. "How many of these canisters can you provide in the next twenty-four hours?" He asked.

Uddin did a quick mental calculation. "We can have two, perhaps three capsules ready," he replied.

"Two will suffice," Mansour told him. "Taking any more than that through Heathrow's customs channels could arouse suspicion, but carrying your inhaler and a spare would be seen as normal for most travellers."

He rose from his chair. "I will return in two days. Please have them ready when I arrive."

The professor considered one more attempt at dissuading Mansour from this course of action, but instead he held his tongue and assured him that everything he needed would be waiting on his return. Mansour paused at the door. "This goes no further than the two of us," he warned the old man. "As far as your team are concerned, you are going to deliver the original virus as planned. Do you understand?"

Uddin nodded meekly, and Mansour left.

Once alone in the office, Uddin slumped in his chair and wiped the sweat from his forehead. Designing the virus for use on their enemies was something he was comfortable with: whether they died from a bomb, bullet or bug was immaterial. What he couldn't accept was the possibility that his creation might be unleashed on the entire world. It

416

would not differentiate between Muslim or Christian, Hindu or Buddhist; it would simply strike down everyone it touched.

Could it be contained within the building Mansour was targeting? Without knowing the layout of the building, the intended release point and the number of exits, he simply couldn't say. Even the counter-biological defences Mansour mentioned could prove to be inadequate, but he couldn't be certain unless he had the chance to look at the specifications.

Uddin wrestled with his conscience for some time, but he knew that if he didn't fulfil Mansour's wish, the only thing he could look forward to would be death. Not just for him, but for his entire family, too. And it wouldn't be as quick as a bullet to the brain. He was certain that he would be made to watch his family die before he himself was killed, and the thought sent a shiver through his body.

With a heavy heart he stood and slowly walked back to the laboratory, suddenly feeling a lot older than his fifty-eight years.

Chapter 9

Sunday May 6th 2012

"We've got the location of the website!"

Veronica Ellis was in the middle of weeding her garden when the call from Gerald Small came through to her mobile, and she was glad of the interruption.

"Where is it?"

"A flat, here in London. Hamad's preparing to take a team to the location."

"I want you to go with them," Ellis said, and hung up. She tapped the phone against her temple as she absorbed the new information, and after a couple of minutes she called Hamad Farsi.

"I don't want you bringing anyone in," she said when the intelligence officer answered. "The person we are after is in South Africa, so anyone manning the equipment has to be an associate."

"Makes sense," Farsi agreed. "What's the plan?"

"Find out if the flats in the building are connected to the gas network. If they are, pretend there's a leak and clear the street, but when you get to the target flat I want you to secure it and keep the occupants there. We don't want whoever is in Durban to know they've been compromised."

The phone went silent as Farsi relayed the instructions and a minute later he told Ellis that gas was supplied to the entire street.

"Okay, so that's your cover. I want you to take Gerald along to analyse the setup and confirm that we have the right people."

Farsi confirmed the order and Ellis told him to forward all the information they had to her laptop. Gardening forgotten, she went into the house to get changed. Once suitably attired for a day in the office, she found the details she'd requested waiting for her.

The council-owned flat was being rented by Carl Gordon, and his record showed one previous conviction for a computer-related offence. He certainly sounded like their man.

She packed her laptop into her briefcase and drove the twenty-minute journey to Thames House, arriving just as Farsi and his team were getting ready to leave the office.

"Gordon's file says he lives alone," Hamad told her as he donned his reflective jacket, "so we don't expect to encounter much resistance."

"Perhaps, but don't go rushing in and spooking the guy. We need his equipment intact." This was directed at Small. "I need you to make sure comms stay open with whoever's in Durban. Do what you need to do to convince Gordon to help you."

The team headed down to the car park and climbed into the van. During the thirty minute journey, Farsi used his smart phone to get an overhead view of the target building. Gordon lived in a side street off the main road, which would make evacuation a lot easier, and as his building was towards the end of the street they wouldn't have to clear too many homes.

His team consisted of surveillance specialists, and he briefed them on the mission.

"The building in question is number twenty-seven, and we're after the occupants of flat three." He selected two of the team and gave them the job of cordoning off each end of the street and preventing people from entering the area. "If anyone asks, an automated system in the pipeline detected a leak beneath number twenty-seven. That should satisfy them if they start wondering who called us in."

He instructed the other three members of the team to go from house to house and clear them.

"Two houses either side should be enough," he told Rob Zimmerman, the surveillance team leader. "Once they're empty, converge on the target. We'll leave his flat until last."

Everyone acknowledged their roles and they did a quick comms check before they arrived in Mercia Road.

* * *

Carl Gordon saw the British Gas van arrive on his monitor but it held his attention for nothing more than a few seconds. He'd installed the CCTV camera to spot the police arriving, not utility vehicles, and he returned to his attention to the website he was working on.

His attempts to sort out an issue with a troublesome web control were interrupted again as another flash of yellow moved across the

419

monitor, and on closer examination he now saw a man in a high-visibility jacket shepherding people towards the end of the road.

Gordon moved from his office to the living room and looked out of the window, where he saw yet another figure extending a roll of tape across the entrance to the street where temporary barriers were already in place. Below him, two more people were heading towards the entrance to his building.

It was obvious to Gordon that the street was being evacuated and his first concern was his equipment. His office was a small second bedroom and one wall was dedicated to servers, which he kept on a purpose-built air-cooled rack. The metal frame of the rack was wired up to a capacitor which could send a massive electric current through every box, frying the hard drives instantly. It would mean thousands of pounds of equipment would be rendered useless, but it was rather that than incriminating evidence falling into the hands of the police.

He hit a few keys to save his recent work to an online storage system before priming the anti-intruder device, something he did every time he left the apartment. Once he closed the door to the office, the device was activated: The next person to enter the room would have just ten seconds to hit the Cancel switch, and they could only do that if they knew about it and could find it.

He walked back to the window in time to see his ground-floor neighbour carrying her two cats towards the cordon, and from behind him came a loud banging on the door.

"British Gas! We've got an emergency and need you to leave the building!"

Gordon grabbed his coat and opened the door, but through habit he left the chain on.

"Got any ID?" He asked through the small gap.

The man in the hallway seemed unimpressed with the request, but he held up the card hanging around his neck. Gordon was satisfied with the comparison, but his attention was drawn to the other man in the hallway, who had his finger on an earpiece which fed down into his collar. At that moment he realised he was facing more than utility workers and he tried to slam the door closed.

It barely moved.

Hamad Farsi had seen the look of panic suddenly appear on Gordon's face and had stuck his steel toe-capped boot into the gap, quickly bringing up the bolt cutters he'd placed beside the door. The thin chain offered no resistance and Farsi shoved his way into the

420

room, drawing his Taser as he moved. His target hesitated in the middle of the room for a second before heading at speed for a door off to his right-hand side.

The electric barb hit Gordon in the thigh just as he reached for the handle and his legs gave way beneath him. He tried to raise his arms to protect his face but they reacted like jelly, and he smashed into the door nose first, leaving a trail of blood as he slid to the floor.

Farsi pulled out a pair of plasticuffs and secured the prisoner's hands and feet, and then dragged him onto a sofa. Two members of the team began securing the tiny flat, one taking the kitchen and bathroom while the other started a search in the main bedroom.

"Now why would anyone react like that to the gas man?" Farsi asked, but Gordon just looked at the three men standing in his living room, his gaze shifting from one to the other. Zimmerman had his Beretta drawn and ready, while Gerald Small stood still next to the wall. This was only his second field assignment but he knew to keep out of the way and not touch anything until he was needed.

Farsi noticed Gordon glancing at the blood-stained door and indicated for the surveillance officer to take a look. Zimmerman nodded, and he had his hand poised on the handle when Small told him to stop.

"He *wants* you to go in there," Small said, having noticed the faintest of smiles forming on Gordon's face. Zimmerman took a couple of steps back and aimed at the door, ready to deal with anyone who came out, while Farsi stood over the prisoner.

"Who's in there?" He asked.

"I want a solicitor."

"I said who's in there?" Farsi repeated.

"You broke my nose."

Farsi grabbed Gordon's hair and pulled his head back, examining the man's face. "Hmm, looks okay to me." He suddenly raised his arm and brought the side of his hand crashing down on the bridge of Gordon's nose. The distinct *crack* was drowned out by the prisoner's yelp.

"Yeah, you're right, it is broken," Farsi said, less amiably. "Now tell me who's in that room."

"No-one!" Gordon spat, blood spraying from his mouth. "Open it and see."

The two men finished up clearing the other rooms and emerged shaking their heads.

"Where's your computer?" Farsi asked, and Gordon nodded towards the bloodstained door. "In there. Help yourself."

"Thanks, but I'd rather trust my colleague." Farsi looked over at Small. "What do you think?"

"I think we should stick a fibre-optic camera in there first."

Farsi agreed and sent one of his men down to the van to get one. While he was waiting he decided to make Gordon as uncomfortable as possible.

"I find it reassuring that the first words out of your mouth were to demand a solicitor," he said. "Most people would have asked what the fuck we were doing in their home, but you seem to have been expecting us to call round at some point."

Gordon said nothing, but his expression told Farsi he'd hit the mark. He let the prisoner stew for a couple of minutes until the surveillance device arrived. Small took it and unravelled the flexible cable, then checked the screen to make sure he had a good image. Satisfied that all was working, he hit the record button and played the cable under the door.

"No sign of anyone," he said as the tiny camera snaked along the floor. "He's got some serious hardware in there, though."

Small used two dials to control the direction of the camera, and as he moved it to the base of the rack he saw the capacitor tucked away on the bottom shelf. The cable wasn't long enough to get in any closer, but he knew what he was looking at.

"Where did you get the capacitor?" He asked Gordon.

"It was here when I moved in."

Unlikely, Small thought. "Okay, what are you using it for?" He asked, although he was certain he already knew the answer. Gordon ignored him, and Farsi seemed confused and asked what the capacitor could be used for.

"Think of it as a kind of re-chargeable battery," Small explained, "but rather than releasing its energy at a constant rate, it purges instantly. They are used on a much bigger scale to replicate lightning strikes."

"How big is this one?" Farsi asked.

"It's not huge, but my guess is that as soon as you open that door, everything in the room gets hit by a couple of thousand volts. Forensics might be able to salvage some of the data on the hard drives, but if he's using SSDs, everything will be wiped instantly."

"SSDs?"

"Solid-State Drives," Small said. "Normal hard drives store data on rotating metal disks, but SSDs are more like chips or RAM, with no moving parts. They are more resistant to shock, such as being dropped, but they are susceptible to power surges. Zap one with a capacitor and you lose everything."

Farsi looked at the prisoner. "Do you think you can wriggle out of this if you destroy the evidence?"

Gordon suddenly found some bravado, more in desperation than anything. "I want to see the search warrant."

"We're here under the Terrorism Act 2000, we don't need a warrant. All that's required is for me to suspect that you're a terrorist, simple as that. No warrant, no solicitor, no bail and we can hold you as long as we like. How does that sound?"

Gordon's eyes grew wide with shock. "I'm not a terrorist!"

"Perhaps not, but while we suspect you are, you're royally screwed. I guess the only way you can prove us wrong is to give us access to your computers."

Gordon's eyes darted around the room, searching for a way out of the situation. He'd thought they were there because of the hacking he'd done on behalf of his benefactor, the man he knew only as B, but as far as he was aware he hadn't accessed any networks that were so sensitive that his actions could be labelled terrorism. There had been a few individuals' computers and perhaps a dozen companies, but none of them were risks to national security.

This led him to wonder just what they were planning to charge him with.

"What is it that I'm supposed to have done?"

"Collection of information of a kind likely to be useful to a person committing or preparing an act of terrorism," Farsi replied. "We know you host a website for someone we're looking for, so you can add helping in the preparing or commissioning of a terrorist act, too."

"That's got nothing to do with me!" Gordon shouted. "I just host the site, that's all. There's no law against it."

"You must have known he was up to no good," Small jumped in, "otherwise you wouldn't have hidden behind a dozen relay servers."

The prisoner bit his lip as he stared once more at his office door.

"If you've got any booby traps in there, I suggest you disarm them now." Farsi said. "You're looking at a long time in prison, so don't add further charges by destroying any evidence. We already have proof that the website is being run from this flat, and that will be enough to convict you. However, if you play nicely we might be able to convince the judge that your co-operation helped our investigation. You might get away with five years."

The prospect of a long sentence was the final straw. He was built to manipulate ones and zeros, not fight for survival in a prison environment.

"I want immunity from prosecution," Gordon whined. "I can't go to prison. I wouldn't last a week."

"Not going to happen. We might be able to push for three years and you'll serve just eighteen months, with half of that out on licence."

Nine months was still a long, long time, and if word got out that his sentence had been reduced because he'd given evidence against someone else, his cards would be marked.

There was also the backlash from B to consider. He'd met the man just twice: The first time outside the court when he'd offered Gordon work; and the second when he'd turned up with his first cash payment. On that occasion his new employer hadn't been as cordial. He'd explained what he needed and asked if Gordon could provide it. The answer had been an easy "Yes". He already had a server relay in place for his own file-sharing site, and setting up another would be a piece of cake. Finding ways into other people's computers wouldn't be too challenging either, Gordon had promised – though it obviously depended on the nature of the information. He could get into the telephone networks or National Health Service in seconds, but banks and government networks were out: Their firewalls and intrusion-detection systems were simply too advanced.

B hadn't needed anything that secure, and the partnership had been sealed with the handing over of the money and delivery of the caveat: "When you take this money, you're in for good. There's no walking away when you get bored, and you never tell anyone about me. If I find out you've opened your mouth I'll hunt you down, and trust me, you don't want that to happen."

With his contact book containing zero entries, Gordon had no qualms on that score, and the weight of the envelope had felt good in his hands. The money would enable him to buy some of the equipment he'd only been able to dream about, and the threat was soon forgotten.

Until now.

Whether he gave up his employer or not, he was facing jail, and that didn't make for an easy decision.

Jeff Campbell helped his wife Anne prepare the evening meal while the Levines dealt with yet another teenage tantrum. Alana was facing her third night in the tent and wasn't about to go quietly.

"I hate it in there," she pouted, arms firmly crossed against her chest. "There isn't even a toilet."

Carl Levine sympathised with her, having spent countless evenings sleeping rough during his time in the Army, but she had a roof over her head to keep the rain out and the inconvenience of having to squat behind a bush just didn't rank very highly in his book.

"It won't be for much longer," he told her for the hundredth time, but when pressed for a firm date he admitted he had no idea. All he could do was reiterate the offer to make amends once things were back to normal.

Alana noticed movement outside the window and suddenly her demeanour changed.

"Okay, but I want a new laptop when we get back home."

"Deal," her father said, glad that there wasn't going to be a scene.

"Can I just go for a little walk?" Alana asked in her sweetest voice, and Levine nodded, but not before reminding her of the rules.

"Your name is Alice and we're here on holiday from Essex, okay?"

"I know, Dad."

She was up and out the door before Levine could say anything else, and his wife took the vacant seat.

"Are you sure about all this?" She asked her husband. "There hasn't been anything about us on the news, and no-one seems to be looking for us. Is there a chance you've misinterpreted the message?"

Carl wondered if it was possible. Had he turned their lives upside-down for no reason? Alana had missed over two weeks of school and the authorities would soon be taking an interest — if they weren't already. On top of that, his wife Sandra hadn't told her employers that she would be taking time off, which meant she would probably find herself out of work once the situation was resolved. Finding another job at her age — given the current economic climate — would be no easy task.

If he'd got the message wrong, this whole mess could have been avoided, but in his heart he knew he was doing the right thing.

"I know it seems strange that no-one appears to be looking for us, but I'd much rather be safe than sorry."

Sandra wasn't about to argue with her husband. She might have if Alana wasn't a consideration, but her daughter was her whole life, and she wasn't about to let anything happen to her.

Levine took her hand in his. "We'll have a family holiday when this is over," he told her. "Somewhere nice and sunny, just the three of us."

"As long as it isn't camping," Sandra said with a hint of a smile.

While the Levines discussed possible destinations, Alana struck up a conversation with the girl from the adjacent caravan.

"You look like you're enjoying this as much as me," she said.

The girl rolled her eyes. "I can't believe they call this a holiday. I'd rather be at school."

"I wouldn't go that far!" Alana laughed, and got a smile in return.

"I'm Melissa," the girl said.

"Alice," she replied, remembering her father's instructions. "So why *aren't* you in school?"

"My dad works away most of the year," Melissa said, "and he's only back for like two weeks. I can't believe we have to spend it here, though."

"Yeah, same here. Dad disappears for months at a time, but I'd rather stay at home than go camping. It sucks, big time."

Alana looked at the girl's handset. "What phone have you got?"

Melissa handed it over. "It's the new Samsung."

"I prefer the iPhone," Alana said, though the one in her hand was very similar. "Would it be okay to text my boyfriend? My dad forgot to pack the chargers, so all our phones have run flat. I haven't had contact with the real world for days."

Melissa said it was no problem, and Alana tapped out a quick message:

Hi Sam. Hope 2 b back soon. Luv U & miss U. No need 2 reply. A.

She hit the Send button, waited for confirmation, and handed the phone back. "Thanks."

"That's okay. I get, like, five hundred free texts a month, so you can use it any time."

426

They chatted for a few minutes about music and Facebook before Sandra called her in for her dinner.

"I gotta go," Alana said. "See you later."

"See ya."

Alana trudged back inside, the thrill of her communication fix wearing off quickly, replaced by the dread of another night under the stars.

* * *

"We've got our man," Farsi said over the phone, "but his equipment is booby-trapped. He'll only give us access if we offer immunity from prosecution and give him a change of identity."

"What about Gerald?" Veronica Ellis asked. "Can't he get access?"

"If we open the door to the room it triggers a device which wipes the hard drives. He said he has a similar detector on the windows, though we haven't been able to check that yet."

"Then go through the wall," Ellis said sternly. "I haven't got the power to authorise immunity. That's down to the CPS, and I wouldn't build his hopes up."

Ellis knew that the Crown Prosecution Service *could* offer Gordon the deal he wanted, but there were no guarantees. They had famously done so with Bertie Smalls back in the 1970s after the armed robber offered to give evidence against over twenty others in return for his freedom and the chance to keep what was left of his ill-gotten gains. The men Smalls helped to prosecute were given a combined total of over three hundred years in prison, but with Gordon it was unlikely that the catch would be so big, meaning the Director of Public Prosecutions would have little incentive to let him walk away a free man.

There was also the fiasco of the previous year to consider. Even though Tom Gray had died, his associates — the very men they were looking for — had been released without charge following a deal done with the Home Secretary. That had come back to bite him on the arse at the subsequent general election, and there was no way the incumbent minister was going to be handing out get-out-of-jail-free cards any time soon.

"If we go through the wall, we still need him to log on to his computer," Farsi told her. "He claims to have encrypted his disks, and if we get the password wrong three times or remove the disks from their housings, they get wiped. Gerald confirmed that this is easy enough to do."

"You're the lead officer on the ground, Hamad. Do *whatever* you need to do," Ellis stressed, "but get him to co-operate. We need to let Andrew know what he's up against."

The phone went dead in Farsi's hand and he stuck it back in his pocket.

"No promises," he told Gordon, "but we'll do everything we can."

Gordon thought long and hard about his prospects, and eventually nodded in resignation. He pointed towards the door. "I'll let you in."

Farsi told Zimmerman to remove the cuffs and stayed close as Gordon made his way to his office.

"Wait here," he said. "Once I get inside I have a few things to do. I can't disarm it if the room is full of people getting in my way."

Farsi nodded to the others to hang back and Gordon opened the door. Once inside, he felt for the top of the frame and then walked to desk, leaned over his chair and drummed out a command on the keyboard. Finally, he walked over to the rack and reached deep into a gap between two servers as if searching for something on the back wall. His shoulder was hard against the rack and he grabbed one of the metal uprights with his free hand.

The procedure had taken seven seconds.

"I can't go to prison," Gordon repeated, and screwed up his eyes in anticipation of the end.

Farsi saw what was about to happen but was too slow to react. He managed just one step into the room when the capacitor vented its charge, sending over a hundred megawatts through the prisoner. The discharge lasted a little over a microsecond and Gordon was thrown across the room, slamming into the far wall with enough force to make a body-shaped dent in the plaster.

Farsi ran over and checked his pulse while Small headed to the computers. The mains electricity had tripped and he sent someone to find the fuse box. In the meantime he unplugged one of the servers and took a screwdriver to the back.

"He's dead," Farsi said.

"So is this," Small said as he noticed the scorch marks on the hard drive. "As I suspected, he was using SSDs. I doubt we'll get anything from them."

"I want you to try," Farsi said. "Load everything into the van and search for any hard copies. Look for a notebook, backup drive, anything that might tell us who's on the other end of that site."

He dug around in Gordon's pockets and found just a mobile phone and some loose change. The phone refused to turn on, obviously affected by either the impact or electrical surge. Farsi handed it to Small and told him to see what he could get off it, and then made two phone calls. The first was to call in a clean-up team, and the second was to break the news to his boss.

* * *

"We've found them!"

The call from Todd Hamilton came through to Farrar as he was entertaining guests, and he excused himself, finding a quiet spot in his study.

"Where are they?" He asked.

"It looks like a caravan park in Dorset. We intercepted a text sent to the Levine kid's boyfriend and traced it back. She wasn't using her normal phone."

"Can you pin-point the caravan they're in?" Farrar asked.

"We narrowed it down to a thirty metre radius, and slap-bang in the middle is one owned by Tom Gray's solicitor."

"I told you to check connections to all friends and acquaintances," Farrar said angrily. "Why am I only hearing about this now?"

"It's registered at the camp in his wife's maiden name," Hamilton said. "We just hadn't dug that far."

The phone went quiet for a while, and Hamilton took the opportunity to deflect some of the blame away from his team. "If we'd drilled down to relatives of friends, where does it end? Relatives of relatives of friends? Friends of relatives of friends? We've had our hands full just looking at known contacts."

Farrar knew he had a point, but wasn't about to let him off the hook so easily. "I want this finished tonight. Get in touch with Matt Baker and work up a plan."

"Baker's a liability," Hamilton objected. "My team can handle this."

"He gets the job done," Farrar replied, hoping the insult registered. "It must look like an accident, you understand?"

"Got it."

429

"Make no mistake, if you don't end this in the next six hours, you certainly will 'get it'!"

Farrar killed the connection and put the phone back in his trouser pocket. His watch told him it was just after eight in the evening, which meant it would be a few hours before the team were in place. Despite this, he wanted to end the dinner party early so that he could get to the office to listen in to the take-down over a secure connection.

After dishing up the meal he informed his guests that an emergency had come up at work and he would have to disappear shortly after dessert. They made consoling noises, not envious of the hours he kept.

Throughout the meal, Farrar wondered whether or not to tell Palmer about the find. There was no longer a need to get the information from Baines and Smart, but it would be satisfying to have them go through one of Palmer's interrogations. Then again, Palmer was a valuable asset, and the men he would be going up against had proven themselves rather resourceful. It would be totally unprofessional to ask Palmer to take on these two as well as Gray when three bullets could solve the problem.

Actually, four bullets, he reminded himself. There was a fourth passenger on the ship, though he had no idea who the other might be. Whoever else was with Gray was obviously a fugitive, otherwise they wouldn't be tagging along. That made them desperate and potentially dangerous.

Farrar decided that he would tell Palmer to simply kill the targets. However, he would wait until his team confirmed that Levine and Campbell were well and truly dead. Given the incompetence shown by his team in the last couple of weeks, he wasn't going to go as far as demanding heads on plates, but he did want to know that they were no longer breathing before signing the task off as complete.

* * *

Alana Levine muttered to herself as she angrily stuffed a change of clothes into her rucksack. Carl knew the night ahead wasn't going to be a pleasant one for his wife, and he apologised in advance, but Sandra ignored him. She wasn't too happy with the new sleeping arrangement, either, but she held her tongue as she finished making the last of the sandwiches.

430

Once the food was packed away, she called her daughter and Anne Campbell, telling them it was time to leave. The men had to forgo their goodnight kisses.

The girls left the men to their own devices and headed out into the night without another word. Carl Levine knew he was going to have to work damn hard to make things right, and was working on a mental list of peace offerings when there was a knock on the door. Instinctively he grabbed for the handle of the 9MM automatic pistol which was strapped to the underside of the table but Campbell waved him off.

"It's just the kid from the next caravan."

Campbell opened the door. "Hi," he smiled. "What can I do for you?"

"Is Alice here?" the girl asked, holding up her phone. "She got a text from her boyfriend."

Campbell was about to say she must be mistaken when Levine joined him in the doorway.

"How did he get your number?" Levine asked, a little too harshly.

"Alice sent him a text," Melissa said, taking a step backwards. "She said her dad forgot the chargers for the phones, so I let her use mine."

Levine did his best to keep his anger in check. "When did she send the text?"

"I dunno. Couple of hours ago, maybe."

Campbell moved past Levine. "The girls have gone out for the evening," he said, smiling. "If you give me the message I can pass it on to Alice when she gets back."

Melissa wasn't too keen on the idea. This was boyfriend-girlfriend stuff — definitely not the kind of thing you shared with parents.

"I think it's best if I give it to Alice," she said, and got no objections. Levine wasn't interested in the content of the message, just the fact that his daughter had disobeyed his instructions.

"No problem. She'll be back late, but I'll let her know and she can pop round in the morning."

Melissa seemed happy with the arrangement and headed back to her own caravan, leaving the men to consider the implications of Alana's actions.

"What do you reckon?" Campbell asked, once he'd closed the caravan door.

"If it *is* the government who are looking for us, they'll have traced either one or both of those text messages, and that means they'll probably be on their way."

Campbell agreed. "Let's grab the girls and go."

"Not so fast," Levine said. "We still don't know for sure that anyone's actually looking for us. If we run now, we still won't know. I say we leave the girls where they are, find an OP close by and see if anyone knocks on the door."

"And if someone does turn up?" Campbell asked.

"Then we'll know we're not being paranoid. I say we grab at least one of them and find out what they want."

"Sounds fine if they send a small team, but what if they bring half the local police with them?"

"I very much doubt it," Levine said. "If the police were going to be involved, we'd have known about it by now."

Campbell saw the wisdom in his friend's words, but he expressed his concerns for the safety of the women. "I'd feel happier if they were out of the area. How about I drive them into the nearest town, park up out of sight and then tab back here?"

Levine asked why the women couldn't just drive themselves, and Campbell pointed out that they hadn't had the defensive and evasive driver training the men had been through in the regiment. "If they're spotted en route, they'll have no chance. It would also be a good idea to change the plates on the car, and there's a Ford showroom in town. I can swap the plates from a similar model and that should give us enough time to get to where we're going."

"Fair point," Levine conceded. "Let's load our gear before we fetch them."

They grabbed what few belongings they had and stuffed them into holdalls, which went into the boot of the car. Campbell trotted off and was back within ten minutes, the three ladies in tow. Their mood hadn't changed in the last half hour, and Levine guessed his friend hadn't yet explained the situation.

"You have to go," Levine said, opening the door to the car so that his wife could get into the front passenger seat.

"Why? What's going on?"

"Ask Alana," Levine said, and glared at his daughter.

"What have I done now?" Alana asked, full of indignation.

"Sam replied to the text message you sent him."

432

"But I didn't use my own phone," his daughter argued. "You didn't say anything about using someone else's."

There was no time to get into a fight, especially with such a headstrong teenager. "Just get in," Levine said. "I'll deal with you later."

Alana stamped her feet like a five-year-old as she trudged to the car, arms once again folded tightly across her chest. She climbed into the back seat and put her seatbelt on, her face still a picture of fury as she failed to comprehend the seriousness of her indiscretion.

"So what was Sam's message?" She pouted, and Levine just stared in disbelief. Her life was in danger, yet she was more interested in a how her boyfriend was doing. He knew he would have to have a word about priorities when this was all over.

He turned his attention to his wife and spoke to her through the open window. "Jeff's going to take you into town. I want you to stay in the car until we come and get you." He looked over his wife's shoulder at his daughter. "That means all of you."

"How long will you be?" Sandra asked.

"I don't know. Maybe a few hours. Just sit tight until we come and get you."

"But what if you don't come? How long should we wait?"

"If we're not there by six in the morning, just go. Drive north for a few hours and find a town with an internet café, but stay off the main roads. I want you to contact the newspapers, BBC, Sky, anyone. Tell them who you are and what's happened, and see if you can arrange to meet up to give them the whole story."

"Why can't you just come with us?" Anne Campbell pleaded with her husband. "We're not cut out for this kind of thing."

"We have to end it tonight," Jeff said. "If we don't make a stand, we'll be on the run forever."

Anne looked pitiful, but Campbell wasn't going to be persuaded otherwise.

"You want things to go back to normal, don't you?"

His wife nodded, and Campbell kissed her on the forehead.

Levine said his own goodbyes and Campbell climbed into the driver seat.

"I'll be tabbing back over the fields and coming in from the East. See if you can find a suitable observation post while I'm gone."

Levine nodded and watched as the car drove out of the caravan park and turned left on the country lane, its lights fading quickly. His

433

watch told him it was nudging nine-thirty in the evening, and if anyone was coming to pay them a visit they would be in the area soon, if not already. He ducked into the caravan and turned the lights off. From the window he could see several of the other mobile homes were in darkness, so it wouldn't look too suspicious.

There were several good spots to set up the OP on the hill off to the north, but rather than just observe his visitors, he wanted to get up close and personal. Confirmation that they were being sought was one thing, but more important was the need to know who they were up against. At the moment they were running from shadows, but once they'd identified their adversary they would at least know the magnitude of the battle they faced.

That was, if anyone actually turned up.

Levine left the caravan and locked the door, then looked round for a suitable place to lie up. The caravan was situated three yards from the four-foot high privet hedge that ran around the perimeter of the camp. Cut into the hedge was a wooden style, a small ladder that granted access to the public footpath in the adjoining field. Levine climbed over, stepping into the darkness.

Off to his right he could just make out the shape of the tent the ladies had been using for the last few days, and it was from that direction that Jeff would make his appearance. Levine turned to his left and followed the hedge, looking for a spot which would allow him a good view of the caravan while also shielding him from sight if anyone wandered too close. The best he could find was a small depression, but the view through the bottom of the hedge was obscured by another caravan, so he retraced his steps and climbed back over the style and into the camp. Even on this side he could find no natural cover, so he would have to settle for squeezing underneath the people carrier parked behind his neighbours' accommodation.

He tried it out for size, and from the side of the vehicle his vision was obstructed by the gas canisters underneath the adjacent caravan. He adjusted his position, peering out between the front wheels. This was a much better view, allowing him to see the door to his caravan as well as the ten yards leading up to it. The moon was full, but Levine was grateful for the cloud cover which reduced its glare and would help to keep him concealed.

His only worry was if the unwanted guests brought night vision goggles to the party. He knew he couldn't be seen with the naked eye, but he would stick out like a sore thumb to anyone with NVGs.

With one position sorted, Levine crawled out and headed towards the entrance to the camp. He walked nonchalantly, just another holiday-maker out for a late stroll. He saw a couple of others braving the mild evening, but most of the residents were settled in for the night.

The heavy main gate was attached to concrete posts on either side of the entrance, marking the end of the hedge, but once again there was little to offer in the way of cover. He wandered out into the country lane and looked at the hedgerow on the other side of the road. There would be no reason for anyone to approach the camp from that field, not when they could simply drive up to the gate or park up nearby, so it seemed a sensible enough hiding place. The gate to the field was just ten yards away, and Levine scrambled over it quickly.

The field had been left fallow the previous year, and long grass grew around the edges. This would help to break up his profile should anyone glance his way, and he lay down to see what the view was like. He had to crawl forward a few feet, but eventually he found the perfect spot, one that enabled him to see through the entrance all the way to their caravan.

Levine got up and made his way back to the road, checking both ways to make sure no-one was in the area. The road was clear and he strolled back into the camp, waving to one of the residents as he headed back to the caravan. Inside, he took the rounds from the magazine to let the spring relax while he stripped down his Browning and gave it a thorough clean: the last thing he wanted was the gun jamming on him if he came to need it. It took him just a few minutes to finish the job and once it was reassembled he headed for the style to keep an eye out for Campbell.

Jeff arrived at a trot just after ten-thirty, barely breaking a sweat.

"You took your sweet time."

"I did some shopping on the way back," Campbell said, holding out a plastic bag. Levine took it and fished out a pair of Pay-As-You-Go phones.

"I figured we'd need some comms," Campbell told him. "They were the cheapest I could find, but they come with hands-free kits."

"Good thinking. Let's get back inside and charge them up."

While Campbell cleaned his own weapon, Levine charged the phones, turned the ringtones off and programmed the numbers into each other's speed-dial facility. He then put ran through the sequence of commands to call the other phone until he knew which buttons to press with his eyes closed. Once he had the combination memorised and he was sure that Campbell had, too, he put electrical tape over the tiny displays so that the light from them wouldn't be visible when they got an incoming call. Campbell told him they only had twenty pounds of calling credit each, which wouldn't last forever, especially with mobile-to-mobile calls, so they agreed not to use the phones until the person observing the gate saw some activity.

"How do you think they'll play this out?" Campbell asked as he reassembled his pistol.

"If they're morons, they'll come in all guns blazing," Levine said. "I doubt we'll be that lucky, though. I expect they'll turn up in the dead hours, probably between one and four in the morning."

Campbell concurred. "We'll let the phones charge for another hour, then get in position."

Levine described the locations he'd found and offered to take the spot under the vehicle. At just five feet nine he was the smaller of the two by six inches, and had a slight build compared to Campbell's bear-like physique. It would be much easier for him to get out quickly when the time came.

"We'll need knives," Levine said, and went to the kitchen. In the drawer he found two which would serve their purpose, though their edges were rather dull. He found a honing steel and sat down to sharpen the blades.

They discussed tactics until a few minutes to midnight. By this time the phones both had a charge of over eighty percent, which was plenty for the next few hours.

Levine pulled the corner of the curtain aside and looked out into the camp.

"Clear."

They left the caravan and Levine locked up before they parted without another word.

* * *

Ben Palmer glanced over at the clock on his bedside table as the monotonous chime of the mobile phone dragged him from his deep sleep.

"Palmer," he said wearily, wondering what was so urgent that it meant calling at close to one in the morning.

"It's James," the voice said. "I was just —"

436

"Wait." Palmer hit a couple of keys on the handset and brought up the next combination of numbers for his private web portal. He read them out, and once he had confirmation that Farrar had written them down correctly he asked if the message was vitally important or if it could wait a few hours.

"There's no rush, but I need you to check your messages tomorrow. We've had a new development here, and in the next few hours there could be a change to your mission."

Palmer was glad that they wouldn't have to discuss business over the phone. There was no internet connection at the farm, so he would have to wait until they drove back to Durban the next afternoon. "I'll be able to get to them in around twelve hours," Palmer told him. "Can it wait until then?"

"Just as long as you check them before you meet our friends, that's fine."

Farrar hung up, and Palmer was suddenly wide awake. He had everything ready for the next evening's operation, and now Farrar wanted to change things at the eleventh hour. It was bad enough having to source a new weapon with every job, what with handguns being frowned upon by the customs people, but Sean had found him a beautiful piece. He'd spent the day sighting his new suppressed Sig P226 and adjusting the trigger tension until he had a weapon that reacted to his liking. In the meantime, Littlefield had gone out early to get the 3-Methylfentanyl and flash-bangs.

Now, with his shopping list complete and the plan in place, Farrar wanted to move the goal posts.

Was he going to call the whole thing off? No, he'd mentioned a change to the mission rather than a termination. Even if Farrar *did* decide to pull the plug, there was no way he was getting a refund.

It could be that there would be more than four people to deal with, or Farrar might want more information from them. Either way, he had what he needed to take care of the situation. The 3-Methylfentanyl he'd asked Sean for is an analogue fentanyl, an opioid analgesic similar to the one the Russians used to end the Moscow theatre siege in 2002, when it was delivered by aerosol into the auditorium. Palmer was sure that any container designed to hold people for weeks at a time would have air vents to allow them to breathe, and it was through these that he would administer the incapacitating agent. If there were no vents, he would open the door and throw in a couple of the flash-bangs, which produce a deafening noise and blinding flash and are designed to disorientate, but unlike conventional grenades they don't produce the large amounts of deadly shrapnel. This would allow him to set the canister to auto-release and throw it in the container. By the time anyone came to their senses it would be too late to stop the contents being dispersed, and with the dispersal mechanism being almost silent, it was doubtful that anyone would notice it even with perfect hearing. Everyone in the container would lose consciousness within a few moments, leaving him the simple task of dragging out the four non-Chinese occupants and loading them into his vehicle.

Satisfied that he wouldn't have to adapt this plan too much, no matter what Farrar had in mind, Palmer settled back to sleep.

Chapter 10

Monday May 7th 2012

Todd Hamilton pulled in behind Matt Baker's Ford Transit at just after one in the morning and killed the engine. His colleague was already out of the van, weapon drawn and hanging loosely by his side.

"Put that away," Hamilton hissed as he got out. "We need to make this look like an accident."

"I know!" Baker responded loudly, and Hamilton wondered how he'd ever made it to adulthood, never mind team leader. Perhaps it was the kill-rate despite his tender years, or his willingness to take on any job. It certainly wasn't down to his tactical thinking.

"Keep your voice down, man."

Two more occupants climbed out of the vehicles and into the brisk evening, doing up jackets to shield themselves from the wind that ran ahead of the rain clouds. A downpour was forecast for the early morning, yet another in what had already been a miserable spring.

Hamilton could have called on all eight members of their teams, but there was little need for that many bodies. It just meant more chance of detection. He'd have happily done it with just Paul Dougherty from his own team for company, but orders were orders.

Hamilton assumed command of the operation despite holding the same position as Baker. The personnel from both teams listened intently as he outlined his plan, happy that Baker wasn't leading the assault.

"I've got a canister of Silane in the back of the car," Hamilton said. "We're going to put it inside the target caravan and release it."

"What the hell's Silane?" Baker asked.

"It reacts violently with air, causing small explosions."

"Great!" Baker sneered. "We're gonna give them a tiny, indoor fireworks show."

Hamilton squared up to him, their faces almost touching. "If you'd let me finish, I could explain that when it's dispensed at high velocity under pressure it results in delayed combustion."

Hamilton took a step to the side and addressed the others, not waiting for a reaction from Baker.

"By the time the canister is empty, the air inside will be soaked with Silane. The resulting blast will blow the caravan to pieces. It should also breach their gas bottles, making it look like one of them failed and caused the explosion."

"What about residue?" Baker asked. "Fire investigators can spot an accelerant a mile away. What are they going to make of this?"

"According to the lab, the explosion and resultant fire should destroy all traces."

"After we deploy, how long do we have before it goes up?" Andy Hill asked.

"We should have around three minutes to clear the area," Hamilton told him. "I've had a look at the overheads and that's plenty of time to get out of the camp."

"Sounds risky to me," Baker said. "How do we get your canister into the caravan?"

"I'll go in with Paul. He's the best lock pick we've got and can pop the front door for me. I only need to open it a few inches so I can place the aerosol on the inner step and hit the release button."

"What if they're still awake?" Baker persisted.

"Then we come back and re-evaluate," Hamilton said, becoming increasingly frustrated with his colleague's attitude. He went to the back of his car and returned with a large can with an air-freshener label.

"This should be destroyed in the explosion, but if it survives it isn't going to arouse any suspicion."

Baker had to admit to himself that the idea was a good one, but was still pissed that he hadn't been included in the planning.

"So what are we supposed to do? Sit here with our thumbs up our arses?"

"Exactly," Hamilton said. "Sit tight, and I'll radio in once the job is completed."

He held out his tablet PC which showed an aerial photo of the camp. "Their caravan is situated near the back, here. We're going to enter this adjoining field and follow the perimeter of the camp until we come to this gap in the hedge, here. That brings us into the camp just a few yards from the target. After I hit the release button, we'll come back out the same way."

"Why don't we just come with you?" Baker persisted.

440

"Because if they somehow manage to get away, they'll do so by car. They've got women and a child with them, so they're not going to make a dash for it across the fields. I've left the keys in mine, so if you don't hear from us within ten minutes, seal the entrance and do what you have to."

"You mean clean up your mess," Baker sneered, and Hamilton was tempted to wipe the smile off his face. In-fighting, however, wasn't going to get the job done.

"I told you to bring the van for just this reason," Hamilton said as calmly as he could. "These guys know their stuff, so don't underestimate them. I'm not, and nor should you."

Baker looked for signs of nervousness but saw none. Hamilton was simply stating an opinion, not making excuses. "If we don't make it, get them in the van and dispose of them."

Baker perked up at the thought of some action if it all went to shit.

"Comms check. Alpha one."

"Delta one," Baker replied.

"Alpha two."

"Delta two."

"Farrar. Are you in position?"

"Setting off now," Hamilton told him, and with a final gesture for Baker to stay put, he jogged off down the road, Dougherty in tow.

"How long is this going to take?" Farrar asked. "I plan on sleeping tonight."

"It should all be over in ten minutes," Hamilton told him, as his eyes swept the side of the road for the entrance to the adjacent field. He saw it a hundred yards from the vehicles and led Dougherty over the gate and into the darkness.

A minute later he reached the hedge enclosing the camp and heard Farrar's voice in his ear.

"Where are you now, Todd?"

Hamilton replied with three clicks of the throat mic and continued onwards, bending at the waist to stay below the top of the hedge.

"Todd, talk to me."

"He's gone silent," Baker interjected. "He's near the target and can't talk."

"So how come you can? Where are you?"

"I'm three hundred yards away guarding the vehicles."

"What the hell for? Why aren't you in there getting the job done?"

"Todd's taken charge of the operation," Baker said, ensuring his frustration was noted. "He had it planned out before we even got here and doesn't want me to go along. He's taken Dougherty, that's it."

Farrar went silent, and Baker knew from experience that this was usually the calm before the storm. He was proven correct moments later.

"You get in there and make sure this job is finished in the next few minutes," Farrar snarled.

Two more clicks came over the air. "That'll be a No from Todd," Baker explained, "and I agree. If he can't pull it off, we have a backup plan."

One that Baker was looking forward to.

Hamilton's idea, even though it had been thrown together at the last minute, was sound on paper. If the targets were asleep, if Todd didn't wake them as he activated his device, and if the gas worked as expected, then it would be job done. However, it didn't have the hands-on aspect that Baker really enjoyed. Given the nature of their work, it wasn't often that he got to look his victims in the eye as he brought their lives to an end, and so he was glad that the next few minutes held so many imponderables.

"I'll leave that call to you, Matt," Farrar eventually said, "but I want this finished tonight."

Baker looked at his watch. "You've got seven minutes, Todd."

Seven minutes, and then Baker would know if the mission was over or it was time to have some fun.

* * *

Campbell hit the Accept button the second the phone in his hand vibrated.

"Movement," said the whispered voice. "Coming from the west, looks like two."

Campbell looked up the road in the direction Levine had given, but saw nothing. Whoever was heading towards Carl must have transport nearby, though.

"Clear here. I'll head in that direction and see if I can spot their vehicle."

There was no objection from Levine, so Campbell rose slowly and made his way towards the gate, pulling off his waterproof jacket as he went. It had served its purpose, and he didn't want to be sneaking up on someone wearing a coat that rustled every time he took a step.

There was no sign of anyone in the immediate area and he dashed past the entrance to the field, choosing to remain inside rather than expose himself out on the road. He stopped every fifteen yards and had a look through the bottom of the hedge to see if he could spot anything, but all the night had to offer was darkness and the usual hoots and screeches as animals went about their nocturnal activities.

Campbell crossed into the adjoining field, taking care to find a gap big enough that it wouldn't create a lot of noise as he squeezed through. As he traversed the edge he kept stopping, hoping to see a sign of life or hear a sound to indicate that he was getting close, but it wasn't until he crossed into the third field and rounded a bend in the road that he came across a likely looking pair.

The vehicles were parked up on the grass verge and two men were behind the Transit van, one of them looking cold and bored with his arms wrapped close to his body. The other looked more focused, leaning against the bonnet of the Ford saloon as he stroked the silenced pistol in his right hand. Every few moments he would glance at his watch, and then look in the direction of the camp.

"I've got a car and a van, about two hundred yards from you. I see two x-rays, one definitely armed. There could be more in the van, though."

Campbell waited for a reply, and when none came he knew the two men Carl had heard were most probably too close for him to talk.

"I'm going to get round in front of them," Campbell said quietly. "If they make a move, I'll stop them."

He slowly backtracked until he could no longer see his targets, then found a small gap in the hedge and squeezed through before dashing across the road. He cautiously made his way back towards the vehicles and stopped when the right-hand front wing of the Transit van was in view.

All he had to do now was await a signal from Levine.

It came moments later.

* * *

Carl Levine watched as the first pair of feet landed silently a few feet from the car he was sheltering under. Seconds later another person climbed over the style, and both men made their way towards

443

the target caravan. Levine watched as one of them expertly attacked the lock, and now that he knew they weren't just fellow campers returning from a night out, he edged out from underneath the car. As he did so, he saw the caravan door open and one of the men placed something inside, closing the door almost immediately.

The men had a quick look around and then started walking back towards the style, but their progress was halted as Levine suddenly appeared in front of them, gesturing with his pistol that they should reach for the skies. Both men did as instructed, shocked at the sight of the man they were supposed to kill standing just yards away.

Levine pointed the pistol at Hamilton and made a gesture with his left arm. Hamilton understood, and slowly unzipped his jacket, revealing a silenced Beretta in a shoulder holster. With another couple of signed instructions, Hamilton got the message to take the gun out with two fingers and toss it towards Levine.

Dougherty followed suit, his agitation showing as his glance shifted from Hamilton to the caravan, and Levine realised that they weren't comfortable being so close to the scene of their crime. They certainly hadn't come to deliver pizza, so whatever they had shoved inside the caravan had to be some kind of explosive device. He quickly gathered up the guns and after checking there was a round in the chamber of the silenced pistol he adopted it as his own, pushing his own weapon and the spare pistol into the waistband of his jeans.

"Move!" He hissed, indicating towards the style, and as the men walked he took up position behind them, grabbing Hamilton by the collar and placing the suppressor into the base of his skull.

"How many, and where?"

Hamilton hesitated for a few seconds, trying to decide whether to bluff or fold. "There's a dozen of us," he lied. "The rest are waiting in reserve just down the road. There's no way out."

Levine cuffed him around the ear with the gun. "Try again, and remember I've got another pair of eyes out there."

"Four," Hamilton said, his ear still ringing from the blow.

"I've got two secure," Levine said softly into his hands-free mic. "Bringing them out now. Looks like four in total." He heard a faint "Roger" in reply, and a glance at Hamilton's left ear confirmed that the man had his own comms.

"Tell your buddies you're pulling back," Levine said, "and don't even think about trying to warn them."

Hamilton slowly moved his hand to his throat mic and clicked it on. "The Semtex is in place. We're on our way back."

"Semtex, eh? You guys weren't planning on taking any prisoners, were you?"

Hamilton ignored the rhetorical question and followed Dougherty over the style, hoping Baker had understood the message. His colleague wasn't the brightest man on the planet, but surely he could spot a warning signal.

"How long until it blows?" Levine asked, and Hamilton told him they had little under a minute to get clear. He was about to tell them to pick up the pace when Campbell's voice came over the earpiece.

"Something's spooked these two. They're heading your way and not hanging around."

Levine jerked Hamilton to a halt and shifted his aim. A single round spat from the gun and Dougherty dropped to the floor before he could make a sound, a small hole on his temple marking the entry point.

"You came here to kill not only me, but my family, too," Levine said, the gun once again pressed against Hamilton's skull. "Don't think I'll hesitate to kill you."

There was a barely perceptible nod in reply, and Levine pulled his prisoner over to the side of the field and forced him down onto his knees. Levine got down on one knee a couple of yards behind him, pistol up and searching for targets.

He didn't have to wait long.

The first figure appeared in his sights just as the explosion lit up the sky off to his left, and it caught Levine off guard for just a second. That was long enough for Hamilton to grab the stone near his left leg and he spun, throwing the projectile as he turned. Levine saw it a split second before it hit, catching him on the bridge of the nose before he could swing the gun around. Hamilton was up instantly, kicking the gun hand away before landing a blow to Levine's head which sent him sprawling backwards. The air was knocked out of him as Hamilton landed on his chest with both knees, grabbing for the weapon in Levine's right hand. He resisted as much as he could, aiming punches at his assailant's kidneys with his left hand, but Hamilton ignored the blows. He pinned Levine's right arm to the ground and began pummelling his shoulder, hoping to dislocate it. After three attempts there was a satisfying crack and a howl from Levine.

Hamilton picked up the pistol that had fallen from Levine's grasp, and he placed it against Levine's chest while he retrieved the other two weapons from his waistband. He turned when he heard footsteps from behind and saw his colleagues approaching.

"Campbell's out there somewhere!" He told them.

"What happened to Paul?" Hill asked, standing over Dougherty's body.

"Levine killed him. Now go find Campbell!"

"Let's get this one in the van," Baker said, "then we can all look for him."

Hamilton didn't see the point in all three escorting the prisoner to the van, especially in his current state. "I'll deal with Levine," he said. "You take care of the other one, and make it quick. We'll have to come back for Paul's body."

Baker didn't like the fact that Hamilton was still giving the orders despite his plan having gone to shit, but the prospect of spending a few minutes alone with Levine spurred him on. He and Hill retreated the way they'd come, weapons up in search of movement. They soon disappeared from view, and Hamilton ordered Levine to his feet.

"Fuck you!"

"I'll count to three," Hamilton said.

"Don't bother, just give me the bad news."

Hamilton was sorely tempted, but he needed to know where their spouses were, a fact not lost on Levine.

"There's no way in hell I'm giving up my family," he said as he got up onto one knee, all the time cradling his useless right arm. Looking up at Hamilton, he let his left arm drop to his side.

"Do it," he said, focusing his eyes on the gun pointing towards his head.

The park was now fully awake, with people shouting and several children screaming. An adjacent caravan, showered in flaming debris from the initial blast, began to burn, adding to the intensity as the fire crept higher into the night sky.

It was only a matter of time before the emergency services arrived, and Hamilton wanted to be clear of the area before that happened.

"Come on, you stubborn bastard..." He grabbed for Levine's collar, and the knife came up with such ferocity that he didn't even have time to register shock before it plunged into his throat and exited through the back of his neck, severing the spinal column on the way.

Levine eased the corpse to the ground and retrieved both the silenced pistol and his own weapon. He replaced his earpiece, which had fallen out during the struggle, then took the dead man's comms unit and placed the receiver in his right ear.

"These two are down, the other two are coming towards you now," he said over the phone.

A quick search for ID produced nothing but a small amount of money. No driving licence or credit cards, not even a library card to put a name to the face. That wasn't too surprising, given the nature of their visit.

Leaving the dead where they'd fallen, Levine jogged towards the road. He slowed as he reached the trees lining the narrow country lane and peered through the foliage, cursing the flames from the camp for ruining his night vision. Shadows danced before him, and he knew he would have to break through the tree line and put it between himself and the fire in order to see anything.

He carefully climbed over the rickety, wooden fence and sought cover behind the largest tree he could find. A glance around the thick trunk told him he was just a few yards from the road, but there were no signs of any vehicles. He guessed he was too close to the camp, so he headed away from it, taking care to minimise the sound of his footsteps.

The van came into view thirty yards ahead, and he could see Campbell kneeling next to it, a gun held to his head. He knew the other one had to be close by, and he realised just how close when the cold, hard steel of the suppressor jabbed him in the temple.

"Move," Baker said, holding his hand out for Levine to surrender his weapons. Where the man had come from, Levine didn't know, but he'd been a silent as a cat. He gave up the guns and stood, receiving a shove in the back to urge him forward.

"Hamilton screwed up," Baker said into his throat mic, "but I've got things under control."

"What do you mean, he screwed up?" Farrar asked.

"His bomb went off but there was no-one in the caravan. I've got the two men and I'll make them take us to the women."

"Hamilton, talk to me. What the hell is going on there?"

"Hamilton's dead," Baker told him, as he ushered Levine forward. "So is Dougherty. I'll report back when we're done."

Farrar wasn't happy that the mission hadn't been wrapped up, but he accepted that it might take a little time to break the ex-soldiers. He told Baker to call him as soon as the job was complete, then signed off comms.

When they reached the vehicles, Campbell offered Levine an apologetic look.

"Sorry, mate. They got the drop on me while I was trying to slash their tyres."

"Shut it!" Hill hissed, giving Campbell a kick in the ribs.

Baker told Levine to lie on the floor and ordered Hill to cover them both while he fetched two pairs of plasticuffs from the van. He returned and went to work on Levine first, wrenching his injured shoulder and pleased to see the signs of discomfort. Levine clenched his teeth as the pain from his shoulder shot through his body, but Baker wasn't in the mood to be tender and he gave the arm another tug for good measure.

When both prisoners had their hands secured behind their backs, Baker gestured for them to climb inside the van. Levine looked over to where Hill had Campbell by the scruff of the neck, and he moved towards the van, hesitating in front of the open door. Baker moved in to give him a shove and as soon as Levine felt the hand on his back, he made his move.

Placing one leg up onto the sill of the van, he pushed back with all his strength, swivelling in mid air and coming down with an outstretched leg which caught Baker on the chin. The strike knocked the man backwards and he fell against the bonnet of the Ford, but managed to squeeze off a round which caught Levine in his good arm. The thud of the impact spun him for a second, but the adrenalin pumping through his body held the pain at bay. He kicked Baker's legs from under him and as he hit the floor, Levine threw himself on top of him. He began using his forehead to pummel Baker's face, smashing the nose and sending blood spraying into the air.

Campbell took this as his cue and raked his heel down Hill's shin. While the man was stunned by the intense pain he took a step away from him and tried to deliver a roundhouse kick, but Hill recovered just quickly enough to deflect the blow and he kicked out at Campbell's groin, knocking the wind out of him. Once he was on the ground, Hill gave him another kick to the head, then went to help his team leader.

Hill grabbed Levine's blood-stained arm and dragged him off Baker, and the resulting scream pierced the night. Baker sat up groggily and climbed unsteadily to his feet, his pistol swinging

448

drunkenly by his side. He gingerly felt for the damage done to his face, and his hand came away a dark crimson in the faint moonlight.

With anger seeping from every pore, Baker approached Levine and pointed the pistol at his head.

"I thought you wanted them alive," Hill said, having seen the look before.

Baker glanced over at Campbell and saw him sprawled out on the ground, alive but dazed.

"We only need one," he snarled.

Carl Levine looked into the small hole of the suppressor and knew that death was an instant away. He'd always known it would come, and a bullet in the head was preferable to other ways of meeting one's end, such as drowning or the lingering agony of a terminal disease, but his thoughts turned to his family. Who would look after them once he was gone? How would —

The sound of the bullet echoed through the trees and Levine flinched, but the anticipated darkness never came. Instead, Baker sank to his knees before collapsing forward onto his face. A stranger came into view, with a pistol held in a two-handed grip and trained on Hill.

"Drop it," the newcomer said with a hint of an accent. As he drew closer to pick up the Hill's weapon, Levine could see that he was of Asian origin, perhaps from India or Pakistan. Another man appeared and quickly cuffed Hill before leading him back down the lane.

"Carl Levine, I presume."

Levine said nothing. While thankful to still be alive, he was too busy wondering what the hell was going on.

"I know this is going to sound corny," the man standing over him said, "but come with me if you want to live."

Levine saw two more men appear. One came over and knelt down next to him, placed a first-aid kit on the ground and pulled out a bandage which he used to dress Levine's bullet wound. The other went over to Campbell and helped him to his feet.

"You mind telling me who you are, and who they are?" Levine asked, nodding towards Baker's corpse.

"We're Five," the man told him. "The name's Hamad. Hamad Farsi."

Levine looked sceptical. "If you're Five, who the hell are these guys?"

He winced as the medic tightened the bandage around his wound and declared him good to go, before calling the other man over to help

449

carry Baker's body. They dragged it to the van and unceremoniously threw it in.

"You'll find two more in the field," Levine told them as he staggered to his feet. "Head towards the fire, you can't miss them."

The two men trotted off and Farsi gestured for Levine to follow him. "We need to get you to a proper doctor."

Levine stood his ground. "You still haven't told me what's going on. Who were those guys?"

"They work for the government, and we believe they're trying to eliminate everyone involved in the Tom Gray episode last year. Why, we don't know."

Levine thought it was obvious, but he didn't let on. He wanted to speak to Jeff alone before he said anything else, so he followed Farsi down the road to where two saloons were parked. Campbell was already in the back seat of one and he climbed in beside his friend.

Farsi climbed into the front passenger seat and turned to face them.

"Are your families close by?" He asked as the first of the emergency service vehicles roared past, sirens wailing.

"They took off hours ago," Levine lied. Until he knew exactly what was going on, he wasn't about to drag his family back into this. "If we don't get in touch with them within four hours, they take our story to the press."

"And just what is your story?" Farsi asked.

Levine and Campbell looked at one another. "Let's get Carl sorted out first," Campbell said. Farsi nodded and told the driver to move out.

"It's a bit of a coincidence that you should show up just in time," Levine said as they drove past the camp. He noticed that the fire now having spread to a third caravan, and was thankful that the girl next door had let his daughter's indiscretion slip. There was no way any of them would have survived the blast or the resulting inferno if they'd been tucked up in bed.

"It was close," Farsi said. "We're guessing your daughter sent her boyfriend a text, but it didn't hit our desk until an hour and a half ago. The night shift didn't realise the importance, otherwise we'd have been here hours ago."

"Is that how the others found us?" Campbell asked.

"We believe so," Farsi said, "and we'd really like to know why they want you dead. Apart from the team that just tried to kill you, we

450

know there's a contractor waiting for Simon Baines and Len Smart to land in South Africa tomorrow evening."

"South Africa?" Campbell asked. "What the hell are they doing there? I thought they were in the Philippines!"

"And what do you mean by contractor?" Levine said. "A hit man?"

"At least one," Farsi told him. "They're on a cargo ship that will be arriving in Durban and we intercepted instructions that sound very much like a kill order. Unfortunately we haven't been able to establish just who will be meeting them."

The news confirmed what Campbell and Levine had thought all along: the government wanted rid of everyone who knew that Tom Gray was still alive.

So why couldn't Farsi put two and two together? Surely it was obvious that the information they had could cause the entire government serious damage. The opposition, who had been ousted in the last election, were responsible for creating the subterfuge, and the current ruling party were complicit by not only maintaining the silence but also sending out kill squads.

There could only be one explanation — Farsi didn't know that Tom was still alive.

"So why are you helping us?" Levine asked. "If the government are looking to kill us, surely MI5 would be involved in the plot."

"You've been watching too many movies," Farsi told him. "Our mandate is to protect the citizens of the UK, not kill them. If someone has committed a crime, we seek justice through the courts."

"Then how come you just shot that guy?" Campbell asked. "You could have tried arresting him."

"Because I knew he'd been sent to kill you, and it was his life or yours. Hopefully that will convince you that we're on your side."

It was a compelling argument, Levine thought. If they were just playing good-cop-bad-cop, burning one of their own to execute the charade was a bit extreme. While Farsi's sentiment about following the proper judicial procedure was noble, Levine wondered how the man would react when he discovered the truth. Would he or his superiors allow Tom Gray to announce his return to the world once they realised how devastating it would be to the credibility of the government?

Levine decided that while he trusted Farsi — if only for the time being — he would keep that particular card close to his chest.

"When you get to the next village you'll see a supermarket on the high street. Our families are in the car park at the rear."

Campbell threw him a look, but Levine assured him it was okay. "There's a loose end we need to tie up," he told Farsi. "The man you shot was due to report in once he'd finished his mission."

"No problem," Farsi said. "We'll take care of it."

Chapter 11

Monday May 7th 2012

The chirping of his mobile woke Farrar from a fitful sleep. According to his watch he'd been asleep for less than two hours.

"What?" He barked into the phone.

"It's Hill. The job's complete."

"Where's Baker?" Farrar asked.

"He's...tidying up," Hill told him.

"I'll give him a ring," Farrar said, but Hill told him not to bother. "During the takedown, Baker got into a skirmish and his mobile was damaged."

"Just get him to call me when he's got a new phone," Farrar said, and hit the End button.

Durban was an hour ahead of the UK, which meant it was just after seven in the morning in Durban. Having woken Palmer just a few hours earlier, Farrar decided to wait until he got to the office before contacting him again. He'd said he wouldn't have access to the website until the afternoon, so there was no point in depriving the man of any more sleep when he had an important hit to carry out.

Despite the abrupt wake-up call, Farrar found himself looking forward to the day ahead. He headed to the shower and began preparing his report for the Home Secretary, which he would deliver once Palmer confirmed his kills.

* * *

Even though it was barely six in the morning, Veronica Ellis found that she wasn't the first member of the team to make it into work. A light from the technical team office told her that Gerald Small had beaten her to it.

"Morning," she said as she stuck her head through the doorway. "What's got you in so early?"

"Just finishing up the website," the technician told her. "I managed to get the source code from Gordon's cloud storage account and the

ISP has graciously agreed to point the IP address to one of our machines."

"So when Farrar uses the site, will he notice any difference?"

"None at all," Small said, "but we haven't been able to crack the encryption algorithm he used to generate the passwords. The best I could do was to pretend to authenticate, but in actual fact it will accept any password the user enters."

"If you have the source code, why can't you figure it out?"

"It relies on a key in the web.config file," Small explained. "It reads the key and uses that as the hash for the encryption. Trouble is, this is his backup version, and the key is blank."

"Surely this would only be a problem if they intentionally entered the wrong password, wouldn't it?"

"That's right," Small told her. "The risk is tiny, but there nonetheless."

Ellis wasn't about to second-guess him on anything technical, and if he said he couldn't do any more, that was the end of the matter. At least they had the site in place, and following the news she'd received an hour earlier, she only expected it to be in use for another twenty-four hours at the most. They already had logs that tied Farrar to the website, and one of his operatives was currently being more than co-operative in a safe house south of London. While compelling reading, Andy Hill's testimony wouldn't be enough to get Farrar into court, let alone convict him. According to Hill, there'd been no written instructions beyond a workup file, which had been deleted once the plan had been drawn up and approved, so it would be Farrar's word against theirs. Farrar would no doubt paint his team as disgruntled, rogue employees and have some high-ranking figures offer testimony on his behalf, so the more proof she could gather, the better.

With that in mind, she thanked Small and went to her own office to let Andrew Harvey know about the latest developments.

* * *

With an hour remaining of the flight to London Heathrow airport, Abdul Mansour carefully adjusted his *burqa*, unlocked the toilet door and returned to his seat. He hadn't spoken a single word to his male companion during the entire flight lest anyone discover the charade that had seen him pass easily through passport control at Lahore's Allama Iqbal International airport. He hadn't really expected any

454

problems leaving Pakistan, but he had to trust Al-Asiri when he said the arrival would be uneventful: That wasn't normally the case when walking into the lion's den.

Thirty minutes later, the plane began its decent. Mansour once again felt for the inhaler in his pocket, and he decided that if they were stopped on their way through the airport, he would set the device off and leave himself at the mercy of Allah.

When they eventually touched down, Mansour and his companion, Ali, joined the throng of other passengers heading towards the immigration desks. Mansour looked for a desk staffed by a likely ally, but Ali guided him to a queue manned by a burly male. He kept his hands inside the *burqa* and removed the canister from his pocket, ready to activate it should there be any trouble.

It took ten agonising minutes for them to reach the head of the line, and Mansour prayed that they would be let through with just a cursory inspection of their documents.

It wasn't to be.

"Lift the veil, please," the border guard said, flicking through the passports.

Mansour pretended not to understand the instructions, and they were repeated with hand gestures. Again he didn't move, but Ali lifted the thin material and Mansour found himself staring into the official's eyes.

He pressed down on the canister and began a silent count of ten, but he only got to two before the guard nodded, handed back the documents and waived them through. Mansour let out the breath he'd been holding and glanced back, but the man was already inspecting the paperwork for the next passenger.

They collected their single suitcase from the baggage hall and made their way to the exit, where they found a man holding a placard bearing Ali's surname. They followed him to his vehicle, which was located in the multi-storey car park. Once they'd cleared the airport, Mansour finally felt he could relax.

"I wish you'd warned me what to expect," he told Ali.

"He has been working for us for quite some time now," his companion told him. "The man has a severe gambling problem, which we feed with a few thousand pounds every month."

"Is money enough to ensure his obedience?" Mansour wondered aloud.

"It usually is. This one was about to lose his house because of his addiction, but we paid off the mortgage arrears and he gets a gambling allowance in cash every month. He is happy with the current arrangement, but he also knows that if he tries to cross us, his precious home will go up in flames while he and his family sleep."

"Sometimes the carrot works, sometimes the stick," Mansour said, "but a combination of both is better."

Ali nodded. "I have been here eleven times, and you are the eleventh wife he has allowed me to bring through immigration control. It has proven to be a valuable route into the country."

Mansour agreed, though he did wonder why he hadn't been told of it on his last visit to England. Hadn't they trusted him? His masters had provided him with a forged passport and let him make his own way there, rather than disclose this more secure method of entry. Perhaps the operation had been so hurriedly put together that there simply hadn't been time to ensure their man would be working when he touched down.

That was a year ago, he reminded himself, and his exploits since had surely demonstrated his loyalty beyond any doubt.

His loyalty to the cause, at least.

In his pocket he had the flash card from the mobile he'd been carrying on his recent visit to Azhar Al-Asiri's home, and embedded on that drive were the GPS co-ordinates of the building. Once they reached the London safe house, he would send someone out to a local toy shop to buy the equipment he needed for the next part of his plan.

* * *

Andrew Harvey removed the magazine from the 9mm Beretta, checked the chamber was empty and stripped it down, as his firearms training dictated. The barrel looked clean and the moving parts slid nicely into place. The well-oiled gun had obviously been properly maintained.

"Thanks, Dennis. Should I ask where you got this?"

"Best not to," Owen smiled.

They were sitting in Harvey's hotel room waiting for a phone call so that they could make a move. The plan was to check out the area around the port exit to see if they could spot anyone waiting for the Wenban haulage trucks to make an appearance. Unfortunately, they still had no idea just how many they were up against.

456

That information, according to Veronica Ellis, had died with Carl Gordon.

The good news was that they had managed to rebuild the website Farrar had been communicating through, though the latest message they'd intercepted an hour earlier hadn't made today's task easy.

Ellis had given Harvey a brief rundown on the events of the previous evening, and it seemed Farrar had believed the news he'd been fed by Andy Hill. On the understanding that Campbell and Levine were out of the way, Farrar had left a curt note on the website:

"Information no longer required. Terminate their journey."

For Harvey, this changed the entire game. Up until a few hours ago he was looking for someone who wanted the people in the container alive, which meant being subtle and choosing the moment carefully. Now, however, the strike could occur at any time, and Harvey and Owen would be the only ones concerned about the passengers' safety.

He would have felt a lot better if he had a full team behind him, but when he suggested the idea to Ellis, she ruled it out. There simply wasn't time to get anyone else in place, and using the local cops was out of the question.

"What happens if you and the police catch some guy in the act," Ellis had said, "and the locals want to take him in? That's only natural, as it's their country. We might lose access to him and our case against Farrar falls apart."

Her reasoning was sound, but it didn't make his job any easier. What did was the recent discovery made by Gerald Small. His eventual success at hacking the Port Authority servers meant they knew that the larger consignment was to be delivered to a small firm to the south of the city. The mom and pop company operated normal business hours, which meant that unless the truck could reach them before five in the afternoon, it would have to park up overnight, and the logical place to do so was the Wenban facility. Small had been searching for further details, such as the offloading time, when the server security systems recognised the intrusion and kicked him out. That information would have been handy, but at least they knew a lot more now than they did a few hours earlier.

Owen's mobile chirped and he hit the Accept button. After the briefest of conversations he nodded to Harvey, grabbed his jacket and headed towards the door.

Harvey tucked the pistol into his waistband and covered it with the Hawaiian print shirt. Owen was similarly dressed in order to create the impression that they were just tourists out enjoying a drive.

In the hotel reception, Owen was greeted by two young blondes from the Durban office who he'd arranged to come along on the surveillance, adding to the pretence. After brief introductions, the girls led them to the car, an Audi A5 convertible. Harvey climbed in the back with Clara while Elaine took the front passenger seat.

On the short drive to the port, Harvey gave Clara a smart phone and was glad to discover she was familiar with the model.

"It's set to record video," he said. "Just hold it up to your ear and make sure you aren't covering the camera lens."

As they drove, Clara pretended to make a short phone call, then handed the phone back to Harvey who looked at the recording.

"All I'm getting is the wheels of the vehicles," he told her. "If you can hold it vertical we should get some good images."

Clara tried once more, this time with better results. Harvey wiped the test video and handed the phone back, then pulled his own from his pocket. After a dummy run, he declared them good to go.

Earlier in the day, Owen and Harvey had studied aerial shots of the port before spending a couple of hours monitoring movement from the main exit, Bayhead Road. They knew that the trucks would turn left onto South Coast Road and head south until they had a chance to join the M4 highway heading north towards their depot.

Following the likely route, both Harvey and Clara set their phones recording, placed them to their ears and pretended to be deep in conversation as they cruised along at a sedate pace. They passed shops and service stations built in the fifties and looking like they hadn't had a lick of paint since. Their job wasn't made easy by the sheer number of vehicles on the road, and though Harvey had a clear view of the occupants of the vehicles parked along his side of the street, Clara's phone was mostly capturing oncoming traffic.

It took almost fifteen minutes to travel the two miles to the M4 on-ramp, where Owen made a U-turn and retraced their route. Once they'd reached their starting point at the junction of Bayhead Road, Harvey uploaded the videos to a cloud storage site and emailed Hamad Farsi, asking him to scan through the images and see if any of the faces captured were known to the service. It was a long shot, but if they could identify their suspect before the truck arrived, it took the targets out of the equation.

"Let's go meet up with Kyle," Owen said.

He drove down Bayhead Road and pulled up at a service station where he'd parked his BMW that morning. Kyle Ackerman was waiting by a Suzuki Jeep and he came over as they parked up. Owen handled the introductions and thanked Kyle for helping out.

"No problem," Kyle said. "Two thousand Rand for following a truck is the easiest money I've ever made."

Harvey wasn't sure that having someone with no field experience on the operation was a good idea, but Kyle was the only person Owen could call on at short notice. When Owen had suggested the idea, Harvey had asked for someone who could handle themselves in a tight situation, and Kyle had been Owen's only option. His four years spent in the Royal Marines would have to make up for his lack of field craft, and hopefully his only task would be to tail a slow-moving vehicle for a few miles.

Owen thanked the girls for their help and promised to treat them when the mission was over, and Clara slipped Harvey a business card and a smile before climbing into the driver's seat and gunning the engine.

"You're a sly one," Owen grinned as Harvey studied the phone number he'd been handed. "She's not usually that forward."

"Hey, I'm as surprised as you!"

"Trust me, that's one call you wanna make."

Harvey was flattered by the invitation, but his first concern was ensuring Kyle knew what was expected of him.

"Dennis said I just had to stay behind the truck and wait for a phone call from you guys," Ackerman smiled. "Not really rocket science."

Harvey found himself warming to Kyle, his easy-going approach making him a likeable sort, but concerns about his ability to pull off the mission pushed those thoughts aside.

"It might get a bit hairy," he warned. "If the first container looks big enough to hold a couple of dozen people, Dennis and I will follow it, otherwise it's yours. We have no idea which one contains the people we're looking for, and we don't know where or when it's going to be hit. We don't even know how many people will be looking for it."

"Lots of imponderables," Ackerman said, as the smile melted away and his demeanour suddenly went into professional mode. "Don't worry, I'm not stupid enough to take on an army all by myself. If I see anything suspicious, I'll let you guys know."

Harvey nodded, his confidence in the man growing by the minute. He handed over the card Carla had given him.

"Take this," he said. "I prefer brunettes."

Kyle screwed it up and tossed it into a nearby bin.

"Been there, done that," he winked.

The ship was due to dock at any moment, but it could be hours before the containers they were interested in were ready to come ashore. Harvey knew they wouldn't be able to park at the service station for long without arousing suspicion, but for a while they would be a lot less conspicuous than if they were to park right on the junction, and the truck would have to pass them on its way to the highway.

They went into the service station and ordered coffee before finding seats near the window so that they could keep an eye out for the distinctive Wenban livery. Their thoughts turned to the mission ahead, and after all the preparation, all they could do now was wait. Owen had prepared passports for both Smart and Baines, and two more were waiting to be processed once they had new photos for the other two passengers. There was still no confirmation that the mysterious Sam Grant was one of them, and Harvey thought back to the file that was currently locked in his hotel room safe.

He'd studied the picture time and time again, and while it still seemed like a composite, the eyes had once again struck him as remarkably familiar.

Hopefully the next few hours would provide some answers.

* * *

An hour and a half later, just as Hamad Farsi was informing Harvey that no matches had been found within the images — either within their own database or Interpol's — Sean Littlefield drove past the service station and continued down Bayhead Road until he reached the junction with Langeberg Road, the arterial route leading from the cargo terminal.

"It's going to be a long wait," he observed as he parked the Mercedes Sprinter van.

Ben Palmer nodded, but his thoughts were on the operation that lay ahead.

Since getting the message from Farrar, he'd been thinking about the take down, and they'd stopped off at a hardware store on the way to buy a few items. He got out of the passenger seat and climbed into the back of the van to prepare his improvised munitions.

With the need for subtlety gone, Palmer had wanted to get his hands on some proper grenades rather than the flash-bangs Littlefield had provided. He didn't know if his targets would be armed, but experience told him that it was always safer to assume they were. Unfortunately, it was too late in the day to acquire the real thing, so Palmer set to work adapting the flash-bangs so that they would be as lethal as fragmentation grenades.

His first task was to cut out a piece of cellophane the same height as the barrel of the M84 stun grenade and long enough to wrap around it, plus an extra three inches. The grenade had a thin aluminium core surrounded by a perforated steel body, which allowed the magnesium-based pyrotechnic to escape and temporarily blind the victims. Palmer's plan was to wrap layers of putty heavily impregnated with small steel screws around the barrel. It was based on the principle that if you set off a firecracker in the palm of your hand, you burn your hand, but if you wrap your fingers around it, you'll never play the piano again.

The M84 produces a subsonic deflagration rather than a supersonic detonation, but by encasing it in the putty the effect of the blast would be magnified, and the screws would be as deadly as any bullet. He'd considered using ball bearings, just like those found in Claymore mines, but the irregular shape of the screws would produce more collateral damage, tumbling as they entered the bodies, tearing flesh and fragmenting bone. The idea wasn't to inflict pain, just to cause as much shock to the system as possible so that the body shuts down.

Palmer used the first piece of cellophane as a template to produce another eight before cutting out slits in each one to accommodate the grenade's handle, then smeared the first three with a thin veneer of the putty. He sprinkled around fifty screws onto each sheet and used the putty tin to roll them flat. Once he'd trimmed off the excess, he wrapped a sheet around each of the M84s, using electrical tape to hold them in place. After waiting a few minutes to let each layer dry, Palmer repeated the process twice more until the grenades were completely encased.

The sun had set by the time the weapons were ready, and the container was still an hour away from being offloaded. Trucks filed past as he climbed back into the passenger seat, some destined for local trading estates, the majority heading inland.

"All set?" Littlefield asked, and Palmer nodded.

* * *

When Arnold Tang's car pulled up to the entrance of the Hong Wing restaurant, the owner was already standing near the entrance ready to welcome him. The visitor was quickly shown to a table near the rear, where waiters were busy laying place settings.

"Are you dining alone?" The manager asked, and Tang informed him that a friend would be along shortly. His henchmen took their positions at a nearby table as Tang sat in a chair facing the door, and a bottle of Remy Martin Louis XIII was quickly placed in front of him.

A few minutes later, Koh Beng Lee arrived with his own entourage. Arnold greeted him and poured two glasses of cognac, and they exchanged small talk until the waiter arrived to take their order. Once he was gone, Lee steered the conversation towards business.

"I have another twenty people from Singapore ready to make the journey west," he said. "When is the next ship leaving?"

"On the twentieth," Tang told him. "How do you want them to travel once they reach Durban?"

Lee knew the options open to him. Tang had two tiers of travel, the first and cheapest being overland from Durban to Morocco. After a short ferry ride to Spain it would be overland all the way to Calais for the short hop to Dover.

The second option cost an extra ten thousand US dollars and meant a plane ride to the north of the continent, shaving fifteen days off the journey and avoiding a lot of dicey border crossings.

As the people making the journey tended to be the poor looking for a better life, very few could afford option two.

"They will all be going overland," Lee told him, and gestured to one of his men, who brought over a briefcase. He opened it to reveal bundles of fifties, and Tang nodded. He wouldn't insult his friend by counting it, and Lee already knew the consequences of being so much as a dollar short.

Tang placed the case on the floor next to his feet and poured another two drinks.

"I trust you heard about Timmy Hughes," Lee said as he savoured the spirit. "He was a good customer of mine. I understand you had...dealings with him, too."

Tang's demeanour shifted instantly at the mention of the name. "What about him?"

"You didn't hear?"

"Obviously not."

"He was killed two weeks ago. Shot in the head, I was told."

Tang rubbed the bridge of his nose as he digested the news, then suddenly banged a meaty fist on the table. One of his men ran over, hand inside his jacket and ready to draw down if his boss was in danger. Tang waved him away and pulled out his mobile phone.

"Where is the last shipment?" He barked. It took a moment for his new lieutenant to find the information, and that got Tang wondering.

Was Hughes' death somehow linked to the disappearance of two of his men a fortnight earlier? They were good men, and had handled the people smuggling operation efficiently before they suddenly vanished. Was another player trying to move into his territory? Had they simply decided to work for someone else, or had they been taken out in an effort to cripple his business?

Anger boiled within him, his face taking on a crimson hue.

The first thing to deal with was Hughes' fare-dodging friends. When his lieutenant came back on the line he was told that the ship had landed in South Africa an hour earlier.

Tang had already given instructions for the passengers to be killed once they'd arrived in England and he'd received his payment from Hughes, but as that money was never going to arrive, there was no point in paying for an unnecessary plane journey. He was going to be slightly out of pocket on the deal, and the passengers would pay for it.

"Call Leng in Durban. Get him to cancel the *gweilo*'s flight, then I want him to take them somewhere remote and dispose of them." He thought for a moment, then added: "Tell him to rape the woman and make the men watch, then kill them all."

He hung up and poured himself a large measure of cognac. The possibility that someone might be making a move on his operation would gnaw at him for days, and the death of the *gweilos* would be small recompense.

Chapter 12

Monday May 7th 2012

"Here we go."

Andrew Harvey saw the blue truck with lightning flashes approach the service station and he grabbed his coat, following Owen out of the door.

"Follow the next one, and be careful," he warned Ackerman, who nodded solemnly.

They allowed several other vehicles to get between them and the target, both men making a mental note of the drivers and passengers. Owen eventually pulled into the traffic and saw the red container roughly a quarter of a mile down the road.

"Don't get too close unless it leaves the expected route," Harvey said, angling the rear-view mirror so that he could see who was behind them.

The truck turned left onto the coast road, retracing their earlier steps, before obligingly hitting the M4 on-ramp which led to the Wenban compound. The road threaded its way through central Durban before heading to Durban Beach and hugging the coast as it meandered north. By now only three vehicles remained between them and the truck, and that soon fell to two. Traffic was disappointingly light at this time of night, and Owen held off the throttle to allow the gap to open up.

After twenty minutes, one of the cars ahead pulled off the M4 at an off-ramp, and Harvey checked the mirror for the hundredth time and saw that their tail was clear.

"That has to be our guy," he said, indicating to the van up ahead.

Owen agreed. "Sure you don't want me to just pull him over?"

"No," Harvey said. "Slowly overtake them both and then stay half a mile ahead of the truck."

He pulled his phone out and prepared the video camera before holding it to his ear. The powerful BMW closed the gap easily and they cruised past the van, Harvey recording the driver's face while simultaneously noting the licence number. By the time they'd eased ahead of both vehicles, Harvey had plenty of footage. He scanned through it quickly and saw the lone driver, a man in his fifties. Not recognising him, he sent the video to Farsi along with a note requesting details of the van's owner.

Owen opened up a lead on the target vehicles before slowing to match their speed.

"We should reach Wenban in about ten minutes," he said.

Having scoped out the route a few days earlier, Harvey knew that there was just one more off-ramp before the highway took them past the compound, and it was just a few minutes up the road. If the truck continued past it, his gamble would have paid off. If it took the turning, it would be another fifteen minutes before they could get off the highway and try to find it again.

His heart beat faster as the BMW slid past the turn off and he willed the truck to follow. He watched the headlights in the mirror as they appeared to crawl along the tarmac and he muttered to himself as the seconds ticked by.

"Come on, come on, a little more..."

He let out an audible sigh of relief as the truck trundled past the off-ramp and continued to follow them.

"Okay, head for the warehouse opposite the Wenban compound. We'll park behind it and see what they do once they get there."

Owen gunned the engine and they pulled away from the miniature convoy. By the time they pulled off the highway and reached the warehouse they were around four minutes ahead of the truck, and Owen parked up around the back of the derelict building. As Harvey got out he noted that theirs were the only fresh tyre marks in the loose dirt, which meant it was unlikely their quarry would choose the same location — anyone worth their salt would have scoped the area out, and this place hadn't been visited in months.

He pushed his way through a hole in the fence and sprinted to the front of the warehouse, where he checked that the front gate he'd oiled on his previous visit moved without making a sound. Satisfied that he could get out of the compound without being heard, he tucked down behind a row of rusting oil drums. A moment later, Owen joined him, zipping up his black jacket as he sank to his knees.

"Where the hell did you get that?" Harvey asked, looking at the R4 assault rifle Owen was brandishing.

"Same place I got your pea-shooter," Owen smiled. "As we don't know the enemy strength, I thought it best to bring it along, just in case."

"Couple that with your muscle car, and you must have the smallest dick in the world."

Despite the banter, Harvey was grateful for the extra firepower.

It was another two minutes before headlights heralded the arrival of the truck. The driver swung the vehicle through the open gates and manoeuvred the flatbed to the back of the compound, where he reversed into a marked bay and climbed out of the cab. Harvey watched him head into the office, and a couple of minutes later he emerged and climbed into a car which sped away into the night.

There had been no sign of the van, and Harvey was beginning to wonder if they'd followed the wrong container when the Mercedes slowly cruised past his hiding place, the driver concentrating on the road ahead while the passenger's attention was focused on the haulage company's yard.

Just as he was wondering where the second person had appeared from, his phone vibrated. Farsi had sent him the file on Sean Littlefield and he quickly scanned through it, sharing the information with Owen. There was nothing to link him to Farrar or any black ops teams, and none of his known associates matched the name the van was rented under.

Harvey was still no closer to discovering who his enemy was, and now he and Owen were facing at least two adversaries. There could even be more hidden away in the van, but he couldn't do anything about that at this late stage. He hadn't even had time to get a snap of the newcomer to send to Farsi, so all he could do now was exercise caution and hope to bring one of them in alive.

* * *

Ben Palmer had spent most of the journey in the back of the van, looking out of the small rear window to see if they were being followed. The BMW had caught his attention soon after they'd joined the highway, but once it had sped past and disappeared into the night, he began to relax.

Satisfied that they had no tail, he climbed over the central console and into the passenger seat.

"We're clean," he said, and Littlefield looked in his wing mirror, seeing nothing but darkness.

They watched the truck pull off the highway and Palmer ordered Littlefield to stop two hundred yards short of the compound. A few minutes later, a car drove out of the gates and roared past them, heading towards the city.

"Do a drive by," Palmer said. "I want to see if anyone's still there."

Littlefield rolled the van forwards, and as they crept past the gates, Palmer spotted a single car parked outside the office building. Lights shone through the windows, and he knew he'd have to wait a little longer to complete the mission.

"Sean, park up further down the road and I'll walk back. Once the last person's gone I'll call you."

His friend drove along until they rounded a corner, where he performed a U-turn and went off-road, parking the van behind a row of trees. Palmer hopped out and jogged parallel to the road until he was within a hundred yards of the perimeter fence, where he took a knee next to a bush, his eyes on the prize. He took a ski mask from his jacket pocket and pulled it over his head, a low-tech solution to the three CCTV cameras covering the target.

The nocturnal orchestra was in full swing, and insects buzzed around him as he waited impatiently for signs of movement. Eventually he was rewarded as the lights went out and the office door opened. A male appeared carrying a bowl, followed by the dog Palmer had encountered a few days earlier. It bounded to the fence to relieve itself, and then ran back to its owner, barking for its food.

As the dog ate, the man climbed into his car and drove out of the gates, stopping at the road side to lock them before heading into town, another shift over.

Palmer waited another few minutes, then called Littlefield on his mobile.

"Bring the van up to the gates. I'll meet you there."

Sean joined him at the entrance thirty seconds later and Palmer rattled the fence next to the gate. The dog came pounding towards him, teeth bared as it growled an ominous warning. When it was within ten feet, Palmer put a silenced bullet between the animal's eyes and it dropped before it could even register the impact.

The final level of security to overcome was the chain securing the gates. Palmer slid open the side panel of the van and pulled out the bolt cutters, which made short work of the lock. He pushed the gates open and Littlefield drove the van into the yard, spinning it around so that the nose was pointing towards the entrance, ready for a quick exit.

* * *

Harvey watched the masked man swing the gates open and the van drive in, and as soon as the driver jumped out of the cab and ran to the back, he was ready to move.

"I'm going in," he said. "Cover me."

He squeezed through the warehouse gate and across the road, his rubber-soled sneakers minimising the sound. When he reached the van he saw that the back doors were wide open and he eased his way to the rear, his pistol extended in a two-handed grip.

Taking two steps to the side, he rounded the door and caught the two men unaware.

"Hands up, nice and slow, and move away from the van."

Palmer froze, one hand on the 3-Methylfentanyl aerosol, one of the improvised grenades in the other. Littlefield had the other two, and he looked over at his friend for guidance. When Palmer gave the slightest of nods, he put the munitions down and raised his hands.

Palmer depressed the nozzle on the canister and showed his hands. He turned to face Harvey, who gestured with the pistol for him to move away from the vehicle. He complied, Littlefield in tow.

"Masks off," Harvey ordered. "Slowly."

Both med did as instructed, and then Harvey asked for their weapons.

"It's in the back of the van," Palmer said, and Harvey backed up to the opening. He glanced in and saw the pistol, then reached in to grab it, his eyes back on his prisoners. Once it was tucked into his waistband he ordered Littlefield to surrender his own gun.

Harvey told them both to unzip their jackets and lift their shirts, and satisfied that they were no longer armed he ordered them to their knees.

Neither man moved.

"Down on the grou..."

The words felt heavy in his throat, and the gun wavered as he tried to focus on the two men. He shook his head to clear it, but all he succeeded in doing was throw himself off balance. He slammed into one of the doors and collapsed to the ground. Palmer was on him in an instant, disarming him and giving him a kicking for good measure. He held his breath as he picked up the canister and threw it towards the fence, making a mental note to collect it on the way out.

"Drag him clear of the gas," Palmer told Littlefield as he grabbed all three grenades. He scanned the area but saw no-one else, and the questions came thick and fast. Who was this guy, and who had sent him? Only two people could possibly know about this mission, and between Carl Gordon and James Farrar, he knew who he trusted most.

It just didn't make sense for Farrar to double-cross him, but having dealt with the man on more than one occasion, he knew he could trust him about as far as he could throw him.

He needed to find some answers, and fortunately that was a field he excelled in.

"Why don't we just kill him?"

"Because he's not a local, Sean. This isn't some guy protecting his property, and I want to know what he's doing here."

Littlefield shrugged and grabbed Harvey's ankles, dragging him towards the office building while Palmer headed for the truck. He got five yards before the shot rang out and he heard the scream of pain.

He swiveled to see Littlefield lying next to the prisoner, clutching his thigh as a crimson stain grew between his fingers, his hand outstretched in a plea for help.

Palmer ignored his cries and ducked behind a flatbed trailer as another round came in, missing his head by a whisker as it ricocheted off the vehicle's frame.

What the hell was happening?

It wasn't local police, he knew that much. They'd have swarmed the place by now. Everything pointed towards it being just one person with a rifle.

He got down on his knee and peered between the trailer's wheels, looking for the shooter.

There!

A flash gave away the gunman's position in the adjacent lot, and he knew his own weapons would be useless at this range. A glance around told him there wasn't enough cover for him to get closer, so he would have to draw the man in.

"Sean!" He shouted as loud as he could. "Throw me the detonator!"

Littlefield was confused. What the hell was Palmer talking about? With his femoral artery shredded, he'd already lost a couple of pints of blood. Combined with the pain, he was unable to think clearly, and he patted his pockets looking for whatever it was Palmer was asking for.

Dennis Owen had heard the shout, and when he saw the injured man searching his pockets he knew he had to stop him handing over whatever he was carrying. He took careful aim, looking to incapacitate him rather than end his life. The first shot flew an inch high, the second catching the man in the shoulder.

That was all the time Palmer needed. With the gunman concentrating on Littlefield, he dashed from cover and managed to get behind the cab of the target vehicle just as a volley followed inches behind him.

Owen cursed, knowing he'd fallen for a feint. Throwing the rifle strap over his shoulder, he drew his Beretta and broke cover, sprinting towards the gate. He stopped when he reached the van, scanning the area for signs of movement but seeing only the prostrate figure of Harvey lying next to Littlefield. He made his way over to them at a crouch, his pistol searching in vain for the other target.

He'd seen Harvey disappear behind the van and emerge a minute later, being dragged to his current position. At first glance he saw no wounds, and after removing the pistol from Littlefield's belt he turned Harvey over. Unconscious but breathing, there was a trickle of blood on the back of his head, although it didn't appear life-threatening.

Owen slapped him a couple of times on the face but all he got in return was a grunt.

"What have you done to him?"

"Gas," the injured man grimaced.

Littlefield was in bad shape. Owen pulled the man's belt free and applied a tourniquet to his thigh. If the other man was willing to use his friend as bait, he was unlikely to cheerfully hand over his weapons and come quietly, so keeping Littlefield alive was their best chance of getting the information Harvey wanted. In his present state he was unlikely to be a danger to Harvey, but just to be safe Owen yanked on Littlefield's index finger, dislocating it and rendering his good hand useless.

"You can still use it to apply pressure to the wound," Owen said, "just don't try anything funny with my friend. If I come back and he's dead, I'll introduce you to some real pain."

Not waiting around for an answer, he dashed towards the truck. He'd just reached the cab when he heard the *clang* of the lock being breached, and a squeal as the rusty door hinges protested at being opened.

Owen rolled under the truck and saw a pair of legs standing at the back of the vehicle. He took aim as he heard the doors slam shut, and squeezed off a shot that grazed the man's trouser material as it flew a few millimeters wide of the mark. The legs suddenly disappeared behind an adjacent truck and Owen was searching for his next shot when the whole world seemed to come crashing down around him.

The first grenade exploded inside the closed container, shaking the entire vehicle. Dirt and rust from the flatbed's ancient chassis assaulted his eyes, and the deafening noise threatened to burst his eardrums. One of the welds burst at it weakest point buckling the side wall of the container, and blood quickly began dripping onto the dusty ground.

Screams of terror began emanating from the container when they were cut off by the second explosion, which caught Owen as he struggled for a breath. He coughed as he ingested a cloud of dirt, choking as the fine particles caked his throat. His lungs refused to co-operate, demanding an inward breath while all Owen wanted to do was clear the mess from his airways. It seemed an eternity before he was able to coax in just enough air to get the natural process going again, then heaved as the contents of his passages fought for a way out.

By the time he'd managed a few short breaths and regained a semblance of control, the cries from the container had died down to just a couple of barely perceptible moans.

Owen crawled out from under the truck and lay panting on the ground, staring at the container looming above him. Through the tear in the side he could see the lifeless limbs of a woman, her skin pock-marked with bloody entry wounds.

He staggered to his feet, anger at the senseless murder gripping him like a vice. He'd seen death in the Gulf War, but that was usually soldier on soldier, not premeditated murder. He tucked the Beretta into his waistband, pulled the R4 off his shoulder and turned to give chase.

And found himself staring down the barrel of a pistol.

"You know the drill," Palmer said, and Owen dropped the rifle and slowly removed the pistol.

"Kick them under the truck."

Owen swiped at them with his foot, and Palmer ordered him to assume the position, hands outstretched on the side of the truck. He expected a quick frisk but instead felt a prick at the base of his skull and moments later his legs gave way beneath him. He scrambled for a hand hold until his arms also refused to obey his commands, and within a minute he found himself lying on his back, staring up at the glacial face of his assailant.

"You and I are going to have a little chat," Palmer said.

He picked Owen up and threw him over his shoulder in a fireman's lift, and then carried him to the van, throwing him in through the open doors. After grabbing a torch and checking that Littlefield was going to make it, he went back to the container to finish the job.

The gas he'd brought along would have been useless if he hadn't already wasted it, given the size of the hole the detonation had created in the side of the container, so he would have to go inside and make sure there were no survivors. He pulled the door open and the fetid combination of coppery blood and cordite hit him square in the face, but he knew the kill had to be confirmed. He climbed in, his feet fighting for grip on the blood-soaked floor, and as he played the beam of light around it was soon apparent that the majority were dead from a combination of shrapnel and blast concussion. He heard a faint moan and moved towards it, where he found a heavily-pregnant woman cradling her bloodstained stomach.

Palmer stepped over her, ignoring her clutching fingers as he searched for his four targets. He moved the light from face to face, until he reached the pile of bodies at the back of the metal box.

* * *

Kyle tapped the wheel of the Jeep to the beat of the eighties classics pumping out of the CD player. Over an hour after Owen and Harvey had taken off, the second truck had left the port and he'd followed it up the M4 until it switched to the N2, heading towards King Shaka International Airport. As instructed, he'd checked regularly for a tail, but the last set of headlights had disappeared from his mirror a few minutes earlier, and the only vehicle ahead was the Wenban Iveco.

With just fifteen minutes before they reached the junction leading to the cargo terminal, it was a bittersweet moment for Kyle. The prospect of easy money for an evening drive was nice, but a part of him had hoped for something a little more exciting than cruising along at sixty miles an hour listening to Billy Idol.

The track ended and he returned his attention to the road, spotting the headlights gaining ground fast. Kyle watched a blue Mitsubishi Evo with a yellow stripe on the bonnet power past him and draw level with the truck, and his heart skipped a beat as it matched the Iveco's pace for a brief moment. Just when he thought he might be called into action, the Evo driver hit the gas and the powerful car sped ahead, its tail lights quickly disappearing in the distance.

Kyle realised his heart rate had jumped by twenty beats per minute, just as it did before combat, heightening the senses and focusing the mind. With the excitement over, he tried to calm himself, skipping a few tracks on the CD until he found a soothing ballad. The clock on the dashboard suggested they would hit the turn off in just over twelve minutes, after which he would return to the city centre and have a beer in his hotel room before heading back to Johannesburg in the morning. Since he wasn't due back in the office until Wednesday morning, he could have a couple, perhaps in a local bar where he could look for some female company…

The truck up ahead suddenly slowed as the brake lights came on, and all thoughts of a relaxing evening disappeared in an instant. He couldn't see any reason for the driver to stop in the middle of nowhere, which told him something wasn't quite right. He flicked off his own headlights and pulled over to the side of the road a couple of hundred yards behind it, navigating his off-road vehicle between two clumps of trees.

Ahead, he saw the driver climb out and walk to the back of the vehicle, then kick the wheels in frustration before digging out a cell phone. Kyle thought about going to offer help, but realised it wouldn't be the same as changing the wheel on his own vehicle. All he could do was keep the Iveco in sight and wait for the tow truck to arrive.

He debated whether or not to call it in, but in truth there wasn't much to report, and he knew Owen and Harvey would probably have their hands full following the real target.

He decided to wait until either the Iveco was repaired and reached its destination, or Owen called him to end the mission. One thing he couldn't wait for was the growing pressure in his bladder, so he climbed out of the Jeep to relieve himself in the bushes. He glanced up and down the road as the plants got a watering, and as the moon emerged from behind a cloud he saw something glint in the road about fifty yards ahead of him.

Kyle zipped himself up and went to take a look, staying in the shadows as he advanced. In the road he saw a triangular tube around six feet long, with metal spikes protruding from every side. He instantly recognised the stop-stick used by American law enforcement agencies to halt car chases. Each spike was a hollow metal tube which embedded itself in the tyre, allowing the air to escape slowly without causing a catastrophic blowout.

He was about to step into the carriageway to retrieve it when the sound of an engine drew his attention to the approaching headlights. He ducked back into the trees and watched as a dark grey van slowed as it neared the truck. A Chinese youth, no more than seventeen, jumped from the passenger seat and picked up the stick, then jogged after the van as it pulled up behind the stricken truck.

Kyle's first thought was that this was preplanned rather than a good Samaritan coming to the truck driver's aid, and this was confirmed when the kid dropped the stop-stick and produced a blade from his waist. The truck driver immediately put his hands up, expecting to have his load stolen, but the boy continued to close on him. The driver backed away, sensing that he was involved in more than a simple hijacking, but as he backed into the rear of the truck, the boy plunged the knife into his stomach.

Kyle watched the man fall to the ground, but the assault wasn't over. He watched the youth strike again and again, hitting the man in the back and head. A shout from the driver of the grey van halted the attack, and the youth wiped his blade on the dead driver's shirt before dragging him into the undergrowth.

Another man had appeared from the van's cab and he approached the driver at the rear of the truck. The youth joined them and got a rollicking in Cantonese from the elder of the trio. Kyle had no idea what was being said, but when the boy removed his T-shirt it was obvious that the blood stains hadn't been part of the plan. The chastised teenager was banished to the van while the other two began opening the container.

Kyle had his Glock 9mm in his right hand while he thumbed through the contact list on his phone. He selected Owen's number and held it close to his ear, but after five rings it went to voicemail.

"Shit!"

Until he knew for certain that this wasn't just a violent robbery, all he could do was watch.

Tom Gray screamed as the pain shot up his leg.

"What is it?" Vick asked, concerned.

"Cramp!" He said, gritting his teeth. He tried pointing his toes to get rid of it, but as soon as his foot went back to its normal position, the pain returned.

"Welcome to the annual meeting of the agoraphobic society," Sonny deadpanned, but no-one was in the mood for laughing.

"At least it smells a bit better in here," Vick said, massaging Gray's calf as best she could.

It was an improvement, but not much. Two weeks of rudimentary bathing facilities and a shortage of shampoo meant her odour was worse now than it had been during her time in the jungle, and the others weren't exactly smelling of roses.

"I'd have happily put up with the stench for a few more hours if it meant I could lie down properly," Gray moaned.

"If you ask me, those guys are going overland, which is why we got transferred into this shoebox."

Gray knew Len was right. The cramped air-cargo container wasn't the ideal way to travel, but it beat another three weeks in the stinking box they'd called home for the past fortnight. According to the research he'd done before setting off from Port Kelang, he expected them to spend a couple of hours on the road, an hour or so in the airport and then a further ten to twelve in the air. After that it would be around three days overland before they hit the ferry to Dover, and he hoped the final leg of the journey would be in more luxurious conditions.

Once they reached the UK, however, their problems wouldn't be over. He still had to deal with Farrar, and over the last week he'd been formulating a plan that relied on one man's help. Guaranteeing his co-operation wasn't a given, but the countless hours spent deliberating had thrown up no alternatives. With the man on board, it would be easier to sway the other players that would inevitably become embroiled, but if he didn't offer his support, Gray's plan would fall apart at the first hurdle.

"Anyone fancy a game of I-Spy?" Baines asked, breaking Gray's train of thought and getting an elbow in the ribs from Vick for yet another poor attempt at humour.

"Can it, Sonny," she said. "Or stow it, or whatever it is you guys do." Her lexicon had grown in the last month to include words such as "tabbing" and "jankers", but she still couldn't keep up when the men were in full flow. One thing she had learned was the camaraderie that existed between them. They might be boastful when recounting their adventures together, and often disparaging towards each other, but their stories always hinted at an altruistic bond not found in other walks of life.

She went back to her daydream, picturing herself taking a long, hot shower in a luxury London hotel, followed by a head-to-toe massage accompanied by a few glasses of champagne. She was just about to slip beneath the satin sheets when the truck juddered and slowed to a halt, shattering her illusion and casting her back to the present.

"Are we at the airport already?"

"I don't think so," Gray told her. "I think we've got a flat."

"Does that mean we'll miss our plane?"

Gray thought it unlikely that it would wait for four stowaways, but he remained hopeful that Arnold Tang would have contingencies in place. If his success rate was as high as he'd boasted, he would surely have people en route already.

"I'm sure we'll be fine," he told her.

Minutes passed, and Gray was wondering what the implications would be if they had to wait for the next flight out of the country when he heard the door to the main container opening. Moments later the plastic sheet of the tiny AKE air cargo container was unfastened and the cardboard box shielding them from view was pulled aside. A Chinese face appeared, giving the occupants a once over, his eyes coming to rest on Vick. The beginnings of a smile crawled over his face, revealing yellow, nicotine-stained teeth.

In an instant it was gone.

"Come!" He ordered. "You come now!"

Gray was the first to crawl out of the tight space, glad of the chance to get his circulation moving once more. The others followed and were shown to the van, the rear doors held open so that they could climb in.

"See, told you we'd soon be on our way," he grinned at Vick as he made himself comfortable on the bare floor. Vick snuggled up next to him, while Len pulled out his Kindle and Sonny sat with his back to the cab.

"Ooh, you're bleeding," Vick said, pointing to Sonny's feet.

He looked at the soles of his shoes and saw fresh, red patches near the heels. He gave himself the once over but found no sign of a wound.

"Must have stepped in something when we switched vehicles," he shrugged. "Probably road kill."

The driver pulled away and within seconds the passengers felt the van turn and bounce across the grassy median, heading towards the centre of the city.

"We're going the wrong way," Sonny said, and despite the van having no side or rear windows, Gray knew he was right.

"Taking a shortcut?" He offered.

"Maybe they're taking us to another truck," Vick suggested. "We can hardly just walk onto a cargo plane."

It was possible, Gray thought, but he wanted to hear it from the horse's mouth.

"Ask them what's going on," he said to Sonny.

Baines turned and tapped the elder passenger on the shoulder. "Where are we going?"

The man blew a cloud of cigarette smoke in Sonny's face and began gesturing out of the front window while rattling off a barrage of Cantonese.

"I don't understand a word you're saying," Sonny said. The teenager joined in, a malicious grin on his face as he looked Sonny in the eye and added his two cents worth to the conversation. He was silenced by a dig in the ribs from his elder.

Baines shrugged noncommittally and went to sit down next to Smart.

"I think we've got a problem," he whispered. "From what little I understood, the kid is looking forward to having his way with Vick before he kills us."

A look of horror crept over Vick's face and Gray quickly pulled her head into his chest, just in case her reaction drew any unwanted attention. He kissed her hair and whispered for her to stay calm.

"I'm not going to let anything happen to you," he promised, and threw Baines a stern look.

"I thought you only knew a few Chinese phrases," Len said quietly.

"I do," Sonny said. "I know when someone mentions sex, and I also know when they want to kill me. That kid ticks all the boxes."

"Even I know that in most languages, words have several meanings," Len said.

Sonny knew the point was valid, but he had an uneasy feeling. "The old guy was carrying a crowbar," he pointed out, "and there was no sign of the truck driver. Surely they would have got him to open the container instead of breaking the lock off."

"You think they killed him?" Gray asked.

"It would explain this," Sonny said, waggling his feet and drawing their attention back to the blood stains.

Gray considered the options, and came up with just two: take the Chinese men on, here, on the road; or wait until they reach their destination and see what happened. If they chose the latter, there was no way of knowing how many people they'd have to face if Sonny had correctly understood the kid's intentions. On the other hand, if Sonny had got his wires crossed, they could end up blowing their only chance of getting home.

With every passing second they were motoring towards option one, and Gray knew they'd have to make a decision. He asked his friends for their thoughts, and not for the first time, they were in agreement.

"It's your call, Sonny," Gray said.

"I know what I heard," Baines said flatly, and the others nodded. Each of them looked around for a weapon, but the van was sterile. They were going to have to use their bare hands, but there wasn't enough room behind the seats for them to effectively tackle the Chinese one-on-one.

"I'll take the kid and the one on the right," Len said. "Tom, you take the driver."

"Aren't we forgetting someone?" Gray asked, gesturing towards Vick. "It'll be dicey while we're moving. Let's see if we can get them to stop first."

The others agreed, and Gray asked Vick to pretend she needed a rest stop. As it wasn't the hardest acting job in the world, she squeezed her knees together and put on a pained expression.

Gray tapped the kid on the shoulder and nodded towards her. "The lady needs to go to the toilet. Can we pull over?"

The teenager spoke quickly to the older man and got a bark in reply. He looked at Gray. "You wait. Go soon."

"She can't wait. She's gonna piss all over your nice clean floor."

The youth ignored him, turning his attention back to the front window. Gray sat back down next to Vick and explained that things might get a little bumpy. The van had a series of webbing restraint straps down each side, and Gray told her to grab one and hold on with

478

all her might. He saw the look of apprehension, but assured her it was going to be okay.

Still uncertain, Vick clutched the nearest strap as tight as she could and nodded. Gray gave her a smile and kissed the top of her head, then knelt behind the driver. Smart got down on one knee, two feet to his right.

The youth felt their presence and was turning around to decline what he thought was another toilet break request when Smart cupped his hands around the elder's forehead and pulled down and back sharply. The crack was clearly audible over the roar of the diesel engine and the man fell forward, his body held in place by the seatbelt, head hanging at an unnatural angle.

Smart turned his attention to the kid, anticipating another easy kill, but the youth recovered quickly from the shock of the initial assault. As he wasn't wearing a seatbelt he was able to swivel and face Smart, eluding his grasp and pulling his knife from the sheath on his belt.

Gray had his man in a headlock and was shouting for him to pull over, but the driver ignored the order and yanked the wheel to the right, trying to unbalance Gray. All he succeeded in doing was to throw the teenager off balance, and instead of the blade driving through Smart's throat, it glanced the side of his neck, drawing blood but doing no serious damage. Smart pulled back, wary of the knife, and the kid turned his attention to helping the driver.

Switching the knife to an overhand grip, he brought it down hard, aiming for Gray's head. Tom saw it coming and jerked away from the blade but not far enough to prevent it slicing through his upper arm. Blood gushed from the wound but he didn't even have time to register pain before the knife came flashing down again. Gray jerked the driver backwards and the van jerked violently to the right once more, throwing the youngster off balance. He fell into the driver, the strike missing everyone and deflecting off the side window. He was righting himself when the van bounced onto the median and he was thrown up against the roof of the van before collapsing in the foot well.

Smart came to Gray's help, delivering a powerful punch that took the last of the fight out of the driver. He went limp and Gray let him go, reaching over him to grab the wheel. He had one hand on it when they hit a huge rut and the wheel tore from his hand. He was thrown upwards, slamming into the roof before collapsing in a heap next to Vick. The van rolled, throwing the occupants about like socks in a tumble dryer as it spun across the grass before ending up on its side.

They untangled themselves and took stock. Vick had a cut on her cheek and a sprained ankle where someone had landed on her. Smart and Baines had minor scratches and a few bruises, but Gray was worst hit. Blood poured from the wound on his arm and he was lying motionless near the back doors, which had torn open during the crash.

Smart went to tend to him, checking for and finding a faint pulse, and he tore Tom's T-shirt and used it to create a tourniquet.

Vick cradled Tom's head. Tears were streaming down her face, partly due to Tom's condition, but ultimately brought on by the ferocity of the brief, chaotic exchange. Her body shook as she fought for control, her breath ragged and laboured. Sonny saw the signs and went to comfort her, trying to calm her down before she went into shock.

Behind them, in the cab, the youth wiped the blood from his face. A three-inch gash in his forehead leaked crimson into his eyes, but his focus was on the four *gweilo*. There was no thought of running, taking flight so that he could live to fight another day, despite being outnumbered. Instead, he weighed up the opposition and decided that the larger man was the more dangerous. He would die first, followed by the by the little fair-haired one and then the female. He wouldn't get his few moments of fun with the woman, but he'd complete the task the team had been assigned and his stock would rise as a result.

He got quietly to his feet, knife in hand, and took two silent steps towards Smart. Vick caught the movement from the corner of her eye but the warning shout stuck in her throat as she froze in terror. The knife hand came up as Baines saw the look on her face, and he snapped his head round as the teenager took a final step to get within range of Smart's back. Sonny thrust a leg out at the side of the boy's kneecap and the snap of bone and cruciate ligament resounded through the vehicle. He collapsed, dropping the knife as he fell. Sonny grabbed it and knelt on the adolescent's arm and stomach, clamping his hand over the kid's mouth.

Taking prisoners was out of the question, and there was no way they could simply let the Chinese kid go. Sonny looked behind him and saw that Vick and Len were watching him.

"Look away, Vick," he said, and Smart shielded her while Sonny administered the *coup de gras*, plunging the knife into the boy's heart and twisting. When the life finally drained from the young killer's eyes, Sonny withdrew the knife and wiped it clean before putting it in his inside pocket.

"We're getting lazy," he said to Smart. "We should have made sure they were all dead before we did anything."

Smart agreed, and it struck Vick just how little she knew these men. She'd listened to their tales over the last couple of weeks, how they'd fought their way out of seemingly countless situations — and taken a Thai brothel apart with their bare hands in one of their less sober moments — but the stories didn't convey the ease with which they could take another human life. Those stories had seemed so...detached from reality, as if she'd been watching a movie or reading a book. Sonny, who she'd thought of as a loveable rogue, had just turned dispassionate killer in front of her eyes and...

Her thoughts were interrupted by the sight of the armed figure standing near the twisted back doors. Smart followed her gaze, and when he saw the Chinese features his shoulders sagged.

* * *

Kyle Ackerman had watched the four people climb down from the truck and pile into the van, and was surprised to see a woman amongst their number. Regardless, he knew these had to be the people Owen and Harvey were looking for, and he reached for his phone, stabbing the preset number. The van took off across the median, heading back the way it had come, and by the time he got to the Jeep he saw the distinctive Evo pass by in pursuit.

It must have been a team effort, with the Mitsubishi setting the trap and the van picking up the pieces.

He climbed into his own vehicle and backed out onto the tarmac, then crossed over into the southbound lane. He was about to turn the headlights on, then thought better of it. He could see the tail lights of the vehicles ahead and there was no point announcing his presence, especially with so little traffic on the road.

He followed for three or four miles, constantly hitting the redial button on his mobile but getting no further than the electronic voice asking him to leave a message. He'd done so once, and that was enough.

Without warning, the van veered into the right-hand lane before correcting itself, and Ackerman knew something was amiss. He toyed with the idea of pulling them over, but he had no idea if they were armed beyond the teenager's knife, and he was outnumbered at least five to one if he included the two in the Mitsubishi.

He was trying the mobile for the umpteenth time when the van skewed to the side once more and bounced onto the grass. He watched it nosedive before bouncing onto its side and rolling half a dozen times.

Ackerman pulled up against the side of the road as the van settled on its side. His first instinct was to get out and go to their aid, but then he remembered the Evo. It had stopped in the inside lane and he saw one of the occupants get out, drawing a weapon and approaching the wreckage.

He pulled out the Glock but knew it would be useless at this distance, and going on foot was not an option as there was no cover to hide behind if it turned into a gunfight. He was wondering how close he could get in the Jeep before they heard him when an idea struck. It was a downhill run to the van, so he put his vehicle in first and gently popped the clutch. It rolled forwards, and once he'd built up enough momentum he selected neutral and turned the engine off, coasting towards the Evo. At the last moment he tugged the wheel to the right until he was on a collision course with the van.

The driver of the Mitsubishi saw him and leaned out of the window, shouting a warning to his accomplice. The gunman heard the shout but didn't understand the message, and he shouted back over his shoulder for the driver to repeat it while keeping his eyes on the *gweilo*.

It was the right thing to do if he didn't want to get jumped from the front, but it still cost him his life.

At the last moment he caught sight of the Jeep barrelling towards him, but there was little time to react. Instinctively he turned and aimed the gun at the windshield, getting off a single, wayward round that flew harmlessly high. Ackerman ploughed into him at just short of thirty miles an hour and the man disappeared beneath the front of the wheels, his body mangled as the combination of ground and undercarriage chewed him up and spat him out the back.

Kyle applied the handbrake and jumped out. He fired off three quick shots at the Mitsubishi and the driver got the message, hitting the gas and speeding off into the night.

With the immediate area clear, he checked inside the van, gun up and ready for any surprises.

There were none, apart from the amount of carnage. Three bodies were quite clearly dead, and one wasn't looking too clever. The three walking wounded regarded him dolefully, as if at the end of their tether.

"You guys okay?" Kyle said, focusing on the lady.

Smart was relieved to hear an English voice, but the questions began piling up in his head. What was he doing here? How did he know they would be in the van? Who was he working for?

"Depends who's asking," he said.

"I work for the government," Kyle told him. He lowered the gun and looked at Gray. "How's he doing?"

"He's out cold and his arm needs attention."

Kyle disappeared and returned moments later, carrying a first aid kit. He began to open it but Sonny stopped him.

"We need to get out of here," he said. "Let's load him into your car and get as far away from here as possible."

Smart liked the plan, and they carefully carried Gray to the Jeep before Ackerman could have his say. Sonny climbed in the back seat and pulled Tom in, then Smart joined him and they rested their friend on their laps.

Vick got in the front passenger seat and fastened her seat belt.

"I'm Kyle," Ackerman said, and the others introduced themselves. "Who's your friend?"

"That's Tom," Vick said.

"It's Sam," Sonny corrected her.

Ackerman looked in the mirror quizzically.

"It's complicated," Smart told him as he extracted a bandage from the first aid box and began tending to the wound on Gray's arm.

Ackerman shrugged. Their names didn't concern him, but the lack of contact with Owen and Harvey did. If he'd found the people they were looking for, and the bad guys were dead, what in God's name had happened to them?

Gray gave a moan and opened his eyes tentatively.

"How're you feeling?" Sonny asked.

"Like I was run over by a train," Gray said, trying to focus. "Where are we?"

"We're heading towards...hey, Kyle, where exactly are we going?"

"I'm going to drop you off at the hospital, then I have to go and help my friends. They went after the other truck and I think they're in trouble. They're not answering the phone."

"Who is this guy?" Gray asked, his head still groggy.

483

Sonny filled him in on what had happened while he was out cold, and asked Kyle to give them the bigger picture.

"Dennis Owen asked me to provide backup for his operation. He and Andrew had intelligence that you four would be on the cargo ship and that someone had been sent to intercept and kill you. They didn't know which container you were in, so they followed the largest one and I was asked to follow the truck you were in."

"Who's Dennis Owen?"

Ackerman explained that Owen was his boss at the Trade and Investment department, and what their real role entailed.

"What's Andrew's story?" Sonny asked.

"He's based in England," Kyle said. "Five would be my guess."

Gray was still trying to clear his head, but the mention of MI5 suddenly brought clarity. He sat bolt upright.

"Are you talking about Andrew Harvey?" He asked.

"That's right," Ackerman told him. "You know him?"

Gray didn't answer. He was too busy trying to digest the news. Andrew Harvey, in Durban? Someone sent to kill them? A Chinese kill team?

He needed answers, and only one man could provide them. "Forget the hospital, we need to find Andrew."

"Are you sure?" Ackerman asked. "That wound looks pretty nasty."

"I'll live," Gray said. "Where is Andrew now?"

"They were following the other container to the depot. I expect they'll be there or thereabouts."

"Then that's where we go."

* * *

After double-checking every corpse, Ben Palmer knew he'd followed the wrong container. He whipped out his camera and thumbed through the images he'd taken on his last visit until he found the itinerary for the other truck. It had been due to leave the port an hour after the first, which meant it would be en route right about now.

Catching it up shouldn't be a problem, but having been surprised by the two men who'd jumped him, he was beginning to have doubts about the whole mission.

Another glance at the itinerary told him the other container was going to the airport, and if it boarded a plane he could lose it forever.

Carl Gordon might be able to get into the airport servers and follow the trail, but he would only pursue that once he'd finished with his interrogations.

Palmer moved to the container doors, stepping over the pregnant woman who once again cried for his help. He ignored her pleas, climbing down and closing the container door. His first stop was the office, where he kicked in the door and found the CCTV equipment. He extracted the VHS tape from the machine and took it back to the van, where he found Owen unconscious.

He realised the gas hadn't fully dispersed, which meant using the van was out of the question. He knew his attackers must have come in their own vehicle, but with both out cold, he could hardly ask them where it was.

Palmer went over to where Littlefield was lying next to the unconscious man. Sean was fading fast, the blood still seeping from his wounds despite the tourniquet. There wasn't a lot Palmer could do for him, but he didn't say as much.

"I'm going to find their car and get you to a hospital," he lied. He would take Littlefield from the scene, but only so the connection between the two men couldn't be established. If Sean's body was found, one of the first things they do was a forensic sweep of his farm, a building riddled with Palmer's fingerprints. Although he religiously wore surgical gloves on every mission, he hadn't used them during his recent visit.

He moved over to the motionless figure and slapped him on the face.

Nothing.

He tried harder and this time got a reaction, a moan and shake of the head. Palmer glanced around, looking for some water to splash on the man's face, then remembered the coffee pot in the office. He got up to fetch it just as the headlights appeared on the road a few hundred yards away.

It wasn't a well-travelled road, just a spur off the highway that led to the industrial units and beyond that a small village a mile or so further on. Palmer had to make a decision, and he erred on the side of caution, sprinting back to the truck where he found the R4 rifle. A quick check revealed an almost full clip, and he carried it back to the front of the rig, staying in the shadows with a clear view of the main gate.

The vehicle cruised past at barely fifteen miles an hour. That in itself meant nothing, Palmer knew. It could be locals being cautious after a few too many beers, or one of the many gangs casing the area for something to steal.

As the vehicle neared, Palmer could make out the driver and a female passenger, though he couldn't tell if there was anyone in the rear as the windows were tinted. The driver didn't seem to be paying the compound any attention, his focus on the blonde sitting next to him.

The Jeep continued down the road until the lights disappeared around the corner and the sound of the engine eventually faded.

Palmer waited a few moments. Once he was satisfied that it had been a false alarm, he ran back to the office and grabbed the coffee pot, which he emptied out and filled with water from the cooler. He took it back into the yard and poured half of it over the supine figure's face, shaking the man from his deep slumber.

Harvey shook his head, which felt heavy, turgid. He opened his eyes but they refused to focus, the world a blur of dark shapes and flitting movement. A dark shadow moved over him and morphed into the shape of a human head.

"Where's your car?"

Harvey fought for clarity, but it was a long time coming.

"Where is it?" The voice repeated.

"I...er..."

Palmer gave him another slap, gentler, just enough to get the man to focus. He squatted next to him, the rifle on the floor replaced by his silenced pistol, which dug into Harvey's ribs.

"I haven't got all night," Palmer said calmly. "Tell me where your vehicle is, or lose a kneecap."

He moved the gun to Harvey's knee and began the countdown, while Harvey frantically tried to get his bearings. Palmer reached four when he raised his hand and pointed towards the gate.

"It's behind that building," he said, his voice sounding alien in his own ears.

Palmer grabbed Harvey's collar and dragged him to his feet, pushing him towards the main road. Bending down to retrieve the rifle, he spotted movement from the corner of his eye, in the direction the Jeep had disappeared. He walked nonchalantly behind the van, then got down to see if he could see anything out of the ordinary.

He saw nothing apart a few bushes swaying in the breeze, but to be on the safe side he let off a couple of three-round bursts.

There was no return fire, and no screams, and Palmer chastised himself for jumping at shadows. He got back to his feet and walked around the van in time to see Harvey stumbling towards the main gate, his legs barely obeying his commands.

Palmer realised this one could be trouble once he fully recovered from the effects of the gas, and decided he could get the information he needed from the one who was still in the van. He raised the rifle and fired a round an inch above Harvey's head, causing him to stop in his tracks.

"Just give me the keys," he said, and Harvey patted his pockets in a vain attempt to find them. It took a few seconds for him to realise he didn't have them. He explained this to Palmer, who responded by raising the rifle.

"Drop it!"

The voice came from Palmer's right, and he moved his head to see the slight figure advancing towards him, a Glock held in a double-handed grip.

"Looks like we've got ourselves a standoff," he smiled, keeping the R4 pointing at Harvey's lower back. "Aren't you a bit young to be out so late?"

"One last chance," the newcomer said, continuing to close on his target.

"That's far enough, sonny. Stand down —"

The first bullet tore through Palmers skull, the second, redundant round hitting an inch lower. He collapsed in a heap and Baines held the gun on the corpse until he was close enough to confirm the kill.

"Only my friends call me Sonny," he said, and then turned to check that Harvey was okay. He seemed a little confused, almost as if he were drunk, and Baines told him to take a seat on the ground.

"How many more?" he asked, but Harvey was still catching up on events, his brain having difficulty maintaining a normal pace. Baines gave up and signaled Smart to join him, indicating that he should use the rifle to help clear the area.

A minute later, two others helped Harvey to his feet. One he didn't recognise, but the other was strikingly familiar.

"Sam?" He asked quizzically. "Sam Grant?"

"Hello, Andrew," Gray smiled.

"You know me?"

Explanations were put on hold as Baines and Smart returned with news of the carnage at the rear of the compound.

"We also found someone in the van," Sonny told them. "He's out for the moment, but no sign of injuries."

Harvey started towards the Mercedes and Gray offered him a shoulder. They got to the rear doors and saw Owen lying on his back.

"We'd better get out of here," Sonny said, and Gray agreed. He asked Harvey where their car was and it took a few moments for him to clear his head and pass on the information. Smart grabbed the keys from Owen's pocket and trotted off while Kyle and Sonny pulled Owen from the van and laid him on the floor.

"We need to know who this guy is," Harvey said, pointing to Palmer's corpse. Kyle checked the man's pockets and came out with a wallet, then pulled out his phone and took snaps from several angles.

"Do you need fingerprints?" He asked, but Harvey decided that what they had was enough.

When Smart returned with the BMW they loaded Owen and Harvey inside, then drove down the road to where Vick was waiting in the Jeep, while the others made their way back on foot.

"Where do we go from here?" Sonny asked once they'd all assembled.

"We've got passports for you and Len in Pretoria," Harvey said, beginning to get his head together. "We also have one ready and waiting for Sam, though we need a new photo. We didn't know who the fourth person would be, but it won't take long to knock one up."

Gray introduced Vick, and it took Harvey a few moments to realise that Vick was the Victoria Phillips he'd been asking questions about a week earlier.

"How on earth did you end up with these three?" Harvey asked, and Vick told him that it was a long story.

"That's fine," Harvey said. "It's also a long drive back to Jo'burg."

They split themselves between the vehicles, with Len driving the BMW carrying Vick, Tom and Andrew, the rest taking the lead in the Jeep

Harvey turned to Gray once they'd set off. "And the mysterious Sam Grant, the complete stranger who seems to know me. What's your story?"

Even as he asked the question, his attention was drawn to Gray's eyes, and when the penny dropped he couldn't believe what he'd stumbled upon.

"Tom? But you're…"

"He gets that a lot," Len said, before Vick could get the words out. "I was actually coming to look for you," Gray told him, "but as you're here, how about I tell you our story and you decide if you're willing to help us?"

* * *

"*Just leave it!*"

Uddin grabbed the bag containing the family ornaments and hurled it onto the bed. "We can only take the bare essentials," he told his wife Fatima. Their luggage already exceeded the baggage allowance for the flight, and there simply wasn't room for sentimentality at the moment.

"But why do we have to leave?" She asked yet again.

Fatima had been preparing the evening meal when her husband had arrived home agitated, and broke the news that they would be taking a flight later that night. When asked how long they would be away, he'd told her that it would be a one-way trip. Her subsequent protestations had been met with anger, and she went about the task of packing with a sense of dread. She knew her husband's work was shrouded in secrecy, and his behaviour told her this had something to do with the laboratory.

"I was given instructions and I...disobeyed them," he told her.

Fatima knew Munawar was an honourable man, so whatever order he had refused must have been in stark contrast with his principles.

"Surely the pharmaceutical company will understand," she said, but the look she received told her this was something more than a squabble with a supervisor.

The steps he'd taken had, he'd told himself, been for the greater good of mankind, but he knew that the driving force behind his decision had been the welfare of his family. Having driven them into hiding, the least he could do was explain why.

"The laboratory I work for doesn't make cold remedies," he said, sitting her down on the bed. He explained who his ultimate boss was, and the kind of product he was tasked with manufacturing.

"The virus they asked me to make was almost ready when a newcomer changed everything. He told me Al-Asiri had changed his mind about the agent to be delivered, but on reflection it didn't seem probable. It was the leader's pet project, and when we met he seemed

489

more than happy with my projections, yet this Mansour was determined to use another, more virulent strain.

"The only one we had was too unstable, with no cure. If it was released before we had a means to control it, ninety percent of the world's population would be annihilated within months. Only the most remote regions of the planet would escape."

"So you refused to give it to him?" His wife asked.

"Whether I gave it to him or my replacement does, it makes no difference," Uddin told her. "What is important is that he not be allowed to use it."

The look Uddin gave her suggested there was more to come, and when he eventually told her the rest of the story, Fatima knew there was no way they could ever return to their homeland.

Chapter 13

Tuesday May 8th 2012

Tom sat across the desk from Veronica Ellis and laid out the plan, just as he'd explained it to Harvey during their journey from Durban back to the UK.

They'd made a brief stop at the Durban office where a doctor took a look at Gray's arm and declared him fit to fly. He'd also given the others a once over and found no lasting damage. After Tom and Vick had their passport photos taken and emailed to the Johannesburg office, they had driven north to collect their diplomatic passports and airline tickets. During the journey, Tom had given Harvey a full rundown of the last four weeks, starting with Farrar's unannounced visit to his Manila home and culminating in their two-week no-frills cruise.

Harvey had reciprocated, giving his account of their successful effort to locate Campbell and Levine before Farrar could dispose of them. Gray had been concerned about his friends' conditions, but Harvey assured him that both men were responding well at a private clinic, and the women were bearing up.

The conversation had turned to Farrar, and Tom had shared the plan he'd been working on for the last fortnight. After Harvey explained that all the evidence they had was circumstantial backed up with hearsay, they'd agreed that Tom's idea was the only way to make Farrar accountable for his actions.

Ellis had been as shocked as anyone when she'd learned that Tom Gray was still alive, and what had started out as a bid to bring Farrar to task had escalated to the point where it that could bring down an entire government. There was no way she could have foreseen this a fortnight earlier, and the decision to help Gray hadn't been an easy one to make.

It had been a battle of conscience over pragmatism. When this broke, any trust the people had in parliament would be destroyed. The Home Secretary would certainly be the first to fall, and it might even reach as high as the Prime Minister himself.

If the current government fell, the opposition wouldn't fare much better. It was they who had made the decision to lie to the world, spiriting Gray away and ordering his subsequent death. That left the fringe parties, none of whom were — in her opinion — capable of running the country.

That said, it was either leave the country in political turmoil, or allow them to continue their dark practices and execute citizens at will, and that simplification had made the decision a lot easier.

Ellis smiled when Tom wrapped up. She liked the way he thought, and given the planning that had gone into his last escapade, she had every confidence in him pulling this one off.

Hamad Farsi entered the room and handed Tom a piece of paper. "Here's the number you asked for."

Gray nodded towards Ellis's desk phone. "May I?"

"Be my guest," she smiled.

Gray dialled the number and asked for Paul Gross. When asked who was calling, he said: "Just tell him it's Icarus."

It took a minute before he was put through, and the voice that came on the line sounded curious. "Hello?"

"Hi, Paul. Remember me? It's Tom Gray."

"I'm sorry, I haven't got time for pranks," Gross said.

"Would it help if I said I once sent an email to your personal email account, and that I threatened to take the story to a rival channel when you pestered me to go on the air?"

There was silence for a while as Gross recalled the incidents. "Say I believe you. What do you want from me?"

Gray gave him a condensed version the events of the last year and explained what he wanted from the producer of the BBC news channel.

"That's a great story, Tom, but what you're asking is far too risky. Besides, I have a DA order which prevents me featuring any story about you still being alive."

"Doesn't it feel a little strange that the government doesn't want you to let people know I survived the explosion last year? What possible motive could they have?"

Gross was silent again as he considered the question. Ellis looked at Gray and offered to take over the conversation, but he shook his head, confident he could wear the man down.

"You make a compelling case, Tom, but the DA notice —"

"Is an advisory notice, or so I've been informed. If you ignore one, you cannot be prosecuted."

"Perhaps not," Gross agreed, "but it could be career-defining."

Gray wasn't convinced. "Only if your superiors came out and said they disagreed with your actions. The Director General would have to go on record as saying the BBC fully supports the government's practice of killing innocent civilians."

Both men knew it would never happen, but Gross still needed more.

"What if I do as you ask, but there's no confession?"

Gray once more explained the plan, and while not as confident as Ellis had been, Gross did think it workable.

"When is this going to happen?" He asked.

"Tomorrow," Gray told him. "There are a few technical aspects to work out, so you'll be getting a call from someone called Gerald Small in a few minutes."

He thanked the producer and hung up. "Can I tag along with Gerald?" He asked Ellis. "I'd like to try out the equipment once it's in place."

"Sure," She said. "Andrew can take you —"

Hamad Farsi knocked on the door and walked in without waiting for an invitation. "Something you should take a look at," he said, handing a file to his boss. She read quickly, her expression giving nothing away, before she put the papers down and turned to Gray.

"Sorry, Tom, but you'll have to excuse us," she said, holding up the file. "Business as usual." She showed Gray to Small's office, then led Harvey and Farsi to the conference room and asked when the news had come in.

"Just a couple of minutes ago," Hamad said.

Ellis read it through again, this time aloud for Harvey's benefit.

"Abdul Mansour will be travelling to England via Heathrow airport in the next few days with the intention of releasing a malevolent variant of the Ebola virus. His target has biological defences against an external attack and he is hoping to use this to contain the virus within the building itself. There is currently no known cure for this particular variant."

"Short and sweet," Harvey noted. "Origin?"

"The British High Commission in Islamabad. A kid delivered it along with those images."

Ellis looked through them but couldn't make head nor tail of the information. It appeared that someone had taken pictures of

493

documents explaining the genetic make-up of the virus, through the hieroglyphs meant nothing to her.

"Is anyone verifying this?" She asked Hamad, who told her that copies were on their way to the Health Protection Agency.

Small knocked and entered the room, explaining that he'd spoken to the BBC technical controller and there would be no problems setting up for the next morning.

"Thanks, Gerald," she said. To Hamad: "The facial recognition at Heathrow should pick him up when he tries to get through immigration. Check through the logs to see if there are any near hits."

"Yeah, right," small murmured, catching Ellis's attention.

"Something wrong with my instructions, Gerald?" She asked, wearing her most indignant face.

"No, it's just..."

Ellis urged him to continue, knowing how little he thought of the technology.

"If I was to go through immigration wearing the most basic theatrical prosthetic, such as a fake nose, it would throw the system off by at least forty percent."

"Possibly," Hamad agreed, "but make-up would easily be spotted by the border guard. Besides, you said yourself that it was the eyes that gave the biggest indicator."

"Exactly, and eyes can be covered up with glasses, eye patches, veils, anything that you would see if you walk down any high street. These things don't raise suspicion and can easily be overlooked.

"Check the logs by all means, but I'm just saying, don't be too reliant on them."

Ellis thanked him for his input and Gerald left them to discuss the latest events.

"Bear that in mind," Ellis told Hamad. "I want people watching all of his old haunts, plus a team at Heathrow in case he hasn't arrived yet. Also, get onto every informer we have and see what they've heard."

She turned to Harvey. "Dig around and see which buildings have the bio-defence mentioned in the note. There can't be that many, but start with high-profile targets."

"The US Embassy has one," Harvey told her. "Perhaps we should give them the heads-up."

Ellis nodded. "I'll let them know," she said, standing and tacitly ending the meeting. "Hopefully they'll share any chatter they've had in the last forty-eight hours."

They split up to take care of their respective tasks, with Harvey doing a search for bio-defence installations over the last fifty years. The list that came back was not substantial, but it did include some high-profile targets. He was prioritising them when Ellis came over to their desks, her face like thunder.

"Cancel the Heathrow team," she told Hamad, "he's already here."

"We've got him?" Harvey asked, but her look told him otherwise.

"It seems our American friends have a new policy: You scratch our backs, we'll piss on your chips and call it vinegar."

Both men were confused, but let her continue in her own time. "It seems they received a card handwritten by Mansour himself, delivered to their embassy this morning. Fingerprints confirm it was handled by him, and ink analysis shows it was written only a few hours earlier."

"Did they tell you what the message said?"

"They told me they couldn't share that information until they'd followed up on it, but we'd hear about it soon enough."

Farsi was suitably unimpressed. "They know that the world's most wanted man is in the UK, but they don't feel the need to share that with us? That's bullshit."

Ellis agreed. "Andrew, you know someone over there who can speak off the record. Any chance they'd know anything about this?"

"I can try," Harvey said. "What did they make of the news you gave them?"

"I didn't tell them," she said. "I got as far as saying Mansour was on his way when they dropped their bomb. If that's the game they want to play, they'll find it works both ways."

It made sense to Harvey, at least from a bargaining point of view. He pulled out his mobile and moved to a quiet corner of the office. Doug Wallis answered on the second ring.

"Andrew, how's things?"

"I'm good, Doug. Can you make lunch today?"

Wallis sensed the urgency in his voice and agreed to meet up within the hour. Harvey thanked him and hung up, then told Ellis about the upcoming meeting.

"I don't know how helpful he'll be," Harvey admitted. "Our arrangement does have its limits."

Ellis was glad to hear it. She wanted to press him on the information they'd previously shared, but decided to save that conversation for later.

Harvey printed off the list of possible targets and gave it to Ellis before helping Farsi with his workload. While Hamad went through the list of informers and undercover operatives, he started on the facial recognition logs.

After uploading the most recent image of Mansour and setting it as the search parameter, he waited for the system to go through all entries for the last seventy-two hours. With over ninety-five thousand passengers arriving each day, the system would have to compare the image with well over a quarter of a million faces. Harvey decided to filter the list to disregard planes arriving from the west, which cut the number in half but still left a huge amount to go through. After setting the match threshold to sixty percent, he hit the Search button and left it running while he went to meet up with Wallis.

He arrived at sandwich shop five minutes early and ordered an egg and cress baguette to take away. When Doug arrived he waited until his CIA counterpart chose a bacon, stilton and cranberry on wholemeal before they headed towards the river.

"My boss is a bit pissed with you guys," Harvey opened the conversation when they found an empty bench. "She doesn't like the fact that you kept Abdul Mansour's arrival to yourselves."

"Thought it might have something to do with him," Wallis said, before taking a bite of his sandwich and taking his time chewing it. Harvey realised he was asking a lot from his friend, perhaps even stretching the relationship, but he had to at least try.

"Not really much I can give you, I'm afraid," Wallis eventually said, to Harvey's obvious disappointment.

"Can you at least pinpoint his arrival time?" Harvey pressed. "We know how he got in, why he's here, and his probable target. If we knew when he got here we'd have a better chance of tracing him."

Wallis was taken aback. "You're kidding, right?"

"Deadly serious, Doug. We even have the genetic make-up of the virus and a good idea of which bio-defence he plans to circumvent, but, as you say, maybe this stuff is above our pay grade."

He had Wallis's attention. The American looked at his watch and did a quick calculation.

"I suppose it will be on the news soon enough," he said. "Mansour gave us the co-ordinates to Azhar Al-Asiri's current home. We have a drone en route to take him out."

It was Harvey's turn to be shocked. "You get a note claiming to be from a known terrorist and you send in the bombers, no questions asked?"

"Don't be facetious, Andy, it doesn't suit you."

"I'm not trying to be, Doug, but if you'd shared this with us you could have got the whole picture. Doesn't it seem strange that Mansour is handing you Al-Asiri on a plate, and shortly afterwards we're given a tipoff that could help take Mansour out?"

Wallis had to agree that it was too much of a coincidence. "Can I share that with my people?" He asked, and Harvey said it would be better if it came through official channels. "Tell your people to contact Ellis and give her everything you have, and she'll share the details we received."

He could have told Wallis that he'd effectively given him every morsel they had, but in order to get the agencies talking to each other he knew he would have to keep that to himself. It meant jeopardising their friendship as well as their professional relationship, but Harvey knew the time would come when he would have a chance to rebuild that bridge.

They parted company, Wallis dumping his half-eaten sandwich in a bin before walking away with his phone to his ear.

* * *

The BBC news channel opened with an announcement that the Bank of England planned to inject another forty billion into the economy in an attempt to kick start the recovery, but still no reports of an air strike in Quetta.

Mansour wasn't particularly concerned as he knew it would take some time for the US government to sanction the hit on Al-Asiri's home. In his note, he'd said that Al-Qaeda's leader would only be at the location for a short period, hoping that the idea of a forty-eight hour window of opportunity would force their hand.

Apparently not.

The sound of laughter floated upstairs, heralding the return of the men from their morning's testing. He went to join them and found the

497

four of them in the living room, surrounded by their new toys. After a quick greeting he asked how their morning had gone.

"It was fun," the younger one said, but his levity wasn't well received by Mansour.

"I didn't send you out to have fun," he said, wiping the smile off the teenager's face. "Are you able to control them using the phone app?"

"It was tricky at first, but we have the hang of it now," another said, as Mansour picked up one of the remote-controlled helicopters. The machine was twenty-four inches long and sturdily built, with a purported range of over five hundred yards, but they told him it was only really effective at four hundred.

"After that, it becomes erratic."

Mansour wasn't concerned. That was more than enough for their purposes.

"How long will it take to fit the attachment?"

They told him it would take less than two hours. "I want you to go out and test them again with the smoke canisters attached. Let me know if it affects performance."

The plan was a simple one. The four men would launch the helicopters a mile from the Palace of Westminster and guide them over the building, where the canisters would release their contents. The yellow smoke would be interpreted as a chemical attack, causing the triggering of the building's defences. Those inside would consider themselves safe from harm, but in fact they would be the only people exposed to his virus.

At the same time as the building was being locked down, he would have his note delivered to the security services, letting them know the fate of those inside.

And what a fine collection they would be. The Queen would be delivering her speech at the State Opening of Parliament, where the Prime Minister and his entire government would be in attendance.

This single strike would be the greatest victory in Al-Qaeda's history, bigger and bolder than anything the organisation had ever attempted, cementing his reputation for all time. Once Al-Asiri was gone, he would assume control of the organisation, and few would dispute his right to lead the struggle towards ultimate victory.

The only part of the plan remaining was to hand the inhalers to the BBC cameraman who would be filming the event, and Mansour would do that personally the following day.

Chapter 14

Wednesday May 9th 2012

The sun had barely shown its face when Andrew Harvey reached Thames House and took the stairs up to the office. He expected to be one of the first in but the place was already a hive of activity as the search for Abdul Mansour continued apace.

He took a seat at his desk and turned on the monitor, then entered his username and password combination to unlock the screen. He saw that the search he'd left running overnight had finished, but the number of matches was low.

Hamad Farsi arrived a few minutes later, armed with coffee and a sandwich.

"Any word from the street?" Harvey asked, but Hamad shook his head.

"No-one's heard a thing. I'm beginning to wonder if the note was disinformation, just to get us chasing our own tails."

"Or to see who we go to for answers," Harvey offered. "Maybe they just wanted to see which cages we rattled so that they could spot those who'd infiltrated their operation."

Hamad agreed that it was possible. "I thought with the CIA confirming his presence on UK soil it was a certainty, but he could have written that note anywhere in the world and had it flown in by a courier."

Despite their own misgivings, and until told otherwise, they had to assume the threat was real.

"I've had no luck with the facial recognition. Closest we got was someone four inches shorter than Mansour, and that's not easy to fake."

Farsi walked round to Andrew's desk and took the mouse off him. He clicked the filter option, selected zero percent for an eye match and ran the query against the current set of results. "Let's see if Gerald's idea pans out. If Mansour really did come through Heathrow, it's likely he used countermeasures to fool the software."

While the search ran, they pored over the chatter coming through the normal channels, but there was no mention of Mansour or a biological threat. Harvey was about to go and grab a coffee when a notification blinked in his taskbar and he opened it to see that the search had finished, producing just thirty-one results.

Farsi joined him as he flicked through them, seeing a blind male but discounting him because of his tender age. Another male was wearing sunglasses, but again, he was too short. Harvey came across a woman in a *burqa* and quickly moved on to the next image. One by one he went through the selection until he came to the end.

"Nothing."

"Go back to the start," Hamad said, and Harvey went to the first image.

"Okay, flick through them until I say stop."

Harvey hit the Next button, then again.

"Stop."

"Hamad, I know you don't get out much, but that's what we in the real world call a 'woman'."

Farsi ignored the jibe. "Got beautiful lips, hasn't she."

"How can you tell when she's wearing...that...veil."

Farsi clapped Harvey on the shoulder. "The boy cottons on fast," he smiled. "Send me the arrival time and I'll follow her through the airport."

He returned to his desk and brought up the airport security system. He set the date and time to three minutes before the flight arrived and then started to fast forward until the passengers emerged from the gangway. While he watched the target make her way through the terminal, Harvey collated the details of the other veiled women in the search results and sent them to Hamad's screen.

"I'll start at the bottom of the list, you take the top."

They studied the recordings for two hours before Farsi called Harvey over.

"Check this one out."

Farsi rewound the footage and they watched the woman walk from the arrival gate through to the immigration area.

"Play it again," Harvey said, and Farsi obliged.

"Definitely something not right in her gait," Harvey noted. "If she gets to immigration and they don't ask her to lift her veil, I'd say we had a hit."

Farsi fast-forwarded to that point, and both were disappointed to see the woman's companion lift the veil and the border guard study the face, comparing it against the passport.

"Damn!" Farsi said, throwing the mouse across the desk. "I thought we had him."

"Me, too." Harvey stood and checked his watch. "I have to go and check on our guests. Let me know if you get anything from the other possibilities."

* * *

The resident security officer at the safe house looked at the monitor and recognised Harvey standing at the front door. She hit the door release and went to meet him in the hallway.

"Morning, Andrew."

He approached the lady and gave her a peck on the cheek. "Morning, Linda. You're looking gorgeous, as ever."

The fifty-year-old gave him a coy smile. "Charmer."

"How's everyone doing?"

"Fine," Linda told him. "Just finished breakfast and they're washing up."

Harvey thanked her and went through to the kitchen where he found Vick with her hands in the sink and Gray doing his fair share with the towel.

"Ready for your big performance, Tom?"

"Hi Andrew," Gray said, almost dropping the plate he was drying. "To be honest, I'm crapping myself."

Harvey laughed, unable to envisage Gray caving in under the pressure. "I'm sure you'll be fine."

"I'm surprised it's still on," Gray said. "You said yesterday that something big was on the cards. I expected that to take priority."

"I checked with Ellis on the way over, and she's happy for this to go ahead. We're at a bit of an impasse at the moment."

Harvey poured himself a coffee. Impasse was an understatement, he thought. The CIA had decided it might be prudent to know what information MI5 had received and had suddenly been keen to share all they had on Mansour.

Their discussions had led to the drone being recalled while they figured out what was happening within Al-Qaeda. Until they could get

501

a handle on what was causing the in-fighting, they thought it best to maintain the status quo.

"Any thoughts as to what you'll do once this is over?" Harvey asked Gray.

"First thing is to get my money back," Gray told him. "I checked the balance of my PNB account this morning, and it was cleaned out a couple of weeks ago. There was over half a million dollars in there, and Farrar is the only other person with access to it."

"I'm sure that once the government's involvement in this is established, a suitable compensation package will be arranged."

Gray shook his head. "I'm not going to take millions in taxpayer's money. All I want is what's mine, and Farrar to get what's coming to him."

"I think that last one's a given." Harvey said, finishing off his drink. "I'll give you half an hour to get in position. Call me when you're set to go and I'll give Veronica the nod."

Gray shook his hand. "Thanks, Andrew, for everything. I know you didn't agree with what we did last year, but..."

"Yeah, I know," Harvey said. "Look, I gotta go. Call me when you're set."

* * *

Farrar was just about to tuck into a chicken Caesar sandwich when his mobile chirped, and he wiped his fingers on a handkerchief before answering it.

"Farrar."

"Hi, James."

Farrar immediately lost his appetite, though he tried his best to be pleasant.

"What can I do for you, Veronica?"

"I know the operation is over, James, but we've come across some information that suggests there may have been more to the Levine and Campbell case than first meets the eye."

"Really?" he asked, trying to remain calm despite the feeling of dread that accompanied every conversation with Ellis. "What would that be?"

"Something about an agreement they made with the government," Ellis said, and Farrar almost dropped the phone.

How could she possibly have known about that? Had one of Gray's cronies left instructions with a solicitor to leak the details if they died, or had one or more of them shared their little secret with a third party?

Whatever it was, he would have to nip it in the bud.

"Sounds interesting," he said. "What kind of agreement?"

"I can't tell you over the phone," Ellis replied. "How about we meet up. Are you free in thirty minutes?"

For this, he would miss his own funeral. "Sure. We can take a walk along the embankment, just like the old days."

Ellis agreed and hung up, leaving Farrar to ponder the next move. Denying any knowledge was a starting point, but Ellis was tenacious, like a terrier with a tennis ball. The first thing he needed to do was find out how much she really knew and how much was speculation. Whatever she brought to the table, he would dismiss it as conspiracy theorists seeking their fifteen minutes of fame and get her to drop it. With Gray and his buddies gone there would be no-one to corroborate any stories, and the DA notices he'd sent to the media would ensure the public never got to hear about it.

Coming up with an explanation for the notice was easy: they had intelligence that a group was planning to claim Tom Gray was still alive in the hope of reigniting the debate on judicial process. This group had been threatening vigilante activity and the government felt it wasn't in the country's best interest to give them the publicity they craved.

He left his office feeling a little apprehensive, but with the i's dotted, he just had to cross this final t to put the matter to rest. When he reached the street he opened his umbrella and sidestepped a few of the deeper puddles, then made his way to the Albert Embankment. Footfall was sparse, save for the few joggers who braved the elements day in, day out. That suited Farrar perfectly. The fewer people around the eavesdrop on their conversation, the better.

His watch told him he was seven minutes early, and he hoped Ellis would be punctual so that he could get out of the rain and back to his meager lunch. He walked slowly towards Lambeth Bridge, the murky, grey waters of the Thames on his left, the snarling traffic crawling past on his right. Coupled with the awful weather, he found the entire scene depressing and promised to treat himself later in the evening. Perhaps an evening in with a bottle of wine and the intern he'd been seeing on and off for the last two years.

Yes, an evening with Michael would cheer him up.

503

"Hello, James."

Farrar spun but a hand gripped his elbow and urged him onwards.

"Keep walking," Tom Gray said. "There's a van ten yards ahead. I want you to get in."

Farrar planted his feet, his jaw hanging open as he struggled to understand how a dead man could be standing next to him. Palmer had confirmed the kill himself, which meant the assassin had either been compromised, or he'd chosen to switch sides. Had Gray offered him more money not to complete the job?

"How...?"

Gray turned to face him. "Come with me and I'll explain everything."

Farrar tried to pull away but couldn't escape Gray's grip. "Don't be stupid, James. You've read our files, so you know what Jeff Campbell can do with a sniper rifle at a thousand yards. Do as you're told, or he'll put a round through the base of your spine, and as you lie screaming on the floor, he'll take out each kneecap and elbow. If you survive, you'll be paying someone to wipe your arse for the rest of your life."

Campbell was alive, too? The news just got worse and worse, and Farrar was overwhelmed by so many revelations in such a short time. One minute he thought the operation had been wrapped up, and now he discovered that his targets were alive and well, not to mention armed.

Gray could see Farrar was finding it difficult to make a decision, so he pushed him up against the embankment wall and pulled his collar mic up to his mouth. "Warning shot, please."

A second later he heard the *thwang* as the 7.62mm round hit the top of the wall an inch away from Farrar's back before ricocheting off into the river.

Farrar got the message and began walking, his mind still straining to come to terms with the situation.

In the car the surprises kept coming. Carl Levine twisted in the driver's seat and smiled with a distinct lack of benevolence.

"Hi, Jimmy. Bet you didn't expect to see me again."

Farrar ignored him and turned to Gray. "So what happens now, Tom?" He tried to sound confident, defiant, but his voice dripped fear as the car set off.

"You're going to record your confession and admit everything you've done over the last thirteen months."

504

After a moment's thought, Farrar began to relax. With the initial prospect of pain and death banished, his mind began to focus once more. He looked out of the window as the city flashed past, and a smile appeared on his face when he realised that once again he had the upper hand. He would play Gray's game and walk away, if not totally unscathed, then at least with his life intact. It would require some clean-up work and a lot of political spin, but those mechanisms were already available and he would make best use of them.

"What's so funny?" Gray asked.

Farrar looked him in the eye. "The irony," he said. "Here we are, a year on, and you're about to parade yet another hostage in front of the cameras. Not a tactic that's worked well for you in the past."

Gray ignored him and gave him a quick frisk search, being none too gentle in his approach. Farrar was unarmed, but Gray took his phone, cranked open the window and dropped it into the street.

They drove for another twenty minutes in silence, both men deep in thought.

Levine eventually pulled up at an old industrial estate in the east end, the businesses long since gone, each falling victim to the global recession. They pulled up next to the door of the last unit and Gray urged Farrar out of the car. He unlocked the chain securing the entrance and pushed Farrar forward, along a corridor and into what had once been the warehouse of a greetings card manufacturer. The fixtures and fittings had gone, but boxes and rubbish littered the floor.

Levine followed them in, but Gray stopped him near the door. "I've got this, Carl."

"Tom, the guy's a snake. I don't trust him."

"Nor do I," Gray agreed, "but I can handle him on my own."

Levine looked disconsolate. "I'll be waiting outside," he said.

"No need, Carl," Gray said, pulling the Browning from his jacket. "I'm armed, he's not. Take the car back to the hotel and I'll join you when I'm done." Levine was about to protest again but Gray put a hand on his shoulder. "Go. I'll walk back." As an afterthought, he called Carl back. "If I'm not there by two, you know what to do."

Levine threw one last, malevolent look at Farrar and left.

Gray waited until he heard the car start and pull away before waving to a chair, which was facing a video camera mounted on a tripod.

"Sit."

Farrar obligingly took a seat, unbuttoning his coat and making himself comfortable.

"You know, there's really not a lot of point in going through with this charade, Tom. No-one's going to let this air to the public, and I mean no-one."

"You seem pretty sure of yourself," Gray said as he stood behind the camera, working on the focus. "What if I told you I had a British news channel ready and waiting for me to deliver this tape, eh?"

Farrar seemed less cocksure. "I don't believe you."

"Why not? Because of the DA notice you slapped on them?"

Gray watched his expression and smiled. "They were more than happy to help once they found out that the person who'd issued the notice would be the one confessing."

Farrar went from uncomfortable to angry in an instant. "You're wasting your time," he snarled, getting to his feet. "You really think anyone will take notice of a confession extracted under duress?"

"They'll listen," Gray said. "They have to listen."

Farrar took a couple of steps towards him. "You really are as stupid as you look, aren't you? You're a little kid playing a big boys' game, and you don't even realise how —"

Gray fired at the floor a few inches from Farrar's feet, the sound of the shot echoing around the room.

"That was your last chance." Gray pointed the gun at Farrar's face and his demeanor turned sour. "You either sit down and answer my questions, or I find another way."

Farrar was about to suggest he do just that when Gray forced him into the chair with the barrel of the pistol.

"And if I have to find another way, there'll be no need to keep you alive."

Farrar held his tongue. The last thing he wanted to do was push Gray too far and overplay his hand.

"Get on with it," he said, straightening his already immaculate tie.

Gray went to the camera and hit the record button and then moved next to Farrar, careful to keep the gun out of view.

"My name is Tom Gray." He paused, more to compose himself than for dramatic effect. "Some of you may not believe me, but I'm sure subsequent audio comparisons with my recordings last year will convince you."

Farrar winced. He hadn't considered forensic confirmation, so any attempt to dismiss Gray as a delusional imposter was not going to fly.

"I have a remarkable tale to tell," Gray continued, "and this man, James Farrar from Her Majesty's government, is going to confirm everything I say."

Gray moved back behind the camera and zoomed in on his subject. Once he was happy with the way Farrar was framed, he placed the pistol on the camera case and pulled a set of prompt cards from his inside pocket.

"On the thirtieth of April last year, it was announced to the world that I had died from the injuries I'd suffered ten days earlier. In actual fact, I was secreted out of Britain on a military transport plane and taken to Subic Bay in the Philippines. The order to do this came from the Home Secretary."

Gray looked at Farrar. "Is that what happened?"

"That is correct."

Gray moved on to the next card, but before he could read it, Farrar jumped in. "I also want to say that I am agreeing to everything because this man is armed and I fear for my life."

"Duly noted," Gray said. "Last month, I was taken hostage by members of Abu Sayyaf and you sent Len Smart and Simon Baines to rescue me. You gave them unserviceable ammunition in order to increase the chances of them being captured and killed. Is that correct?"

Farrar again acknowledged the statement as being true.

"When we managed to escape from the Philippines, you found out which route we were taking and you hired a hit man to intercept and kill us in Durban."

He looked at Farrar, who nodded. "Correct."

"The same hit man who killed British national Timmy Hughes in Singapore two weeks ago."

"Yes."

"You also sent a hit team to kill Carl Levine, his wife Sandra and their daughter Alana, as well as Jeff Campbell and his wife Anne. They were staying in a caravan in Dorset, which was recently destroyed in an explosion."

"That's right."

Farrar noticed that Gray was becoming complacent, strolling around the room as he made his accusations, and he'd taken his eye off the pistol near the camera. Farrar didn't yet have an opportunity to grab the weapon as Gray was still too close, but with a handful of cards still to be read, there was still time. He calculated it to be three steps, so even a two second start should be enough.

He kept his focus on Gray, deliberately keeping his gaze off the gun, just in case he telegraphed his intentions.

The next question, when it came, caught him off guard.

"Why did you do it?"

"I don't know what you're talking about," he said. "You're the one who invented this nonsense. I can hardly be expected to explain what goes on inside your mind."

"Then how about I give you the theory presented to me by Jeff Campbell?"

"By all means, go ahead."

Gray read from the card, explaining how the government had made a deal with the six surviving men in return for their silence, and how Farrar had been instrumental in trying to eliminate everyone involved.

"Does that sound right?"

Farrar waved a dismissive hand. "Whatever."

Gray strode purposefully towards him, his face ending up inches from Farrar's, the venom in his eyes palpable.

"Don't give me whatever!" He shouted. *"Is that what happened?"*

"Yes! Yes! Exactly like that!"

Gray straightened up. He turned his back and walked away, studying the next card in the pile. Farrar watched him take two, three, four steps, still concentrating on the next question, and he saw his chance.

Gray heard the sound of the chair leg scraping against the floor as Farrar made a bolt for it, and by the time he looked at where his captive had been, he'd already reached the gun. Gray started to charge towards him but the pistol came up, pointing at his face. He stopped dead.

"The safety's still on," he said, hoping to get Farrar to take his eye off the target.

"Nice try," Farrar said. "I know my way around a Browning and that's the first thing I checked. I also know there's a round in the chamber."

Farrar ejected the magazine, the gun never wavering. The clip was full and he rammed it back into the grip. "Turn the camera off."

Gray moved slowly over to the recorder and hit the stop button.

"Give me the tape."

Gray ejected it and threw it on the floor near Farrar's feet. "Now what?" He asked. "Are you going to shoot an unarmed man, a delusional imposter?"

"Enough games, Tom."

"Oh, so now you acknowledge that I'm Tom Gray. Too much of a coward to admit it to the world?"

"I said *enough!*" Farrar shouted. He tried to gather himself, concentrating on turning this in his favour. "Tell me where the others are."

"That's not going to happen and you know it," Tom spat. "If I don't meet up with them in thirty minutes, they'll disappear."

"Tom, I'll give you one last chance. Tell me where they are and I'll make it a quick death, otherwise…"

Gray laughed. "You know, when you try to sound intimidating it just comes off as desperate." He sat down on the chair. "And just what would you do if you found them? Apologise for the inconvenience you've caused over the last year or so? You've sent teams to kill them and they failed. What makes you think you can get it right this time?"

"I'll do it myself if I have to," Farrar said.

Gray snorted. "You haven't got it in you. You're happy to sit behind a desk and let others do the dirty work, but you're nowhere near man enough to pull the trigger yourself."

Farrar took two steps towards him, the gun aiming at the centre of Gray's face. "I'll give you one last chance, Tom. *Where are they?*"

Gray ignored the question. "What are you going to do when this gets out, James? You can't bury the truth forever, you know that."

"Very apt choice of phrase," Farrar said, "because that's exactly what I intend to do, starting with you."

Gray just smiled back. "It's over, James." He got to his feet and started walking towards Farrar. He had three paces to cover, but only managed one before the trigger sent the firing pin smashing down on the percussion cap of the next round in the chamber.

Click!

Farrar looked stunned. He ejected the round, thinking he had a blockage. He tried the next round, and the next, both with the same result.

Gray grabbed the gun from him and pushed him to the floor. He removed the clip, then extracted the top bullet and pulled a penknife

509

from his pocket. He eased the bullet from the cartridge and tipped the contents onto Farrar's chest.

"Sand," he said, dropping the empty brass casing into Farrar's hand. "Seems to be happening quite a lot these days."

Farrar scrambled to his feet, his fists clenched, but Gray ignored him and walked over to a pile of boxes covered by an old tarpaulin. He dragged it aside to reveal a television set, which he switched on.

Farrar looked at a picture of himself, streaming live to the nation via the BBC news channel. He raised a hand, and a moment later the figure on the screen did the same.

Gray waved to the four corners of the room. "Fibre optic cameras and state-of-the-art microphones, courtesy, ironically, of Her Majesty's Government."

He clicked his throat mic. "All yours, Andrew."

* * *

Harvey entered the room accompanied by two armed police officers. "Don't forget to read him his rights," Harvey told them as they forced Farrar to the floor and cuffed him.

Farrar was dragged to his feet and marched out of the building. Harvey and Gray followed them, and Tom watched his nemesis take a seat in the back of the unmarked car.

"We got some great footage," Gerald Small said, handing Gray a tablet PC. "You ought to be on the stage."

"Can I get a copy?" Gray asked, handing over the comms kit.

"Already done," Small smiled. "I'll get Andrew to drop it off at the safe house later today."

Gray thanked him for his help and joined Harvey in the Ford saloon. They drove away from the city, heading for the quiet residential area which housed the four-storey building Gray and the others would call home for the next few days.

There was no telling what immediate effect his transmission would have, though Gray knew the Prime Minister's spin doctor would no doubt be working overtime to play it down. The next step was to get a live interview on the BBC and give his side of the story before the political machine had a chance to bury the story as a hoax. Paul Gross hadn't been convinced that he'd be allowed to broadcast a live interview, but Gray would simply take it to the other news outlets if the BBC hierarchy refused to play ball, and he'd already created a home video that would hit the top dozen social media sites if no broadcaster was willing to run the story.

Harvey's phone chirped and he put it on speakerphone. "Hi, Hamad."

"Andrew, we may have found Mansour."

"Abdul Mansour?" Gray asked, perking up on hearing the name, and Harvey suddenly remembered he wasn't alone in the car. He went to take the phone from its dashboard mounting but Gray stopped him. After all he'd been through at Mansour's hand, he thought he was entitled to hear this.

Harvey saw the look of determination, and decided not to make a fight of it. "What did you find, Hamad?"

"Remember the lady we followed through the airport this morning? The one we thought was walking strange?"

"Yeah, but we discounted her. She showed her face to the border guard."

"I know, but there were no other hits, so I went back to her. If the guard hadn't seen her face I would have been certain we had our man, so I checked him out. Turns out he had over thirty grand of gambling debts until three years ago, then they were suddenly paid off. He's been debt free since."

"That's not unusual," Harvey said. "Maybe he just stopped gambling."

"That was my thought, but I checked with the casino he used to frequent. He still goes there six days a week, and spends an average of two hundred pounds a night."

"Doesn't sound like something you could do on a border guard's salary."

"I know," Hamad said. "Someone's been giving him a shitload of cash each month, and you'd expect him to be giving something in return."

"Such as turning a blind eye now and again," Harvey agreed. "So assuming it is Mansour, where did he go once he left the airport?"

"We tracked his car through the Highway Agency's network of cameras to a place in Stratford."

Harvey pulled over and asked for the address, which he typed into the satnav. "I can be there in twenty minutes," he said, and pulled out into the traffic.

"SO15 won't be there for another thirty," Farsi said. "They're in the middle of an operation at the moment."

511

"Okay, I'll hang back when I get there."

Harvey steered the car through side streets, trying to avoid the main arteries of the city that would be clogged at this time of day.

"Abdul Mansour is here, in the UK?" Gray asked, incredulous, and Harvey nodded. He explained that they'd received intelligence and were working it up, though he didn't go as far as telling Gray about the specific threat. "We think he came in dressed as a Muslim woman and was helped through customs by an officer on the take."

They arrived at the target street seventeen minutes later. Harvey parked close to the junction and told Gray to wait in the car.

"I'm going to do a walk past," he said, taking the phone from its holder. "I want you to stay here, Tom."

Gray nodded. It wasn't his operation, and the last thing he wanted to do was antagonise Harvey after all he'd done for him.

* * *

"Abdul, we may have a problem!"

Mansour had just finished taking a shower and he went to the living room to see what Mohammad, the house owner, was concerned about. He found the man looking through a small gap in the net curtains.

"What is it?"

"A stranger in the street," Mohammad said, and Mansour watched the man walking slowly past the house. He was on the other side of the street and didn't seem to have any particular destination, simply ambling from one end of the street to the other.

"He could be a salesman, or an estate agent. How can you be sure he's a threat?"

"Because he parked his car down there," Mohammad said, pointing to a Ford, "and there's someone in the passenger seat."

Mansour could see the occupant of the car, but couldn't make out the facial features. He asked Mohammad for a camera and he used it to zoom in on the car.

His heart almost stopped. He instantly recognised the man from his time in the southern Philippines and a strange, alien feeling washed over him.

It took him some time to realise that it was fear.

Mansour was torn between confronting the man and running, and prudence dictated he choose the latter. He took a photo of the man and handed the camera to Mohammad.

512

"You are right," he said. "I must leave, but I want you to find out who this man is."

"What of the operation?"

The cameraman was due to arrive in twenty minutes to collect the virus, but Mansour knew it was too late. Somehow they had found him, which meant it was time to disappear again.

"It is postponed." He ran up the stairs and threw on the *burqa*, then collected the inhaler and spare canister and put them in his pocket. He left the passport as it had probably been compromised, but he grabbed the cash on the dressing table.

When he descended the stairs, Mohammad was waiting in the hallway.

"I haven't seen anyone else arrive," he said, and gave Mansour a slip of paper. "You can stay here for a few days until the heat dies down."

Mansour committed the address to memory and handed it back. "Can you distract them while I go out the back?"

"Of course. Go, and may Allah watch over you."

* * *

Gray watched the man appear from the front of the house and cross the road on a collision course with Harvey.

"Hey! I know you! You stole my bike!"

Harvey turned to see an angry looking man bearing down on him. The last thing he needed was a scene, so he tried to walk away, but the stranger grabbed his collar and swung a punch. Harvey easily avoided it, but the man kept coming and he tried talking his way out of it.

Gray was watching the drama unfold when a flash of movement caught his eye. In a gap between two semi-detached houses he saw a figure in black hurdle a fence and disappear into the next garden, and he knew instantly that Harvey's attacker was a distraction.

He jumped into the driver's seat but the ignition was empty: Harvey must have taken them with him. He debated helping, but he knew that with every passing second, Mansour's chance of escape increased exponentially.

Harvey seemed to be holding his own, and with the armed police due in the next few minutes, he decided to take up the chase.

By the time he climbed out of the car and reached the end of the road, Mansour had cleared the garden and was running towards an

513

alleyway, his *burqa* flapping around his legs. Gray followed a hundred yards behind and hit the alley just as his target exited the other end, turning to the right. He'd closed by ten yards, but Mansour still had a healthy lead.

When Gray got to the end of the alley he saw the black clothes disappear around another corner and sprinted to catch up, the exertion already beginning to tell after weeks with no proper exercise. When he reached the main road he saw a sea of pedestrians parting as Mansour barged his way through. An elderly lady was knocked to the floor but Mansour didn't give her a second thought as he dashed across the road, narrowly avoiding a van which just managed to slam its brakes on. The driver of the car behind wasn't as quick to react, and she ploughed into the back of the van, but Gray didn't break stride as he ran between the two damaged vehicles.

He was beginning to close on his target, and Mansour could sense it. He turned and saw the pursuer less than fifty yards behind him, and his first thought was to find a weapon. He saw a hardware store and dived inside, scattering customers as he search for the aisle containing the knives. Mansour grabbed two from the shelf and turned to the front of the store, only to find his way blocked by an employee. He ripped off his headpiece and gave the teenager a look which offered two options: get out of the way; or die.

The young man got the message. He stood aside and Mansour ran out of the shop.

Where he found the mystery man waiting for him.

They stared at each other for what seemed a lifetime, oblivious to the crowd gathering around them — albeit at a respectful distance.

"Drop the knives," Gray said, his voice tinged with anger.

Mansour ignored the command, instead trying desperately to think where he'd seen the man before.

"Who the hell are you?"

Mansour may not have recognised him, but a few of the shoppers had seen the BBC news transmission and knew exactly who they were looking at. Whispers of 'Tom Gray' began to grow, and when they reached the terrorist's ears he wondered if it could possibly be true.

He looked Gray in the eyes, and at that moment, he knew.

He'd tried to kill this man twice, but this time he wouldn't delegate responsibility to someone else. He gripped the handles of the knives until his knuckles turned white and took a step towards his opponent, expecting him to move backwards.

514

Gray held his ground.

The attack, when it came, was lightning fast. Mansour raised his right arm and brought it down hard, aiming at Gray's head. That blow was easily blocked, but the simultaneous jab with the left punctured a one inch hole in Gray's side.

Mansour danced back, bobbing on the balls of his feet, while Gray put a hand to the wound. It came away covered in crimson.

"You'll have to do better than that," he said, adjusting his position to move closer to a street light.

Mansour came again, this time thrusting at Gray's face, but he was ready and caught the knifeman's forearm in a vice-like grip before slamming Mansour's knuckles against the steel lamppost. The blade clattered to the floor, but Mansour had another and he swung it, aiming for Gray's kidneys. The move was telegraphed and Gray easily avoided further injury by backing into his enemy and switching his attention to the knife hand.

Mansour tried to bring the blade up to Gray's neck but his strength was no match for the ex-soldier, who held his wrist tightly while slowly pivoting so that they were once again face to face, the knife poised delicately between them.

Both men heard the sirens approaching, and Mansour knew his time had run out.

But there was still time for one last, defiant action.

He brought his knee up sharply into Gray's groin and pushed him away, sending him sprawling to the ground, but instead of finishing him off, he put his hands into his pockets and brought out the inhalers.

"The difference between you and me," he said to Gray, as he pressed both canisters into their housings and held them in position, "is that I am willing to die."

The crowd, thinking he was holding a detonator, scattered in all directions, screaming incoherently and trampling each other in their bid to clear the area.

...two, three, four...

The first of the armed response vehicles pulled up and two officers decamped, shouting for Mansour to get to the floor as they aimed their single-shot MP5 rifles at his chest.

...five, six, seven...

"Allahu Akbar..."

"Drop it, now!"

...eight, nine, ten.

Mansour closed his eyes just as the rifles spat, and the inhalers fell from his dying grasp. One of them rolled towards Tom Gray, and he felt a breeze on his face as the canister dispensed its entire contents.

Epilogue

Monday June 17th 2013

"Push!"

Vick Phillips screamed and dug her nails into Tom's hand, hoping to cause him as much pain as she was experiencing.

"You're doing well, darling," Tom said through gritted teeth. In truth, she'd been in labour for over thirty hours, and neither was at their peak.

Vick did her breathing exercises as best she could, but all she could focus on was the seven pounds of human trying to navigate a four centimeter passage.

"Do you know the sex of the child?" The nurse asked, trying to take Vick's mind off the pain.

"No," Tom told her. "We wanted it to be a surprise."

"What about names?"

"Vick wanted to do the celebrity thing and name it after the place it was conceived, but there's no way I'm calling a kid Machu Picchu."

The joke was lost on the nurse, but Vick showed her appreciation by squeezing his hand with enough force to draw blood, and Tom wondered if she'd had her nails sharpened just for the occasion.

"Just kidding," Gray winced. "We chose the names weeks ago."

The obstetrician, sitting at the foot of the bed, saw the crown of the baby's head appear.

"One more big push," he said, and Vick obliged, her face contorted as beads of sweat coursed down her crimson forehead. She produced a scream befitting a horror movie, and then it was over.

The umbilical was cut and the baby taken away to be weighed and checked over, before it was wrapped up and placed on its mother's chest. Vick looked down at the screaming, purple bundle and thought it the most beautiful thing she'd ever seen.

"Congratulations, you've got a beautiful little girl," the nurse told her, and Vick cooed over her daughter.

"Hello, Melissa." Vick shed a tear, but finally one of joy rather than pain.

Tom Gray gently traced a finger down her tiny wrinkled face and his thoughts turned to little Daniel, stolen from him at such a tender age. His son may be gone, but he would never be forgotten, and Gray made a silent promise to give his daughter enough love for two.

The one thing he was truly grateful for was that she could at least lead a normal life.

The political fallout hadn't been as bad as some commentators had predicted, with just the Home Secretary and a couple of his minions giving way, awaiting a decision as to whether or not they would face criminal charges. Farrar, for his part, had already been charged with multiple counts of murder and attempted murder and was awaiting trial, along with the remnants of his team.

While those bad guys had been taken off the streets, Gray was pleased to know that there were still many more out there. Viking Security Services had nosedived since he'd sold it to the venture capitalists, who had increased their prices and lowered salaries to the point where those staff who hadn't fled to sign up with Timmy Hughes had been demoralised. The effect on the company's reputation had been quick and harsh, with contracts drying up. They'd been at their lowest point when Gray walked into the office and made them a generous offer, which had been readily accepted.

With Gray back at the helm and Hughes gone, his staff had come back in droves, as had the customers, and he knew he would be able to give his daughter — not to mention his new wife — a more than comfortable life.

Melissa wouldn't be spoiled by any means. At least, that's what Gray told himself, though he knew it was going to be hard to say no, just as it had been with Daniel. All he wanted was for his daughter to grow up with the same morals as her father, and he'd consider that the perfect foundation on which to build her life.

The obstetrician checked mother and child over, and happy that they were doing well he left to complete the paperwork.

He also decided to check with the Department of Health to see if any other maternity hospital had gone a whole calendar month without delivering a single male child...

THE END

CPSIA information can be obtained at www.ICGtesting.com
Printed in the USA
BVOW072259230613

324101BV00001B/40/P